QUEENS' PLAY

THADY BOY BALLAGH, his ollave

PIEDAR DOOLY, his servant

THERESA BOYLE, an Irish widow resident at Neuvy

OONAGH O'DWYER, her niece

HÉLIE and ANNE MOÛTIER, relatives of Oonagh resident in Blois

CORMAC O'CONNOR, heir to Brian Faly O'Connor, captain of Offaly

GEORGE PARIS, an agent

These, by birth, service or adoption, are the French:

HENRI II, KING OF FRANCE

CATHERINE DE MÉDICIS, his Queen

DIANE DE POITIERS, Duchess de Valentinois, his mistress

FRANCIS, Dauphin of France, his heir, affianced to Mary Queen of Scots

ELIZABETH and CLAUDE, his young daughters

MARGUERITE OF FRANCE, his sister

ANNE DE MONTMORENCY, Marshal, Grand Master and Constable of France

FRANÇOIS, second Duke de Guise, brother to the Queen Mother of Scotland

CHARLES DE GUISE, second Cardinal of Lorraine, his brother

CLAUDE DE GUISE, Duke d'Aumale, his brother

DUKE DE LONGUEVILLE, French-born son of Mary of Guise's first marriage

JOHN STEWART, Lord d'Aubigny, former captain of the Royal Guard of Scottish Archers in France, and brother to the Earl of Lennox

ROBIN STEWART \
LAURENS DE GENSTAN } members of the Royal Guard of Scottish Archers

JACQUES d'ALBON, Marshal de St. André

LOUIS DE BOURBON, first Prince of Condé

JEAN DE BOURBON, sieur d'Enghien, his brother } Courtiers

FRANÇOIS DE VENDÔME, Vidame de Chartres

ARCHEMBAULT ABERNACI

PIERRE DESTAIZ } Keepers of the Royal Menageries of France

FLORIMUND PELLAQUIN

THOMAS OUSCHART (Tosh), a funambulist

MAÎTRE GEORGES GAULTIER, a usurer of Blois

THE DAME DE DOUBTANCE, astrologer, of Blois

RAOUL DE CHÉMAULT, French Ambassador in London

JEHANNE DE CHÉMAULT, his wife

And these, by birth, marriage or adoption, are the English:

JOHN DUDLEY, Earl of Warwick, Earl Marshal of England

MATTHEW STEWART, Earl of Lennox, brother to Lord d'Aubigny

MARGARET LENNOX, *née* Douglas, his wife, and niece to the late King Henry VIII and to Sir George Douglas

WILLIAM PARR OF KENDALL, Marquis of Northampton, Lord Great Chamberlain of England and leader of the English Mission to France

THOMAS BUTLER, Earl of Ormond, an Irishman resident in England, also of the Mission

SIR GILBERT DETHICK, Garter King of Arms

SIR JOHN PERROTT, illegitimate son of the late King Henry VIII

SIR JAMES MASON, retiring English Ambassador in France

CONTENTS

PART ONE

The Vulgar Lyre

1

PART TWO

Dangerous Juggles

95

PART THREE

London: The Excitement of Being Hunted

195

PART FOUR

The Loan and the Limit

289

The chapter headings are taken from the Brehon Laws, the ancient laws and institutes of Ireland. The Senchus Mor itself was written in the 5th century, A.D.

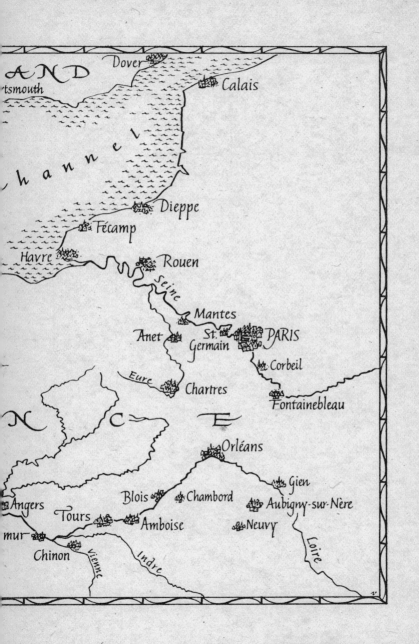

ENGLAND

Portsmouth
Dover
Calais

Channel

Dieppe
Fécamp
Havre
Rouen

Seine

Mantes
Anet
St. Germain
PARIS
Corbeil

Eure
Chartres
Fontainebleau

FRANCE

Orléans
Gien
Blois
Chambord
Aubigny-sur-Nère
Angers
Tours
Amboise
Neuvy
Saumur
Chinon

Vienne
Indre
Loire

PART ONE

The Vulgar Lyre

My son, that thou mayest know when the head of a king is
upon a plebeian, and the head of a plebeian upon a king.

The Fork is Chosen   3

  I: *Silent in the Boat*   5

 II: *Dieppe: The Pitfalls and the Deer*   12

III: *Rouen: The Nut without Fruit*   28

IV: *Rouen: Fine, Scientific Works without Warning*   43

 V: *Rouen: Fast Drivings for the Purpose of Killing*   62

VI: *Rouen: The Difficult and the Impossible*   76

The Fork is Chosen

The cauldron is exempt from its boiling when the food, the fire and the cauldron are properly arranged, but that the attendant gives notice of his putting the fork into the cauldron. That is, but so he warns: 'Take care,' says he. 'Here goes the fork into the cauldron.'

SHE wanted Crawford of Lymond. His nerves flinching from the first stir of disaster, the Chief Privy Councillor understood his mistress at last.

Regal, humourless, briskly prosaic, the Queen Dowager of Scotland had conducted the audience with her usual French competence and was bringing it to its usual racing conclusion. She was a big woman, boxed in quilting in spite of the weather, and Tom Erskine was limp with her approaching visit to France.

To the most extravagant, the most cultured, the most dissolute kingdom in Europe the Queen Mother was shortly to sail, and her barons, her bishops and her cavalry with her. And now, it appeared, she wanted one man besides.

The Queen Mother was a subtle woman, and not Scots. The thick oils of statesmanship ran in Mary of Guise's veins, and she rarely handed through the door what she could throw in by the cat's hole. So she talked of safe conducts and couriers, of precedents and programmes, of gifts and people to meet and to avoid before she added, 'And I want intelligence, good intelligence, of French affairs. We had better place some sort of observer.'

Her Privy Councillor had never found her foolish before. From the Duke de Guise downwards, every member of that privileged family, with its quarterings of eight sovereign houses, its Cardinals, its Abbesses and its high and influential posts at the French Court, might be wordly, might be charming, would almost certainly be a congenial gambler; but would never be foolish.

These were the Queen Dowager's brothers and sisters—good God, where better could she go for intimate news? Granted, it was now twelve years since, a young French widow, she had come to Scotland as King James V's bride, and eight years since he died, leaving her with a war, a baby Queen and a parcel of rebellious nobles. True, again, that she would be watched, by her Scottish barons no less than by the enemies of her brothers in France. Only, for a French King, however friendly, to find an informer at Court would be disaster.

3

Erskine said aloud, 'Madam . . . you are supposed to be joining your daughter, nothing else.'

'—Some sort of observer,' she was repeating, quite unruffled. 'Such as Crawford of Lymond.'

With an elegant yellow head in his mind's eye, and in his ears a tongue like sword cutler's emery, Tom Erskine said bluntly, 'His name and face are known the length of France. And I'm damned sure he'll not be persuaded.' Notoriously, at some time, every faction in the kingdom had tried to buy Lymond's services. Nor was the bidding restricted to Scotland, or to statesmen, or to men. Europe, whenever he wished, could provide him—and probably did—with either a workshop or a playground.

The Queen Mother's manner remained bland. 'He is possibly tired of trifling at home?'

'He isn't dull enough to commit himself to a contract.'

'But he might come to France?'

Oh, God! 'To entertain himself,' said Tom Erskine warningly. 'But for nothing else.'

The Queen Mother smiled, and he knew that he had misjudged her again, and that, as usual, streets and palaces and prisons beyond anyone's grasp lay under her thoughts. She said, 'If he is in France for the term of my visit, I shall be satisfied. You will tell him so.'

Tom Erskine thought briefly that it would be pleasant to fall ill, to be unable to ride, to become deaf. 'It will be a pleasure, madam,' he said.

4

I

Silent in the Boat

If there be a hand-party there, and a rowing party, and a party of middle-sport, the hand-party is the swamping-party, the middle-sport party is the rowing party, and the spectators are they who are silent in the boat.

ON the last Thursday in September, and the fourteenth day out of Ireland, the wind dropped to a flat calm, forcing the galley called *La Sauvée* to approach Dieppe under oar.

The best ships, the reliable crews and the senior captains had just brought the Scottish Queen Dowager to France. *La Sauvée*, built in 1520, was only fetching some Irish guests to the French Court, a common errand enough. But her captain, an able courtier, was no seaman; her seamen, through a misplaced concession, were far from sober; and her bo's'n had been taking hashish for months. Thus, two hours off Dieppe, the flags and streamers lay ready on deck, a little too early; the oarsmen, capping shaved heads, were resting and re-engaging oars; and the pilot, involved with banners, was far too busy to attend to the wind.

Robin Stewart, baulked of small talk, had found a chair in the poop beside the fat Irishman, who was asleep. There were three of them, and it was Stewart's task as one of the Royal Guard of Scottish Archers in France to bring them safely to Court. For a century and a half, Scottish Archers had guarded the King of France day and night, had crowned him, fought with him, buried him, and were looked on, by others as well as by themselves, as the élite of the men-at-arms who served the French Crown. Thus Robin Stewart was used to odd jobs; ferrying the King's less sophisticated guests to and fro was just one of them.

Ahead was a reception party on the quay, a speech, a meal at the best Dieppe inn, and a good night's rest on a bed before the ride inland to deliver his guests. Nothing difficult there; but little to earn him money or fame either. Heir to nothing but an old suit of armour and a vacant post in the Guard, Robin Stewart had always been deeply interested in money and fame, and had for a long time been convinced that in a world of arms, skill and hard work would still take you to the top, however doubtful your background.

It had only latterly become plain that success in the world of arms ran a poor second to success in the world of intrigue; and that while no one worked harder, a good many people seemed to be more skilful than Robin Stewart.

This was palpably impossible. He applied a good analytical brain to discovering how other people managed to give this appearance of excellence. He also spent a good deal of time trying to breach the stockade between reasonably paid routine soldiery and the inner chamber of princes or of bankers, or even at a pinch of the fashionable theologians. At the same time, he could not afford to lose ground in his regular job, however irritating its calls on him.

He looked round now, counting heads. At his side, the Prince's secretary was still asleep, in a poisonous aura of wine, his black head bound like a pot roast by the sliding shadow-pattern of the rigging. Whether from panic or habit, Thady Boy Ballagh had been asleep or stupefied for two weeks.

Further off, Piedar Dooly the Prince's servant was just visible, fitted into a recess, like something doubtful on the underside of a leaf. And beyond them was the Prince himself, their master, and his third and most important charge.

Phelim O'LiamRoe, Prince of Barrow, son of Milesians, descendant of Carbery Cathead, of Art the Solitary, Tuathal the Legitimate and Fergus of the Black Teeth, cousin to Maccon whose two calves were as white as the snow of one night, was thin and middle-sized, with a soft egg-shaped face thatched and cupped with blond whiskers. And at this moment, Stewart saw, he was bent double in fruitless converse with a coal-black bow oar from Tunis; thereby closing the main thoroughfare of the galley to seamen, oarsmen, timoneers, soldiers, warders, ensigns, lieutenants and captain alike.

The sweating Moor, bearing down on fifty feet of solid beechwood, crashed back regularly and wordlessly on the five-man bench like a piston, rowing twenty-four strokes to a minute, while the voice of The O'LiamRoe, Chief of the Name, Prince of Barrow and feudal lord of the Slieve Bloom in the country of Ireland, warmly cordial, went on and on.

'. . . And it would be queer if we didn't agree, with leverage itself the great wonder of the world, as my own father knew, and my grandfather twenty-two stones and bedridden. When they came from sluicing him down at the pump they would lay the coffin lid over the turf stack next the bed and sit my grandfather at one end. They had a heifer trained to jump on the other. When the lid was nailed over him at the end my grannie was blithe, blithe at the wake; for she got a powerful lot of bruising when he landed. . . .'

Robin Stewart winced. He had had two weeks of it. At Dalkey, Ireland, he had had his first sight of the great man, as The O'Liam-Roe had shinned ineptly and eagerly up the ladder, to stand revealed on the tabernacle of *La Sauvée*, a carefree, mild and hilarious savage in a saffron tunic and leggings. His entire train, for which Mr. Stewart had cleared a compartment, consisted of two: the small wild Firbolg called Dooly and the comatose Mr. Ballagh.

Robin Stewart had been mortified: not by O'LiamRoe's looks, or his dress, or his simple enjoyment of useless knowledge, but because he not only invited questions, he answered them. As a student of human nature, Stewart enjoyed a long, difficult analysis; his on-slaughts were memorable. A man talking amicably about the art of the longbow would find that, by means known only to Mr. Stewart, this led straight to God, his total income, and where his schooling had taken place, if any. In one day, the Archer knew that O'LiamRoe was thirty, unmarried, and resident in a large, coarse Irish castle. He knew that there was a widowed mother, a string of servants and five *tuaths* filled with clansmen and the minimum wherewithal to sustain life with no money to speak of. He knew that, in terms of followers, O'LiamRoe was one of the mightiest chieftains in English-occupied Ireland, except that it had never yet occurred to him to lead them anywhere.

Watching the lord of the Slieve Bloom straighten and move happily off, tripping over an old pennant with a salamander on it, the Scots-man was moved to an irritation almost maternal. 'And anyway, what in God's name's a *tuath*?'

He had said it aloud. A voice replied in his ear. 'Thirty ballys, my dear. And if you ask what in God's name does a bally do, it holds four herds of cows without one cow, desperate lonely that they are, touching another.' The fat Irishman in the next chair scratched his black poll and recrossed his hands over his comfortable little stomach 'Surely The O'LiamRoe told you that? Bring in any little fact and O'LiamRoe will wet-nurse it for you.'

Mr. Ballagh, asleep or drunk, had so far escaped the Archer's attentions. In the dark-skinned, slothful, unshaven face he thought he saw disillusionment, intelligence, the remains of high aspirations perhaps, all soaked and crumbled into servitude and cynicism. He said easily, 'Ye'll have been a long time with the Prince?'

Mr. Ballagh's answer was succinct. 'Three weeks.'

'Three weeks too much, eh? You should have made enquiries about him beforehand.'

'So I could, then; but who would answer me? The fellow lives in a bog and devil the person has laid eyes on him from one end of the country to the other. I heard from a friend of a cousin of a cousin,' said Mr. Ballagh on a little wave of wine-coloured confidence, 'that he was wild for a true-bred ollave who could talk in French for him, and here I am.'

The O'LiamRoe had no French. That he had English was a welcome surprise. France, from the lowest of motives, had entertained not a few of the powerful leaders of her downtrodden neighbour, and had sweated over their plots and counterplots in Gaelic and Latin. 'What's an ollave?' asked Mr. Stewart.

Master Ballagh recited. 'A hired ollave is a sweet-stringed timpan, and a sign, so they say, that the master of the house is a grand, wealthy fellow, and him for ever reading books. An ollave of the highest grade is professor, singer, poet, all in the one. His songs and tales are of battles and voyages, of tragedies and adventures, of cattle raids and preyings, of forays, hostings, courtships and elopements, hidings and destructions, sieges and feasts and slaughters; and you'd rather listen to a man killing a pig than hear half of them through. I,' said Mr. Ballagh bitterly, 'am an ollave of the highest grade.'

'Well, you're wasting your time here,' Robin Stewart pointed out. 'You should be getting grand money for all yon, surely. And what made you take up poetry anyway, for heaven's sake?'

'Grand money, is it; and everyone forced by legislation to speak the English?' snarled Mr. Ballagh. He calmed down. 'The O'Coffey, who ran the bardic school near my home, had a hurley team would make your mouth water and the blood come out at your ears. I was the fifteenth child, and the nippiest, so why should I object to what my father and The O'Coffey might arrange? The fifteenth. And the nippiest . . .'

Master Thady Boy Ballagh smoothed the doubtful black of his pourpoint, flicked the limp grey frills of his cuff, and wrapped the stained folds of his robe over his knees. 'Hand me that bottle, will you?'

And by then it was too late. The squall was already coming, a streaming blemish over the water, and lying over before it the *Gouden Roos*, a three-masted galliasse caught with every rag on the yards. For a moment still, *La Sauvée* slid peacefully along. Claret flowed from the leather down Master Ballagh's throat. Stewart, his arms folded, watched O'LiamRoe's head bob and the fifty blades rise, catch the red sun and fall into glassy green shadow.

They rose again, but this time the shadow remained. The whole galley disappeared from the sun in the fair blue waters of the English Channel as a thousand tons of galliasse drove at them broadside on.

She was Flemish and foul-bottomed, her sheets paid out on a lee helm so that the westerly squall had caught her and was spinning her leeward on top of them, hurled on by wind pressure on sides, sails and gear. Then the wind caught *La Sauvée* too. Master Ballagh's bottle fell from his hand; the chairs in the poop slid, and the galley heeled, her shrouds whining and the long lattice of her shells spiked and quilled along its 150 feet by the oars, clenched, thrashing or rattling loose. The shadow of the galliasse darkened and the captain jumped, shouting, on the gangway. The oarsmen on the starboard side were on their feet. Spray hissed and then clattered on the bared benches, and for a moment the stentorian voice of O'LiamRoe, sliding with twenty others in the mess of pennants and tenting around the open holds, was heard bellowing: 'The key! The key for the leg irons, ye clod of a Derry-born bladder-worm!'

Stewart, out and gripping the handrail, heard that, and saw that the galliasse, white faces fringing the prow castle, was close-hauling at last, pulling the sheets hard in and bringing up the tiller to head her into the wind. She was a heavy ship, and badly handled. She turned beamside on to the galley and pointed into the wind, her sails shaking, but she was already moving too fast to leeward. The leaping water between the ships shrank and vanished; there was a moment's shudder; and then wood met wood with a grinding scream of a crash. Twenty great oars to starboard stubbed to needles with the impact, and as the top side of *La Sauvée*'s low freeboard gave way, twenty shanks in vengeful hunger closed on blood and muscle within, pinning Christian thief and pagan pirate alike with polished beech and spliced lead. The world stopped as the boats locked; then the *Gouden Roos*, obeying the helm, lurched off as the sea leaped into the hole in *La Sauvée*'s side.

Horror, panic and ignorance held Stewart fast to the ship's side. He saw that the undrilled crew, leaderless, shocked and decimated, had no idea what to do. The bo's'n had vanished. The captain, wet with spray, was clinging hard to the mainmast and mouthing at the heaving galliasse. There was no sign of the Irish party; then the Archer, taking a step on the jumping, slippery deck, saw O'LiamRoe disappearing down the poop ladder and two black-headed Celts capering down the main gangway closing hatchways and hurling the tangle of pulped bunting in the sea.

La Sauvée began to settle. On her port side she was dry and firm yet; on the roll to starboard she took in green sea with a slap and suck. The galliasse, her timbers buffed and splintered, pitched still at their side. The helmsman had brought the *Gouden Roos* up to the wind, but with the impact she had lost all her way. She lay clumsily in stays, helpless to sail out of the galley's hapless path, and the September wind, pranking from side to side, gripped her broad upperworks and began grimly to drive her again, backwards and up to the flank of the stricken galley once more.

The O'LiamRoe, crowbar in hand, appeared for an instant under

Stewart and vanished to starboard into the pit of overturned flesh. It seemed a futile errand of mercy. Ashamed of the thought, Stewart leaped down himself and was belaboured like a log in a millrace. The free men, silent with terror, were fighting towards the single spare boat, followed by the first of the unlocked slaves. As he was dragged, twisting with them, a sea broke and hissed on the rambade. They cowered, and then scattered screaming. For the last time the galliasse overshadowed the clotted and struggling ship.

It was then that the whistle blew. It blew twice, and the second time they heard the order, clear, succinct and calm. '*On va faire voile. Casse trinquet! Timonier, orse!*'

There were just enough sane men left to obey; and Robin Stewart was one of them. With violent purpose they leaped for the running tackle of the furled staysail, high above them. Willing hands unclewed the rope; and in the very throat of all the malignant crab-gods of the ocean, they mustered in fright and foreboding the mighty snap of a tug needed to break the sail from its withies and gather the wind to their rescue. The hemp snaked and crashed as they pulled—and the sail stayed hard-tied to the yardarm.

Stewart, glaring swollen-eyed at the masthead, dragged with the others a second time and a third at the sheet. Nothing moved. The galliasse nudged nearer. To leeward the sea suddenly bobbed with a cluster of heads; then more. The skiff, freed on a starboard roll, fell badly and overturned. The slap and crash of the sea, louder than wind-voice and wood-groan and the air-swallowed scream from the injured, rose to a thunder as the ships neared. Stewart, the burrowed skin white and red off his palms, pulled again in heart-gouging unison in vain.

Round, compact and shining with salt, a scrubby figure whisked up the loose foremast rope, its wind-torn black flying, its unclean hands warping the wind-scoured skies to its chest. Master Thady Boy Ballagh, ollave, poet, professor, the fifteenth and the nippiest, climbed straight to the yardarm, made his way to the peak, and sixty feet up over a listing deck, knife in hand, probed the lashings. He used his blade sparingly and with care; then sliding quickly back to the masthead, gave a signal. They pulled.

With a slithering crack, 400 yards of canvas dropped from the arm, swelled, and went tight. *La Sauvée* shuddered, throwing every last man of her 400 flat. She shuddered; she steadied; then, leaning softly from the wind, the ship raised her broken side from the sea, gathered strength, and heeling round the gross stern of the galliasse, drew tranquilly off. Behind, the *Gouden Roos* began to pick up the swimmers.

Robin Stewart, feeling faint, and with his hands in his armpits, was counting heads. He had just found Piedar Dooly, chopping off leg irons, when a golden head rose from the benches and addressed the red evening sky.

'*Liam aboo!*' screeched Phelim O'LiamRoe, Prince of Barrow and lord of the Slieve Bloom, in princely paean to his fathers.

'*Liam aboo!*' returned his ollave concisely from the yardarm, and like a soiled raindrop, slid down to the deck.

II

Dieppe: The Pitfalls
and the Deer

As to the pitfall of the unlawful hunter; the deer which he
rouses and the deer which he does not rouse come equally to him.

DIEPPE, city of limes, was asleep. On the walls, at the bridge, on
the broad city ports, the watch kept guard. The fishing boats had
moved out. In the river, lanterns flickered where the galleys lay like
whales, prow to quay, and the lighthouse shone over the bar. Inside,
the streets smelt of herring and the new paint still fresh from the
Scottish Queen's visit; here and there an overlooked flag fluttered
darkly, with the de Guise emblem on it.

All these dignitaries had now moved inland. Tomorrow the Irish
guests of the King of France would follow them; but tonight the
comfort of the Porc-épic's mattresses claimed them after the rigours
of the sea, and the windows were dark.

La Pensée, the beautiful house of Jean Ango, late Governor of the
Castle, was not lit; but at least one man there was awake. Unmoving
by the quiet fountains of the terrace, looking down on the moonlit
river through Jean Ango's bowers, glimmering with the marble bones
of Attic deities, Tom Erskine waited without impatience for a visitor.

The uneasy peace lately fallen on Europe had meant hard travelling
and harder talking for Scottish statesmen. Erskine was here now on
his way to Flanders because he was his nation's chief Privy Councillor, and because his common sense was the needle and the
battering ram which Mary of Guise could trust him to use.

Common sense had not brought him out here on the terrace, but
curiosity to discover what path his visitor would take. He lingered in
the mild September night, square, good-tempered, reliable; but like
the artist of quiet movement that he was, the other man arrived without sign or sound. There was somewhere a breath of laughter and a
stirring of cooler air, and a pleasant, familiar voice spoke from the
shadows. 'How delicate, love! Shall we dally?'

12

'Are you there?' Tom Erskine turned quickly, searching the darkness. 'Where are you?'

'Sitting, as it happens, on Clotho's distaff and keeping an eye out for the scissors. One of the rarer benefits of a classical education.' And indeed, on one of the nearer pieces of statuary a dark shadow moved, swung, and dropped lightly to the ground. A cool hand took his arm.

'Enter the wily fox, the widow's enemy. Let's go indoors,' said Crawford of Lymond.

Lymond was masked. Slender in black silk, the bright hair hidden by cap and caul, he suited the room like a piece of Ango's Florentine silver. He pulled off the mask, and Erskine was caught in the heavy blue gaze; saw again the ruthless mouth; the thinly textured fair skin neatly tailored over its bones.

Not for a moment, carrying the Queen Mother's request, had he thought that Lymond would agree. Not for a moment, bringing back Lymond's ultimatum, had he expected the Queen Mother to accept. And yet the absurd relationship, neither of employer and employee nor of allies nor of partners, had been born. Here, reporting his presence as a free agent, was Crawford of Lymond, who would remain in France for the winter of the Queen's visit, and who would tell her as much or as little as he chose of the world of plots, of secrets and of intriguing he had undertaken to enter. On the other hand, the Queen Dowager owed him nothing, and least of all protection if he were caught. It was an arrangement, it appeared, which pleased them both.

Lymond and Tom Erskine had little in common, and their personal exchanges took no longer than the pouring of two cups of the King of France's wine. As they sat, Tom raised his in elaborate salute. 'Welcome to France.'

'Thank you. I gather our excellent Queen Mother arrived safely.'

'Last week. The French King is outside Rouen, waiting to make one of those damned ceremonial entries. She's off to join him, and they'll install her in Rouen for the festivities. Then the whole Court goes south for the winter.'

'While you go to Brussels: there's no justice.' There was a little silence, occasioned by the Special Ambassador wondering, rather despairingly as usual, how much Lymond knew. He was on his way to Brussels and Augsburg to conclude a peace treaty with the Emperor Charles, or with the Queen of Hungary on her absent brother's behalf. It was a treaty not much wanted in Scotland, whose abler mariners liked to be able to raid Flemish galliasses in peace. But under French pressure, the Scottish Governor had agreed; and for that agreement, no doubt, the Queen Dowager of Scotland would receive due reward in due time from France.

13

It was a peace of which the Emperor himself, at Augsburg, was also wary, and of which he would be warier still if he knew that Tom Erskine was coming to him fresh from London, where he had just opened negotiations for a treaty with England, the Emperor's current enemy. No peace treaty had yet been signed between Scotland and her neighbour, only a truce. Erskine could say, hand on heart, at Brussels, that there was no trade or contact between England and Scotland without safe conducts; that the Queen Dowager's visit to France meant nothing more than a mother's natural anxiety to see her daughter the Queen; that his own visits to France now and after this embassy were merely to satisfy himself for the Government as to the welfare of Mary of Scotland.

He hoped to God that Lymond believed so too; from the malice hardly concealed in his face he doubted it. But Lymond himself merely said, 'And Mary Queen of Scots, our illustrious princess?'

'With her mother.' Erskine hesitated to go on, distrusting the other man's tone. In the stiff ceremonies at Dieppe it had been one of the picturesque moments of the Queen Dowager's arrival: the meeting with her child Mary, now seven, cheerful and self-willed after two years in France. Queen and Queen Mother had been in tears; the Dowager's visit was limited, after all, and when she left Mary would still be in France, and in six or seven years would marry the King's heir. She was the reigning Queen of Scotland, and had forgotten most of her Scots.

Lymond said, 'And now, tell me: which of your charming colleagues came with the Queen Mother from Scotland?'

Erskine's face cleared. 'By God, Francis, that's a pack of weasels she has in her train this time . . . the whole Privy Council, pretty nearly. All the rogues she can't trust at home. You'll need to be careful.'

There was a little inlaid spinet in the corner. Lymond had put down his wine; getting up, he wandered over to the instrument and perched before it. 'They won't know me. Who?'

Erskine reeled them off. The Earl of Huntly was amongst them; and Lord Maxwell, and Lord James Hamilton, heir to the Governor of Scotland. He added, watching Lymond, 'And two Douglases. James Douglas of Drumlanrig and Sir George.'

Francis Crawford and the Douglas family were old opponents, and he looked pleased. 'This is promising. Anyone else?'

'A pack of Erskines.' Tom was grinning. His family, father to son, were among the staunchest next the throne. Margaret his wife was here as a lady of honour; Jenny, Lady Fleming, his wife's mother, was the little Queen's governess; his wife's young sisters and brother were her playmates. His own two brothers were in the train, and his father, now invalided and absent, small Mary's guardian since she came to live in France.

He went over the dispositions, and Lymond listened and remarked, 'And with Erskines so plentiful, what am I doing here?'

'Playing the spinet,' said the Special Ambassador. 'Too damned well.'

The neat and tingling flow of notes continued. 'It will cover our voices. None of your friends realize how gifted you are.'

'Practically all of my friends know I can't play on that thing. What else do you want to know? You don't need to be told what the French court is like. It's the most—'

'It's a hand-set maggot mound,' said Francis Crawford. 'I could teach you more than you would want to know about it.' His fingers running over the keys, he spoke without rancour. 'The universities, the prisons, the boudoirs and the brothels, the palaces and the paintings, the serenades, the banquets, the love-making, the hoof and hair of a heretic frying. Bed-talk and knife-talk and whip-talk. I know where it breeds. If there's danger, I'll find it. —I must go.'

Rising at the same time, Erskine controlled his impulse to protest. Lymond had engaged to report his presence in France, and no more; and he had come promptly to his appointment. Tom said, 'Have you been waiting long in Dieppe?'

He caught Lymond's raised brows; but the answer was perfectly matter-of-fact. 'Five hours, that's all.'

Comprehension, like a searing stir in hot water, ran stinging over the skin. 'Christ . . . you didn't come in today with that boat with the hole?'

'Come in?' For a moment Lymond showed genuine feeling. 'I damned nearly paddled in with the thing in my teeth. There was a catastrophic collision in the roads; the tavern flooded; nineteen dead and twenty-five injured; the master a ninny and the comite with enough bhang inside him to float an anvil.'

In his excitement, Erskine strode to the windows and back. 'I saw it. Saw her come in on her ear with the cannon all to port and her anchors rigged abeam, dammit. Rammed by a galliasse, weren't you? Nine-tenths bad seamanship, they said, and one-tenth filthy luck.'

'The *Gouden Roos* thought it was bad luck, I should think,' said Lymond, amused. 'After all, she was paid off to sink us.'

Erskine sat down. 'Are you sure?'

'Yes.'

'Has it occurred to anyone else?'

'I doubt it. You've heard the accepted version of the crash.'

Roused, Tom Erskine's verdict was blunt. 'This Irish masquerade is madness. How can you work if you're being assaulted before you've even begun? Do I take it you are using the name of an actual person?'

'Yes, of course. But one whose appearance is little known. Credit us with a little intelligence.'

15

Lymond's Irish sister-in-law Mariotta would have helped. Erskine exclaimed. 'And so you are proceeding to the French Court to be indoctrinated by the French Crown on how to kick the English out of Ireland.' He broke off. It was, he had always felt, the scheme of a power-drunk idiot. But he did not say so, and received the rare compliment of an explanation.

'Yes. It remains,' said Lymond, 'a simple way of reaching the inner circle unidentified. My guess is that King Henri will allow O'Liam-Roe a long, luxurious stay in which to savour the delights of an alliance with France. I hope so.'

Erskine's voice was still sharper than he knew. 'And what about this attack? You can't ask French protection and have a bodyguard dogging your heels. Who's behind it?'

Lymond's voice was pure malice. 'Won't it be amusing to find out? What do you think the Queen Mother fears for most—her alliances or her life?' He withdrew the bolt from the shuttered windows.

'Without French troops and French money, she thinks Scotland will never fight free from the English.'

'And there is a faction in France, they say, which disapproves of the de Guise family sending good French money abroad. I hope,' said Lymond opening the window, 'that nothing serious occurs. My intentions are purely frivolous.'

Standing beside him, Erskine put a blunt question. 'Why did you come here? Not because the Queen Mother asked it?'

'The Queen Mother,' said Lymond, 'as you and she are well aware, has suggested this entirely as a means of committing me to her party, and is going to be disappointed. She has a hundred informers to hand.'

'And every one of them watched,' said Tom Erskine dryly. 'Including my wife.'

'I am aware,' said Lymond distinctly, 'that I am expected to do nothing in particular but raise the devil with ten pitch candles and a pipe of dead children. But I am prepared to spread my small benignities among my friends. I have time to spare.'

There was a pause, heavier perhaps than either man intended. Then Lymond raised his hand and laid it, unjewelled and unfamiliar, on the Councillor's broad shoulder. 'Go to Flanders and your contracts, and leave the orgies to me.' He withdrew his gaze and turning, slipped over the window-sill. 'Sweet Clotho, where are you?'

The night was dark. Tom Erskine, leaning out, saw the grim goddess suffer a flamboyant embrace; then the shadows moved, and the affronted fates were alone.

*   *   *

Later that same night a watchman, passing the Porc-épic, saw one of its latticed windows glow red. He hammered on the door; the

16

kitchen boys roused the house, and cooks, ostlers and turnspits surged upstairs to The O'LiamRoe's room.

The bed hangings were a whispering curtain of flame, and seams of fire had begun on the panelling. With brooms and carpets and pails they rushed to the bed, the bitter smoke in their eyes, and hurled the flaming cloths wide.

The bed was empty, but for a shrivelled, untenanted nightshirt.

The stabler himself, with Robin Stewart, led the wild search which went on while the fire died. They found Master Ballagh fast asleep in his cupboard bed reeking of aqua vitae; and left him there. They discovered The O'LiamRoe in the loft, curled up in the straw next to Dooly. He viewed with mild surprise the circle of lamplit faces above him, and as the agitated tale unfolded, slipped in his graceful condolences to the stabler. He had felt, he explained, a touch of cold between sheets, and had climbed out to join Piedar Dooly in his nest where, praise be, they were sleeping in no time as cosy as two new-laid eggs. He rose and, wrapped in his salt-splashed frieze cloak, went to look at the damage.

The cross-questioning, the accusations, the polite enquiries went on for an hour between the servants, the innkeeper, the night watch and O'LiamRoe before Stewart finally forced the incident shut and sent everyone off to bed. Two things only had emerged from it. The inn staff were probably guiltless, and were convinced that some wild Irish practice had started the fire. The O'LiamRoe had no idea who started it, and was enjoying the excitement too much to care.

When the throng had left him in his room, alone with a new bed and Thady Boy, aroused at last, to share it with him, Phelim O'Liam-Roe threw back his golden head, yawned, and letting the frieze cloak fall where it would, climbed into bed. The ollave's dark face watched him. 'Saints alive! Was that the one nightshirt you brought to the fair lands of France?'

'True for you. And wasn't it the lucky thing I didn't have it on me at the time? D'you think that was an accident?' said O'LiamRoe from the pillow.

'I do not.'

'Oh, you don't? And,' said the Prince of Barrow, one mild blue eye unexpectedly open, 'did you think the sinking this afternoon was an accident?'

The sweet-stringed timpan hardly bothered to look up. 'I doubt it,' he said, and drawing his outer garments carefully off, rolled them into a ball. 'Your quarrels are your own affair. But I would say there is a lad or two anxious that you should not reach the King of France.'

The Chieftain stretched, clasping his hands behind his uncouth head. 'I was wondering,' he agreed. 'Yet can I think of a single slieveen who would work at it the like of that. Take a peck at me, maybe, with a morsel of steel on a black night; but it's mortal lazy the worst of them are in the Slieve Bloom.'

'What about the English?' suggested Thady.

'True for you. They're the boys for being uncivil at sea. But I think,' said O'LiamRoe, grinning quietly on the pillow, 'that the English would rather have me on their side, and alive, than two rows of teeth on the underside of a boat. How would you fancy a free stay in England as well?' And as the ollave shrugged, Phelim added, 'Come here, lad.'

Slowly, Thady Boy approached the bed. O'LiamRoe leaned on one elbow, and for a moment his blue eyes studied the dark, self-contained face of his secretary. Then he said, 'Regretting you took the post, is it?'

'Not yet.'

'You are so, Master Ballagh. A spruce, tender prince of a master the like of a dead sheep for quietness would suit your book better, would he not?'

The ollave did not move. 'Are you turning me off?' he said.

'God save you, no,' said O'LiamRoe hospitably. 'Would I live with one eye? It's no secret that I haven't a word of French and my English sprains its elbow now and then in the rush. Stay by all means if you want.'

The ollave's attentive face relaxed. He turned, and shying his coat neatly into a chair, continued to undress. 'If Piedar Dooly has managed for twenty years, I can subsist, surely, for a matter of months,' he said.

'Piedar Dooly's a born liar. Never look for a true word out of a man with his two front teeth crossed. It's a poor omen when his very dentures are scandalized with the tales of him. Did you hear his latest?'

'Was it worth hearing?'

'It was, too. At the time of the fire, our Piedar heard someone open a window, and he cast about outside afterwards for traces. You know the false sea they're putting up in the market-place?'

'I remember.'

'Our inflaming friend in a hurry did not. He fell into it, and left great muddy footprints all up the street until Dooly lost him.'

'If he lost him, it was hardly worth telling.'

'True for you, except for this thing: the footprints were of a man lacking the right heel.'

'Or with his heel hurt?'

'If you had set fire to the bedcurtains of a guest of the King of France and were running away, there would be a time or two when even a sore heel would hit the ground; and his did not. I wonder,' said O'LiamRoe thoughtfully, 'why he didn't just stab me outright, now.'

18

'Because you weren't there?' suggested the ollave, with a certain acidity.

'I have a notion,' said O'LiamRoe comfortably, 'that it was a fright only they were hoping to give me,' and turning over, he closed his eyes.

There was silence. Thady Boy brooded. Then he scratched his dusty curls, ran a soot-blackened hand over his chin; considered, clearly, having a wash and thought better of it; and then, lifting up the ball of his jerkin, delved into a recess and brought out a bottle of spirits. He glanced across at O'LiamRoe. O'LiamRoe was fast asleep.

'And devil the splash of fright there is on you, you great marmalade puss,' said he. 'And for an Irishman, you have the sorrow's own want of common sense. So.'

And he blew out the candles.

*   *   *

The next day at breakfast, they had flattering news. A Court dignitary was arriving that morning to escort them, with Stewart, to Rouen. O'LiamRoe was pleased and interested. He had already admired the inn, the food and the Archer, whose padded silver and white, with spotless collar, fine hose and soft riding boots filled out a figure far from robust.

No thought of his own attire, clearly, had crossed O'LiamRoe's cloudless mind. The carpetbags, when pulled out to the linings, had produced one change of clothes; but though whole and clean, the Prince of Barrow's dress was as bizarre as before; and Mr. Ballagh was in threadbare black and one or two smears from his breakfast. Only Robin Stewart appreciated that their appearance and manners constituted an emergency, and knew that Lord d'Aubigny had been called in to deal with it.

Before he arrived, O'LiamRoe was asking eager questions. Would his lordship, for example, have the English?

'Yes. He's a Scotsman by origin,' had said Stewart painstakingly. 'Of the same surname as myself.' He wondered how much about John Stewart of Aubigny he could suitably tell. That he was a cultivated gentleman who had once captained the King's Garde de Corps of a hundred Scottish men-at-arms, but was now a Gentleman in Ordinary of the King's Chamber, with a company of sixty lances to his name?

John Stewart had once been his own captain. He was still, in a sense his superior—on duty the Archer was answerable, more often than not, to the behests of the King's Gentlemen. So he could have told the fools more than they wanted to know of this Stewart, of royal name, whose ancestors had been Kings of Scotland. One branch of the family had remained in Scotland, and as lords of

Lennox, had been among the greatest in the land. The other had married in France—powerful marriages, which made John Stewart now the relative, if only distantly, of both the Queen of France and the King's mistress, Diane. And they had served France brilliantly in war, captaining the King's Bodyguard for generations and giving France a marshal as famous as Bayard: services rewarded with position, money and land.

All this, the Great John, present Lord d'Aubigny, had inherited, and it had done him as much good as Robin Stewart's old suit of armour. For his brother the Earl of Lennox, having failed to marry the Queen Dowager and obtain the power he wanted in Scotland, had defected to her enemy England, with 10,000 stolen French crowns in his pocket, and had thereby forfeited all his Scottish estates. Brother Matthew, as it happened, had come out of all that little the worse, having had the forethought to marry Margaret, King Henry VIII's niece, which brought him wealth and asylum in England, and the promise that one day he would govern Scotland on Henry's behalf.

But the King of France, where young Lennox had grown up, had been in no mood to be charitable, especially about the lost money; and since he could not touch Lennox, had seized his brother, John Stewart of Aubigny, instead, and thrown him into prison, deprived of office and honours. From there the present King had released him, on coming to the throne. The incarceration, in Stewart's view, had not done his former captain much good.

'A Scotsman!' O'LiamRoe was saying. 'Then roll out the Latin, boy! Air your astronomy! We mustn't let down the old country before the great chief ones, with the silver buttons like mill wheels on their shirts!'

Very soon after that, Lord d'Aubigny arrived, very creditably got up in blistered velvet, with a curled beard, and a diamond or two, and a neat, small cap on his head, sewn with pearls. With him were two young noblemen and a priest.

Stewart smelled the scent even before they came in, and knew which of the boys had come. They had amused themselves dressing in full court style, with their fans; as the introductions were made he saw O'LiamRoe's eyebrows shoot up. The priest, master of the hydrography school, started to bow and considerately stopped; the young men, with joyous accord, bowed three times each, right knee bent, bonnet low in the left hand, gloves gripped at the stomach in the right.

O'LiamRoe smiled widely. Lord d'Aubigny sketched a bow, advanced steadily and kissed the Prince of Barrow on both cheeks.

'Man, you smell nice,' said The O'LiamRoe appreciatively as they sat. 'I see how it is. The O'Donnell, God save him, came back from France the very same, tasselled like a cushion and with a particular smell. Excuse me.' And grasping his secretary, he drew him into the circle. 'My travelling ollave. You'll forgive him. He had the manners all bled out of him in the water, and is dead sober on me today besides. He can talk Greek itself when he has the drop in: I got him to sing at the milking and every cow in it gave off pure alcohol.'

Lord d'Aubigny was not quick-witted. For a moment he was wordless, the big handsome face reddening under the pearls. Behind, the two gallants were scarlet; and it was the priest who stepped in, his eye twinkling. 'We are all glad to see you; and sorry to hear of the shocking voyage into harbour.'

'Shocking! A Flemish galliasse. You can't trust them. Criminally poor seamanship. Letters have been sent,' said Lord d'Aubigny sharply, to reduce the levity he sensed behind him and suspected in front. 'The King himself will make amends.'

'Ah, no apologies,' said O'LiamRoe, his oval, soft-whiskered face alight with freckles and good humour. 'If you'd seen Thady Boy saving the navy: a kick, step and a lep and his hocks over the yardarm like a handful of syboes. . . .'

Master Ballagh stood for a good deal; but he brought that to a halt. He said sourly, 'The O'LiamRoe is sensible of course, my lord, of the honour done him by his grace the King in inviting him to France. Ireland is not a country of wealth naturally. Our crops are few and our roads are bad, so that—'

'—Damn you!' said O'LiamRoe with surprise. 'There's a fine bothar road to the Slieve Bloom alone that two cows would fit on, one lengthwise and the other athwart.'

'—But the Prince of Barrow is as consequential and scholarly a man as you would be hard put to it to see in a city. And I am not saying so,' added Thady painstakingly, 'for the pay he gives me, for you would quarter yourself looking for it did you drop it from between your finger and thumb on a white sheet at midday itself.'

There was an explosion, hardly covered, from the young men, but Lord d'Aubigny grimly persevered. 'You and your principal know a little, I take it, of the present Court of France? You will be presented shortly to King Henri, and to the Queen who is, of course, Italian born. There are five young children. . . .' He described, as plainly as he could, the public faces of the Crown and its suite, without a hint that the King's wife and his mistress were at loggerheads; that the King's friend the Constable supported the Queen; and that everyone distrusted the de Guises, who held the King's love and most of his higher offices apportioned between them, and at altar, campaign or council table were first with their advice.

'It is,' said Lord d'Aubigny, 'a gathering of people who cannot fail to impress you. A blossoming culture. A taste for beauty and

21

considerable wealth. And consequently a certain state; a formality; a feeling for polite usage of some sort—'

'We are not,' said a bored voice from behind him, 'permitted to duel'.

'—And the wearing of hair on every part of the face,' said its neighbour suavely, 'is not now acceptable.'

Without looking round, his lordship went on. 'Fashions change, of course. But the King himself decides style and colour for his gentlemen, and it is usual for those at Court to conform. Please do not hesitate, if in need of a tailor, to seek my advice.'

As an appeal to the aesthetic leanings of O'LiamRoe, it was a dead failure. 'Ah, faith, is he one of those?' said the Chieftain with pity. 'The late King Henry VIII of England thought the same: that every drop of us should dress, talk and pray like the English, and shave off the face hair as well. It was a grand thing for my father that the hair grew on him like wire; and did he shave off the moustaches at night, there they were, glorious as ever, by morning.'

A brief silence fell, honouring this speech. O'LiamRoe, unaffected by it, glanced round. 'Are you not for making some remark, Thady?' And to the priest: 'The tongue on him is green-moulded for want of exercise. There's nothing he'd like better than a word on the hydrography.'

The ollave's black face turned, stamped with affront.

'Hydrography, is it? It's hydrography we were wanting last night, God help us, and the smoke curling like an old, dried cow out of your nightshirt. I'm clean out of my nerves entirely, with your burnings and your sinkings; and "talk here" and "talk there" on top of it.'

'Have I offended you?' said O'LiamRoe, looking narrowly at his ollave.

'Burnings!' It was Lord d'Aubigny's exclamation.

'You have, so.'

'But a small sup of wine, now, would put the extremities back into your bloodstream, Thady?'

'It might, so,' said the ollave, sulkily.

'Burnings? What's all this, Stewart?'

So, to the Archer's chagrin, the news of the night's unfortunate incident was prematurely unfolded, while Lord d'Aubigny's handsome, high-coloured face set in extreme irritation. The fat fool and the thin fool, with their scarecrow wardrobe, were clearly of no consequence. The accident, obviously, had been slight; the guests of the King of France had been discomfited in no way that mattered. He cast a chastening glance at Stewart, uttered a few routine words of regret and began to move. The party was actually on its feet, its baggage collected, scores paid and horses engaged to take them to Rouen, when Lord d'Aubigny recalled Madame Baule.

He stopped dead. 'Before we leave, O'LiamRoe, we've a call to make first. There's a countrywoman of yours in the house, a charming lady who's going to Rouen for the Entry. She hoped to see you before you left.'

'Oh?' said O'LiamRoe.

'Madame Baule, she's called. Married a Frenchman years ago—he's dead—and keeps a most unusual house in Touraine. A delightful person, an original; cherished, I assure you, in every well-bred home she visits. But of course, you know her,' said Lord d'Aubigny, sweeping the two Irishmen incontinently into a side passage.

'Do I?' said O'LiamRoe weakly.

'From the lady, I certainly assumed so. Here, I think.—Yes, the lady herself certainly knew all about you. Come along.' And he scratched at the door. It opened, and he pushed the Prince of Barrow inside. 'Here he is: The O'LiamRoe, lord of the Slieve Bloom, and his secretary. Madame Baule, late of Limerick. You two, I'm sure, are acquainted.'

Had he known it, Lord d'Aubigny was being amply rewarded for his embarrassments of a short time before.

On the wreathed marmalade figure in the doorway fell the pinlike scrutiny of two round, pale eyes in a firm, weatherbeaten face packed with teeth. There was an impression of piled, plaited hair, caterpillar-heaped with ornaments, of a square neck filled with nooses of jewellery. A broad hand gripped his lordship's silvery sleeve. 'Boyle!' screeched a voice high as a bat's, thin, jolly, encouraging. 'Boyle! You can call yourselves d'Aubignys all you want, John, my darling, but keep your expatriate, hand-licking tongue off a good Irish name. . . . O'LiamRoe!'

'Madam,' said O'LiamRoe politely, and quite subdued.

The ropes swung and jangled. 'You've the sorrow's own whiskers on you, have you not?'

'There's worse at the back of me,' said O'LiamRoe apologetically. 'It's two great-six-nights since I was clipped.'

'Hum! I would never forget those whiskers,' said Mistress Boyle in a light scream. 'They would put nightmares on you, the moustaches alone. O'LiamRoe, we have never met, but here's my hand to you. You may kiss me.'

It was a sight; and Robin Stewart, had he been there, would have been afraid to see the woman hooked there for ever, in uncurried skeins round his clavicles, had they not come suddenly apart, Mistress Boyle saying with composure, 'Whirroo, that's Irish blood you've brought with you past the ninth wave. . . . We were worn thin as a cat's ear waiting for it . . . *o'n aird tuaid tic in chabair*, as the old tale has it. And who's the *cailleach-chearc* there at your back?'

'Ah. . . . 'Tis a bard out of Banachadee. My little, weeshy ollave, Mistress Boyle.'

'Death alive! What's your name, man?' she screamed at Thady Boy. The secretary edged away. 'Ballagh, mistress.'

'One of the tinker tribes, surely. And you take no offence at the name *cailleach-chearc*?'

'Buddha,' volunteered Thady Boy unexpectedly, 'was born in an egg. A fine duty, *a mhuire*, to lay on a henwife. The henwives are queens and kings, to be sure, in that country.'

'But that country, *a mhic*, was not Ireland.'

'Indeed, when was a god born that way in Ireland?' said Thady politely. 'With the loud-mouthed hens there are, and the folk with their two keen ears, one engaged for the hen and the other for the boil on the cooking water?'

She screamed like a kittiwake. 'Oh! Oh! You have a sharp knife at your hip here, O'LiamRoe, and God attend you; for it's the quick tongue and the clever tongue that's all these poor French worship, the heathens, and heaven knows the Leinster pudding-brains that have shamed me this year. Sit and tell me of home. Is your mother well?'

So, innocently, was ushered in a formidable interrogation on the social history of Limerick and Leix. Stewart of Aubigny, half-listening, thought that between them, the two seemed to know more of genealogy and gynaecology both than any Scotsman would admit to. He had known Mistress Boyle for many years; did not dream of stopping her as she worried O'LiamRoe unstintedly about next, his corn, his fishings and his cattle. The Chieftain's answers were quite cheerful, even when she went so far as to question them.

'The Cross o' Christ about us,' said Mistress Boyle at length, sinking back in her chair. 'But the great, gorgeous butterfly you'll be among those quiet worker bees up at Court.'

'Not so quiet,' said Lord d'Aubigny, reasserting himself. 'Ante-chamber's full of Scotsmen, arguing like the damned. Half of them have seen Mason already.'

'Mason?'

'Sir James Mason, the English Ambassador. That small girl will be lucky if the Scottish throne waits for her to grow up. There are some of her mother's nobles who would prefer a fine post under England to a shabby one under a Scottish queen. Are you uncomfortable, O'LiamRoe?'

'No, no,' said the Chief, sitting up quickly. 'Only there is a kind of glitter in my head that has come straight off my eyeballs. Is there a dryad in the room?'

A woman had come in from her chamber. All her life, she had made men dumb by her presence, and she was young yet. Pausing, not shy, she stood by the rain-drenched window, and you could see she was Irish as a *Murrúghach*—not the wide-shouldered, fair

Milesian, but dark and neat-boned, with neck and shoulders a single stem for an oval face, wide at the cheekbones and light-eyed, with the black hair piled in pillows and coils about her crown and ears, and on the nape of her neck and down her back. She was dressed in dark blue, with no jewels; and when she saw them all on their feet, curt-seyed to Mistress Boyle and Lord d'Aubigny, and stood waiting again.

Stewart of Aubigny, his fingertips together, watched her with a connoisseur's eye. Thady Boy, liverish and morose, stared, unloosing his dark, stubbled jaw. Nor did O'LiamRoe acquire any pretensions to grace, but he rose, and his long-lashed blue eyes were wider and steadier than before.

'Ah, the devil, bad end to the girl!' screeched Mistress Boyle, spinning round, and ropes swinging, skirts swaying, she pounced on the newcomer, her face hot with delight. 'Pay no heed to them, Oonagh. It's a party of Irish come to Court; the very same kind of silly fowl you left in Donegal. You're not to look twice at them. Gentlemen, my niece Oonagh O'Dwyer, over from Ireland to stay with her old aunt awhile and pick the flower of the French Court for a husband if I have my way. Oonagh, my child, The O'LiamRoe, Chief of the Name—ah, don't curtsey too close, you'll step on his whiskers . . . and Mr. Ballagh, his secretary. You should hear him. He can rhyme rats to death like Senchan Torpest himself.'

With a soft flush of blue wool, the girl sat, her calm gaze on the Irishmen, and said in Gaelic, speaking impartially between them: 'They have been sparse in the woods, the ollaves, for this time past. Is the season on us again?'

With the change of language, the warmer impulses of chatter were halted. In a little silence, Master Ballagh coughed, and as O'LiamRoe glanced at him he plumped down, settling his shiny trunk hose in his chair, and said politely in English, 'The ratio, now I think of it, is one ollave per inhabited and manured quarter of ground. Do you miss them, it may be that the other conditions are lacking.'

The young woman's light eyes turned to O'LiamRoe. 'The Prince of Barrow, as I heard it, had a bard called Patrick O'Hooley.'

'You heard right,' said O'LiamRoe composedly. ''Tis like the *Birach-derc*, now. Put Patrick O'Hooley on a boat and show him the blessed Saint Peter himself, and it would stretch four stout men with hooks to lift the lid of his eye.'

She was contemptuous. 'He gets seasick.'

'He does, too, and him a bard only, without lawful learning but his own intellect; whereas Master Ballagh here is a comely professor of the canon, a stream of pleasing praise issuing from him, and a stream of wealth to him. But would you grudge it, and the epigrams pouring off him like a man straight from the Inishmurray sweating-house?'

The talk was straying in these dangerous shoals when Robin Stewart came to the door, seeking permission to borrow or buy replacements for O'LiamRoe's saddlery. On top of sheer old age and neglect, the salt air of the journey had completed its ruin; and in its present state no one at all could travel to Rouen.

Thankfully, Lord d'Aubigny left, taking O'LiamRoe with him, and the Irish accents rolled back along the passage, giving an untrammeled account of some fantasy-life of his horse harness. Mistress Boyle pulled in Robin Stewart and shut the door. 'Come in, for the sake of God, and the two of you tell me something of that champion of the Slieve Bloom, that would fetch his price cut into two hairy hearthrugs and cured. I heard tell he was queer, but not as terrible queer as all that.'

She had poured them wine, and Thady Boy, working diligently, was almost restored to his normal condition. He relaxed. 'You've seen him. What else is there? It was O'LiamRoe's misfortune to be born a prince with a smart lot of followers instead of a little, mad-like professor with a wife and a pension and a shining day-long circle of pupil-philosophers; not a one over twelve. I met him at his castle, a great slab of wet rock with rats in it. He will talk you dry on any subject you wish; it's all in his head. And, of course, he is the unhandiest thing in life. Not one finger of him is on speaking terms with the next.'

Stewart grinned. Thady Boy raised his wine in faltering salute to the girl, whose gaze had not moved from his face, and slammed it back on the chair arm as Mistress Boyle said, 'You are nippy enough yourself, we were hearing, and a terrible smart fellow up a rope. Are they putting games on you, in the long training you have, now?' And she shrieked with laughter. The girl did not smile.

'And teaching us to run like the wind too; 'tis fundamental', said Thady Boy sourly. 'And when serving such as the Prince of Barrow, it would be a great help and comfort to be invisible as well.'

Oonagh O'Dwyer got up. Silent as a cat, she walked over and removed from Thady Boy's lax hands his dry cup. 'Why come to France with him?' she said. 'To set your epigrams pimping for a little free drink?'

'Free, is it?' said Thady. 'I thought I was paying for it.'

''Tis a little polished living the fellow is after,' said Mistress Boyle comfortably.

'Polished living! With The O'LiamRoe stuck on me, and the jaws of him going like the leper clappers?'

'Ballagh's here for asylum,' said Robin Stewart, grinning. 'He'll tell you he's come for the money, but it's woman trouble, mark me.'

'And O'LiamRoe, has he woman trouble too?' asked Oonagh O'Dwyer of Thady.

Mr. Ballagh was exasperated. 'Have I the second sight? I was one week at his castle, and there was no woman in it barring his ma and the kitchens; and two weeks at sea when he passed his time on his two knees splicing ropes like the wind in the barley fields. I never caught him so much as wink at the figurehead.'

The older woman sat back in her seat, chuckling; but Oonagh O'Dwyer spoke like an ancient goddess in her black hair. 'He doesn't mind being laughed at?'

'Not if he can laugh first.'

'Well, cock's blood,' said Robin Stewart with annoyance. 'He was asked over to discuss ways and means of throwing the English out of Ireland. Is it a joke, just?'

'Oh, he's got a brain in him. He'll talk all you want,' said the ollave, wildly airy. 'And maybe the King'll get one or two good ideas off him, if he can stand him at all. But first and last and in the middle, The O'LiamRoe plans to treat himself to a small private survey on how the rich live . . . and it paid for by somebody else.'

Mistress Boyle shook with laughter and Robin Stewart was delighted. But the black-haired girl turned on her heel and walked out of the room.

III

Rouen: The Nut without Fruit

Thou shall not bind anyone to pay in kine . . . who has not kine;
thou shalt not bind anyone to pay in land, who is wandering; . . .
thou shalt not bind a naked person to pay in clothes unless he
has got raiment: it is as a nut without fruit to adjudicate in
this manner.

VULNERABLE as a crab at the moult, The O'LiamRoe rode,
mild, unwashed and hoary, into the splendid bosom of Rouen.
And by the grace of all the old and mischievous gods, his arrival, with
Thady Boy Ballagh and Piedar Dooly, passed that day unremarked
by the townspeople. For four days, the Sacred Majesty of the Most
Christian King of France, the most magnanimous, powerful and
victorious King Henri, Second of that name, would enter his Norman
capital for the first time in the three years of his reign, and the
preparations for that joyous Entry had worn the Rouennois into
tatters.

They were lucky to miss the Court, which had blocked the Rouen
road all that morning, settling into the Priory of Bonne-Nouvelle
across the river to sit out the days till the Entry. Lord d'Aubigny, who
had escorted the Irish party from Dieppe and last night had secured
them an unexceptionable inn for their comfort, took his leave there
with his lances to join the gentlemen about the King, leaving Robin
Stewart with his small retinue to see O'LiamRoe safely lodged in the
city.

They had reached the suburbs in the plain of Grandmont when a
whale came out of a house on a trolley and crossed the road, with
four men pushing it. Every horse in Robin Stewart's party snubbed
its owner and O'LiamRoe's mare reared. The Chieftain was nothing
if not a good rider. He bore her down, the horsecloth all over him,
and instantly bestowed his fond attention on the situation. 'Dhia! I
see you have a great care for your fishing industry, to improve them
with wooden legs. Will you look at that, Thady?'

Mr. Ballagh leaned over. The whale at their feet, its plaster sides
sweating in the sun, clapped open its jaws and a jet of Seine water
hit the air. The horses, thoroughly shaken, plunged and danced to

the tune of Scots swearing, and O'LiamRoe this time very neatly fell off.

It was a scene of unqualified extravagance. Before them lay the lit walls of Rouen veiled with rigging; the crowded bridge and the yellow, slapping water; but the city was all but masked by the white canvas of tents and marquees sprung like land-ships on the near bank before them. A half-finished pavilion covered with crescents and fleurs-de-lis stood by the roadside, crawling with joiners, and behind, a square of horse lines was busy with men, and a knot of six or seven soaked geldings being rubbed down. Someone had left a streaky chariot in the mud, a trident stuck by a wheel; and inside one of the tents, where a city archer gossiped on guard, a dozen fresh green canvas fishtails were drying in a row.

The sandy mud of the banks boiled with dripping men and small boats; the islands were messy with erections; and somewhere a rather poor choir was practising hard. The air was filled, like birds flying, with shouts and hammer blows and arguing voices, and at the entrance to the bridge a woman halfway up a ladder with a bow under her arm was screeching at a painter curled on a pediment high above, decorating a niche. The four men, no doubt regretting their exuberance, had disappeared with the whale to the water. Leaving his horse blithely loose, and with never a glance at his surroundings, O'Liam-Roe followed.

Robin Stewart, of the King's Bodyguard of Scots Archers, gave a hard-pressed sigh and turned to share his despair with his bowmen. Instead, the acid, droopbrowed face of the ollave caught his eye.

'*France, mère des arts, des armes et des lois*,' observed Thady Boy, without altering a muscle. 'I take it you wish to enter Rouen. Unless you divert O'LiamRoe's mind instantly, he will feed on his whale like a prawn on the seethings of drowned men.' Robin Stewart opened his mouth.

But the diversion came from another direction. Over the bridge before them, two women came riding, satins fluttering and furs blowing; and the servants mounted behind were all in a livery Stewart knew as well as he knew the redheaded owner in front. It was Jenny Fleming.

Janet, Lady Fleming, was pretty, and Scottish, and a widow. She was a natural daughter of King James IV of Scotland. She was also royal aunt and governess of Mary Queen of Scots, whom she had brought to France two years before as a little girl of five, and whose mentor she had been ever since.

'Governess' as applied to Jenny Fleming was the most irrational of terms. Mary had her teachers for every art and science, and her faithful Janet Sinclair for nurse. Jenny, who could govern nothing, and least of all herself, was her companion in mischief. A king her father, an earl her grandfather, her dead husband a great and wealthy Scots baron, she had been born like a honeycomb moth into silk and soft living; and despite seven children, had preserved in her thirties the vivid, autocratic and expensive sparkle of her youth.

Now, leaving her escort by the bridge, she plunged down with her horse to the shore, her companion following. She waved to Robin Stewart as she passed and Stewart flushed and waved back, and wondered who the quiet, plump young girl behind her might be. He did not know Margaret Erskine.

'A whale! Does it swim? Does it spout? May I look at it?'

The enormous creature lay in the shallow water. As its attendants grinned and chattered, an impossible jaw dropped and the whiskers of O'LiamRoe rose, tadpole-like, from the Leviathan depths. He bowed, and smiled like a sickle. ''Tis better still inside: the Eighth Wonder surely, but a small bit damp for the very Rose of Jericho like yourself.'

She laughed at him, her firm, dimpled face sparkling. 'You're the Irishman!'

'One of them. The other's behind you.'

She turned. The unkempt figure of Thady Boy Ballagh stood gloomily waiting. 'He's angry. What's he angry about?' she said.

'He wants to get to Rouen and start his drinking. But there was a serious situation here, will you note, to be dealt with first. . . . You're a Scotswoman, surely. Do you stay here?'

Jenny was alight with mischief; had been joyous with excitement from her flaming hair to her cork-soled shoes since she arrived. She opened her mouth, but Margaret Erskine's quiet voice forestalled her. 'We stay at Court. Perhaps we shall have the pleasure of seeing you there. Mother, we must go.'

'Yes, but we must introduce ourselves first. You are O'LiamRoe— I can tell. And this? Aren't there three of you?'

'The richest soil,' said Mr. Ballagh's cutting voice from behind, 'is known for its three weeds. An old Irish saying. You will excuse us. We are expecting an audience with the King.'

A square body; a quiet voice; brown eyes in a plain, country-woman's face—Margaret Erskine, twice-married at twenty and with a son of her own, controlled her mother as no one had done since her father died. She drew her now from this dangerous amusement as she had done many another; and gave no hint, as she and Jenny remounted, and called greetings, and moved off, that she knew whom she was facing.

The O'LiamRoe barely watched them go. He turned, rubbing his hands, to Thady Boy. 'Is it not like the Great Fair of Carman, which the forty-seven kings came to?'

'Would it strike you that the kings now and then ate?' said the ollave. 'Here's Master Stewart waiting for you like Job, and Piedar Dooly with the eyes in his face set with glassing bands. And where will you be if the King sends and you are not yet in your other frieze cloak?'

'This is—' began O'LiamRoe, and broke off, mildly annoyed. 'There's a powerful lot of fussing about the clothes on me.'

'Faith, well,' said Thady Boy patiently. 'But it's a prince he's expecting, man; not a Water Sheerie.' And they set off side by side to the horses, leaving the riverbank, the whale and the four men, one of whom, as any inquisitive passer-by might see, had no heel to one foot.

*　　　*　　　*

The party from Ireland, it was understood, was to be struck by the magnificence of the King of France, and by the wealth and loyalty of his subjects, as a prelude to any personal talks which might follow. So a bedroom and a parlour had been put at their disposal in the Croix d'Or, a large new inn off the Place du Marché; and that, as Robin Stewart remarked, was just about worth the monthly returns of Notre Dame, accommodation being what it was at an Entry.

He saw them settled in before leaving for Bonne-Nouvelle over the bridge. They had three days to wait in Rouen before the festivities. He had given up thinking too much about their habits and their clothes. He had been told to come each day and look after them, show them the sights, and fulfil their reasonable wishes. When the Entry was over, they would move with the Court to its winter quarters and the serious business of the visit would no doubt begin.

Robin Stewart, who above all things was fascinated by success, found no particular enjoyment in handling his Irishmen. He introduced them to the innkeeper, made Piedar Dooly acquainted with the kitchens, and left. As he rode out of the street a Gentleman of the Bedchamber rode into it, bearing a message for Phelim O'LiamRoe, Prince of Barrow, from His Most Christian Majesty Henri II of France. He welcomed the party, in the heartiest terms, to the hospitable shores of France, and invited The O'LiamRoe to visit His Majesty at noon that day in the Priory of Bonne-Nouvelle, *dressed for tennis.*

'Dear God,' said Thady Boy Ballagh, when the courtly messenger had bowed himself out; and lowered his round form on the bed.

There had already been a remarkably sharp argument about what to do with the half-footed man: O'LiamRoe allowed that without proof they could make no accusations, but had decided in the end that Piedar Dooly might well be asked to keep an eye from time to time on the maimed Jonah and his whale. And now—'Dear God,' said Thady Ballagh, 'you can barely walk as it is in that lather of

31

saffron and pig's hair you've got on. How the tatteration will you lep about with a racquet, and those leggings, and the little wee ball that's in it?'

The sun, bright for autumn still, fell on O'LiamRoe's head as he stood at their parlour window looking down. Heads hooded and bare passed and repassed below; a scarlet plume in a man's cap tossed, and satin gleamed; then white gauze and blue velvet from a woman's head and cloak as she passed with her servant. A cart went by, full of beer kegs, and a maid with her trailing skirt black-wet came along from the fountain with a pail in one hand. A man strolled past and leaned on the doorpost opposite, stroking his black beard.

'Ah, you're a faint-heart,,Thady Boy. If a man can give a breeze-fly a clap in a byre, he can smite a great baby's plaything like that. But it's a strange, heathen way to welcome a guest.'

'He's offering you the privilege of a friendly meeting before the formal courtesies,' said his secretary patiently. 'Dress as neat as you can, for the sake of us all, and stay outside the nets streaming flattery like a honey cane on the hot roof of the world.'

'Look at this,' said O'LiamRoe, instead of answering. Outside, the bearded man had moved. Taking off his plain black brimmed hat, he scratched a head of thick dark hair, while his gaze roved the roof-tops with idle vagueness; the sun, patched with stack-shadows, fell on his opaque white skin and straight nose, and the black plangent eyebrows. He had a short, white coat, plainly cut and showing dark full sleeves and a coarse doublet under; but they lay on a big, heavy-shouldered form vaguely familiar. Bad drawings of the man were everywhere, and the coins in their two purses had his likeness.

'It's the King,' said Thady Boy. 'No, it can't be.'

'Then it's his double,' said O'LiamRoe.

There was silence, then a crooning sound broke from Thady Boy. 'It is so,' he said. 'Of course. The terrible show on Wednesday they're so full of. Was there not to be a chariot all done up with the double of the King and his family for the procession?'

He was right. Looking closely, you could see that a rough likeness had been emphasized by the exact trim of hair and beard; the man was a natural for the part. Unaccountably, O'LiamRoe was ruffled. 'I'd have said it was damned dangerous to have two kings in a hare-brained country like this one.'

The man darkly preening in the doorway, if he had had notions of practising a kingly fantasy, had quickly abandoned it. A child had hopped round the corner, a girl of seven perhaps, and flung herself with audible grief on her father. They could not hear what she said, but the black-haired man, rehatted, bent hastily and shook her, and as the ear-piercing whine continued, seized her arm and hauled her

32

off with the look of all fathers with publicly importunate young. Of the regal bearing of a moment since, there was no trace.

'Thady Boy, you are right,' said O'LiamRoe. 'And you are maybe worth your hire to me after all, for all the expense you are. Let you go downstairs and have a sup with Piedar, and I shall see what cloth I can put on my back for a game with those bloodsucking clegs in their gold lace, bad cess to them. Is he good?'

'Who?'

'King Henri. Is he a fair man with a ball?'

'Middling good. He's the best athlete in the kingdom, or thereby,' said Thady Boy cruelly, and went out.

*   *   *

He did his adequate best. Since he left the Slieve Bloom, O'Liam-Roe had never looked so memorably neat. The saffron tunic abandoned, he had sent out for breech hose, brought in at Thady's back, and a holland shirt, and a doublet of near fit and bold colour. Not to waste money on slippers, he had pulled his half boots on top, but cleaned, and had got a small cap with a feather which sat flatly on his combed yellow head. Only the beard, unregenerately floating, hinted at the rebel inside the silk cords.

When the latch rattled, he thought it was Ballagh. Cursing under his breath, his hat under his arm and cloak over it, he strode to open the door. He was very late, and the King's Gentleman, back on the hour, had been waiting some time for him below.

On his threshold stood Oonagh O'Dwyer.

O'LiamRoe stood still without speaking, the latch in his hand. It was his visitor who showed her surprise, unexpected colour flooding her brown skin and revealing the light, limpid eyes. Then she said shortly, 'It's wonderfully grand you are this day. I feel enough of a prostitute as it is, without standing side by side with you on your doorstep. Will you let me pass?'

She was alone; something unheard of in a young woman of standing. He shut the door, stood still as she marched past, and made no comment until she turned to face him. 'I am not in the habit of doing this,' she said.

'It is not a bad habit, now it's started,' he said. 'If you confine it to one person.'

It was the worst line he could have taken; he recognized it instantly. Her lips went hard, her body tautened; and for a moment he expected a blow. It did not come, but when she spoke he realized that in her mind she had closed a human relationship and opened a business meeting.

'I have just come from Bonne-Nouvelle. My aunt is there with a friend who is in the Queen's train. I have a word from her.'

33

'Have you so?' He did not offer her a seat.

They were of a height and otherwise utterly in contrast: the hand-fuls of hair under her hood were wood-black where his were tortoise-shell to the pellicle. She looked him straight in the eye, and her small, round mouth curled. 'They are an idle cageful of mockingbirds; always fresh for a new victim.'

He knew then. His bearing relaxed a little, and he leaned back against the painted panelling, his blue eyes attentive on hers. 'Let them laugh till it sends the Adam's apples on them up and down like cerbottana balls, my dear. It won't hurt me.'

Her strong, soft brows stayed level. 'However, you have spent some money on yourself, I see, this day?'

'Yes,' said O'LiamRoe calmly. 'That was a mistake. I am thinking that I shall just change back to the saffron. Is there an ostrich of your acquaintance would like a tail feather?'

She ignored the flourish of his hat. 'It does not affect me, O'LiamRoe, one way or the other. I came to tell you that the Household are having sport with you. You will get a summons that is not from the King.'

He smiled a little, among the flosslike whiskers. 'The like of an appointment to meet his double?'

'How did you know?'

He turned from her wide eyes, and gestured outside. 'He stood there for a while to get our view. A dark man with a beard.'

Oonagh O'Dwyer said dryly, 'Yes, that's likely. Some of the younger Court mignons have hired the man who'll play King in Wednesday's procession. Your fame preceded you from Dieppe. They are hoping to confront you with the false King and make the world's fool of you.'

Not in the least upset, he said merely, 'A dangerous game, surely, to put a discourtesy on the King's guest the like of that?'

'Would you have the courage to complain to the King?' she said impatiently. 'You maybe would, but they think you would not. They think that since peace has been made with England, and a new cool-ness with the Emperor, France is not so hot to appropriate Ireland, and would hardly be troubled if a lordling, offended, took the first galley back home.'

'I am tempted,' said O'LiamRoe.

For a moment longer she studied him; then with her square-tipped boy's hands pulled her green cloth hood forward. 'That is all. I promised to tell you I hope,' she said pointedly, 'that your phil-osophy does not leak on you under stress.'

'Do not distub yourself,' said the Prince of Barrow, and the sun-light carried his raw shadow and laid it like a plinth at her feet. 'If they come close to tickle, they can't complain of the fleas. Is Thady Boy expected to join in my folly?'

34

'No. He speaks French. It is you alone they are baiting. I am sorry,' said Oonagh O'Dwyer unexpectedly, raising her light grey eyes straight to his. 'It is not the sweetest news from a woman.'

'No,' said O'LiamRoe slowly. 'No, it is not. There must be vanity in me somewhere yet. But it was not an easy errand you gave yourself either, and my thanks to you and Mistress Boyle.' He opened the door as she moved forward, his oval, whiskered face quite benevolent. 'But God help me, I was raised on all the wrong sports in the Slieve Bloom,' said Phelim O'LiamRoe.

*   *   *

An hour later, in his saffron, his leggings and his frieze cloak, Phelim O'LiamRoe, Prince of Barrow, walked into the royal residence at the Priory of Bonne-Nouvelle, hairy as a houseleek; and the thick cream of French *espièglerie* closed over his head.

It was a young, supple Court, with the sap still in its veins. Henri, absolute lord of nineteen million Frenchmen, was thirty-one; and of the ten de Guises in whose hands half the power of ruling France lay, the eldest, the Queen Mother of Scotland, was only thirty-five. It followed that the courtiers, too, were mostly young. Those of an older generation had been born into the world of Henri's predecessor Francis I, the enchanting rake, the Caesar, the Sunflower, who did not care for dreamy, sullen, sleepy children and had committed his two sons without a thought to the prisons at Pedraza in his place when he lost his Italian war and his liberty at the battle of Pavia.

Henri came back from Spain an uncouth eleven-year-old, unable to speak his native language; and the gay Court noted him in passing —'M. d'Orléans, a large, round face, who does nothing but give blows, and whom no man can master.' When he was King, he kept a court still of marzipan and kisses, but a tough, esoteric, gamey core also persisted: the patronage of scholars and master craftsmen; the habit of good talk and private accomplishments, with the poet and the professor familiarly at the elbow.

But although the personal triumphs of the sullen, sleepy prisoner were now established, not without pains; although the swiftest runner, the best horseman, the finest lute player in France, was her King; although he had ended the English wars successfully, regained possession of Boulogne, would have Scotland when his son married the little Queen, and was in a fair way to frightening the Emperor with his league of German princes—in spite of all these, Henri of France kept two things from the world of his father as a child keeps its cradle rag: his beloved Montmorency, shrewd old warrior whom Francis had exiled from Court; and Diane de Poitiers, for fourteen years Henry's mistress.

Too wealthy, too powerful, too blunt for King Francis's liking,

35

Anne Duke de Montmorency had been none the less one of the bulwarks of the kingdom; and it was not until the old King's latter years, when Montmorency was already nursing the young heir, that the final clash came, and Francis threw him into the exile from which King Henri rescued him.

Diane, widow of the Grand Seneschal of Normandy and familiar with courts, had come, at thirty-six—some said straight from the old King's pillow; and with wit, address and a natural kindness perfectly disarming, had begun teaching the future Henri II, then seventeen, his roles of lover and prince. It was unlucky that before his father died, Henri had become too attached to Diane his mistress, that Montmorency had become too helpful to Henri his prospective master, and that Henri had talked a little too freely of the appointment he would make and banishments he would cancel when his father was dead . . . selling the skin, said the Court, before the bear was killed. Francis did not like it; and it was as well, on the whole, that Francis had died when he did.

O'LiamRoe, who was well informed in his magpie way, needed little or no material briefing from the Gentlemen of the Bedchamber who had waited with remarkable patience for two hours to take him to the presence of the King. He received an unbelievable amount of information about etiquette; about bowing, about titles, about the gentlemen he might meet—for, as the interview would take place in the tennis courts, ladies were unlikely to be there. He listened with a thoughtful tolerance as he was handed through the guard posts into the Priory, pricked with golden fleurs-de-lis and busy as a Michaelmas market. Archers, steward, equerries, pages came at him in waves, and keeping him off the main corridors, channelled O'LiamRoe and his escort into a side room, a side door and a grassy courtyard where someone had hastily pinned up a net. The Gentleman of the Bedchamber, who was red in the face and sweating slightly under his satin, gripped O'LiamRoe's sleeve with soft fingers and said, 'Here you are. Wait. There is the King.'

The square had a look of disuse. Built up on three sides, it was overhung by nothing but shuttered windows. Benches, hung with fine cloths, had been put up hastily on its paved edges with food and drink laid out, and there were stools and one or two chairs, with a doublet or a racquet left lying. Because of the height of the building, the sun was nearly off them, but the four or five men talking at the far end of the court were in shirt sleeves. In the centre a man, big, broad-shouldered and black-bearded, stood listening, with an arm on either shoulder of the flanking players. He was dressed entirely in white. 'The King,' repeated The O'LiamRoe's guide; and pointed.

The O'LiamRoe's oval face craned forward. 'Do you tell me,' said the Chief, fascinated. 'He'll be at them for the scrofula.' Two of the men in the group had been with d'Aubigny at Dieppe: the scent of them carried downwind.

The Gentleman of the Bedchamber, whose English was not quite perfect, opened his mouth, thought better of it, and ended by saying, 'He has seen us. Come forward, my lord prince, and I shall present you.'

'Faith, he's complete,' was O'LiamRoe's next remark, as they moved forward, 'and as black as a crow. I heard he'd greyed early; does he dip it, now? There's a fine receipt of my mother's: two pottles of tar to a pottle of pitch. From the hour we put a brush to it, we lost never a sheep. And is this the King's grace?'

The two parties had met. In a loud voice, the escorting courtier made the introductions; and as his titles hung quaintly on the warm air—Monseigneur Auleammeaux, Prince de Barrault et Seigneur des Monts Salif Blum—O'LiamRoe stood like an amiable chaffbin, the day's merciless noon on the dreadful nap on his frieze cloak and the dreadful lack of it on the saffron tunic below; like an exercise in the assembly of rubbish, to be dismantled shortly and given away to the poor. He stood at ease, without the shadow of a reverence, and when de Genstan of the Royal Guard of Scottish Archers, slipping forward, hissed in his ear, 'Sir, it is customary to bow,' he merely widened his disarming grin and said, 'Do you tell me. And here am I born like the devil with my knees at the backs of my legs. What's he blathering on about, the poor man?'

M. de Genstan, with the faintest sign to his allies, slipped into the role of interpreter. 'His Majesty is welcoming you to France, sir. He would have had you meet their graces the Duke and the Cardinal of Guise, and the Constable Montmorency as well, but they have pressing business to attend to.'

'Ah, devil take it; and I had made up my mind that wee little one there was the Cardinal,' said O'LiamRoe agreeably. 'Will you tell the King's grace he's a happy man, surely, with the kingdom running itself while he can lep about after a ball. What's he saying?'

Speaking through an interpreter imposes its own languors and strains on an encounter, and this one was in any case, with astounding clarity, failing to take the course expected of it. The sieur de Genstan, his face flaming, was trying hard to prolong the interview by censoring his translations. The man in white, at least aware that some of the courtesies were lacking, was still a little at a loss. In a slow, carrying voice he addressed his interpreter. M. de Genstan said to O'LiamRoe, 'His grace asks you to be seated and take wine with him.'

'Ah, now,' said O'LiamRoe comfortably. 'Thank his grace, will you, and say I'd ten times sooner see him finish his fine game of ball. It's plain to see he's as nimble as a pea on a drumhead, and the nearest I've seen to it was a priest fighting-drunk with a censer.'

To this, expurgated, the King replied with a question. 'Will you play with him?'

The blue eyes twinkled. 'Dressed like this? God help us, I'd be mince-boiled in my sweat like a deer. At home we have the one dress, suitable for all occasions, and that is all.'

The black-bearded man replied cautiously, through M. de Genstan. 'You do not have this sport in Ireland?'

Wholly at ease, O'LiamRoe sat down. Round the courtyard a sigh ran like the flight of a shuttlecock. Cheerfully aware of it, he went on 'Sport, do you say? Pat-ball is not in it; no. But sport we have, surely and many a good man has died on the field of it with his honour bright, bright as the sun. Hurley for instance. Do you know it?'

They did not.

'It is played with a stick, then; and dress is no matter, for you have to trouble about the one thing only, and that is getting off the sportsfield alive. And whatever dress you came on with, there will likely be none on you at the end. It's a good way of filling in time if there are no wars. I don't play it myself, being a peaceable man. But go to it; let me see you,' said O'LiamRoe with unfeigned interest. 'It is never a fault to see what other folk do.'

Because they were at a loss, because they could not immediately see what had happened, because, finally, anything was better than continuing to talk, they took him at his word. As The O'LiamRoe lounged at ease, one elbow on the velvet table at his side and the speechless courtiers beside him, the bearded leader chose a single partner, without ceremony, and launched into a hard game.

They were both excellent players; and being excellent, they took risks, and sometimes suffered from them. There was no netted ball, no fruitless leap, no dropped racquet, no lonely stance, mouth agape while the ball landed neatly behind, which escaped the soft undertone of O'LiamRoe's commentary. Excruciating, unforgivable, fluent, unerring, pitched to the trembling octave of Straw Street irony, he noted the clouted thumb, the missed serve, the sweat, the split in the seam and the single, hissing, green-bottomed slide on the turf. He noted the uncurling hair, the throttling dive at the net; he observed and reported, serenely and without mercy until under the pressure of it de Genstan, who was listening and softly translating, laughed aloud, and the infection of it burst the decorum of the rest. There was a bellow of laughter. Already sensitive to the undercurrent of two voices, the players turned, their faces printed with anger; and with a glorious, earsplitting crack, the tennis ball shot through a window.

The mild, Irish voice had at last ceased, but they were still laughing, in small helpless sobs, when the man in white, flinging down his racquet, seized his partner by the arm and strode over. The laughter stopped. O'LiamRoe, his fair brows raised, looked up at the sieur de Genstan, who from red had gone suddenly white. 'And now,' he said comfortably, 'supposing after all that you get the fellow here, and we talk.'

That they obeyed was the result of sheer self-protection. They had aligned themselves by their laughter on the wrong side of the fence. The players were clearly furious, and from a distance, M. de Genstan could be seen inventing explanations and excuses far more plausible than O'LiamRoe could have produced, if excuses had been anywhere in his remotest thoughts. He waited, rising, grinning as the black-bearded one, still flushed, left the crowd of men and approached him at last.

'I'll take that wine now, if it's offered me,' said O'LiamRoe cheerfully, 'and give a word in your ear to go with it. For, God save us, you're an insular lot, you Frenchmen; and it's time you learned a thing or two about your more cultured neighbours such as the Irish. And translate it all, de Genstan me boy, this time; none of your three words to every three hundred, *divina proportio* and a wink and a shrug for the rest of it.'

Crested cups were being filled. 'His Majesty says,' said the harassed interpreter from behind the bearded man's chair: 'He says that he would wish the differences between Ireland and France to be less.'

'Ah, never mind the English in it,' said O'LiamRoe. 'We've had them lording it over us these three hundred years and swallowed them whole, same as you did, though the ones that came from Normandy were devils for taxes the same as yourself.'

'His Majesty asks,' said de Genstan, 'if you are comparing his rule by any chance to that of England?'

'Faith, would I do the like of that?' said O'LiamRoe with his freckled smile. 'And it so superior. There's the Concordat, now. Why destroy yourself making out you're the world's head of the church when your Concordat lets you whistle up the abbeys and the bishops and the archbishops to your liking; all found money and a pet of a way to make friends?'

There was a pause. 'The King says,' said M. de Genstan, 'that these subjects are not a matter for discussion at this meeting, which is only meant—'

O'LiamRoe's smile had malice in it. 'Not a matter for discussion! My dear boy, in Ireland the midwife uses one hand to hold the baby's best fighting arm from the font water, and grips its jaws with the other lest the child goes to litigation about it.' He put down the cup and rising, laid a commiserating hand on de Genstan's shoulder. 'Scrub off the civet and spit out the sugar plums and the next time. choose an arguing, manly violent sort of king for yourselves. Sure, if that one's hair were shaved off, like Bandinello's Hercules, there's not enough skull in it for his brains, so.'

There was a deathly silence. The bearded man, rising also, glanced in turn at The O'LiamRoe and at the interpreter, who had gone even paler. De Genstan, appealing helplessly to the blank faces of his fellows, muttered something.

The man in white drew a deep breath, curled his fist, and brought it down on the table with a thud that brought the cups cracking on their sides. A stream of red leaped on the velvet. '*Traduisez!*' he exclaimed. And the young man, stumbling, began to translate.

Listening, Blackbeard snapped his fingers. Pages ran. A surcoat was slipped on his shoulders, and fastened with gold knots. A chain was brought, and laid over his head. A pair of embroidered slippers was put on his feet in place of the plain shoes for tennis; and white leather gloves and a plumed hat were put in his hand.

With the entwined crescents of his monogram leaping with his ill-compressed, angry breathing, Henri II, Elect of God and Most Christian Majesty of France and her peoples, heard O'LiamRoe's translated words falter to a close. 'If his hair were shaved off, there's not enough skull in it for brains,' said the sieur de Genstan; and looked anywhere but at O'LiamRoe.

For a long moment, many things hung in the balance, and not the least of them O'LiamRoe's life. But Henri was not quite committed to an alliance with England. His need of Ireland might return. And royal dignity, in the long run, mattered more than royal vanity. He prepared to speak.

O'LiamRoe's face, as realization struck him, went quite blank. Then he drew himself quietly together, his fair skin hotly red, his blue eyes steady; and by a visible effort of will, detachment, cynicism, amusement even flowed back into his bearing as, slow, heavy, measured, the King's words proceeded, shadowed by the light, hurried English of de Genstan.

'You claim a culture. You speak of a common ancestry. You call yourself the son of a king. You show scorn for our customs and make fun of our person.'

'It was a mistake,' said O'LiamRoe.

The King's hands were clasped behind him; his voice continued unchanged. 'We are aware of your poverty. We are aware of your claims to learning. We are aware of the racial distinction of your people. But we had expected certain courtesies of the person and of the tongue. We were prepared to entertain you at our Court as an equal; and without offering you or dreaming of offering you the insult of our compassion. You had better, Prince of Barrow,' said the King, and the gilded gloves in his hand were wrung like a rag, 'you had better think well and invite that insult from us now.'

O'LiamRoe looked round the circle. Shocked and shaken, they avoided his eye. The Prince's fair face hardened. Rubbing his nose with one finger, he cast a mild blue eye on the controlled and angry figure before him. 'Dear, dear,' said O'LiamRoe in concern, in contrition and with, at the back of his eyes, the faintest unregenerate spark of joy. 'Dear, dear. I have fallen into a small error of judgment. I thought the King here, you see, was a play-actor.'

There was another silence. Then, with an explosion of disgust, Henri strode off, pacing the court, and de Genstan seized O'Liam-Roe's arm. 'Go now. Quickly,' he said.

With a strength quite unlooked-for, the other man resisted. 'Not at all, so. It will never do to be losing our heads.'

'My God,' said de Genstan, who had lost his a good time ago. 'You'll come to table tomorrow with an apple in your mouth.'

'Not at all, now. Wait. Here he is,' said O'LiamRoe, as the King swung to a halt before him. 'Ah, bad cess to it, it's a damned heathen language, the French. What's all that about?'

De Genstan translated. 'Since you have proved your ignorance in these matters, it might please you to study the monarchy of France and her peoples in their great moment of accord. His grace desires you to stay in Rouen at his expense until and during the celebration of his Joyous Entry on Wednesday. On Thursday you and your party will be escorted to Dieppe and at the first fair wind a galley will be at your service to return immediately to Ireland. Between now and Wednesday, his grace expects to hold no further communication with you.'

O'LiamRoe had flushed again; but beyond that, there was no trace of anger or of chagrin on the disingenuous face. 'Tell him I agree so. Why would I not? The Emperor is the King of Kings, so they say; the Catholic King is the King of Men, and the King of France is King of Beasts, "therefore whatever he commands he is instantly obeyed." And who am I, a mere gentleman, to deny him?'

He waited, to do him justice, until it was translated; he bowed three times in the doorway like the unrolling of some primitive carpet, and he departed. Thus Phelim O'LiamRoe, Chief of the Name, Prince of Barrow and lord of the Slieve Bloom, left his audience with the King of France, his principles firmly unblemished amid the smoking shambles of his personal impact, and his deportation pending.

*   *   *

The O'LiamRoe had no pressing wish to tell his henchmen of the event. As it turned out, he had no need. Profiting by his chief's absence, Thady Boy had visited every alehouse in Rouen, picked up the rumour, and returned rocking slightly to hear the details.

He bore these with more philosophy than Piedar Dooly, who,

41

enthralled with his new role of bloodhound, could hardly wait, said O'LiamRoe, to see him half-assassinated another time. 'But I doubt,' he added, 'that there will be no luck in it for him, for who'll bother himself with me, now I'm leaving? *Ochone, ochone*,' said the Prince of Barrow, who, to finish it off, had taken a good drink himself. 'For it will be dull, dull in this town from now till Thursday, and with nothing happening and no one killing us at all, the spoiled souls.'

IV

Rouen: Fine, Scientific Works without Warning

In the case of all fine, scientific works which can be done without being seen or heard, it is required by law to apply the rule of notice and removal: warning is to be given to sensible adults; beasts and non-sensible persons are to be turned away, and sleepers are to be awakened; deaf and blind persons to be removed.

THOUGH none of the King's circle, naturally, would tell tales out of Court, the whole city of Rouen had the news of the royal baiting in the tennis court in an hour, and like Leo X, said O'Liam-Roe, who came to power like a fox, reigned like a lion and died like a dog, the rise and demise of Ireland in the bosom of Father France was not without note.

Very soon in the afternoon, a drift of small boys began to appear outside O'LiamRoe's lodging, and to pass observations on the traffic therein. A man called Augrédé whose brother had died in the salt tax revolt called on the Chief, and had to be shown out incontinently. A Scotsman spoke to them in the street when, unwilling to lurk at home like a malefactor, O'LiamRoe had insisted on strolling out; and another one, young and speaking good French, had accosted Thady Boy in a tavern, and after a good deal of double talk, hinted that he could get O'LiamRoe an interview with the English Resident, Sir James Mason. Children followed them, and a man or two smiled discreetly, but no fellow Irishmen darkened the door.

After some thought, O'LiamRoe sent a letter to Mistress Boyle with a lighthearted account of what had passed, forestalling visit or apology, and courteously taking his leave. They had, after all, to live in the country; Oonagh, after all, would marry a Frenchman.

The Queen Dowager of Scotland sent for Tom Erskine. There was no idle laughter this afternoon in the Hôtel Prudhomme, where the Queen had lodged since her State Entry, waiting as the Irish party

43

were doing, though in considerably more state, for the King's own Royal Entry on Wednesday.

It was only a week since Mary of Guise, the Queen Mother of Scotland, had re-entered her native France on her first visit for twelve years, and already she had lost weight, so that the long sleeves dragged on her large-boned, hollow shoulders. She was the Queen Mother of a sister kingdom which France had just helped to rescue from the hands of the English. She was the oldest member of the de Guise family, the most powerful in France and dearly cherished by the King. But she was also a twice-widowed woman who, in the space of a day, had been reunited with the son of her first marriage, the pale Duke de Longueville whom she had not seen for a decade; and with Mary, the seven-year-old Queen of Scotland and the only child of her second marriage, whom King Henri had brought to France two years since as the betrothed of his heir.

For a motherly woman, which the Queen Dowager was not, a double meeting of distressing joy. For a politician, which she was, an extra agony of behaviour to confuse the already terrible complications of her visit. For she was not on good terms with all her late husband's subjects. The war with England was over, but England was still giving shelter to disgruntled Scots; and reminding others with promises and pensions of her ancient claims to the Scottish crown. The Earl of Arran, ruling Scotland in the little Queen's stead, was weak: half-wooed by England and the Reformed religion England stood for; easy game for the powerful families eager to oust him and control the Regency. And France, having poured men and money and munitions into Scotland to help her win the late war, was reaping a fury of wounded pride and growing resentment as her reward. Looking at their forts, their castles, their streets and their beds stuffed full of idle, boasting, quarrelsome French, the Scottish half of the Old Alliance was coming very close to a wholehearted upheaval which might send both the foreigners and their ancient religion flying out of the window.

She had thought of all this. She had met that danger as best she could simply by removing the worst elements of danger and carrying them with her. But even so, before even she came to Dieppe, the powerful and violent men in her train were nipping and kicking and plunging at one another and at the ribbons which held them.

And in the face of this she must move correctly, with haughtiness and with splendour through the excessive and appalling round of ceremony that had been prepared for her; must behave to the King and his Court, to her own family and their rivals and the ambassadors of every nation in Europe who came to pay court to her, as if she had come merely to visit her child, and as if, given her own way, she would not have smashed the gilded bubble of dance and laughter

44

with a blow, so that these damned lackadaisical, self-important, rich, preening men would be hurled by circumstance round the conference table, where she would have them, to discuss with all the gifts in their power, the future policies of France and of Scotland.

So she sat restless in the Hôtel Prudhomme after a morning of state receptions, with Lady Fleming and Margaret Erskine at her side; and said abruptly, 'Madame Erskine. I wish to speak with your husband.'

The page found him when he was paying his last calls before leaving, on Friday, for Flanders. The Chief Privy Councillor had also heard the rumours. As he hurried back to the Hôtel Prudhomme, Tom Erskine knew very well he was going to be asked about Lymond.

It was hurled at him as he stepped over the threshold. 'I hear the Irishmen are being sent home. What does this mean?'

Since Dieppe, he had heard nothing. He wished he had not told her of Lymond's identity. Now, in the presence of his wife and his wife's mother, he attempted to reason with the Queen. With so much else, God knew, to harass them, she could not afford to pursue indefinitely this curious whim, or allow its failures to distract her. Lymond's visit had no vital purpose; he was not her agent. His presence or his absence would make no difference.

But the Queen Mother's patience had run out. 'For whom is he working?'

'Himself. No one.'

'And whom will he be working for in a year's time?'

There was a silence. Then Erskine said, 'He won't be committed. He told me himself.'

Mary of Guise checked her temper, waited and then spoke in an even voice. 'You call yourself his friend. Consider him then. He has now his reputation, his possessions, his wealth. Yet at home his future is uncertain. It is his elder brother Lord Culter who has the barony, and the child which Lady Culter is expecting will oust our friend Lymond from his inheritance and even from his title, if it is a son. . . . He is idle then; he has no attachments, no dependants, no followers; he is ready, my dear Chancellor, for the dedication. In one year's time,' said the Queen Dowager of Scotland explicitly, 'I want his allegiance to be mine. I need it. But far more than that, the Queen will need it. This is the moment most critical in his life and ours. If I do not seize him now, we shall never have him. And now, now is the moment; for I mean to take this man in his failure, Master Erskine— in his failure, and not in his success.'

As she spoke, the door had opened on a scratch, and a page entered, bending double in silence. 'Bring him in,' said the Queen Dowager, and turned her cold eyes on Tom Erskine and the two women. 'I suspected there was only one way to find the truth; and so I sent for him,' she said. 'M. Crawford of Lymond is here.'

The page scuttled; the door shut. The masked man in black, whom Tom Erskine had last seen at Dieppe in Jean Ango's moonlit garden, stepped delicately from the shadows. He appeared to be quelling a strong impulse to laugh.

'I must apologize for these damned entrances,' said Francis Crawford of Lymond. 'I feel Tom here never knows if he should send for a bishop or start a round of applause.' And lifting finger and thumb, he slid the mask from his face, disclosing the intelligent, sardonic features of Thady Boy Ballagh.

*   *   *

It was late when Lymond returned to his lodging, walking silently under the rocking lamps skeined sagging over the crooked streets. Behind him lay an interview remarkable for its courtesy, its cool vigour and, from the Dowager's point of view, for its total lack of success.

Tom Erskine might have warned her, had she given him time, that it was a mistake to allude to O'LiamRoe's shortcomings. Personally he shared her doubts about Lymond's choice of travelling companion. Whether or not the sinking of *La Sauvée* had been an attempt on O'LiamRoe's life, O'LiamRoe's present actions had certainly led to his and Lymond's dismissal from France. About the Prince of Barrow's innocence in all this Tom was perfectly confident: Lymond had not only studied the Chief in that preliminary week in the Slieve Bloom before sailing for France; he had set on foot an investigation of appalling thoroughness into O'LiamRoe's character before ever O'LiamRoe was approached.

And Lymond had been right. O'LiamRoe was the one man in ten who would look with amusement and even enthusiasm on the prospect of duping his royal hosts by passing off a foreigner as his Irish secretary and bard. Unhappily, it was this very irresponsibility which had brought the scheme to a halt.

The Queen Dowager only got halfway towards speaking her mind about that, when Lymond stopped her. She turned next to the future, and to the prospect of closer cooperation, object unspecified, between the Master of Culter and herself. The Master of Culter simply reminded her, with unvarying deference, that what he did in France or out of it, by their mutual agreement, was his own affair and not hers. For Lymond, who could explode into fire and brimstone when he chose, could be equally formidable in the language of etiquette; and had already managed to give Jenny Fleming a chaste verbal trouncing for her morning's work at the bridge, unnoticed by either Tom or the Dowager.

It was at this point that the Queen Mother played her master card, and startled even her Chief Privy Councillor. 'And what,' she had said, 'if the Queen my daughter's safety were in question?'

In the ensuing silence, 'Is it, ma'am?' had asked Lymond.

But already, she was retreating. 'Of course, we know of nothing. Where could the child have better care than among our dear friends in France? But if her life were threatened, by some madman, let us say . . .'

'Then double your bodyguard, madam,' he had coolly replied. 'They are not in your confidence either, but they are in your service.'

They let him go after that, with something like relief; and after he had gone, Margaret Erskine was very silent, counting up in her mind the frequent illnesses and the unexplained accidents that had befallen Mary Queen of Scots, during her sojourn in France. Her thought had reached her husband. Tom began a single, hazy question, 'Does your grace suspect that. . . ?' and received the snub of his life for his pains. Her grace was visibly regretting that the subject had ever been raised.

To Lymond, presumably, the interview meant no more than an irritation brushed aside. Retiring, exploring, the swinging lights as he walked lit an emotionless face.

The streets were not empty. Light shone from most houses, seeping in slits round baffled shutters where shields were painted, swords burnished, jewels embroidered in the great, consuming fever of the Entry. A troop of the de Guise household went quickly by, banner held at thigh and wrist, and the lamps tripped and rocked afresh as the silver eaglets of Lorraine, the quartered lilies of Anjou and Sicily, the crimson bars of Hungary and the double cross of Jerusalem brushed by.

A girl stepped back out of an open doorway, laughing, and Francis Crawford sidestepped softly and went on his way. More even than Lyons, than Avignon or Paris, Rouen's women were notorious. A mocking voice called after him, and below the mask, momentarily was the twitch of a smile.

Very soon after that, he vanished altogether for a moment; and when he took the cobbled crown of the street again, it was in the portly, potbellied, unmasked and alcoholic person of O'LiamRoe's secretary.

Robin Stewart saw him wander along the Rue St.-Lô, pass the Palace of Justice and stop looking up at the newly finished tower of St. André. The church lantern shone on the ollave's Adam's apple and upturned, stubbled chin and Stewart himself glanced up at the tower. He laid a hand on Thady Boy's shoulder.

His purpose, in a muddled way, was to give comfort; his need was to receive it. Thady Boy Ballagh turned round slowly, and said, 'Well,

47

well, Mr. Stewart. The Orcades flowed with Saxon gore this day, and Thule became warm with the blood of the Picts, and icy Erin wept for her heaps of slaughtered Scots. We're to take the next boat home on Thursday, you'll have heard.'

'If I had my way of it, those dewy young madcaps at Court would hang like catkins on a willow tree. It's plain to anyone the insolence was unintentional.'

'And yet, do you know, I have an awful feeling that O'LiamRoe himself had a wee, little suspicion, a hint, a first trickle of a notion, that it was maybe the King he was facing after all,' said Thady Boy placidly. 'He wasn't very sure of being courtly, but he knew he could make a smart success of being outrageous.—Were you going somewhere?'

Robin Stewart recalled suddenly that he had been struck before with this man. 'I was going just a step up the road,' he said, 'for a word and a drink in the back parlour of a friend of mine. Would it interest you?' He grinned with sudden candour. 'You'll need to make the most of your days left in France.'

Which was exactly the opinion of Francis Crawford of Lymond, accepting.

*   *   *

The house to which he had been so impulsively invited was not far off: a handsome, dormered merchant's mansion behind a high wall, entered by a door recently widened. Outside, Robin Stewart stopped dead in his bony, marionnette's walk to discuss Master Ballagh's religion. 'Have you strong views, maybe, on Lutherism and all yon trash?'

Thady Boy's eyes were twin pools of maidenly blue. 'I have strong views on nothing at all, *a mhic*, save women and drink, and maybe money. I can content me barefoot or bareheaded, and keep Lent or Ramadan, such little weedy views on religion do I have.'

'Aye, well. The fellow we're to visit is a sculptor. A retired sculptor. And an inventor. He whiles invents machines, you understand.'

'Like Leonardo.'

'Like Leonardo,' agreed Robin Stewart with great promptitude, and knocked on the gates.

They were not admitted at once. There was a whispered colloquy, and a short wait; then a man with a lantern appeared and led them through the inner courtyard and into the house, talking amicably in good English as they went. They passed, at his direction, up a narrow wooden staircase and at the top stood dazzled in the light of a door already open. Two powerful hands reached for them; two powerful arms hauled them inside; and a rolling bass voice intoned, treading strongly, like monks at a vintage, on the mangled accents of Paris and

48

Perth: 'Robin! My sweet conscience, my great buck in velvet, touch me at your peril. I'm all swelled like a foxglove with the gout, and damned glad to see you. Bring him in, whoever he is, and sit down.'

Michel Hérisson was a big man, with loose white hair lit by the spare wax candles behind, and powerful hands rubbed by the hafts and handles, the wood and metal and stone of his profession into premature cracked monuments of themselves. Shouting cheerfully, he made them free of a comfortable, chair-scattered room with a fire at one end, where three or four Scots and French, already gathered, rose and offered their welcome.

The room looked what it was: an unofficial club, where men of like mind and diverse background could meet away from the hubbub of public taverns. The greetings over, Stewart pulled Thady apart and seated him. 'He's a good fellow, Hérisson—a brilliant artist in his day, before the gout. His brother in London was one of the best friends I ever had.' He picked up two tankards from the deep sill at his side and got up. 'We help ourselves. Get your drouth in good order, Master Ballagh. It's a grand wine Michel Hérisson serves, and he doesna measure your mou'.' And he walked away, leaving behind him for five minutes the competent gaze of Crawford of Lymond.

One of the group before the fire was a minor member of the Queen Dowager's train; he was talking, in fluent French, about Tom Erskine's present embassy. From the number of used tankards, the circle had recently been much bigger; and yet the fire was quite fresh, with no long-seated bed of ash. Also, below the talk and laughter, and the chink of wood and metal on stools, there existed a rhythm that was no sound, but a pressure on the soles of the feet. No sooner had it made itself felt than it stopped; and Robin Stewart came back.

He spoke abruptly, after the first pledging draught. 'Thank God O'LiamRoe isn't to stay. I canna thole the man, Master Ballagh; and that's the truth.'

'It's fairly dispiriting, I know,' said Thady Boy, 'when he makes a virtue of the very things that you would be after being sorry at him for.'

Stewart's voice slid, aggrieved, into its common note. 'Shambling here and yon, looking at the Seven Wonders of the world as if they were pared from his toenails, and making such a parade of his poorness and silliness that no man of feeling could bring himself to discomfit him. And all the while you've got a gey queer feeling that he thinks you're the fool and he's the wise, tolerant fellow laughing up the holes in his sleeve.'

'Whereas it's yourself is the wise, tolerant fellow,' said Thady Boy; and ignoring the Archer's sudden flush, he stirred a wine ring on the table with a long slender finger. 'Tell me, since he's such a wise, scholarly fellow—and he is, make no doubt of that—why he's brought an ollave to France?'

49

'Oh, to add to the splendour of his train, surely,' said Stewart sarcastically.

'While parading his lack of polish and his poverty? O'LiamRoe brought a secretary although he is a fairly good humanist, my dear, because he was afraid he mightn't be quite good enough. He brought his saffron and frieze—'

'That I respect,' said Stewart. 'I can see that. It was a matter of principle because the English proscribed it.'

'The English proscribed it, true for you; but devil a man, woman or child in the whole of Ireland is paying any regard to it. The O'Liam-Roe himself has six silk suits in his wardrobe, but none so grand, let you see, as the gentlemen have in France. Detached irony about the world's work is O'LiamRoe's rule; and that is where he is to be pitied, if you are dead keen to be pitying us some way.'

A calmness had come to Robin Stewart: a calmness wrought, had he recognized it, by a man used to dealing with men, who had taken time to feed the lions of envy, curiosity and aggression with these titbits and set them temporarily asleep. He said suddenly, watching the fat man's dark face, 'You're a great one for dissecting, I can see. What do you make, I wonder, of the likes of me?'

'Ah, the touch I have is only for Irishmen. You've no need of an outside opinion, surely. You know yourself, Robin Stewart.'

'I know myself,' said the Archer, and his bony hands tightened white on his tankard. 'And I don't need to like what I know. But, God, do we know other people?'

'Who is it—d'Aubigny?—that you dislike? You needn't see much of him, surely?'

'He knows the secret of a good life—'

'Has he taught you it?'

'I can learn,' said Stewart with the same suppressed violence. 'I haven't a title—I haven't money or education—I've not even a decent name. I've got to learn; and I tell you this: I'll work like a dog for the man that'll teach me.'

'Teach you what? Success?'

'Success—or how to do without it,' said Robin Stewart bitterly.

The ollave lay back. The waxlight shone on the black, lightless hair, the stained gown limp on his stomach and the hand, idly playing which still lay on the table. The trace of wine, like a jewel on the timber, was tremulous with a hundred wax lights. 'And the best way to success—or the other thing—is an illegal printing press?' said Thady.

By speechless instinct, the Archer's hand moved to his sword. Then his face relaxed; his hand dropped. Here was a decent, drunken crony who would be gone in three days. The presses were not normally used at this hour; he had never contemplated Mr. Ballagh detecting

50

them. But Dod . . . what harm could a man do who would be thrown out on his ear if he so much as breathed on the King's boots? Most of his thought lingering all too clearly on his face, he rescued the pause, just too late; saying, 'How did you guess?'

'Blubbering Echo, hid in a hollow hole, crying her half answer . . . In the cellar, is it?' said Thady Boy. 'I've heard the sound of night printing in Paris. What students of religion pay to read isn't always ripe for a Faculty of Theology certificate; and a retired artist with a fancy for machinery is surely God's gift to the theologians. Is there a great prejudice against ollaves of the more heathen sort; or could I see it, do you suppose?' Master Ballagh enquired.

*　　　*　　　*

Stuffy, stinking, choked with tallow smoke and reeking of humanity and hot metal, the cellars of the Hôtel Hérisson resembled nothing so much as neap tide in a nailmakers' graveyard. The half-cut sinews of monumental grey gods nursed tottering towers of type frames; from its seething copper, varnish fumes wreathed the eyelids of some armless oracle; a muscular goddess, hand outstretched, had a bucket of fresh-mixed glue on her arm.

And everywhere, like inky bunting, the wet, new-printed sheets hung; while presses chattered and clanged, supervised by Michel Hérisson, who, gouty leg notwithstanding, was turning out proscribed theological literature with one hand, and arguing its obscurer points with a ghoulish gusto the while. Milling, laughing, drinking, arguing around him, squashed and wadded among the litter, was the cheerful company which had left its traces in the parlour upstairs.

Robin Stewart was already running down the stone stairs to join them. Thady Boy, pod-shaped behind him, paused a moment on the landing, his heavy-lidded blue gaze on the gathering. No one from Court, obviously, was there. There were some richer tradesmen, one or two evident lawyers and a good many students. Somewhere German was being spoken, and somewhere, Scots. He saw Kirkcaldy of Grange, whose name he knew perfectly well, and who had made the afternoon's clumsy approach in the tavern. There were some resident Franco-Scots, another Archer and Sir George Douglas and his brother-in-law Drumlanrig.

For a second Lymond paused, the thick smoke surging in the draught. The House of Douglas, splendid, ambitious, once the greatest in Scotland next to the King's, had recovered once already from a long exile in the 'twenties when George Douglas and the Earl of Angus his brother had been forced to abandon their plotting and hurry to France—where they were no strangers. More than 130 years before, Archibald, Earl of Douglas, had been created Duke of Touraine for helping to drive the English out of France, and many a

Douglas was among the Scottish veterans who settled in France with him then.

But it was a long time since then, and still longer since King Robert the Bruce had sent the Good Sir James Douglas to carry his heart to the Holy Land. The Douglas's most recent crusades had been largely to do with cradle-snatching. Angus, head of the family, had seized his chance after Flodden to marry Margaret Tudor, widow of the Scots King James IV, and sister of King Henry VIII. The marriage was less than idyllic in practically every facet, and the resulting child, Margaret, had gone to England, married the Earl of Lennox and besides being a possible contender for several crowns, was embarrassingly prone to demand her father's allegiance to England at moments when he was being made by main force to prove his loyalty in quarters quite different.

The Earl of Angus and his brother Sir George had tried to control the childhood of the late King James V, and of the present young Queen Mary; but despite English bribes and English pensions, they had failed. Now Angus was old, and there remained only Sir George, smooth, clever, nimble-witted; of dwindling account in the world of affairs, but with a son whose heritage he was guarding and for whom he snatched at what honours he could. And there was something else. In a fertile jungle of treachery and betrayal, George Douglas and Lymond had more than once matched their wits. Of all the Scots at Court except Erskine, Sir George alone knew Francis Crawford of Lymond really well.

There was still time to retreat. Robin Stewart turned round, enquiring, at the foot of the stairs. A rare smile flickered over the ollave's dark face: and he ran downstairs lightly to join him.

Down below, the climate was scholarly, part-inebriated and wholly sporting. Michel Hérisson seized them both as they tussled through the back-thumping crowd, ale in hand: Stewart's white silk shoulder was scarlet with claret and Thady Boy, squeezing in grease-spattered motley past a man killing himself on a double-bellows, was exuberant: 'Ah, dear God: how The O'LiamRoe would come into his own here now. But'—as Stewart's face froze—'how could we risk it, and him born with thumbs on his feet: you would find him flat in the very next edition of Servetus, folded duodecamo.'

Michel Hérisson winked broadly at the Archer. 'How's your learning, Master Ollave? Have you Latin?'

'Are you asking an Irishman? Do we breathe?' said Thady Boy, and bent over the printed pages. 'Ah, *dhia*, he was a woeful fool that one; and the words coming off him like a dog shedding mud. . . .'

The more precocious uses of a portable printing press held no interest for Michel Hérisson, whose cheerful and disrespectful exploit it was; but an attack on one of his authors was Nirvana. He and the

52

ollave plunged in, tongues flailing, while Robin Stewart stood by, full of proprietorial pride and black jealousy. In the end, he broke in. 'You've a cellarful tonight, man. How in God's name can you work in this crowd?'

'They're here for the fun. There's paper coming.'

It was the kind of recklessness that Stewart could not stand. He raised a prickly eyebrow. 'Getting a bit cocksure, aren't you? You're taking in paper tonight, with the King at the gates and the whole place heaving like an anthill?'

'Why not? They'll think it is another patch for the Pegasus Arch.'

He was probably right. His paper mill was twenty miles away; his arrangements were typically neat. The cart would arrive at Rouen, bearing his marble or his clay, his new furnace or his fuel; and in the false bottom lay the quires, ready to drop by grille and chute straight into the cellars while the cart stood, innocently unloading, in the inner courtyard. In the cellar, there were cupboards everywhere: in the base of a vast sculpture, with the armatures showing like the ribs of a bog-corpse; in the floor; in the bottom of the paste trough. Stewart thought he would take Thady Boy home.

Thady Boy had gone. Instead, a tall man in handsome blue lounged at his side. 'Hullo, Stewart. Who's your portly friend?' It was Sir George Douglas; and Stewart reacted typically.

'I wouldna call him friend, just. It's Ballagh, one of the two Irish I'm bear-leading till Thursday.'

'You ought to keep an eye on him. He's over there with Abernaci. Does he talk English?'

'Oh, aye, and Irish and Irish-French and Irish-Latin for good measure, the times that he's not snoring drunk. All you can say for him is that he's under no illusions about his master. They're going on Thursday.'

It happened to be news. Sir George said, 'Oh, they're going?' and immediately lost all interest in whatever speculation had inspired his enquiry. He moved off, and Stewart pressed on to where he knew the turbaned head and talbot-hound features of Abernaci would be crouching.

He was in his usual place, with Thady Boy Ballagh seated before him, the worse for drink. Thady's breeches were stained with vermilion, and his idle gaze was focussed on Abernaci, cross-legged on the floor, his dark face hidden and his long, brown fingers curled round a knife. He was wearing robes, finely laundered and brilliantly printed, and a jewelled turban on his head. From a block of pearwood in his left hand the shavings were falling, tender and curled in the light.

'Woodcuts. He's fair away with himself making pictures,' said Stewart ironically, towering over Thady's right shoulder. 'Hérisson found him doing it one day, and asked him over to see it on the press. It'd surprise you sometimes what these natives can do. You wouldn't credit him with a thought barring slitting your throat one dark night for your buttons. Wait till you see the face on him. Abernaci!'

The carver looked up. Under the fine turban, the brown face was small and seamed like a walnut. Years of Indian sun had dried a skin possibly middle-aged to look like the sloughed hide of a serpent; his nose was broken-backed and ignoble, and he had a scar, running from brow to cheek, which clenched one eyebrow unnaturally high. He glanced at the two men, and then resumed his carving without a word.

'Will you look at yon!' said Robin Stewart, who was no longer feeling so remote from his guest. 'And he can take a drop, too. Abernaci!' He bent over the silent figure. 'Drink—good, yes?' He made a motion of drinking. 'More?'

Within the black beard, the thick lips moved. 'More,' said the man Abernaci gutturally; and Stewart, laughing, turned away.

In an untidy, stained heap on his hocks, the ollave remained, watching.

The carver looked up. The knife, razor-sharp, lay still in his hand; but his grip suddenly had changed. On the opposite wall a leather ink bottle hung with a table just below it, and on the table Robin Stewart's white jacket lay.

The hand with the knife moved. There was a flash, a hiss, and the blade, arching slim through the air, slit the fat-bellied bottle clean through. Ink, in a thin black stream, began to issue and splash on the table. The brown hands clasped, the robes were still, and Abernaci was passive once more, his dark eyes resting on Thady.

There was a knife in Thady's hand, too, although no sign of how it came there. He turned, balancing it thoughtfully, waiting until he might be unperceived; then he judged it, and threw. It was a more difficult target than Abernaci's. The knife hurtled straight to the bottle cord, and parting it, let the spouting ink flask fall free to spill its black pool harmlessly on the floor. Black eyes met blue in mutual speculation; and Lymond, speaking softly, said, 'More?'

And then the shouting began.

The voice of Hérisson's steward began it; a door banged, and his calling rang suddenly through the packed cellar. The paper cart had reached the Porte Cochoise and was entering the city. Stewart, fighting back to collect Thady, watched for two minutes while the scene dissolved into pandemonium, with Hérisson in the middle sonorously making his dispositions to take the illegal consignment. Then he hurried Thady outside.

It was the ollave, cheerful with much drink, who wandered immediately from Stewart's side and was found presently halfway up the adjacent scaffolding. And it was Thady Boy, rocking slightly on the steeple top, oblivious to the Archer's angry hissings below, who spotted the spark of gorget, the glint of arquebus and the bristling shadow of pikes under the housetops in the Rue aux Juifs.

They raised the alarm in the Hôtel Hérisson as the cart arrived from the north. The grille was lifted, the base unbolted, and the bales were sliding into the cellar while the city guard was two streets away. Bouncing like a cork, Thady Boy ran downstairs to the cellar; and when Stewart, scrambling, got there after him, the ollave's voice, raised in charitable zeal, was already making drunken, flamboyant and shatteringly practical suggestions on how to deal with an imminent raid,

*   *   *

For years after, in Hérisson's circle, they told the story of that night: how with a cordon round the whole house the bailly and his sergeants burst into the cellars to find nothing worse going on than an uproarious, a scurrilous rehearsal for part of tomorrow's great Entry, with charade following monologue and lampoon following charade under the direction of a potbellied, black-headed Irishman representing the Spirit of France, suspended gently swaying above the packed audience from the blocks and pulleys on the roof.

And when, reluctantly at length, the city guard tore themselves away, the entertainment was only beginning, for they had forgotten to let down the Spirit of France and that fluent person, not at all willing to be ignored, had captured the hand bellows and, declaiming, was coating the seething heads below with black varnish.

It was Michel Hérisson himself, draped half-naked in a sheet and almost helpless with laughter, who jumped for the cable operating the hook and let go, so that Thady Boy hurtled down through the air, past the dais under which lay the portable printing presses, past the bales of paper disguised behind scenery and the bales of paper disguised as scenery, and straight into a full trough of paste. A wall of white porridge three feet deep rose with a glottal smack and dropped in knackery-haunted gouts on the company.

It was as if a divine signal had come. The audience stood to a man. Into the nameless, lung-scouring gas which replaced air a clay ball shot; then another; then one with lead in it knocked someone out. Benches began to rise. The Delphic Oracle, tackled low, sagged with godlike indifference and stuffed her august nose at last into the copper. Abrupt as an overtaxed weight lifter, other deities fell. Someone whirled a stone elbow, skirling; paste-soggy clothes ripped; and in the glorious, semi-inebriated whirl of pounding flesh, the thicket of flailing arms and belling throats and the shouts of damnable hilarity, blood and ink became one.

*   *   *

They delivered Thady Boy, damp, clean and singing at the Croix d'Or at three in the morning.

Not a few people heard him arrive. A door banged after repeated farewells, and an uneven satisfied chanting ascended the stairs interrupted by innumerable thuds and clatters:

> *'Cows, pigs, horses, sheep, goats,*
> *Dogs, cats, hens, geese—noisy goods—'*

The O'LiamRoe heard it. He awoke from his fireside snooze in the parlour and turned a speculative blue eye on the door.

> *'—Noisy goods,*
> *Little bees that stick to all flowers:*
> *These are the ten beasts of the world's men.*
> *The reason I love Derry . . .'*

'Death alive, the world's only liquid chapbook,' said O'LiamRoe.

> *'—The reason I love Derry . . .'*

The solemn voice was outside the parlour. There was a prodigious fumbling, a scrape, and the door shook.

'The reason I love Derry is for its quietness, for its purity and for its crowds of white angels. Still up?' Thady Boy Ballagh strolled in, locked the door, slung a spattered cloak on a chair and stuck out his tongue at a mirror. 'God, I'm full of sour wine and cows' feet and you could make scones from my underwear.' His voice was pleasant, without accent, and clear as a bell.

O'LiamRoe, while philosophic enough about a reverse of his own, did have a conscience, and had been out of temper ever since Lymond's summons from his Dowager Queen. Addressing his prodigal ollave, his voice had an edge to it. 'The Queen Mother of Scotland surely has a queer style of entertaining?'

'Oh Lord, no. I spent the evening elsewhere. Playing at paper games. With your admirer Robin Stewart.'

'In Ireland,' said The O'LiamRoe shortly, 'that man would be put into petticoats and set to milking the goats. He's a terrible let-down to his sex. . . . So the royal audience was brief? Fruitless her corn, fruitless her rivers, milkless her cattle, plentiless her fruit, for there was but one acorn upon the stalk, and it failed her?'

Quickly, methodically, Lymond was stripping. Under his soaked shirt the false stomach sagged in its leather covers. He unbuckled it, his face unruffled, and examined it before laying it by the hearth. 'She has her worries. No need to concern yourself.'

'What did she say?' asked O'LiamRoe, driven to being explicit.

Lymond paused. His black hair, damply curling, showed a tinge of gold at the roots; and only the dye ingrained in his skin disguised the gold stubble of his beard. In the slack-lidded eyes lived an echo of something hilarious and vital. O'LiamRoe felt a sudden obscure drag at his entrails. If he could, he would have withdrawn the question.

'What did she say? "I have brought you to the ring—hop it if you can." Quotation,' said Lymond.

O'LiamRoe stood up. 'My life for you, it's another master you're needing. Is there not a smart, orthodox rebel of an Irishman that would do? There's young Gerald of Kildare now; but he's in Rome and maybe a thought too small for the hire of an ollave. Or Cormac O'Connor, then. His father's between four walls in the Tower of London and Cormac is wild, wild to kick the English out of Ireland; Henri would see that he came to Court and sat soft in the crook of his arm, and his ollave too. You would need only another name, and pink hair maybe.'

Lymond glanced at him, and picked up a towel. 'What'll you wager I can't enter the royal circle as Thady Boy Ballagh?'

'Before Wednesday?' O'LiamRoe spoke sarcastically, the exaggerated ease out of his manner.

'Or Thursday.' Below the collarbone, Lymond's skin was surprisingly brown, and the contouring was neat-muscled and shapely, despite the flawing of scars. He added, glancing up from his towelling, 'If I achieved a foothold at Court, would you stay?'

O'LiamRoe's freckled face gleamed as he enjoyed the idea. 'As your ollave? Let you not be tempting me.'

Lymond flung a bedsheet round his shoulders and hugged his knees, his gaze on the hot charcoal, and this time gave his mind to it. 'As O'LiamRoe. This nonsense will sort itself out. And after the pleasure of berating the King's Majesty, it might be pleasant to spend the winter at his expense.'

'Ah! The powerful old women there are in it,' said O'LiamRoe. 'This nonsense is to be sorted out, is it? And Francis Crawford of Lymond needs a sponsor, if that awkward clod of an Irishman will drop his pretensions to pride?'

Lymond was not drunk. But even taking a tenth of what he appeared to take, his head was not at its clearest to deal with O'Liam-Roe in this mood, and he knew it. He said finally, 'You'd better play tennis with them on Tír-nan-óg, my dear, if you're going to call thirty-five old. The Queen Mother isn't going to stir a little finger in this affair; and I'm not at all sure that I want to meddle in hers. I suggested a sporting wager; but if you're bored with France or with myself, no doubt you'll take ship on Thursday.'

The marmalade head was cocked on one side. O'LiamRoe felt like being difficult. It was the other man who was in his debt. He had brought the fellow to France as his secretary to please his cousin Mariotta, who was also Lymond's sister-in-law. He knew Lymond was Scots and not Irish, and he knew he was here with a mission. Indeed, it was out of a kind of schoolboy amusement that he had offered to help the deception. He therefore grinned, stretched, yawned an ear-cracking yawn and said, 'Will I stay, now, if someone kindly gives me a chance? Who knows? Ask me after the King and yourself have had a talk about it. . . . And that puts me in mind of a thing. Piedar Dooly has a morsel of news. You recall our half-footed friend of the whale?'

This time he had the other man's full attention. 'Who fairly spoiled your one nightshirt? Yes.'

'Well, now. He's called Pierre Destaiz, it seems; and plaster whales are a passing concern. He's one of the royal keepers at St. Germain. He's an expert on elephants.'

Lymond's eyes narrowed. His gaze, suddenly impersonal, rested thoughtfully on the accustomed idleness in O'LiamRoe's soft face. Then he buried his face in his sheet, laughing noiselessly. His voice, muffled, came to Phelim. 'And he's come to Rouen for the *collier à toutes bêtes*. Go on.'

'He's been sent from the Royal Menagerie as he's a native of Rouen—'

'—And the elephants are to be used in the procession. With the enemies of France painted on the soles of their feet. With a dugong, a pill-rolling beetle, and a full squadron of horse of three pashas. And the little bees that stick to all flowers,' said Lymond, laughing harder. 'Ah, my simple orchidaceous, rotten, fertile, maimed, beloved fool of a France. Tomorrow,' he said, sitting up with an effort, 'tomorrow we go, web-footed country cousins that we are, to see the elephants.'

'Tomorrow,' said O'LiamRoe placidly, 'we stay in this room. And on Monday. And on Tuesday. By urgent request of the authorities. The Elect of God has had enough of visiting natives, and them not using their handkerchiefs and leaving marks on the walls, and we are confined to this building henceforth. "Achieve a foothold at Court" is it?' said the Prince of Barrow cordially, raising a limpid blue eye. 'Well, well. Busy child, I think I shall just take that wager up.'

*   *   *

They had three days to pass indoors before the Entry on Wednesday. They spent them drinking, arguing and nourishing a concatenation of visitors.

Their first, on Sunday morning, not too early, was Robin Stewart. Lord d'Aubigny was the official watchdog, but besides finding the task uncongenial he was involved in the day's dreadful events. Stewart had been told not to let the Croix d'Or party out of his sight until Wednesday, when he and his lordship would take them, under leash, to the great Entry before shipping them post haste for Ireland.

He took the job eagerly. Slit-eyed and thickheaded, he arrayed his numberless ball and socket joints on the Croix d'Or fireplace and analysed Thady Boy's recent performance. But still, after all his questions, it was hard to find out why to Mr. Ballagh inspiration seemed to come easily, and to Robin Stewart it came not at all.

Then Michel Hérisson arrived, his coat streaked with clay and strained across his broad shoulders, his white hair plastered wet from a sobering water jug. He leaped at Thady, his outstretched hand a flat boulder of cracked and cooled pumice; and thumped him mightily on the shoulder blades. 'Man, man, I wouldn't have missed that if it had cost me my presses instead of saving 'em. . . .'

The O'LiamRoe and the sculptor took to one another. If the Irishman was surprised by his secretary's exploit he did not show it. He launched forth at some length on a parallel adventure and set the older man laughing so that Stewart was able to concentrate on Thady Boy once again.

The callers that day were largely members of the previous night's audience. They did not come empty-handed, and among other things brought a lively account of the Earl of Huntly becoming a Knight of the Order of St. Michael, with thirty-odd members of the Chapter trailing about Rouen clinking with what Thady Boy had irreverently described as the *collier à toutes bêtes*, or Every Quadruped's Free Chain.

By Monday a small court had sprung up, with the Irishmen at its centre, and patronized by those of a liberal or unorthodox turn of mind who were willing to risk royal displeasure—a minor risk, for Stewart was discreet. The O'LiamRoe, expanding in a climate he knew, was outrageous and entertaining at his ease; and Thady Boy, while visited by no wild inspiration under the eye of his master, produced *sotto voce* at intervals a caustic commentary which the newcomers cherished. On Tuesday afternoon there were some half-dozen there, including Stewart, sitting cross-boned in the corner cleaning his nails, when the door opened to admit a small party which included Mistress Boyle and Oonagh, her dark and singular niece.

O'LiamRoe greeted them, his freckled face alight with pleasure dimmed by the merest crumb of a fret. Her headdress askew, her cloak pinned with three different brooches and long, unsuitable earrings wagging like some hair-controlled scale for hysteria, Madame Boyle beat into the room. 'Will ye look at him! He no sooner sets foot on the land than he ups and gives the holy King of it the desperate scold that a cow hand would be sorry to get. . . .'

She flung back her head, emitted a peal of laughter, and lowering a face wiped clean of levity said, 'O'LiamRoe, I've been fairly bothered out of my senses with that thing. Had I never sent you a message, you would have behaved like a dove and be sitting at Court with your two shoes on the white neck of a lady-in-waiting, with respect and deference and fine meals and a sweet kiss in a corner to keep you warm this winter.'

'Indeed; and it's quilted frieze I prefer,' said O'LiamRoe politely, beginning the introductions. 'And with Thady Boy at the criminality too, we have fairly enjoyed ourselves putting a blot or two in the terrible rule books they have.'

'Sweet, sweet is your hand in a pitcher of honey, my jewel,' said Mistress Boyle, sitting. 'But I'll not count myself pardoned till I hear the whole tale; and what the King said; and what our pretty de Genstan got out of his mouth, and the hairs on him stiff as a hog brush with fright.'

As O'LiamRoe told it, it was a rollicking story. While her aunt howled and chortled, mopping her eyes, Oonagh withdrew to where Robin Stewart sat, grinning, beside Thady Boy, who was engaged puff-eyed and scowling over a solitary game of cards. Acid in her low voice, she addressed the secretary. 'The tale is beneath the notice of an ollave of the highest grade?'

He picked up a card and laid it down doubtfully. 'The novelty, I would say, is the least thing worn off. But the first time I heard it, surely, the balls of my eyes set to whirling like mill paddles from fright.'

She was cold. 'Why? You had nothing to lose.'

'A man with a deficient helmet is not called to pay forfeit,' said Thady Boy calmly. He shuffled the cards.

'A man who helps to hide printing presses might have to forfeit more than he bargained for,' said Oonagh. 'You flatter yourself, my jolly boy.'

For a moment he was quite still. Then he lifted his head. Oonagh O'Dwyer, cold, hard-wrought with unleashed storms and eaten with pride, looked full into his eyes. The heavy gaze, warm, cloudless and deliberate, held hers as long as it needed, and tossed it aside. Deep lines of mischief and laughter sprang to Thady Boy's dark face. He laughed. 'No. I flatter you, my dear, don't you think?' he said, and returned placidly to his game.

Her breath beating unregarded in her throat, she got up then, her hands taut, and looked down on his bent head. In Irish, she said, '*Thady Boy Ballagh:* would you not expect the name Boy on a yellow-haired man?'

O'LiamRoe heard it. He gave a quick glance at his ollave; but Lymond's Gaelic was adequate, he was certain, and the black hair had been re-dyed that morning. Thady answered in English.

'I pushed up through the sod yellow as a crocus, they tell me, and so they christened me after Papa. *Boy* was all they ever knew of his name; but he left the English version well accredited and they had no reason to disbelieve him in Gaelic. Oh, bad end to it!' He glanced up, gathering together the cards. 'Ah, the dear sympathy in that sweet eye . . . I haven't the least objection, mind; but it's fairly taking my mind off my game.'

Her voice was quiet. 'Women grow in the fields of France like turnips. Don't you care for them?'

Thady Boy smiled, running the cards lightly through long fingers. 'Experiments have been a little restricted by the curfew.'

She watched his hands too. 'La Veuve at Dieppe will be sore to the heart. Won't you miss her down there on the Loire?'

The cards danced without a pause. Behind them, amid the laughter and talk, O'LiamRoe had become quiet. Thady Boy took his time. He dealt himself a hand, turned up a card, and drew one from the pack before he said, 'No. A dear, neat little soul like a pot of strawberries, would you say; but hard, hard on the purse.' And he paid no more attention. She turned on her heel.

It was a long time before she and her aunt left, and still longer before the other visitors followed, and at last they were left alone with their Archer as guard. For once O'LiamRoe sat silent, hunched by the fire, his eyes straying to the dark, withdrawn face of Francis Crawford. They were sitting there still when the bell spoke, announcing midnight, and the morning of Wednesday, October first, 1550: the day of the Royal Entry of King Henri the Second into his good town of Rouen; and their last day in France.

V

Rouen: Fast Drivings for the Purpose of Killing

The following are fast drivings and unlawful drivings for the purpose of killing: Driving into the sea; driving into a puddle; driving into mud; driving with malice and neglect, by which some are lost. . . .

The wounds of beasts are as the wounds of human beings, from death to white blow.

TWO scented red heads, fresh from morning worship, hung cheek by cheek like two peonies in a garland, window-gazing at the crowds.

Mary Queen of Scotland spoke first, dreamily, her face cupped in warm palms. 'I regret,' she said in English, 'that I bit your marmoset, my aunt.'

No regret was visible on her lucent, seven-year-old face. On one of her fingers was a small piece of bandage.

'Don't apologize,' said Jenny Fleming, lifting her firm, pretty hand from the little girl's shoulder. 'Our nerves aren't what they were; and the brute had the last word anyway. Glory, child, if you get the rabies on top of today's little gadding, they'll bring the skin up over my ears like the widow did to the Judge.'

Turning, the Queen eyed her favourite aunt for a long moment. She said piercingly, 'You're afraid! You're afraid we'll be caught!'

Although a good many in despair had accused her of it, Jenny Fleming had never been afraid in her life. Her soul was fanned with peacocks' tails and nourished with stardust; her appetite for excitement was a child's. Children loved her. Mary, future bride of the Dauphin and treasure of the royal nurseries, was her own special care; but the six-year-old fiancé Louis himself was an ally, and the small French princesses Elizabeth and Claude were her fondest admirers.

Thirty-seven children were being reared with the Children of France, to serve them and play with them and bear them company, and mischief and measles broke out in the nurseries with equal facility. This month one of the smallest princes was ill—was dying, had they known it—and the great household of babies, with its 150 officials and 57 cooks, was at Mantes. So that instead of the paralysing sea-growth of maids of honour, grooms, pages and ladies-in-waiting, Queen Mary was here at Court with her mother and with only her aunt and her aunt's four Fleming offspring to look after her.

And today, not even these. James, Lord Fleming, fifteen, sandy and solemn, was to ride with the King in his Entry. Margaret Erskine, with her husband, would watch the procession from the state pavilion with the Queen Dowager's retinue. And here, at a magnificent window in the Faubourg St.-Sever, Mary Queen of Scots was to see it with her aunt Jenny Fleming, with her two small Fleming cousins and with no nurse, groom or page other than two members of the Royal Bodyguard of Archers outside the door. A situation with many attractions for Jenny Fleming, and which she had planned for some days to use to the full.

Now, half an hour before the procession was due to begin, she glanced at the clock, jumped up and began distributing cloaks. 'Caught! Lord, we shall be if we're late!' And catching their hands, she ran for the door, the three children spinning behind her.

Outside, the Archers stared straight ahead as the muffled figures emerged, although one of them winked at the trim, unmistakable Fleming back. My lady the Queen's aunt could make surprisingly effective arrangements when she chose; and today as always, her wishes were law. In making historic Entry into his loyal town of Rouen, the *très magnanime, très puissant et victorieux Roy de France, Henri, Deuxième de ce nom,* was, unwittingly, to be royally supported. Nothing, uniformed or not, was going to dissuade a parcel of irresponsible redheads from the iron path of a whim.

*   *   *

At dawn the same morning, leaving Piedar Dooly behind, The O'LiamRoe and his secretary left the Croix d'Or under strong escort to cross town and bridge and take up their stance outside for the Entry. Lord d'Aubigny, in a dress of unbearable magnificence, had collected them, and Robin Stewart, highly polished to the best of his conscientious ability, was at the rear with a handful of men.

Already the streets were all but impassable. Half Normandy was taking part in King Henri's processional Entry and the other half had turned out to watch. The streets had been crammed to the crown since midnight and the processional route, the Rue Grand Pont, the Cross, the Rue St.-Ouen, St.-Maclou, the Pont Robec and the Cathedral, was lined with tapestries and flowers, and the draped and garlanded windows were thick with heads.

Somewhere a trumpet called, threadlike above the trampling, and the pace suddenly quickened. The trumpet sounded again.

'God, we're going to be late,' said Robin Stewart; and Lord d'Aubigny, hearing, swore. The mistiming was his, not the Archer's, but his place for the procession, unlike theirs, was public and prominent. 'There's a cart,' said O'LiamRoe mildly.

The stresses of the journey had made speech so far impossible, but both the King of France's guests had seemed more tickled than impressed by the occasion, although The O'LiamRoe, industriously craning, had twice tripped and been saved by his armpits from being trodden flat underfoot.

The cart he had noticed held the last of the cortège: a huddle of garlanded nymphs clutching baskets; several men with cardboard castles on poles, or with antique trumpets or amphorae; two gloomy mock-captives with their hands tied; and three withdrawn figures in square-necked Roman costume and bare knees, burdened each with a struggling lamb. 'Come on,' said O'LiamRoe, and scrabbled diligently at the side of the vehicle. Thady Boy gave him a heave and followed, and Stewart and his men piled after.

Lord d'Aubigny hesitated. The decision was not his, but he could see no alternative. He had no intention, however, of personally riding in the cart. He had a brief, charming conversation with the nearest embroidered young man on horseback and was helped up to share his saddle. In a short while he had disappeared.

The cart with its habromaniac burden trundled on. The O'Liam-Roe, wound like the Laocoön on a trumpet, raised his voice in amiable strictures on victory processions that were a dead copy of the Ptolemies, and one of the dryads crushed close to an Archer gave a giggle. Yellow light burst from the sun. Shadows sprang fresh and lively over the crowd; gilt shone and paint sparkled, and cold, neurotic, bad-tempered faces warmed and coloured and relaxed. There were bursts of laughter, and bursts of cheering, and a surge of noise from behind them as the cart, reaching the gates, rumbled on to the bridge, and the fresh river air greeted it.

The Seine was covered with ships. On their right, the big merchantmen were crowded to the yardarms; and on the left smaller boats, brightly painted and pinned all over with armorial shields, darted backwards and forwards. On the far shore Orpheus waited by the Triumphal Arch chatting to Hercules. Beside them on the beach Neptune, a cloak over his blue robes, was sitting huddled beside a Seven-Headed Hydra which was lying on its back and eating a sausage. Beyond that sat three men next to a plaster whale.

The noise, the splashing, the flag-strewn spread of colour beyond, where the whole pageant wheeled and formed and shifted ready to move, like some private army conscripted by gods, jewellers and theatrical costumiers, was too much for the lambs. They broke loose. One got over the side of the cart. One, struggling, was hooked by O'LiamRoe's trumpet, and the third was silenced, threshing, by a pot on its head. To laughter, shouts, bleating and a shower of triumphant toots O'LiamRoe arrived at the muster point like chariot-borne Dionysus with his Pans, Menads and Satyrs but without Thady Boy Ballagh who, to Stewart's rib-squeezing chagrin, was no longer there.

There was no time to search. A fanfare sounded. Running, they reached the pavilion as the drums rolled and the voice of the *Georges d'Amboise*, over the river, declared the King in his chair.

O'LiamRoe and Stewart found their obscure benches and sat. With glint, twitter, rustle, like the flight of small costly birds, the Court of France and its guests settled around them. Silence fell, into which, quavering, rose the *Exaudiat te Dominus* of the first advancing procession.

Bedded in scent and blinded with cloth of gold, The O'LiamRoe watched with the rest as, blackhooded, tall crosses trembling, a file of clergy appeared and paced slowly towards them. The Triumphant and Joyous Entry had begun.

*   *   *

The Chariot of Happy Fortune was in the middle of it, after the councillors and the corporations and the parliamentarians and two overdecorated floats. Drawn by unicorns and surrounded by nymphs, spearmen and halberdiers, it represented King Henri, enthroned, with four of his children at his feet, and a winged figure loftily poised at his back, offering a paper crown to his bonneted head.

It received a great welcome. Phalanx after phalanx of worthy bodies, however splendid, had had time to pall. The unicorns, led by costumed grooms, were behaving well about their horns, and the painted rhapsodies all round the cart were more than flattering while the pseudo-king, sceptred in ermine, was positively handsome, as well as resembling the real one quite a lot. The small boy acting as the Dauphin, was obviously his son. It was easy to guess that the angel and the other three children, demure on tasselled cushions, were also related. Reminded by the red heads before her, the Queen Dowager spoke absently to Margaret Erskine. 'I must tell your mother to destroy that marmoset. Mary teases it, and it bites.'

Her gaze, resting idly on the float, suddenly focussed, slid down a familiar small body, and stopped at a hand adorned with a small piece of bandage. The Queen Mother of Scotland drew a long, shuddering breath and brought her fingers hard down on Margaret Erskine's soft wrist. 'It isn't possible!'

Jenny Fleming's daughter, pressing her lips tightly together, caught her husband's eye. There must be no scene. But, of course, except in private, there would be no scene. The Dowager's hand was already relaxing. 'It is, you know,' said Margaret Erskine. 'Look who the angel is.'

The Chariot of Happy Fortune reached the Pavilion. It paused; king bowed to king, flowers were thrown and cheering broke out; then the unicorns took the strain and it rumbled on in its turn, bearing with it, unnoticed by its less observant French audience, Lady Fleming, Mary Fleming, Agnes Fleming, and Her Majesty the Queen of Scotland.

The O'LiamRoe was very taken with it also, mentioning to his neighbour that it would be a grand cart for market day, and the hens fairly cross-eyed peering and marvelling at the pictures. The elephants which followed, tasselled, crescented and harnessed, pacing in three pairs between their turbaned attendants, fascinated him even more.

Long trunks docile, brush tails lightly twitching, they patiently paced with shaky replicas of ships, forts and captured castles on the mighty massif of each back. The finest beasts led, a monolithic pair with the noble head and bright hazel eye of a healthy animal in the prime of its life. The bull elephant, with a certain amount of planned forethought, carried on its back four bronze ewers smoking with scented oils. On its high brow there lay a broad and shallow serenity, and its small, searching ingenious eye was irregularly gay.

They passed, and the foot cortège came, and the mounted Children of Honour. As the end of the procession came in sight the King rose, the princes and peers of his retinue with him, and prepared to mount and follow his burghers into his good city of Rouen.

The head of the procession reached the bridge and began to cross it. In silence the trample of hooves and the tread of feet rumbled over the boards. Gaunt and splendid in the October air, the Cathedral bell spoke. It rang in great strokes, beating on the wind as the Court, glittering silver and white, moved in a drift after the long laborious ribbon of the pageant. The *Marie d'Estouteville*, high and sweet, joined her voice to the *Georges d'Amboise* and from church to church and belfry to belfry the pealing anthems of pomp and tribute sprang to life. From the Grosse-Horloge itself *Rouvel* and *Cache-Ribaud* swung and vied until the crack of gun salvoes told that the King was nearing the bridge.

From all the theatres, music rose and fluttered like flags beyond and within the crowds. A burst of cannon from the river told that the water pageant had begun. The crowds cheered, debris floated, and a firecracker, mistimed in the excitement, coughed, exploded and sparked under the bellies of the Queen of Scotland's four unicorns as the Chariot of Happy Fortune entered the bridge.

Another went off. The leading horse, sweating, jerked its head, horn askew, and with a plunge whipped its bridle free and turned round. The harness jangled, the wheels rumbled and skidded, and the groom, losing grip, ran forward and shouted just as the horses, jammed flat on the rail, came to a stop in a tangle of traces. The Chariot, swinging behind them, struck the float in front, split, and stopped broadside on the bridge, with four startled children upset on the floor and a king, prostrate, with a descending angel in his arms.

The six elephants hesitated. By the great bull at their head a man in Oriental dress spoke sharply. There was a pause; and in that small instant, unnoticed by the crowd, a plaster whale at the bridge end ran up on quiet wheels. Swift, white-faced and gruesome, it sped towards the last pair of elephants, and as their eyes whitened and their vast loins gathered, it opened its jaws and ejected, squealing, bloody and blinded, the one missing lamb. Like blown paper in a grey, petrified forest of limbs it hurled itself, insane, among the elephants; and the elephants, screaming, began to lumber away.

There was only one way for them to go; and that was forward to the bridge. The man, woman and children in the jammed cart, the watching crowd and all the impacted mass of the procession filling the far bridge watched them come in a trance of fright. The turbaned men began to run; the great beasts gathered speed. There were perhaps ten yards of road, densely lined with spectators, between the bull elephant and the bridge when the chief Keeper, running lightly, caught him with his iron hook.

It might have been a fly whisk. The bull brushed past, great feet thudding, housings swaying; and there was a crash as the powerful hind leg, lashing out, found the drifting side of the whale and made it powder. The Keeper dropped the goad, and laying hands on the crupper straps, tried to mount as the beast passed, but was shaken off, hands bleeding, before he could find a hold for his feet.

On the bridge, the trapped float rocked and crashed as its horses, frantic, splintered and smashed the bridge rails. Lumbering steadily, the six elephants made straight for the threshold, the bull leading, eyes white, tusks alight in the sun, burning oil jars rocking spilt on his back.

On the arch over the bridge, something moved. Plump, nimble, fluttering black, light as leaf on lind, a man dropped from the pediment and clung firm among the upset, steaming urns on the bull elephant's back. Then, gripping the harness with one hand, he plunged spur and knife both into the animal's right flank.

The bull raised his taut, dripping trunk, screamed, and stopped dead like a log in a jam. With a shuddering thud, his harem ran into him. For a moment they plunged, trumpeting, edging and thudding on to the bridge; then the bull's rider used the goads again quickly, shouting, and the Keeper, running up, added his strange gibberish to the noise. Frantic, infuriated, blind with fright and seared and scalded by the oil, the bull heeled like an undermined fortress and made for the river.

Thady Boy Bailagh, filthy, blistered and smelling like an in-season civet cat, slid off the bull elephant's back as it went under. A turbaned figure, sleek as an eel, with one eyebrow pulled high by a scar, passed him running and got to the great back before it submerged. The elephant ducked, and the Keeper, with the ease of long practice, wrapped his fists round the harness and prepared, standing, to be taken for a swim. The other five followed; and with heaving flank and spraying trunk and bright eyes turned suddenly from panic to pure mischief, began to put the fear of God into the mermaids, the monsters, the little boats and Father Neptune himself in the Seine.

For a moment Thady Boy watched; then streaming river water and perfume he turned, a little stiffly, to wade back to the shore.

He was still in the water when they reached him, back-slapping, shouting, talking, exclaiming, streaming down from the road. He was hustled from the beach to where a heavy, grey-bearded man in his fifties waited on horseback, a sword of ceremony stuck temporarily in his pommel. The rider bent down. 'You, sir!'

Behind them, the procession was jerkily resuming its way; the wreckage was being cleared, and the shocked performers had vanished. Thady Boy was white, but his voice had a lilt in it. 'Your lordship's servant.'

'Your brave action was marked by the King's Majesty. He desires to thank you.'

'It was nothing,' said Thady Boy with modesty. 'A middling piece of invention, all patched up with cat and clay.'

The royal party was beginning to pass. The Constable Montmorency brought his horse to the side of the road, and Thady Boy followed. 'His grace desires to do your courage honour. I am commanded to ask your name and designation and to invite you to sup with the King and his friends at St. Ouen tonight.'

'Indeed, now, isn't that kindness itself?' said Thady Boy. 'And I would think shame to refuse, except that the King himself was for having me leave the city this night. Thady Boy Ballagh is my name, and I am paid secretary to The O'LiamRoe, Prince of Barrow; and himself unlucky with his small chat the other day.'

There was a short silence. The Constable cleared his throat. 'I am sure that your departure can be deferred for at least a day. You will be advised. I am to tell you also that clothes will be sent to replace those you have spoiled.'

'Ah, *dhia*, the sweet generosity that spouts from his heart's veins,' said Thady Boy. 'And the loving forgiveness. And then Sir Gawaine wept, and King Arthur wept, and then they swooned both. Mallory might have had this very thing in his mind.'

'I am not empowered,' said the First Christian Baron, Marshal and Grand Master and Constable of France, Knight of the King's Order and of the Garter and First Gentleman of the Chamber and Governor of Languedoc, 'to invite the Prince of Barrow.'

'And that is a power of good news in itself,' said Thady Boy with composure, 'for it would take an elephant, no less, to persuade him to come there.'

The procession was moving quickly now, and the Swiss Guards were almost on them. Montmorency sat back in his saddle, gathering the reins, his small shrewd eyes above the squat nose and rough beard outstaring the ollave. 'But you, my friend, have no objections?'

'May I be struck by a mallet of lightning like Lewy if I lie. You couldn't stop me,' said Thady Boy Ballagh.

*   *   *

Long after the Court had gone, crowds still jammed the roads and access to the city was blocked for an hour. The affair at the bridge, seen by them merely as a distant upheaval, had by that time been detailed ten times to O'LiamRoe and Robin Stewart. While the Irishman seemed only mildly amused, Robin Stewart, red-faced and a little upset, was avid to discover Thady and explore every nuance. They made the attempt to get back eventually, pushing through the picnicking crowds; but although they met plenty who had seen him, Thady Boy himself in his temporarily restored dignity was not to be found.

*   *   *

Alone on the plains of Grandmont, disgraced in the trampled grass and litter, far from the celebrated procession, the six elephants stood, roped each by the foreleg side by side in the vast thirteen-foot tent put up several days since for their comfort; their trunks peacefully swaying as the cowardie scuttled back and forth with limp forkloads of hay. Small puffs of steam came from their mouths. Their breath was sweet, filling the sun-warmed, crisp air; and their hides, soothed, clean and lustrous from the water, lay calm on their great hips like the skin of the moon. Only at the end of the line the great bull stirred a little, the towering back swathed and padded and the knowing eye blurred.

Lymond, who had been standing quietly at the entrance, moved a little; and the workboy, pulling his fork out of a bin, saw him and whispered in Urdu. 'M. Abernaci?' said Francis Crawford.

The boy was frightened. He walked sideways for three steps, saying nothing; then suddenly scuttled and vanished. Within the Keeper's own tent beyond, the door flap in his hand, a silent, turbaned figure stood watching. Scarred, bearded and withered, the brooding Djinn of the printing presses, Archembault Abernaci, head Keeper of the King of France's elephants, smiled, displaying gapped, broken black teeth, and summoned with a noiseless raised hand. Lymond passed the elephants and went in.

Inside, it was comfortable, with a bench and several stools, a small chest and a mattress in one corner. There was a cloth of coarse saye on the floor and a stove with the remains of somebody's meal beside it. Against the canvas was a stand of weapons: a hook, a spear, a sword, several knives and a mahout's wristband, the five lead-heeled tails hanging limp.

Abernaci stood now by his armoury, immaculate in the high-collared coat, his face within the shining folds of his turban like one of the jewelled crocodiles of Arsinoë. The black eyes stared unmoving at Lymond.

Lymond, weaponless, tattered and damp, gazed back, his head tilted. Then, still silent, he slipped his hand inside the scaly mess of his clothes and brought it out holding a square block of pearwood. It was the block Abernaci had been carving four days before.

The dark man's eyes flickered. There was a pause; then he broke the silence at last with a soft exclamation in Urdu.

'I trust,' said Lymond pleasantly, 'that the sentiment was polite. You guessed, I should imagine, who had taken it.'

The mahout bowed.

Amusement, irrepressible, pulled at Francis Crawford's long mouth. 'God keep us from gyrcarlings and all long nebbit things from the East. There is no need,' he said, 'to be so cautious, my butty. I'm from Scotland myself.'

The scar lifted, the black eyes narrowed, and the dreadful teeth within the curling black beard were exposed. 'Christ. It's yourself, Mr. Crawford,' said Archembault Abernaci, Keeper of the Menageries of France, in the purest cadences of Partick, Glasgow, Scotland. 'It's yourself; and here I never said sids for fear I was wrong—heigh, heigh.' And the mahout sank down on the bench puffing and cheeping like a hen with a cold. 'Heigh, heigh; and the grand head ones of France with a scrape or two where they hadna an itch, but for twa clever lads from the Clyde.'

Lymond laughed aloud; and spinning the block of wood in the air, let it impale itself on the razor-sharp spear, engraved side uppermost. The arms of the house of Culter, crudely peeled from the wood under his eyes by Abernaci in the murk of the sculptor's big cellar, stared down at them both. Abernaci, his head cocked, studied it fondly, and Lymond said, 'You left it lying at Hérisson's, for me to take. How did you guess who I was?'

'We fought together, you and I,' said Abernaci, and grinning, hauled off the silk turban. Underneath was a fringed head, trimly bald. Below that, by some alchemy, the nutlike face was pure Scots. 'When I was between jobs. Ye willna remember. But my brother ye knew. A grand man at arms in his day; and he was with you and your men a good while. He's dead, I've heard tell, but whether it was the drink or the English I never found out.'

Lymond's voice was sharp. 'What's your name?'

'Abernethy. Erchie Abernethy,' said the King of France's mahout, his face blithe.

'So Turkey Mat was your brother . . .' said Lymond, and went on with barely a pause. 'He's dead, yes. He died in my service. I can tell you about it if you wish. And then I'll go. I'm not proposing to make it a family custom.'

The athletic small figure jumped to its feet. 'Christ, man, there's nothing more I want tae hear. He was going anyway: what better way would he want it? . . . I formed my ain opinion of Crawford of Lymond, I'll say to your face, yon time I served with you; and Turkey formed the same. It was the only time in our two lives we ever agreed about anything. . . . There was a scar or two ye had then that ye carry now, and I was nine-tenths sure of ye. Sure enough to give a hint that there was a friend handy at least . . .

'. . . Fegs,' said Erchie Abernethy in a vexed voice. 'Fegs, I'm right buffle-heidit—sit down—I'm that pleased tae see ye I forgot the state you'd be in. I'd a chancy half hour with yon big bull in there, I'm telling you. A nicer, kinder-hearted big bairn of a beastie you'd be hard pushed tae find. Heathens! Foreigners! I'll have the law on them, so I will . . .'

Hopping, chattering, his arms full of cloths, he came to rest at last. 'Sit down, man. It'll pass off. I'll ease it for you in a minute. Man or beast, the treatment's the same. But I'm ettlin' tae know,' said Erchie Abernethy, tenderly lifting the ruined cloth off Francis Crawford's shoulders, 'I'm fairly bursting tae ken how ye guessed I spoke Scots?'

Lymond looked up. Superficial pain, withstood or ignored for quite a long time, had made his eyes heavy, but they were brimming with laughter. 'Well, God,' he said. 'In the water, you were roaring your head off at a bloody bull elephant called Hughie.'

*   *   *

Skilfully doctored and done up in balm and bandages, Lymond slept on Archie Abernethy's pallet like the dead and woke up fresh, collected, and in command of a stream of cool, sarcastic invective.

71

The Keeper was impervious.

'Ye needed it. It was part of the treatment. Ye ken the tale of the lassie and her pastille of virgin Cretan bhang—'

'Whereof if an elephant smelt a dirham's weight, he would sleep from year to year. Quite,' said Lymond. 'But I am not Ali Nur al-Din and you, save the mark, are not Miriam the Girdle-Girl. I can stand twitching my tail like Hughie any damned day of the week. Meanwhile, my time is short.'

The Keeper had unbuttoned his brocade coat, displaying a wonderful silk shirt and breech hose beneath. Sitting hands on knees, he studied his fellow Scot with a cracked black-stumped grin. 'I heard you were with the Irish prince, him that's soft in the heid,' he said. 'And under guard these last three days forbye. How would you be so sore short of sleep, I wonder? Picking locks, maybe, of a night?'

Sitting on the low pallet, Lymond picked up Abernaci's dress scimitar and made a cut at the air. 'No need. The guard was Robin Stewart.'

The walnut face filled with a malicious joy. 'Och, yon speldron. King Harry's prize Archer, all sense and no wits. He'd let a mouse out of a mousehole if it put on drawers and a mask. Anything byordinary, and Robin Stewart's fair flummoxed: you can dodge him blindfold, I suppose. They let him in to Michel Hérisson's, ye know, and lay wagers on what he'll do next.'

'Do you go there often?'

Archie Abernethy rose. He caught the scimitar deftly in midair by its handle and hung it on the stand with the rest. 'I enjoy the carving. And whiles I like to hear Scots spoken—a lot of exiles, and English too, go there.'

'I noticed as much. The English Resident calls it a hotbed of intrigue.'

'Och, it's a cheery crowd of irreligious rascals. They don't care. You've been making night calls on Sir James Mason then? And you the guests of the King of France?'

'The estranged guests. We antagonized our host so much that one of Mason's men was bold enough to approach me next day. Our English friends are interested, of course, in attracting O'LiamRoe's alienated affections. O'LiamRoe hasn't given it a thought. But I have been discussing it on his behalf. I wanted to find out, and quickly, whether it was myself or O'LiamRoe someone is trying to kill.'

The Keeper's dark eyes were entranced. 'Why should anyone want to kill you?'

Lymond said ruminatively, 'That's what I wondered until today. I have an unspecified commission from the Queen Mother to be on hand during her visit to France. Which is why I am formed so fowle.

I now know why she wants me, by God. Did you see the float on the bridge?'

Abernethy shook his bald head.

'Mary, Queen of Scotland, was in it, my merry mahout,' said Lymond coolly. 'And her aunt and two of her cousins. A private prank which one person too many knew about. Someone tried to assassinate that small child today, and it was the same person who tried to kill either O'LiamRoe or myself. Who is Pierre Destaiz's employer?'

Well past its zenith, the October sun shone red into the grain of the canvas, spilling curious shadows on the wall. Beyond the flap, an elephant could be heard siphoning hay with a dry rustle over her back, and whining breathily as the cowardie checked her.

There was a silence. 'I am,' said Archie Abernethy at length. 'When he's here to employ.'

'Who is he?'

'A Rouen man. He was at the St. Germain menagerie when I went there in '48, with two others. They had one animal each—Dod, think of it!' said the Keeper, showing his teeth. 'The beasts they had in the old King's day: hundreds of livres' of them—lions, ostriches, bears, birds. Peter Giles did nothing but travel around and send him stock. And then the old King died, and what was left? A lion, a bear and a dromedary. That's what was left. I'm telling you,' said the mahout, rocking himself, 'it was pitiful.'

'What brought you?' asked Lymond.

The Keeper shrugged. 'I'm getting old. But after Constantinople and Tarnassery I couldna see myself in a bit hutch in some lady's garden, looking after a wee puckle peacocks, or an old done lion and some doos. Giles told me King Henri here was building a grand new place at St. Germain and restocking, so I got the elephants together and came. You can't beat experience. I was in charge of them all, the birds and the hunting cats too, in six months. Yon one Destaiz didn't like it.'

'Did he know you were Scots?'

Abernethy spat. 'Would I get a job, would I keep a job anywhere with elephants, if it was known I was Scots? I'm Abernaci of St. Germain, the King's Keeper and Hughie's mahout; and in the whole of France, the only ones who know different are one or two travelling showmen, a moneylender, and a woman who lives in a house called Doubtance and kens not only my name but my soul, if I have one.— And yourself.' His shrewd eyes turned on the other man. 'I know I can trust you, but you've only my tale to believe. You've been gey confiding for a man of your sort, Crawford of Lymond.'

'You don't need reassurance,' said Lymond. 'And neither do I. You identified me at Hérisson's and told me so. You ran your guts

73

out with those elephants today. You're Turkey Mat over again without your nightcap; and I remember you more clearly than I want to for a murderous, reliable Partickhead rat.—But I wish to God you'd tell me all you know about Pierre Destaiz. He's attempted arson and bulk murder both in less than a week.'

'I've done you a good turn you don't even know about,' said the Keeper complacently. 'I told Sir George Douglas I'd met you in Ireland, passing through five years since. He was giving you a gey queer look in yon cellar. But what with the tale and the hash I made of it with my English, he was ready to laugh himself into fits and forget it. As for Destaiz . . . He was heading for trouble. I never took to him. He was in the procession with me, but he'd put in days helping his friends with yon damned whale, and he'd disappear for twenty-four hours at a time. But if he was working for someone else, I never heard of it.'

'He was,' said Lymond mildly. 'But he knew he was being followed. Piedar Dooly's enquiries the first day possibly put him on guard. . . . Destaiz filled the urns and strapped them on Hughie's back?'

'He did. And would Piedar Dooly be a wee, dour black fellow like a goat, that was haunting us all day Saturday, and upsetting the elephants?'

'It sounds like him. He's O'LiamRoe's servant,' said Lymond gravely. 'They both know who I am.'

'By God,' said Archie Abernethy. 'He nearly got served with a kick on the bottom. I was nearly sure Destaiz was plotting something myself, and then he turned as cautious as a dog with his first flea— Are ye wanting to see him?'

'I have been trying,' said Francis Crawford, 'to indicate as much for ten minutes.'

'Yes. Well. There's a wee difficulty,' said Archie Abernethy; and standing, he began to button up the gorgeous silk of his coat. 'There's a wee difficulty. He's deid.'

'You surprise me,' said Lymond dryly. 'How?'

'Oh, drowning. He got dragged in this morning, and he was no swimmer, poor chap. We had to send the elephant back in after him.'

'May I see him?' asked Lymond.

The Keeper hesitated. Then he said, 'Oh, aye. Come away. He's just next door', and led the way through to the elephants, nimble fingers resetting the turban on his head. In the darkest corner he bent, and hauling back a layer of sacking, disclosed the undignified and sodden corpse of a man with half a foot missing. 'That's Pierre.'

He had probably drowned as indicated; but he had certainly been knifed first. Proof or none, Hughie, the kindhearted big bairn of a beastie, had been swiftly avenged.

Crawford of Lymond, looking down, kept his counsel, and the man Abernaci, equally wordless, softly replaced the sheet. They walked together outside, and faced each other.

'Aye. It was a pity he drowned,' said Archie Abernethy, a genuine frown on his face. 'For I fancy if they're after the little Queen, someone else will have a try.'

'Yes. Unless we find out who it is.'

'*We?*'

'I thought I might rely on your benevolent eye—and that of Hughie,' said Lymond. 'How strict is your secret? If I send friends of mine to you, will they have to speak Urdu?'

'If they're Scots, and you trust them, then I'll take my chance,' said Abernaci. 'Tell them what you want, and ye can count on me if ye need me. Of course the Irish, I've always held, are a different matter . . . but I'm willing tae make an exception for your Doolys and such—provided, ye understand, it doesna spread. But, man— ye're leaving France yourself tomorrow, are ye not?'

'My dear Archie, were not you and I and Hughie all that lay between the King's triumphant Entry and a sad calamity today?'

'Even so—'

'And has not the King invited me to appear at his supper at St. Ouen tonight?'

'It's the least he could do. But still—'

'There is a saying of my adoptive ancestors. Though he performs a miracle, or two miracles, if he refuses the third miracle, it is not as profit to him. I shall dine at the Court of France tonight, and in the course of that evening, acquire the royal consent for O'LiamRoe and myself to stay as long as we please. For, to be perfectly frank,' said Lymond, gently reflective, 'to be perfectly frank, I can't wait to sink my teeth into the most magnificent, the most scholarly and the most dissolute Court in Europe, which so lightly slid out The O'LiamRoe, Chief of the Name, on his kneecaps and whiskers.'

VI

Rouen: The Difficult and the Impossible

The difference between the difficult and the impossible is as follows: the difficult is troublesome to procure, but though troublesome it is still procured; whereas the impossible is a thing which it is impossible for a person to procure, because it is not natural for anybody to get it at all.

ONE of the pleasures of Lord d'Aubigny's fastidious middle age was to see the Court dine, properly served, housed and habited. In diamonds, music and spice, in good talk, in good taste, in the secure knowledge that nearly every man present was of a higher rank than his own, Lord d'Aubigny felt that his life was worth while; that the great deeds of his forebears and the high honours of his brother Lennox were being outstripped by the splendour of his days; and that winged Comus was his bedfellow.

In all this glory, the promised presence of an Irish princeling's toadlike secretary was a blight and an affront. At Court, his distaste was shared. And when after Mass the Court resettled itself finally into the Abbatial Logis of St. Ouen amid a roar of talk in which with irony, with ridicule, with parody, with ruthless observation, the municipal efforts of the day were analysed, the cruellest and the wittiest quips concerned the King's forthcoming reluctant discharge of his elephantine obligations.

Meanwhile, the ollave, of course, was still missing. It was one of the occasions when Lymond asleep wrecked the peace of mind of more people than Lymond awake. Lord d'Aubigny was if anything relieved. Robin Stewart became very short-tempered, but was persuaded to allow The O'LiamRoe, unruffled as usual, to take advantage of the relaxed atmosphere to visit his friends under guard. In the smouldering ruins of a major explosion, which left the child Mary's face swollen with angry tears and Jenny Fleming in bed, boiled to rags in the seething vat of the Queen Mother's rage, Tom Erskine was trapped by the Dowager's remorseless determination that nothing whatsoever should prevent Thady Boy Ballagh from making the most suave, the most accomplished and the most glittering debut of the century at the French Court that night.

So, in the utmost secrecy, there was despatched to Thady Boy's lodging a case of soaps, scents and jewels, a sword, a sword belt, a dagger, a paper for a horse of up to 150 crowns, and a set of garments stiff with gold buckles and embroidery. It lay sealed in his room all afternoon beside a similar parcel, of a soberer kind, containing a selection of garments from the King of France's tailor. O'LiamRoe, returning at five from a successful series of visits, beginning with Michel Hérisson and ending with Mistress Boyle, found both boxes locked and untouched in the empty bedroom at the Croix d'Or, and beside them a litter of tattered black clothing.

Thady Boy Ballagh had returned, had climbed into his spare and salt-stained black suit, and abjuring even the modest standards of grace and hygiene enjoined on O'LiamRoe, had trailed off on foot to the Abbey Lodging of St. Ouen looking, as Piedar Dooly observed, like a potboiling of chimney sweeps' handkerchiefs. For, where The O'LiamRoe had an obstinate humour all his own, Francis Crawford of Lymond had genius.

*   *   *

Each in its nest of gauze and gilt thread, of tissue and taffeta, swathed in silver and satin, in velvet and white fur sugared with diamonds, each face painted, each brow plucked, hair hidden by sparkling hair of raw silk, the well-born of France sat in waxlight and flowers like half a hundred candied sweets in a basket. Last at the last table, soggy gristle next the sugar plums, sat Thady Boy Ballagh.

Coming in with the Queen Mother's train, Erskine had seen him at once, and noticed by the hardening of her face that Mary of Guise had also been taken aback. He sat, taking care not to meet his wife's eyes, or the carefully restored face of Jenny Fleming. He was familiar up to and beyond the point of boredom with these affairs. Plain food was his preference and plain clothes his unfulfilled dream; below his solid face, fresh as prawn butter, the whitest velvet looked slatternly. He sat; rose again for the royal entrance; noted Lord d'Aubigny's miraculous bow and the trumpeter who had drunk a little too much. There was a second, more brilliant fanfare, and the supper began. Erskine's eyes, irresistibly, travelled once more down the table.

A weed in the fairest orchard of France, Thady Boy had been placed, with a malice both deadly and deliberate, next to the curled and painted, the earringed, the chypre-strewn young person of Louis first Prince of Condé. Brother of the Duke of Vendôme, Condé was at that time just over twenty, a Bourbon of the blood royal; spare, sallow and of an extraordinary agility despite the crooked shoulder which he quite simply ignored, having no need of either an incentive or an excuse. The Prince of Condé was a younger brother with the tastes of a king. Below the paint lay the potential greatness which was marking him already as a man to watch in the field. Idle, he was a force to be reckoned with, one of the four men in the King's circle about which happily scandalized gossip most frequently flew.

The second was his older brother, Jean de Bourbon, sieur d'Enghien, olive and beautiful, who sat at the same table, newly back from London with one of the younger de Guises, with his favourite love lock dyed rose. No wealthier than Condé, d'Enghien liked a mode of life equally self-indulgent, a shade wilder, and decidedly more eccentric in its scope. It was difficult not to like him, and few people tried.

In London, d'Enghien had left the third gallant, François de Vendôme, Vidame of Chartres. A favourite of the Queen Mother of Scotland, the Vidame combined brilliance and charm with the subtle mind of a diplomat: if treaty making with an elderly queen was in question, the Vidame was the man to send. In London at this moment he was enchanting the ladies of England with four-thousand-crown parties into which even the stiffer noblemen of the Court threw themselves with abandon—d'Enghien had brought to France a highly witty rendering of the Duke of Suffolk at one of the Vidame's parties, dressed as a nun. Lively, superstitious, enthusiastically scheming, the Vidame was the best company of all.

And lastly, close to the King stood Jacques d'Albon, seigneur de St. André, Marshal of France; soldier, courtier, wellborn son of the Governor of Lyons, who was twenty years older than these three young men; rich, adventurous and at the height of his power.

Fourteen years before, when Henri became heir to the French throne, St. André had been brought to his side to make of him a king of courtiers and a commander of armies, where Diane had been installed to instruct in the gentler arts. As with Diane, the growing love between the Dauphin and his tutor earned St. André the dislike of King Francis. As soon as Francis was dead, the new King Henri made of St. André a member of his Privy Council and a Marshal of France, appointed him Chevalier of the Order of St. Michael, and First Gentleman of the Bedchamber, and later gave him his father's post as Governor of Lyons. Shrewd, courageous and intimate friend of the King, St. André shared with these three men, with the younger de Guises and with the other quick-witted, cultured and happily immoral lights of the Court, a talent for profligate luxury which was a byword in Europe.

Of the four courtiers, three had suffered the displeasure of the old

King; a matter of near poverty to men like Condé and the Vidame, who had survived on a pittance of twelve hundred crowns yearly as chamberlains-in-ordinary to Francis. They had used their wits, and contrived: the Vidame by refusing to marry Diane's younger daughter, which had endeared him to the Queen; and the Prince by judicious friendships among the married ladies at Court. Since taking his place tonight, for example, Condé had expertly avoided the eye of Madame la Maréchale de St. André, and instead lavished all his public attention on the handsome, arid presence of the Princess de la Roche-sur-Yon on his right. Divining with a sure courtier's instinct the King's dilemma and his desires, the Prince of Condé carried them out as best he could by presenting to Thady Boy Ballagh without courtesy or compromise, a permanent view of his round, jewelled back.

Thady Boy paid no attention. He sat like a blackbird in cold weather at the table end and applied himself with both hands to his food.

There were nine courses, served feathered and ribboned by good-looking pages in cloth of silver to the interminable blasting of trumpets. Knife in hand, nose to plate, Thady Boy muttered from time to time. ''Tis marvellous, surely. One toot for the ham, and another for the capons; and wouldn't you think it, at the third you get attacking the pages.'

Louis of Condé faltered only a moment in his chatter. He was far enough from the royal table to exchange a little current gossip; philosophic dialogues with Marguerite of France were well enough in their place, but with the Princess he could relax. They had finished discussing the sale of chastity belts at the last St. Germain fair, which had temporarily doubled the locksmiths' trade before the unfortunate salesman had to flee the Court gallants, and were now into a little triangular affair of some years before between d'Estouteville, his mistress and a young widow of a Rouen Parliamentary President which was still having repercussions.

A recipe for chestnut hair was bandied about, causing a good deal of laughter, some of it high-pitched as the strong Hungarian wine went round; and a conscientious consort of assorted wind and percussion followed the lutenist in the gallery. In a fleeting lull, the voice of Madame la Princesse de la Roche-sur-Yon was heard saying suavely, 'And what is this I hear of our dear Constable and the Lady Fleming?'

'Nothing, I fear, that can be repeated at table,' said the Prince of Condé, presenting her with a piece of wrought marzipan. 'Remember our friend on my left.'

She peered round him, her silver wig spooled, veiled and jewelled, her long buckram bodice coated with satin and jewels. 'The Irishman? Is he alive, my dear?'

The Prince neither looked round nor lowered his voice. '*Vivit, et est vitae nescius ipse suae.*'

Having just enough Latin to recognize an expression of contempt, the Princess gave out a peal of laughter. Against the whine of the music, the roar of chatter and the clatter of sugar almonds bleached and milling in his teeth, the ollave droned comfortably on to himself: '*De una mula que haze hin, y de un hijo que habla latin, liberanos, Domine!* . . . Tell me,' said Thady Boy, swallowing busily as the Prince of Condé whipped round, 'is it the King's fool, the fellow in black and white by the top table there?'

There was a little silence. The lazy eye of the Prince fell on the replete ollave, travelled from his black-rimmed hands to his mud-splashed boots and rose again. 'Yes. That is M. Brusquet. Allow me to invite him over,' he said smoothly, and spoke to a page. His eyes, and those of the Princess, were wide, vacant and impersonal. Further up the table, someone pressed a fan on someone else's arm and smiled.

The last course had been served. Soon the boards would be removed. Meanwhile the players had given place to tumblers. They came up the centre carpet springing and whirling and took their stance, the acrobats before the royal dais, the jugglers at the other end. The royal fool Brusquet, a hard-working man, strolled down from the top table and placed a privileged hand on the shoulders of Condé and his Irishman. 'Welcome, Master Ollave, fresh from the kingly castles of Ireland. Can we hope to match them in splendour at this poor Court of France?'

The Irishman thought, chewing. 'Well, at home, 'tis not the fools only who make converse at table.'

Before Brusquet could reply, Condé's dark, painted face turned. 'You would teach us how to be courtiers?'

Thady Boy bowed meekly. 'I would leave that to Madame la Princesse.'

Urgent with epigram, Brusquet rushed in, as the lady exchanged raised brows with Condé. 'The courtier's task, like garlic, sir, is to flavour his master with his own wit and skill.'

Thady Boy licked his fingers and wiped them fastidiously on the sleeves of his gown. 'Do you tell me now. I would put it nearer the surgeons', M. Brusquet: to bring together the separated, to separate those abnormally united, and to extirpate what is superfluous.'

'And what, sir,' said the fool silkily, 'has proved superfluous in Ireland?'

'Ah, did I say we needed courtiers in Ireland?' said Thady, surprised.

A light had come into Condé's eye, but the King's fool, his colour high, was again first. He was acid. 'We had forgotten. If you can manage one elephant, no doubt you can manage them all.' He lowered his voice suddenly. A page, sent from the top table, requested silence for the tumblers. Up and down the room, conversation and laughter fell to a mellow buzz.

A resounding hiccough pock-marked the silence, like an arrow in the gold.

Thady Boy apologized. 'Strange, strange are your ways. In Ireland, now, princes are not known as elephants, and them walking about with their castles on their backs.' The glance he gave at Condé's superb satin was politely fleeting. 'But there is a saying. A fool, though he live in the company of the wise, understands nothing of the true doctrine as a spoon tastes not the flavour of the soup.' He choked, but failed to stifle another shattering hiccough.

Condé said softly, forestalling Brusquet, 'The spoon has compensations. Of washing thrice daily, for example.' He had an audience of perhaps half a dozen, and at the hiccoughs more were turning.

'Not in Ireland,' said Thady Boy, his blue eyes innocent; at ease from his tangled black crown to his fine, dirty hands. ''Tis not the gentlefolk but the beans that we put into water, so that they swell and go soft. . . . To turn to these hiccoughs, now. There's a thing you do with a cup to stop them?'

'What?' The Prince of Condé, drawn into extraordinary tête-à-tête, was momentarily at a loss. Another report like a pistol shot escaped the Irishman's glottis, and more heads turned. Distantly, by the King's chair, Lord d'Aubigny moved restively. The tumblers, leaping, looked resigned.

Diamonds flashing, Condé picked up his silver drinking cup and offered it to the sufferer, his face suddenly contorted. Thady Boy shook his head, exploded and explained. The cure sounded incredible. The Princess said, 'Give him water!' She was amused, and in a lifetime of boredom, the moment was worth keeping. A laugh rippled up the table, and Condé jerked his head.

A page, misunderstanding, brought a fingerbowl, the rose leaves still floating, and Thady Boy, between two explosions, had his chin in it when Condé pulled it away. A silver tankard was brought. 'Oh, Jesus, no!' said Thady Boy, and hiccoughed. 'Two ears, the thing must have. . . . It's clean infallible. Ah, wait you now. There she is!' And rising, The O'LiamRoe's ollave tipped the royal flowers from their tall vase before him, lifted it, and inserting his chin, attempted to suck the far rim. Brackish water poured round his ears. It soaked his jerkin and streamed on the cloth, and jellied leaves, slipping through, came to rest on Condé's white satin. From about them, there was a muffled round of applause and a low cheer; and opening watery eyes Thady acknowledged it, before exploding like the tuck of a drum. '. . . Infallible,' he was heard to say; and his two hands grasped the handles again.

Three people pulled him back from it, and as many more offered advice, some less sober than others. 'Something cold.' 'A key.' 'A coin.' 'Madame de Valentinois,' said someone else, *sotto voce*.

The Prince of Condé, who had started to laugh, opened his purse on the table and then stopped. He was too late. Thady Boy's long fingers had already darted inside the mesh. 'The very thing, so!' And he held up a key: a very fine one of silver gilt, with leaves and flowers and a crest on the stem. Condé snatched. Madame la Maréchale de St. André was not watching—she was deep in low talk with de Lorges. But her husband, from across the carpet, stared at the pretty key with his thoughts plain on his face. The eyes of the two men met; and the limpid blue gaze of Thady Boy, after dwelling on them both, turned and surveyed his audience. One eye closed, then both, in the most stupendous upheaval yet, and he slipped the key down his spine and wriggled. 'Although, *dhia*, you are all wrong; it is for a nosebleed, so. . . .' From along the table, Jean de Bourbon's silvery laugh rang out.

With practised ease, his neighbours softened the pause. They chattered to Condé; they called gentle advice; they summoned pages to mop up the water while their perceptive senses descended like locusts on the immediate conduct of Condé, of St. André and of his wife. At the top table, the King sent to know the reason for the flurry. In a low and private whisper the details, discreetly censored, began their journey up the scented tablecloths. A sense of tolerance and even of indebtedness began to settle on the Irishman's neighbours. Condé was perhaps a little quiet; but the others, drawling, vied with each other as the tables were removed in trying to cure Thady Boy's hiccoughs; and Condé's brother, smiling, watchful, had begun to flicker his fan.

It was then that the jugglers got involved. Ignoring the laughter, eyes snakelike, arms whirling in particoloured costume, they sent blunt-edged daggers in a stream to each other, their hands a pink blur in the slipstream of silver. Thady Boy exploded, his arms full of remedies, and somehow a two-handled vase flashed alien into the glittering stream. Cramp-fingered and incredulous, the first juggler waited for it, changed grip desperately, and sent it back to his partner in a shower of knives. The next convoy of daggers brought a key; and then a cup appeared. The juggler caught it and hurled it to the side, where Thady Boy with no apparent effort received it.

Swift, timely, in perfect position, one of the juggler's little knives came back from the same quarter; then another; then the cup. His embrace slipping with objects, Thady Boy seemed to have acquired a whirlpool of possessions in mid-air: dishes and salt-cellars began to join it. His object seemed to be to regain possession of the amphora; but instead a stream of incoming knives began mysteriously to shoot at him. With combined and deadly malice, the jugglers had begun to incorporate Thady Boy in the act. From knives, they fed the rest of their stock into the air. The knives turned to balls, the balls to rings, the rings to eggs. He returned them all.

By now the whole room was watching. From a rustle of amusement rose a few cheers; then the King, leaning forward, was seen to smile, and the cheering became louder. From the top table Lord d'Aubigny, his handsome face on fire, strode down to the ollave; then backed a step as an egg, mishandled, landed, thickly soggy, in his shirt. Another, slipping badly astray, splashed M. Brusquet, talking hoarsely and unheard in what was approaching a din. The jugglers themselves began to suffer.

Their clothes were not cheap. To preserve their garments and the shreds of their professionalism they with one accord moved backwards, out of range and towards the end of the room. The alien objects—the cup, the key, the vase—dropped to the floor. A last tremendous hiccough shook Thady. Clothes streaming with egg yolk and water, hair erect as the crest on a jay, he leaped and fell on the amphora in the exact moment that Condé leaped and fell on the key. There was a squelching collision. Thady Boy tripped, rocked and collapsed, and falling, snatched at the carpet. Far off at the end, in front of the dais, the pyramid of tumblers, wreathed in dazzling smiles, planed a moment, genuflected and shot into space.

The King of France laughed. And like the well-bred bone and tinkle of an ancient and imperial sepulchre on the eve of All Hallows, the bored and over-refined flower of French civilization gave way to its mirth.

*   *   *

The tumblers had gone; the mess had been cleared up, and in the muted, end-of-meal light, diamonds flickered, caught like stars in quick water, as the company talked and laughed, and the King summoned Thady Boy to his chair.

As Lymond walked past without a sign, Tom Erskine at last allowed his eyes to meet the Queen Dowager's with gentle triumph in his gaze. Thady Boy's face was childlike in its innocence, and the wide, fringed blue eyes met the King's with confidence, with a trust perfectly endearing. Henri of France addressed him in his deep, pleasant voice. 'You have made chaos of my supper and a shambles of my supper room, sir. Are dinners so conducted in Ireland?'

'We repel sadness if we can. It is a duty of our profession.'

'You were not invited, I believe,' said the King, 'to repel sadness.'

'I was not invited, I believe, to repel elephants,' said Thady Boy with serenity. 'We turn our hand to whatever we may.'

The royal eyes searched for presumption and found none. The royal face relaxed a little. 'It is true, both your endeavours today have made you remarkably damp.'

'It is not my favourite element. I had no choice.

> '*A la fontaine je voudrais*
> *Avec ma belle aller jouer.*

'*Ma belle* being a cow elephant called Annie.'

'Ah, you quote poetry,' said Henri. 'But you prefer horseplay to music?'

'It depends on the music,' said Thady Boy with the gentlest gravity.

Beside the King, Catherine, Queen of France, had made leisurely study of him, her nimble mind and blanched cultures weighing his answers. She now spoke, her voice muted. 'You dislike the King's lutenist?' The consort, she was aware, had been unspeakable.

'I should be proud to have trained him,' said the ollave.

She sat back and a little drift of comment ran along the table, with a laugh. The King was smiling. 'You think you could do as well?'

'It is my profession.'

'As well as elephant riding and juggling?'

'These are my field sports.'

Without looking round, the King snapped his fingers. Lord d'Aubigny, blank and deferential, stepped forward. 'Fetch Alberto quickly.' To Thady Boy Ballagh, the King spoke slyly. 'We have heard the buffoon; show us the bard, Master Ballagh. Play for us, sing, perform as well as M. de Ripa, and you shall have a full purse to take back to Ireland tomorrow.'

Slowly Thady Boy shook his black head. 'Money, now, that is not the price of a song. The reward we would ask, O'LiamRoe and myself, is leave to enjoy a little longer the wonders and delights of your country, and to atone for the innocent mistake which led the Prince of Barrow, to his sorrow, into such misfortune the other day.'

There was a silence. 'I cannot,' said the King at last. 'I cannot under any circumstances have your master here at Court.'

'The O'LiamRoe,' said Thady Boy delicately, 'is not accustomed to Court life. He asks only to remain and study the grand country it is.'

The King hesitated. De Ripa had come in, looking startled, and carrying his lute. Further along the table, the Dowager of Scotland chatted softly to her neighbour, ignoring the little audience. The Constable of France, excusing himself, rose and bending over the King's chair, murmured in his ear.

Henri turned, collected the unspoken agreement of his Queen, and said pleasantly to the Irishman, 'If these are the only conditions under which you will play, then we must of course agree. But we wish it understood that we propose passing the winter at Blois, and that none but the finest in each profession accompany us there. The lute is my own instrument. Her grace the Queen, my lady sister, and my sweet sister of Scotland besides M. de Ripa and myself will judge you.' Somewhere under the white and silver, there was an amiable spirit. 'In Ireland, the standards for such things may be different. Do not be disappointed. You will not leave the poorer,' said Henri of France.

The bundle of wattle and daub which was Thady Boy Ballagh straightened up. His gaze wandered past the King to the Queen Mother, to Erskine, to Margaret, to Jenny Fleming, to Lord d'Aubigny behind them, and down the long tables to Condé and the Princess, d'Enghien and St. André—all the bored, chattering faces. Then he turned and, bowing elaborately, accepted the challenge.

*   *   *

In the softly lit hall the command was passed; the noise died. Heavy with food and wine, warm and weakened with laughter, and laden with visiting dreams of the night hours ahead, the predatory and feckless flower of France lay wreathed in its velvets, and the Bodyguard, in sparkling white, stood silent behind.

There was a low chair for the player, and a stool for his foot. Thady Boy took the satiny, pear-sliced lute from the Italian and smiled at him; the dark eyes were inimical for a moment longer, then smiled back. Drowned in the coloured darks of the floor, Thady Boy sat with the frail waxlight over his head, bearded stubble and obesity sunk in the darkness. From his right hand came a hardly heard brushing of sound; then he spoke in his skilful, velvety Irish-French.

'To the ladies of France, who win music and love as their birth-right. To the ladies of France, the tale of the King of Kerry's daughter whose greenan was thatched with eagles' wings, and their breasts made her pillow.'

For years he had commanded men and knew the trick of controlling and throwing out tone. He knew others too. His fingers flowed over the shining wood, plucking, snapping; dipping the phrases into acid and wiping them pure again. Then Thady's voice joined the music, and the spare, tragic story was told, reaching into the carved room where the silence was the same as the night silence of a deep Kerry meadow. Moving to its end the music was strict and steely light; the pull at the heart extraordinary. In that company wholly spoiled, wholly self-centred, ruthless, neurotic, worldly-wise, more than one woman bit her lip to avoid tears and ridicule.

It ended; and there was silence, and then a rattle of cautious, genuine approval; and Marguerite of France, her jewels running like light over her dress, rose and knelt by the ollave. 'I pray you . . . play Palestrina for me. And sing me this.' And she stayed, watching his hands, as the fastidious music was made, watching his face as he sang the words she had requested.

'*Si la noche se hace oscura,*
y tan corto es el camino,
¿ cómo no venís, amore? . . .
Cómo no venís, amore?'

The stamp of her approval, the vivid attention on Henri's face, the concentration on de Ripa's, broached the brittle defences of pride, and opened the golden floodgates of fashion. During the poem, someone sighed. Towards the end, the Duchess de Guise pulled out her handkerchief. As it finished, a wave of sensitive acclamation engulfed the singer and, charmingly, other ladies surrounded him. He glanced at them thoughtfully, and roused the strings this time to gentle satire. The song was new, and it pleased them. He sang again, settings by Jannequin and Certon; *Il n'est soing que quant on a fain*; Belle Doette, *Mout me desagree*; and songs even older. He sang in Gaelic, *sirechtach* music; and drawn like the tides by the wordless drag of the pain, they wept this time and were proud of it. And later, he sang them songs which were spicy as well as romantic, and they laughed and cheered and joined in with the catch phrases. But he took no risks, yet.

They were all, or nearly all, his patrons. Condé, for dignity's sake, was his loudest admirer. Marguerite of Savoy addressed him softly between songs, and Jean de Bourbon, sieur d'Enghien, thoughtfully fluttered his fan. The two senior de Guises smiled with tolerant approval. Did they know who Thady Boy was? Erskine thought it unlikely. The risks were too great.

Only two people reacted differently. Margaret Erskine sat in silence, as she had done the whole evening, her candid gaze on the ollave. Only when he sang, her face changed to something very like pain. And Brusquet, angered, had left.

Towards the end, when the circle about the singer overflowed, and people were moving freely, talking, singing and drinking wine, Sir George Douglas leaned confidentially on Thady Boy's shoulder as he sat, head downbent, tuning the lute. 'My dear man, how fortunate that your friend Abernaci was in charge of the elephants.'

The implication was obvious. The Bourbon beside him looked up. 'You're wrong this time, my Scots Machiavelli. Abernaci would never permit the big Ué to be fried—not for His Holiness himself.' And Condé chimed in, yawning. 'The scents must have been worse than usual. They ruined the poor creature's skin. Let that be a lesson to you, my dear.'

It was the oldest woman there who took the point. Diane de Poitiers, Duchess de Valentinois, was not easily moved, but she was intensely curious about the newcomer; and had no intention of competing with the flattering circle on the floor. Neither Condé nor his absent friend the Vidame was a favourite of hers. She moved coolly to remove their protégé to rarer climes. 'If the elephant was hurt,' said Madame de Valentinois, 'did M. Ballagh not suffer injury?'

Like a thunderclap, watching Lymond's taut back, Erskine realized that she had hit on the truth; and further, that this was no part of the evening's improvisations. His personal state, both spiritual and physical, was Lymond's own affair; and injury, if he were injured, spelled nothing but inefficiency within his creed. Nervously, Erskine saw the idea spread among Thady's admirers; heard the mellow cries of well-bred curiosity; and saw St. André, more than a little in drink, lay hands on the ollave's soiled shirt.

Lymond sprang to his feet.

He's going to throw it away, thought Erskine. Step out of character, wreck the whole evening's work. He's going to turn round and treat them like bloody servants . . . Christ! For Lymond's sharp blue gaze, swinging round, had caught the stiff face of the Queen Mother of Scotland. With every nerve end in his body, Tom Erskine willed the Dowager to school her face. The shadow of a threat, the shadow of an appeal, the slightest effort to prompt him, and she had ceded the evening; she had lost Thady Boy Ballagh; and she had lost Lymond for good.

The Queen Mother stared at Lymond, the sea-cold gaze without focus, and, scratching her nose, turned to ask her neighbour a question. But already the danger had passed. Lymond, standing, had looked beyond her and caught the flare of pure anger in Margaret Erskine's brown eyes. His own narrowed. He hesitated for a second; then turning, allowed St. André without protest to claw open his doublet.

Under the egg-stained shirt, the burns were obvious where the acid had caught his shoulders and back. Madame de Valentinois rose. 'Bring M. Ballagh to me.'

From the high chair the King spoke to Lord d'Aubigny and his lordship moved also towards the ollave. John Stewart's manner had undergone a slight change. A wit, a poet, a singer of sorts who had caught the imagination of the Court, was a different proposition from the shabby bundle of sops he had chivvied from inn parlour to inn.

He halted by Master Ballagh. 'The King wishes me to say that he had of course no idea of your hurt, or he would not have thrust this entertainment upon you. He bids me say that you are welcome to join his Court for its winter sojourn on the Loire; and that if he so wishes, the Prince of Barrow may remain also in France. I am to offer you a bed in this lodging for tonight, and to give you the King's permission to retire.'

He had won.

*   *   *

He also had, by any standards a memorable couchée that night in the King's Lodging of the Abbey of St. Ouen, painted with egg yolk and turpentine and bandaged under the supervision of the Duchess of Valentinois herself, until at length, unrecognizable in borrowed night robes, he had his bedroom to himself.

When, late that night, the knock came to his door, Lymond was by no means asleep. His occupation since the last servant left was shatteringly clear from his too-steady gaze and his less than steady hands. Wrapped in a furred bedgown, he had been drinking seriously for a long time. Behind him, the little room was cracklingly neat: a characteristic of his own which was quite foreign to Thady Boy. What he had expected as he opened the door no one could have guessed. What he saw made him stop short, vigilant and more than half sobered.

Outside was Margaret Erskine.

Shapeless, brown-eyed, rather pale, neat as a nun in her day dress, with a single good jewel pinned to her breast, Jenny Fleming's daughter seemed quite composed; visiting wild younger sons in their sleeping quarters might have been a nightly occupation.

A smile, bracketing his still mouth, spread like bane over Lymond's pale face. 'Come in, sweeting. I have a friendly bed.'

She disregarded it, entering prosaically and shutting the door at her back. 'Why drown your victories?' she asked. 'You have succeeded, have you not? You need not leave France.'

For answer, Lymond tossed the tangled hair back from his eyes and broke into an accurate parody of the Queen Mother's fractured Franco-Scots. 'I mean to take this man in his failure, Master Erskine —in his failure and not in his success.' He shook his head, mourning. 'I have succeeded; but unless I'm careful, by God, the Dowager will have me trussed and indented as her servingman yet.'

Margaret Erskine drew out a chair and, sitting, looked up at the sweat-beaded, sardonic face. 'You heard that. I'm sorry.'

'Like The O'LiamRoe,' said Lymond with a large and positive gesture, 'I feel I deserve a little amusement at someone else's expense. That is all. I have worked for it. I have paid for it. And I propose to have it. Don't you approve of me?' His voice mocked her. 'I had a

88

suspicion back there tonight that you didn't want me to quarrel with our playful friends.'

Her own voice was quite level. 'Will you really find it enough to fill the next months? Sharpening your claws on them between fool-hardy pranks? . . . The women were already drawing lots for you when you left.'

'And you won?' His eyes matched his words.

She bit her lip, the first sign of discomfiture she had shown. 'I came because a visit from Tom would be dangerous. Whereas a visit from myself would be merely . . . compromising.'

'God, how patriotic,' said Lymond. 'And considering the relatives you have, what fool would imagine you'd come to talk politics.—Damn it,' he added with a sudden interest. 'Only the ladies?'

Her voice remained level. 'No.' She drew a deep breath. 'If you will not serve the Dowager, why are you troubling to stay with the Court?'

He had roved away from her, kicking the preposterous velvet skirts out of his way. He turned, unnecessarily expansive, interested in nothing as yet except being difficult. 'Because in this sweet realm of France, my dear, lives a small, venal animal who will drown a ship-load of men or trample a gathering of women and children to death on the strength of a whim; and I mean to peel his knees with his backbone before I leave.'

Pale, persistent, she outfaced his restlessness and his boredom. 'I know nothing about *La Sauvée* except what I have heard from Tom. But today's accident—Tom, my mother, the Dowager, are all sure of it—was an attempt to kill or injure the Queen. It has persuaded the Dowager to tell us plainly what you guessed, perhaps, when she talked to you last. There have been other accidents to Mary, and other coincidences. It was because of these that the Queen Mother asked you to come to France. Openly, she dared say or do nothing without seeming to question the good faith of France, or their capacity to look after the child. . . . Instead, she relied on you.'

Against the far wall, the window shutters were open. Lounging between them, Lymond took no time for reflection. 'Why interfere?' he said airily, over one velvet shoulder. 'Why interfere? The Dauphin may have plans to marry again.'

A personal attack, this, against her own marriage, following so fast on the death of Tom's first fiancée, Christian Stewart, killed tragically in Lymond's service two years before. She knew, and Lymond knew, that only after Christian had gone did Tom Erskine notice the plain person of the widowed Margaret Fleming, who for years had been his silent admirer. She had not been prepared for such a challenge, but she was equal to it. She said quietly, 'You hate me because I am Christian's successor—even if inadequately; even if only in Tom's eyes. But you didn't love her. You know that perfectly. Love has never struck you yet, and you should thank God for it. Be honest, at least. You are not refusing to help because of me.'

She waited, while Lymond stood looking out over the quiet cobbled courtyard and the lantern-lit trees of St. Ouen. Then, stepping back, he closed and flicked the latch of the shutters, and turning, faced her again. 'I'm tired,' said Lymond,' of funerals. Show me a project, and I'll promise you that before it is ended half my so-called friends will have thrown their illusions, their safety and their virtue into the grave. There was Christian Stewart, about whom we need not speak. There was a man called Turkey Mat. And a number of others. I have refused to become a royal informer, my dear, to spare my associates the pains of paying for it.' There was a difficult pause. Then his cold blue stare softened. 'I am not really fit to talk to you,' he said. 'I think you should go.'

'But I have something more to say,' said Margaret Erskine placidly. 'And I could say it more easily if you were sitting down.'

This worked. After a moment's hesitation he walked forward, and finding a fireside seat opposite hers, dropped into it and propped his head on his fists. Margaret, watching, chose her moment. 'You made the point I thought you might make,' she said. 'It's none of my business if you choose to raise a poor kind of monument to your friends. They might well deny, were they alive to say so, that Mary's life is worth your care. But you are already committed, surely, to your precious project? You want to find a dangerous man, who has the inclination to kill. For that you will need friends; how will you preserve them? And surely, if this man has designs on the little Queen you are likeliest to find him while you are protecting her? Or is she merely the bait in your philanthropic trap?'

He did not stir. 'Of course not. The Queen Dowager's purposes and mine are the same; but you must excuse me from promises. This time at least I am quite free. Anything I set out to do I can abandon— and if need be, I will.'

'And if,' said Margaret Erskine in a careful voice, 'I stand surety for your promises? If I say, kindle your fires for us, let them burn freely and light up what they will, and I shall do my utmost to see that no innocent bystander is burnt? Would you accept from the Queen Mother, through me, the task of protecting the young Queen, and trust me to watch over your friends? . . . Or being Tom Erskine's second choice,' said Margaret, her round, unremarkable face pale, 'am I forever beneath your notice, as well as your trust?'

At which Lymond swore without apology, dropped his hands and fixing her with a stare of numbing austerity remarked, 'I can grasp the situation without being bludgeoned over the head with either rhetoric or hangman's humility. However. I gather I have been lecturing you. I apologize. It was a matter of irresponsible timing on your part. As far as your offer goes—'

Margaret had recovered her placidity. 'Tell me later. You may feel differently,' she said. 'But I really shouldn't let the Queen Dowager drive you to drink. Did Madame de Valentinois make any advances?'

'Considering,' said Lymond with a little constraint, 'that she is twenty years older than even the King. . . . No. But then she had a large escort with her. She was surprisingly effective, as it happens. And most thoughtful. Is it likely to continue?'

'On an intellective level, I believe. She nurses all the royal children. And Lord d'Aubigny is also liable to take you up now. You will visit La Verrerie, admire Goujon and Limousin, take wine with the professors of the College, take lessons in drawing from Primaticcio, listen to readings by the Brigade and recitals by Arkadelt. You will be expected to like Chambord.'

'I am prepared to like anything,' said Lymond, 'except his lordship of Aubigny. But he did me a service tonight with his glum, heifer's face. There was a moment when I thought they were going to throw me out. And now—'

'And now?' She could not keep the hopefulness out of her face.

Jaded, nervy, sober at last, he watched her with a bleak amusement. 'Yes. The game is yours. It seemed rather likely from the beginning that Her Highness would win. We shall merely hope that under your sheltering wings, no fingers will be burnt other than my own in protecting this one child from her fate.'

Over the turbulence within, 'My natural place is by the hearthstone,' said Margaret Erskine dryly. 'No one will notice me there.'

'They will be the losers,' said Lymond; and as Margaret looked down, her skin red, altered his tone. 'Very well, my lady. If we are to protect the young Queen, there are some pertinent questions to be asked. About this rumour linking Montmorency and your mother, for a start. Tell me: is Jenny the Constable's mistress?'

It was a subject on which, in adult life, Margaret felt nothing but a resigned tolerance, or an amused exasperation, depending on her mother's current fancy. Irregular relationships among a royal family and its adherents were a matter of course; often a matter of business; and only occasionally a matter of love. The arrangement, temporary or otherwise, was usually public and acknowledged when at the highest level; only when it was clandestine and conducted to the injury of legitimate relatives did it become untenable in the oblique moral eye of society.

But such considerations only applied on home ground. As guests of foreign royalty, the Scottish party's behaviour was required to be impeccable. So exasperation informed Margaret Erskine's quiet voice as she replied. '*Montmorency?* Heavens, no. The *Constable* isn't Mother's bedfellow,' she said. 'Mother's lover is the *King*.'

For the first time in his restless evening, Lymond genuinely shouted with laughter. 'Oh, God, oh, God. Why didn't I guess? Oh, for Christ's sake—the Chair of Happy Fortune. . . . Isn't she a priceless, beautiful, giddy queen of a woman?'

He dissolved into silent mirth. 'If Diane finds out she has a royal competitor—if the Queen finds out he has *two* mistresses—' He stopped suddenly. 'Who else knows?'

She had flushed. 'The Constable. One of the King's Gentlemen. My mother's maid. And me.'

'She has dreams, of course, of establishing herself in the aging Diane's place. Are you sure Queen Catherine doesn't know?' asked Lymond more soberly. 'For unless you're sure, I should strongly suspect her of throwing Jenny and her husband together. It would be a stroke of genius. In one move, ousting the permanent maîtresse en titre, discrediting Jenny and the Queen Mother, reducing Scotland's worth as an ally, and weakening all the related de Guises in France—'

'—And also,' said Margaret, 'throwing doubt on the little Queen's moral standards and general fitness to marry the Dauphin. . . . This is habitual. Mother flutters her wings, and every institution within sight tumbles flat.'

'She must put a stop to it, I'm afraid. Tell her. No, I'll tell her myself. Then I'll want some help. You'll find you're being watched by the King's people quite apart from our conjectural friend with designs on the Queen, and nothing we do, naturally, must seem to question French goodwill or French security.' He added suddenly, 'Whom does the Queen Mother suspect?'

She had come hoping for help, and was beginning to realize, to her anguished relief, that she had called in a professional. For a moment she stammered. 'I—don't know.'

'Someone at Court, obviously. Or she would have confided in the King, or at least in her own family. Who, I wonder. The possibilities are interesting. Queen Catherine? She hates the de Guises. The Constable, or his nephews? He's said to favour a different marriage for the Dauphin; they wouldn't mind a snub for the de Guises, and there's a rumour they wouldn't mind a change of religion either. Have any of the King's other close friends a motive? Or what about some of the Scottish nobles . . . I shouldn't trust the Douglases or their relations, for example; and some of the others lean towards England and Lutherans rather than a Scotland allied to Catholicism and France. The Dowager would hesitate to call in a Frenchman to deal with a situation like that. . . . Now what else? Which of the child's maids of honour are Scottish? Whom can we trust absolutely? Can her food be privately supervised? Her play? Her lessons? Her travelling . . . ?'

Exhaustingly, it went on. At length—'Has it struck you,' said Lymond suddenly, 'that everything that has happened so far, barring the elephants, has been directed at O'LiamRoe? The fire at the Porc-épic was in his room, not mine. The tennis-court frolic was devised to get O'LiamRoe into trouble. The *Gouden Roos* which tried to sink us off Dieppe was captained by a well-known adventurer who was paid to do it, and told on no account to bring back O'Liam-Roe alive.'

'How do you know?'

'I asked. For reliable information, apply to a lawyer, a barber or prostitute. My informant hasn't found out so far who paid the captain.'

'But she will,' said Margaret, her face grave.

'I hope so,' he said with equal gravity, and continued unshaken. 'It is possible that these attacks are purely against O'LiamRoe. It is also possible that O'LiamRoe is being frightened or driven back to Ireland in order to remove me as well. But not likely. I might remain; I might assume another identity. No attempt has been made on my life, although God knows I've given them enough chances. And really, no one with any information about my concerns would attempt to do me damage at sea. Which leaves only one other possibility.'

'What?' Her deadened brain attempted to keep track with his.

'That O'LiamRoe is being attacked *because someone has mistaken him for me.*'

There was a silence. His composure was quite unchanged. In face of it, Margaret struggled to remain matter-of-fact. 'Of course. That must be it. But . . . the elephants stampeding was no accident? How can that be accounted for?'

'It was organized,' Lymond said. 'The man who planned it was killed before he could speak. The man he paid to push out that hell-begotten whale knew nothing beyond his orders and will trouble us no more. . . . Which reminds me. O'LiamRoe and Dooly, as you know, are aware at least who I am. But if you, or Tom, or Jenny, or anyone connected with protecting the Queen should need help and you cannot find me, go and see Abernaci, the King's Menagerie Keeper. He will do what he can. Meantime, we've two forms of incredibly careless plotting: one against O'LiamRoe, and one against the small Queen. In both, Destaiz, the dead man, was used. Every-thing has been done at second or third hand, and on a ridiculously distorted scale; as if by someone who had no means of scouring the alleyways for the usual paid assassin. A Destaiz presents himself, or some rogue of a captain; and the hint is dropped. If it is successful, so much the better. If it isn't, there is no hurry, and plenty of money for next time.'

'It may not be a person,' said Margaret bluntly. 'It may be a nation.'

Lymond smiled. 'It leaps to the eye, doesn't it? The obvious inspiration for both kinds of attack—anti-Irish, anti-Scottish—is England, and I've kept close to Mason to feel my way there. But he's too patently anxious to have O'LiamRoe on his side; and anyone can see he'd be more valuable to England alive. Which leaves us in delicious confusion, with one good thing to look forward to, and one bad. It's going to be hard to detect any attack on Queen Mary, because it won't be blatant; every attempt so far has been made to look like an accident. On the other hand, O'LiamRoe is staying, which is helpful. Someone is bound to try to murder him again.'

It was said seriously, but she caught the glint in his eyes, and laughed. Then she sobered. 'But are you sure The O'LiamRoe will choose to stay in France? Won't he find it too humiliating? You will be with the Court, and he will be on the fringes.'

'It needs a little energy to be humiliated,' said Lymond dryly. 'He will stay.'

Margaret was on her feet, making at last for the door, blind with fatigue. He was committed to help the Queen. She could report it thankfully to Tom before he left, to the Dowager, to her mother, and to all those in the Queen's inner, most trusted circle with whom he would be working henceforth. Lymond had risen too, still talking, his face fine-drawn with tiredness.

Margaret Erskine spoke abruptly. 'I seldom quote Tom, but not because he isn't capable of producing hard common sense. He thinks you're mad to tie yourself to O'LiamRoe. The Prince may be a wag, but he's lazy and foolish and unreliable to boot. Tom says he's so damned harmless he'll kill you.'

'Nonsense,' said Lymond. 'Why should I suffer moral blackmail and The O'LiamRoe escape unfettered? He is an educated man. He has a brain. He shall be made to use it. I shall make him drunk on the palm wine of power,' said Lymond sweepingly, 'until he falls out of his tree.'

PART TWO

Dangerous Juggles

The person is exempt who multiplies the juggling spears up, or the juggling balls up. If they be dangerous juggles, there is a fine of foul-play for injuries for them. 'Dangerous juggles' means all juggles in which pointed or edged instruments are used.

I:	*Rouen to St. Germain: The Inexpugnable Drone*	97
II:	*Blois: Red Tracks in the Wood*	113
III:	*Aubigny: Boldness of Denial*	128
IV:	*Blois: All the Mean Arts*	139
V:	*Blois: Wickedness is the Rule*	148
VI:	*Blois: The Forfeited Feast*	171

I

Rouen to St. Germain:
The Inexpugnable Drone

It is not easy for Brehons to decide concerning bees that have
taken up their lodging in the trees of a noble dignitary; with
respect to which it is not easy to cut the tree.

THE news of Thady Boy's unlooked-for success was brought
his employer the next morning by Robin Stewart, who had risen
very early for this privilege. O'LiamRoe, listening, scratched his
feathered golden head.

At the end, he looked pleased. 'Ah, 'tis a tearing fellow, a noble
champion itself. To the devil with your pearldrops and your parroty
manners. A filled mind and an apt wit will earn you all the respect any
man has the means to deserve.'

'*Man, ye canna trust them.* Look how choosy they were with you
thon day at the tennis. And now they expect you to sit here on
suffrance while the wee smart fat ones go about arm in arm with the
dukes,' said Robin Stewart, employing tact much as O'LiamRoe
employed fine clothes as a blandishment.

His cheekbones grinding, the Irishman yawned. 'If Thady Boy is
desperate to squeeze kisses on to princesses, my dear, O'LiamRoe
won't begrudge it.'

'You'll scour France at his shirttails, and sit behind the closed
door? They'll have him at every supper like physic. I've seen a fancy
take them before.'

'I believe you. He'll be clean worn down and fit to pass through a
dog stirrup before he sees Ireland again. What of it? I'll not lack
entertainment.'

Quarrelling with the Prince of Barrow was like fighting a curtain.
Robin Stewart gave up.

*   *   *

It was a busy day for O'LiamRoe. His next caller was d'Aubigny,
bearing the King's deferential request for the continued company at

Blois of the Prince of Barrow's gifted ollave, Thady Ballagh. No mention was made of O'LiamRoe's mooted departure, but the letter implied, and Lord d'Aubigny confirmed, that he himself would be at O'LiamRoe's service, and that on the journey south and beyond, he need have no worry about tolls, fares or fodder, or about his nights' lodgings. O'LiamRoe was delighted. '*Dhia!* It's like being cuckolded.'

With Lord d'Aubigny was the small, red-haired, pretty woman O'LiamRoe had first met at Rouen on the other side of a whale. Jenny Fleming had seized the excuse to survey him.

The Prince of Barrow's interest in Lymond's affairs was minuscule. But he knew wilful curiosity when he saw it. She and d'Aubigny seemed on good terms: he was, after all, also of royal Stewart descent; their forebears were the same. Her liveliness and her graces fitted elegantly into the fiddling pattern of her kinsman's behaviour The reservoirs of his speech flowed freely for her entertainment; his voice mellowed. Listening, you could guess how he had impressed the gauche boy who became King.

O'LiamRoe amused her with Irish nonsense, let her tease him, and contrived one or two exchanges with his lordship which almost reached the dignity of serious conversation and probably startled both men. In fact, a shade of puzzlement occasionally crossed d'Aubigny's face and once, unexpectedly, he addressed Lady Fleming less than civilly.

She had been talking of home; but at the tone she lifted her clear eyes to his lordship. 'John, if you wish to leave so badly, you may wait for me below.'

And huffily, to O'LiamRoe's mild astonishment, Lord d'Aubigny left. As the door closed behind him with unnecessary firmness, Jenny, triumphant, turned to the Irishman. 'And what do you make of our darling?'

She had come, breaking every prohibition, to talk about Lymond. O'LiamRoe, amused, picked up her furred cloak and said, 'Thady Boy? He'll be in crumbs in a year, with all that scurrying about; but he makes a middling good Irishman.'

'Then don't show me a bad one. He came to my room and read me a lecture this morning—' She broke off. It was no part of Jenny's technique to destroy her own charming image.

Affairs of status meant nothing to O'LiamRoe. He hitched the cloak round her straight shoulders, and patted it, dispatching her. 'He's a quaint fellow, to be sure; but dead lucky with women.'

She must have realized then that no confidences would be forth-coming. He was simply not interested.

At the door, she paused. 'Don't tell him I came. Or he'll do it again.'

O'LiamRoe, who knew a little more about Lymond than she

bargained for, noted that occasionally Lady Fleming had a conscience. 'I don't need to,' he said. 'It'll be all over Court by nightfall, surely.'

*   *   *

He was right. Tom Erskine was among the first to hear it, and the news added to a certain uneasiness which already tinged his confidence in Thady Boy Ballagh. The situation made him hesitate, but it was nearly time to leave on his embassy to Augsberg. He made his final calls, formal and informal, and at the end of them lost his escort and slipped unseen into the room where Thady Boy Ballagh as guest of the kingdom of France had spent his interrupted night.

Hindered by visits from the Constable, from Madame de Valentinois's matron of honour, and from the Queen's page, Lymond was preparing, among the ruins of an uneaten meal, to return to the Croix d'Or, where he and O'LiamRoe were to stay until the Court left. At the click of the latch he looked up.

'*Sacré chat d'Italie!*' said Francis Crawford. 'The wife, the wife's dam, and now the husband. Let's have the Schawms of Maidstone in a pack on the doormat. Secrecy was your idea, wasn't it?'

Erskine might bow to a superior brain, but he had no patience with temper. 'The visit to Jenny, I understand, was initiated by you.'

'My dear Thomas,' said Lymond, 'any man can visit Lady Fleming without comment. Unhappily she formed a low opinion of the night's events, or lack of them, and took her complaints, I suspect, to O'LiamRoe. The much revered mother of your wife needs to be turned on her stomach and bladed on the back of a captured Bacchante.'

Erskine was sharp. 'I've been taking formal leave of the King. And it was d'Aubigny who took Jenny to visit O'LiamRoe.'

'Why?'

'They get on well together.'

'Well, get her away from him. Tell her it's incest. And keep her apart from O'LiamRoe as well. She would have her work cut out anyway. He could thigh you a pigeon and disfigure a peacock and unlace a coney, but I'm damned sure he couldn't undress a—'

'—Particularly as he knows just who Jenny is, and no doubt, admires your restraint more than she does. This is rubbish. You're talking as if she were someone from the Pont Truncat. We'll interfere with you as little as possible; have no fear. Remember that you also have accepted an obligation.'

'Oh, yes,' said Lymond. 'Margaret worked very hard last night; you should be proud of her. I gather that if our deceased friends and lovers could see us, they would be proud of us. Even including, she seems to believe, Christian—'

99

Erskine's face stopped him. For a moment their eyes met; then Lymond turned away, his lip curling. 'All right. You're leaving for Brussels and Augsburg and Margaret stays. You'll be back when?'

'After Christmas. Then home via England. Meanwhile, the little Queen, so far as we can manage it, will stay with the Queen Mother and not the royal children. All the safeguards you suggested will be applied. Everything she eats and everything she does will be watched; there will be a day and night guard. It can't be complete, for above all, we must work invisibly. It mustn't look as if we don't trust her safety in France. That is our work. Yours is outside.'

Lymond said nothing. He had finished his sketchy packing and was lounging discouragingly by the door. Erskine wondered if he knew what was ahead of him. He said, 'It'll take God knows what time to get to Blois. You'll go mostly by river, stopping off at lodges and palaces and staying exactly as long as the game lasts in each place. Nothing in this lunatic country matters as much as the hunt. Fifteen thousand people, this man's father went about with, their beds, their clothes and their furniture on their backs, signing state papers on horseback and heralds running after him yearning in couples. They never stayed above fifteen days in one place, unless they were at war, and every ambassador in Europe hated hunting for life.'

It was a favourite subject; but something in Lymond's manner made him stop. 'But of course, you know France quite well.'

'Once,' said Lymond, 'when I had too much money, I laid out some of it here. Sevigny is mine.'

Nicholas Applegarth of Sevigny was a friend of Tom Erskine. He began cautiously, 'But Nick—'

'—Is a tenant of mine.' The tone of voice was dismissive. 'And how will the Queen Mother's coup d'état prosper when you go?'

It was then that Tom Erskine, finding a mine at his feet, temporarily lost his wits. The Queen Dowager's purposes in France were many, but only one of them could properly be called an attempt at a coup d'état, and that so far was strictly secret. It must be obvious enough, God knew, that the Scots lords were being honoured: that pensions were hailing down indiscriminately like rice at a wedding, while Governor Arran's heir, without a syllable of French, was now captain of the Scots troops in France and drawing twelve thousand crowns a year.

But no one could know for certain what he knew: that a meeting between the Queen Mother of Scotland and Henri of France would presently settle once and for all whether France would help the Dowager towards her greatest ambition—to oust the Earl of Arran from the Governorship of Scotland, and to rule as Governor herself for the rest of her daughter's minority.

The Queen Mother wanted Lymond, and Lymond suspected the

truth. Now, if ever, in this delicate matter of state, was the time to engage his concern. But she wanted him, as Erskine knew, for his sword-arm, not his mind. In her tortuous ways, a trained and meddlesome intelligence was the last thing she sought.

So, his hands tied, Tom Erskine hesitated, and delivered the fateful rebuff. 'The Queen Mother's affairs are her own, as you probably know. We can trust her, I think, to do what is best. In any case, there is really no alternative.'

Crawford of Lymond raised his delicate, dyed brows. 'There is union with England.'

He had guessed, then, what was afoot. 'There is suicide,' said Tom Erskine, his voice flat.

'Not while you may come to me,' rejoined Lymond, and rising elegantly, sketched a sardonic bow. 'And buy a fit of mirth for a groat.'

There was nothing to say. Erskine didn't need that to tell him that, somehow, at some level too subtle to be understood, he had not done quite well enough by the Dowager, and perhaps in some way by Lymond himself. In his heart he knew that if Lymond had not chosen to speak coarsely of Christian, his impulse would have been different. It did not help to guess that Lymond's words were not a matter of impulse at all.

*   *   *

Robin Stewart arrived, just after Erskine had gone, to escort Thady Boy to the inn. He was the picture of cynical amusement. 'You'll be fairly joco this morning?'

'I am, then.'

'Dicing for you all night, they tell me.'

'So I've been told three—no, four—times. No one mentions the only aspect that interests me. Who won?'

'I believe,' said the Archer stiffly, 'it was the sieur d'Enghien,' and watched disapprovingly as Thady Boy choked with laughter. 'In some circles, vice doesna matter,' said Robin Stewart. 'Some people will do anything to get into a certain type of company, never mind is it coarse as cat's dirt.'

'It's little I'd know,' said Thady Boy, his eyes guilelessly clear. 'I've not been at either end of this trade up till now.'

The austere voice softened. 'Some people,' said Stewart, 'get carried away when the women behave yon way, and think their fortune's made, and that from now on they're something special. They don't know French ladies. I've seen them turn in a night, and what they fancied before they'll fling in the moat. You'd be as well to understand—'

'I understand,' said Thady Boy concisely, 'that I have a headache. Come along.'

Lymond, as it happened, spoke the truth. Looking narrowly, Stewart launched the theme which was to dog Thady Boy, in tenor and soprano, for four stricken months. 'Man, you'll need to watch that! You'll need to cut down the drinking! They'll egg you on for sheer devilment and it can fairly strip your inside. . . . Did ye get those burns looked at?'

'Yes. My tail is plaited like a Barbary ram. Do you want to see it? Mary Mother, *come on*.'

At the Croix d'Or, having shaken off the solicitous Stewart, Lymond arrived at last at the door of O'LiamRoe's room and stepped inside, closing it quietly behind him. The silence, as the two men stared at one another, was fat with danger. Then a smile pulled at the corner of O'LiamRoe's whiskered mouth and he gave tongue mellowly.

'Busy child, if I read it right, there is the father and mother of all headaches on you which you surely deserve. Sit down. As you may have forgotten, in the long dereliction from your duty, I had better remind you that Phelim O'LiamRoe is the unnatural sort of fellow who has no need to be handled and who can even on occasion hold his tongue. I hear you are the finest lute player since Heremon. You can prove it to me tomorrow.'

'Thank God for that,' said Lymond. He passed by, resting his hand for a moment on the other man's shoulder, and dropped limply into a chair. In five minutes, he was asleep.

*   *   *

In the ten days still left in Rouen, they learned the rudiments of Court routine which would affect them both, willy-nilly, for four months. The King rose at dawn, held his levée, read his dispatches and talked them over with his Privy Council before ten o'clock Mass. Then the privileged traffic began: the secretaries and couriers and ambassadors and heralds and diplomats and soldiers and clergy with news and courtesies and gifts and complaints.

Routine reports came in: from the master masons on the King's building work, or Madame Diane's; from St. Germain about a valued bird fallen sick; a gentle reminder, routed through the Constable's kind offices, that someone had been promised a present of wine, and someone's butler had come for it; news of the children, with a painting. News of a death in Paris that left a benefice vacant; you could see by the new face lined up waiting who had already bought that titbit of news from the dying man's doctor. Gossip about a new lawsuit in Toulouse, brought by an ambassador anxious to ingratiate himself; and you could tell by the needy face absent at supper who had borrowed enough money to go there and try to buy it.

Dinner was at noon. After it, the General Council might meet, but not now with the urgency of the days when France still had high hopes of Italy, and when, triumphant over England, they were engaged in tweaking Boulogne from her tail. Not that the prospects for next year were particularly serene, in spite of the nominal peace with England's little King; the new Pope and the Emperor Charles, France's traditional Hapsburg enemy, were too friendly for that.

At the beginning of his reign and his freedom, Henri had found it intoxicating to fondle his favourites. Diane, the Constable, St. André, d'Aubigny and the rest had half-emptied the treasury among them. But the proper exercise of the King's divine power, obviously, was to encourage upheavals in Germany. By linking arms with Protestant and pagan—German princeling and Turkish infidel—he might defeat Charles. Unfortunately, the money was lacking. All the General Council could propose was prevarication—prevaricate with his dear sister Scotland; hold off his eager Irish friends; and make a cool social gesture or two in the direction of England, herself split in two with the old story, the struggle for baronial power during small Edward's minority.

Henri of France could prevaricate without even thinking. He attended the Queen's evening parties, gave large suppers, spent what time he could, which was quite a lot, with Diane; and in rare moments of privacy could be heard practising his lute. The rest of the waking hours, for these ten days at Rouen, were filled with ceremony.

The capital of Normandy, perfectly capable of turning down flat a Grand Sénéchal wanting an Entry on the eve of vacation, was prone by the same token to extract the last ounce from a really royal occasion, once they had set their minds to it; particularly with Lyons to outshine. There was the State Entry of Queen Catherine; the speech-girt presentation of vase and saltcellar and other tabernacle-like trifles; the solemn dinner and the lugubrious farce by one of the two Rouen burlesque societies, torn between pride and a natural anxiety to do with the disappointed company.

There was a solemn procession to the Palace to hear a case on the King's Bed of Justice which gave Brusquet his only real chance of the visit. After a morning of well-rehearsed speeches by the advocates and the King's procureur-general—'Levez-vous: le roi l'entend'—and an equally well-rehearsed judgment thick with classical and flattering allusions, a private burlesque of the whole thing was performed extempore by the King's fool in the empty chamber for the benefit of the royal ladies in their box.

They laughed, but not quite enough. The King changed his clothes, made appearances diligently, patiently and with charm, and entertained himself and his Court in privacy with the music of Thady

103

Boy Ballagh, his breath sweet as a rose chafer and his lyrics strenuously unexceptionable. Thady Boy was working quite hard.

O'LiamRoe was amused. As rumours of the long evenings of romances eruditos and romances artísticos reached him, he was heard on occasion to express a left-handed pride that the sweetest finger that ever slid upon a fingerboard here should be Irish. At length the King left to make his State Entry to Dieppe, and then, by Fécamp and Havre, back to the River Seine for the water journey south.

Five Kings had wintered on the shores of the Loire, as it flowed wide and sandy through central France from Orléans to the Atlantic with castle and palace, town and village and vineyard, mill and fishery and hunting lodge on its mild chalky banks. For twelve hundred years pilgrims had gone by river and river bank to Tours, the holiest shrine in Europe after Rome; and the Gallo-Romans had built their villas there, and the Plantagenets for a while had made it English until their overthrow, when a grateful France had replaced them with Scots.

But it was a long time since a Douglas had ruled in Touraine. The Kings of France had developed a taste for the country and made it their centre. They governed from Blois and Amboise and Plessis and came back there from their wars to plant their booty and rear their children and try out their notions of modern building. The Chancellors, the Treasurers, the Admirals and the Constables built their houses there too; park and chase and garden were laid out; and even when, latterly, Henri's father had turned aside to use Paris and Fontainebleau more and more, the well-worn journey was still made: Rouen, Mantes, St. Germain, Fontainebleau, Corbeil and Melun; overland to Gien like a migration of guinea fowl, cart, mule, horse and litter, the packs of servants and gentlemen, the endless baggage train, the men at arms, the filles publiques whose prescience about morning moves was both marked and relied upon.

And from Gien, through Châteauneuf, Orléans, Amboise, Blois, the barges floated them home. Pleasant, equable, healthy and full of red deer, the valley of the Loire was a place where many an unwanted embassy had grazed its knees and barked its knuckles and gone home unhappily neither satisfied nor affronted. The Court of France was going there to spend Christmas.

It started off, but amoeba-like, before it arrived its one cell had split into two. Louis, the King's two-year-old son, died at Mantes. The royal household and the officials involved stayed or returned. The staff, the grooms and the younger element of the Court, among whom was the Irish party, continued to St. Germain-en-Laye.

As guide and conductor, vice Lord d'Aubigny, of Phelim O'LiamRoe's trio, Robin Stewart had sensed, long before then, that the mignons were out for Thady Boy's blood. O'LiamRoe as a garrulous and discredited foreigner they ignored. But Condé and de Genstan and St. André and d'Enghien, with their friends, had taken cool note of undue diligence among the monarchs. Stewart, who had discovered Thady Boy before anybody, watched sardonically as d'Enghien, young, witty, ambitious, lightly unfaithful even to the fortunate succession of friends who maintained him, decided calmly to teach his prize a small lesson. Thady Boy Ballagh was to be given, rumour affably reported, a good bob with the bag.

The bag was the quintain, a wooden Saracen on a post, to be charged on horseback and hit three times with a lance. A poor hit, because of its pivoting arrangements, gave the rider a crippling clout on the ear. It was a popular spectator sport.

How Thady Boy was brought to compete, Stewart never knew. But on a mild grey afternoon in October The O'LiamRoe and the Archer and every idle sophisticate on the premises turned their backs on the newly renovated castle of St. Germain, on its wide terraces above the flat panorama of the Seine, and strolled off to the tilting ground to see the courses.

Far from being technical, the talk in Stewart's vicinity was largely about someone's new boots, straying lightly now and then into the recent boudoir history of the combatants. But whatever they sounded like, they were soldiers judging soldiers. There was some wit on the changes which other times and other alliances had brought to the quintain itself: instead of the Turk there hung a crude painted barrel with eyes, nose, chin and a string midriff to mark the points of high scoring.

It rocked slightly in the light wind, causing a moment's alarm to those in the plot, who had gone to a great deal of trouble to struggle it off and fill it up to the brim with cold water.

And of course, the first rider selected by blind fate to try his three stabs at the wood was Thady Boy Ballagh, hatless and gently fuddled on what appeared to be the highest peak of a very tall horse.

There were a hundred paces of a run up to the barrier. At the far end the barrel gaudily swayed; the circle of judges and spectators was suspiciously wide. Thady Boy stuck his heels into the tall horse; along the fence the hoofbeats redoubled; beyond the fence the stout post with its burden lay in wait.

The squat, black figure reached it, raised its lance, aimed and thrust. So far from scoring, the mark was not even over the belt. The lance nocked into the wood, with a thud which could be heard, and came out fast as Thady Boy ducked to dodge the swing of the pivot. A great and derisive cheer rose into the clear air of the St. Germain plateau, and Jean de Bourbon, sieur d'Enghien, flushed. No icy douche had soaked Thady Boy from the gash. The barrel, inexplicably, was dry.

Three times Thady Boy Ballagh ran the prescribed course, and the mignons applauded the cheerful constancy of his incompetence and rallied Condé and his brother in the same merciless breath on the collapse of their scheme. Since no other entertainment offered, the tilt continued. D'Enghien himself trotted up as Thady Boy came back, and spurred into the first course.

Slender and dark, with his pretty lashes and red, Bourbon lips, the sieur d'Enghien was an expert jouster. The lance, aimed true and straight, transfixed the very nose on the staves. There was a thud, a hiss, a light puff of steam, and from the stab in the wood a trembling arc of hot water started to play on the noble rider below.

They made him run the three prescribed courses before cutting down and examining the barrel. It had been floored midway and top-filled from a copper; Thady Boy, he remembered, had aimed consistently low.

Music, seeping out from the lounging throng of his friends, told Jean de Bourbon where to find his ingenious prize. His fur weeping, his boots full of water, d'Enghien for a moment looked like sinking his teeth, like the Archbishop of Pisa, in his neighbour. On second thoughts he bent, arm on elegant knee, and said, 'For that, my dear, I shall want my revenge.'

Thady Boy looked up. Garlanded with young men, he sat squat on the grass, boots crossed, expression pure as a halcyon hatching an egg. '¿Con que la lavaré, La tez de la mi cara...?' he sang, and smiled at the unfolded hair and the sleek, wet painted face. '... That depends on the sport.'

They all stayed five days at St. Germain, and St. Germain would as soon have suffered a plague. From the quintain they passed to rovers, played with hackbuts until someone's page came out at dusk to complain of the noise. They reverted, all contrition, to their bows and resumed silently at dawn, with whistles tied to their barbs. The graveyard screech that unfurled every sleeper was a deathless victory for Thady Boy.

They roamed the neighbourhood. Sightseeing in Paris, they stopped at the Pineapple and ordered the first ten men they met to eat pork and mustard in their gloves. De Genstan left the Pineapple on a ladder. The rest were more fortunate, but lost Thady Boy, who was removed by Lord d'Aubigny for a quick cultural tour of the city. After St. Denis, Notre Dame and the unfinished Louvre, Stewart reclaimed him for display at the Mouton, but before he could be primed sufficiently to sing, his lordship was back to escort him to see the jumping at Tournelles. Stewart sulked. He could tolerate the mignons and Thady Boy's half day at Anet. But Lord d'Aubigny's patronage roused him to rage.

On the last day at St. Germain, Thady Boy put himself in Stewart's hands for a visit to the menagerie. Lymond handling a disciple had all the address of a surgeon.

With Thady went Piedar Dooly and The O'LiamRoe who, like Maximilian's pelican, followed him everywhere except into the royal presence and who, in private, uproarious sessions in Gaelic, was evolving a brilliantly bigoted new philosophy to meet the occasion.

It was a mild, damp day, with a haze over the valley, beading the cobwebs, and with grit and bladdered leaves underfoot. Stewart led the way, his starched collar limp on his cuirass, and the three Irishmen followed through the castle park to the Porte au Pecq. The kennels by the Parc des Loges were empty; the famous pack of black and white hounds had gone south. The Falconry too was denuded.

The elephants were not travelling yet. Abernaci, warned beforehand by a call from Stewart, met them with his primitive English at the barred gates, bowing softly in his turban and silks. Not by a flicker of his opaque black eyes did he betray interest in either O'LiamRoe or his ollave. The Keeper's words were blandly welcoming, and at Stewart's prompting, he led them inside.

This building was new, a hollow square two storeys high enclosing a courtyard. On the ground floor were the cages, each divided into two compartments by a door operated by chains from above. Upstairs, stores, offices and sleeping quarters gave on to a gallery running round the entire court. The Irish party, looking down from the gallery, were shown the arena where the animals exercised and fought; and at their feet the traps, one for each cage, where the meat was thrown down to the lions and bears and hunting cats far below.

Robin Stewart had seen it already that morning. While The O'LiamRoe, all honey hair and plum-coloured vowels, went off to sink his teeth into zoology, Robin Stewart was waiting edgily by the door with a groom. He established, automatically, what the local butcher wanted for mutton, and whether a keeper's monthly wage matched his oncosts. He asked if the groom's wife approved of his work, if he had ever caught anything off the beasts, if he'd been clawed.

The man was reluctantly opening his shirt when O'LiamRoe interrupted. There was an empty lodge just below which he wanted to see. The groom, relieved, scuttled away and Stewart took the Prince down, while Thady Boy remained to watch Abernaci wind the chains.

It was difficult to tell afterwards how the mechanism stuck. Stewart and O'LiamRoe entered the windowless rear half of the cage and Abernaci shut the door from above. There it remained immovable for some considerable time. As every ablebodied man on the premises worked cheerfully with crowbars to release the two men, Thady Boy and Abernaci watched from above. Then, 'Aweel,' said Archie, pushing back his turban to scratch his bald head.

'They'll be some time at that. Come on away ben where it's comfy. I hear you're having a grand time playing Roi Ca'penny at Court.' And firmly shutting the door of his sanctum, he gave the ollave a broad and confidential wink.

Lymond's dark face was amused. 'I am being fattened like a thrush on flour balls and figs.' He hitched a stool to himself neatly and sat on it. 'I hear you are going to Blois with the cats and Mary's little menagerie. Who goes with you?'

'Two men I can trust. And there'll be more there. The travelling trainers aye come in when the court arrives. It's a grand fraternity; ye can trust them. I ken them all. Tosh'll be there. D'ye mind Tosh?'

Lymond shook his black head. The place was a store. On one side of him was a sink, and at his elbow a high cupboard and table flap loaded with bowls and mortar, spoons, gallipots, balances. Stretching an arm, he took down and opened a stone jar, and sniffed it cautiously. 'Christ, Archie, you could blow up the whole tedious stewing of them if you wanted to, and establish a Court of Beasts. Who's Tosh?'

'Thomas Ouschart's his name. Tosh they called him when he was a builder's laddie in Aberdeen, and a good friend you'll find him at need. He was fairly born in the shape of a ladder; he could lift the whiskers out of a gallant's beard-box without giving a tweak to his chin. Tosh'd take the meat off your foot.' Abernaci rocked, incandescent with gossip.

'He'd to get out of Scotland in a hurry, of course, but you should see him now with his tightrope—a rare act he has, him and his donkey. Gets its horoscope read whiles in Blois by the woman I told you of, that lives at Doubtance by the moneylender's; but you won't get him to tell you much about that.' He broke off, his gaze following Lymond's, and added in his matter-of-fact voice, 'I saw your eye on these pots at Rouen. Ye ken that stuff, do ye?'

Carefully Lymond put another stoppered jar back. 'Yes, Archie. I thought your range was a bit startling when I was being washed in warm water by Sakra-deva's diamond hand. What drugs do you keep?'

In the withered face, the darting black eyes were steady. 'All the ones you're thinking of. If you knew elephants, ye wouldna be surprised.'

'Such as—?'

'Belladonna for their coughs, and sweet oils. You had them on you at Rouen. And soap and salt and Aak ka jur Mudar . . . that's a narcotic. Bhang, ganja and kuchla when their bowels are upset.' The wrinkled face filled with compassion. 'Awful bad with their bowels, some of them can be.'

'I can imagine,' said Lymond. 'What else?'

'Well. Lime water—that went on Hughie's back. Opium for a sedative. Resin and beeswax against the flies; arsenic and nux vomica for a tonic . . . that's the most of it. You can see it all. There's big supplies,' said Abernaci informatively, 'because elephants is big beasties.'

Below, the banging had become intermittent and joined with occasional noises of rending. Lymond was thoughtful. 'How many people know of these poisons?'

'The whole Court, I should think,' said Abernaci. 'We had to lock up the hashish and the opium in the end—they were aye daring each other to try it. The worst of the pharmacies hand it out. Bordeaux, Bayonne, Pamplona—they all sell freely. And they get it when the spice ships come in, if only from the seamen and their women. If you've money, it's not hard.'

'All the same, don't lock it up any more ' said Lymond. 'Don't lock anything up. We want it to be easy.'

'It *is* easy,' said Abernaci simply. 'Since I checked them this morning, a hundred grains of arsenic have gone.'

In the silence, the brazen blows from below sounded Ogygian: some ritual call to intercession. Then Lymond said, 'Who has been in? The keepers? The carters, for example?'

Abernaci shook his head. 'Not the keepers. They're my own lads. And not the carters; not with the cats ready to travel. They're excited enough without a wheen of heavy-footed labourers stirring them up. We had the joiners to look at the travelling cages, and the butcher's cart, and the man with the buckets, and fifteen bushels of hempseed for the canaries; but they all stayed outside, and had one of my men with them forbye. As for the ones we let in . . . there were your four selves, and the Prince of Condé, to see a bear he's betting on, and the children—Queen Mary and the Dauphin and the aunt Lady Fleming and her boy, and Pellaquin, a man of mine that looks after the wee Queen's pets—'

'Why did they come?'

'It was about a leveret, a sick leveret that needed a dose. They're aye giving her wee things. Pellaquin's about daft with it, because she won't turn them off when they're full grown. He's having a grand time, I can tell you, with a full-sized she-wolf the now . . . Oh. The Marshal de St. André was with her, and his wife. The leveret was their present. Nobody else . . . No. I'm telling a lie. George Douglas came to pass the time of day and speir whether I knew my friend Master Ballagh was the sensation of Rouen. The midwife should have clipped yon one's mouth with black ants.'

'The Queen Mother's very words. What a pity; they've got the gate open. That's Stewart's carping tract of sweet Berla-speech, I'll swear. And that's the final tally? How very competent, Archie.

109

Unless someone simply wants to put down some mice, we have at least a list of possible culprits.'

Abernaci grinned. At the door he said, 'Well, look out. It's tasteless, and there's just about no known antidote.'

For a moment Lymond, irritated, did not answer. Then he said succinctly, 'Every crumb the little Queen eats has been tested first, from the time she left Rouen.'

The Keeper snorted. 'What d'you test it on? Her aunty?'

'One of your animals. If you're dead keen, I'll make it the she-wolf,' said Lymond. 'In Brehon Law, they call it setting the charmed morsel for the dog. We want to see them try out that arsenic. Because then, with a little luck, my dear, we shall know who they are.'

*   *   *

They were packing the monkeys in baskets as, returning, the three Irishmen and Robin Stewart passed the little garden of pets. Mary was helping, a piece of bandage on her other hand, and her red hair streaked over her face. The she-wolf was still in its cage, and a bear, together with a wild pig and the female parent of the leveret, wearing a small, gold-chased collar. Its name, Suzanne, was picked out visibly in stones uncommonly like emeralds. The twenty-two lapdogs now whirling in squeak-girt and telepathic unrest in the castle were collared also, Robin Stewart informed them, in precious ore. His grimly ossified face relaxed, however, when the little girl turned, and he answered her questions as readily as acute uneasiness would allow. Robin Stewart was unused to children.

'Vernom-tongue of Loughbrickland,' said The O'LiamRoe to his secretary, 'you did not tell me she was a pearl in a clear glass of mead.'

Her grace the Queen of Scotland was not much interested in O'LiamRoe, although he got a practised smile and a fine-grained, downy wrist to kiss. She said immediately to Thady Boy, 'It is you who throws eggs in the air?'

Thady Boy's hands were still over his small, shoddy stomach. 'Question me, doorkeeper. I am a sorcerer.'

She instantly flung back her head and looked down her stained nose. 'I am no doorkeeper.'

'It would be a terrible presumption, would it not, to call you so. I was speaking of an old tale, noble person, which you may hear one day.'

With Janet Sinclair behind her, and the little girls standing waiting Mary dropped like a twig on to a pile of sacking and folded her hands. 'Tell me,' she said.

'Please your noble grace,' said O'LiamRoe, his face solemn. 'But it is a terrible long tale, that one; and I hear the juggles of him are the wonder of the world. He is better than Aengus the Subtle-hearted, that drew live frogs out of his ears.'

Lady Fleming had come across to the group, and with her, her son and the Dauphin. Sallow and ill-grown, smaller and feebler than his red-haired fiancée, François of France crossed to ask her a question. She answered him in her disconcerting Scots-French and, gabbling absently through the courtesies, pulled him peremptorily down beside her. Jenny retreated to the nurse's side and Robin Stewart, backing also, attached his joints to the small menagerie fence. If anything went amiss, he couldn't be blamed.

'Juggle,' commanded Mary.

In two minutes Thady had what he wanted: some oranges from the monkey house; the Dauphin's scabbard; a fan. On the wild red hair was a small brimmed hat, very smart, with a feather curling at an angle; and he got that from her too. Then he began to juggle. He caught the oranges a foot from their upturned faces; he dropped the hat neatly on the little Queen's crown, to scoop it up the next moment; he sent fan, scabbard, spheres vivid as fish in the grey air.

Her face scarlet, Mary was squealing with pleasure. The Dauphin hunched his shoulders a little and Jenny, laughing beyond them, applauded sharply with her two plump palms. Cross-legged in the mud, O'LiamRoe watched, a forgotten grin on his face.

When the bell rang for Vespers they had found how to make the fan unfurl descending, and were experimenting, hazel eyes and blue gazing upwards, Thady's hands flying just above Mary's ruffled head. Then the bell clanged and instantly he sent his implements flying; oranges lobbed each child on the skull, the fan struck Jenny Fleming and the hat dropped precisely on Mary's own head. Warm with pleasure, forgetful, she swung on his arm, ignoring her nurse's purposeful moves. 'Master Thady, Master Thady, do you tell me a riddle?'

It was the first time, thought Robin Stewart, amused, that he had seen Thady Boy pulled up short. Anyone can seize a child's interest for a moment. To keep it needs rather more than one trick.

Thady Boy looked down at her, her weight on his arm, swinging her a little while he thought. 'It is time to go in. Ask your lady aunt about the three thousand monkeys of Catusaye who came at bell stroke to take their supper by hand. Is there a particular riddle you want?'

They were moving out of the paddock. She turned back, pulled François to his feet, and returned, holding his hand. 'Anything. A new one.'

Jenny Fleming had come forward. She laid a hand on Mary's shoulder, a glint of mischief on her face. 'Don't bother folk, child. You know all the riddles there are.'

'True for you, lady,' said Thady Boy Ballagh, 'but there is no woman so great that she knows all the answers there are. There is the one on the monks and the pears, now, what about the like of that? The answer you must work out for yourself.'

It was new to Stewart as well.

> *'Trois moines passoient*
> *Trois poires pendoient*
> *Chascun en prist une*
> *Et s'en demeura deux.'*

Later, without success, he tried to get the solution out of the ollave; it annoyed him to be left out. He became irritatedly aware that he had to add the royal children to the list of his rivals. If O'LiamRoe had not been there, Stewart would have tried to quarrel with Ballagh again.

But Thady Boy was extraordinarily forbearing; and O'LiamRoe was silent all the way back to the castle, pricked for the first time in his life by the terrible innocence of childhood.

The next day they resumed their journey, and Thady and his patrons were restored to adult pursuits. They raced. They shot. At Fontainebleau they set fire to a birch grove and hurled their mounts through it. At Corbeil they paid the boatmen to exchange clothes and in blue caps and wide breeches towed the women's dress boxes to a side stream and held them to ransom.

By that time, the gaming was at a fairly high level. Between Melun and Gien, Thady lost Piedar Dooly as his last stake at the tables; and stark sober and hissing the little Firbolg was in pledge for ten days, eating black bread and beans. None of the others was approaching sober, except O'LiamRoe. Surprised and interested, and gifted by nature with no compelling urge to join in, he understood that this, in an unfettered form, was what Lymond meant by taking a holiday. When shortly before Gien, the all-night escapades on strong wine bowled the last of them over, O'LiamRoe captured a donkey, loaded his ollave into a pannier, and paid a boy two silver carlins to see him on to a boat. There Lymond, who was by no means incapable, curled up peacefully and slept.

II

Blois: Red Tracks
in the Wood

The dog that follows a woman and that has on a tested muzzle,
and the dog that follows on the red track of a stark naked man
in the wood, and the lawful hunting dog, and the lawful stag-
hound, and the dog with time and notice: all these are fully
lawful dogs.

SAFE and untouched, Queen Mary also reached Blois, with a
fresh piece of bandage and the monkeys. The household staff and
O'LiamRoe were already in, with some of the courtiers. The Queen
Dowager and her Scotsmen arrived in the same fleet of barges, and
the Duke de Guise and Madame de Valentinois came later. Only the
royal suite and the Constable had not yet travelled south.

Home and birthplace of kings, Blois was rich; Scotland had
nothing so precious. Robin Stewart had watched, along the waterway
from Gien, as the blue roofs and white towers slid by at every turn of
the Loire, and the flaming swords of Charles, the porcupine of Louis,
the cord and ermines of Anne, the salamander of Francis and the
double crescents of Henri franked every stone. Then landing, he
climbed with the rest to the basse-cour of the castle and saw the
familiar château before him diced red and white, the dormers high
as rose mallows, and through the deep arch the inner court, through
which every man but the King must walk on foot.

Round the hollow square inside, Charles of Orléans, Louis and
Francis had each built a wing, each the best of its day. Everywhere
the eye was beguiled by griffins and crockets, puttis and niches; by
the strange crested staircase, and the stone worked like brocade.

To most of the Scots there, it was too familiar for comment. They
entered, and after the usual interval of chaos, settled into their
quarters. The Queen Dowager of Scotland used the suite set aside for
the de Guises, in the Louis XII wing, overlooking the basse-cour. Her
brothers, who were at the castle most of the day, slept in the Rue
Chemonton and her lords were farmed out, among hosts willing and

unwilling, throughout the town. In the opposite wing, the old Charles of Orléans block, were the Irishmen.

Finding them was no trouble. Setting off some days later, Jenny Fleming simply followed the far sound of music across the inner courtyard. Her hood held tight over her traitorous hair, she picked her way across the paving and up the staircase on its southwestern side, and her excellent hearing led her from there.

The thick door, carved and painted, opened into a comfortable room. The maître d'hôtel, in the end, had been generous to O'Liam-Roe and his entourage. The floor was tiled, the white walls pinned with tapestries, and the pillared bed, Lady Fleming was charmed to see, envisaging Thady Boy and O'LiamRoe side by side on the feathered bolster, was of tortoiseshell and ivory. There were several coffers and a secretaire; two benches and a heavy chair, several stools and a prie-dieu; a balcony; and a cabinet off, where Piedar Dooly sat and slept.

There was also a spinet, bearing Diane de Poitiers's monogram, at which she could see Thady Boy's back, a split across the main seam. He was playing steadily and correctly, his mind clearly elsewhere. When the latch clicked he said, unmoving, 'Go away.'

Jenny, Lady Fleming, shut the door, alive to a ravishing situation. 'You don't know who it is.'

Still he made no effort to turn. 'I do. Go away, Lady Fleming.'

She smiled, and swinging her little cosmetic case on one finger, moved in and tapped him with it. 'Do you know that you are alone? Soul as the turtil that hath lost hir make.' And still smiling, Jenny Fleming walked round him, rested her arms on the spinet, and, holding the open case between her two hands, communed with her reflection inside. 'My sweet ollave, you have lost O'LiamRoe again.'

'*Plan, plan, ta ti ta, ta ti ta, tou, touf, touf; boute selle.* . . . He can go to hell.' One finger parodied the drums for alarm. 'I'm tired,' said Lymond, 'of playing cache-cache with O'LiamRoe.'

Leaning there, she studied him. Last night's stubble was still there, and the faint slackness of high living. The uncombed, dyed hair, tumbling forward, had robbed the face of any distinction. 'You look a little overdrawn on sleep,' she said.

'I could sleep in a candle mould.'

'I thought you were supposed to be at O'LiamRoe's hip, booted to the groin, whenever he moved.'

One long finger remained pressed silently on the last key. 'Then you would lose the pleasure of telling me where he is.'

'In the kennels.'

'Dripping like a clepsydra with useless information. Ollaves' powers are unconscionably limited. I could recite an aér before breakfast and he should break out in bolga by dinnertime. But get him to remain in one room I cannot.'

'Is he nervous?'

'Not as far as I know.'

'Then he ought to be, my dear, if only of you. . . . You thought I was d'Enghien, didn't you?'

'No. He uses a different scent. I think you should go.'

He had curbed his tongue, always, when dealing with Lady Fleming; and she was far too expert to court the unforgivable. Instead, she turned the mirror towards him, so that he faced the dregs of his elegance; then closed the little case with a click. 'There is no need to be nervous,' she said.

He waited until she had gone, and then laughed at the sheer effrontery of it.

*   *   *

That same afternoon, O'LiamRoe lay on his back in the grass, fending off a loosely upholstered, unkempt mat of a deerhound called Luadhas.

It was a sweet, well-nourished day with a ruddy sun and crisp air and an early shower of rain which had soaked the Prince's breeches and shoulder blades black from the grass. He was alone. The dogs were out, rolling, yapping, scampering in the paddock: tumblers and lurchers; spaniels for hawking and fowling; the hare-hounds, light and nervy; the mastiffs with their flop ears for boar; the flat-headed, vicious allaunts and the white, fleet children of Souillard, the famous Royal White Hounds, which never gave tongue without cause. With them were the wolfhounds, Luadhas and her brother, each three feet high; 120 pounds of big-boned, brindled dog with thin muzzles and arched loins and mild flat-browed noble heads, who could catch and slaughter a wolf.

Tuned to the din, O'LiamRoe and his deerhound heard the footfalls at once. Shaggy brindle next to hispid gold, the two Irish heads turned as Thady Boy Ballagh strolled over the grass. Mildly and inaudibly, O'LiamRoe swore. For Luadhas, he had found, was for sale, at a price. And he had just bought her as a present for Oonagh O'Dwyer.

When his secretary was near enough therefore, the Prince spoke softly, a glint in his gentle blue eye. 'Busy child, you've been a middling long while finding me this time. I could be killed, dried and folded flat in a drawer like Callimachus' corpse and no one the wiser.'

'A little co-operation would help,' said Thady Boy, and dropping on his haunches, picked up Luadhas's big paw, with its strong, curving nails. He spoke without heat. It was his self imposed task

115

to keep O'LiamRoe in sight. O'LiamRoe was free to put whatever value on his own life he chose.

'My grief,' said that person with interest. ''Tis a hard time you have, with those delicate interests besides. Modify your enthusiams, busy child. France is a dangerous tutor. What joy? What laughter? Let us recall the everlasting burnings.'

Lymond said, smiling down at the grass, 'Their arguments get more heated than yours do, that's all.'

Beguiled as ever by the sweet pipe of a theory, O'LiamRoe pondered. 'True. There is one thing that you Scots and this kindle of latter-day Romans have got that the angry lads back home with the hatchets will miss sorely if they break out against England. And that's Royalty to lead you: the divine vessel of kings that cannot err. Bring on the Vice-Regent of God, and you've enlisted a nation. Bring on Sean O'Grady from Cork, and you've merely got Cork.'

Thady Boy, careless also of the wet grass, was flat on his back, taking leisurely soundings. 'And what about the cult of the full man? How do you fancy life lived in the round?'

'Forty-one million livres' worth of coats from Italy and the rest? Ah, 'tis as old as the world,' said O'LiamRoe. 'From the Celtic Kings downwards you have it: high power and high living; art and sculpture and music; strong campaigns, hard sport, splendid talk. Three of the fine lords good at it; or maybe four; and all the others worked up to look very creditable, unless you get them to yourself for too long on a wet day; and then all the artists start cutting their throats. Half of them,' said O'LiamRoe mildly, 'could do with a dirty big scrub on the flat before they lay a hand on the round.'

'Stewart thinks it's perfect,' said Thady Boy idly. 'The joy unspeakable, the comfort inestimable, the pleasure without murmuring, the hilarity without care. He can't get into it—that's his only complaint.'

'He could have my room. . . .' The former owner of Luadhas came round the corner of the paddock, a promised leash in his hand. 'I'm after buying the Irish wolfhound there,' added O'LiamRoe quickly.

'Why in God's name,' said Lymond, 'do you want a dog?'

And, studying O'LiamRoe's pink face, answered himself instantly. 'Of course,' said Thady Boy. 'To corrupt a lady of gentle bearing, vide Frère Lubin. . . . A formidable wooing, my dear. I'm willing to wager the O'Dwyer kennels are awash with wolfhounds; but please yourself. Does the creature run well? You'd better let Piedar try her for you tomorrow.'

The wolfhound Luadhas rose, lifting her long, Byzantine face. Shoulders bunched, forelegs taut, flanks shuddering, she stretched; and collapsing, shook herself. O'LiamRoe sneezed. There was a peal of laughter from Thady Boy. The great bony mat of a dog, stalking forward, gazed anxiously at the Prince of Barrow and licked his hand. O'LiamRoe was pleased, and rather touched, and not a whit embarrassed, now the story was out.

Robin Stewart, who was viewing the progress of O'LiamRoe's glacierlike wooing with some private pleasure, also derived some entertainment from the news of the purchase. It was he who, passing Neuvy, mentioned to Mistress Boyle that the Irishman and his intended gift would be on display at the chase the next morning. The girl he found unstirred to the point of impatience; but not Theresa Boyle, who, ablaze with jolly malice, made instant plans for herself and Oonagh O'Dwyer to be invited to hunt the king of venery, the melancholy hare, next morning from Blois.

*   *   *

The chase was launched from a little wood, white with dawn frost, threaded with rimed oak and hornbeam, and one or two wide-girthed chestnuts.

It had been a sharp night; but now the early sun, glaring cross-grained through the branches, laid fresh black contours, thinly prowling, over the people below.

They wore grey velvet under the pewter trees; and they laughed, dismounted, and warmed themselves at the braziers patched red like salamanders here and there in the white dusk. Grooms, pages, kennelmen, muleteers, wheeled and whisked through the throng; low tables appeared under the trees, and crested hampers began to yield up their patties and wine while the dogs, tongues lolling, tails swaying, were chased off the cloths.

Margaret Erskine was late, as was all the little Queen's entourage. Mary had been sick and Janet Sinclair and she had been up half the night until, hot-eyed, they had seen her drop into slumber. Rising at five this morning, seeing that James and Agnes were awake, soothing Janet, getting a sleepy child dressed and out to the courtyard, and finally collecting Tom's brothers and their grooms, together with their own equerries and pages, had been a formidable task, made no sweeter by the thought that Jenny, retiring radiant for the night in clouds of musk and lynx trimmings, had planned to sleep late and avoid the hunt. Whatever fascination Lymond held for her mother, it had no power at five in the morning.

Francis, Duke de Guise, young, splendid, finely bearded, with his pleasant, full-lipped smile and long nose, was master of the day's hunt. A jewel mine of courtesies and a living casket of diplomacy, he would in any case have paid tribute to the King's mistress by asking her advice. Today, by mutual consent, both Diane and the Duke treated the small Queen as their patron. Kneeling, her uncle gravely discussed where the forms were, which hares to chase, and where to establish the stables where the berners released the fresh hounds should the prey come their way. Then Margaret saw the little girl mounted, unmarked by the night's languors, and went off herself to her Brittany hackney, arranging her looped grey skirt with both feet on the board.

Despite herself, she looked for the Irishmen and found them, Thady long-stirruped on a jennet whose belly tickled the grass. Above him towered O'LiamRoe on a mouse-dun stallion. The Archer Stewart swung off to mount beside a pack of his colleagues. Bit by bit, the coursing dogs vanished to take their place in the relays. The picnic, dismantled, had gone. She saw O'LiamRoe bend down to speak to Dooly, who was moving off with two whining couples hardelled in his fists. Then a rustle of brushwood, a chime of metal and a scriech of greeting announced the Irishwomen from Neuvy.

Quilled like a porcupine, her hood leaking grey hair, and her strong, crowded teeth active in the leathery face, Mistress Boyle knew how to make her apologies to a de Guise. She soothed him, amused him and left him, pulling Oonagh's horse with her own.

At O'LiamRoe's side both horses stopped dead, under the idle, observant eyes of every waiting soul in the wood, while Theresa Boyle gazed at the mounted huddle of frieze and the matted, calf-high dog at his side. 'Father in heaven. I'd not have believed it, though 'twas the buzz of the court. They did say that splendid great prince O'LiamRoe had bought a dog was the most handsome thing ever made; more beauteous than the sun in his wheels of fire, so they said. And whatever do you want with a fine thing like that, Prince of Barrow?'

The two pairs of eyes, dog and man, turned to Mistress Boyle and the young woman at her side. The waiting horses, impatient, trampled a little in the quiet; and far off you could hear the berners, speaking low to their greyhounds as they went. The lymhounds, trained to silence, sat and scratched.

Margaret Erskine, who knew O'LiamRoe from the river bank at Rouen, and from her mother's sophisticated hilarity, felt her face harden with anger, and leaning over, spoke to the Queen, her back to the clear, expressionless profile of Thady Boy's face.

Into the silence, only a little flushed, O'LiamRoe spoke evenly. 'She is not Failnis itself, but she is sweet-mouthed and fleet, so they say. Her name is Luadhas, and she and I had great hopes that you and your lady niece would accept her.'

Like a tall sea goddess, stonelike on her horse sat Oonagh O'Dwyer, her black hair blowing a little, the only moving thing, on her trailing mantle. Mistress Boyle, releasing a thin scream, leaned over and dug her fingers in the girl's quilted arm. 'Is he not the darling knight of the kennels, and shy too, with the two little blushes on his cheeks? Thank him, Oonagh. *Ná buail do choin gan chinaid*, they say.'

It was doubtful whether any part of this speech reached Oonagh O'Dwyer. At the first words she had pulled off her glove, leaned down, and cracked her long, boy's fingers once. The wolfhound turned its flat head and, trailed by a sullen Dooly, first walked and then trotted to her side. The long, hairless white arm caressed the dog briefly; then she straightened, drew on her glove and renewed her firm grasp of the reins.

'A fair beast and a good purchase, Prince of Barrow,' she said, straight-faced and straight-backed, and clear as a bell. 'Now let us see how she runs.' And with her movement, as at a signal, the company, circling, swinging, trampling, returned to its affairs. With the rustle and pad of perfect control, the Duke trotted past, and into the lead. With him went the Duchess and the Queen, their entourage following. Then they paused; the Duke turned, and they saw his arm raised, and heard the ululation of the horn.

Taut, merry, nervous, expertly mounted, exquisitely clothed, haughty in their bright youth, the chevaliers of France poured from the dishevelled clearing. Sunlit, all that morning, they spanned the glittering woods: diamond on diamond, grey on grey, riches on riches; bough and limb indistinguishable; skirts and meadows sewn in the same silks; skulls in antique fantasy knotted with rhizome and leafy with fern frond. Webs, manes, beards, spun the same smoke-like filament; rime flashed; jewels sparked, red and fat, on rosebush and ring. Earth and animals wore the same livery. Jazerained in its berries, the oak tree matched their pearls, and paired their brilliant-sewn housings with low mosses underfoot, freshets winking half-ice in the pile. O'LiamRoe's mild face was suffused like a god's; Diane's alert, sweat-bathed cream; Margaret's and the child's a bright, comely red; and the Duke de Guise, like the sun, threw off splendours and had majesty at his command.

There were many hares. Four miles she might run at her best, the lovers' creature, the God-given Hermaphrodite; and thirty grey hounds might she still outpace. Fast, keen-nosed, cunning, jack or puss, they leaped from form or feeding ground as the lymhounds came. Big-jointed, white-tailed, they ran, jumped, doubled as the three motes rang out mellow behind them and the first relay of hare-hounds left the liams.

They hunted not in an enclosed park, but in a chase; in woods and scattered covert of nut tree and beech, poplar and ash, and in scrub and heath with elder and alder on the ground, gorse and blackthorn and the stubble of reaped corn. There the great hares started, with three years of cunning behind them, ears and scut couched, leaving the form cantering, not yet at full stretch. Then the running dogs would pass the slow lymers, the leader opening a single note as the hare ran and the '*Laisser courrer*' sounded. Other hounds doubled and trebled their tongue as the hunt swept uphill, horns stuttering du grêle, the yeomen berners addressing the dogs.

The O'LiamRoe, Prince of Barrow, golden hair streaming on streaming wool frieze, with his queer, inbred instinct had chosen his dog well. In the third relay, the best, the parfitières, ran Luadhas with her great bones and long back swaying, swimming; the flat brow and Roman nose high and delicately held. O'LiamRoe watched her, his soul in his eyes, and did not even know that Oonagh O'Dwyer was watching him in her turn.

Nothing in the situation escaped Robin Stewart. Pounding along, never quite abreast of the hunt, he caught Thady Boy's eye at last and heavily winked. Thady Boy, who had pressing concerns of his own, took the first chance to spur his pied jennet and draw off.

The next hare was a fast one—eight pounds of her, grey in her winter coat, but with the wisdom to spare herself, squat when she could, and exhaust the dogs seeking her, questing, yearning in circles. They headed her at last to the stable where the last relay stood, and O'LiamRoe was not the only one who, elated with the sun, the cold wind, the warm saddle, the music of hunt horn and voice, strained to see the noble, waiting head of his lovely dog Luadhas.

She was there, but tight in hardel as were all the braches in that place, the rough hair lifted stark at her spine. Next to her stood a royal groom, a great thong round his wrist. And among the grey-yellow dusty filaments of last year's flowering weeds was a low spread of dappled fur, staunch elbows, and great pads laid flat, and, above them, motionless in the quiet grass, a shallow, masked head. In a moment you could see the wide-spaced, tufted ears, the bottle nose, and the cheetah's lyre mark sealing ancient secrets round the white muzzle. One of the hunting cats had been brought.

It was not hard to tell who had engineered it. Through Robin Stewart, mischievous in his jealousy, O'LiamRoe had already been forced to present his lady prematurely with his self-conscious gift of the hound. So much Thady Boy had already ascertained. Now the display of Luadhas was destroyed at a stroke, and Robin Stewart, who had laid his plans well, admitted as much buoyantly, with his knowing smile seeking Thady Boy's eye yet again as they stood arrested, the tired dogs hard-leashed, the horses still. In the bare field before them, nothing moved but the hare.

The Duke de Guise raised a hand. The groom, bending, whipped off the cat's mask. There was an arc of something pale-spotted, all shoulder and leg; then the plushy shoulders and weird, thick-jointed shanks worked silently through the long grass so that it leaned a little and stirred, as if a snake had passed through. The blemish sprang

120

across the wide field like a shadow, and then stopped. With a thin scream, the big hare died.

Oonagh O'Dwyer knelt by the groom, her pale eyes blazing, as the cat drank its reward and, masked and manacled, leaped in a flash of white fur on its keeper's crupper. Soon, pleased with their new toy, they were galloping at full stretch again; and the sun at its height patched the white shadows with colour and lit them like a book of hours in vermilion and gold as they streamed through the little woods, black-fanned by tree shadows. On the boldest horse, erect and still, masked like an executioner, sat the cheetah. Nearest to him rode Oonagh, her black hair freed and streeling in the wind, her mermaid's eyes green-lit and intent as the cat's. The running dogs, leashed, were still with them, but they were not used again. The reign of Luadhas had been short.

The check came with the last hare of the day. The mechanical killing, the silken violence of the cat, had added a fulsome excitement to the hunt but drained it of skill. A good while before, O'LiamRoe, without comment, had dropped to the back; and immediately the pied jennet also had slackened its pace.

This hare had waited in her form till unharboured and had left it like a thunderbolt, running hard in the open for over a mile before clapping; and then trying every trick. She doubled over gates, bobbed along a boundary wall, leaped long-short, long-short on the straight for a while, and then, jumping at right angles to her own track, made off in a fresh direction. In a little while she began to run mostly straight, and they knew she was lost. Then the scent, weakened over the stubble by the morning's bright sun, suddenly redoubled, fresh and strong, and the lymers quickened, tongues lolling; and then checking, flung here and there searching. She had come back on her tracks, doubling scent, and then vanished. The riders stopped and the horns blew the ritual bewilderment of the stynt.

They were not sorry to stop. In twos and threes, they gathered at the edge of another wood, steam rising from riders and horses. Before them, a wide mole-combed meadow unrolled, dipping distantly to a grey, ice-clogged stream and rising beyond in the same rolling yellow grass and gorse, with low bushes and a rare copse beyond.

Waiting, they chatted. Margaret Erskine, pausing briefly at his side, complimented O'LiamRoe pleasantly on his dog; but he wanted to speak of the little Queen, who certainly rode well, even boisterously, for her age. St. André on foot at Mary's side was checking a saddle girth. The horses chafed a little, sidling as the cold penetrated; and O'LiamRoe, his face thoughtful, looked down at the ollave heaped at his side. 'Thady Boy, between this and no one murdering me at all, it's a poor day you've had.'

'Ah, be still. The day is not over. There are worse off,' said Thady, acknowledging the unexpected thrust neither in dark face nor flat voice. 'Look at Piedar, and the legs on him like honeybags.' Then the horn, blowing the rights, told the hare had been found, and like split pulses the party tumbled apart.

A beaten hare, far from landmarks, forgets to run in a ring. A beaten hare runs uphill; and if she is old and shrewd and there is a fresh young hare at hand, she will clap and lie by the young one, and let her spring up first, if she will, so that the simpler braches, the pups, the addlepates, would bob and babble after the different scent.

It happened here. But the older hare, rising, fled the meadow with half the company following, as the braches in the wood gave tongue after a different prey. For a space, two hares held the field and split the pack between them, one crossing the open in great bounds with the leaders—the Duke, Diane, the little Queen, the Neuvy party— after her, and the other skirting the wood, with the dogs in full cry.

It was bad hunting and improper coursing, but the day was ending and etiquette relaxed. The rival hunts swept after their respective hares, neither knowing nor greatly troubling about which pack was following the original prey, and which was hunting change. Then, with the width of the meadow between them, the de Guise party killed.

The ironic whoops, the waves, the horn blowing from the ridge, reached the less fortunate party down below; the second hare, now patently a fresh one, was far ahead, and both horses and riders were tired. But St. André, riled by the shouting, followed grimly, with O'LiamRoe at his elbow. And behind, among the running berners and the leashed dogs, the cheetah rode stiff-legged on its cushion, the mask dark above the silent muzzle.

They had no break for horn blowing now. Stream and ridge far on their left, they raced along the wooded edge of the meadow until the turf turned to a weedy tilth and began to show the bones of the underlying lime. Small quarries, holes and underworkings patched the distant ground; and it was apparent that they were now very close indeed to the banks of the Loire. Stewart, loose-seated in the middle, could hear O'LiamRoe swearing. Once into the broken ground, their hare was as good as lost.

Then their luck turned. Out of the ground far ahead materialized a man, a middle-aged man dressed in working clothes who waved his woollen cap and shouted and jumped so that his breeches clapped in mid-air. It had perhaps been worth a crown to him once before, and it certainly earned him as much again. The hare veered, hesitated, and then altering course grimly, began to forge back over the meadow.

It lay before them, a long field of close grass rolling uphill, dipping to the stream, rising to the ridge where the others waited, black and derisive against the frosty blue of the sky. If they chased her, they would simply drive her into the Duke's hands.

St. André's arm came up. They halted, sweating, jolting, behind him, the latecomers padding through the crumbling lime; and at an order the groom thrust past with the silent cat. The Marshal spoke. Fast and smoothly, the thong was slipped, the mask peeled off; and the cheetah's peat-brown eyes, glassy full, were directed to their prey. Then with gloved hands the man lifted the cat by its flanks and flung it to the ground. For a moment the cat crouched, pale-spotted, furry, the tufted ears pricked; then the spine rose thin and raw like a lash, the thick joints folded. and the cheetah launched itself, clinging, inescapable as a dream and, undulating, began to cross the wide field after the hare.

Softly as she went, the sound reached the hare. Her thews responded, flinging her forward in great jumps, eight feet and nine feet between her pricking, her dark-tipped ears surging above the high grass. She jumped; and from the short fur on her neck a blaze of green flared into life and died again in the shade.

St. André suddenly froze in the saddle. On the pied jennet, Thady's blue eyes narrowed. But Robin Stewart, closer to the household than any, knew at once what it was. As the hunting cat, smooth as lava, unfurled to the rhythm of its most perfect pace, Stewart flung his horse forward, shouting, the words floating thinly through the ice-clear, sunny air. 'Damn you. It's the leveret! It's the Queen's hare you're hunting!'

They heard on the ridge. On both sides of the field, for a single second, no one moved. An outsider looking at the flushed faces would have seen fright and irritation and anger. The death of a royal pet was not the best way to win favour. Of all the faces beside St. André, only O'LiamRoe's showed pity. Thady Boy was as still as the cheetah on his leashed pillion had been. For clearly the little hare was doomed. Already, it had swum, big-headed, bobbing, over the stream and was halfway up the long meadow; and already, far behind, the long spine and the padded, working shoulders of the cat, yellow like smoke, smoothly loping, had begun to narrow the gap. And hopelessly behind on a tired horse, Robin Stewart was going to be too late. For no horse on either side could now reach Queen Mary's pet hare before the cheetah did.

The hare was tiring. Little lovers' gift, consecrated to Venus, fed on wild thyme and summoned by flutes, the young puss with her emerald collar was unused to enemies, had had no dreams of the bamboo forests of the Ganges and the glib death lurking there. She ran white-eyed and unbreathing, sensing the thick soft pads closing and feeding horror from every sense to her loaded heart until, clear above the sifting grasses, the far-off barking, the distant beat of a tired horse, the voices muted and uneasy and the tinkle of bit and hardel, a familiar voice cried, a little porcelain mare started forward, and someone with a familiar smell and look and shape called '*Suzanne!*'

With all the strength in her bleeding paws, the little hare turned from the open, unyielding horizon and made for the small Queen. Far behind, the cheetah turned too, and pinned its mesmeric, passionless gaze on the white scut and the little palfrey and its red-haired rider beyond.

On the ridge, the Duke de Guise, his spurs instant and cruel, hurled his horse after his niece. Below, helplessly, the mounted and unmounted surged forward in their fear. But before that, a hand like steel closed on O'LiamRoe's wrist, and Lymond's clear voice said 'Luadhas.'

For a second the silence lay between them, aching. Then O'Liam-Roe moved and spoke. Unbelieving, the little Firbolg heard, bent and, slipping the fine shackles, sent the wolfhound Luadhas hurtling after the cat.

She was a noble bitch, high in heart and honest after her calling. She could overthrow a wolf, but the alien, wicked beauty slipping through the grasses ahead was of an element she had never known. She raced uphill, tail streaming, rough hair blown and parted with her speed, loping high on her long legs; and fast as the gap was closing between cheetah and hare, the gap between dog and cat began to close faster still. The hazel rod in O'LiamRoe's right hand broke in two.

The hare was at its end. Thrashed by its heartbeats, suffocated with exhaustion and fear, its thick sight blinded, it was running by sound alone to its mistress's voice, the fortune on its neck winking and sparkling in the unsparing sun.

And the porcelain horse, with the lightest and smallest of riders, had flown, skidded, stumbled downhill faster than any. Within yards of the creature Mary kicked her feet from the planchon and slid to the ground as the Duke's gelding reached her. She rushed forward; the little horse fled; and her uncle, one-handed, snatched at her cloak.

Mary stumbled. She was weeping, her hair tangled about her hot face, the tears rushing off nose and chin. The leveret gave a mighty, last leap and stopped, rigid, in the naked ground out of her reach. Mary tore herself from her uncle's grasp and flung herself forward as, in the distance, the grass shook and parted.

In an act as brave as any in his whole young, foolhardy career, the Duke de Guise leaped from his horse, seized the girl, and scooping up the leveret with one hand, flung it to the nearest rider. Robin Stewart caught the inert, warm, fatigue-sodden weight in his arms as the Duke flung the child on his plunging horse and followed her into the saddle.

From above and below, horses were rushing towards them; but the cheetah arrived before them all. The grasses stirred and he was there: lyre-marked face and strong forelegs and silken, yellow-white belly. He came upon the big gelding as the little girl clutched at the saddle and the topaz eyes followed the red head. He did not even pause. Cheated of his rightful prey he landed, turned and sprang. The Duke, the child in his arms, dragged the terrified horse sideways, but the spread needles did not reach them. Instead, a matted, brindled shape breasted the grass. A slender, pointed muzzle struck the air; long legs, rough-haired and uncombed, paused a little; and then the deerhound Luadhas, with the courage of her inheritance, gathered her powers and sprang on the cat.

It was a fight well remembered for years afterwards by the company who gathered there to watch it that day. No weapon existed which could now separate cheetah and dog, and no man could hope to pull them apart. As the child, sobbing, was swept to safety, the rest in terrible fascination stood and looked.

There was never a doubt as to its end. As O'LiamRoe had known, as Lymond had known, the dog had no chance. Hound and cheetah rolled over and over, compacted silk hair and rough, mean, triangular head and long-nosed Byzantine; then Luadhas, lips bared, would seek a grip on the spotted spine and the sinuous snakelike fur would unroll and untwine; the heavy soft paw would flash, and on the skull of the dog the brindled hair sank, wet and dark, as the deep lifeblood welled.

She was a brave dog. As she bled she bit, her strong teeth sunk again and again in the dirty yellow-white plush. She shook her head and the cat, blood-spotted and scarred, wrenched free and staggered a pace: a dancer tripped, inelegant and baleful. There was a pause. Then, his haunches tightened, the cheetah called on the great muscles of thigh and hock and with all his power sprang quiet, curved and deadly into the sunlit air. The soft body fell and its great paws, needle-sharp and fatal, sank into the great cords and vessels of Luadhas's neck and spine. The bitch screamed, rolling over; and on the squeaking, flattened grass her great body opened and shut, the soft fur like a woman's twined about it, the cat's claws deep in her back. She threshed for a long while, panting in her blood and whining softly, but the cheetah's grip never relaxed; and after a while the whimpering stopped and the pointed muzzle opened, and the cheetah withdrew its claws.

Its keeper, white with the premonition of royal doom, leaped down, chain in hand and, cajoling, approached the cat. The flat brainpan, the haughty lyre, the chestnut eyes turned, and he stopped. Delicately, in a high remote ecstasy of some icy bloodlust, the cheetah stalked by. Fastidiously he stepped over the heaving thing of torn fur,

125

bloody on the crushed ground, and his topaz eyes, roving, saw the wide circle of faces and of horses which, unbroken, encompassed him. One horse was nearer than the others and there, forgotten, was his true prey. Evilly, without warning, like some eerie familiar, he sprang at Robin Stewart where he sat, the leveret gripped in his cold hands.

The Archer's elderly mare could suffer no more. As the hot fur brushed by, she neighed shrilly, reared, and throwing Stewart hard to the ground, galloped wildly downhill. On the trampled grass the cat crouched, watching Robin Stewart as he lay, the forgotten leveret tight in his arms, the mature amusement, the detached contempt quite disappeared.

Urgent and quiet, a voice said, 'Throw it.' But that would be professional ruin. In a kind of petulant stupor born of fright, Stewart lay and watched as the cat gathered its limbs for a jump. Then it was airborne. In the same kind of trance, he saw its belly above him, smelled the blood, saw the sun spark on the claws. And saw, torn from his dream, sick and fiery with hope, something hit and enfold the scarred, arching body, swaddling the spare head, muffling the peaty eyes, twisting and trapping the powerful limbs.

It was Thady Boy's saddlecloth. As the cheetah, hurtling threshing against them, began to fight its way free, the ollave's strong hands jerked Stewart, staggering, to his feet and, one steadying hand under his elbow, made him run.

With stones, with rods, pulling the horses as near as they dared to separate victim from cat, the others did what they could; but they were not quick enough. Insane for its baulked blood, the cheetah drove through them, wet with fresh wounds, and settled into its stride in the tracks of the two running men.

It reached them as, sprinting, jumping, twisting over uneven ground, Thady brought the Archer to the edge of the meadow where turf gave way to scrub and rank grass and the pitted limestone banks of the Loire. A wisp of smoke, the dying breath of some oracle, rose for a moment in the bright air and died away. Stewart turned, his bony hands tight on Suzanne's fat body; and in a flash of torrid fur, the cheetah rose.

At that point, the automatic obedience which had brought Stewart so far came to an end. He could run no further. He couldn't fight a hunting cat with his bare hands, nor could Thady. He began to duck, in pure reflex action, but in his mind was only a dead wilderness which did not even anticipate pain. Then something took him by the collar. As the cat was in mid-spring, Thady Boy ducked, twisted, and hurled Stewart forward with all the strength of his shoulder into the ground.

And the ground gave way. In a kind of trauma of exhaustion and fright the Archer felt himself falling not merely forward on his knees in the scrub but sucked downwards, blundering, banging hip, knee and elbow on unyielding surfaces, losing his breath, and not merely from concussion; losing his sight, and not merely from panic. Slipping, sliding, skidding, in utter amazement, Robin Stewart tumbled head over heels into darkness.

There was a lung-flattening jolt, a burst of light, a choking flurry of smoke, and a scream. The Archer opened his eyes. He was sitting half-disgorged from a twisting stone chimney, on a hearth with a little wood fire: a discovery he made painfully and fast as Thady Boy, tumbling down on his tracks, landed plump on his lap. In that age-old limestone landscape, all colonized with caves, he had dropped on to the troglodyte hearthstone of the man with the cap. And ringing in his ears was a soft voice which had surely just spoken, back there in the field, before the bed of the fire burned his seat. '*For O'LiamRoe's sake, my dear,*' it had said, '*you deserve to fall first.*'

Before they left, the Archer got Thady Boy by the arm. 'You saved my life,' he said. 'You'd no need to do yon for me.' Then, being Stewart, he spared a glance for the little hare. Her eyes were open and her soft ears laid back, but already her brown fur was cold.

'She died of fright just after you got her,' said Thady Boy Ballagh. 'I told you to throw her.'

A less worldly society would have cheered their reappearance from the cave. The Court of France cheered the cheetah, laughed, and went about their business. Someone brought up Thady's jennet, and Stewart, sitting tenderly in the saddle, posted stiff-legged after the rest. The cheetah, masked and leashed, sat rock-still and silent once more on her groom's crupper; and strung out, the horns speaking their message, the hunt was making for home. Long ago the Queen's party had gone. The younger men trotted beside Thady; and St. André himself held him in light conversation, his hand on his knee. The leveret hung from his saddlebow, the jewelled collar winking green.

Back in the field, one horse still stood waiting; one man was not quite ready to go. Mistress Boyle noticed it, glancing over her shoulder; lightly she skirled, and winked at her friends. 'Ah, Oonagh, there goes the fine present our noble friend was after making you. Is it paid for, do you think, or will he be needing to ask a loan of us next?'

There was a long laugh. It rolled clear over the crushed stalks and bruised grass, the smeared weeds and wet earth to where O'LiamRoe knelt, his golden hair blowing, by the shuddering rags of the dog Luadhas, and drew his knife in charity along her long throat.

III

Aubigny: Boldness of Denial

Four things sustain crime: temptation, consent, urging, and
boldness of denial.

THAT autumn, Margaret Erskine wrote to her husband, 'Your
lantern lissom of light is possessed of devils'; and far off in
Augsburg, with its vineyards and walnut trees, its sandy, stony
terraces and its ageing, weakening Emperor, the Ambassador, knowing
Lymond, wondered what barbaric enfranchisement of soul or of
body he was devising for himself and for his sponsors now.

Before the cheetah hunt was a week old, the full Court arrived at
Blois, streaming uphill from the river to the broad court of the
château. The sun on the King's mail splashed through the dark
archway, slid over the thick, eely salamanders on his father's great
wing and winked from the stony case of the stairway as the Court in
silver, satin and jewels was sucked up in his wake, as O'LiamRoe
observed, like crabmeat in a gullery.

With King, Queen and Constable had come the nursery. Mary was
delighted to see them. In the old days she had enjoyed sleeping with
Elizabeth and Claude, but she liked sharing her room with Aunt
Fleming even better and was looking forward to mentioning it.

The death of the leveret had been a two days' agony. After it, on
her charming uncle's advice, the small Queen was taken, her face
still white with crying, to see and thank O'LiamRoe.

She was only seven. Halfway through, the speech came to an end;
and she stood before him, breathing heavily, her lip transfixed by her
teeth and a tear in each lid. The Prince of Barrow, who had been
suffering an embarrassment almost as acute, instantly knelt, stumbling slightly, and said, 'What is on you, Princess? There goes Luadhas, hunting with the old gods and the noble champions at the great
Feis of Samhantide, with golden Cormac himself, without blemish or
reproach; and after, Bran and Luadhas and Conbec lie all at the
King's feet, fed and sleeping. For this day, to be sure, the wolfhound
and the little hare have shared the two sides of a dish of new milk;
and when we have years and years on us they will be running yet

128

up there on the blue speckled Curragh, with their pink tongues and their sharp, young, white teeth. Thady Boy there will tell you.'

Lymond did not speak. Watching O'LiamRoe from the fireplace, he and Margaret Erskine, who had brought her, had already exchanged all their news; she had no wish to provoke him further to speech. The towering, icy rage of the Queen Mother after the hunt had been easier to bear than Lymond's smooth tongue. Here was another attempt to endanger the Queen and her friends. On the face of it, a travel-split cage explained the hare's escape from the menagerie; coincidence explained its presence there in the woods. It was Lymond, combing the bushes on his own, who had found the anonymous game bag afterwards, not far from where the hunt had paused during the final stint. Stiff, roughly perforated, offensive with crotel, it showed by a torn buckle where someone had wrenched it off in his haste, and then abandoned it. So the hare had been carried throughout the chase, it now seemed, its bag probably cloaked; and had been released just there, deliberately, to do what harm it could. And but for the dog, braver than anyone could have calculated, the trick might have succeeded.

Since that day, the tourniquet of their duties about the Queen had tightened. By Lymond's laws they were bound now, in an unbreakable fence about the Queen. There was no second of the day when an Erskine or a Fleming was not at her side. Only Jenny, popular, resilient, was exempt, while they waited for the shadow of death or accident to fall again.

O'LiamRoe, silent on the subject of Luadhas, struggling perhaps himself with an unaccustomed need for privacy, was ignorant and content to be ignorant of his ollave's affairs. And since Mistress Boyle, in her positive, eccentric way, had apparently forgotten the whole episode, he resumed his relationship with the lady and her niece, adopting with pleasure their wide circle of friends and finding in Oonagh, now and then, a trace of courtesy lacking before.

Fresh, night-long cronies from the Franco-Irish circle at Blois in turn visited him, and so did the English and some of the Scots. The big room shared by Prince and ollave was seldom empty of convivial company disputing hotly in French, Irish, English, Latin. Occasionally Thady Boy's sardonic voice was heard, and O'LiamRoe's face would admit a certain avuncular pride. Thady Boy could talk. And he was a pet of a listener as well.

Barred himself from the ultimate presence of the sovereign, the Prince of Barrow missed the solid hard work which was making Thady Boy indispensable at Court. At levée and reception, at ball and after sport, during meals and after supper parties, Thady was expected as a matter of course. His playing had become as fashionable as a drug. He made music in public and in private for them all:

the King, the Queen, Diane, the Constable and Condé, d'Enghien, the de Guises, Marguerite, and already they thought nothing and less than nothing of how he looked. Then, that goal reached, he hardened his long fingers in their entrails of icing and sugar and started to twist.

It was then that O'LiamRoe, coming back to his chamber now and then, found the door locked against him and a woman's voice, sweet and unrecognizable, spoke once when he rattled. '*Non si puo: il signor è accompagnato.*' The next time the voice was a man's; but it ceased as soon as O'LiamRoe rapped.

Only Robin Stewart upbraided Thady Boy, and then on the eve of their sole journey: a two-day visit by ceremonial invitation to Lord d'Aubigny's home. Since Thady Boy's first, carefree days in France, Lymond had kept his finger lightly on the pulse of Robin Stewart's troubles, for little reason other than habit. Attention to weaker vessels had been for years a fighter's necessity. It was also the sign of a born teacher, although this was not an aspect of Thady Boy which leaped to the eye.

On Stewart's side through all this, a grudging admiration had succeeded distrust. Even before the hunt he had started to seek out Thady. After it, aggressively, he showed signs of haunting him, and Thady Boy, who by this time had his own reasons, did nothing to stop him. Faced now with one of the Archer's more popular tirades, Thady Boy listened patiently, unrolling a doublet and beginning to put it on. Stewart's lecture ended, and his bony hand rubbed over his face, stirring his already disordered hair and flicking his shirt collar awry. Unnoticing, he said suddenly, 'Ballagh—why d'ye stay with O'LiamRoe? Any God's number of dukes and lords here would be blithe to employ you, if it's money you want.'

Thady Boy pulled shut the paned windows. 'I thought you'd got O'LiamRoe out of your pate. What's wrong with him now?'

The Archer said brusquely, 'I don't know.' Then bending, he picked up his cloak and swung round, his face red. 'It's not worth speaking of. But . . . hell fry them . . . there they sit in their fancy clothes, with their lapdogs and their boy friends and the carbuncles bluff on their pinkies; and unless you're Michael Scott or Michaelangelo, or Duns Scotus or Bayard, or a six-headed sow that can play prick-song on a jew's harp, they've no use for you.'

Thady Boy, too, had slung his cloak over his shoulder and was standing, legs apart, hands clasped behind him, watching. 'And which of O'LiamRoe's spanking successes is irritating you?' he asked. 'Being turned off the tennis court or your cheetah clawing his wolfhound to death?—That hurt, by the way.'

'I'm pleased to hear it,' said Stewart viciously. 'You'd never know it. He's mediocre, and he doesna care. He doesn't even bother with—' He stopped.

130

'With what? Women? That remains to be seen. You may think you've endeared yourself to the Boyle family, my dear, but I doubt it. And *is* he mediocre?' asked Thady Boy. 'He upsets your philosophy by being happy; but I find him irritating for other reasons entirely.'

'Then why stay with him?' Blundering, Stewart renewed the attack. 'Do you think you owe him loyalty? Do we owe àny jack of them loyalty? If you made one slip yourself, they'd have your liver under their nails.'

His voice was thick; Thady's, mellow and cool as the Liffey. ''Tis yourself, my fellow, who needs to leave this fine country. Quit off and go back to Scotland. Why not?'

Robin Stewart drew a deep breath. The waves of heat from the hearth oppressed them both, fully dressed for the journey. Stewart's coarse skin was moist with heat; the brows indented, line upon line, where the fretful pressures of his spirit squeezed into his flesh day and night. 'I'll be sorry I said it,' said the Archer suddenly. 'But I'd liefer you knew. I would have left many a long week ago, if it wasn't for you.'

Neither surprise nor pleasure showed on the dark face opposite, only hard-held patience and something else so efficiently suppressed that Stewart missed it altogether. The ollave loosed his clasped hands and laid two fingers on the latch. 'They are waiting for us. I hope you will regret nothing you do from this out. But because of me . . . because of me, gallant man, I think you should leave.'

For a moment, in silence, they faced each other. Then, without waiting for an answer, Ballagh opened the door and moving quickly and lightly, ran downstairs to the horses.

*　　　　*　　　　*

On a little river south of Orléans, at the eastern edge of the rolling green fens of La Sologne, lay the moated town of Aubigny-sur-Nère, given to John Stewart, High Officer of the Scots Army fighting in France, by a grateful nation a century and a quarter before this. Twice burned by the English and once by accident, it had risen on its ashes neat, prosperous and comely, with its statue of St. Martin, its shops, stables, gardens, houses, smithy, fountain, worksheds and its elegant castle where, beneath the lions and salamanders of a bygone Stewart the present owner, lordly in silk, welcomed the arrival of O'LiamRoe, Thady, Dooly and their guide Robin Stewart. And with Lord d'Aubigny were his two Scottish relatives by marriage, Sir George Douglas and Sir James.

Blandly, the visit began.

*　　　　*　　　　*

Once before, John Stewart of Aubigny had been surprised by the range of O'LiamRoe's interests. Now, displaying his treasures to the trained mind of the ollave, he found again an unwilling kinship with the ollave's queer master. O'LiamRoe could and did alarm with unseemly fables of the Gobbam Saer; but Delorme, god of masons, could reduce him to silence; and the names of Limousin and Duret, of Rosso and del Sarto, Cellini and Da Vinci, Primaticcio and Grolier rose familiarly to his lips. With Robin Stewart sour and Thady discreet behind him, he wandered happily though Castle Aubigny and, next day, through Stewart's other beautiful house on the Nère, touching silverwork and embroidery, admiring paintings, savouring gem-bound books and tapestries, imported tiles and Milanese beds and Florentine marquetry, the frescoes and the grave, Italian marbles. The houses were large; the staffs—stewards, equerries, ladies-in-waiting to his wife, tutors and pages for his son, chambermaids, waiting women, priest, surgeon, butler, cook, gatekeepers and porters, baker, cobbler and baron-court sergeants of the wards—were immense.

Watching d'Aubigny, his big, firm hands turning over a piece of enamel, his cultured Scots-French voice expatiating on the Pénicauds, it was hard to imagine him in the field, his company of arquebusiers mounted behind him, the smell of horseflesh drowning the pomades. Yet he had fought; he had been in prison, if for political reasons only; he commanded a company. And judged by the unfairest standards, set against a scourging aesthetism bloodily acquired, his tastes were easy and his appreciation oddly slack.

He showed them, at La Verrerie, a Cellini saltcellar given him by the King. 'Some years ago now, of course,' said Lord d'Aubigny. 'He has certain other continuing drains on his income. It isn't easy for him to be as generous as he would like. Except in some quarters. Chenonceaux—have you seen Chenonceaux? Prettier than Anet, in my view. She's hardly ever there. Thirteen thousand aubergines, she has in the garden; and nine thousand strawberry plants he sent her last year. It will be a pity if she spoils it. They like throwing money about. Have you seen Écouen and Chantilly? It's a pity when the taste isn't there. They talk a lot of the Queen—these pearls from Florence, the furniture she has there at Blois. Of course, Florence was at its height very recently. She married at thirteen, a cradle between two coffins—you won't remember the phrase—and learned all she knows about a court under François au Grand Nez. And we know what *that* means. . . .'

Behind them, on their tours, sauntered the Douglases. Once, as Thady Boy leaned his idle weight on a table, a hand came down sharply and silently on his wrist, pinning it on the rich wood where the flexible fingers lay exposed in relief. Holding it thus, 'Don't you sometimes regret, John, that something like that can't be bought?' said George Douglas. 'Or can it, I wonder?'

After the first second, Thady Boy's right hand lay relaxed in his grip. The others all turned to look. O'LiamRoe grinned, but Stewart, forced to look at that elegant hand, found rising within him a profound and inexplicable annoyance. He said nastily, 'They're not so bonny on the other side, are they? I doubt Master Ballagh caught a few knives wrong end up when he was learning to juggle. . . . Yon's the arcade his lordship was speaking of.' Lord d'Aubigny cleared his throat; Sir George, smiling, loosed his hard grasp; and the little party, dismissing the scene, shuffled after.

And once, when Lord d'Aubigny touched with a certain wit on Stewart's recent ordeal by fire, Sir George smiled. 'Life at Court seems to be uncommonly risky. I hope, Stewart, both you and your rescuer had read your Pynson. You know it? *The Art and Craft to Know Well to Dye.*'

The greater part of his audience looked amiably blank. O'LiamRoe picked up a piece of rock crystal and whistled. The book Douglas mentioned, he seemed to remember in the unfiled rubbish heap of his mind, dealt not with mortality but with tinting. A grin of pure joy lined the smooth, egg-round face; and the Prince of Barrow, returning the crystal, addressed his ollave over his shoulder. 'Busy child, you have surely read that.'

'Ah,' said Thady. 'The Douglases are expert on titles. I would never contradict them.'

And paid for it that same evening when, neatly noosed by courtesies and polite insistence, he was drawn alone into Sir George's room and heard the door close crisply behind him.

'And now,' said the most intelligent of the Douglases, removing his superb cloak and smoothing his doublet, while watching the fat, sweep-headed creature before him. 'And now, Francis Crawford of Lymond, let us talk.'

From his black head to his scuffed mockado shoes, Thady Boy was relaxed. A point of light from the fire danced under his lids. 'You are speaking, maybe, to the fairies?'

Moving with grace, Douglas dropped into a tall tapestried chair and put his fingers together. 'You forget. I know your face, my dear Crawford. I know it better than any of my colleagues do. I had the pleasure on several occasions of causing you trouble, and I bear you no grudge for having on occasion made use of me. At times, as I remember, we have even helped one another. For the future. . . . Who knows?' His eyes rested thoughtfully on Thady Boy's calm face. 'I thought the Queen would have had you at today's meeting. Doesn't she trust you yet? Or is it the other way round?'

The room was exquisitely furnished. Detaching himself in all his bleary satin from the door, Thady Boy took from the wall an Aztec mask fiery with jewels, its nose and ears of beaten gold. He put it on.

The bone teeth grinned, and his voice came hollow through the metal. 'Quetzalcoatl, Lord of the Toltecs.'

Sir George waited, but the voice added nothing more. 'Shall I spell it out, then?' he said. 'The Queen Dowager of Scotland and her brothers had a meeting with King Henri this morning. They reached an agreement, as a result of which our dear Scottish friend the Earl of Arran will be asked to give up the Governship of Scotland, on the promise that if little Mary dies childless, he will rule Scotland as King. And in Arran's place the new Governor of Scotland in Mary's minority will of course be that well-known Frenchwoman, the Queen Dowager Mary of Guise. . . . Interesting?'

'Very.' The mask had descended.

'So that at all costs the little Queen must be kept alive so that her mother, during the minority, may run Scotland as she wishes; so that Mary in time may marry the heir to the French throne; and so that the Dauphin may in time become King of France, Ireland and Scotland, with the entire family of Guise at, if not on, his right hand. This conception of the future is not universally popular in the kingdom of France.'

'Do you tell me?'

'No. Diane, it is rumoured, is becoming a little jealous of the de Guises, and did she know what, for example, some ladies of my acquaintance suspect, she would be very angry indeed.'

'They're easy vexed, so, the women here.'

'On the other hand, the Constable is said to favour reducing the power of both the de Guises and Diane, and marrying the little Queen off to a lesser duke instead of to the Dauphin as planned.'

'There does be a power of scheming among the grand, high folk there are,' said Thady Boy humbly.

'—Finally, Queen Catherine, we know, dislikes sharing her husband with Diane, with the de Guises, and even with his old crony the Constable, though she's capable of allying with the Constable at a pinch. She dislikes England intensely. She has seen to it that d'Aubigny here, for example, will never rise in the hierarchy since his brother Lennox, my revered relative who hates you, my dear Lymond, so cordially, is at the English Court and a strong contender, if not a strong favourite, for both the English and the Scottish crowns. He, we must not forget, is descended from Scottish Kings, and his wife—my niece—was niece also to the late King of England. No one shakes the King's loyalties lightly. The Constable was made to release d'Aubigny from prison because the King loved d'Aubigny. The love has perhaps weakened, but the regard is still there. Neither Catherine nor the Constable can injure d'Aubigny; but they will see that he is kept out of the royal mind.

'The King has other favourites besides the de Guise family. You know them well. St. André. Condé and d'Enghien. The absent Vidame. Each in turn hates his or her rival; nearly all without exception hate the de Guises. So that if someone is trying to kill the little Queen, the little Queen's mother is in quite a predicament. The foreign assassin is soon dealt with. But the assassin within the Court is another matter entirely. For example, if it were Queen Catherine herself?'

With a smooth rustle, Thady Boy slid down his stool, settling his potbelly on his knees and gazing at the segmented ceiling.

> '*A Madame la Dauphine*
> *Rien n'assigne*
> *Elle a ce qu'il faut avoir*
> *Mais je voudrais bien la voir. . . .*

'Or Diane?' said Thady Boy. '*Vieille ridée, vieille edentée?* As you see, I know a verse about her too. . . .'

'I have no doubt you do,' said Sir George, his voice grating very slightly. 'Do I have to be more precise? The Queen Dowager has to protect her daughter. And she must do it covertly, without knowledge of King or Court. So the man she chose, unknown to the King, is pranking at his very table. *Are you listening?*'

The ollave's blank stare, very slightly unfocussed, dropped from the ceiling. 'Am I not here sober, celibate and buttoned like a March stag? What must I do else?'

'Dance,' said Sir George succinctly.

A smile, starting somewhere on the scalp, crawled downwards over the dark, slovenly skin. Thady brought his chin down and his hands up, and sketching an unmistakable gesture, replied. 'The answer is a doux Nenny, my dear.'

A refusal, sweet or otherwise, was no use to Sir George. He sat up. 'You understand at least what I'm talking about?'

'Devil a word,' said Thady Boy cheerfully. 'But three months in this fair land have taught me something, surely. Five words, to be precise. A doux Nenny, my dear.'

For a moment Douglas was silent. But he was not of a race easily daunted. He said pleasantly, 'You would find it helpful to have the friendship of the next Scots Ambassador in France.'

The smile, remaining, matched the abandoned lilt in the voice. 'Does the Queen Mother know who the next Ambassador is to be?'

'She will, when you have told her,' said George Douglas. 'Myself.'

'Otherwise—?'

'Otherwise Henri of Valois, Second of that name, will be told why Queen Mother of Scotland has brought a spy with her, and who he is.'

Thady Boy's soft voice was sad. 'It all sounds terrible unlucky.

Would it not be a better thing, surely, to put the problem to the Queen Mother yourself? Or would the tale, maybe, fall faint on her ears? I doubt you have axe-land to cultivate there, my hero.'

'It wouldn't fall faint, I dare think, on the ears of King Henri,' said Douglas comfortably. 'As you are aware, the Queen Mother will disown you instantly.'

Thady Boy shook his head. 'Logic, logic; why then should the lady ever agree to your wants?'

'It wounds me to say it, but for quite a sound reason I believe,' said Sir George Douglas. 'She disapproves of me, I do believe; but she wants Lymond more.'

There was a thoughtful silence, filled with the hiss and crack of the fire. Thady Boy stirred. He rose to his feet, picked up the Aztec mask, and clapping it on, Janus-like, back to front, surveyed Sir George who also had risen, not quite so smoothly. ''Tis a neat, pretty scheme; but you overrate friend Quetzalcoatl here and underrate the Queen Mother. If his stock were as high as you think, he would have been at this meeting you speak of, surely. And to exert pressure and still be refused would be intolerable, would it not? So that it is lucky that there is no Quetzalcoatl, but only a Druimcli of the seven degrees with a simple negative in his mouth.'

He strolled away, replaced the mask, and turned to the door. Sir George Douglas followed him. They understood each other. Lymond knew that Sir George would take just as much as he could snatch, this side of danger; and Sir George knew that Lymond had quite cheerfully called his bluff. The situation, however, was still full of plums for the picking. He said mildly, 'The seven degrees of self-confidence, I take it. You deserve to be made a little uncomfortable, my friend.'

'*Dhia*, you are forestalled,' said Thady Boy absently, his hand on the latch. 'I will add, however, a true piece of advice.

'The country is stronger than the lord, noble Douglas. Stronger than the lord and equal to the power of her songs—Do you sing, now?'

Sir George did not sing. He turned to Quetzalcoatl, empty-eyed on the wall, and as the door shut, exchanged a bald grin.

*   *   *

The Douglas was sufficiently piqued to retaliate next day, when maliciously he dragged the small talk to Scotland, the third baron Cutler and his Irish wife, and the third baron's brother and heir, Francis Crawford of Lymond, Master of Culter.

The secret of Lymond's identity, Sir George believed, was his own and O'LiamRoe's. But surprisingly, O'LiamRoe with a flood of animated questions was his ally. Drumlanrig, who disliked the

Culters, was typically gloomy and the Archer Stewart looked merely angry and bored. But Lord d'Aubigny, surely, knew that Lymond was a notorious enemy of Lennox, his brother in London, his name even having been linked with Margaret, Lennox's wife.

Yet far from slandering the Culters and unwittingly giving help with the baiting, Lord d'Aubigny listened almost without comment, and only once contradicted. 'The fellow's yellow-headed, surely; the same as my brother. That's why my dear Matthew found it infuriating when Margaret—' He broke off. Margaret, he had perhaps remembered, was George Douglas's niece.

It was what Douglas had been angling for. 'Yellow hair can be dyed, John. They say the man is now somewhere in France.'

There was a dreary silence; to his irritation he felt the topic founder at his feet. Lord d'Aubigny said with surprise, 'My dear George . . . must we pass the whole day talking about a provincial adventurer, a galley slave even at one time, I believe? The man Ouschart is coming, and I was hoping Master Ballagh here would play for us.'

'Ah, tattheration. Any day of the week you can hear Thady Boy; there is nothing like a good, stout tale of a rogue.' O'LiamRoe, elaborating, was not going to let his private entertainment lapse.

Prone on the window seat, his instrument on his stomach, Thady Boy took no part in the discussion. Later, after some brilliant rope dancing by Thomas Ouschart, whose other name was Tosh, Thady Boy beat O'LiamRoe unmercifully at backgammon, gave a brief and unquestionably fine recital for his host, and then in company with O'LiamRoe, Robin Stewart and Piedar Dooly took his departure for Blois, the visit ended.

They were to break their journey at Neuvy. Sir George Douglas, who was returning to Blois via Chambord, along with Sir James and Lord d'Aubigny, returning to duty, let the ollave go without comment.

On the journey, Stewart edged up to Thady. 'Your Prince was awful interested in this fellow Lymond.'

The ollave was patient. 'Your Lord d'Aubigny is terrible interested in Italian silver. 'Tis the same thing; only O'LiamRoe collects useless facts.' His eyes were on Stewart's bony, tight face. 'Don't you agree?'

'Italian silver! *A small trifle by Primaticcio*,' mimicked Stewart viciously. They had all caught the edge of a flaming row conducted behind closed doors between Lord d'Aubigny and the Archer. 'What would he do, faced with a hunting cat in the grass? Throw a bracelet at it?'

*　　　*　　　*

Then they came to Neuvy. Mistress Boyle's modest, pretty château

137

where they broke their journey that night was stretched to the jowls with relations and visitors and rocking these two days with the news that the great Cormac O'Connor himself was coming to stay with them. Francophiles and Anglophobes to a woman, the Boyles and the O'Dwyers would always worship a rebel. O'LiamRoe, ollave and servingman, stepping into the ferment, were welcomed with the bursting of kisses and passed a night there that never hinted at a pillow through midnight to dawn, so fierce were the arguments. Thady Boy shone; O'LiamRoe spoke fitfully. Oonagh was not at home. She had gone to Blois itself two days before, staying with a second cousin, to attend a function at Court.

Next morning, dressing, Thady Boy was unduly entertaining on the subject of O'LiamRoe's reticence.

The Prince of Barrow, putting on his snubnosed boots, got up, stamped each foot with great care, and spoke with some deliberation to his ollave. 'It would be a great saving for everyone, would it not, if you passed a little time on your own affairs, before you came interfering with mine.'

Shocked, Thady Boy looked round. ''Tis my affairs I am returning to Blois for, surely.' And then, after a moment, added indulgently, 'But to take heed to the luck of another, Prince of Barrow, 'tis a true friend you are.'

'I'm happy you think so,' said O'LiamRoe dryly. Behind him, the eyes of his ollave were tenderly blank.

IV

Blois: All the Mean Arts

Musicians and sport-makers in general, viz. equestrians, and chariot-drivers, pilots and conjurers, and companies, and scarifiers, and jugglers, and buffoons, and podicicinists; and all the mean arts in like manner. It is on account of the person with whom they are—it is out of him they are paid: there is no nobility for them severally at all.

THEY returned to Blois to find the Court full of women. The King, together with Lord d'Aubigny and his officers, was boarhunting at Chambord. To the ladies at home the arrival of Thady Boy, all pale acid and invention, was as welcome as the warty toad with his ruby.

Tired of walking in the frosty labyrinths and exchanging stale barbs round high fires of rosemary and juniper, tired of the tumblers, tired even of watching Tosh and Tosh's donkey in their wooden harness skimming from steeple to steeple, they closed around him in clouds of patchouli, and peeled his brain like a walnut. O'LiamRoe found Oonagh at her friends' house, riding, hawking, playing chess with her suitors, and attached himself, jocular and uncomplaining, to their number. He had bought her a new wolfhound. It was good, but not a Luadhas.

Just before the King returned, Queen Catherine invited O'Liam-Roe to one of her afternoon entertainments. The offence of the tennis court, it was clear, had been nearly effaced by his ollave; soon the last ban might be lifted. He attended, pink, smiling, verbose. The tumult of luxury entertained him: the blasts of chypre from the birds, the hissing farthingales and Hainault lace, the net stockings and gem-stuck pumps, the headdresses starched and spangled and meshed and fluted, the plucked eyebrows and frizzled hair, the lynx, genet and Calabrian sable stinking in the wet, the gauzy cache-nez drawn over nose and chin in the gardens and referred to in the careless vulgarity of the mode as *coffins à roupies*. Thady Boy, absent on this occasion, translated after.

Afterwards, he was presented to the Scottish Dowager. The meeting took place in her own rooms, and only Lady Fleming and her daughter Margaret attended. O'LiamRoe, who had been stubborn about changing his saffron for one of Thady Boy's clever old women, was conscious, under the lightly detached calm, that she hadn't even noticed the frieze cloak. The interview was formal and pleasant. At the end, with a suddenness which alarmed him, she thanked him in her firm, strongly measured English for creating and preserving the *alter ego* of Crawford of Lymond.

The Prince of Barrow had drawn a certain mild amusement from the idea of flouting authority. He had preferred to forget that if Lymond was the Queen Mother's busy tool then so, to a certain degree, was he. As if guessing his thought, Mary of Guise said, 'I am sorry he has proved a little . . . unorthodox.'

'But, ma'am,' said O'LiamRoe, touched on his dearest theory. 'When a man draws the blood out of his heart and the marrow out of his bones to make an art, there's little sense in bemoaning the frayed suit or the poor table or the angular manners. 'Tis the liberty of mind, and annulment of convention and a fine carefree richness of excesses itself sets the soul whirling and soaring.'

'You've certainly hit on Thady Boy's receipt,' said Lady Fleming with asperity. 'I should think his soul is whirling and soaring like a Garonne windmill. His habits are low enough.'

O'LiamRoe smiled, but the smile turned a little absent on his face. He had noticed a rag doll left asprawl on a cabinet, its linen split, its hair torn, its head limp. And in his stomach, smooth, clean, washed in wholesome juices and diligent as the churns in a dairy, something altered in beat.

*　　　　*　　　　*

Next day, the King came back. Archembault Abernaci stopped fussing with his cages in the outer reaches of the château gardens and retired to the town lodging he shared with his assistants, several bears and the saltimbanque Tosh. The donkey, foreseeing hard days ahead, brayed irritatingly from the castle terrace. Oonagh O'Dwyer, on her second last day in Blois, received her second last visit from O'LiamRoe. And the brothers of Bourbon and the other young gentlemen, released like puppies from the whalebone of Chambord, raced upstairs to Thady Boy.

By now, they expected something more than his music. He gave them freely an idea which had occurred to him at Neuvy and they embraced it instantly and fell to planning.

What he proposed was a race in pairs, from the cathedral hill to the castle, following a route determined by clues which some of the King's Guards could lay. News of it spread uncommonly fast. By evening, with the Court settled to watch its after-supper wrestling, the Guard alone was seething with it; and Lord d'Aubigny, one of

140

the few men on duty with long experience of such things, was clearly suspicious of the general air of vivacity. An Archer was brought in with a broken leg, and the hilarity increased. The King had not been made aware of the project—a natural precaution in this sort of race. It was Thady Boy's idea that they should run it at nightfall, over the housetops of Blois.

The evening wore on. The wrestlers ended. The Queen rose; the King retired; and half the French Court, with torchbearers, Archers, men-at-arms, servants and a few discreetly cloaked women, melted out of the château precincts and uphill to the highest region of Blois. At its head, along with the Marshal de St. André and the Colignys and the young Bourbons and the young de Guises and the musicians, trotted Thady Boy Ballagh explaining, to their polite applause, why he wished to break his journey halfway in order to deliver a serenade.

*   *   *

The Hôtel Moûtier in the Rue des Papegaults, with its turrets and dormers, its fountain and its orange trees, its courtyard paved with Venetian mosaic and its small-paned windows with the marble sills, was built high in one of the precipitous lanes which plunged downhill from the Cathedral on the far side of Blois. All the way up from the Carrefour St.-Michel the walled houses faced each other, leaning together so close over brick paving and worn steps that dormer breathed into dormer and the inlaid chimneys mingled their juniper-scented smoke. Sometimes a man of property might bridge the street with his own windowed gallery. Behind the moving shadows of the trees, gargoyles and griffins and painted cherubim flickered in the lantern light from the courtyards. Here the rich merchants lived, the town officers, and the great officers and their families from this Court and the last. Condé's own house was nearby; and the de Guises lived further down the hill nearer the foot of the castle plateau.

Although thickly crowded, the Rue des Papegaults was not noisy. Late at night, horsemen were rare. The sound of the hooves would patter like sea spray off the brick paving and walls; three streets away a group of riders would sound like the muted rumble of a storm. But most people kept inside after dark, or walked with swords and torchbearers; and a party intending to launch a serenade or run a race, if they valued privacy, would travel on foot.

Hélie and Anne Moûtier were leaving Blois next day to winter in the south, as was their custom; and Oonagh O'Dwyer, accordingly, was on the point of returning to Neuvy and her aunt. All her suitors free of duty at Court had come to the Hôtel Moûtier for her last evening in Blois, together with a good number of the friends of her host and hostess. Among them was Phelim O'LiamRoe, proving himself capable of a questionable branle and endless good-natured obstinacy.

By midnight the dancing was over, the wine had been drunk and the guests had departed. All except O'LiamRoe. Before the hissing, murmuring fire where Hélie sat, mouth open, hands clasped on unlaced doublet, fast asleep beside his young wife, O'LiamRoe stretched his mud-splashed shanks beside the brocade table and raised an eyebrow at Oonagh O'Dwyer, her black hair tumbled by the dance, who sat dreaming in a high chair. The firelight winked on the silver on the cloth at his elbow and touched on gilding and well-kept wooden panels, waxed against heat and smoke, and slid over the carving of the high chimney cope. Hélie Moûtier, even half-undressed looked what he was, a prosperous mercer; and Anne, now frankly asleep at his side, had her sleeves set with pearls.

O'LiamRoe turned. Oonagh, her head laid back in the deep velvet, was handsomely gowned too, but she wore it all like sea riches, prodigally and carelessly, leaving the rack to bring her fresh gifts tomorrow. The fire, merciless in its glare, printed two sleepless arcs in a face otherwise vacant of moulding. It was the first time since the Croix d'Or that he had ever had her undivided attention; and he spoke quietly, not to waken her cousins. ''Twas a queer thing, now, to come to France to pick a husband; and all the splendid Saxons and the susceptible Celts and the endless mixtures of the one and the other ye might come across in Ireland?'

In the revealing firelight a small muscle moved; but neither irritation nor animation showed in her voice, and she did not stir when she answered. 'It is a better thing, surely, than sitting in a mud hut with salt herring and garlic and kale boiled in a soup bowl between your two knees? Why else are you here?'

'My grief, for the change of company, surely,' said O'LiamRoe. 'Ever since our great lord Henry the Eighth of England and Ireland went to his account, it has been a thought crowded in the green fields, with the secret French emissaries, and the secret Scots emissaries and the secret Papal envoys, all anxious to lead the old country into the rare pathways of independence and light.'

Her head turned. 'You have no truck, yourself, with independence?'

'My own self?' said O'LiamRoe, shocked. 'No, no. Politics are for the politicals, and the sons of Liam are content with a castle and a spread of heather and the chance of a good talk over a dried cod in the Slieve Bloom—leavened, you understand, with the occasional gadding to neighbouring heaths.'

Her black brows drawn in thought, she turned from him to the fire and, her grey-green eyes on the flames, considered the phenomenon. 'You are happy under the rule of English Viceroys and the Star

Chamber. It doesn't disturb you to know that you can be sent to London and executed or imprisoned untried. The Scots occupy Ulster from the Giant's Causeway to Belfast and James MacDonnell himself rules the Glens of Antrim beside ten thousand Hebridean Redshanks. You have no care. You are content with the garrisons and the debased coinage and the fact that no Parliament has sat in Ireland for seven years?'

There was a pause, broken by O'LiamRoe's mild voice. 'The last supreme King of Ireland, *mo chridhe*, was three and a half hundred years ago. And *ríg-domna* I am not.'

The blood, rare under the white skin, suffused her face unexpectedly to the eyes. Hélie, sunk deeper in his chair, had begun to snore. Oonagh's retort, across the rich table, was necessarily low. 'You have no care for your country, none at all? I find it hard to believe.'

O'LiamRoe was gently reproving. 'Ah, with all the great brains and fine lords fussing over it, what for should I add to the noise? Caritas generi humani I can understand; if you press me, I'll lend it my passive support. But where would balance, where would detachment, where would proportion end up did no person stroll here and there outside the fence, and put his chin on the gate from time to time, to click his tongue?' His tone was severe. 'There's no chance of inciting me, my dear. As the Pope said of Hippolito, "He's crazy, the devil; he's crazy. He doesn't want to be a priest."'

He was unmistakably sincere. There was a blank interval, then she said accusingly, 'Then why stay in France? It must surely be obvious—'

He broke in quickly. 'It is obvious. But I have a plan to present you, between now and your wedding, with seven hounds with chains of silver and a golden apple between them—do I ever get them to you alive—so that when you race through the woods and fell your deer and see him undone and brittled there, you will bethink you of O'LiamRoe.'

The words were wry, but the tone, with whatever effort, was one of lightest amusement. Her mood opened to him suddenly, the white brow patterned with fine, dry lines which had not been there before, and her eyes searching his. 'I have had dogs enough, O'LiamRoe; and lovers enough.'

'You have no friends,' he said, 'man or dog. I had thought to be a small bit of both.'

'What happened to Luadhas,' said Oonagh, 'is what happens to my friends. Your place—you have said it yourself—is outside the fence. Did I like you or did I love you, I would tell you the same.'

O'LiamRoe said, his voice light and his face rigid, 'And do you like me or do you love me at all?'

Which was the moment Lymond selected to set the drums rolling.

The skull-splitting crash rocketed bumping along the walled street, shaking the high houses into light. In the Hôtel Moûtier it sent Hélie tumbling, snorting to his feet; wakened his wife Anne with a gasp; and gripped Oonagh O'Dwyer like saltless frost in her chair, the moment, the mood, the answer all gone.

O'LiamRoe was the first to thrust his way to the balcony; the first to peer over the yard, where the little trees trembled black in the yellow lantern light and where the narrow causeway beyond was packed with young men, thick as seedlings, their diamonds, their boredom, their wit outrageous below upflung windows. The side drums in their midst rattled like cannonball and then stopped. There was a brief pause, a mighty inhalation; and the cog-mouthed trumpeters from the Marshal de St. André's own suite split the night with a fanfare ripening like the Bishop of Winchester's organ into a prodigy of praise.

Anne Moûtier saying 'What is it?' could hardly make herself heard; but O'LiamRoe answered directly, his voice neither mellow nor amused. 'Several trumpets, a hautboy, a fife, a viol, two side drums, a trio of flutes, and that rare youth of two parts for whom the hazel trees stoop, Master Thady Boy Ballagh.' Under the worldly stare of the Court, the pitiless serenade to Oonagh O'Dwyer was under full way.

Even then the blandly sportive intent did not strike home until she saw Thady Boy himself, conducting his clangorous consort from a gatepost. Her furious plunge into the house was stopped short by Hélie Moûtier's wise arm. 'No, child. If it's not meant as a compliment, it's meant as a test. Either way, it calls for good nature. Stay and smile.'

'*Smile!*' She stared at him, cold outrage sleek in her eyes. 'At that pack of incompetent sow-gelders?'

'There is no need. I shall stop him,' said O'Liam Roe.

'And make us both the butt of the palace?' Her voice rooted him to the floor. 'If I need a champion, you fool, I'll choose someone better than the fat, white-fronted cat of the Breasal Breac.' He fell back; and the music went on.

Brumel they played, and Certon, Goudimel and de Lassus, Willaert and Le Jeune—all badly. The watch put in an appearance and hurried away, gold in hand. A word, an appraising glance from d'Aumale, from St. André, from d'Enghien, were enough for the angriest sleeper. O'LiamRoe, from the shadows, watched Oonagh's straight back as she stood on the balcony listening. Presently she turned to him and, without apology, asked him for a service. He complied gravely out of his wisdom, honouring the impulse as he had once seen Luadhas do. Embracing the gatepost down below, Thady Boy was carolling in Gaelic.

144

> *'To whomsoever of women we arrived*
> *Of Scotland and of Ireland*
> *She is the goat-haired woman*
> *She is the rambler among rocks. . . .'*

Her eyes flickered then; and O'LiamRoe, silently watching, was filled again with his rare, slothful anger.

Shortly afterwards she left the balcony, and the gates of the Hôtel Moûtier swung open, with good grace, to admit the performers to the courtyard for soup and wine. With them came the thirstier servants, some men-at-arms and several hopeful passers-by. The courtiers, losing interest, had moved on.

Exposed to all that crowded, craning street, Oonagh walked through the courtyard, giving soup with her own hands, the steam white in the moonlight. So, with the veil coiling between them, she met Thady Boy.

Smiling, flickering in the lamplight, his face was Quetzalcoatl's again, maliciously observant. She set the bowl in his palms and spoke evenly. 'Thank you, Master Ballagh. I was wondering how to bring the great folk of France to take notice of me.'

He dipped a long finger in the soup and held it up. 'Larks' tongues, is it? Ah, 'twas a cultural triumph for Ireland this night. Three flutes we had, mark you, and a flute is not at all cheerful at being out of his bed after nine o'clock at all, I can tell you. . . . Was that a whisker of O'LiamRoe I had a sight of up there?'

'It was.'

'My own lord and master. He will be a proud man this night. Is he not for coming down?'

'He is not; and it is better for you, I can tell you, that he is not. Do you think he is pleased?' said Oonagh.

Thady Boy's actor face was crestfallen. 'Is he not?'

'*He is not,*' said O'LiamRoe's curt voice at his elbow. The Prince of Barrow, his back squarely to his ollave, went on: 'Your cousins kindly pressed me, but after all I'd liefer not stay. There are things to be done and said which are better done at the château.'

Oonagh took one step after him and then halted. Thady Boy did not even do so much. When she turned back he was buried, intoning, in a pack of drunken trumpeters, and two of St. André's men, dispatched from the road end, were trying to hurry him into the street. The race was due to begin.

Oonagh heard of it from a viol player, morosely returning his instrument to its bag. He was cold, tired, and humourless, and had no intention of waiting to see young men run over housetops from the cathedral hill to the château in the dark. 'They're mad,' he said. 'They're drunk,' he added. 'They'll break their necks.'

'That,' said Oonagh O'Dwyer dryly, 'would be an excellent idea.'

*   *   *

The bald, moonlit square above the Rue des Papegaults was heaped with people, sliding and darting like iron filings stirring under a magnet, the smoke shadows and copper glare of the torches streaming across the face of the half-finished cathedral. Older Blois, hearing the noise and watching the gallants laughing below, had stuffed its ears and turned back to bed, muttering; but sycophantic Blois, and working Blois, and gambling Blois, as well as all the rival followings of the twenty competitors, were here in the square to see the race begin on the blue slate roof of the Inn of St. Louis.

Robin Stewart, returning unsuspecting from an errand for Lord d'Aubigny, was caught in the updraught and swirled to the top of the hill before he could stop himself, there crashing into the soft black spread of Master Ballagh. He found his arms gripped. 'What Moses, I pray, called you? What God's minister bade you rise?' Thady Boy had spent some time in the inn. 'I thought you were on guard.'

'I am. I'm on my way back. What's this rubbish they're telling me? You're never going to run that damned steeplechase in that state?'

The dark, sweaty face was reproachful. 'What state?'

'And at night. You'll kill yourself. My God, don't you know how the King loves St. André? If he falls and it was all your fault . . .'

'If he fallsh—falls,' said Thady, releasing him, 'there's a lady every five paces to catch him.'

'Well, *you* don't want to be killed. *You're* coming with me,' said Robin Stewart, and took firm hold of the ollave in his turn.

There was a wrench and a twist, and an empty doublet sagged from his hand. From the vine-covered walls of the inn Thady laughed, swung, and climbed until his untended, tousled head appeared black against the broad moon-washed sky. He called to Stewart. 'Come up. I need a partner up here.'

'Don't be a fool. Come back.'

'Afraid?'

The Archer tightened his thin lips. 'Come down, you fool. Let the others be killed if they want to. It's not your damned country.'

'Or yours. Show them what your country is like. Come on up.'

A crude catcall from below reached them both. Stewart began to say, his upturned eyes white in their horny sockets, 'It takes a lot more courage not to do a crazy thing than it does to fall in with the—'

Crisp, pod-shaped and fiend-inspired on the ceiling of Blois, Lymond kicked off his shoes in two shining arcs into the packed causeway far below. Then he knelt, hand outstretched. 'Friend Robin. . . . Come running with me.'

He went.

It was a night Robin Stewart would recall all his life. It was a night memorable too for the Prince of Barrow, striding home with Piedar Dooly at his back, struggling with a new emotion and an untoward rebellion of the mind, and unmindful of the shadows shifting unseen in corners. Memorable for Jenny Fleming, in her pretty room at the castle, where she was not lying alone. And memorable, at last, for Oonagh O'Dwyer, sitting alone and unseeing for half that long night in the Hôtel Moûtier before a dead fire.

V

Blois: Wickedness is the Rule

The King is exempt from liability for accidents caused by a
chasm that he may have in his green. If the chasm be one that
could have been made safe by levelling or filling up, but was not,
wickedness is the rule respecting it.

FEW of those running ever finished the course. But ten pairs
started, moonlit and insubstantial as fawns on the slanting roof of
the Inn of St. Louis, in their white shirts and long hose and brief,
elegant trunks. Below, the narrow streets were knee-deep in discarded velvets, and the gutters sparkled with shoes. Then St. André
leaned over and shouted for torches.

Like fireflies they sprang into the air, the red sparks jerking and
darting below; and the young men on the roof caught them, cursing
and laughing, and sprang erect, each pair with a cresset held high.

Thady Boy caught his last. Within the sluttish casing, the indulgently fat body, Robin Stewart recognized the white blaze of vitality
which had struck at his manhood at Rouen, at St. Germain, at Blois.
It drove him to make one final attempt. Stone sober—alone of the
twenty—he stretched out an arresting hand. At the touch, Thady
wheeled, read his face, and without listening to a word that he said,
drew the Archer's wide-brimmed hat from his head and set fire to it.
'You won't need that. *Gare le chapeau!*' And holding it between
finger and thumb, he dropped the flaming thing into the street as
d'Enghien's hand, this time, held him fast.

'Set fire to the rest of him, my dear, and drop him below.'

Thady's teeth shone white, and his eyes blazed with drink and with
laughter. 'Robin is my partner, monseigneur.'

The ringed fingers on his shirt tightened. 'You are racing with me.'
In his smiling, sleepless face, d'Enghien's eyes were black and
glittering. 'You're very drunk, my dear. Entrust to me those beautiful
hands. We must not risk a fall.'

Lymond, staring back, did not move. 'Find yourself a new *lám-
dhia*. My hands are for the only fellow among you who has not had
the drop in him since suppertime.'

Jean de Bourbon, sieur d'Enghien, no more vicious than the rest,

148

had his own style of wildness. He answered the rebuff quite simply by a neat jab which knocked Robin Stewart staggering down the roof. At the gutter he fell. As the edge struck his back Thady Boy flung himself full length in the gulley and brought his arm hard down on the somersaulting body. Then a hand beneath his head gave Stewart the leverage he needed. He swung himself half round and, using a gargoyle at his hand, threw his weight up and back to the roof. Thady Boy gave him a parting shove and sat up, rubbing his grazed palms and gazing sardonically at d'Enghien who was standing still, breathing rather hard.

Of the rest, only St. André was clearheaded enough to have noticed. He gripped the young man's satin arm, speaking briefly, and d'Enghien answered tartly; then, staring at Robin Stewart, made a three-word apology and turned his back. St. André, catching Thady Boy's eye, smiled and shrugged and then, to a roll on the side drum, bent in the sudden silence to catch a white packet thrown up from below. In it were the first clues. The rules they knew. To set foot on ground level was to be disqualified. Each clue would lead them to a fresh house. In each house was a new clue and a word they must memorize. The couple to reach the château first, over the rooftops with the whole message, would be the winners.

On the roof, in the red glare of pitch torches, the heat was surprising. Below them, splayed, crooked, jostling, the impacted rooftops of Blois like some dental nightmare sloped down from the hill to where the plateau of the château rose blue-black against the green-black of the sky, iced and prickled with lights. On their left, beyond serried chimneys, the river Loire lay like pewter, braided with dark trees. Above, it was cool, sparkling and silent: a gracious winter sky below which earth's younglings could rest. With a roar that rattled the windows, the steeplechase began.

At first the danger lay in the numbers. They ran shoulder to shoulder, pushing, joking and jostling for position along the flat-topped sloping roof, twisting past the hot chimney, and sliding down the blue tiles. The next house, a yard away, was lower. Stewart hesitated but beside him Thady Boy leaped into space and landed, bouncing on the crown of the thatch. Stewart jumped, was caught, and ran.

For the space of three houses, the levels were uneven, but just feasible. At the fourth they were faced with a blank wall, a brick and stone house a full three stories above their heads. It was just possible to get a toehold among the packed bricks. Thady Boy watched the leaders start to climb. Then he looked up at the sky, glanced back at his partner, and backing a little, deliberately put out his torch. Turning his face to the street, he started to run. Stewart saw him launch into his jump from the gutter, arms outflung, hurtling across the narrow gap of paving below. The width was not excessive; the roof opposite was flat. Tumbling, he landed on the edge, somersaulted forward and leaped up as Robin Stewart, elbows flailing, arrived smash in his wake. When the Archer got to his feet Thady Boy, running lightly, was already halfway down the street. Stewart followed, his teeth clenched and a splendid schoolboy bravado burning bright in his breast.

They re-crossed further down the road and found by the bobbing torchlight they had gained two housetops by the manœuvre. Then they were in the Carrefour St.-Michel, and next to the high sloping roof of Diane de Poitiers's town house.

She was not there; always at Blois she slept at the château when the King was in residence. The clues they sought, one for each pair, were in the attic. It was a tricky climb round the twisted columns of the dormer and on to the carved sill. Thady Boy moved in like a marmoset while Stewart waited, anxiously watching the torches; and the next two competitors arrived as the ollave climbed out and up. He gave de Genstan a deft flick with his toe as he went, so that the young Franco-Scot, shouting, dived neatly into the room; and then, grinning, joined Stewart on the rooftop to read the clue by the bright moon. He stayed for some moments—too long for Stewart's liking— before saying, 'All right. Come on . . .' and hurling the crumpled paper to the street. Stewart followed blindly. Acrostics in French or acrostics in Hebrew were still Greek to him.

The Rue des Juifs led out of the square, and this time the house they wanted was at the far end. Their lead now was much reduced. Three couples were hard on their heels: d'Enghien, with his brother Condé as partner; Tom Erskine's brother Arthur with Claude de Guise, Duke of Aumale; and St. André, running with Laurens de Genstan. More distantly were two others, and behind that four more partners were following slavishly, having failed either to enter the attic or interpret the clue. These alone now kept their torches; the leaders, like Thady Boy, had preferred to trust to darkness. And lacking the word cypher the others had memorized, they had no chance of winning, although they might be ready to run for the sport.

Below, their audience ran too, lamps swinging, torches streaming, and shouted insults and encouragement. Sliding, jumping, Stewart hardly saw them. Once, when a cat sprang, spitting, from a corner, he stopped with a gasp; and once, as a tile broke loose under his foot, he froze, gripping the gutter as the thing clanked and slid to drop tinkling below. 'Good God, there's no time to spit,' exclaimed Thady, passing his shoulder; and grinning, Stewart picked himself up and ran after.

Then, minutes ahead of their rivals, they stood high on the pinnacle of some merchant's house, looking across a twelve-foot gap to the roof slope of the house they next wanted, soaring high over their heads to the fretted, stalk-chimneyed ridge and plunging below to inaccessible gutters, below which was the only window in the whole facing wall. It was a large window, with a small balcony, and the balcony rails ended in spikes. On either side of the two men, the roof they were crossing planed down, blue and silver in the moonlight, to overhang the packed street. It offered a standing jump across twelve feet to a gradient too steep to walk on; and it was impossible.

Stewart, clinging to his side of the chimney and breathing fast, found Thady Boy had hardly hesitated. Sliding, slipping, using his hands as brakes, he made his way down the overlapping Angevin tiles to the roof's edge and with infinite care swung himself over. Then, his fingers in the gutter, his shadow moving and jerking on the cobbles far below, he began to move along the timber face of the building.

Stewart followed. He let himself down, found a toehold in the wood, and instantly found what Thady Boy had seen from above: a window facing out across the gap they must cross, with a balcony. To reach it meant leaving the gutter: for some steps their only foothold and their only grasp would be the uneven surface of the wood. Stewart, spread-eagled, his heart cold, saw the dark head turn towards him and something gleam. Then Thady Boy, pressing his soft bulk against the building, felt downwards with one shoeless foot, found a toehold and began to transfer his weight. Then there was another spark of metal, a thud, a spiderlike flurry of movement; and Thady Boy was on the balcony. In the moonlight, the haft of a knife glinted, deep in the timbering: he had left a new-made handhold for Stewart.

Years of summer expeditions, of interminable chases, of public tournaments and duty matches with bow and stave had made the Archer physically as adept as his shambling frame and harried spirit would allow. With thought bludgeoned from his brain he concentrated on crossing to the balcony, foot here and here and here as Thady had done; and did the extra thing that last week, last month, last year he would never have dreamed of: he clung sweating to the wood and jerked the knife out, taking it with him in his last spring.

He arrived. The balcony windows were open, the shutters gaped and inside, very close, a woman's voice said '*Ah!—Ah! Assassin! Voleur!*'

'O faix, be quiet, woman dear,' said the voice of Thady Boy Ballagh, cheerfully drunk. 'For if you let out but one weeny screigh you'll have eighteen of us here; and yourself with your teeth on the table and your hair on the bedpost and your sense just nowhere to be seen at all . . . God bless this good house and all belonging to it.'

Then, under Stewart's horrified gaze he emerged, a halo of auburn curls straddling his black head and under his arm a prodigious roll of somebody's tapestry.

The crowd below had reached the house now. Torches jogging they swarmed round its foot, their heads upturned to the night. With a flap and a crack the canvas flew out, to drop and fix itself on the spiked balcony. Then, as Thady held it secure, the Archer half scrambled, half slid down the soft matlike bridge to the balcony as leaping figures poured over the skyline.

D'Enghien began to descend the roof in their wake just as the Archer clenched the spiked slack in his fists and nodded. After one swift glance upwards, Thady gripped the strong cloth at either corner and dropped.

Like some forgotten flag, the tapestry with its load plunged between the two houses, stretched taut, kicked, and swung back with the strain. Above, hoarsely ripping, the fabric gave way at one spike. The others held. Jerkily, hand over hand, gripping the cloth with knees and feet, Thady began to climb up; and a moment later Stewart seized him. As d'Enghien and the Prince of Condé, dropping on to the balcony opposite, met a screeching beldame, bald as an egg, the ollave ripped the cloth free and flung it into the street. A moment later he was indoors and the window was empty but for the auburn curls of a wig, fluttering free on a spike.

The clue was easy to find. Thady Boy read it, grinned, and led the way upstairs. 'Pierre-de-Blois next. How is Condé?'

'Across. They've got some rope from his own house nearby. They ringed a spike with it and then pulled it in after them.'

'Do you tell me,' said Thady Boy, and under the sleek lids his blue eyes were graceless. ''Twould be an uneasy day in Heaven, now, if two mortal sinners such as that had the good of it much longer. Do you agree with me, Robin?'

Light, well-knit and agile in spite of the drink they were carrying, the Prince and his brother were capable of making expert use of their ropes; and each high-born gentleman, for his own reasons, was coolly intent on taking the lead in this race with as little obvious effort as possible.

The rope made for speed. The Rue Pierre-de-Blois was lined with a jumble of houses. Turrets and gables, flat roofs and sloping, balconies and galleries, machiolations and turrets met one another in a confusion of angles and levels sometimes easy, sometimes accessible by crawling, sometimes by leaping from chimney to chimney, and sometimes only feasible by rope.

Where the others, Thady and Stewart among them, had to make use of the bridges which now and then crossed the street, or descended a storey or more for a foothold, Condé and his brother swung across, looped to grilles, to chimneys, to butcher's hooks straight to their object.

This time they were first at the clue. Reading it where they found it, by an inside window in the dim moonlight, they heard nothing of the soft footsteps entering overhead. Only when they made fast their rope and throwing one end out of the window, prepared to climb down, were they dumbfounded when the rope-tail dangling under them was whipped out of their grasp, hooked from above by the long shaft of a candle snuffer. Above their heads a blade flashed, and the frayed stub of one of their two great cartwheels of immaculate cord sharply expired at their feet. Thady Boy, from the window above had captured the rest.

At the third clue, with ten to go, the two leading couples had a coil of rope each, three couples had dropped out and five were still following, with St. André partnered by Laurens de Genstan leading Arthur Erskine and Claude de Guise. Running softly for the Place St.-Louis, his hand on Stewart's arm, Thady Boy spoke in his ear. 'My dilsy, I foresee trouble now. We are too even, and some fine fellow is going to try and set that to rights. Go as quiet as you can. If one is held up, the other goes on. There is a word with each clue to memorize, as certain proof we have seen it, and you have a stark sober mind to hold them. *Honneur*, *Espérance* and *Noblesse* are behind us, and were I to choose, I would surely nominate Régurgitation the next.'

It was, in fact, *Renommée*, nestling with its clues in the carved frontage of a draper's house in the Place; and when the next, in the Rue du Palais, turned out to be *Justice*, Stewart saw what he meant.

Ballagh had been right also about the horseplay. They were all on top of one another again, and it was both drunken and rough. Ropes were hacked at without mercy for those suspended; gutters kicked down and tiles dislodged; elbows, knees and feet brought brutally into play. Stewart, tripped up neatly from the shadows, had a fall of twenty feet, ultimately and safely ended in thatch. De Genstan, who perpetrated it, was caught, as he ran along an exposed upper gallery, by the contents of some sleeper's slop bucket, hurled with a soft Irish benediction full in his face.

Stewart himself saw it, his eyes shining. Outside himself at last, he had no fear. Even when hurtling down among the chimneys he had an absolute belief in his own salvation, and rose unharmed and unshaken.

It was as well, for a new challenge was appearing. As much as a steeplechase now, it was hide and seek. Their brains were well matched. The subtleties of the acrostics gave them pause more than once, but only briefly. The real test was one of agility and ingenuity and pure stamina.

153

And here, taking over as the Constable's nephews, the Colignys and the de Guises—tripping each other up, exploding into laughter, clattering down the rooftops on tin trays and pelting one another with eggs from some long defunct nest—began to lose the sharp sense of contest, were Jacques d'Albon, Marshal de St. André, and de Genstan his partner. Courtier, diplomat and fighting man, hated by the King's father and most dearly loved by the King, St. André was trained to an inch, sinew, muscle and brain. As windows lit behind them in street after street, as the spectators, the admirers, the rabble coursing below them along the route roared their acclaim; he began to press forward.

Many of the locations properly vacant in the daytime were far from so in the middle of the night. Ten little girls in a convent dormitory giggled, squealed, or hid under the bedclothes, as one by one, the window was darkened by six or seven gallants, each in turn dropping to the floor and subjecting the fireplace to a search. The Mother Superior arrived running as the last well-muscled leg shot round the shutters and, trapped in a fog of hysteria, did not find until morning the discarded shift blatant on the highest finial of all.

It was about this time that St. André and de Genstan passed them and Thady Boy, who had prepared for the circumstance two streets ago, cracked a jar of rose attar and lobbed the contents at the Marshal as he went. The crowd yelled; the victim swore, choking, in rivers of pomade; and Robin Stewart laughed till he cried.

Then it was their eleventh call, in the market square near the quays, with the Loire running black under the arches of the bridge. Above and behind them loomed the high town they had left. They were nearly home.

The Hôtel-Dieu in the Place Louis XII had an orchard behind. They crossed from tree to tree like Saurians and pelted each other with apples until, from shed to storehouse to attics, they took to the rooftops again. There, the youngest pair made a discovery, and two more, exhilarated with exercise and drink, knelt with them and cheered loudly and sardonically at a lit window whose light suddenly went out. In the shadow of a gable end Thady Boy landed softly and rose to his feet. Stumbling, Stewart was beside him. 'Where now? D'Enghien's ahead of us. And St. André.'

'There's not the least hurry in the world.' The liquid cadences comforted. 'Let you take breath a little. My life for you, in a little short while it will be *either* d'Enghien *or* St. André who's ahead of us—but not both, *a mhic*; not both.'

Four o'clock on a weekday morning was no unusual time for the public roaster to begin his work. Red in the scented glare, with grease spattering his apron and sweat spreading in his neckcloth, he worked half-sleeping over the crackling spit, while a thin-shanked child in cotton shirt and bare feet cranked at the treadle. And inside his shop was the last clue but two.

For all the attention he paid, he might have been deaf to the noise outside his door as the crowds surged and swayed, moving with the dark figures, jumping and scrambling far over their heads. Heavy as it was, the wagering among the contestants was nothing compared to the money which had changed hands in the streets. Half the Scots Guard off duty, as Stewart well knew, were among the brawling, struggling mass down below.

Lying hidden in the shadows beside Thady Boy, Robin Stewart prayed only that he might reach the castle and the last clue before Laurens de Genstan. It was the happiest day of his life.

Jean de Bourbon, sieur d'Enghien, was the first to force open the steamy roof-light on the roaster's house and drop cautiously through.

There was a shelf running high along the wall, from which in the daytime hung the sides of beef, the sheep and the poultry bought and waiting to be cooked; and below that, a table on which d'Enghien and his brother Condé could step without touching ground and thereby infringing the rules. D'Enghien, his curling hair plastered over his dirty face, silk doublet gaping and hose ripped and blotched black, green and white from lime and tar and moss-grown copings, was aware that St. André and St. Genstan were almost on him and in no mood for waiting.

As the roaster tipped a pool of hot fat over the meat, put the ladle carefully down, wiped his hands on the limp stuff of his apron and turned, the young man hopped from table to stool, from stool to dresser and from the dresser to the neighbourhood of the fireplace. Built into the stonework, ridged and scored by the honing of generations of knives, was the salt recess. In it was absolutely nothing but blocks and boulders of drying salt.

The roaster, porklike arms akimbo, his round beard a wet fuzz of grease, watched him without sympathy. 'You seek some papers, monseigneur?'

Above, the roof-light rattled as St. André attained it.

'Yes, you fool. They should be here. Where are they?'

The roaster turned his head and the boy, who had stopped cranking, mouth open, hurriedly began again. He turned back. 'They were put in the fire. What a pity. An accident.'

'*An accident!*' Behind, there was a scuffle. The Prince of Condé, as tattered as his brother, was back on the shelf, gripping the roof entrance fast shut against the onslaught of the two men outside. Urgently d'Enghien harried the roaster. 'Can you remember what it said? What was the clue?'

His red face blank, the man gazed up. 'I have a bad memory.'

155

Feverishly, d'Enghien dug into his purse. Gold gleamed. 'What was the single word, then? You must at least remember that?'

The roaster caught the coin, bit it, and allowed himself a brief smile. 'The word was *Obédience*, monseigneur.'

'And the verse?' Meeting the same vacant face d'Enghien, empty-pursed, gritted his teeth. Foursquare on the grease-splashed floor, the man could defy him indefinitely. 'Louis!' he called; and the Prince of Condé, turning, snarled in reply. 'I have no money, idiot!'

The answer cost him his post. In that second's inattention, the two on the roof, lunging, flung open the trap, and St. André dropped beside his rival on the shelf. 'But I have. Where's the Irishman?'

'Not here.' The Marshal had remained within a step of the trap-door and Laurens de Genstan was kneeling on the roof, looking in. It was patent that as soon as the vital words had left the roaster's lips—if he ever remembered them—St. André and his partner would have a head start.

But he also had the money. Impotent, d'Enghien watched him slip the whole purse from his belt and throw it, sagging, into the roaster's powerful red hands. The big man opened it, and grinned.

'*Obédience*, like I told you, was the word one had put there. For the rest, there were only five lines. Like this, as I remember...' And above the hiss and spit of the fire, he raised his hoarse voice in elocution.

> *Marie sonne*
> *Marie ne donne*
> *Rien sinon*
> *Collier et hale*
> *Pour la Sénéchale.*'

In Blois there was only one church bell named Marie: the tenor bell of St. Lomer.

As the words left the roaster's mouth, Condé sprang. But the Marshal was ready for him. An arm jerked, a strong hand pushed, and caught off balance in the cramped place, Condé shot forward.

It was no purpose of St. André's to crack the man's skull for him. As the roaster, the gold stuffed into his shirt, plodded thoughtfully to the great doors of his shop and, wheezing, began to unbolt them, the Marshal caught Condé under the armpits and thrust him, hooked by his collar, on to the stout prongs below, transferring the coiled rope as he did so to his own shoulder. There the Prince kicked, livid as a newly caught heifer, while d'Enghien, cursing, swung himself up to free him.

But the shelf was built to withstand the hanging weight of dead carcases, and not as a springboard for live ones. It creaked once as d'Enghien's two hands clutched it, groaned as he swung his feet round, and collapsed with a rending crash as he landed. The heaving, shouting throng in the street, bursting through the half-open door to see the state of the race, saw only the Prince of Condé and his brother d'Enghien battered, bruised and disqualified on the floor amid the debris of the roast shop.

St. André hadn't waited. De Genstan helping, he shot through the roof window on to the tiles and took a hasty casting look for possible rivals. Behind was no one. In front, the torchlight from the street lit a tattered once-white shirt and glittered on the crescent of an Archer, flying batlike towards the tall huddle of spires that was the Abbey of St. Lomer.

'It isn't possible!' wailed de Genstan.

St. André flung himself forward. The red, squat mouth of the roast-shop chimney loomed before them, belching smoke. Jacques d'Albon, Marshal de St. André, slapped it as he passed with a furious and masochistic intent. 'It *is* possible . . . if they were lying listening at the lip of *that*.' For a moment they were both silent, negotiating the chasm between one building and the next. Then, slipping short-legged along the spine of an almshouse, St. André spoke again. 'The last crossing will be from the bell tower to the château. Whoever climbs the château wall first is certain to win.'

In both their minds was the same picture. The church of St. Lomer with its high bell tower stood between the château hill and the Loire, its highest spire just below the lowest part of the castle wall. The space between spire and château was three times as long as the ropes which both parties now carried; but this had no bearing.

For the chasm was bridged already by the stout cable put there a week before by the saltimbanque Tosh, down which he slid, torches flaming, to the cheers of the crowd. The moon had set, but dimly, behind the black bulk of St. Lomer, that thin sickle of rope could be seen, up which the victors must climb. There was the means of victory; and there at St. Lomer was the crux of the race. For whoever crossed the rope first had only to cut it, and the last clue was theirs.

A long time ago, the crowd had discovered Thady Boy; or Thady Boy had invited the attachment of the crowd. In the last stages of the race, the excitement was frenetic. The whole of Blois was a network of light. Catcalls, screams, jibes, encouragement and insults were flung at them all; but Thady Boy received the compliment of laughter.

None of them now was either fresh or sure-footed. After a chase equal to a hard climb at speed up the most difficult mountain he had ever attempted, Stewart's knee muscles were on fire, his shoulders ached and his heart burned in his chest. Thady Boy could hardly have fared better, but his inbred sense of the ludicrous never failed. Someone far below played a guitar, and he trod a half measure with a chimney. Of the three clocks they had passed, none was ever straight, timely or decent again. Shutters were for swinging on and roof gardens for plucking and bestowing, nymphlike, on unsuspecting persons below. One angry gentleman, complaining from his window, was mysteriously smoked out of doors three minutes later by his bedroom fire.

As window after window in the quarter lit up and opening doors threw their light golden on the running Blésois below, hands waved to the dark figures slithering by. Someone reached up a hot sausage on a stick, and a trio of tousle-headed kitchenmaids, kicking bare heels at an attic window, passed up and tossed them a stolen bottle of wine, and received three kisses, at speed; and three more, alarmingly, from a hilarious Stewart.

Thady and his partner drank the wine as they scrambled on, St. André and de Genstan two houses behind. Then they were among the Benedictines' sloping roofs and ahead of them was the squat, foursquare tower of St. Lomer.

It was an outside climb, vertical from base to belfry, with no unbarred window which would admit them. Nothing they had attempted so far had been a tenth as difficult. It was Thady who, speaking soberly for once, insisted that they should be roped together. 'Lean inwards, keep your hands low and use my footholds Let me make the pace. If you're worried, use the free rope to belay yourself and give a shout. Forget the audience. A hay ladder is all they could climb.' He smiled suddenly, a carefree, friendly, uncalculated smile; then turning, black head upflung, began the ascent.

Sometimes in nightmares, Stewart re-created that climb. The tower was three hundred years old, and its weathered fabric offered crevices; but by the same token nothing—gutter or stringcourse, cornice or coping stone—could be taken for granted. A parapet, firm under one foot, might crumble under the other; a louvre break beneath the fingers. To the upturned faces in the street, the two climbers moved infinitely slowly. To St. André, leaping and stumbling over the remaining roofs, it was faster than he thought possible. Eyes stinging with sweat, he strained to watch every foothold. When he and Laurens climbed, it would be quicker. Then the other two had to find the word to be memorized, and the clue, and disentangle it. If he or de Genstan could so much as lay hands on the funambulist's rope before it was cut, they stood a chance. No Scots Guard, no Irishman, however mad or however drunk, would cut it while St André was crossing, and send the King's friend to die on the rocks.

Shoulder to shoulder with Laurens de Genstan he climbed the rooftops that cluttered the south shoulder of the church, and the crowds at the foot of the façade, with its three great doors, its arcades, its twin towers and rose window, surged round to watch. Then,

reaching the sloped roof of St. Lomer itself, the two men scrambled
to the base of the tower and started to climb.

Between Thady Boy and Robin Stewart the rope hung slack. The
fat man was moving gently, testing foot and handholds half seen in
the dark, and Stewart crawled up after, paying rope in or out, the
night air cold on his body. Directions, clear and precise, came now
and then from above. Once Thady Boy, secure on a ledge, was able to
lay hands on the rope and draw the Archer bodily up to his level.
Breathing was difficult; the cramp in his fingers, the stitch in his
side, were agony; but looking down was no hardship. The church of
St. Lomer rose like a lighthouse from a silting of faces, winking,
glinting, shifting in the radiance of lantern and torch. Their own
shadows, grotesquely, had climbed the first twenty feet of tower
before them. Now they were in darkness above the black equator of
night. Across the hollow was the cathedral on its hill, and the crooked
down-running streets they had just toilsomely left; and beyond the
chimneys, the flat black pool of the Loire, the houselights from the
bridge caught there trembling.

He had taken his eyes from his leader to look at it; had failed to
watch Thady's movements and to match them with precautions of his
own. The first he knew was a crack of a stone at his ear which disappeared chattering into the void. There was a quick movement, then
the sound of a breath sharply drawn and then held. The linking rope
whipped and swayed.

He looked up. Faced with a space of sheer wall, Thady Boy had
done the only thing possible. He had flung the free end of his rope to
noose a stone crocket high above his head near the belfry, and
bringing his weight to bear slowly on the doubled rope, was climbing
the open face with its help.

The crocket bore his weight. It was the rope which, fraying on
some unseen neck of the spire, had given way, bringing him slithering
down to the fine ledge of his starting point. And under the sharp
impact of his foot, the stone had broken.

Horrified, Stewart watched. Thady Boy had saved himself, for the
moment, by throwing himself inwards, hands flat on the wall, feet
arrested in inadequate cracks; but he had almost no purchase, no
belaying projection within reach and no safeguard but the remaining
intact rope linking his waist with Stewart's. And Stewart, cramped
like a moth himself to the stonework, nails dug into crevices, could
not support another man's falling weight.

Lymond knew it too. Economically, using as little as possible of
his vanishing store of balance, of energy and of time, he cut the rope
between himself and the Archer.

Thought that night came godlike to Robin Stewart; dilemma and
master plan appearing from nowhere printed themselves on the wax

tables of his brain. In the half minute before the fat man fell, he knew exactly what he must do.

There was a barred window on his left, just out of arm's reach. For a moment, each in turn had rested on its sill, looking longingly at the inaccessible staircase inside. Stewart had no time to wonder if the stone was rotten there too, or if the bars would hold. To reach it, he must leave hand and foothold and jump: a jump of life and death, with below him the gaping chimneys and the blue slates and the waiting bricks of the streets.

He turned his back on Thady Boy and leaped. As his bony hands, like a grip from the tomb, closed hard on the cold bars, his feet swung free over the void; then his knee found the sill, his shifting elbow the bar, and ramming body and arms like some iron throttling plant within the lifesaving cangs and cavities, wearing the window like a harness, he spun the dark rope through the night, unfolding the coils he had held spare in his hand, sending the hemp hissing along the stone surface level with Thady Boy's head.

In his turn, Lymond took the life-or-death chance as had Stewart. Loosing all his inadequate, sliding grip, he watched the dim rope coming, and jumped.

Stewart braked his fall. The bars, though he didn't know it till later, squeezed his arms black; and the rope running harsh through his hands left raw flesh, whipped and bloody, behind it. Then came the drag at his body he was waiting for, the pulsing strain at his waist rope as the man below swung and span at the bottom arc of his fall. Stewart braced his aching body across the width of the window and gave his whole strength as an anchor. And the bars held.

The rope had stilled. Then, as if his ears were unstopped after deafness, Stewart heard a roar rise from the sunken radiance of the streets, and the strain on his back and pelvis lifted. Thady Boy had found a foothold and, using the rope as sparingly as he could, was climbing back up.

Presently, black against the black night, the unkempt head appeared at his feet; the light, acrobatic bulk gave a wriggle and a twist, and Thady Boy, breathing hard, was sitting beside him. Thady snorted. 'Dear God, is that all the distance you've got? I could have been up and down the damned thing twice in the time.' In the dark, his teeth flashed in a smile. 'I told d'Enghien you were worth ten of him.'

Then they were climbing again. As he watched the Irishman above him moving steadily, delicately exploring, there stirred in Stewart something life-giving: a surprised gratitude for what Thady had tried to do; a fierce pride in what he himself had done. Strong, confident and free, for one evening envious of no man, Robin Stewart followed his leader up and into the belfry.

160

By the reaction of the crowd St. André also knew that something had occurred. The route he and de Genstan had chosen gave them no very clear view; but seeking footholds presently round a corner he realized that in spite of the setback the other two must be already inside.

Fingers bleeding, bruised and grazed by the stone, he was quite unaware of discomfort; only of the need to reach the belfry fast . . . at the very worst, before the rope-crossing from church to château had been completed. He gazed upwards, impatient of the noble Franco-Scot labouring in his wake.

Above his head, trailing, abandoned and God-given, was a length of rope. Upwards it wound, above his head, as far as he could see, and disappeared, if it ended at all, not far short of the belfry itself. In two steps he had reached it and, firmly straddled, had tested it with one hand and then both. Then, slowly and cautiously, he began to edge up.

It bore his weight without difficulty. After a moment, accepting the calculated risk as calmly as in battle, he brought his feet to grip the rope also, and climbed up.

Far below in the street they watched it; saw the free end whip beneath him and the rope sway and jerk over the uneven stones of the tower. Far above their heads, something moved in the night air, something mighty and echoing, as if a hollow wind had passed over and, passing, sucked in its breath. It came again, a shaking of the air, a word spoken a universe away by an awful and inhuman tongue.

They saw the white face of Laurens de Genstan look up, and St. André himself pausing, a foot on the stone to keep steady. The rope jerked, and the mighty bass bell of St. Lomer bawled out over the sleeping vale of the Loire. The rope swung, and again the bell spoke. St. André, close enough to be deafened, looked up frantically, and then down at his partner. Then he pronounced a stream of curses, heard rarely on land or sea, but properly suited to a position halfway up a cable lashed to the hand rope of a church bell. The choice was simple. They could lose the race, or climb the bell rope for all Blois to hear.

The Marshal de St. André did not even hesitate. Fist over fist he sped up the rope, and de Genstan after him; and as the great tocsin boomed and bellowed over the country, the remaining lights of Blois sprang to life until town and palace on their two hills sparkled in the black night like an oasis of pleasure, a queer winter revelry of some antique city of vice. With pikes rattling the town guard answered the alarm. Streaming with them, nightcapped, sheeted, quilted, the citizenry sank through the streets to St. Lomer like fussing aphids set awash in a flowerpot. The château blazed.

The belfry was empty, but for the silent tenor *Marie* and the great moving mouth of the bass bell, lumbering to a halt. On the floor, the penultimate paper gave them their key word, and their final clue. To win, they had to reach the château, and the Archer on duty outside the King's suite.

A wooden platform had been built out, extending the size of the bell chamber, and a small handrope railed it. A metal post, strutted into the stone, held one end of the cable which rose upwards before their eyes, shining in the new light, above the ravine separating the church of St. Lomer from the château on its rock. Two-thirds of the way along, arms scissoring, legs swaying, an angular figure was moving, suspended above the vault. A second was already over, climbing the crowded wall, busying himself, distantly and mysteriously, on the far side. Three yards, or four, and Stewart would have landed also.

St. André reached the platform and ducked under the rail. As on the far side Stewart struggled off the cable to the blessed safety of the château wall, the Marshal de St. André bent, found a grip, and swung off into space.

Short of murder, the cable could not now be cut. And there was a chance—a slim but real chance—of snatching the lead in that crowded courtyard where, as he could see, the huddle of bobbing heads had not parted even to let Thady Boy and Robin Stewart through. St. André was three arm spans from the church wall, and de Genstan was just stopping to grip the wire when a roar of acclaim —a double roar—reached his ears. Hung in black space, arms cracking, palms hard on the rope, he looked to his right.

On the wall of the château a queer, misshapen bulk had appeared. On its flanking harness holstered torches spluttered and burned. Under its knees and haunches a wooden platform was bound. Between its heavy ears, black and gross in the wild, smoking darkness, were two rolling eyes and a lip that curled back, showing long teeth and an open throat that lanced the cheers, the screaming, the laughter, the remembered beats of the great bell, with an ear-splitting bray. Tosh's donkey, untied and in full working array, was about to make its solo celebrated cable-swoop on the church of St. Lomer. With all the power of his shoulders St. André set himself, grimly, to race back to the safety of the church.

It was Tosh's donkey's finest moment. With a whine and a hiss she left the wall and, torches streaming, tail flying, ears laid back and braying fit to drive back the waters of the Loire, whizzed over the abyss on smoking timber to plunge, hot, hairy and kicking, into the crowded belfry of St. Lomer.

What St. André said was never recorded. What the donkey said rang from wall to wall and spire to spire and house to house of Blois. Robin Stewart, watching filthy, exhausted and triumphant from the walls of the château, cried tears of laughter at the sound until he found himself swung off his feet and riding shoulder-high side by side with his friend through courtiers, colleagues, well-wishers, failed competitors, over the courtyard to the castle.

John Stewart, Lord d'Aubigny, on duty in the King's cabinet, came out at the noise, already sufficiently irritated by his overdue Archer. But the scene in the wide guardroom had in it such a flamboyant smell of success that his lordship paused. His Archer and the Court's darling, Master Ballagh, in a state only describable as revolting, led a vociferous and excited crowd, struggling to tack up on the beautiful woodwork a paper which Robin Stewart had just finished writing, in his round, difficult hand, to the ollave's dictation.

> Honneur
> Espérance
> Noblesse
> Renommée
> Justice
> Diligence
> Equité
> Vérité
> Amour
> Libéralité
> Obédience
> Intelligence
> Sapience

His lordship of Aubigny smiled, and moved forward to congratulate them.

Much later, when the wine was finished and the songs were wavering, Robin Stewart, half-clean in borrowed clothes, went back to duty, still a little tending to pant, a stressful ache in his larynx and throat base and a shrunken cabbage inside his ribs.

All the rest of him was happy. He had attempted to analyze the night's events with Thady Boy, but the ollave had cut him short. 'You did a good thing or two this night, Robin Stewart. A few small exploits more, and you have this Court eating out of the palm of your hand . . . do you never want to see your fingers again.'

He had been embarrassed. 'If the King ever hears of it. According to d'Aubigny he's been out the whole night, and came in the back way only just now with his nose white; and the Constable behind him with his nose red. The lady didn't suit him tonight, I jalouse.'

'He'll hear of it.' Thady, trailing his recovered doublet, was at the guardroom door. Stewart suddenly wanted to stop him. 'Ballagh, listen . . .'

Patiently the fat man turned. 'I have been making terrible free with the Robin, so you had better put your tongue to Thady Boy.'

Full of drink and success and his new, frail, fledgling trust, the Archer stood over him. 'Leave O'LiamRoe. Leave him,' he said. 'Yon *serena* was gey funny, and he fairly needed the lesson, but it isn't enough. Leave him. He's no good. They'll spoil you, the lot of them —och, it's recognition, I know, of a sort: the kind I once thought I was desperate to have. But it'll wreck you, body and mind. Better find an honest master and do an honest day's work; and if success comes, you can be proud of it.'

His friend Thady Boy was able, at least, to put something of its proper value on this newborn and unwanted solicitude. After a second he said, 'The O'LiamRoe and I will part soon enough in Ireland. We talked of this once before. If you dislike the Court so much, why not leave?'

Stewart's unpractised, eager emotion carried him forward too quickly. 'And come to Ireland with you?'

There was a pause. Then, relaxing, Stewart heard what he had wanted to hear. 'If you wish to,' said Thady Boy slowly, and bearing Stewart's inarticulate pleasure with patience, won his way at last out of the room. Presently he lost the last of his escorts and was able to make his way straight to Jenny Fleming's pretty room.

*   *   *

She was not in bed; not even surprised, it seemed, to see him, although it was nearly dawn and the paint on her face, over the feathered bedrobe, was cracked and moist. 'Francis . . .? I gather you have sounded the tocsin and ruined the sleep of every living person in Blois. Margaret will be beating her breast.'

He stood stock-still inside the door, his doublet thrown over one burst and filthy shoulder. 'Pray tell me, Lady Fleming . . . Why is no one on duty outside the Queen's door?'

Jenny Fleming never shirked an issue; she enjoyed it. Backing up the velvet steps to the great bed, she perched on the end. 'Do I need to tell you?'

His eyes and voice remained bleak. 'No. The King has been here, and probably the Constable. Is the child always unguarded when the King comes?'

Mary's room adjoined hers. Lymond's voice had been quiet. Even late hours could not make Jenny's smile less than delicious. 'You would like me to have Janet, and James, and Agnes in chairs round the room? The doors from the Queen's room to mine and to the passage are both locked. And the King's valet and the Constable are usually in the anteroom.'

'But not always. What happened tonight?'

'Happened?' Her fair lashes rose like stars with the stretching of her brows. Then as Lymond's stare stayed immovable, she laughed.

164

'The Duchesse de Valentinois surprised the King leaving my room. She accused the King of being unfaithful, and the King was hurt to the quick at the lady's lack of faith. "*Madame, il n'y a là aucun mal. Je n'ai fait que bavarder*".'

Her laughter, light as it was, had the finest edge to it. 'Are you wondering if he cut her off after fifteen years? If so, you are wrong. He apologized.'

'And Diane?'

'Accused the Constable of procuring. There was a considerable scene, with some high language, at the end of which the Duchess and the Constable were not on speaking terms. The King promised not to see me again. He also promised'—she laughed—'not to tell the Duke or the Cardinal of Lorraine.'

'And,' said Lymond, 'where were you all this time?'

'Here,' said Jenny simply. 'At the keyhole, listening.' She rose lightly and, drifting down the steps in a shiver of satin, came close and caught his two wrists. She clicked her tongue. '*What* a state to come visiting in. It was rather silly, and very amusing. Margaret will laugh. No, perhaps she won't. But in point of fact, it doesn't matter. The maîtresse en titre was a little late. Whether he likes it or not the King will have to admit, I fear, that he did a little more than gossip.'

And holding his hands, she laid one over the other to her heart. 'Feel it beat strongly, my dear. It rings out like your tocsin for a son or a daughter of France.'

The violence of his disengagement staggered her. Strong wine and stretched muscles disregarded, Lymond strode to the window and stayed there, gripping his anger hard until he could speak.

' "A girl of spirit need never lack children," as was said on another celebrated occasion. You are with child by the King of France. It will be born when?'

Straight-backed she eyed him. 'In May.'

'Do you imagine, after what happened tonight, that the King will install you instead of Diane?'

The red hair fell streaming over her silken robe, and her brown Stewart eyes shone. 'I think,' said Jenny Stewart, Lady Fleming, 'you are forgetting who I am.'

Fat, battered and dirty, a hireling, an adventurer, a guest in her room, he showed not one shred of the mercy he had shown to a Scots Archer.

'You are a bastard,' said Francis Crawford. 'Your son will be a bastard. Who is the Duchess? A cousin of the Queen. The wealthiest woman in France. The finest huntress in Europe. The patron of every high official at the Court. The ruler of Henri's lightest action for fifteen long years. The virtual ruler of France for three years. Her boudoir is the political axis of the kingdom; the Cardinal dines daily

165

at her table; the children of France are her creation by training, if not by bearing. Her position is known, recognized, assured, accepted in public, long accepted by the Queen, free of scandal, stable, built into the King's daily routine. There is no woman alive, were she Guinevra herself, who could eject her now.'

She stood by the bedpost listening to him, her eyes sparkling with anger, and one blue-veined arm caressed the ebony. 'Will you take a wager?' said Jenny.

Levelly, Lymond answered. 'You will be sent back to Scotland with a pension, my lady. That is your fortune. But first, nothing can now stop a scandal. And every name the bourgeoisie of France chooses to call you will attach itself, in double measure, to the Queen.'

'Nonsense.' For Jenny, her voice was sharp. 'We are not touching on hay parties and inn wenches and simple fun in a close, my dear. Things are arranged a little differently at Court.'

'Do you think,' said Lymond softly in a voice which recalled, suddenly, many things—'Do you think I don't know *exactly* how they are arranged?'

There was a long silence, and it was Jenny's gaze which dropped first. He said, 'How often are the pages and the maids of honour dismissed?'

'Once or twice a week. She couldn't possibly come to harm.' She paused, and said sulkily, 'It won't happen again, in any case. He won't come back here.'

'—You will go to him. By all means, if you want to. You can hardly do any more harm. Within the unguarded doors, what could be tampered with?'

She was already a good deal exasperated. 'They were locked. And the Constable—'

'I heard you. Every locksmith in the kingdom knows how to make false keys. Do you keep drugs here?'

'No.'

'Drink of any kind?'

'No.'

'Oh, for God's sake,' said Lymond, and flinging from the window, caught her by her two shoulders. 'Think. You want Mary to die; and you can get access secretly to her room and to the cabinet. What harm might you do?'

Jenny's eyes flamed back at him. 'Nothing. She's perfectly safe; has been always. Do you think we shouldn't hear. . . ?'

'No,' said Lymond brutally. 'I don't. Think. *What could be done with that arsenic?*'

From below his fingers she dropped to sit, her hair fallen, her back straight as a rod in spite of all she had been through. She had never looked more a King's daughter than now, when her face told its own story.

'I suppose . . . there are . . . the sweets: the cotignac,' she said.

Eight-year-old, sweet-loving Mary. The Duchess de Valentinois had forbidden her sweetmeats and Janet, Lady Fleming, had made them for her; giggling together over a midnight fire: the Queen, the small maids of honour, James and Jenny. From Chastain, the apothecary, they had the cinnamon and the sugar—four pounds of it, at ten sols a pound. Nothing was too much trouble. Jacques Alexander had supplied the boxes. The kitchens, secretly, had provided the fruit. Peeled, quartered and cored, the quinces had been boiled and strained and pounded in a stone mortar with the sugar and spice, all the children beating in turn; and then the paste was boxed and, after a little, cut into strips.

They had done all that a long time ago. The boxes, stacked in Jenny's garde-robe, full of thick fingers dusted sugary white, had become fewer and fewer, until less than half a dozen were now left.

With Jenny silent beside him, Lymond pulled out box after box, piling them opened on the floor. All looked innocent and all looked alike. From the last one he lifted some of the sweetmeat, marked the lid, and closed it. Then he left the room and Jenny could hear his voice, two doors away, and one of the loyal grooms, Geoffrey de Sainct, answering. Her son James, whom she had sent away earlier in the night, suddenly appeared, sleepy-eyed from next door, and she made him go back. Then Lymond returned.

'Put the boxes away in your own coffer, and lock it. Tomorrow, search everything in these rooms and tell me if anything has been disturbed. We shall know shortly if the cotignac was touched.'

'How?' Her face, drained of its vivid daytime colour, was still pretty and positive.

'The old lapdog has been given some. You needn't weep for him.' The hostile, soft voice made not the slightest concession. 'He deserves an end to his misery.' He paused. 'You realize, of course, that the Queen's life is in danger; that poison is known to be missing; and that every morsel she has eaten since she came to Blois has been protected, tested and passed as safe first, except for your cotignac? Do you expect your *love child* to inherit the throne?'

Roused, she answered with asperity. 'If we are to be serious, we still needn't be silly. If you think something has gone wrong, then do what you can to put it right. I shall help as far as I can. But to be frank, I think this commotion is a little foolish. You have no shadow of proof that the cotignac or anything else has been touched. . . .' Her voice softened. 'The romantic trappings of leadership are hard to give up, are they not? Francis?'

He had not even listened; had only paused, half turned to the door, to run his eyes for the last time over her possessions: the table, the bed, the coffer, the shelves, the prie-dieu, the chairs. Between his eyes, a thin line of sleeplessness showed.

Jenny said again, 'Francis? I am going to need help. I don't want to quarrel.'

'Are we quarrelling?' said Lymond.

'We were insulting one another like brother and sister.' She paused. 'I must go to bed, my dear. Am I forgiven?' She had laid her hand, still endearingly young, on his steady arm. Now she slid her fingers up, and drawing him gently downwards, kissed him full on the mouth.

Under hers, his lips were taut and wholly inexpressive. But her own kiss was warm and loving, and she held him lightly, so that he breathed in her natural freshness, her costly scents and her human harmlessness.

She had thought, if she had thought at all, that he was tired enough to respond. But his fingers opened and he stepped smoothly back, boredom and a jaded, forbearing courtesy dry as meal on his face. 'I ceased discriminating a long time ago. Good night, Lady Fleming,' said Lymond; and in the precise pressure on her name and her title she glimpsed at last the chasm that lay and always would lie between them. Then the door closed at his back.

Behind him, as he crossed the courtyard, the night sky was already aware of the dawn. Beside the black coil of the staircase, the guard-room windows were lit, and opposite, men's voices stirred from the chapel. The guards, appointed at every door, paid no attention. Thady Boy's nocturnal habits were nothing new; and ignorance, at this Court, was often best.

He climbed the staircase to his own wing automatically and blundered once, blindly, crossing a passage. Robin Stewart had remembered it with pleassure; Jenny Fleming as yet knew nothing about it; but Lymond had lived that evening with the memory of Oonagh O'Dwyer's serenade and the knowledge that there awaited him in his room neither sleep nor peace but the Prince of Barrow.

Outside his own room he rested for a moment, his palm on the door, and for a moment looked neither brutal nor romantic nor indifferent. Then he heaved the door open and went in.

Inside, the storm was waiting for him; but it was not of O'Liam-Roe's making. The candles were burning, the fire was lit, but the room was empty except for Piedar Dooly, his black eyes venomous, the rawhide flanks of his face blotched with passion and prickled with the onset of his overnight beard. Thady Boy shut the door, and the fumes of strong wine from his clothes, stiff with spilled drink and dried sweat, filled the room. 'Where's His Highness?'

O'LiamRoe's indifference to his ollave's double identity had never been shared by his little Firbolg retainer. Dooly's Wicklow accent was silky. 'Isn't it troubles enough you have without bothering yourself over O'LiamRoe? I hear you and the great gentlemen have been walking the length of the stars in your woollen stockings, and came back with the universe set in a ring.' He broke off.

Thady, moving swiftly, stood over him. 'Where is he?'

Between double lids, the Irishman's eyes were full of hate. 'You had wrestlers at Court this evening, I heard tell. A power of strong lads they must have been, and a terror for horseplay. . . . They jumped on O'LiamRoe, on his way home from Mistress O'Dwyer's.'

'And you were there?' said Thady Boy.

'Just behind. He'd been asked to stay at the house, Master Scotsman. He only left to discuss a certain thing with yourself.' Again he stopped.

Thady Boy, leaning hands clasped over the back of a chair, said quietly, 'There is no mark on you. So I have a fair idea, you see, that O'LiamRoe is not much hurt. But I think you should tell me.'

The colour high in his face, Piedar Dooly said, 'There was a party of men in the next alley who heard us, and turned back to help. Two of the wrestlers were killed and one ran away—the Cornishman, we thought, but no one could swear to it. O'LiamRoe himself took a slash on the arm, and it pouring blood more than was correct for it; so he walked back to Mistress O'Dwyer's.' He paused. 'I left him there. She has asked him back to Neuvy, tomorrow. I was to tell you that in the course of a piece maybe, he'll be back.'

'It would be better,' said Thady Boy, 'if he stayed at Blois.'

The Firbolg's face had resumed the impassivity of leather. 'He assumed you would say that. I was to tell you that, after looking at it this way and that, he preferred to go tomorrow to Neuvy. And the lady sent to tell you the same.'

Thady Boy's voice was soft. 'How did the lady put it precisely?'

'Mistress O'Dwyer? She sent to say there was a welcome for you, the kind you might expect, at Neuvy; but did you prefer to stay with the Queens, she would look after himself for you. So she said.'

Finishing, he was aware of being subjected again to that dispiriting blue scrutiny. Then Ballagh said, 'Is she fond of him? How fond?'

The irony on Piedar Dooly's hollow-boned red face eased into contempt. 'What call have I to discover a fondness between ladies and gentlemen? Yourself she don't fancy at all. That I can swear to; but that will be no news to your lordship. God save us, 'tis a high-road at your front door this night. Someone is scratching.'

Lymond had heard it. He got to the door, unlocked it, and had already made up his mind when young Lord Fleming, entering and shutting it, asked permission with his eyebrows to deliver his message.

'Go on,' said Lymond. He had returned to the fireplace and put his elbows on the stone, his grazed and battered hands hanging limp. 'Tell all. The ineffectiveness of my measures is no news to Piedar Dooly.'

Jenny's son, wooden-faced and straight, made his report. 'The dog is dead, sir.'

'I see.' Lymond did not stir. 'So a hundred grains of arsenic would have been taken by the Queen before she left Blois. Who do you think did it, James?'

Lord Fleming avoided looking at Dooly. 'Anyone could have. There was no guard.' He hesitated, and then went on doggedly, 'I was to say: she is exceedingly upset. *She is, sir.* And to ask you what to do.'

Lymond's uncomfortable manner slackened, and straightening, he dropped his arms. 'I know she must be upset. Tell her to burn the cotignac and the boxes, that's all. I'll do the rest.'

'What will you do, sir?'

His eyes were shining. Francis Crawford turned his head away, letting his gaze dwell instead on the saturnine Irish face at his elbow. 'Tell The O'LiamRoe from me, friend Piedar, that I wish him Godspeed at Neuvy, for what it is worth. . . .'

Dooly had risen to go. Fleming, lingering, was hoping still for an answer. Lymond rubbed his strained eyes with the back of one filthy hand, and measured the distance between the fireplace and the bed. 'As for me: there have been enough scapegoats, and a damned nuisance they are. From this time on, God help me, I shall be my own bait.'

They left; and as dawn lit the scuffed, the tileless, the broken and well-trodden rooftops of Blois and pricked at the eyelids of its weary sleep-ridden citizens, Francis Crawford of Lymond at last rolled into bed.

170

VI

Blois: The Forfeited Feast

There are three banquets: godly banquets, human banquets and demon feasts; i.e. banquets given to the sons of death and bad men; i.e. the lewd persons and satirists and jesters and buffoons and mountebanks and outlaws and heathens and harlots and bad people in general; which is not given for earthly obligation and is not given for heavenly reward. Such a feast is forfeited to the demon.

AT Neuvy, O'LiamRoe's arm healed. He stayed there longer than he had intended; rode, hunted, argued and played chess with Mistress Boyle, with Oonagh and their friends, and was not further molested. When Cormoc O'Connor did not arrive as expected, he was far from disappointed, but wise enough not to take undue advantage of the vacancy. He sent word, by a fellow house-guest, that he would come back to Blois within the week.

The message was brought to Blois by George Paris, a rangy Irishman gifted with considerable powers of intrigue, who happened to be on his way home to Ireland. But first he had an interview with the Constable; and another with the King, accompanied by the Duke de Guise, who charged him with errands of a diplomatic sort, and promised him Robin Stewart as escort.

For some time, Stewart was ignorant of this. He had not carried out his threats to leave the Court and now knew that as long as Thady Boy was there he was unlikely to do so. But the decayed brilliance that had infected the Court since the moonlight steeplechase that night was beginning to frighten the Archer, as it had already frightened Margaret Erskine. Tom, returning fresh from the Low Countries with a peace treaty signed and a six years' war ended, had been disquieted, though he did not say so, by the disciplined strain on his wife's face; and when he spoke lightheartedly: 'I've brought you herbs, as you wanted, for your fiend-sick patient,' she said, with a grimness new to her, 'Have you brought enough for the whole Court of France?'

At Court, everything halted for Christmas. Financial worries might be pressing, but at least both the season and the threat of penury made it unnecessary to think of war. Honour could be sought in other fields: in wrestling, in leaping, in tilting at the ring, in jousting and casting the bar, in hunting and hawking, in shooting at rounds and at rovers, in tennis and pall-mall and bear fighting and dancing, in dressing as gypsies and Greeks and Arabian knights.

They gambled and sang and made love lightly and expertly. In all they did, they were experts. The men about the King were chosen for their grace and gifts in the arts of sport and chivalry as well as for diplomacy and war; and the King used them as touchstones for his own manifold skills.

Henri of France was a moderate man, but short of disrespect for the throne, licence at this feast time was nearly boundless. Copied, encouraged, cosseted by the younger Court, Thady Boy had now the amused applause of the royal family; and on the King's orders some-one, generally Stewart, was always at hand at midnight, at dawn, or whenever the wayward day ended, to roll Thady Boy out of the pothouse, the ballroom floor or the gutter and see him safely to bed. Solicitude, of one sort or another, was remarkably widespread. Completely charming, completely drunk, completely irresponsible, he accepted it all.

The Scottish Court watched him do it. The Erskines and Jenny, a little subdued, observed in silence. The Queen Mother, retreating gratefully from her state discussions, continued to smile superbly at her hosts, in a bold effort to deny the billowing and tramping behind the curtains, where the ambitious, half-bribed lords of her retinue were quarrelling like henwives. And Sir George Douglas took time to write an anonymous letter to the Queen of France, suggesting that one Richard, Lord Culter, should be invited to Court. Catherine de Médicis received it next day.

It was the day, chilly with sleet and early dark, that they danced a pavane on horseback in the Gran' Salle, weaving between the bright pillars, fire sparking from the chipped tiles. The clatter of hooves drowned the music as they moved, laughing, through their paces, and Thady Boy, threading sideways, plucked the candles from their brackets one by one and threw them, juggling, to his scorch-fingered partners, swearing, laughing and plunging, until hysteria and ultimate darkness crowned the exercise.

Leaning watching on the fretted balustrade, the King read the letter his wife had given him, while the large, shallow Médicis eyes marshalled the scene. 'Does this wildness distress you?'

Glancing up from the letter, he followed her gaze. 'Art roots in mouldering soils. I suppose that is always the answer.'

'He is of a fresh and original talent, even when outside himself, certainly,' said the Queen. 'But I had thought lately that even the bloom was becoming a little tainted. What do you make of the letter?'

Henri scanned the paper. 'The name is a famous one. But who exactly is Richard Crawford of Culter?'

Catherine's lashes lay discreetly on her coarse-grained, powdered cheek. 'I enquired of Madame the Queen Dowager. He is the third baron of the name, with considerable power and money in Scotland, and a supporter of the young Queen. The story runs that he has remained behind until his wife should be brought to bed of an heir. . . . By now the child will have been born. Since he is free, we might well suggest to Madame the Queen Dowager that it would delight us to see him.'

She was right. France had promised to do all in her power to install Mary of Guise as Regent of her daughter's kingdom. It was only common sense, given the hint, to inspect whatever influence, for good or for evil, she had found it politic to leave behind her at home.

Below, sleeves flying, fringes swaying, the riders streamed past. The King, leaning down, snapped his fingers; and Thady Boy, lifting his eyes, sent a torch flying with a flick of his wrist. Henri caught it, raising it a little in salute; and turning, held the flame thoughtfully to the edge of Sir George Douglas's letter.

*   *   *

Three weeks after that, Robin Stewart heard that he was to travel once more to Ireland, this time with an agent, to bring back Cormac O'Connor. It precipitated one of the great crises of his life: the day he stood up to John Stewart of Aubigny.

Robin Stewart had been seconded to his lordship in order to help with the O'LiamRoe visit. For his extra work with the Irishman, and for all the special services he had rendered Lord d'Aubigny for far longer than that, Stewart had expected one day to receive an appropriate reward: a minor household post, perhaps with the promise of advancement; maybe even a captaincy later on . . . something at least, which would lead him at last towards the inner sphere of influence and the high life.

All these were in d'Aubigny's power to give, but all Stewart had received so far was money, and that sparingly. And now the conceited fool seemed to be indicating—but could not be indicating—that he had no further use for Stewart's special services, and that he was turning him off to some routine duty abroad.

Lantern jaw jutting, Stewart stated his case. 'I've already been to Ireland, your lordship. I understood I was to assist you for the whole of the Irishmen's visit. I believe that so far I've given satisfaction.'

A buckle of his cuirass had come undone, and his hair needed cutting. Noting these things irritably, 'Do you?' said d'Aubigny. You botched their arrival at Dieppe. You botched one of them at Rouen.

You let O'LiamRoe's dog run wild for some petty purpose of your own, and made a thorough fool of yourself falling off your horse like a fisherman and bolting next down a rabbit hole.' He yawned. The couchée had been long and boring last night. 'It's my own fault ultimately, I suppose. For this kind of work you need a touch of breeding, a little finesse. You will feel happier, I'm sure, with more familiar tasks. When O'Connor comes, I shall see to him myself. One of the men—perhaps Cholet—will help.'

He *was* turning him off. And Stewart suddenly thought he saw why. In ugly patches, the angry blood stained the Archer's gaunt face and neck, and turned his ears scarlet. 'I've noticed you can hardly bear to be civil since we won yon night steeplechase. It's hardly my fault he chose me to run. . . . And remember this, my lord. The name Robin Stewart means something to the King and his courtiers now.'

Opposite, the handsome, thick-skinned face was merely contemptuous. 'More than d'Aubigny, do you think? One more word out of turn, Stewart, and I'll be the first, believe me, to put it to the test. Threats to a friend of the King in this land come very near treason, you know.'

It was not the insubordination that made d'Aubigny's hand shake on the onyx inkwell before him; it was the crude mirror held up to his bright-eyed stalking of Thady Boy Ballagh. That Stewart should regard himself as a rival had never entered his head, and he resented the intrusion of brutish feet in the precious gardens of his conoisseurship.

He stood up, shuddering a little in his displeasure. 'There is no point in searching out your weaknesses, Stewart; we are both, I am sure, quite aware of them. You have done the best that you can, and I am grateful. But you should be content now with the duties laid upon you. You will not find me ungenerous.' Bending, he drew from his desk a hide bag and laid it, clinking, between them. 'That will, perhaps, enable you to buy some aqua vitae or pleasant evenings with your friends in Ireland.'

Years of training, of poverty and repression had stolen the secret of spontaneous anger from Stewart, leaving him without the courage even now to fling his career in the other man's face. But something newly nurtured within him baulked at walking to the table and picking up that limp rawhide bag. 'Keep it,' he said shortly. 'And buy a new inkwell with it for yourself. You've gey near cracked yon one in two, playing Almighty God in your fancy new necklaces. I'll go to Ireland. Cock's blood, I will. And,' said Robin Stewart furiously, producing the worst threat he could think of, and hitting with the the only weapon he possessed at Lord d'Aubigny's indifference and complacency, '*And I'll take Ballagh back with me.*'

It was a boast he had hardly hoped to realize. But Thady Boy had looked at him, as narrowly as he could out of eyes that did not focus very well, and said that he was beginning to think the Court of France was overrated, himself, and that he would consider it.

He had had, it was clear, no breakfast apart from some strong wine before the day's sport; and was unlikely to bother with supper. Stewart, bitterly aware of the amusement roused by his missionary zeal, stopped himself in the midst of an angry and solicitous tirade. Whether Thady came with him or not, they had only one more week of each other's company left here in France.

*   *   *

That day, Thady Boy hunted three-quarters drunk and came back with a slashed hand. It was Stewart, who, off duty, crossed the gardens to the postern and called at the house of Dame Pillonne to beg some balm from the keepers.

Abernaci was away. In his place, one of his friends in the trade sat in the jar-laden room above the brown bears, and returned Stewart's greetings, and added, at the sound of his accent, a genuine welcome in the broad chanting vowels of Aberdeen. Detached from his donkey, Thomas Ouschart was a gentlemanly little man, with small bones and a pale face in spite of a lifetime of travelling. He had a cough which spoke sometimes of rough-dried bricks in a builder's yard, and his calf muscles spoiled the particoloured set of his stockings. Stewart, his need riding him like a parcel of fleas, sat down and sent off a straight volley of questions about his personal attitude to ropewalking and the monetary expectations therefrom.

Tosh, a good-humoured man, answered plainly but was not in the least backward with a negative when the Archer touched on matters best left private. They got on well together; and the Aberdeen man, who had turned his hand to many things other than tightropes, mixed a very competent ointment from Abernaci's store for Thady Boy's hand, and then went rummaging neat-fingered for an empty jar in the piles of papers, bottles and wood shavings which covered every available surface.

Stewart, rising to help, said, 'Mind, if there's a scar on Thady Boy's lute finger, you'll have to answer for it to three Queens. So put the best you know into it, for God's sake.' He found a jar, cleared a space with a sweep of his arm, and sat down again.

Tosh, filling it, laughed. 'If you believe Abernaci, there's hardly room on him for a fresh-made scar anyway. You've seen his hands. And the galleys fairly made a show of his back.'

Robin Stewart sat still, his hands on his knees, his feet planted apart on the littered floor. After a pause he said, 'I never heard he was on the galleys.'

'I don't suppose he'd go about describing it,' said Tosh with

passing irony. 'But he's got the brand on him. The cowardie saw it at
Rouen, for one.' He glanced at Stewart's frowning face and grinned.
'A queer customer, Thady Boy Ballagh. But aren't we all? You'll
need to get him into a rowboat and see if he'll show you his paces.'
He finished packing the balm jar in linen and turning, studied the
Archer, lost in meditation. 'It's likely no secret. The fancy bitches up
yonder'd find it thrilling, I shouldn't wonder.'

He had no need to put Thady Boy in a rowing boat. Crisp in
Stewart's ears rang that decisive *On va faire voile* which had commanded the struggling half-wreck of *La Sauvée* four months ago. He
said, making his voice pleasant, 'What else do you know about our
Irish friend?'

But Tosh had only met the ollave through Abernaci, and told
Stewart nothing else that was new. From the litter on the floor, the
Archer selected an old, used woodblock and fiddled with it. He had
assumed that Thady Boy's history was all his, as well as his friendship. The ollave had been far from overflowing with his confidences,
as The O'LiamRoe was, but he had not been reticent. And this
violent and blighting episode in his life, for so it must have been, had
not been entrusted to Stewart.

The Archer, stirring from his insubstantial dream of mutual
confidence, waited for the familiar plucking of pain at his guts. Tosh
was still talking when Stewart got up and, taking his leave a good deal
more abruptly than was polite, strode off, forgetting his ointment.

When he went back for it later he found, to his relief, that the blunt
little Aberdonian was out.

The Archer's first impulse had been to go up and have it out with
the ollave. Instead, he went directly to Lord d'Aubigny and presently
got himself a mission which took him away from Blois for the six
days before he was due to leave with George Paris for Ireland. A
message, bald in the extreme, was sent to Thady Boy announcing the
date and time of his departure.

Puzzlement, as he read it, showed briefly through the disordered
rubbish-heap of Thady Boy's face. Then he brushed it aside, and
swept into the bizarre and engrossing activity of the moment.

*   *   *

Then, at last, O'LiamRoe was on his way back to Blois.

He had his last ride with Oonagh the day before, jogging out
through the park at Neuvy, the new wolfhound loping at their side.
It was one of the few times they had been alone together since the
unfortunate night of the serenade, when O'LiamRoe had appeared,
dogged and apologetic, his arm streaming blood on the Moûtiers'
threshold. Now they trotted, shoulder to shoulder, finding silent
pleasure in the stinging air, the thin woods worn dry and silver with

wind and ice, the spent grass rustling at their knees. Soon they reached open ground and the horses pulled unchecked into a canter, and then a gallop, racing neck and neck, his frieze billowing alongside her black hair and her furs.

Side by side they jumped ditches and followed dykes, and fled at last down a dry-tussocked hillside full in the yellow sun, leaving their breath white behind them, the blood whipped bright under the skin. Then, at the edge of another copse, they drew rein in pity for the sweating horses, and he walked them and then hobbled them while Oonagh flung herself among the bracken and the thin, dead spokes of bush and branch and bough which nested the ground.

There was a flask at his saddlebow. Kneeling, he offered it and she drank deeply, like a man. When he had drunk and laid it by, he came back and, finding a boulder at her side, leaned on it looking down at her. Throughout the morning, against the whole grain of his being, he had hardly spoken. Now it was she who broke the silence, her green eyes watching him. 'I have news for you, O'LiamRoe. Your ollave is leaving you.'

'Is he now?' He waited. They had never discussed Thady Boy, or spoken of the serenade.

'I heard today. Robin Stewart leaves for Ireland on Friday, and has threatened, it seems, to take Ballagh with him. The attachment I gather, is a little one-sided, so you may preserve your suite intact yet. On the other hand, Thady Boy may simply be waiting to persuade you to go, too.'

'He would sooner help to ship me off, I am sure, and stay on here for ever, indulging himself. Has he wearied so soon? The life must all have run out of him with his songs.'

'Or maybe he has a sense of responsibility?' suggested the black-haired woman. 'Ah now, but I forgot. You believe there is no such thing at all. Only a fool's craving for power, the dream of the officious, the corruption of the mediocre. There is no natural leader alive who should not have this throat slit directly he has led.'

'You have a bully of a memory,' O'LiamRoe agreed peacefully. 'I never knew a being on two legs yet that got a pennyworth of power and so much as treated his hound-dog the same. Or his women.'

She almost did not answer; but she could not quite keep her temper from showing. 'Men have taken up that particular burden who would give their souls to be able to shed it.'

O'LiamRoe's retort was mild and sunny and disbelieving. 'Who? Who has there ever been? Do you know such a one?'

The wild colour had come up under her skin; couched in it, her two eyes looked like clear, green-grey water. She said, 'You cut Luadhas's throat for the sake of a Queen who is no more than a senseless baby, and a foreigner at that. Are your own people worth less to you?'

His head cocked, he was revolving on his knees his broad, helpless pink thumbs. 'Now that you mention it, I had never thought of the King of England's sheriffs as so many cheetahs.'

She raised herself on one hand and swung round to lean her back on the rock where O'LiamRoe sat. Her head tilted back, she watched him, her expression not unfriendly. 'You feel for the man you can see; not the nation you cannot.'

'You may have the right of it,' said O'LiamRoe. It was not the wittiest of ripostes. Against the rock, her head was very close. He could by moving his arm have brushed the warm, heaped, blue-shining black of her hair. He tried again. 'I find it difficult, for example, to feel for the Kingdom of France. You peel it away, as you might an artichoke—the music, the sculpture, the pictures and the palaces—and there, soggy at the bottom, are hereditary parliaments and absolutism, a dumb States-General, the primitive taxes, the gifts, the favouritism. England breathes a coarser air, but it seems healthier to me.'

Lazily, she replied. 'Do not delude yourself, Phelim O'LiamRoe or me. Were you faced with eternal night and chaos you would poke up the fire and theorize till your blood itself boiled under the skin. Why stay if you no longer enjoy it? Go back to your heathery nook on the Slieve Bloom, where Edward's sheriffs pass you by; and take Ballagh with you. If you have a new master, someone doubtless will tell you.'

O'LiamRoe's gaze, for once, was unreadable. He said, 'I didn't say, I believe, that I was wearying. I told you once why I intended to stay. . . . And I asked you a question, but we were interrupted.'

'Then ask it again,' she said.

There was a long silence. At the side of his neck, in the baby's skin, a pulse was beating, although outwardly he was still perfectly tranquil. '*And do you like me or do you love me at all?*' he had asked, that night in the Hôtel Moûtier. 'If I were fifteen years old again, I might,' he said. 'But now I know the answer.'

'Do you? I think you should know,' said Oonagh, 'that you are not alone in your view of the artichoke.'

Looking down, he could see her high brow, her thinking eyes, the firm body under the piled, thick folds of her robe. He said innocently, 'That might make it awkward when you take a French husband.'

One angular, boy's wrist lay on her lap; the other hand was tucked under her head. He saw the tendons sharpen suddenly, and was not surprised when she said, 'I have had dogs enough.' There was a little interval; then she added, hearking back still to their previous talk, 'I have reached a queer conclusion. There is a thing or two worse than sitting in a mud hut with salt herring and a kale bowl between your two knees.'

O'LiamRoe did not know that he himself had turned rigid. He said only, 'I always said it. It depends on the company.'

She did not remove her eyes. Instead she gave a little twist so that instead of her back, she had one elbow on the rock, the other hand laid idly on the grass. Dead leaves, like flotsam on a web, scattered her fur. Unbelieving, he read in her eyes a kind of testy, unassumed kindness. 'I like you, Phelim O'LiamRoe. For my own good, I ought to love you.' She scanned his face. On it were small unaccustomed marks; of strain, of some measure of need or defence. She said with wholly unexpected anger, 'You are the very soul of detachment, are you not? Can you do nothing to make me love you, since you are so wise?'

There was a racking silence. Then he slipped to one knee beside her, crushing her dress, and, catching her idle hand, drew her into his arm. She came lightly, holding up her face for the kiss.

It was a strange embrace. The woman, it was clear, was the more experienced of the two; and she made no effort to hide it. O'LiamRoe's own simple nature came to his rescue. At this ultimate moment he felt no awkwardness; nor did he strive for a sophistication beyond his means. Instead, his own basic qualities, his speculative mind, his adventurousness, his essential decency, all brought to that first kiss something perfectly well integrated, of its kind; and to Oonagh O'Dwyer, quite new.

So new that for a moment it confused her. He sensed something wrong and broke away, his whole face shaped in a queer, unaccustomed way; then found her hand on his back had hardened disturbingly. She brought her other hand up, the heavy sleeve falling back, and drew his head down to her own. During this kiss she let him know, without speaking, that what he wanted, he could have.

Humility . . . intelligence . . . insecurity: one of them spread its message through his brain, and then his nerves, and made his hands slacken, his head move, his eyes open. She did not realize it. She lay lithe in the grass, where she had slipped, and said in a gentling voice, her brogue broadened and warmed, 'Are you afraid of bankruptcy? I'm not asking the impossible, my dear. You will go to Ireland with Stewart and wait for me. This is a beginning; not an end.'

He sat back on his heels. Among the silken down of his hair, the features were still not his own, and oddly held, as if broken against some unheeding obstacle, and clenched again into defect and misshapen pain. 'You are very kind,' he said; and it was impossible to tell whether or not he was being sarcastic. 'But as it has not begun, it can be neither a beginning nor an end.'

He had moved himself out of her field of vision, whether for her relief or his own, she did not know. Lying quite still, her taut gaze on the sky, she said, 'What is it? You had better tell me what it is.'

'Nothing,' he said. Her outflung arm was very white. On it, he could see the impress of his rough frieze, a pink trough of interlocking chainwork, where she had gripped him so hard. Her own dress was so fine, he bore no marks anywhere. He said conversationally, 'It is the first time, surely, that my poor, negative principles have brought me anything so charming. I doubt I couldn't bring myself to collect a revenue on them. I had thought them worth something less, or something more.'

Then she sat up; and he saw that she was pale, her brain behind frowning eyes following the possible burden of his. 'I have nothing more to give that you would take.'

'I would take honesty,' said O'LiamRoe. And after a pause, 'Or should I change my principles and turn firebrand first?'

He had been right. Her impulse had been kind. But it had not been selfless, and she was exceedingly proud. Her first reply to him died on her lips. Instead, she said, 'Change them if you want to; why not? No one will ever notice the difference, and the exercise will surely do you some good.'

On the way home, she did not speak at all. Nor did O'LiamRoe make any attempt to put it right. And no one but he knew that under the thick frieze cloak, he was shivering.

*   *   *

By next day, he and Piedar Dooly were back in their old room at Blois.

Thady Boy, when they arrived, was out, fêting up river with the Court. Stewart's ambitious plan to remove him had all too obviously come to nothing.

O'LiamRoe was aware that he himself had not been helpful. He could understand the exasperation, of even the dislike which he supposed had prompted Thady Boy's ill-natured riposte of the serenade. It was the abuse of Oonagh's good name and hospitality which he found regrettable. O'LiamRoe, from his detached side of the fence, rarely thought of anything as unforgivable.

So for the next few days he stayed in his room, seeing few people, quietly coming to terms with himself, and only smiled a little at the irony when a Gentleman of the King's called to invite him to a royal banquet on the following day. Recognition had come at last. When the puppetry had palled and no reason but pride was left to hold him in France, the innermost door, long forced by Thady Boy, had opened to him also.

That same afternoon Stewart came back, rattling in his caked spurs and yellower in the face than usual. Finding Thady out he remained only briefly. He and Paris were leaving on the first stage of their journey to Ireland next day.

Then the Court returned, late at night and hilarious. O'LiamRoe was wakened by the arrival of Lymond with a whole drinking party, introduced thickly and meticulously, who then stayed until dawn. O'LiamRoe gave him Stewart's message when at first light the rabble tumbled at last through the door, and Thady Boy kicked off his boots.

'Oh God, yes of course. You took your bruises to Neuvy. I could almost hear them begging you to go home with me before the end of it. What did she offer you to leave her?'

He couldn't have known. But the foul taste of it, the casual accuracy of the guess, made him feel suddenly physically ill. So far from being detached, with another man O'LiamRoe might have blundered into violence. As it was, he left the room abruptly, without seeing the sudden stillness on Thady Boy's face.

*   *   *

The next day, Friday the 16th of January, opened quietly. Blois slept late these days, for the King, never privileged to share his own father's council, gave his own the least possible regard; and during a season of sport or fêting abandoned it with relief to the de Guises, to the Constable, to the Marshals and the cool, overseeing glance of Diane, who never slept.

This year, the pleasure seeking hid more than the King's ingrained resentment and his wish to please and renew the love of his friends. Beneath the surface were new tensions, no less disturbing for being petty. About this time rumour, unavoidably, had begun to play about the appearance of Lady Fleming. She, moving serenely about her daily adventures, was undisturbed; but the rift between the Constable and the Duchess de Valentinois was now perfectly patent.

It could be guessed also, without pretence of secrecy, that the Queen Dowager of Scotland was finding it harder to harness her unruly nobles. Honours, pensions, ready money in the purse, had done nothing but sharpen their hunger. Failing the bribery they were worth, their minds turned again to power and to their duty to their religion, belligerently recalled. Tom Erskine, lingering on his way back from Augsburg and cumbered with transactions to do with papal legations and bishoprics, and with arrangements for the French garrisons and armies at home, was still there, doing his best to doctor the mess, while waiting to leave in due time to complete his last treaty of peace back in England, and to return to Stirling and Margaret's small son at their home.

The invitation to Richard Crawford, which it had been totally impossible not to send, was now a month old. Lymond had been told, with extreme circumspection, that his brother had been sent for, but it was hard to say if he either listened particularly or understood.

181

The entertainment for this evening had been designed by the Constable and Queen Catherine, not with a new guest in mind, but in an effort to rationalize the feverish gaiety in the castle, and to reduce the tension. It was to be a private festival held by the inner Court for itself, and the only guests apart from the two Irishmen would be less guests than pensioners: the professors and scholars and scientists and wits who came by invitation to Blois, and sitting at the King's elbow, turned somersaults for him in the swept galleries of thought. From Paris, Toulouse, Angers, not all of them had heard of Thady Boy. The King, amused, did not enlighten them. The new toy, wound up, clicking and jumping, was to be set among the pedants unawares.

For this reason perhaps, Thady Boy was not much in evidence during the day. The O'LiamRoe saw him twice only. The first time, as the ollave was dressing, he had sat himself astride a chair and said mildly, 'In my day, as I remember, it was customary to ask permission before leaving one's employment—The Lord guard us, are these all the clothes you have?' And flinching aside from the shirt and trunks and doublet the ollave was donning, Phelim had opened the clothes chest. Piled and screwed up within were the other costumes, jewelled, embroidered and beribboned, given Thady Boy by the King of France. They had all been handled like rags.

Lymond was ready, in a hurry, and not interested in O'LiamRoe. 'You've no need to believe every tale I tell Robin Stewart. It was the only way at the time to get rid of him. He's welcome to sail back to Ireland and stay there, if he wants to. I'll go soon enough . . . in better company than that.'

He hadn't mentioned, but Piedar Dooly had, the incident of the arsenic. Watching him now, lute in hand, hurrying off to Diane, or to d'Enghien, to St. André, to Marguerite, or any of a score of his acolytes, masters, or mistresses, O'LiamRoe was conscious of a sourness in his mouth which recalled suddenly the taste of other wretchedness recently endured. He had to force himself to remember that the creations of an original mind were seldom bought nor were they offered without a price.

The second time, coming to dress for the banquet, he heard Robin Stewart with Thady. He had come at the wrong moment. The conversation, to begin with, must have been a stumbling one. The Archer by now was at his most abrupt and nervously aggressive, his voice splitting a little as his feelings ran beyond it. O'LiamRoe heard that; and heard Thady's voice in a tone he did not at first recognize, quiet and clear-phrased and sane. He was still, he noticed, using his Irish accent. He spoke for some time; then Stewart replied, but a good deal of the edge had gone. Then Thady said something quite brief, and there was a little silence. It was getting late.

O'LiamRoe, feeling that he had done more than enough for Scotland, pushed the door open and went in.

Thady Boy was sitting on the edge of their decorated chest, rather still, looking with calm attention at Robin Stewart's face. The Archer, evidently just risen, had come forward and had laid a hand, gingerly and enquiringly, like a nervous schoolboy, on Thady arm. Then, without seeing O'LiamRoe, he dropped to his knees.

O'LiamRoe made the next step a heavy one. The Archer looked round. His long-jawed face, hollow with hard work and recent travelling, went scarlet, and then white. He jumped up. Tired of the limp and foetid atmosphere of badly controlled emotion, the Prince of Barrow sailed across to his side of the bedroom, and sitting down, began to fight off his boots. 'Ah! Don't let him have you deceived, Stewart. How would he leave? He's supping with the Cardinal tomorrow, and hunting the day after, and playing quoits with the King the day after that. Let you make haste to make your own plans with friend Paris and leave, for it's that gay he is, there's no knowing where he will stop. But, by God, if there was any sense in me, I'd come with you myself.'

For a burning second, no one said anything. Then Robin Stewart, all the sting returned to his voice, said shrilly, 'God's curse, I hope not. For five months I've had Irishmen falling out of my clothes like lice. I can't wait to get done with them.'

He saw Thady shake his head; whether at himself or at the Archer was not quite clear. He had time to experience a happy sense of fulfilment before the door burst open and half Stewart's comrades-in-arms tumbled in, tired of waiting to give him his send-off, and seizing the excuse to capture a better prize at the same time.

By invitation, O'LiamRoe went along with them and, dressed in a brave creation of pastel silk, a little niggardly at the seams, drank mulled wine and added his mite to the loud laughter and wild invention set afloat in the copious backwash of hot mace and ginger. Stewart, who had very little to say anyway, had no need to speak a word. Thady Boy, at his elbow, haunted possibly by his forthcoming exhibition, tipped down the thick, scented liquor, choked, swore, and was the first to stalk off when pages brought the early summons to supper.

From his discreet afternoons with the ladies, O'LiamRoe had sized up the great Court of France and considered that he had its measure. He stepped into the blazing Salle d'Honneur that night, and the reality hit him like a blow on the head.

About him were all the famous, high-browed faces pink-flushed in the firelight, the little pearls and crystals winking in every ear as the restless, chattering heads turned. Tonight, the colours were all different, heaped, tangled and flowing one on top of the other:

velvet orangé, tanné, green, cendré, blue, yellow, red cramoisie, white, gold, copper, violet. In her high chair the Queen had thrown back a cloak of white fur sewn with gems; the King was in cloth of gold, Brusquet and the Archers and the dwarfs in attendance.

Everything was here that he could not help but know was beautiful: a good taste made better by wealth, but which would have managed without it; intelligence on a scale which made him remember ruefully his once cynical words; and a brittle, assured and scholarly wit as detached and ironic as his own. He recognized that in pursuit of his theories, he had nearly fallen over the most remarkable signpost he was ever likely to meet. And while nursing the barked shins of his amour-propre, O'LiamRoe was still capable of honest admiration.

His neighbours he found pleasant, in a casual way. There had been no place yet for serious conversation, but it was well within his powers to make them laugh with him; and he supposed he did not care if they laughed about him afterwards. In any case, the ear of the Court was pitched, not to him, but to Thady Boy.

During supper, the ollave had been asked to sing, and did so readily, unprepossessing but reasonably clean, and almost quite sober. Palestrina and the caquet des femmes O'LiamRoe enjoyed; but he had not expected the purities of the *Gen-traige*, the *Gol-traige*, the *Suan-traige*. In what nether vert Thady Boy had learned the great music of the bard he did not know; but he played in the austere tradition of the monasteries, stretching from Pavia to Roth, which once made the music of Ireland free of every harpstring in Europe. Whatever he was, the justification was there in his art. The familiar music, precisely chosen, decorated the beautiful room as if it had been a painting, and O'LiamRoe, his heart tight, thought, This is my country. Whatever she may become, she has conquered the world. Then the meal ended, and the singing; and the other entertainments began.

These were pleasant enough. Nothing, in fact, hinted at a change in the tenor of the evening until the display of the savages was reached— a dance by some captured Brazilians, sent down from the latest expedition in charge of the Keeper. Abernaci, in a cloth of gold turban, was amongst them, supervising his men as they bustled the confused captives in. Suddenly the entertainment had changed from the civilized to the freakish: was that why the Scottish Dowager's face was immovable; and Catherine fidgeted a little, as if prepared for imminent boredom? But the men of the Court on the contrary had come alive. The King, leaning away a little from his gathering of scholars, had caught St. André's eye, and a smile of common understanding had passed. O'LiamRoe counted six men and one woman who had obviously had too much to drink. The rest, presumably, could hold it better. This surprised him too, for he had expected the standard of behaviour here at least to be rigid to the point of fussiness.

For the Prince of Barrow, the urgency and beauty of the dance, in their own way, complemented the handsomeness of the setting no less than the music had done. The dancers were all men, black-haired and naked. Copper-skinned, they whirled and padded on the smooth tiles, bare feet slapping, the swinging blue-black curtain of their hair blown sticky on to their jerking, round muscled arms. Sweat, gold in the firelight, slid down the smooth channels of breastbone and spine, between the flat bronze pads of the breasts and round the taut horseshoe of the rib cage. Their eyes, cut round and small above the taut cheekbones, were hot and blank.

At first, O'LiamRoe and those around him heard only the music from the embrasure where the small drums thudded and the flutes whistled. Then under that, he began to hear laughter and exclamations, and one familiar voice; and between the leaping, silent, shifting figures he began to see three in particular, directly in front of the King, whose bearded mouth showed suddenly a flash of white laughter. Between the curled toes and knotted calves, a little flurry of feathers dived out, glinted and changed direction, like small, silvery fish in a shoal.

A rustle passed along the cushions. The ranks of dancers suddenly cleared to give an excellent view of Thady Boy Ballagh giving a spirited rendering of New World agility, flanked on one side by a nude Brazilian and on the other by an Archer, stripped to his netherstocks and crimson with shame and a violent determination to win the wager undoubtedly in the offing.

The Brazilian, who probably had hopes of a square meal at last, was making the best job of it, and in any case could not understand the braying Archers by the wall. But he was nearly matched by Thady Boy. Glassy-eyed, light as a spider, O'LiamRoe's ollave kicked and flung like a maid shaking a mop; and at every stamp, a forest of feathers would fly fighting out of his boots . . . stuffed full at some point today, or yesterday, or the day before, against the cold and never removed.

O'LiamRoe gazed. This thick-faced Silenus, pouch-eyed, diligent, was something he had glimpsed in the privacy of his room, but had never, even in nightmares, expected to witness here. He felt the hairs of his neck rise, and his stomach lodged in his throat. Then he took in the fact that the King was laughing.

The figures came nearer. The dancers, shuffled into bewildered disorder, had already made way. In a vortex of ecstatic improvisation Thady Boy led, scraping a phrase from a snatched fiddle, dousing the steaming Archer with a wine jug, directing a figure from a table top; dancing suddenly in a flicker of parodied styles which brought each its calls of recognition and laughter. He began to dance a Volta

with the Archer. Then, grasping an arm each of of his acolytes, Thady
Boy whirled them faster and faster and then set them at each other.
Helpless, captive and Scot cracked together in a ringing of skulls
and slithered bemused to the floor. Thady Boy sat straight-legged,
looking up, the blue, blurred eyes unfocussed; then he closed his
mouth, climbed into one of the dog baskets and fell firmly asleep.

He may have thought the performance sufficient, but the courtiers
did not. O'LiamRoe, watching dumbly, saw St. André and someone
else slide the basket to the door and shake him awake, the black head
joggling back and forth on his shoulders. Thady Boy came to life
suddenly, with a snort, and burst into song.

> '*I cannot eat but little meat*
> *My stomach is not good;*
> *But sure I think that I can drink*
> *With him that wears a hood. . . .*'

In O'LiamRoe's ear, his lordship of Aubigny had hardly ceased to
pour a stream of amused comment, tolerant, civilized and worldly-
wise. He seemed not in the least put out by anything they had just
witnessed; he gave more the appearance, in fact, of enjoying within
himself some enormous private joke. O'LiamRoe, his nerves on
edge, found it intolerable. Did they imagine that this was how Ballagh
ought to behave? Or think that he knew no better? Then he saw that,
during the act which followed the dancers, Thady Boy had been
taken into the King's own circle.

They were just within earshot. The earlier part of the evening had
been made memorable for O'LiamRoe by the famous faces pointed
out round the King: Turnèbe and Muret from Bordeaux and Paris,
de Baïff, Pasquier the lawyer and Bodin the philosopher. Already, on
the edge of their conversation the Irishman had heard, without being
near enough to share, the stir and swirl of ideas; through the condition of human society, the nature of liberty, the purpose of law, to
the topical sciences: astronomy, medicine, natural history. They
spoke in Latin, so that all might understand; but the quotations they
flung at each other were Greek and Hebrew, Turkish, Persian. At the
mention of Budé, caps were touched.

But they had accorded Thady's music the perfect compliment of
silence; and produced for him, when he joined them, a genuine
interest which expressed itself in a patter of dry, courteous and intellectual questions about his art. It evidently annoyed Thady Boy to be
questioned about his art. Selecting the oldest and the most persistent
of his enquirers, the ollave replied politely in a phrase off the streets.

More than taken aback, the professor glanced first at his colleagues, then tried again. Thady Boy's answer this time was coarse;

but wittily coarse. Even the King smiled inadvertently and Thady Boy himself dissolved into laughter. Almost immediately it became apparent that no one thought it necessary to rush to the scholars' defence. Vinet, finding St. André at his elbow, said dryly, 'The catgut has got into their manners, I see. A pity. The years of English rule have stamped something out.'

As the King's guest, the Prince of Barrow had to stay. He sat through the short farce, and a cushion dance, where Thady invented the forfeits, and some impromptu versemaking which defined the tone of the evening more harshly than anything so far had done. Thady Boy gave no sign of remembering that his employer was there. In between bouts of frenzy his bloodshot eyes were now perfectly glazed. He sat in disarray, regurgitating wind and brushing off minor, well-meaning helpers until a burst of vitality stirred him to movement again. Through it all, consistently, he drank.

It seemed unlikely that this could go on indefinitely. Yet there was no move to stop it; and O'LiamRoe suddenly had the feeling that all this had happened before, and that the evening was to be exactly delineated by Thady Boy's capacity. By now everyone was restive, roused by the neurotic gaiety. Even with the coolest temperaments— Queen Catherine's, Charles de Guise's—some degree of involvement had been reached. The young men suddenly had become wild, and a series of violent Italian games had started. Thady Boy, now showing a marked tendency to slip quietly to the ground, was shaken awake and made to play. Sallow faced and unsavoury he clowned, his feet tripping each other, until presently he turned a somersault in his wine-soaked satin, fell, belched, and rolled soggily at O'LiamRoe's feet.

A nimble, glowing, sleepily loving little person, springing out from among the heaped cushions, caught the ollave's threshing arm, and with her own two white hands began to tug him to his feet. 'Master Ballagh, juggle for me! Master Ballagh, I know your riddle!' Lulled to sleep by the music, Mary, Queen of Scotland, had sunk nodding and forgotten by Jenny Fleming's generously cut skirts and had awaked, rapt-eyed, to find her mountebank delivered clean at her feet.

With immense trouble, Thady Boy got on to his feet. He took a step, paying no attention to the little girl. He took another, and lines of worry engraved themselves on his lathered brow. '*Dhia*, my best right leg's broken.'

She clasped her hands round his arm and swung on it, as she had at St. Germain, forgetting, in the sleepy strangeness of the hour, to bother with her royalty. 'The monks and the pears? You said each took a pear and there were still two left?—I know why.'

Stiltedly Thady Boy was progressing down the room, one leg buckling short under him, worry crumpling his face. 'My leg is broke . . . that's for sure.'

Upturned to his, the pointed, fresh face lost the first brightness of her joy. She loosed one light hand to brush the red hair coiling at her brow and said, a thread of appeal in her broken childish French, 'One of the monks *was called Chascun*. Am I not right? So that only one took a pear?'

He paid no more attention than if she had been a ewer-servant. Margaret Erskine, moving swiftly forward, caught the little girl by the shoulders and turned her completely away.

Thady Boy continued on his agonized march. His face hollow with worry, he plodded short legged to his friends, fell over, got up, was sick, was set on his feet, prodded, given more wine and made to walk. Limping, lurching and whining he knocked over a torchère, crashed into royal chairs and flattened a royal dog while Fernel, the royal physician, was sent for.

This was likely to be, O'LiamRoe saw, the accepted end of the entertainment. There was no doubt that they thought of him as their protégé: round him as he lay whimpering on the floor was a close circle of women and more than a few men, all eager to help. Catherine remained in her chair, faintly smiling, but the King, genuinely concerned, walked with his doctor to the injured man.

Fernel, his nightshirt showing underneath his doublet, displayed commendable patience. The shortened leg was examined all over and the boot drawn off, without finding anything amiss. Then the other leg was first prodded, then raised. Something red beaded to the rim of the leather and trickling, soaked into the dirty stuff of the hose.

With a deft movement, his face grave, Fernal slipped off Thady's boot. The ollave, craning, started to moan. Then with his knife the physician peeled off the soaked stocking and, cleaning his way gently down the crippled limb, revealed every inch of it to be intact and enjoying the most unsullied good health.

There was a blank pause. It was d'Enghien, idly fondling one of the mastiffs, who sensed the canine worry in the air. Fastidiously he lifted the bloody calfboot; ruminating, he peered into it; and triumphantly he plucked out and held high a nice portion of giblets, squeezed quite flat by the bardic toes. The mastiff barked.

As the shrieking laughter seared through the air, O'LiamRoe damned etiquette and escaped. He was in his room when by considerate royal command, twenty drunken young men, raucous and singing-merry, swept out of the Salle d'Honneur with Thady Boy limply weaving in their midst, and set out to take his ollave to bed. John Stewart, Lord d'Aubigny, was among those who watched, standing at the tall windows as the chosen escort surged down the twisted staircase and across the broad courtyard outside, screeching, struggling and swaying, and letting down all the cross-hung oil lamps as they passed in order to drink from them one by one.

And it was Lord d'Aubigny, shaking his handsome head, who pronounced the epitaph on the evening. '*Per qual dignitade*,' said his lordship sorrowfully to anyone who would listen, '*L'uom si creasse*.' Margaret Erskine was among those who heard him; but she could not trust herself to reply.

*   *   *

By the time Thady Boy was brought to his door, O'LiamRoe was completely packed.

Piedar Dooly, summoned brusquely from the kitchens, had found the carpetbags open on the bed, and their meagre belongings heaped on the floor. When the stamp and slither of a score of unsteady pairs of feet, a volley of bumps and a cackle of uninhibited laughter arrived outside the door, and then burst through it, he was finished. With a jerk of his combed golden head, O'LiamRoe dismissed Dooly, with saddles and bags, and addressed the incoming party. 'Leave him and get out.'

They revolved round him like Bacchantes, screeching, and one whipped off the bedsheet and, draping himself in a rough copy of O'LiamRoe's tunic and frieze, released a squall of synthetic Erse. They sang, harangued one another, and vomited, clinging to the bedposts and the prie-dieu; they scuttled round the room in search of more wine and, finding it, poured it over each other and attempted to pour it over him. Then they aimed roughly at O'LiamRoe's door and fell through it.

The door slammed shut, leaving the Prince of Barrow in the stinking wreck of his bedroom, standing alone over Thady Boy, heaving drunk on the floor. In a voice unrecognizable even to himself, he said, 'Get up.'

He had to repeat it twice before anything happened, and then, conquering a disgust which possessed him like a sickness, he had to touch him, to wrench him by the defiled and oozing stuff of his sleeve. Then Thady Boy lurched to his feet, spluttering, his eyes oily black under slack lids.

Without turning, O'LiamRoe unhooked the Irish harp from the wall and flung it. It struck the other man, jangling, and fell uncaught to the floor. Thady Boy, blankly aggrieved, sank after it, precipitated into his most undignified spasm yet. 'Take it up, then!' said O'LiamRoe. 'What about the *Prelude to the Salt*? Sing me the *Riding of O'Neill*! Are the great, epic songs not to be in it tonight? . . . Mother of God, Francis Crawford of Lymond, you've made a slut of your art, have you not, as well as a whore of yourself?'

Through the harpstrings, like an inebriated jackdaw's, one

distended eye cocked skittishly at O'LiamRoe; but the next moment Thady Boy had lost interest, was on his feet and single-mindedly setting off somewhere else.

There was a keg of wine in Piedar Dooly's cabinet. O'LiamRoe in two calm strides barred the way as his ollave tacked towards it. One hand on both his wrists was sufficient to hold Thady off. 'Tell me a thing. Why did you ever come to France? Can you recall?'

The two wet hands twisted in his. 'To see how the rich people live.' Below the dyed hair, his face was blotched with crimson and lard. O'LiamRoe, his pulse hammering, could not take his eyes from its ruined intelligence. Thady Boy began to buckle gently again. Even the frenetic gaity had now evidently worn off, and his closing eyes showed a sort of sluggish content. O'LiamRoe pulled him erect. 'You *are* rich. Or so they tell me. Have you forgotten who you are? What is your name?'

The sodden mass hung obedient from his hands. 'I don't know,' said Thady Boy.

'You are the Master of Culter, God forgive you and all who made you. Why are you here?'

There was a long pause. 'I can't remember,' said the drunk man very courteously.

O'LiamRoe let him go. 'You don't recall a child who is liable to be killed?'

There was a long silence. Then Thady Boy Ballagh and Lymond, the one at last fused into the other, huddled loose in his haphazard corner and sighed. 'Richard will look after it.'

O'LiamRoe said, '*You bloody plague's meat*,' and stopped himself short, to resume in measured tones. 'Your brother is a marked man,' he said. 'He can do nothing.'

'Neither can I, then. I'm busy,' said the satisfied voice.

'You are indeed,' said O'LiamRoe cuttingly. 'You are busy destroying. What hope has a soft, vain, inward-looking society against such as you?'

Like river water coming smooth down a dam, Thady Boy began to slide down his wall. 'I can't make music and live like a choirboy,' he said.

A memory of the divine theory of self-expression floated through O'LiamRoe's head, followed by another about the universal sanctity of high art. He said flatly, 'You weren't hired to make music. If you're going to abuse the power it gives you, then you'd better not make it at all,'

Lymond started to giggle. With an effort, O'LiamRoe stuck to the important thing he had to say, his breathing passionately fast, his face pale. 'Your job is with the young Queen. Maybe there is a man or a woman alive who can wring the wine from your guts and send you back there to do it. Myself, I can see no need to help. I am for leaving tonight.'

Sitting on the floor, Thady Boy was laughing so hard now that he made himself retch. When he could speak, '*Leaving the other bitch to cut her own throat,*' he said.

There was a cup half full of wine at O'LiamRoe's side. He flung it like a stone at Thady Boy's head. A wash of pink malmsey, like rain on a window, slipped over the ollave's sickly, glistening face and Thady Boy, staring open-eyed through it, heaved with laughter and the vaulting admixture of crude oil and wine and rich food.

There was a fair store of liquid in the room, both water and wine. O'LiamRoe gave Lymond it all, in shock after icy shock, hurled two-handed into his face; pursuing him with silent savagery as he rolled and paddled and scraped on all fours over the floor, stopped again and again, choking, panting, convulsed with idiot laughter as the next bucketful caught him like a blow.

Then, as suddenly as it had come, the blistering rage died away. Suddenly cold and shaking, O'LiamRoe lowered his pitcher.

Huddled like a water rat at his feet, Thady Boy was laughing still, in the high, whistling gasps of near hysteria, and at his movements ripples ran out over the floor. A finger of water, hissing, fled into the fire. The dark stains of wine joined, in moist red falls, over bed-clothes and tapestries; the ivory and tortoise-shell posts were streaked and beaded; the secretaire dripped. The smell of food, of sweat, of stale and fresh wine was unbearable.

So were his thoughts. Driving leaden feet over the splashing, slippery floor, O'LiamRoe strode, and nearly ran, from the room. Behind him, the laughter came to an unsteady halt, and was replaced by a cracked and insalubrious voice.

> '*They shall heap sorrow on their heads*
> *Which run as they were mad*
> *To offer to the idle gods.*
> *Alas, it is too bad.*'

There was a brief silence. Then, 'Alash, it is too bad,' said the voice again, reflectively; and giggled; and said nothing more.

*　　　*　　　*

Margaret Erskine arrived white-faced half an hour later. The floor had begun to dry by then, in islanded patches in front of the big lively fire. She moved through the room like someone running a race, checking neither at the stench nor the gross usage exposed all about her. There was only the firelight to see by, since someone had put out the candles: the room was filled by shadows, running back from the great hearth. The atmosphere of the place stirred chokingly like some

191

deadly tide, to the disordered rhythm of the fire. It was clammily hot.

During wars lasting as long as she could remember, through two young marriages and all the familiar and malodorous all-night sessions of the peer and the bonnet-laird, she knew with precision what to expect, and with resignation what to do about it.

But this was going to be different. Thady Boy had been travelling about since O'LiamRoe left him. That much was obvious by the overturned chairs, the avalanche of bedclothes, the rucked tapestry all pressed into service to keep him erect.

This persevering activity had now ended. It was quiet—too quiet. Flouting her fears, she hoped stoutly that he could at least recognize her, and somehow manage to move. She could not lift him alone.

In all this, she had forgotten that Lymond simply might not have heard her. In fact, he was standing, held up by two chairs, in the shadows beyond the fireplace, most of his sodden clothing thrown off, and his dripping, tangled head turned to the wall. The long fingers of one hand, cramped fast on the wood, were clearly picked out by the fire, and she could hear the thick force of his breathing.

Then he must have sensed she was there. The tortured nerves of his stomach, raw to the point where a thought, a perfume, can be cathartic, revolted as he swung round. He doubled up, closing his arms over his head, but before that, she had caught a glimpse of his dilated eyes, and the queer surprise on his face. He had, she realized, expected to endure it alone.

She pushed the chairs away and gripped him like a nurse, with a practical and impersonal firmness. Then, when it was over, she said in her sensible voice, 'You know you've been made to drink poison. You must walk, my dear.'

The pupils of his eyes were vast and black; in a bright light he would be virtually blind. On her arm his weight was unconsciously relaxed. He said serenely, 'I don't need to walk any more.'

'Oh, yes, you do,' said Margaret Erskine sharply, and taking a double grip of the reeking shirt, forced him to move. He was full of nightshade, his brain drugged with it. While he could, he had done a good deal himself to get it out of his system. It was her task somehow to keep him roused sufficiently to finish the job.

She bore his full weight during that first turn of the room. Then, blearily, he began to relieve her of the burden, to take a leaden step of his own accord and then, stumbling from wall to wall, with her help to keep moving. She did not look at his face; and afterwards was glad, when she saw his nail marks bloody on his own palms. He had been nearer proper awareness than she had believed.

At the time, he seemed frighteningly distant; and then, when the stupefaction wore off, exhausted by the unending nausea to a point far beyond speech. Presently, in this blind state he came to a halt and, steadying him, she looked and saw what the belladonna and his own extravagance together had done to Francis Crawford. And she also saw that she could not afford the luxury of tears, for now he had reached the end of his resources. Whether any poison remained or not, she had to let him rest.

She brought him to the hearth, where she had made a rough bed; and he lay breathing fast, racked by dwindling spasms. His eyes, in their chasms of bone, were sealed shut. When, thus immobile, he spoke, her heart lurched with the shock. '*Mignonne*,' said Lymond placidly, '*Je vous donne ma mort pour vos étrennes*.'

Even in this extremity, damn him, the quotation hurt. 'I don't want your death for my dowry,' said Margaret. 'Give your rewards to Master Abernaci. He saw you from among the Brazilians, knew at once what was wrong, and came to me.'

'Nightshade,' said the quiet voice. 'Put, I suppose, into the mulled wine. They put it on elephants for a skinned bottom,' said Lymond, and laughed suddenly and incautiously; then pressed his hands, sweating, against his face.

After a moment she said, 'If you recognized it, why didn't you get help? O'LiamRoe—'

'O'LiamRoe has gone.' The statement was laconic. 'If someone is going to be disappointed tomorrow . . . they may as well believe it to be drunkard's . . . good luck.'

Silence fell. The huge fire had roared and flamed its way down to a great, silky pillar of heat, and the burning air shook. The floor had dried. In the steady red light the mired and fingermarked walls, the upset furniture, the ravaged bed, looked urbanely dramatic, as if done in stained glass. Nothing had sublimated the stench. It would have made a fitting tomb, she supposed, for Thady Boy Ballagh. That it was fitting for Francis Crawford she would not believe.

His eyes were shut. On its shadowed side, his face gave away nothing. His profile was rimmed with light, convincing in its purity; reflected light touched the underlid, and the highest part of the cheekbone, and the thick muscle joining cheekbone to jaw. In the darkness, the rest was mercifully lost.

Margaret sat without moving until the first, finest sounds told her that somewhere people were dressing for a new day. Then she stirred, and learned for the first time that he was not asleep. His eyes opened, heavy-lidded but blue, and he said, 'Yes, you must go,' and paused, then added, dry-voiced, 'As a family, the Erskines always seem to be saving me from myself.'

Her own shaken nerves shied from emotion quite as much as his disordered ones. She wondered how much stoicism it had taken to continue playing the fool, knowing the poison was working, and trusting to drink, to oil, to God knew what other impromptu expedients, to preserve his life and also his appearance of ignorance. Understanding, she had made no effort to tidy the room.

Now, there was so much to say and so little it was possible to put into words without going beyond her control and his own. In the end she bent, adjusting the blanket underneath his head, and said, 'I told you my role was to sit by the hearth.'

Under his eyes, the light deepened. She had never seen a conscious man lie so still. He said, 'My role has been less to light fires than to extinguish them, it seems. I was sorry about the little girl. But it couldn't be helped.'

He had seen Mary's face, then. She said, 'You will be able to put it right one day,' and knew sinkingly that she must bring herself to go, even while he looked like this. And he was alone; there was no one she could confide him to. . . . God knew what abuses he would lay upon his strength tomorrow, next week, next month—whatever murderous terms this abominable undertaking would occupy. Out of her despair, resting irresolute by his pillow, she burst out, 'If only Robin Stewart, even, were here. Who will look after you?'

Even without looking, she felt beneath her the little shock of his surprise. Then he gave a stifled sound not far distant from a laugh, arrested it, then unfolding his arm slowly, like a man in a dream, touched her hand and then lightly held it. His fingers felt cool and insubstantial, and thoughtlessly indulgent. 'But, my dear,' said Lymond. 'Robin Stewart is the murderer.'

PART THREE

London:
The Excitement of Being Hunted

The excitement of being hunted takes half off it; just as the excitement of being ridden takes half off the horse, when it is a sensible adult that excites both.

  I: *Blois: The Mill in Motion*   197

  II: *Amboise: An Accident Happens*   217

  III: *Blois: Distress is not Released*   228

  IV: *London: Wolves All Around Him*   240

  V: *London: The Intentional Betrayal*   254

  VI: *London: The Nettle and the Venom*   267

  VII: *London: Pledge to Fasting*   281

I

Blois: The Mill in Motion

As to the mill, however, inasmuch as it could not do anything illegal if it were not set in motion; it is right that the person who set it in motion should be responsible for it.

IN the weeks that followed, Margaret Erskine found herself sorely tried. Stewart's journey to Ireland and back could take a month, even without a delay there on his mission. A month to wait, and observe Thady Boy's return to carefree excesses. A month to watch Jenny, glorious Jenny, coolly set out to build a court for herself, dazzling her admirers; drawing the benefice seekers to her side. The royal child, Margaret's half-brother or sister, was due in less than four months, and Margaret knew how the women about the King were reacting. Jenny herself paid no attention. She had never demanded deference. She simply assumed, once the news became public, that they would defer.

But in much less than a month there came the check on Lymond which Margaret was silently praying for. Sooner than they had thought possible, Richard Crawford, third baron Culter, with his short and glittering train, answered his summons to Blois.

Early that day, John Stewart of Aubigny also came back to Court, after a spell at his castle of La Verrerie, and heard for the first time a mildly surprising item of news. As soon as he could, he sought out Thady, taking George Douglas with him, to ask why O'LiamRoe had gone.

The ollave had been on the terrace, with a small and exuberant party, playing quoits. Sir George's speculative eye, looking him over, noticed the suffused eyes and the softer weight and the decisive air of abandon. He also noted, privately, that this young man had been sharply ill, and was not yet quite recovered.

Thady Boy answered his lordship, however, with unfettered buoyancy. 'Are you not for believing all you're told? He had an urgent message from home. Or that's what he said.'

'I know,' said Lord d'Aubigny quickly. 'But—'

''Tis a real student of humanity you are,' said Thady cheerfully. 'But, of course, he got no such message. Sickly, impotent, inable and unmeet was Phelim O'LiamRoe. The lady of his heart upset all his plans, and he could think of nothing but home. Oonagh O'Dwyer was all that was keeping O'LiamRoe in France; surely all the world knows that thing.'

'All the world knows, of course,' offered George Douglas politely, 'of his ollave's famous *serena* last month.'

Lord d'Aubigny, relieved, paid no attention. 'I'm glad. I had a notion, Ballagh, it might have been something Stewart had done. He's a good man, Robin, but unstable, you know. A little erratic. He took a fancy to you, I expect you know; was threatening one day recently to leave and go with you back to Ireland. Then he went quite the opposite way. Last time I saw him, he was consigning every Irishman to the devil. Unstable. So I hoped nothing had been said. . . .'

Thady Boy's dark smile grew. ''Tis a fine Archer you have there, true, but a thought clinging. No blame to him that O'LiamRoe went. Quite the other way. It was O'LiamRoe telling him to his face that I had no intention of going with him to Ireland—a true word, but I would have put it more sweetly myself—that put the pot on the boil. I saw Robin myself before he went. I doubt, my lord, that you won't see that fine fellow again.'

Lord d'Aubigny showed no signs of sorrow at this. He said kindly, 'And what of you, Ballagh? I hope you're staying?'

'As long as the King wants me.'

'Then you must come to La Verrerie again. I have some friends who want to hear that fine playing.' Objets d'art were Lord d'Aubigny's business. 'You're staying at Blois, then?'

Part of the Court was moving upriver shortly. 'So they say. I go where I'm taken.' The silken arm of d'Enghien suddenly encircled his shoulders. Jean de Bourbon, smiling cursorily at the others, said, 'You're holding up the whole game, my dear. Are you feeling well?'

Sir George Douglas's smile was quite masterly, and almost won a response from Francis Crawford. Sir George said, 'He'd better be, after challenging that Cornishman.'

Thady Boy's surprise was guarded. Discovering his quoit, he hooked the iron abstractedly on d'Enghien's high-bred hand, then queried, 'What Cornishman?'

There followed the small silence of the faux pas. Then d'Enghien said, 'You're going to the Cardinal's tonight, Thady? But of course you are. Everyone is.'

Sir George Douglas continued for him. 'He is having wrestlers after supper. The story is that you challenged one of them to a bout. Is it not true?'

Surprise, annoyance, acceptance and a wild and untrustworthy enthusiasm informed the ollave's sallow face. 'No, it isn't,' said Thady Boy cheerfully. 'Someone, I would guess, is wanting to contrive a piquant sauce for the dish—probably that very Cardinal Charles. But it's a matter, you know, of a challenge; and *dhia*, I never refused a challenge of any kind yet.'

He did not, as it happened, know that as he uttered the words, his brother had ridden into the open courtyard beyond the quadrangle at his back, and dismounting, had entered the château.

*   *   *

Because her dear brother the King had made certain, quite properly, that the Scottish Dowager and her friends would be watched, no one in her suite was able to warn Lymond that Lord Culter had arrived. In any case, while his lordship was being welcomed by the Constable, taken to the King, and confronted, in the royal presence, with the Dowager with tranquil assurance on both sides, Lymond was launching a fruitless search for a wrestler.

By late afternoon, the Cornishman had still not been found; a fact significant enough in itself. Lymond wasted no more time on it. He went straight to his room and, lying flat on the tortoise-shell bed, forced himself to rest for an hour. There, after making an inadequate toilet for the Cardinal of Lorraine's supper party, he was collected by a party of fellow guests, already too talkative and exchanging aqua vitae and bad puns. Then, avoiding the official party which included the royal family, the Constable and Diane, they set out for the Hôtel de Guise. The Cardinal's sister Mary, Queen Dowager of Scotland, was already there, together with her brother the Duke, the Erskines and Lord Culter.

By then Richard Crawford of Culter knew all that he needed to know about his younger brother.

Erskine had prepared him, as best he could, with a swift narration of all Lymond had done, followed by an unadorned account of his conduct. Lord Culter heard it with complete calm; at one or two points his mouth twitched. At the end he said, 'Well, Tom; you know Francis as well as I do. Your confidence isn't shaken, surely?'

Erskine's answer had no hesitation. 'No. But my God, Richard, be prepared.'

'A fan, and his clothes hung with bells?' Then, as Erskine hesitated, 'No. Obviously. One of his grosser deceptions. It would be irresistible, given the Court of France and O'LiamRoe.' Richard Crawford's grey eyes were amused. 'Thank you, Tom. I am amply warned.'

This steadiness, this quality of tough-minded tranquillity which could sometimes seem stolid, was balm to the disease of danger and unrest which was preying on them all. In this was Culter's great strength. Now in his mid-thirties, quiet, stocky and unremarkable, he was still nearly unique for his time in that he was perfectly reliable.

199

It seemed as if he had set himself since boyhood to outweigh all the wanton recklessness of the younger brother; and had brought to it much the same deliberate power. Where Francis had ranged Europe in blazing notoriety, Richard had stayed at home, husbanding his wide estates, fighting for them when he must. Beyond this, and the joy he now possessed with Mariotta, his dark Irish wife, there was nothing more he desired.

When, black-headed and sardonic, Lymond had departed for France, Lord Culter and his mother had been, in their different ways, thankful to see him set off at last, wholly on pleasure bent. For family reasons, Richard himself had not wished to go with the Queen Dowager to France. She, in turn, had been as anxious for him to stay: one of the few watchdogs she could trust. So that the bare, censored terms of her message, arriving at Midculter with the King of France's pressing invitation, were enough to confirm that the summons was not of her seeking, and that her reactions to it were being watched. They had even included an invitation to his mother. Lord Culter had hesitated a moment; then, ashamed, had taken it to her.

All the fair delicacy which had been Lymond's at birth could be seen in Sybilla. White-haired, pink-cheeked, blue-eyed, she read the two messages and said instantly, 'Francis, of course, embarking on some nutritive project, while all within hearing drop prone and their matins madly say. . . . Do you think they expect me to appear unworldly and strongly maternal, like a Scotch clocking hen? It will be a pleasure to refuse.'

Long ago it had been recognized by all who knew Sybilla that, though she doted on her two sons, her astringent soul belonged to the younger. Richard did not grudge it. He had sufficient happiness at home here in Midculter not to deny Francis any comfort he could snatch. And always, as she had proved yet again, Sybilla's quick mind and formidable intelligence kept her impulses controlled and her judgment sound.

She was watching him. 'Such a pity. Not a time to be away.'

He was thinking, too, of Mariotta. And it was because of her that he said, almost before his mother stopped speaking, 'Either the Queen is in trouble, or Francis . . . or both. The sooner I go and find out what that fool of a son of yours is doing, the sooner we shall both be back.'

In all her long life, Sybilla had perfected a blithe self-control which was absolute; if she had gone, the watchers, whoever they were, would have learned nothing from her face.

But she knew, who knew him through and through, that they might have learned something from Lymond's.

But Richard, obviously, was another matter.

A good quarter drunk, the Bourbon party arrived in the Rue Chemonton, Thady Boy in its midst, and swept into the wide, low-ceilinged room in the Hôtel de Guise where their host's scarlet gown glowed by the silks of his sister.

Margaret Erskine saw them come; saw Culter's grey eyes rest on his brother, flatten and glance smoothly away; saw Lymond's blue gaze return and look and continue unbroken to deposit its bloodshot burden of greeting on his major ecclesiastical target. In neither face was there a trace of recognition. They were a capable pair.

The meal was a princely one, perfectly served. Lord Culter without evident effort created small talk in an impeccable flow, and only Margaret, her senses unnaturally raw, saw that he was watching his brother throughout. Lymond's behaviour, as always, went to the limits of polite usage and then hurtled off into space. Bursts of laughter rose like cannon-shot from his side of the table, and his voice was blurring, as it always did by this time. When the boards were drawn, he had drunk enough, and so had most of the men, to be ready for whatever outrageous feat of inventiveness sprang into his head. No one had troubled to ask him to play.

At this point, judging the ollave's condition with skill, the Cardinal signed to bring on the wrestlers.

Jousting, fencing, fighting with staffs—this kind of knockabout combat was an old distraction; fresh, lively and painful, boisterous, sometimes malicious, they rejoiced in it to a man. Only Margaret, it seemed, was aware tonight of the queer tension in the air; only to her mind had the breathing space of good company and laughter suddenly shrunk, as if a door had shut in some lukewarm brood chamber, and something uncouth and organic had started to grow. Rumour had it that the chief wrestler, the Cornishman, had been challenged by Thady. True or not, the ollave seemed to be ready to wrestle; as the first exhibition bout started she saw something like eagerness on Lymond's slackened face. It disturbed her. His mind was never, as a rule, so simple to read.

During the bout, her uneasiness grew. One man, the smaller, was quite new. The other, the Cornishman, had fought already at Court on that December night when Thady had roused all Blois with his race. He was a big man, over six feet and solid, with the vast limbs and the cream and rose-flooded flesh of the sandy-haired. His head was shaved, like his partner's. They were both in soft boiled leather, a second skin sewn on them, body and limbs, and their clipped feet slapped bare on the tiles. The weapons were as usual: the cudgel and the shield with the iron prong at its foot. The straining, thinly gloved muscles glistened with oil; as the bodies groaned and grunted and collided and gasped the firelight varnished them, dripping, bald, squat and scarlet as Burmese teak.

Watching, Margaret became aware of yet one thing more. Whenever the Cornishman's attention was free, the white-lashed eyes turned towards Thady. In them was very little of intelligence and nothing of amity. They expressed scorn, she thought, and excitement, and something else she could not properly name. Only Lymond, close by the two men, plainly saw in the pale, pink-rimmed eyes a pleasurable anticipation of murder.

The present bout was soon ended. It had been reasonably exciting. The mild applause, the circling wine, the little stir of gossip and change filled the moment that was suddenly on them, on all those that knew and were concerned, like a burden of unbearable weight. Then the floor was clear, and on it was Thady Boy, portentously solemn, stripped to creased shirt and fat, silk-puffed haunches, club and shield in his hands. Long ago, the stuffed and elaborate clothing he wore had let him dispense with additional padding; his way of life was bringing illusion near enough reality, for the rest. Opposite him now, loosely bent, waited the supple-skinned ox of a Cornishman, the fire red on his skull and his eyes and the silver spike of his shield.

Margaret, feeling her face grow cold, and therefore white, looked away quickly. Beside her, the square, short-nosed profile of Richard Crawford showed no kind of change. No muscle altered; no apprehension showed in his eyes. Margaret wondered briefly if he felt any warmth for his brother or only a sense of duty, doggedly preserved.

The bout began at great speed, because the Cornishman wanted quickly to disarm his opponent. The rubbery hulk of him pattered in, lightfooted; but there was less still of Thady Boy. He blew like a windball, vagrant on the periphery in untraceable patterns, and the heavy cudgel, thrashing hard through the air, whined empty on the place where the ollave had been standing. Behind him, Thady Boy whistled; and as the Cornishman turned, hit two melodious notes from the wrestler's own shield and set words to it, before he had to skip fast to shelter.

He was busy then for quite a few moments, for the Cornishman, annoyed, was impatient. The cudgels cracked, on the shields and on each other, but adroitly missed flesh and bone. That would come. They were fresh as yet, although the ollave's breathing was thick and fast; and Erskine, who had seen him, weightless, fight his brother tempered like a sword, watched with a troubled face all this blunted skill. Then Thady Boy ran backwards, his round shadow swift before him, and without an instant's warning hurled his shield away from him with all his strength.

You could hear the impact of the blow. It hit the wrestler's leather wrist, fell, bounced, and wheeled straight to a dark corner, skidding the Cornishman's dropped cudgel with it. Thady now had his club only; and the wrestler nothing but his shield.

The wave of comment stopped in mid-flight. The circling had begun again, but this time more slowly. The wrestler's white-lashed eyes had narrowed. He moved, crab-legged, his right hand splayed and his oil-sleek muscles shifting until he had the other within reach. Then, like a snake striking, a foot flashed upwards to Thady's groin. As the pounded flock filling his preposterous breeches took the blow, Thady's cudgel swung out. The wrestler jerked his head—in vain.

For the club was aimed, not at his head, but at the uppermost rim of the shield. It landed. And splitting it with a high crack from end to end, it drove the spike underneath into the Cornishman's own shin, With a sharp, strangled grunt the wrestler hopped back, clutching his leg, and Thady, the sweat sparkling on his face, grinned and tossed up his baton. The grunting stopped. The hubbub of laughter and talk died away. In a growling silence, elbows out, hands beseeching, the Cornishman began to advance crouching on Thady.

The Cornishman was now quite unarmed. But he had assets Thady lacked: a hug that could kill and an ungreased body to seize. Above all, he was a professional: a dangerous man, a thug, and not quick witted, but with all the tricks of the game sunk deep in his battered bones.

He advanced, feinted, and double-feinted. His solid, well-trained body answered him this time a fraction quicker than the abused one of Thady's. Lymond guessed right once, but not twice; even so, dodging, his cudgel touched the other man's shoulder. The resilient, thick-knotted muscles accepted the blow. The Cornishman grunted, but continued unshaken. The jaws of a rocklike embrace advanced, hovered and snapped shut. Then the Cornishman pressed; and Thady Boy, held tight as a parcel, was lifted slowly into the air.

It was a perfect move, spoiled by overconfidence in the end. In the instant before the big man drew breath to hurl him wholesale to the ground, Lymond flung his weight forward. His legs alone were quite free. With the last ounce of his breath, the ollave lunged with one foot and brought it sharply, heel down, on the back of the other man's knee.

A lighter man would have fallen. The Cornishman stumbled, opaque surprise on his face turning to anger at the orthodox, classical reply. Already the ollave was half-free. Sheer rage lending him speed, the Cornishman recovered first. He could not, as he planned, smash his opponent flat on the ground. But he twisted, heeled, and diverted his own stumbling weight so that they collapsed together, the ollave underneath, shoulder pinned to the floor. Thady Boy had yielded first fall.

Then they were circling each other again. To win, Thady would have to throw the Cornishman twice. And he still had the cudgel.

He used it now, to keep the other man off. Although the lead-paned windows were flung wide to the night, the room was suffo-catingly hot. It had a stuffy smell, left over from the liver and ginger and the pastries and the venison with Milan cheese; and the company, pressed back in their crumpled satins against the fine, split-oak wainscotting and watching in well-bred passivity, brought to mind nothing so much as a cageful of moulting sparrow hawks. Lord Culter, passing a box full of sugary sweetmeats, had to speak twice before Margaret even heard. Then he turned back calmly to watch.

Any wrestler in his senses would have made it his first aim to seize Thady's club. The Cornishman set out to do it with no nonsense: after all, the ollave might be in poor trim, but the wrestler had fought one bout already. So, dodging and ducking the whirling wood, he took one swift step and, grasping Thady's right arm, twisted. It was perfect. In inescapable reflex, the ollave's hand opened and the cudgel flew out and hit the floor, skidding, as Thady wrenched himself free. In the same moment the big man turned and dived for the weapon himself.

As the sole of his receding foot came up, Lymond struck it viciously with his own, and the Cornishman, hand still outstretched, came down hard on one knee. Then the ollave's hands gripped his ankle, found leverage, and heaved. Eighteen stone of Cornishman rose in the air and fell crashing to the ground. Second fall to Master Ballagh.

The pure shock of the experience held the wrestler prone, if only for seconds. It was long enough for Thady Boy, breathing wildly and dripping with sweat, to upend three boxes of marzipan, over him. Emitting a thick roar, the first voluntary sound he had made, the wrestler rolled over and got to his feet, closely covered in a kind of sparkling white suede. At last, with his oil coated in sugar, he was susceptible to his opponent's mischievous hands.

In the utter silence, as they faced up again, the Cornishman's whistling grunt was queerly disturbing. It continued, at the back of his throat, all the time that he circled. With one fall each, this time they were equal, with no weapons but their hands and feet, their speed, and the tortile strength of their muscles. Thady, periwinkle-gay in the silver cloud of spilled sugar, had become smoothly taut. The Cornishman, soft-footed, ranged round and gently round; the pink-rimmed eyes, like a butcher's, probing and thoughtful. Then, with a sudden, double hiss of forced air, the two men came to grips.

One of the toughest of sports, it could be the most brutal, and the Cornishman knew every trick. A spatulate thumb, sliding into the eye, was his answer to Thady's quick knee lock, and as the ollave's head jerked to protect himself, the wrestler's hard foot flashed up and in, and his hands, deep in Thady's black hair, jerked his scalp hard to the ground. Lymond's hands, outspread, met the tiles a split second before his head. He somersaulted, and his stockinged legs,

204

swinging up, scissored the Cornishman's neck and hurled him off balance backwards.

It was a good escape; but no more than that, for Thady Boy landed first, and on his stomach at that, with the wrestler on top of him. Then they were up and close-grasped again. Beneath the dyed skin, Francis Crawford was livid, and breathing in fast, retching gasps. The Cornishman set his joints. Then, twisting, tearing, wrenching, kicking, he fought for one thing and got it. He trapped Thady at last in the cage of a full hug and without attempting to throw him, set himself, to his whining monody, to burst the lighter man's ribs.

The pressure mounted, bit by bit. Flat against the hot, sticky leather Thady's face looked darkly congested. His hands moved weaving behind the Cornishman's back. They moved till they rested on the fleshy pads of the ribs, and then gripped and wrung, through leather and skin. Shaken, the big man grunted; and in that second, Lymond hooked his inside left leg with his own right. It was not enough, by a long way, for a fall; but enough to shake the intensity of the hug. The Cornishman changed his mind. Slackening his own hold, he spun round so that he was underneath Lymond's belly and prepared to throw him bodily over his head.

From that height, and on those tiles, it meant possible death. As soon as the grasp on him slackened, Lymond changed and tightened his own. When the wrestler applied his leverage, it was counteracted by a lock which not only equalled his but bent him double, as he crouched, until he knelt on the floor. Then the grip under his arms began to shift and extend. There was a grunt, a twist and a deep, shaken sigh. The next moment Lymond's two clasped hands met at the back of the Cornishman's neck.

The knuckles whitened. A vein, rapidly beating, appeared in the dark skin of his temple. Then, slowly, the thick-jointed shining bald head started to bow, to sink, to press lower and lower, to be pushed inexorably into the wrestler's great chest, pushed with the last, deadly, unanswerable thrust that drives bone asunder from bone.

It was then, in the small, breathing silence that was theirs, in the midst of the rustling ring of their audience, the cries, the murmurs, the rapt and riveted gaze of the Court, that Thady Boy spoke to the Cornishman.

What he said could not be heard by the spectators. But the wrestler understood; the veined eyes glared white and the sweat dripped, greasily warm, as he listened. Then, squeezing the words from compressed throat and chest, he answered. 'They're lying. *Ils mentirent, donc.*'

Thady Boy addressed him again. Under the long and pitiless fingers the glittering head was sinking still, the sandy skin darkening to purple. Again, patently the answer was negative.

What happened next was a matter of idle dispute afterwards among all those who watched. The ollave spoke, and this time relaxed his pressure a fraction. The wrestler answered, his voice stifled and raucous, and after another exchange Thady seemed satisfied.

He loosened his grasp, shifted, and as the Cornishman drew a first, shuddering breath, Thady's arm flashed under his chin, gripped, tightened, and pulled up and back. There was a click, clearly audible all through the engrossed room. Then the great bulk of the wrestler, his eyes white and open, his mouth ajar, his neck queerly awry, heeled with momentous precision and, slumping, slid prone on the tiles.

Thady Boy rocked on his hunkers and sat down, looking at once pleased, alarmed and vaguely apologetic. 'Ah, clumsy fellow that I am. Would you think it: I've killed him stone dead.'

It was delicious, the climax of the evening. You could sense their satisfaction and their lack of surprise as the exaggerated laughter and bravas filled the room. They had assumed that their blissful sluggard would pay for his drink in good coin. Rimed and sparkling with sugar, the wrestler lay like some child's flaccid sweetmeat in death, and the dogs licked his eyelids.

The evening was soon over. The King and his suite left, and then the Queen; but Thady Boy Ballagh, full of spirits, scraped precariously through his obeisances and stayed on with his flask and his admirers. Then Mary of Guise rose to go, and at the same moment Thady got to his feet and went pattering unsteadily towards the Scottish Court.

Unbelieving, Margaret Erskine saw him approach, saw him favour her with a tipsy smile, and then pass by to tug at Lord Culter's fine sleeve. Richard Crawford, his face rigid, found himself looking straight into his brother's blue gaze, the stink of sweat and wine and drunken humanity rising to his nostrils.

Thady Boy's sibilants were precocious, but his sentiments were candidly warm. 'Come and see me, if you want to, my dear. One day soon, before you leave us for Amboise.'

Margaret saw Richard's grey eyes flicker, checking. No one else within earshot; but the exchange was obvious, of course, to all who cared to look. Richard said, carefully, 'The sieur d'Enghien is watching you.'

'He's jealous,' said Thady Boy, and giggling archly, showed signs of moving off.

Smiling, speaking quietly in the same even voice, Culter said, 'People will talk. How can I come?'

A long, unclean finger caressed him under the chin. 'How *prudent* you are,' said Thady Boy plaintively. 'The only people who matter know now exactly who I am. But you may show me and them

206

marvellous stratagems, if you like. Sleep well, my sweet, and have modest dreams. . . .'

He drifted away none too soon, for Madame Marguerite had come to claim him, and then d'Enghien brought him more drink. Margaret Erskine did not see with whom he went home.

*   *   *

Next morning, as the Scottish Court of Queen Mary of Guise was preparing to shift to fresh quarters at Amboise, Thady Boy, under pressure, moved to occupy more accessible rooms in the vacated wing.

He was half-packed by midmorning when Lord Culter arrived at his door. On the threshold he stood still. Lymond, left to speak first, said agreeably, 'Quite so. I, King of Flesh, flourishing in my flowers. Come in. I am sensible, sober, and have no designs on your virtue.'

Richard's reserve, so swiftly noted, broke and vanished. Smiling in return, he shut the door and came forward to give Francis his embrace. Beneath his hands he felt the extra flesh and was sorry. And as his eyes took in the dry, blackened hair, the unresilient skin, the shortened focus of far-seeing eyes, reduced and reddened by late nights and smoke—'You *are* a devil, Francis,' he said.

He had expected to find this difficult, but in fact talk came quite easily. He gave the family tidings, answered some light questions and noted that Lymond was in reality much less interested in the new building at Midculter than he was in the political news.

They talked of Scottish affairs. Outside, a black winter's rain had been falling all morning. The dismantled room was untidy and dark, and hardly cheered by a new fire full of whimsy and smoke. The open box at his feet caught Lymond's attention. Rising, he disappeared into the little cabinet next door and returned, after a space, with a towel and his baggage straps. He added them to the general litter, then shutting the empty coffer and sitting on it, said, 'What about the Morton inheritance? George Douglas is ready to be bought if she needs him. He wants ambassadorial power, but that would be madness.'

There were three claimants to the earldom of Morton, and Lord Maxwell and George Douglas's son were the only two that mattered. Richard said, 'I hear he has threatened to expose you,' and regretted it, for his brother looked surprised and said, 'Oh, Lord, that was nothing. Mischief. He's the ingenious conspirator who had you sent for, I should be fairly sure. He always appears to be maintaining great structures of intrigue, but half the time if you subtracted George Douglas the erection would stand just as before. Stronger, probably. But he would come to her for Morton and she needn't lose Maxwell. He has power enough. He'd be perfectly happy with money.

She'll need all the support she can get to cancel the crass stupidity . . .
You've heard of Jenny's little exercise?'

Richard's mouth twitched. 'Scotland is ringing with it. It must
have caused quite a stir.'

Lymond got to his feet, tardier in his movements than once he
had been. 'Oh, it did. Fair Diana, the lantern of the night, became
dim and pale. The Constable has retracted, and so has the King.
And Catherine, of course, is simply waiting her chance to send Jenny
home. All most desirable, of course.'

'Tom and Margaret did their best to put a stop to it. I know you
did, too.'

'Oh yes,' said Lymond mildly. 'She was flattered. I had to fight,
positively, for my reputation.'

He again began to pack, talking intermittently as he did so.
Richard listened to a quiet and dispassionate analysis of leading
members of King Henri's court. It was exceedingly funny and tear-
ingly precise; it rang true, alarmingly, as if the wax tablets of the
Recording Angel were being leafed through on a lectern. They had
not touched at all on the business which had brought Lymond to
France. In the middle of it Lymond said, without a break, in the
same conversational tone, 'Wait a moment, will you?' and went off,
swiftly, through the same door as before.

The lack of fuss for a moment deceived even Richard. Then he
saw the unpacked litter and realized that for five minutes he had been
watching a private rearguard action of Francis's own. In two strides
he was out of his chair and across to the other room.

The attack this time had been a bad one. There had been no real
hope of disguising it, as Lymond must have known. Even Culter,
who had hardly led a sheltered life, had seldom seen a man so
mercilessly sick. His breath coming hard, Richard dropped to his
knees at his brother's side and supported him until it was over. Then,
smoothly powerful, he lifted Francis in his arms and carried him
expertly through to the fancy tortoise-shell bed.

Lymond's eyes were shut; the dead man's pinches, like freckles,
blue on the skin. His face, in the clearing light, was as Margaret
Erskine had said. Last night, in the kind glow of the candles, it had
been possible to recall, comfortably, his impudent talent for acting.
When presently he stirred, Richard hanging over his bed spoke with
something near malevolence. 'You damned young fool. I know you,
remember? I suppose that was just something you ate; or are you
bloody well pregnant as well?'

Lymond waited a long time, apparently unwilling to take a breath,
and then said, 'Richard. Rescues on the hour, like one of Purves's
clocks. Would you bring me—?'

'No.' Richard, pitiless, answered him.

'—Only a twopenny pint of claret?' For an instant, his driving need was visible behind the coolly brazening eyes. Then he resigned from Richard's grey stare and drank, without further comment, the water which was all Richard brought.

Presently he sat up, with caution, embracing one string-gartered knee. 'Forgive me. My guts are unmantled and my sinews unmanned. God knows, it's an offence against decent living; but it will go.'

'When,' said Richard, face and voice quite unaltered, 'did you last taste solid food?'

'Liquids,' said Lymond. 'I thrive best on strong fermented liquids. Saffron milk, like the fairies.' He laughed a little, and then sobered. 'I don't starve, I promise you. If Nicholas the hermit could do it, so can I. It isn't for long.'

'How long?' Ruthlessly, Richard was coursing evasions. 'The Erskines believe you want proof of Stewart's guilt in case he comes back.'

Lymond's stained hands were still. 'Partly true. The proof I have would be quite hopeless at law. A prostitute from Dieppe. A Scotsman posing as an Indian. Another Scotsman passing for Irish. We need something better than that. But as for Stewart . . . I don't think he'll come back.'

'In that case—' With some trouble, Richard controlled his temper. 'Getting evidence is a simple matter. Leave Erskine to do it. I'll help. There is no need whatever for you to stay. If you are perfectly sure, we can deal with him, if need be, without a trial.'

'A plain killing? No, I won't have that, Richard. He was born into gall like a fly in an oak tree. He tried quite hard to get free.'

Richard was sarcastic. 'Like the Cornishman?'

There was silence from the bed. Then Lymond said, 'O'LiamRoe was in danger most of the time he was here, largely because someone took him for me. You know about Abernaci. He has friends, a man called Tosh among them. Wherever O'LiamRoe went, Tosh or someone else or several of them followed. They were only needed once, in an ambush one night at Blois here. The Cornishman was one of the band who attacked O'LiamRoe. He killed two of Tosh's men.'

Richard said carefully, 'A little dangerous then, surely, for the Cornish wrestler to show himself here again?'

'The only person who saw him was a man who later died. He came last night to rid himself of me, too. I didn't challenge him.'

For a second, Richard didn't see it. Then he said sharply, looking into Francis's quiet face, 'How could he know that you were concerned?'

His brother smiled. 'Because Robin Stewart knows who I am. Obviously. Why else should he poison me?'

Obviously. Richard said evenly, 'How did he find out?'

'Stewart? It's a long story. We had to make it easy for him, in the end. He isn't very clever, you know. If you are interested, we sent Stewart on a pretext to the Keeper's lodging, where Tosh shattered his simple faith by revealing that Thady Boy had been in the galleys. This was not only suspicious and alarming, but it linked up with an incident at Aubigny where his lordship had made a graceful reference to the Master of Culter as a provincial ex-galley slave. Don't let it disturb you. It is, after all, true. That; and we let Stewart pick up a wood block Abernaci had made with the Culter arms on it. I hope friend Robin assumes it is a commission. . . . The block has a certain rough vigour, by the way. You should get Abernaci to sell it to you.'

It had been a long journey from Scotland, and he had not slept very well last night. Raising a hand, Richard rubbed his tired eyes. Then he dropped it and said, 'You *wanted* Stewart to find out who you were?'

'I thought I did,' said Lymond, a tinge of irony in his voice, and paused. After a moment he went on. 'I knew, you see, that he was trying to kill Mary, and he had to be stopped. The supposition was that he would come to me. Or lead us to any accomplice he had. Or at worst, leave the country. In fact, what he did was go straight back to the Keeper's lodging, steal some poison, and attempt to rescue his self-respect by dosing my hippocras . . . I must say I hadn't quite bargained for deadly nightshade. An error of judgment. Sown east and west at the wrong time of the moon. Although to be fair, Stewart did come to me before administering the poison, but O'Liam-Roe came in at the wrong moment and matters went astray. Not O'LiamRoe's fault either. I didn't have my wits about me, or I should have expected it.'

Solid, intent, Richard did not lift his eyes from his brother's face. 'You say you *knew* that Stewart was attempting to injure the Queen?'

'Oh, well,' said Lymond slowly, 'it had been a strong possibility for a long time. Margaret Erskine may have told you about the poisoned cotignac. During Jenny's little weekly escapades, she dismissed her own guard on that door. Anyone could have got in during the six weeks or so the stuff was there, and smothered it in arsenic. But no one easier than an Archer of the King's own personal Bodyguard. The arsenic for that, Richard, was stolen at St. Germain. Apart from the Queen and the Dauphin, whom we can exclude, and Pellaquin, whom Abernaci trusts absolutely, only six people were admitted to the menagerie that morning before the theft—Condé, St. André and his wife, Jenny and her son and Sir George Douglas. And—Abernaci forgot in his reckoning—Robin Stewart, who had of course called earlier to warn Abernaci of our visit.

'Now, the next real attempt was at the cheetah hunt . . . I assume they have also told you about that. The Queen's pet hare was carried to the field and released by someone travelling with the hunt, during a pause before the final run. Of all the people I've mentioned, only Stewart and St. André were both at the menagerie and at the hunt; and St. André was in full view adjusting a girth during the entire wait. Besides, neither St. André nor his wife has any real motive. He is doing better under the present régime than he could hope to do anywhere else; he has nothing to gain.

'But Stewart could have organized the fire-raising at the first inn we stayed at. He could have stolen the arsenic. Only Madame de Valentinois and a few huntsmen and he knew before the hunt that the cheetah would be brought—I made enquiries and found that, as indeed he hinted, the silly fellow, he had suggested the cat. So who else could have known to arrange for the hare on that day too? And finally, he was exactly the man I should have looked for: hard-working, friendless, restless, miserable; longing for Elysian fields of power and admiration, and getting very little return from his present duties and masters. The news we gave him the other day at the Keeper's lodging through Tosh would have meant nothing to Stewart unless he already knew that a man called Francis Crawford was here secretly, and why. So that by stealing that poison from Tosh, he actually gave us the final proof of his guilt. . . . Anyway, he has gone.'

The conclusion was unavoidable. Richard had felt it in his bones all along. 'Therefore,' he said slowly, 'if the Cornishman really meant to kill you . . . someone else must have sent him?'

Lymond had both elbows on his updrawn knees, his forehead on his wrists. Studying the mattress, he said, 'Robin Stewart isn't a leader, he's a web looking for a spider. He found one. A man who wants to kill Queen Mary and who thought O'LiamRoe was me. He knows differently now. What's more, with any luck, he knows that the Cornishman spoke to me before he died.'

There was a pause. 'He spoke all right,' said Lymond shortly. 'He had to. He thought his breastbone was going. He told me all he knew so that I would spare his life.'

In Richard's ears there sounded again the click, the dry snapping of bone, as the Cornishman's neck was broken. 'Clumsy fellow that I am,' his brother had said, and laughed. Flatly, Lord Culter asked, 'And what did you learn?'

'Nothing,' said Lymond, and laughed unguardedly, lifting his head. 'Oh, God, I'm going to be sick again. Nothing. *That's why I had to kill him.*'

There followed a silence. The man in the bed was holding his breath, his head averted on his crossed arms, his muscles hard. He had always been able to drink without showing it: the whole furnishing of his body must be in rags. Richard waited grimly, keeping perfectly still. How often did this kind of thing happen? And how could he possibly take his place at Court in this state?

Answering the unspoken thought, Lymond spoke without moving. 'It's mostly only at night. Then the soles of my feet come up like Empedocles' sandals. Guts six shillings the dozen.' He had apparently got himself under control. Richard waited a moment, then said, 'You were telling me that Robin Stewart had an employer, and that the employer thinks you learned something that matters from the Cornishman. Therefore he will try to kill you again. And that is why you are waiting in France. The turtle dove bound in the ivy. Your favourite role.' In spite of himself, his helpless anger was showing.

The Queen Dowager's eminent observer replied reasonably, as he had done throughout. 'Tell me another way.'

There was a handkerchief rolled tightly in Lymond's left hand, which he had used to stifle the coughing. With a brusque movement, his brother pulled it away, and wordlessly flattened it between his brown, capable fingers. In streaks and patches, the linen was stiff with fresh blood. 'Dear God, Francis,' said Richard Crawford, his voice suddenly stifled by the agony in his throat. '—Dear God, dear God, what do you want of me? Must I choose between my own child and you?'

He stopped. The silence stretched on. After the first moment of shock, Lymond's face was unreadable. But his voice when he spoke was deliberate and undramatic. 'I have promised to ride in the Mardi Gras procession two weeks from now. On the following day, I shall go home. Will that do?'

Richard did not at first reply. Whatever he had expected, it was not a surrender, clean and complete, of this sort. In three sentences, Francis had abandoned his mission, his hopes of trapping a murderer, his justification for killing a man waiting for mercy. It was a brutal gift, and one which, without compunction, Lord Culter meant to accept.

Considering Lymond, flat now on the bed in wordless communion with the ceiling, Richard spoke. 'My dear, you are only a boy. You have all your life still before you.'

On the tortoise-shell bed, his brother did not move. But there was no irony for once in his voice when he answered. 'Oh, yes, I know. The popular question is, For what?'

*   *   *

Mardi Gras was two weeks away. Next day, the Queen Dowager and all her train moved off to Amboise. Shortly afterwards Thady Boy, a little less noisy than usual, crossed the bridge too, to call on Mistress Boyle and her niece Oonagh at Neuvy. The aunt was away, but relatives and house guests, as usual, filled the rooms. After laying before them, like cherries, all the gossip of Blois, entering into a satisfactory, hard-drinking argument with a party of guests and skilfully avoiding a meal, Thady got Oonagh O'Dwyer to himself; or she got him.

'Well?' They were in the little oratory, their voices echoing from the cut stone, their clothing coloured by the handsome windows. There was an organ he had to see.

'A pet of a lady,' said Thady gratifyingly, of the organ. 'See you to the bellows, now, while I try her.'

Oonagh O'Dwyer did not stir. She had ridden that afternoon, letting the wind whip her coiling black hair, and had left it to hang free, silky-swinging on her furred brocade. She said, 'And so Phelim O'LiamRoe has gone. You had better luck with that fellow than I had.'

Thady Boy's face, looking up from the keys, was innocently clear. 'He disliked me more,' he said gravely. 'A stout child, O'LiamRoe. Between us, maybe, we did him a little good. Is there any message you have I should tell to him?'

Her lips parted, but she did not speak. Instead, she stepped up on the platform and taking the bellows, glanced at him through the glittering pipes. 'You are going home, then?'

'By Shrove Tuesday. I haven't put my two hands round my mouth with the news as yet. Indeed, formal leave-taking is a thing I don't care for. Explanations are far better left unsaid. Faix, girl, it's a positive organ. Your blowing would be just fine for a standpipe of mice.' And as, irritated, she gave the two bellows a sudden, bad-tempered beating, he put one finger hard on the keys.

An acute, tinny buzz, mercilessly sustained, seared at her nerves. She sat back on her heels, bellows loosed, as the sound drily expired. They eyed one another. Thady, hatless in a soiled concoction of yellow, performed a silent arpeggio up and down the dumb keys, and launched into a memorable parody of the chapel organist's politely faded technique. After watching judicially for a while, she gave him air for it. The organ sang out, filling the church, while she looked down at his hands on the keys and the sliders.

She had known he could play. She knew also, or guessed, how much of his mind it occupied. As, abandoning parody, he wandered abstractedly through quiet passages, some familiar, some not, Oonagh, facing him beyond the lead barrier of the pipes, her hands ceaselessly working, said, 'Do you imagine, now, that Robin Stewart will ever come back?'

Unhurried, Thady Boy played two bars of a lament. 'I do not, the silly creature that he is. I told him myself he had every reason to get

213

out of France.' Two used blue eyes looked at her over the smallest pipes. 'Is it pining you are?'

The air died on him. A silence fell, explicit of impatience and anger; then, whistling an air of supplication under his breath, Ballagh changed his fingering and accompanied himself on the silent keys until, relenting, she pumped again. 'I thought,' he said above it, 'that with O'LiamRoe gone, there might be hope for me.'

The melody hesitated, then acquired such volume that the silver candlesticks rang. 'Where you're concerned,' said Oonagh O'Dwyer, 'O'LiamRoe gone makes no difference at all.'

'Does it not, so?' Thady Boy was unperturbed. 'Strange news, my dear. You are moving in high circles, it seems.'

She did not answer. For a time, he played and she pumped in the thought-filled silence. The little, arched room was empty; though beyond the robing room and out in the passages the normal stir of the household could be heard. The quick notes of the organ ran about the oratory, over the white stone and the Ghent tapestries and the polished wood, then vanished all at once. She had the bellows still working automatically in her fists, but Thady Boy had taken his hands from the keys and was watching her in the wheezing silence.

Her arms were aching, and she knew that the red showed, rising, under her thin skin. She rose, standing over him from the advantage of the table. 'And we are to lose all this steaming banquet of wit? Why so set on leaving us now?'

Thady Boy, sideways on his stool, was hugging his knees. 'As the song says, "A grey eye looks back towards Erin; a grey eye full of tears." 'Tis a queer thing, for a creature so silly, but there's a craving on me that won't be gainsaid, to set eyes once again on Robin Stewart. On Ash Wednesday I go; and between now and then is all the time left for this great land to produce its best to impress me. Would you say,' said Thady, his eyes bright, 'that I have a chance of being impressed?'

Her hands on either side of the gilded posts, she looked at him with a closed face. 'I cannot say.'

'Can you not?' said Thady Boy, and reaching up, freed her wrist-lace from a beading. 'It's no manner of use, is it? What a pity.'

She snatched her boy's hand away, and unaided sprang down from the platform. He rose. 'I told you. O'LiamRoe made no difference,' said Oonagh. Facing him, she was breathing fast from the jump. 'Do you think I haven't escorts enough? That I can't take my pick, then? I hear there's a fine lord come to Court now, rich as they are made, to take his young brother back home. Nursemaids must come dear in Scotland these days.'

Thady's hand on the keyboard didn't move. 'He will succeed, no doubt,' he said, a small thread of amusement barely kept out of his voice. ''Tis a dour race for certain sure, but his lordship is a tolerable specimen, with a taste for Irishwomen, withal. You might do worse than trust yourself to that one.'

If he had expected to bring her into the open, he failed. Her eyes were contemptuous. 'That's a futile custom if you like. Lord Dung-hill's heir is never plain Billy Dunghill, but the Master of this, or the Master of that. Lord Culter's heir, I believe, is called the Master of Culter, who cannot even master himself.'

Francis Crawford, once Master of Culter, pondered a moment on this piece of sarcasm. At length, gravely—'A pity,' he agreed. 'But people do make allowances. And after all, the Master of Culter, my darling, is lying there in his cradle at Midculter, just seven weeks old.'

He had risen as he spoke, and lingered, smiling angelically at the arched door, now opened. 'So whatever you do,' Thady Boy said, carefully explanatory, his smile sweeter than ever, 'it makes no odds to the Culters, you see.' And turning, he went.

The door closed. Tight-faced, Oonagh O'Dwyer watched it; and heard nothing until a blow took her, like the clap of a shovel, first on her right cheek and then her left, rocking her back among the spindly gilt stools. 'You greedy, beef-witted slut,' said Theresa Boyle from behind her, her face blotched, her hair wild. 'Did I bring you here to come jolly into your season at the first taste of a man?' The loud, able, jocular figure of the Porc-épic at Dieppe had quite gone. But in Mistress Boyle's face, with its vizored teeth, its reddened, weather-glazed skin, its staring eyes, its grey spiky hair about the strong jaws, there was visible the brisk malice of the cheetah hunt on the day that the little hare died.

It was, obviously, a foray in what had been a long battle, with sores on each side. Oonagh, recovering with a twist of her body, laid her hand to the altar and would have retorted, violently, with one of the candlesticks had not her aunt caught her wrist. Oonagh said, in a strange voice like thin foil, 'I should be careful.' Then, after a moment 'You have the mind of a cockroach. If anything pulls us down in the mire, it will be you. I told that fellow nothing. You would hear that, devil mend you, since you were listening.'

'I was watching also,' said Theresa Boyle. 'And my two eyes gave me news. It was a fine welcome, that, after the journey I have had.'

Released, the younger woman sat down; then, finding the candle-stick still in her hands, replaced it. 'You went to see our honourable friend?'

'I did.'

'And he knows that Ballagh is Crawford of Lymond?'

'Naturally he knows. He sent a message for you.'

Oonagh's eyes, frowning, were on the strong, embattled mouth. 'Why for me?'

Mistress Boyle laughed, a familiar, wholehearted screech. 'Did you get comfortable with the notion that I would take all the blame? "Oonagh O'Dwyer deceived me," he says. "Oonagh O'Dwyer let me believe that Lymond and Phelim O'LiamRoe were one and the same man. She deceived me unwittingly, she says. Then let her prove it, by God."'

There was a short silence. Oonagh said, 'How?'

Smiling, Theresa Boyle turned, and with a broad, horsewoman's hand, slapped the wood of the organ. An uneasy sound, muffled and metallic, answered back. 'Thady Boy Ballagh will be dead in two sennights.'

'The plan is to go on?' The oval, pale-skinned face showed nothing now.

'The plan to deal with your musical friend is to go on. And if you warn Master Ballagh, or divert him, or if he escapes in any way, whether with your help or not, you and our cause, Oonagh O'Dwyer, are both lost.'

The broad, brown fingers with their grained nails were lying spread on the keys. Oonagh glanced at them; then rising, turned to the door. 'What are we now?' she said bitterly, opening it to the warm bustling world just outside. 'We and our cause?'

II

Amboise:

An Accident Happens

If a sensible adult brings a horse to the structure and an accident
happens, a fine according to the nature of the case is due from
the sensible adult.

CHARACTERISTICALLY, the plan to brush Lymond finally
from the path was so expensive, so wasteful and so baroque that
no one guessed it or anticipated it, and Francis Crawford himself was
neither warned nor, certainly, diverted.

He had not, patently, told his brother all he knew, and Richard
did not press it, trusting to his promise that in two weeks he would be
gone. In Scotland Lord Culter was known, with cause, as a good man
to find beside you in trouble. He took from the Erskines' willing
shoulders the burden of safeguarding the Queen and set a watch on
all Lymond's movements.

Of this last, Lymond was ignorant. They met once, on the eve of
Richard's departure for Amboise, long enough for the ollave to
observe, in passing, 'You may relax, my dear, No elixir à successions
as yet in my soup.' He looked magnificently lightheaded, trapped in
his own image like a fighting fish attacking a mirror. After that, they
did not meet for two weeks.

The Scottish Queen Dowager's sojourn at Amboise, together with
her son and daughter and their attendants and all her seething parcel
of nobles, was an expedient hit upon largely by the Queen of France
and the Constable for several excellent reasons, the first being the
anomalous and burgeoning presence of Jenny Fleming at court. This
removed her from the physical presence of the royal household, if not
from its delighted thoughts. Catherine was sleeping for Maecenas,
and nobody else.

A second consideration had to do directly with George Paris's
errand to fetch Cormac O'Connor, and with a little uneasiness
growing in Blois over the less disciplined of the Scottish Dowager's

noblemen. And lastly, having interviewed Richard Crawford and found him uncompromising, uncomplicated and personally likable, Catherine de Médicis had been content to dismiss him to Amboise with his Queen and a discreet observer to hand. Anonymous advice was always better investigated, but Lord Culter's presence in France seemed unlikely to bring either profit or anxiety to the crown, and the letter which inspired it came, no doubt, from some private malice.

In this Queen Catherine was right. She was also right in guessing the incident closed, although she could hardly know why. For motives all her own, the Queen Dowager had forestalled Lymond's suggestion and had granted Sir George Douglas what he wanted: the earldom of Morton for his son. Sir George had enjoyed thanking her in suitable terms, but had not so far made the decision public, even to his closest relative in France, since he took pleasure in encouraging Lord d'Aubigny's occasional mild hysteria on the ingratitude of princes. It amused him to listen to his lordship comparing with acrimony the rewards brought him by a life of devotion to the arts, and the attention being showered by the Court of France on the head of Thady Boy Ballagh.

Sir George, too, had noted how, during all those wild weeks of festivities that lasted from Candlemas up to Shrove—the revels, the pageants, the masques and the balls, the baiting and tournaments and battles of oranges—the gay, crude libidinous life of the private parlour and supper table began to lick at the stiff, sugary edges of etiquette.

The Vidame de Chartres arrived, fresh from conquests in London, where he had spent half a year, along with d'Enghien among others, as nominal hostages for France's final payments on Boulogne. D'Enghien and d'Aumale had put in a formal few months, made the most of the festivities, and had come home. The Vidame had stayed, to charm the young King, to entice the Marquis of Northampton's handsome wife, to attend weddings, give banquets and visit Scotland, as he pleased.

The Vidame, an ally of Mary of Guise, called on her at Amboise and Châteaudun, and entertained the rest of the Court with tales of his boudoir. He also cast his large, practised brown eyes on d'Enghien's new ami, and gently made himself known to Master Ballagh.

However tumultuous the ungartered life of the Court, the old King had never allowed vulgarity to penetrate the Throne Room. Now, under the debilitating impact of Thady Boy and the relaxations of the season, affairs were being made to wait which could not wait, or were going by default. The historic half-cast of political frivolity in the fine eye of France had become something like blindness.

It was a bad February. Although never doubting that Lymond would keep his word, Richard had said nothing of it to the Erskines,

218

to Lady Fleming or to the Queen Mother. This was a promise undertaken to his brother. With Lymond gone, and the Special Ambassador due home very shortly, the mantle of protector would have to fall on himself, and he knew well that the Queen Mother was as anxious for him to go back to Scotland as he was to return. It would go badly against the grain to keep him here in France to look after young Mary. But whom else could she trust? Moreover, he had no illusions about the danger. The assassin, if he still remained, knew quite well who Thady Boy was. All he had to do was transfer the attack to Thady Boy's brother.

Richard understood that all this would be even clearer to Francis. Hence the guard. His flourish of renunciation notwithstanding, Lymond would, his brother knew, use every means in his power to provoke an attack during these two weeks, keeping silent, even to his patrons, about his impending departure. And until Lymond was out of the way, the small Queen was probably safe.

In fact, the days passed and no attack was made on Queen or ollave. Marguerite, the two Bourbons, St. André, the Vidame, the young de Guises and their wives and the bright fraternity of the Archers nursed, scolded, and encouraged to fresh excesses the fuelless blaze which was Thady Boy Ballagh, living tumour-sick on his nerves. Then, without warning, came the message he was waiting for.

It reached him at eight o'clock on a raw night on the Saturday before Shrove, when dressed in John Stewart of Aubigny's mask and a cloak of green feathers, he rode with a party of twenty Aztecs and as many Turks led by his lordship to the inn on the Isle d'Or, outside Amboise.

That day, the jousting had ended early because the King had an attack of toothache. It was the only ailment which ever troubled him, and he met it as always with the frightened anger of the robust. The afternoon's revels were cancelled, and the Court was left disguised in turban and feathers with a collective explosion of unused energy to let off.

The day had been reasonably fair. Mounted on their heterogeneous coursers and cobs, robes flapping, feathers streaming, gourds rattling aloft, the two jousting teams, Turks and Aztecs, flew calling along the Amboise road, jumping, chasing, belabouring one another, ducking the discourteous in the flat Loire and drying them with gold pieces. It was dusk when they came to the first leg of the double bridge over the Loire, and crossing to the little island in the middle, stormed into the Sainte Barbe for hot food and wine. Astounded by the costumes but flattered by the presence of all these young lords, the staff fled to obey. Thady Boy threw his mask on a table, drank a solid tankard of strong wine straight off, and led the rendering of a new song he had just devised. Then, the pain not deadening at all, he waited until all eyes were on the Vidame, in feathers, attempting a clog dance, and wandered restlessly outside.

It was a still night and very dark, with a thin, wet mist rising grey from the river and turning yellow in the window lights from the two bridges to right and to left. Behind, the roof of St. Sauveur showed black, and there were lights in the cottages grouped round the inn, showing fitfully the strip of white beach and the water parting, smooth, oily and black, round the creaming shoal of the isle.

The mist hid the far shore. He could see only the spires of St. Florentin and St. Denis, the tops of the town wall, its towers and the belfry, with all the huddled chimneys within. The outline of tiled roofs slid down into the misty cleft of the River Amasse, then emerged on the far side as a great bastion of rock, overlaid and braided and terraced by the cameo-like intricacies of the King's castle of Amboise. Above the fog, the ranking windows were lit, and the trees in the long garden glimmered with lanterns. The Queen Dowager was in residence.

It was cold. Lymond wondered prosaically if he were going to faint; and again, with clinical interest, whether his health would give out before either the term of his promise or the assassin completed the task.

The shiver of metal, striking sweet on the ear, revived him like cold water. He wore his sword, as usual, on his skin dress. Drawing it, he slid from the white wall and felt the stable hard at his back as another chink, this time of spurs, sounded to one side. He had his hand on the stable door when the crack of swordplay shatteringly broke out in front.

Lymond stopped breathing. Somewhere in the dark, the spurred unknown, abandoning silence, drew his sword with a whine and thrust past, his footsteps sharp and light on the small cobbles. A man shouted, then bit it off, and in the inn someone opened a shutter, solving the problem instantly with a latticed trapeze of bright light. In a corner of the stableyard a small man, heavily muffled and splashed to the hatbrim, fought for his life against two others, one of whom wore spurs.

The same light fell on Thady Boy. As the inn door banged open and his shadow sprang black on the loosebox door, the small man cried again. They had him by the collar by then, his sword gone when Lymond reached them, his skin boots making no sound, and threw the spurred man off with a twist to the shoulder that made him gasp. The other turned too; and in the second of grace, the beleaguered traveller ducked, twisted and ran.

The attackers took one step to follow, and then halted as Lymond just above the threshold of sound, requested them searingly to stand still. Voices came from the inn door. Someone shouted, and someone else answered. There was a pause, as the silent night was consulted. Then, without troubling to hunt unduly for trouble, the speakers went in. The door banged, and shortly after the shutters closed, plunging the yard into darkness.

'*Now?*' said Lymond. 'Jockie's Rob from Hartree and Fishy James from Tinto. Lord Culter's orders?'

The broad feet on the cobbles didn't shufflle; merely remained stolidly firm. 'Yes, sir.'

'You imagine,' said Francis Crawford of Lymond, 'that something five feet two inches tall with a rapier is going to disturb my pattern of life?'

'No, Master. That's to say—' Jockie's Rob was peevish enough to make that point. 'No, sir.' He didn't need the warning pressure of Fishy James on his arm. The small, soft edge on the dressed-up man's voice was enough. He had rarely met the younger one, back at Midculter, but he had heard about him. It beat him how the Master . . . how young Crawford knew their names.

'Well,' said Lymond pleasantly. 'You'd better find him for me, hadn't you?'

In the darkness, they looked at one another, and got no support. 'For to question?' hazarded Fishy James weakly, at length.

'In order,' said Lymond smoothly, 'to apologize. And to receive from him, if he is now in any condition to give it, the message he has come here expressly to deliver.'

They found him in the horse box, quiet under the straw. He had a thin cut on one shoulder. Lymond dressed it while his two protectors, strangely subdued, kept lookout. Then, soothed, comforted and assuaged with linen and gold, the traveller made his succinct report.

'Landfall safely at Dalkey, sir, the Prince of Barrow leaving direct for his home. Mr. Stewart accompanied Mr. Paris to O'Connor's house, but O'Connor was away. They split two ways to find him, and after a while Mr. Paris comes back unsuccessful, having found out O'Connor is in the far north, and not due back for a week. Mr. Stewart didn't come back at all.'

'He was still searching for O'Connor?' Lymond's voice was merely disposing of an improbability.

'No. He had taken a post-horse and got a ship. Mr. Paris thought he was making probably for Scotland. Then—'

'Then—?' said Lymond, and all the sharpness had left his voice.

'Mr. Paris found that another ship had put in, off Dublin itself this time, and taken The O'LiamRoe on board, with a great trumpeting and bonnet-sweeping and twittering from the poop deck. There was a row of soldiers on the jetty to see himself off, and the sea gulls

221

saluting their breastplates, it was a scandal to see. And O'LiamRoe in his best silken suit, an honoured guest.'

'—Bound for London,' said Lymond suddenly, hilariously, his blue eyes alight in the dark.

'—Bound for London,' agreed George Paris's messenger sourly.

*   *   *

As always now, the reaction was almost more than he could bear. It took a major effort of will, after the messenger had gone and he had dispatched his brother's two abashed nursemaids, to return to the inn for the drink which would smother it and let him go on. When he got there, braced for the buffeting jocularity which would greet his return, Francis Crawford found a fresh idea had already caught fire.

St. André had challenged the Prince of Condé, who led the Aztecs against the Turks, to swim his team from the Isle d'Or to Amboise: a challenge which, if you knew the currents under that smooth river, added an intriguing new chapter to the story of the key and the Marshal de St. André's wife.

To this Lord d'Aubigny, leader for the day, had added refinements. The route was to be reversed. Mexicans and Turks, heralded by a nearly sober young captain with curling hair, would seek admission to the King's castle of Amboise, would foregather at the top of the Tour des Minimes, and racing down the spiral carriage ramp for which the Tower was famous, would debouch over the drawbridge on to the shore and across the near arm of the river to finish midstream at the Isle d'Or, where they now were.

The nearly sober young captain, who had to ingratiate himself with the Queen Dowager and the King's commander, had gone; and to keep him nearly sober, an Archer called André Spens had gone with him.

In due course the rest of the grotesque party followed too, howling, over the second bridge, Thady Boy in the thick of them. He was not, by then, thinking very clearly, part of his mind being distantly occupied with analysing the significance of what he had just learned. Another part, philosophically, recognized that the crisis he had been waiting for was probably on him, and that he had sent his brother's men home. The rest of him did not care; for by then he was blessedly, exceedingly drunk.

He retrieved the mask from Lord d'Aubigny who seemed, with reason, to have lost his fancy for it, and tried and failed to order his vagrant senses as they rode up the incline from the bridge and through the Lion Gate into the castle.

By then, the mist had risen higher, glooming off the dark river like pillowed figures. Mattresses of fog lay round the castle and behind them the lanterns showed faded, with cannibal rainbows, hazy

222

and parched, all around them. Below, the river stirred, black and sluggish in the raw night air.

But no one crossed the Loire swimming that night. The tragedy happened in the castle itself, where all the Scottish Court gathered under the great awning outside the King's lodging to watch the cavorting, careless delinquents of the King of France's train.

The two processional towers of Amboise, up which carts and gun carriages could crawl, climbing the steep, cobbled slope, winding round and round a newel post itself nearly thirty feet wide, could take four horsemen abreast on its slopes. Tonight, it was empty. All down the steep ramp, coiling from palace to shore, torches flared beside the tall windows, night-black slits in the twelve-foot walls, hung with arras, and the fog, curling up from the river, past the convent, filling the moat, drifting smokelike through the wide, crested door, climbed the damp walls below with soft fingers.

At the top, the horses jostled in the wide courtyard, lining up, breaking line and reforming. The still-lanterns made fireflies of their jewels; the cloaks swung, hissing, like thick-winged birds; a scimitar flashed; the awning cords, draught-borne, lifted weblike as quipus; a conch blew, and St. André's face, earringed and turbaned, melted in the queer, slanting glare into an eminently fungoid growth, throwing disjointed shadows.

Richard, watching in silence beside the Queen Mother, his face disciplined to be still, saw the Vidame, nearly too drunk to ride, thickly rallying his forces; Laurens de Genstan, heavily scented in red brocade, groping for his gelding's dropped reins; Lord d'Aubigny, half wishing himself elsewhere and half pleased to be exercising his higher sensibilities; and last, merging into the night, an odd and gruesome mask at his saddlebow, the slack form of his brother being thrust forward to Condé's green feathered side.

A handkerchief was raised. As it went up, Lymond turned, vaguely, towards the faceless body of Scots and raised a hand in a perfunctory wave. In the obscure light his face was both fuddled and strained, as it had been two weeks ago in his room. He looked half-stupefied; but impulsively Richard waved back. Then the white linen dropped, and the surging body of horsemen leaped for the ramp of the Tour des Minimes.

Like heifers pouring, knee on shoulder, through the Martinmas hurdle, like dolphins soaring, back under belly, in a jubilant pack, like Aztecs, like Muslems, like rich and wanton young men, the horsemen choked the wide gateway and rushed over the lip, manes, hair, cloaks flying, to drop down the steep slope of the ramp.

Crushed by flank, saddle and stirrup, rough-dragged by the stone wall, jamming the broad spiral from wrenched arras to arras, the riders flowed down, skidding, struggling in a sluggish miasma of damp and ordure and sweat. And as the open night flashed behind them, and the thick walls curled, and the high, groined roof whirled twisting from their feet to their heads, the noise deadened all thought.

Unknowing, every man shouted. Bits clinked, harness jangled, horses neighed; hooves, striking out, clashed on stone or metal or flesh and rattled fiery on the cobbles below, knitting with their own echoes a mesh of unendurable sound to drive the mind mad. In the lead was an Archer, followed by Condé and de Genstan. Thady Boy came next, riding by instinct in the tumbling avalanche; and d'Enghien, who had been watching him, pressed to his side. The Vidame and St. André followed, and a dozen others. D'Aubigny, his handsome face concentrated, flew with the remainder behind.

Already, stumbling, slipping, thrust over-violently from the way, some riders were down. As the staircase unwound, yellow, hazy with fog and smoke, steeper and steeper, faster and faster, impelled by the loosening fabric of their numbers, by the ramrod of impetus, the wild young blood of France on its splendid horseflesh flew like peacocks, short-reined, teeth bared, saddleback hard on the spine, the thick air swirling at their backs.

The rope was stretched across before the last bend. Laurens de Genstan, leading, could never have known why he fell. His hands spread, he was hurled sideways, one foot still trapped and hit the wall with an impact whose violence, in that inferno of sound, was all in mime. He died, his powdered face shining with blood; but his horse lived to kill the next man who hurtled downhill into his great, threshing shoulders and his iron foot. Then, like a torrent lipping a rock, the oncoming horses smashed uprearing against the heaving barrier of the fallen, and fell broken and sliding down the ramp.

Among them, his reins running hot through d'Enghien's snatching hands, was Francis Crawford of Lymond: crashing, rolling, sliding to lie broken-slack, a mess of scarlet-stained feathers, like a week-old kill in some queer, spiral mews.

In the falling douche of horse and humanity, the torches in one entire volute of the stair had gone out, abandoning it to night and the white fog. Piled like marionettes, splintered men on broken horse, the last were luckiest except for those, rushing down in the dark, who somersaulted over the thick and struggling mass and slid below, ricocheting and crumbling at each bend. The debris, human and material, stretched downhill a long way.

Richard was among those who, in the flickering hazed light of new torches, began the heart-stopping work of rescue from above and from below. Richard saw them all taken up, one by one; dragged, carried, laid on improvised stretchers. St. André, the precious St. André, had fallen soft, cushioned by a rival's green feathers and the dead rump of a horse, and had a gashed leg; that was all. The

Vidame, groaning, was taken off half-unconscious with a broken collarbone and a wrenched knee. De Genstan was dead. D'Aubigny was unconscious, his clothes bloodstained, but his pulse was steady; d'Enghien also was badly bruised, but otherwise safe. The Prince of Condé had fallen nimbly enough, but had been crushed twice, once by his horse and then by St. André's. His hip was broken, and one of his arms; whatever else could not be learned, as he fought off any effort to help him, half-unconscious and screaming. Two more men were taken out, their faces covered. Richard bent over them both, and lifted the cloths. Both were strangers.

At some point, Tom Erskine had appeared at his side. As, one by one, the horses were dragged off and killed and the riders in all their blood-soaked disguises were pulled and shifted, Richard and he worked unsparingly, looking always for one man. More torches were brought. They lit what was best left unlit: the sodden marc of the avalanche; the horsemen who had borne the full weight of the fall. It was Richard who knelt and took the dead hands in his, the unremarkable hands, square and bony and plump, cut by their own jewels, and then laid them each time gently back in their place.

The last horse was removed. Men with candles turned over the looming bundles of cloth, the cloaks, the horse trappings, the over-robes which littered the slopes, black and greasy with blood. The lackeys came out and gathered these up, and the Tour des Minimes was empty but for the fog and the blood: empty, although they visited it again, disbelieving, after climbing up to look again among the rows of hurt, of dying and of dead.

In the end, dirty, stained and exhausted, they and all Lymond's wild young disciples understood only one thing. Thady Boy Ballagh, who had been seen to fall hurt by half the riders about him, was no longer there.

Gone too was the man who, looking down at the death lying about him, had exclaimed, unheard in the uproar, contempt in his reflective, soft voice, '. . . *Ta sotte muse, avec ta rude Lyre!* The devil give you his bed now, Master Thady Boy Ballagh!'

*   *   *

Every doctor and every apothecary in Amboise was at the castle that night; and next day the Constable came too, sitting, thick-veined hands over straddled knees, listening to St. André's white-lipped account. For this time the assassins had been careless. The planned accident, the perfect picture of a chance stumble bringing inevitable result, had been destroyed at the very start by the fact that the murderers, frightened, had abandoned the trip rope stretched from side to side of the ramp.

225

While suspicion grew, faint and thickening like the river fog, Richard and Tom Erskine searched in vain for any trace of Thady Boy. With infinite care, preserving at all costs his masquerade, Richard visited the mahout Abernaci. The Keeper had been all night at Blois and knew nothing.

Then, five days after the disaster, Tosh appeared, pulling his donkey and trailing his ropes, and a group of Scotsmen, leaving thankfully behind them the makeshift hospital that was Amboise castle, walked down to the bridge where, watched by a throng, the lower end of one of the funambulist's great cables was being lashed.

Richard was not among them. It was George Douglas who after a while returned to his lodging, and catching Culter just back from one of his tiring, unexplained rides, said casually, 'Relax, my dear man. Your teeth will rattle like sounding-bones if you wear yourself out in this fashion. Leave your obscure pursuits and go and see Ouishart. He is quite a remarkable man. He ought to be wearing the mask instead of that unfortunate donkey. Quetzalcoatl, lord of the Toltecs.'

'The *donkey*'s wearing a mask?' This was, he knew, the Douglas method of imparting information; but even so, he felt himself redden with the shock. 'An Aztec mask, good God?'

Sir George smiled. 'A great, grinning thing in mosaic, with gold ears. It used to have inlays and teeth too, by the look of it, but someone's tried hard to smash it to bits. Presumably the donkey. Go and see it. You'll laugh.'

He went; but hardly to laugh. Struggling through the crowd, he found the grotesque thing, bound crudely to the beast's furry head, cracked and blackened with the glaze of some stain. It was the mask Lymond had had at his saddlebow, at the start of that fated night's race.

And Tosh's news, delivered with practised discretion, was disastrous. For he himself had found that much-advertised mask that morning—not in the castle, not in its precincts, not in the town of Amboise at all. He had found it in Blois, trampled underfoot by spectators like himself, in the crowded courtyard of Hélie and Anne Moûtier's empty house. And before him, a roaring torch, hidden in sheeted flame forty feet high, was the Hôtel Moûtier on fire.

No one could have entered then and lived. Tosh, after searching fruitlessly in the neighbourhod for any traces of Thady Boy, had sent messages to Abernaci and had set off himself to the Scottish Court at Amboise with the news, bearing the mask as his grim badge.

That night, Erskine used all his powers short of physical force to prevent Richard riding openly to Blois. And he kept vigil at his side as Lord Culter sat, sleepless before the red fire of his fine chamber at Amboise, trying to fathom the truth. Witness after witness among the riders in the Tower had told how Thady Boy had been injured. How then had he found his way from Amboise to the Hôtel Moûtier in Blois? Had he in fact gone there to hide? For if so, it seemed probable that he had died there, in that inexplicable fire.

III

Blois: Distress is not Released

For there are residences in which a distress is not released.
If carried into concealment, if carried into a wilderness, if
carried into a wood, if carried into a dark place; for these are
the residences of thieves and outlaws. Until every distress is
brought into light and manifestations, it is not released.

A VOICE, somewhere, was speaking. What it said was not easy
to follow. Indeed, thought the man in the bed, it would be stupid
to try. Beyond the barrier of understanding were wakefulness, frus-
tration, even pain: a world as remote as the remote, unremitting voice
which seemed to repeat itself, over and over again.

It was a voice no one could have called soothing, an impatient
voice, an acid voice even. 'Your eyes are open,' it said sharply. 'Look
at me. You can see. You can have opium again later, if you want. . . .'

That, thought the man in the bed sardonically, was kind. Memory,
pricked into action by pain, recalled vividly just what had happened
at the Tour des Minimes. Condé's horse, he remembered, had
plunged towards him as he fell. There had followed a series of
memorable impacts and, he had assumed, death.

He did not appear to be dead. His leg was splinted, and it hurt him
to breathe however, and there were bandages, he could feel, round
his ribs. Through the aftermath of strong drugs he could recognize
the irritating torpor of bloodlessness. God. Richard, or Tom Erskine,
or whichever waxen-faced nursemaid was going to patch him up this
time would have to work hard. . . . Sheer anger, sudden and life-
giving, fought with his weakness and mastered it. Explosively,
Francis Crawford of Lymond turned his head.

Above him, misty in a grey daylight, her hair like a veil, her own
eyes caught wide, was Oonagh O'Dwyer. Had he looked, he could
have seen his own reflection, startlingly, in her mirrored gaze. As it
was, the voice had stopped. For a breath or two, there was silence;
then she moved, and he saw a painted ceiling in the place where she
had been. Then, reflectively, she resumed somewhere out of his sight,
her movements sheathing and unsheathing her voice.

'And are you not the stubborn man to awake?' she said. 'And I
longing to know how it feels to be feeble, and in my debt?'

Oonagh O'Dwyer. And as she knew, he would meet that kind of challenge in any state short of dissolution itself. Pitching his voice for clarity and not for strength, 'To be vigorous and in your . . . debt would be nicer. Did you bring me here?' he said.

She came back and looked down, her voice crisp. 'I dislike being coerced. I decided that if you lived, I should bring you away. You were fortunate, lying near the foot of the Tower, and I had a boat waiting in the fog, and two to help me.'

'How long is it since then?'

'Have you really no idea?' She laughed. 'You have been helpless for five days, Mr. Crawford.'

Five days! His brain recorded the surprise, and then deadened under the thundering onslaught of pain. The room had gone again, and the face above him was queerly detached, the painted leaves filling her hair. But he met her contemptuous stare and held it as long as he could, until he began to cough, the iron stale in his throat, and the dark came quickly and coldly again.

*   *   *

The next time he woke to the light of a different day. The straps round his body were still in place; but the windows were wide on a sunlit balcony and the candles, sourly smoking, had been freshly doused. From the violent paradisaical dreams he remembered, and the heavy, throttled sense of incipient pain, he knew that the taper fumes had been used to keep him asleep.

The peace it had brought him was probably the best treatment his abused and broken body could have had. But it had been done, of course, for her own ends. Nothing had ever deceived Lymond about Oonagh O'Dwyer. He watched her now as she sat, unaware of him, by the fire where she and O'LiamRoe had talked before his own unforgivable serenade, her cheekbones shadowed, her high, full brow bright with clear light; the two fine half-arcs of sleeplessness, of high-tempered strain, like a tread in snow beneath her two eyes; her hard, mobile lips shut. He said, his voice carefully preserved, 'Who are you waiting for? Your aunt?'

Her hands closed together, a cage of white bone. Then, leaning back, she settled her gaze on the low, temporary bed, the bracing only visible in the brittle line of her jaw. Worn by solitariness and unconceded fears and an absence of sleep she was more than ever a beautiful woman with no time for beauty. She said, choosing her words this time with cold care, 'If it were, you would be dead.'

There was no sound from inside the house: no clanking of pails, no kitchen chatter, no footsteps on the stairs. It was an empty house, then, and her aunt did not know. Beyond the balcony, the cast of the rooftops was familiar. He thought of the Tour des Minimes and wondered what the tale of injured had been; but decided against wasting questions. He said, 'You and the gentleman attempting to kill me have parted company?'

Oonagh smiled. 'You might say that we disagreed on a minor point,' she said. 'But don't run away with the idea that you're going to be freed. For his purposes and mine you are as well imprisoned as dead; and what he doesn't know won't hurt him.'

Lymond lay still, trying to think. A long time ago, in Scotland, Mariotta had told him about Oonagh O'Dwyer. Even before Rouen and O'LiamRoe's shame in the tennis courts he had been wary; yet she had resisted every effort to draw her, while hardly troubling to conceal that she knew who Thady Boy was. The man she had wished out of the way had been O'LiamRoe. Robin Stewart and his master, too, had tried to assail O'LiamRoe in the belief that he was Lymond. She knew better, but she had not enlightened them.

But then, Stewart had been allowed to discover Lymond's identity and, it must be assumed, had told his principal; the accident at the Tour des Minimes had resulted. And Oonagh, who disliked coercion, and whose prevarication over O'LiamRoe had just come to light, knew of the scheme and had decided in advance, typically, not to save him . . . but to rescue him if he lived. So that the gentleman whose demands she resented, and Robin's master, were the same.

Who? She had not said. Think again. Her aunt did not know of the rescue. If he himself was lying, as he guessed, in the empty Hôtel Moûtier, Oonagh could not be free to come here very often. And the only servants of her own were an elderly maid and two grooms. She did not propose to risk freeing him, yet now he was awake, how could she keep him? Delicately he tried her. 'Are you not afraid that your gentleman friend will discover your act of mercy and even trace us both here? My disappearance from Amboise must have had its element of mystery. Dead bodies don't walk.'

'Sick people talk too much,' said Oonagh. 'And so do the habitually intemperate. The mind of my gentleman friend, as you call him, works on well-defined lines. He thinks you have disappeared, I would guess, because your own people have taken a step or two to protect themselves from exposure. He would think it an act of God in his favour.'

'Do I take it,' said Lymond, 'that he will transfer his attentions now to my brother?' He was not employing much finesse.

There was, he noted the briefest pause. Then she said, 'He is unlikely to move in any direction until he has traced Robin Stewart.'

And that meant that Stewart's disappearance had surprised his own principal, surprised and worried him. Was he afraid Stewart would betray him? Or had he merely been counting on Stewart to blame if any future scheme went wrong? And how had this unknown gentleman—God, he must beg this woman to tell him his name—how had he learned that Stewart had vanished?

The pain, drawing together its forces, began to concentrate in a kind of white haze. He said disingenuously, 'But Stewart, surely, should be due back by now?' and knew instantly, by her face, what her rejoinder would be. She smiled. 'Oh come, my dear. George Paris serves anyone who will pay him. Did you think your little interview at the Isle d'Or was going to be exclusive?'

Her voice was thin; the sunlight darkening. There was not much time. Sacrificing everything to precision, his voice spiderlike in his own ears, Lymond said, 'If this man is exposed, he will drag you down with him. If he is not, he will turn on you sooner or later in self-defence. Tell me his name and let me deal with him. This is my training and my vocation; and no one else can do it. I promise you that. Give me your discretion. You have a unique power. You can do something here and now that will give you in hundreds and thousands the posterity you will never have of your own. If you wait, you lose everything. I promise you that, too. And losing it, what will you be?'

She had risen as he was speaking, a lighted spar in her hand. Shielding it with her palm she crossed to one side of the pallet, then the other, and delicately lit the fine tapers. A sweet and sickly odour stirred in the room. Then she stood, head tilted, and looked at him, the heavy coiling black hair all bronzed by the light.

'. . . What shall I be? *Like Thady Boy Ballagh, surely,*' she said in her worn, bitter voice; and lying open-eyed and still under the smoke, Francis Crawford did not reply.

At the door, Oonagh turned. 'I would sooner let Phelim O'Liam-Roe deal with any secret of mine than I should entrust it to you. You will stay here until I bring someone to see you, and whatever he thinks fit will be done. If you escape to your Scottish friends, I shall inform the French King where you are. If you escape to your French friends, if you are seen abroad in the street, if you move from this room, you will be tried for heresy, theft and high treason. The catch-thieves have been searching Amboise and Blois for you since last week. Every boat leaving Nantes has been watched. They have indisputable proof that the trip-rope accident at the Tour des Minimes was conceived by you. They have found royal jewels in your room and are already questioning your identity. Even without further evidence, the slightest investigation into your credentials will be enough to have you hanged for a spy. A fascinating situation. Think it over next time you are awake. . . . Good night. Sleep well,' said Oonagh O'Dwyer.

She had made only one error. The news she had just given him roused nothing but a sense of challenge and an instant, reluctant

231

admiration. But what she had said just before had set free his cold, quick, terrifying temper. His legs and left arm were strapped down to the bed, but his right arm, slung because of the collarbone and wrist, was quite free. Violently, belabouring the pain for one instant back from his senses, he pulled the arm from its sling and struck the nearest torchère at his side as hard as he could.

It succeeded better than he had blindly hoped. The floor had been left piled thick with dry rushes. The oily tapers, rolling, bestowed a rosy carpet of fire which lit all the bright waxen wood, and the wrench of the cracked clavicle, sagging with its own weight, forced him, gasping, into blackness. Oonagh, no more than two steps from the door, saw the dark head buried in the dragged linen, the hand falling, lit by the fire. Then she screamed, once for her groom, and plunged back into the room.

The flashing pain, as they cut his strappings and dragged him free, roused him for a moment; and he opened his eyes on her angry, feverish face and laughed. Then they had him through the door. Behind, the room had become golden red, a fierce and beautiful monochrome, with detail of bed and chair and table, hangings and woodwork in frail skeletal tracery of gold on gold, red on red. The fire, as they came downstairs, was beginning to show on the ceiling below.

The house was built of wood, and so were many of its neighbours. Already the street was roused: from the burning balcony black smoke rolled over the courtyard. Outside, someone smashed the lock of the gates and, bucket in hand, ran for the well.

The house was supposed to be empty. Oonagh could not be found there with Lymond. Nor, carrying him, could they escape unobserved. Under cover of the thickening smoke they abandoned him near a door, in a wing untouched as yet by fire, with Oonagh's cloak for a blanket. In a heap, flung there where she brought him from Amboise, were the clothes he had been wearing that night. For a moment she checked, then picking up the Aztec mask she tossed it into the courtyard, to influence fate as it would. Then breathlessly she turned, and slipping through the thick smoke, escaped unseen with her servant to melt into the gathering crowds in the streets round about.

Behind her, Lymond lay still. Oddly, he could hear very well: a single, conscious sense left to him, like the threadlike limb of a crane fly, trapped under a stone. As he lay on the stone flags every sound from the courtyard reached him with great clarity: slippered feet running on the cobbles, the squeak of the pulley, the thin, silvery sound of spilled water jolting from a full pail. Voices shouting. Windows creaking. The rumble of a handcart bringing more water, at speed. A dog barking, very high and fluting, like an owl.

232

And near him, the hollow roar of the spreading fire, spitting and exploding on its fissile diet, extinguishing the home of Hélie and Anne Moûtier.

Just before the roof fell, two pillagers bolder than the rest managed to enter the Hôtel Moûtier from the back, and found what they took to be a fellow plunderer overcome by smoke. Kicked awake out of a simple curiosity, the stranger offered them what appeared to be an excellent proposition: a large sum of money in exchange for a private trip in their handcart to a certain address.

Since there was nothing worth taking, the two men lost no time in arguing; which was lucky for them. Between them they had no trouble in getting the fellow doubled up under sheets in the cart, and were trundling off down the packed street, away from the fire, just as Tosh, without seeing them, picked his way up it.

*　　　*　　　*

The house called Doubtance in the Rue des Papegaults had no signboard; its trade was well known.

Above the usurer occupying the ground floor, lived the Dame de Doubtance, of whom he was her keeper, some said, or her owner; an unredeemed pledge like the others which heaped and lined all his rooms, naked and mouldering like picked mice in an eyrie.

The Dame de Doubtance was old; but her private world was even older: the world of France three hundred years before when chivalry was in flower, and the troubadours sang. Moving, in her mediaeval robes, from books to lute to embroidery, she never emerged into the raw, humanist light of sixteenth-century Blois; but many people came visiting her for the out-of-the-way things she could tell them, if she chose. Sometimes, if she did not choose, they came stumbling down the steep stairs of Doubtance with a scratched arm or the graze of a thrown vase on one cheek. For she was not a mouse; but rather a tall, half-plumed predator, pale-spot eyes glaring, mouth flatly downturned into the jaw. And she had a temper.

The usurer Gaultier she never assaulted. Periodically, his clients repaired the deficiency. It was a risk of his trade. Small, opinionative, shrewd, he was no more rapacious than any merchant in Blois, and loved the rough and tumble of business with a passion almost Italianate. He also had a true eye for workmanship; and a fine piece of statuary, once in his hands, rarely found itself redeemed.

It was his treasures which he first thought, naturally, of saving, that grey February day when fire broke out at the top of the road. With his clerk and an apprentice to help, he began loading his wheelbarrow, stopping often to engage his clerk in raucous arguments about workmanship and costing. Soon the wheelbarrow was full and dispatched down the steep road to the river, already crowded with the womenfolk and possessions of the richer and wiser residents.

It was the only conveyance he had, and he could do nothing until it returned. Maître Gaultier went back alone to his dark nest of bric-à-brac and, fierce-eyed, began to cull his other favourites therefrom. As he emerged for the sixth time to his threshold, bearing a clock dear to his heart, he saw a miracle coming towards him in the flurried bustle of the street: a four-wheeled handcart, propelled by one heated individual and steadied by another, which bumped down the steep incline of the street, headed straight towards Doubtance and stopped flat beside Master Gaultier's astrolabe clock as if scenting its destiny.

Almost before the owners of the cart had pushed it into the fore-court and had uncovered and explained the unconscious man inside, Georges Gaultier had bought the cart and its contents and had dis-missed the disreputable pair. He had no time just then to consider the implications of what they told him, or even to do more than compare briefly the face of the man they had brought with a descrip-tion once given him by Archie Abernethy. The moneylender was accustomed to job lots. Drunk or not drunk, the less important item could wait. With a deft heave, Georges Gaultier removed the senseless man lumbering the bottom of his precious conveyance, and stowed him out of the way under the stairs to recover.

Stacking the handcart after that, Georges Gaultier from time to time looked all around him; he at least had no quarrel with his fellow men.

Once, imagining a stirring behind, he turned his head on his shoulder and said practically, for the benefit of anyone who might be listening, 'My friend, you will need to put on a better face than that before your wife sees you. If you go upstairs, Madame will clear the fumes from your head. The fire will only come this way should the wind change, and men walk faster than clocks.'

In the end, he snatched time from his labours to turn indoors, and grasping the man's singed and dusty cloak, lifted him six steps out of the way to the first quarter landing. The fellow opened his eyes. Master Gaultier grinned, and raising his pebbly voice, addressed the inhabitant upstairs. 'Madame! A visitor!'

They were the first coherent words Francis Crawford understood since leaving the burning house up the street. Dimly, he remembered the plunderers who had carried him out; the bargain he had made in the hope that Gaultier, knowing his history from Abernaci, might pay; the subsequent bumping journey in the cart to this house whose address Abernaci had given him, long ago. And now a voice, hoarse and offhand, bawling, 'Madame! A visitor!'

And by then Lymond, with a kind of brutal persistence, had got

234

himself upright. His good hand, groping, felt the cold wood of a stair rail. He leaned on it, all his weight on his serviceable leg, and looked up, straight into the pouched eyes of a woman, whose papery skin, in soft, unfolded swags, hung from her brittle, down-peering bones. Two long braids, thickly plaited and impossibly gold, dangled gently swaying from a wimpled headdress out of fashion a century ago. Her robes were long, flat and flowing, without a farthingale, and her nostrils above the creased and confident mouth were antique and wide.

There was a pause, which Lymond occupied at some cost by standing straight and still, his head thrown back and his breathing nicely controlled. The Gothic face in the gloom far above him seemed to smile. '*Aucassins, damoisiax, sire!*' the Dame de Doubtance observed, in brisk mediaeval quotation; and *Christ!* thought Lymond, thrown into mild hysteria by the greeting. And hazily he sought an apt quotation in return.

He never did recollect much, except in nightmares, of the subsequent exchange; although he never felt quite the same again about the ballad *Aucassin and Nicolette*. At one point out of dire necessity, he was driven to saying, '*Hé Dieus, douce créature.* . . . If I fall, sweet being, I shall fracture my neck; and if I remain here, they will take and burn me at the stake.'

And after a moment, thinly autocratic, her voice had observed, 'Aucassin: *le beau, le blond.* . . . You are hurt: *le sang vous coule des bras.* You are bleeding in fifty places at least. . . .' And at last, collecting her skirts with smooth deliberation, the woman began to move downstairs towards him even as he spoke.

> '*Douce suer, com me plairoit*
> *Se monter povie droit*
> *Que que fust du recaoir*
> *Que fuisse lassus o toi!*

> . . . How I wish to be up there:
> Up there with thee!'

Afterwards, he remembered looking up at her, the brocade robe hooked over her arm, her old, ribbed ankle in its pointed slipper two steps above. Remotely entertained, even then, by the crazy parallel between his affairs and the ballad, he remembered trying very hard, halfway into a thorough faint, to pay her the obvious compliment: '*And thus the pilgrim was cured.*' He did succeed in saying it, but that was all; and of his final journey upstairs to the Dame de Doubtance's bed he had no recollection.

He wakened twice: once out of a feverish dream to the sound of virginals. He was then in her chamber, a dark, thick-walled cave filled with old books and embroidery, watching her yellow, high-nosed profile as she played. He seemed to be strapped up again; under the bandaging the pain already, surely, seemed to be less.

He saw her finish playing and, rising, come over. A reader of horoscopes, Abernaci had said. Hazily, other things one had heard about the Dame de Doubtance came back. Uncannily well-informed, endlessly inquisitive and unnaturally detached, they said. In her day, she had been accused of practising the black art, but nothing had ever been proved. . . . Certainly she seemed to have no interest in acquiring money or power for herself. Her charts were her children; her life was devoted to collecting the facts with which to plot them. Unshockable, old in years and in wisdom, her philosophy of life was just, they said, but harshly just. All the troubles of the soul, after all, were merely a line upon a chart.

When she was close enough, Lymond spoke: a sentence of thanks; a sentence asking her to tell Abernaci of his presence.

Stupidly, he had used English. The old face on its long, gristly neck was attentive, the thick braids still. Then her groined, flamboyant right hand, heavy with queer rings, touched his lips, sealing them. '*Or se chante,*' she said, 'Rumours fly. They are searching from house to house. Speak your own tongue to me or Gaultier if you must, but to no one else. . . . What was the day and hour of your birth?'

It was the English, mauled and unregarded, of a person who spoke many languages and left them broken-hinged and crumbled like clams, solely attacked for the meat. She had not asked when he was born. When he told her what she wanted to know she stared at him for a long time with her squinting, intense gaze, and it came to him suddenly that she knew this already. As the thought entered his head she smiled, the narrow, rubbery cheeks crushed apart, the mouth wide, authoritative and tight. 'You are perceptive. I knew your grandfather,' she said. 'Sometimes he speaks to me still.'

Lymond said, 'He is dead.' That was true, of course. The first Lord Culter, his brilliant grandfather, beloved in Scotland and France, after whom he was named, had died many years before. Only, spoken to her, the words were foolish; he had uttered them as a defence. Somehow, he realized, she had known his grandfather. Certainly she had known he was dead. What else she knew he could not guess. But in the stillness he could sense her mind, firm, powerful, grotesque, scaling the ramparts of his.

He did not know how long the silence lasted, their wills interlocked; but somewhere someone let out a long breath, slowly and nearly inaudibly, and the grey, crocketed fingers lay again for a moment on his brow. 'You keep your secrets well,' she said. 'Make my compliments to Sybilla.' Then, as if a gentle harness had collapsed, he lost all sense of her and of the room once again.

The next time was brief. He was not in bed, but lying cold on some sacks, sharing a minute closet with a little treasury of precious articles; and the room outside the closet was being searched.

He heard stiff questions and unaccustomed civilities: the men at arms and their lieutenant were a good deal in awe of the Dame de Doubtance. A peephole, through which he had no strength to look, threw a single arc of blue light. With idle fingers, Lymond touched the mother-of-pearl and the bronze, the little lacquers and the bracelets so close to his head.

Then the searchers had gone, apparently satisfied; and the door of the little treasure house opened, and he was carried from his hiding place back to bed. For a moment he had the illusion that it was Oonagh O'Dwyer bent over him, with long, incongruous gold hair; then he realized that it was the Dame de Doubtance herself, with the little usurer's head at her shoulder; and behind that, smiling, the dark, turbaned face of Abernaci.

And now it was simple. All he had to do was frame the instruction which had been gripped clearly in his mind since he wakened, the four words he had rehearsed over and over to say.

Jammed by God knew what tensions, by fever and drugs, by lacerated muscles and an exhaustion of mind and body, his voice would not answer him. For a moment, in the stress, sight vanished too, and he was left in a void, silent, blinded, able to communicate nothing.

But he must. But he would.

His eyes shut, Lymond lay and forced panic out of his brain; freed his mind and found, waiting, a block of clear, untrodden thought standing silent for his message.

There was a pause, which to the watchers round the bed seemed interminable. Then the Dame de Doubtance, an odd light in her faded eyes, turned from the silent bed and addressed the mahout in brisk French. 'Take him to Sevigny,' she said.

* * *

The next day, demolishing the Hôtel Moûtier for safety, they passed through the stone-flagged basement and found the stained clothing and the ruined feather cloak. The rest of the house was destroyed and if, as rumour said, Thady Boy Ballagh died in its ashes, there was no other trace.

For a day and a half, his brother, his Queen, Lady Fleming and the Erskines believed with the rest that Lymond was dead; and Erskine, desperately sorry himself, became afraid of what, behind the white numbness, was growing in Richard's blank face. Then Abernaci's message came, with its bare command. Lymond was at his own home of Sevigny and was to be approached by no one—not by Richard nor by the Erskines or their friends.

February wore into March and the weeks passed, but no new message came. Richard rode past Sevigny once as the trees were beginning to bud, and saw its white towers above the mist of dark pink and chrome; but its walls were too high and its wooded gardens too wide to offer more. He had not known it existed. The next day, moving in some endless, purposeless void, he went with an irresponsible young party to an astrologer in an eccentric building called Doubtance. It was a woman. She cast his horoscope and gave him only one piece of advice, regarding him with an irritating kind of tolerance down her high-nostrilled nose. 'Spring is pleasant in France. You should stay.'

Tom Erskine was going home at the end of the month. And it seemed very likely, despite her confidence, that Jenny Fleming would be going, too. They would stop in Paris and then would cross the Channel to England where Erskine would pause to pay his respects to the monarch before going north. By sea or litter, Jenny's journey would be more direct.

Richard wondered whether he should join them. Even before today, he had no desire. He had no wish, he realized, to face Sybilla without news to give her; or with news of such a kind. And yet he had exhausted every approach to the mystery here that his mind could devise.

He had taken over the safeguards for the young Queen, but nothing had happened for weeks. Lymond was not, could not be dead, or Abernaci at least would have told them. But how badly he must be maimed, to enforce this isolation, this enervating silence, was a thought carried bitterly, day and night. And any reappearance had been made impossible by this new attack: the extraordinary revelation, in the most circumstantial detail, of theft and perfidy.

To Richard, at least, that condemnation, astonishing as it had been, had brought a queer kind of relief. In some respects, at least, Francis was safe, if only from himself. And it was proof incontrovertible of something he and Erskine had sometimes doubted: that Stewart's sponsor was not overseas; nor had Stewart been working alone in the hope of selling his services unsolicited. It was proof that there was another mind here in France behind Stewart's and that of someone actively concerned with the plot.

With Erskine eagerly at his side, he had followed every possible clue. They went to Neuvy to see the Irishwoman, Oonagh O'Dwyer, whom Thady Boy had serenaded in the house so mysteriously burned. She was not there. She had joined the Moûtiers, her aunt informed them, in their southern home; and firmly she refused to give the direction. 'Is it not enough to be pitied they are, and their house burned by vagabond jugglers from over their heads?'

She and Oonagh had been living at Neuvy all through the Tour des

Minimes accident and later; the Moûtiers, it seemed plain from their neighbours, were unequivocably harmless and well known. For all they knew, Richard bitterly recognized, Lymond might have struggled there by himself, knowing the house was deserted, guessing for some reason that he was about to be exposed or maligned. They were hamstrung by their ignorance, as Lymond himself must have planned. For in their ignorance lay their safety.

Meanwhile the Queen Mother, the young Queen at her side, made no plans to return to Scotland; and the French Court, with impenetrable charm, continued to make her harried stay pleasant.

It was not the lustrous pleasance it had been. No one in Blois put the whores on cows' backs again and whipped them through the town. Lent passed at Blois and Amboise and ended, still, sour and withered, without laughter or lampoon or quick, scurrilous song. Thady was dead and better dead; and every occasion lacked him.

Everything they did wore a different cast. What had been vulgarly clever, in the light of bare exhumation looked bleakly coarse; what had been vivid looked vulgar; what had been witty looked common; what had been forthright looked outrageous. Etiquette—edged etiquette—came heavily back into place; there were ripostes which were overwitty and reactions which were over-sullen. A sense of acute spiritual discomfort hung over the flower of France, the aftermath of its brilliant flare of indulgence. If Thady Boy had come back—a Thady Boy even absolved from the treachery imputed to him—they would have had him beaten from the room by their valets.

IV

London:

Wolves All Around Him

A cow-grazer of a green is a man who grazes his cows upon a green on every property, between wolves all around him; and this is his wealth.

LIKE St. Patrick, who requested the protection of God against the spells of women, druids and smiths, The O'LiamRoe took instant remedy for his ills. Flinching from the unkind pastures of France, he retreated home but found there only a mirror for the amour-propre so fundamentally hurt. The Lord Deputy's offer came pat. England was glad to invite him—rumours of French invasion were at their height again. It seemed, for a moment, a sardonic triumph to carry his patched self-esteem into the world of affairs on the opposite side.

To begin with, he had been delighted. Englishmen, he found, differed remarkably from the French. Here, the King was a boy. The undercurrents at Court dealt less with the naked clash of cold temperaments and fiery ambition than with opposing factions of barons who were no less ambitious, but who added to their ambition a concern, on some days more serious than others, for the land, for the people, for religion.

To his own startled amusement, he was staying in the Hackney mansion of the Earl and Countess of Lennox. Shuttling curiously between Whitehall and Holborn, Greenwich and Hampton Court at the tail of the Court, O'LiamRoe had more than once met the pallid, pouch-eyed Scottish Earl, with his light hair and his air of faintly bewildered suspicion. Then, a little later, he had met Lennox's wife Margaret, too, and she had suggested that he should come for a spell as their guest.

At the back of O'LiamRoe's mind lay something he had once heard about his late ollave and Margaret Douglas, Countess of Lennox. He made no effort to pursue it; for together with France, O'LiamRoe had abandoned Thady Boy and all his affairs.

In the forefront of his mind, however, was one other vivid fact. Matthew Stewart, Earl of Lennox, was older brother to John Stewart, Lord d'Aubigny. And thus, at second or third hand, O'LiamRoe might have news of the only person in the whole Court of France for whom he felt sympathy—the threatened Scottish child Queen Mary. He had gone, therefore, to Hackney with the Lennoxes.

It had disappointed him. The family were often away. Like himself, they were summoned regularly to Court, in spite of their religion, which he suspected was stubbornly Papish; for Margaret was a full cousin of the boy King and indeed, had she not been disinherited by her uncle King Henry, might have had a strong claim to be next heir to the throne not only of England but of Scotland, where her mother had been Queen, and where her husband's great-grandfather had also reigned.

There were other difficulties. The busy barons at the Court, while polite, had no spare time for him; the Irish he met were all busy lisping about their pensions and their farms; and he was tired of amusing himself with brisk, politically minded Englishmen with prejudices to sell.

Even now, riding through Cheapside to vist the Strand, he was distressed, unreasonably, because among the bawling, huckstering, hurrying crowds, no heads turned as he passed. For England he had abandoned his saffron and frieze, and with it the raffish, engaging detachment which had served him so well had somehow slipped away. It was too late now to aspire to the splendid hauteur of the wealthy chief ones whom he had diligently baited all his life. Under the soft body and the sandy pelt there lurked horrifically, transparent as a jellyfish, a grey, inferior personality, with whom he might have to live all his days. The O'LiamRoe had sloughed off Francis Crawford, but he was not happy in his new skin.

Among the rich mansions backing on the Strand, with their bowered gardens running down to the river, was the little house rented by Michel Hérisson's younger brother, with its elegant door, its tall, paned windows and its striking rooms betraying the static elegance and oddly edgy effect of a house furnished for entertaining, not for living in.

To this house, followed by Piedar Dooly, the Prince of Barrow was riding, in a last effort to find in this famous city of London a warm, uninhibited and friendly face to give him relief. With him he carried a letter from the big Rouen sculptor.

Arriving, he was amused and in no way chilled at first by the contrast between Brice Harisson's style of living and the openhanded carelessness of the sculptor, with his boisterous unofficial club and his illegal printing. He saw Piedar Dooly and his two horses led off quickly and quietly to a splendid small stable; and after a succession of liveried encounters, found himself waiting in a leather-hung parlour for his host.

What little O'LiamRoe knew of this only brother of Michel's was promising. Scottish by birth, unmarried, adventurous, Brice had been brought up, like Michel, in France, and like Michel had no philosophy other than the cultivation of his own talents and prejudices in whatever soil could best accommodate them.

Brice's gift was an ear for languages. Able to mimic anything, he could remember dialect like music, idiom like the phrase of a tune. He had met Edward Seymour, Duke of Somerset, when the future Protector of England had been stationed with the English army on the north coast of France. And when Somerset returned to London, to lead England during the first years of the boy King Edward's reign, Brice Harisson went with him, as interpreter and congenial, if junior, member of the Somerset secretarial staff.

Now Somerset's power was in eclipse, and he had ceded control of the nation to the Earl of Warwick. So Harisson had leisure, a little money saved, a house not too far from Somerset's palace and time to introduce the Prince of Barrow, O'LiamRoe hoped, to the more intimate circles of London life.

So, when the door opened and Brice Harisson came in, his brother's letter of introduction in his hand, O'LiamRoe's only concern, as he rose smiling, was whether to clasp hands or use the double embrace, as Michel habitually did. His host stood in the open doorway, small, dark, spare, dressed in thin-legged black with a high collar closely goffered to the ears—ears widely hinged, and for that reason covered on one side by a fall of thick, flat grey hair.

'The Prince of Barrow, I understand?' said Brice Harisson, in a voice in which disbelief struggled with boredom. 'My brother, I fear, always rates too highly the time to spare in a busy Court such as ours. I have an appointment almost immediately. May I be of service to you first?'

Something had happened, clearly, to put him out of temper. O'LiamRoe had seen Michel, foiled in his plans, carry just this high colour, though with much less restraint. He said peaceably, 'There is no reason to trouble you at all, at this minute. I will come back another time, surely, and we could settle down to a fine evening's talk. There is a tavern up the street that could give a sup to us both.'

The door stood ajar, and the other man neither closed it nor made any move into the room. Impatience had added itself to the boredom; but even so O'LiamRoe was unprepared. Brice Harisson said, 'If you will tell my steward precisely what you are selling, he will give you an answer to your lodgings. An introduction to the Duke, I am afraid

242

I cannot contrive. He does not care for Irish hides and finds your cheeses a good deal too coarse. Roberts!'

There was a pause. Then, with the footsteps of the approaching steward in his ears, O'LiamRoe spoke, his vowels prodigiously round. 'Isn't that a Scot for you, now: never a new acquaintance but he looks for a bargain from it, as the mermaid said to the herring fisherman. I was here for friendship's sake, and with news of your brother, that is all.'

The steward had reached Harisson's elbow. He didn't send him away. The brown eyes owl-like under high, brief tufted brows, he said, 'I have no money to lend, either. Forgive me. My appointment is pressing. Roberts?'

At his side, the steward snapped fingers. Sword, cloak, gloves, were brought. He was booted already, and a flat hat, discreet and feathered, lay on his smooth head. Dressed, he stood aside so that O'LiamRoe had room to leave. 'I shall get the case from the study, Roberts, myself. I am sorry, Prince, to disappoint you. I fear my brother and I parted company some time ago now and he outwore my patience before that with his procession of supplicants. I hope your stay in London is a profitable one.'

'Ah, God save you, I make what profit I can out of the experiences that come my way,' said O'LiamRoe. 'That big boast of a man Michel would have knocked the head off me did I not sample the hospitality of his small, clever brother that has all the strange tongues so pat. And devil mend it, I would say you use your own tongue in the strangest way. The nearest I heard to it in nature was a retired street-walker in Galway protecting her virtue.'

And, opening his purse, O'LiamRoe took out an écu and pressed it into Brice Harisson's neat hand at the door. 'Drink my health in a noggin on the way to your appointment,' he said. 'Our hides are stinking and our cheeses unkempt, but our loving hearts are strong and golden and shining like kingcups in the peat, and you look lonesome, little man.' Only when he reached the stables and found his two hands hard clenched, did O'LiamRoe realize that he had been prepared for actual physical assault.

Piedar Dooly had been looking for him. As he entered the comfortable, manured warmth of the stables the Firbolg sank one wiry hand into his shrunk satin and, hoarsely whispering, tugged him aside. O'LiamRoe, intent on leaving Brice Harisson's premises before Harisson himself entered the yard, cut him short in terse Gaelic.

Then he saw where Piedar Dooly's free hand had pointed, and the meaning of it reached his brain. There were four animals in that stable: his own, a mule, a fine mare in Harisson's colours, and a hack, whose mended harness and saddle, accoutred for campaigning, were as familiar to him as his own. He had ridden behind it from Dieppe to Blois, had stared at it, sliding next to his own on shipboard, down the Seine and the Loire, had watched it at the ill-fated cheetah hunt and had accompanied it to Aubigny and back. It was Robin Stewart's.

O'LiamRoe, who seldom disliked anyone who could supply him with amusement, had found it unusually hard, even before the day of Luadhas, to tolerate the Archer's uneasy ways. Unsettled at present himself, he would have abandoned the ménage with some firmness had several thoughts not come into his head.

First, the sheer unpleasantness of the scene in the house had recalled that other scene over two months before in his ollave's reeking bedchamber at Blois. He had told Oonagh O'Dwyer that authority made monsters of mankind; but he had seen what authority abandoned could do.

Robin Stewart had been sent to Ireland with George Paris to bring Cormac O'Connor to France. Instead, he was here in London with one of Somerset's men, who was at great pains to conceal it. England and France were not now at war; but they were hardly close friends; and certainly not close enough to account for an Archer of the Guard in intimate talk with a Government official, albeit one at present slightly outmoded. Harisson, of course, was Scottish like Stewart; and he was, O'LiamRoe remembered, certainly one of Stewart's old friends. But then, what part in all this did O'Connor play, whom Stewart had been directed to fetch?

It was this last irresistible question, in the end, that led Phelim O'LiamRoe, Prince of Barrow, never a man to hoard dignity and always trusting to a bright tongue to make his queerer paths smooth for him, to ride noisily out of the yard, followed by Piedar Dooly and the sharp eye of the steward, and, dismounting down the street, to leave the horses with his follower while he slipped over two walls and down an alley, soothed an inquisitive dog and dodged at last into the garden behind Brice Harisson's stylish Strand house.

There, by a process of elimination, he located the study window. It was open, and there was a porch roof just below it. In the purple gloom presaging a brisk March downpour The O'LiamRoe seized a barrel and, tearing his stockings, ripping his breeches and sticking an elbow clean through the skin-tight silk of his sleeve, hitched himself up and made ready to listen.

They were speaking in Gaelic. Stewart, nearest the study window, was not sure of his; more than once he stumbled, filling in with French or with English. Harisson's was impeccable. O'LiamRoe could hear him lightly questioning, commenting, occasionally dissenting. His manner, in staggering contrast to his reception of the Prince himself, was quiet, intimate and understanding; and in the very aptness of its handling of all Robin Stewart's quirks argued a very long friendship indeed. He said now, his singing Gaelic nostalgic to O'LiamRoe's listening ears, 'All the same, Robin, why the boat? The Thames itself is a public place to speak with a man like Warwick. It was sure that he would refuse to hear you.'

Stewart swore. 'Did I not try every other way? The messages never reached him. I knew he was sailing to Greenwich that day. The rest was easy.'

Harisson's voice was still agreeable. 'Were you plain with him?'

'I said I had news for him that would do great good to England, and that because it was secret, I wished that he would speak to me alone.'

'And—?'

'He said he did not mean to discuss anything forced upon him by intrusion. I was to think myself lucky not to be put in the river and carried to Newgate; and if I had had anything to say, I would need have written him in the proper way. But he was interested.'

'He does not sound interested.'

Stewart's aggressive voice was smooth with complacency. 'He was, then. I lifted the edge of my cloak and showed him the Archer's insignia.'

For the first time, Harisson's voice sharpened. 'Who else saw this?'

'Not anyone. Good God, is it foolish I am? The boat was full of servants and officials—not anyone who knew me at all. Then they waved to a ferryboat and threw me off. But the next letter I will write, by God, he will read.' His voice, in his excitement, had risen. 'Now is the time. I know it. A fresh message, Brice. We shall ask him to speak to us. And if he will not do that, we shall suggest place and time for a meeting with any man he may appoint. He cannot refuse. And once he knows what we offer, our fortune is made. That brat Mary married to France would mean a French menace at the Scottish Border for all time; whereas if she were dead Arran would likely rule Scotland, and Arran favours the English and could be got for a groat. Warwick might even get them persuaded to let Lennox rule— he's got a good enough claim.

'As it is—' Stewart's voice, hoarse with enthusiasm, pounded on. 'As it is, Mary's a downright threat to the English throne. If the Catholics came back into power, France might well incite them to push her claims here to the crown. She's the granddaughter of Henry VIII's sister. Considering the mess he made of his marriages, you could say her claim was as strong nearly as his daughter Mary's.'

'Or that of the Earl and Countess of Lennox?' Brice Harisson mused. 'I was thinking you had taken your offer first there.'

'Well, then,' said Stewart. There was a long pause, during which the Prince of Barrow had time to think that the tiles below him would begin to drum under the lashing of his heart. Then Stewart said, with

245

uneasy brusqueness, 'I said something once, as I remember. But I don't have a kindness for the family, and that's the truth.'

'Oh, I agree.' And, his voice amiable and unchanged, Brice Harisson used an expression about the Lennoxes which O'LiamRoe had heard in the gutters of Dublin. Then without pausing he said, 'Then we shall write to Warwick; that I agree, too. Give him time to consider, and a place to meet. A bookseller's is always useful. There are too many ears at an inn. . . . Would you think of letting me go? I have, to my cost, a long experience of this Court, and I think they would give me a good hearing. No one would question your standing, but your name, naturally, is not so readily known.'

'I was going to say the same,' said Robin Stewart; and in his capitulation O'LiamRoe read relief disguised as intelligent realism. Then they fell to discussing time and place for the suggested meeting and, this done, began the preliminaries of parting.

It was then, when O'LiamRoe was preparing to leave, that his own name was spoken. Harisson was answering a question. 'They went off—I told you. And he won't be in it again. I made sure of that too. He couldn't be knowing you were here. It was purest chance; my fool of a brother had sent him.'

Stewart's voice, thin with worry, said, 'I can't understand it. I left him in Ireland.'

'My dear Robin,' said Harisson dryly, 'he wouldn't be the first man to wish to change masters. If the man you called Thady Boy Ballagh were alive and in London, you would have had reason to worry.'

'Well, he isn't,' said Stewart quickly in English; and his roughened voice, like succeeding strokes of a bell feared and half-heard on the wind, beat its intimation into O'LiamRoe's sense. 'How often do I have to say it? I put enough nightshade into him the evening I left to kill him outright. Folk like that, I hate them. . . . They go through life sure of everything, meddling with people. Why don't they leave them alone? No one asked him to interfere. He had land, and plenty of money—everything easy from the day he was born into a dry silk towel by the fire. Why did he want to come meddling with me?'

'So you said. You would think sometimes, Robin, that he was the first man you had killed. Forget him. It was well done, and it is past. Now—'

The interview was ending. O'LiamRoe slid off his roof and escaped to where Dooly awaited him in the street, his body chilled, his stomach tight with the recollection of a sick man hurled to the ground under bucket after thrown bucket of water, of his dilated eyes and the free sound of his laughter.

It was a long ride back to Hackney, and The O'LiamRoe did not make it at once. He chose to go to an inn, a good long way from the

Strand; and in the solitude of its common room in midmorning, with the rain beating on the oiled linen, did some elliptical thinking which came closer and closer, as the consoling tankards went down, to the vulnerable point he knew in his heart he would reach.

There, at last, he found his inexorable decision staring him in the face. His blue eyes vacant with solitary communion and drink, The O'LiamRoe mutinously recalled why he had gone back to Harisson's house in the first place. 'By Bridget, and the Dagda, and Cliona of the Wave, and by Finvaragh whose home is under Cruachma, and Aoibheal and Red Aodh and Dana the Moth—Cormac O'Connor, you have a power to answer for!' said Phelim O'LiamRoe. And getting up, he found Piedar Dooly and in two hours' hard work made all the necessary arrangements for his Firbolg follower to take ship to France, there to inform the Scottish Queen Dowager that Robin Stewart, the Archer, the likely author of all the attempts on her daughter and the murderer of Francis Crawford as well, was now in London seeking English help for a further attempt.

He sold Piedar Dooly's horse and his own to raise ready money for the trip and saw him off by post-horse on his way to Portsmouth before setting off himself on the long, wet walk back to Hackney. Lady Lennox met him as he came in and commented, with her double-edged humour, on his state. He made some excuse. He had money enough in his room to buy a new horse; and he was not conspirator enough to be sure of smoothing his face at the moment before either of the Lennoxes, so disparagingly discussed by Robin Stewart and his friend.

Margaret Douglas, Countess of Lennox, tall, splendid and tawny niece of King Henry, who had been a conspirator all her life, looked after the muddy, horseless figure, unattended by lackey, and changing her direction, moved into her boudoir. There, she summoned Graham Douglas, who had been with her from birth, who would spy for her and had killed for her, and told him pleasantly to follow every movement of O'LiamRoe's.

*   *   *

Three weeks later, the Prince of Barrow, leaving a tedious Court function at Whitehall, rode through the red brick gate, past the tilting yard, round by the Cross at Charing and into the noble precincts of Durham House, the official residence of Raoul de Chémault, French Ambassador to the Court of King Edward, where he had himself announced.

Considering that he had been nearly flung out of France in the first place, and that he had since exchanged French hospitality for English with quite unseemly speed, it required a good deal of moral courage to accomplish this.

At the back of his mind was the plain hope that the Ambassador would refuse to see him. In this he was cheated. M. de Chémault, a thick, olive-skinned Latin from southern France with black hair and short legs, was nervously incapable of selection and saw everybody, even at night. O'LiamRoe was shown into a stolid English room entirely furnished from France, like a leather trunk full of butterflies. And like a harassed caterpillar who could not achieve his metamorphosis, the Ambassador held out a short, inelegant arm, and seated him. Then he talked about the weather.

It was O'LiamRoe, who could tell more stories about the weather than anyone south of Antrim, who cut him short in the end. 'The business I have is a queer one for an Irishman,' said he. 'But live comfortably with myself I could not, until I had told one of you. There is a man I met in France, a Scottish Archer called Stewart, who is now in England offering to do away with the young Scottish Queen when he gets back—and it would not be his first effort at that. And the Earl of Warwick himself, the clever fellow, is near accepting it.'

The Prince of Barrow, who had a low opinion of any kind of officialdom, had been ready for disbelief, or a cursory politeness which would have shown him the door. But Raoul de Chémault owed his finicky alertness to a lifetime of commissions, agencies and embassies over Europe, and knew better than to discount information from however unexpected a source. The doors were closed on himself, O'LiamRoe and the Ambassador's secretary, and O'LiamRoe described, with wonderful brevity, the meeting he had overheard between Stewart and Brice Harisson, the letter Harisson had proposed writing to Warwick, and the meeting which had come of it. At that meeting, held at the Red Lion in St. Paul's Churchyard the previous day, Warwick's appointed agent had met Harisson, who had put the Archer's proposal. And Warwick's agent, so far from being indifferent, had brought Warwick's command that both Stewart and Brice Harisson should come before him to discuss the plan further.

To overhear that had taxed all O'LiamRoe's inventiveness. The wry pleasure he took from his success was mixed still with a fearful irritation: from time to time his clean, pink fingers wandered to his face. The fine baby skin of chin and upper lip was naked. Had Brice Harisson, idling in a book-filled corner of the Red Lion, met O'Liam-Roe face to face, he would hardly have recognized him; for all the waving golden whiskers had gone. To that, and his long robes and the black, ear-covering hat of the professor, borrowed blithely from the physician at Hackney, O'LiamRoe owed his triumph.

He had heard Brice Harisson meet Warwick's man, and had heard all that mattered of what they said. He had then watched them severally leave, and had left himself, only to be retrieved by a breathless shopkeeper laying claim to the new book absently tucked under his arm.

All this the French Ambassador heard. At the end, in his good English with an unexpected aptness of thought, he thanked O'Liam-Roe, and complimented him. 'All this will be made known to the King my lord, who will express his thanks better than I.' He hesitated. A flicker of a glance passed between de Chémault and his secretary; then the Ambassador said, 'You may guess our interest, monseigneur, when I tell you that M. Brice Harisson has already honoured us with a visit.'

The sandy brows floated. 'Brice Harisson's been *here?*'

'Yes. Seeking my aid, and my interest with the Queen Dowager of Scotland to enable him to escape from his English employment and return to some well-pensioned office in Scotland or France. I assumed from what he did not say that he guessed Somerset's day was reaching an end. In return,' said de Chémault, watching his secretary marshal the stack of papers on which O'LiamRoe's words had been taken down, 'he has offered to sell me an unspecified political secret of some value.'

'In other words,' said O'LiamRoe, a rare disgust in his voice, 'Harisson is planning to betray Robin Stewart to the French?'

'From what you say, it seems likely. I have told him to give me time to make enquiries, and return. Now that I know what is behind his offer, I shall make it as simple for him as I can; thus the affair will solve itself. As soon as Harisson gives us positive proof of what this man Stewart has done, the Archer can be arrested.' He rose. 'You are to be in England, monseigneur, for some little time?'

He was due the courtesy of a fair answer, at least. O'LiamRoe mentioned that he was the guest of the Earl and Countess of Lennox, and would remain there at least until the affair was cleared up. If his evidence was required, M. de Chémault had only to call.

M. de Chémault made no comment. At the door he took a serious farewell, and laying one broad, brown hand on the Irishman's sleeve said, 'You know your own business best. But should you wish to go back to France, there would be many who would welcome you for your own sake only. And whatever your conclusions or your policies, the friendship of the French Court can be assured.'

'Ah, no,' said Phelim O'LiamRoe, smiling. 'I was never easy with ghosts; and France there is bursting full of them. I shall never go back—God save us, no. . . . I might meet the shade of Phelim O'LiamRoe face to face.'

That afternoon, Piedar Dooly came back. He had delivered his master's message with some trouble to the Scottish Queen Dowager, and had been provided with more than enough money to cover the double journey, and an obscurely worded message of thanks.

He also had news. Stewart's attempt on Thady Boy Ballagh's life had not been successful . . . but a later accident had. From Piedar Dooly, in Gaelic with spectrum-like detail, The O'LiamRoe heard the story of the Tour des Minimes at Amboise, of Lord Culter's investigation and of the burning of the Hôtel Moûtier with Ballagh inside.

That night the Lennoxes, chaffing lightly through the supper courses from their heavy, crested gold plate, found him erratic and even unresponsive to their quips. Margaret, her dark eyebrows raised, more than once caught her husband's eye over the sensationally cropped silky head, and afterwards redoubled her solicitous concern for her guest, expressed in the cool voice with which Margaret Douglas's sentiments were most often presented, ice-fresh and bloody, like newly caught fish. She made little headway. O'LiamRoe, clearly, had other things on his mind.

*   *   *

Robin Stewart, who dared not be seen by any man, Scot, Frenchman or Londoner, was hiding in the brickfields at Islington, and making the rarest visits to the Strand. He did not know that on the morning before the momentous interview with Lord Warwick, his faithful friend Brice rode round the corner to Durham House and, passing through courtyards hazy with young green, was closeted ten minutes later with the French Ambassador and addressing him in fluent French. 'M. de Chémault, I hope you have news for me. I come to tell you that tomorrow I shall be able to give you information of some considerable value.'

This time there were three of them in the room: de Chémault himself, seated at his fine desk, an undersecretary, and someone's herald, deep in conversation with them both. They were all speaking French. Harisson meticulously did the same.

M. de Chémault heard him out. At the end, he said, 'We have not been slow, sir, in extending our powers to help you. The gentleman beside me is Vervassal, herald to the Princess Mary of Guise, Queen Mother of Scotland. Address your wishes to him. On the other matters you have just mentioned we should of course be interested to hear more.'

Harisson was sure they would. But he wanted to find out what they would pay, first. He bowed. The man called Vervassal smiled; then picking up a handsome, light stick, came over and sat down beside him. The discussion began.

The conversation was conducted in French. Brice Harisson's requirements were soon told, confined as they were to simple matters of land, money and security, and a safe haven in Scotland. The herald, dealing with them point by point, was excellent, quick, accurate and fair; and his powers of treaty seemed to be unlimited. Harisson, no novice at bargaining, could admire his skill while jarred by something underneath the words.

Twice, he found himself caught out in a foolish error of grammar. To Harisson, this was staggering; as shocking as if he had become partially undressed. Indeed he, always penguin-neat, felt ruffled beside this elegant person, fine as a fan stick carved under warm water, from pale hair to the pale, moving light of his rings. Harisson did not care for his eyes.

He did his business, which was to obtain a firm promise of satisfactory reward from the Queen Dowager of Scotland, and in return he undertook at midnight the next day to bring information of the most pressing importance to the French and the Scottish Crowns. More, he utterly refused to say. De Chémault indeed pressed him almost beyond his patience, but the other man had sense at least to say nothing and wait. And by midnight tomorrow, thought Brice Harisson, he would have evidence—if all went well, even written evidence—which would dispose of Robin Stewart for ever and earn him a fat Commendatorship in Perth.

The thing had gone just as he wanted. In spite of that, he took out a perfect handkerchief and wiped his brow before remounting his horse, and trotting back up the Strand.

*　　　*　　　*

Back at Durham House they watched him go, from the tall windows of de Chémault's library.

'Alecto, Megaera and Tisiphone attend you, and may you be embalmed with the guts of a civet-rat,' said the man called Vervassal pleasantly, in English; and walking over, opened a door. When he used the stick, especially, the hesitation in his walk was hardly noticeable. 'Come in, Tom. Harisson propissimus, honestissimus et eruditissimus has gone.'

And the Master of Erskine joined them, the distaste which they all felt on his face, but his practical good sense already discounting it. 'No sense in cursing the man. You'll have to pay him and use him. We can't find Stewart without him, and we can't arrest Stewart without his evidence.

'Officially, we know nothing of Warwick's share in the plot, and for the sake of peace, we want to know nothing. Let Harisson come here tomorrow night and betray his partners ten times over. All that matters is that we should be able to get hold of Stewart and quietly take him to France, with Harisson's unshakable testimony to convict him. Your obligations there, Francis, are ended.'

M. de Chémault had the sensation of being surrounded. The transaction had demanded speed. After Harisson's initial approach the Ambassador had written immediately to Panter, his Scottish counterpart in Paris. His reply had not yet come when Erskine, the Scottish Councillor and Special Ambassador, appeared in London on his way home from France, and de Chémault thankfully turned to him.

Erskine had helped swiftly and effectively. Messages crossed the Channel, back and forth. Within a matter of days, the Scottish herald Mr. Crawford had arrived, accredited by every kind of document to the Court of the Queen Dowager of Scotland, and with full powers to treat.

It was excellent service, and under other circumstances, M. de Chémault would have accepted it with surprised relief. But Stewart had been an Archer in the company of John, Lord of Aubigny; and Lord d'Aubigny and his wife Anne had been the firmest friends of the de Chémaults for many years.

So, nibbling now at a biscuit and pouring wine for himself, his secretary and his two dynamic guests, the Ambassador watched, with divided feelings, the burden being removed from his shoulders. Or more particularly, he continued to watch Mr. Crawford, Vervassal Herald, as he talked. 'Don't count too much, Tom, on a tidy conclusion. Stewart, I would remind you, is a lamentable conspirator, and Harisson is a lazy fool. His arrival just now in broad daylight would strike any qualified spy with the ague.'

But the Councillor belittled it. 'He's Somerset's man. He has the entrée anywhere. . . . My God,' said the Master of Erskine, 'why have I to go back to Scotland? What I would give to see Robin Stewart's face when he finds out you aren't—'

But the man Crawford rose, the knuckles sharp on the silver knob of his stick, and broke in without haste. 'Will they not be expecting you at Holborn if you are to set off north today?'

Reminded of his own business, Tom Erskine hurried to take leave of the Ambassador. Vervassal, who was staying now at Durham House, went with him to the yard. Outside, the Councillor turned and met the neutral eyes of his companion, who had once been Thady Boy Ballagh and was now, openly, Francis Crawford, herald, in a solution so simple that only Francis Crawford had thought of it. Tom Erskine said quickly, 'Do you think you can make Stewart speak?'

'Yes,' said Lymond, in the same pleasant voice.

'Because if you don't, it must be done in France, by whatever means they can find. Whoever employed Robin Stewart in the first place must still be in France, and you owe him a debt. I understand that. Go back to France after Stewart's taken if you must—you can go quite openly as Crawford of Lymond, the Dowager's herald. No one will connect you with Ballagh except those who know already.

252

And if you've no wish to go, you can trust your brother to do what is best. He'll stay with the Dowager until it's all over. . . . You should be rather pleased,' said Tom Erskine, 'with O'LiamRoe?'

'Well. Yes. He got drunk on the palm wine of power,' said Lymond dryly. 'That was all right. But it was I who fell out of the tree.'

*   *   *

At twelve o'clock on the following night, Monday the 19th of April, the French Ambassador waited again, behind the tall shuttered windows of Durham House, for Brice Harisson and his promised betrayal. With him were Lymond, de Chémault's senior officials, and his secretariat.

They waited in vain. Half an hour passed of the new day, and then an hour, and no Harisson appeared. At three, taking a risk, de Chémault sent a junior to go on foot to the Strand. He came back at dawn, to where Francis Crawford and the Ambassador waited alone in the library under splayed candles; eyes, throats and minds thick with long conjecturing and the consuming heat of the fire. He brought the news that at half past eleven the previous night, Brice Harisson had been arrested on Warwick's command.

By midday, they knew that Harisson had been taken with two servants and lodged in the private custody of Sir John Atkinson, one of the two sheriffs of the City of London—a mark less of respect for the prisoner than for his nominal employer Somerset. By early afternoon, they knew the ostensible reason: three letters, written by Harisson to the Queen Dowager of Scotland and to two of her lords had been confiscated in transit. In them, Harisson had expressed his gratitude for the Queen's promise to take him into her service, and had begged them all for their continued interest so that on leaving England, where he had handsomely benefited from the King, he would have means to live in the service of his gracious Queen.

One further item of news was forthcoming. The incriminating letters had been seized and taken to Warwick by one of the Earl of Lennox's men.

V

London:
The Intentional Betrayal

Every betrayal, intentional or with concealment, is false: there
are equal fines for the theft which is concealment, and the concealment which is robbery.
Thou shalt not kill a captive unless he be thine.

HAD he been trapped by a peasant walking on all fours in a
goatskin, Brice Harisson couldn't have been more confused. His
jostling languages littered chipped and useless in his mind, he passed
his first days of polite captivity in Sir John Atkinson's best room in
Cheapside in a state of raging anxiety almost equalled by his burning
wrath with the Lennoxes.

Matthew Lennox he had always disliked. Somerset had distrusted
him, and had shown it; Margaret Lennox had crossed him again and
again, and in the bank of ill will which now lay solidly between the
two factions, Harisson had had his full share.

But who would have expected Lennox to intercept these damnable
letters, and to have betrayed him in this way to Warwick? And,
thought Brice Harisson, pacing round the packed furniture on Sir
John's polished floor, how could he hope to persuade Warwick that
his correspondence with the Scots was to disarm suspicion only?
Long before the apprentices' bell in the morning, the two liveried
bodyguards outside Sir John's parlour door heard the secretary
inside, exercising his worries.

When, late in the afternoon, the door opened on Sir John Atkinson
accompanied by the herald Vervassal, Harisson's sheer, frozen panic
could have been axed in the cask and sold off by the pound. He dared
not even burst into recriminations before the sheriff's cold eye. John
Atkinson was a merchant, a guild master and accustomed to judging
cloth and men. It was in fact Lymond's tailoring, although the sheriff
may not have known it, which led him, after a brief and minatory
preamble, to allow the herald to interview his prisoner alone.

Today Lymond wore the tabard of his office. Before the armorial blaze of blue and red and cloth of gold Harisson was aware, for the second time, of his own imperfect state: his immaculate grey hair unkempt; his linen unchanged. Cap in hand, the herald was assuring the sheriff that he might call on the resources of his nation to clear up this unfortunate and unauthorized attempt to change allegiance. Then, as the sheriff left, Vervassal pulled on the crimson velvet hat turned up with ermine and, shutting the door with his stick, addressed Harisson with the clear fluency he remembered.

'Since neither of us is the host, we may as well both sit down. Spare me your fury. I know I have ruined your defence; but at least I have rescued your skin. My lord of Warwick is perfectly aware that you have promised to betray him to the French Ambassador, and the French Ambassador is quite aware that the secret you promised to sell him concerned Robin Stewart's plot. The confiscated letters were only a pretext. Warwick wants you out of the way until he finds out how much de Chémault knows.'

Vervassal paused. He had spoken in English as excellent as his French had been. Harisson realized, as his brain darted shrilling among the impossible obstacles of this fresh landscape, that this man, whose own name he did not know, must be not French but Scots. He sat down.

'Better,' said Francis Crawford, and choosing a high chair, seated himself quietly, the links shivering on his broad chain. An idea struggled in the chaos of Brice Harisson's mind. '*Lennox!*' he said sharply. 'Lennox has told Warwick these things?' And, as Vervassal inclined his head, 'But how the devil could he know?'

'It's a long story,' said the herald calmly. 'But the Prince of Barrow, it seems, understands Gaelic; and the Earl of Lennox is suspicious enough of his guest to see that he is followed. O'LiamRoe was at the Red Lion.'

He waited until Harisson had finished swearing and said, 'Quite. The fact remains that, so far as Warwick knows, he has only to rid himself of you, and he may proceed with the scheme without the French Ambassador or anyone else knowing what secret you were about to confide. An excuse for death or life imprisonment won't be hard, I fancy, to find. In fact, he has already found it.'

It was coming too fast now for Harisson. The cold was in every dapper limb, and his face and posture spelled their fear unregarded. 'But you say de Chémault *does* know.'

'Unofficially only.'

'Warwick will deny his interest. He'll lie about it.'

'Of course.'

'Then how could he touch me?' cried Brice Harisson, harried by this clear-eyed messenger of fate into perspicacity. 'A false charge against me would only admit his own guilt. He should be begging *me* to protect him!'

'That is why,' said Lymond gently, 'you are here, and not in Newgate. He is waiting to see how much de Chémault knows. It is for you to make sure, here, now, publicly and through me, that the French Ambassador knows everything, and that Warwick is aware that he knows. Let me call in Atkinson and tell the whole story of Robin Stewart to us both. You will be free by the morning.'

Momentarily discarding the picture of himself confessing publicly to a sheriff of the City of London that he had attempted to sell to France the most intimate details of an English-inspired attempt to poison a future French Queen, Harisson seized another ghoul by the hind leg and flung it to the fate snapping at his heels. 'Free to get a knife in my back from Robin Stewart. How long do you think I'll live once he knows I've sold him to France? De Chémault would have had him under lock and key before he knew it, if this hadn't happened.'

'The Ambassador can have him safely under lock and key still,' said Vervassal, 'if you tell me now where he is.'

There was a silence. Harisson suddenly felt exhausted, physically battered as if he had been fighting; his hands, knotted between his calves, were tensed, ready to fling out, to strike the table, to sweep through his hair as fresh evils appeared. He needed help, and he had nowhere to look; for Somerset, walking in the shadow of the block, couldn't protect him. 'Get me out of here, and I'll tell you,' Brice Harisson said.

Vervassal's reply was perfectly tranquil. 'I can do nothing for you that would impute guilt of conspiracy to my mistress. Only Warwick can free you. And then only if you publicly confess.'

By now, it was too much. 'If he's arrested me on suspicion of going to de Chémault,' said Brice Harisson sarcastically, 'he'll be damned sure to free me when he knows why. . . . I'll get out of it somehow.'

'Do you think so?' said Vervassal. 'Then your mind is not very quick. I have shown you the only way. Warwick is unlikely to stir until he thinks he has de Chémault's position clear. You have one day's grace, perhaps two. When you have considered what I have said, send for me. In the meantime I make you this offer. I cannot contrive your escape. But the Ambassador and I from this moment will use all our powers to have your offence mitigated on the grounds of these letters, and will try to prevent Warwick bringing forward any charges more serious. In return we must have the means of preventing Warwick's share of the plot going further. *Tell me where Robin Stewart is.*'

The comfortable room, with its wood and tapestry and leather was growing dark. In the jewelled light from the fire the herald's gold tissue glistened flatly, and the Scottish leopards in their silken pastures, rising lean from the shadows, offered haunch, head and claw to the glow.

'No,' said Harisson.

'You wish Stewart and Lord Warwick to pursue this plan to their joint profit?' continued the light, ironical voice from the darkness.

The word Harisson used to describe Robin Stewart escaped unwanted from his congested mind, and was not in Gaelic. It was then, indeed, that not only his logic left him, but the thin veneer of accomplishment which had handsomely covered a soul and mind much less than handsome. 'God damn Robin Stewart to hell,' said his friend furiously, the pliant voice sliding high on the thin scale of hysteria. 'I want to get out of here alive—that's all I want!' And to the voice of irony and reason he simply repeated, higher and harder, '*No! No! No! No!*'

Vervassal waited no longer. He rose, dim in the near-dark, and bending, lit a taper from the fire and carried it delicately to the sconce by the door. A branch of silver candlesticks sprang to life, sparkling on his tabard and the feathered gold of his hair round the red velvet cap. His face was shadowed.

'I shall be back in two days,' said the herald. 'Send to de Chémault when you want me.'

Like a bird's, Harisson's two hands clung to his chair, and his skull and ears, undisguised, made a foolish patch of shade on the back. 'I don't want you,' he said. 'You devil, whoever you are, I don't want you.'

Beneath the golden light the other man's face was luminous as alabaster. 'Dear me, you are appallingly ignorant of affairs. Haven't you found out?' said the herald gently. 'The Ambassador knows—it is no secret, I assure you. My name is Francis Crawford of Lymond. My brother is Culter. I am not, of course, an officer of the Lyon Court. But temporarily Herald to the high and mighty Princess Mary, Queen Dowager of Scotland, in absence of better.'

On Harisson's chair, the small, wishbone hands had sprung open; in the darkness the round, desperate eyes strained. 'That's the man—' Harisson broke off, then, raggedly, gave a high laugh. '*You're* Lymond? My God, did he even bungle that one as well? *You're the man Robin Stewart thinks he murdered!*'

'Not one of his most resounding successes, then, we must admit. You see therefore why I should like to meet him. Also, as you may know, the Earl of Lennox is an old and dear enemy of mine, and by now he also should know where I am. Which means that he will do all he can to encourage Warwick to preserve Robin Stewart and to foil the Ambassador and myself. Think out all I've said, my dear

Harisson. Your choice is France; or Warwick, Lennox and death.'

For a moment longer, Vervassal remained in the doorway, his head a little bent, his expression strict, as if condemning the dramatic vulgarity of this speech. Then with a kind of shrug of impatience and distaste, he opened the door and went out. The bodyguards outside shut it and Harisson, crouching, remembered not to put his head in his hands and disarrange his hair.

*　　　　*　　　　*

To de Chémault, the account by Lymond of this affair was retiary in its lack of substance. In effect, the herald said only, 'I am sorry. We have lost him. I rather think I mishandled it. I was counting on some metal in the core, like his brother, but he collapsed like wet fruit. He'll do precisely what Warwick tells him.'

He had discarded the bright tunic on returning. Now, as he moved to a chair, de Chémault noticed that the hesitation in his walk was after all quite a serious limp. The Ambassador said, 'It would have served well to have this confession, but no great harm will come of it. It needs only a hint to Warwick that we are aware of the plot. We have no evidence, true, except at second hand, but a hint would deter him. Of that I am sure.'

'Oh, God, so am I,' said the man Crawford with the first hint of impatience de Chémault had seen. 'Even Harisson might have guessed as much if he had had control of his wits for two minutes. The loathsome little muck-worm can confess or hold his tongue, as he likes. I just want to lay hands on Robin Stewart before anyone else does; that is all.'

*　　　　*　　　　*

Brice Harisson did not send for Vervassal. But when two days later Lymond went as he had promised for his answer, Harisson greeted him with smooth affability, and ran on, light as stucco, sparkling with handfuls of Spanish and German, to inform the herald that on second thoughts he had confessed.

And to prove it, he confessed again to the herald, to the sheriff, and to anyone who would listen, the complete tale of his plot with Stewart, his association with Warwick, and of his attempt to sell out Stewart to France. He told it firmly, bravely, and with a masochistic enjoyment which clearly baffled the sheriff, who could hardly understand this sudden eagerness to brand himself traitor. There was a glibness indeed about the whole thing which confirmed Lymond's own suspicions. In the end he had five minutes only alone with the delicately contrite predicant. He had no need to speak. Harisson did all the talking.

'I fear,' said Brice Harisson, 'that you must think me very stupid.

The sense in what you said struck me directly you had gone.' He gave his unexpected, high laugh. 'I think the poor sheriff was quite startled when I began to tell him. It has gone to Warwick already, and now they will know, of course, that I have told you. It will all be very simple. Now I was to tell you about Stewart?'

'Yes.' His left arm always had to bear the weight of his stick; he moved a little, so that the wall took some of the strain.

'He's at the brickworks in Islington. You go to a certain place, and whistle and a boy will fetch him.' Graphically, Harisson described the place. There was nothing to do but note it, and leave.

Lymond went alone to Islington, and on horseback—something not easy for him yet; but though he whistled, no boy arrived; and though he searched, Robin Stewart had gone.

*   *   *

The bare fields, the lime kilns, the mud and the rubble of Islington had fitted Robin Stewart for all these weeks as an ancient landscape frames and nurtures its fossils.

Flung in grating revulsion from Thady Boy's perfidy back into the caustic stewardship of his lordship of Aubigny, Stewart had accepted the hated commission to travel to Ireland, and had reached with his lordship the tacit understanding that on his return, he would be tolerated in his lordship's vicinity.

On board ship, this arrangement lost most of its attraction. Stewart suffered George Paris's bland self-confidence all the way to Ireland. There was no future with Lord d'Aubigny. There was no future with any of the gentlemen whom he served and envied and criticized so bitterly. What he had to sell, he would market in England.

The violence of the decision was in itself a deliverance. He held to it through all the difficulty of getting to London: the curricle; the fishing boat up to Scotland; the horse bought with the gold provided by the Kingdom of France to pay for the journey of Cormac O'Connor.

Once in London, he had found Harisson, and he was no longer alone. The plotting he had enjoyed. He had always found it satisfying, since his earliest efforts in France, quite apart from the rewards he hoped it would bring him. When, stepping ashore at Dieppe, Destaiz had brought him the news that O'LiamRoe was a danger to them and was to be removed, he had decided on a casual gesture, as flamboyant as Thady Boy's ascent of the rigging, and with Destaiz had arranged for the fire at the inn.

That had failed. Someone else had got O'LiamRoe into trouble over the tennis court meeting with the King, and he had kept out of the affair with the elephants. But he had found the hunting of the Queen's hare exhilarating. He could still picture O'LiamRoe's face when the woman O'Dwyer had arrived and he had been forced to

259

present her with the dog. And when he saw the cheetah arrive. That had not been difficult to arrange: a respectful suggestion just beforehand to the old mistress had been enough.

So there he was, with a very good chance of involving both O'LiamRoe and the child Mary before the day was over; his only worry, to keep the scent of the leveret he carried from the dogs. How was he to know that O'LiamRoe's bitch would actually tackle the cat?

After that, he had begun to think that he might do better on his own. He had the arsenic he had stolen at St. Germain—he had told Harisson about that. He had mentioned also that the way was open, now and then, into Mary's anteroom, where the cotignac was. There was no harm in Harisson or Warwick being aware of his special chances, and also of his special ingenuity. He said nothing, discreetly, of having doctored the tablet already; nor of the discovery, made just before he left, that all the poisoned sweetmeat had gone. He was only beginning, in bloodshot snatches of retrospect, to realize the part Lymond had played.

The name of Thady Boy Ballagh he could barely bring himself to mention. Nor, with belated wisdom, had he betrayed the fact that nearly all he had done had been done under direction. He wanted Harisson to admire his proficiency. And he felt, common sense struggling dimly through the smoking wreck of his ardours, that Brice, tender friend that he was, would be less likely to aid him find a new sponsor if he realized that, back in France, was an employer he had abandoned already.

All that he put behind him. He might find it difficult to explain abandoning O'Connor in Ireland, of course. He might have to return anonymously, and work and bribe under cover. But that would be easy. He would have money from Warwick; he knew the weak links, the irresponsible guards, the kitchenmaids. And once the thing was done, he could leave France for good and find prestige, wealth and security at Warwick's fine English Court.

No one suspected him. Lymond might have come to it—sullenly, you have to recognize the man's perverted skill. But Lymond was poisoned and dead. The arrival of O'LiamRoe, left safely in Ireland, had shaken him, disturbed his precarious confidence. But there had been in it nothing ominous: a typical piece of foolishness by a foolish man.

Thrusting these thoughts behind him, Stewart smiled. Someone else might even attack the small Queen before him. And that would be even funnier. For Warwick would surely give him credit for it, just the same. No one else was likely to come forward; that was sure.

In the weeks he spent alone, or during the rare, discreet visits to Harrisson, the image of Mary, the living child he was to murder, never took shape in Stewart's mind. His half-set, vulnerable emotions, trodden underfoot too hard and too early, had become a cage lined with mirrors in which daily, nightly, he could examine the shrinking image of himself. And the people he met who spoke to him through the bars, and pushed him, and directed him, and exercised him, were his food.

Much of this, in his queer way, Harisson must have understood. In Scotland, long ago, he had endured Stewart's pricking aggression without riposte or impatience: on a creature as confined in his way as the Archer, Stewart's shafts had simply missed their mark. Also, as a matter of vanity, Harisson happened to enjoy, from time to time, using his neat-fingered charm. Coming back to Harisson, for Stewart, had been like returning to a private, mossy plateau after wading rotting through the treachery of some infested swamp.

When Harisson had concluded his interview with Warwick, he was to send for the Archer. The summons came: the rendezvous was not at Harisson's house, but in Cheapside. Full of firm, purposeful efficiency, Stewart pulled his bonnet low over his long, bony face, and set off.

*   *   *

Just past the High Cross of Cheap, next to the rich gables of Goldsmiths' Row, the sun gay on its sinewy carvings, the painted balconies, the gilded statues, was the house Harisson had designated. Cheapside was thronged. Its sparkling conduits, its church spires, its inns, its calling apprentices ('What d'ye lack?'), its thrusting bustle of men and women, cheerful, noisy, decently dressed, were all kindly to Stewart's eyes: a fat token of promise for the leisure to come. He dismounted at the gate; a boy ran forward to take his horse, and he was conducted instantly to the sunny parlour overlooking the garden, where he found Brice Harisson waiting.

Excitement, suspense, pleasure, had never altered the middle-aged smartness of Brice's face. He was dressed as usual, with extreme care, his doublet braided and his cuffs showing, a slit of frill above the small hands. He wore a dark puffed cap on his brushed hair, and the flat of his cheeks and his thin nose shone.

He represented success, amity, excitement, and a haven from the brickfields of Islington. Stewart grinned, his Adam's apple moving untidily, before he noticed that Brice was not alone. Beside, him in black and scarlet robes and the gold chain of his office, was a sheriff of the City of London, with his usher and clerk.

By God, thought the Archer, and paused, controlling his delight. By God, Warwick is with us. We've got a sheriff to deal with the affair. Next it'll be the Mayor, Alderman and Recorder. But naturally he won't risk getting the Council openly involved. An intermediary, this would be. And a very nice house, thought Robin

Stewart, looking round appreciatively, to conspire in. There were two men standing at the door.

'That is the man,' said Brice, the pliant voice flat, not taking time to answer the grin. Stewart looked round, but no one had come in. Instead the sheriff, a stout man marbled in puce, unrolled a paper, depressed a firm pink underlip as overture, and read, 'Robin Stewart, late of the Royal Guard of Scottish Archers in France and now in London and in no known abode: know ye that I, John Atkinson, Sheriff of the City of London, am bid and empowered to seize and hold you on the charge of conspiring against the body and person of the high and mighty Princess Mary, by the grace of God Queen of our dear sister kingdom of Scotland, while under the roof and domicile of the Most Christian King and our dear ally, Henry II of France. And until instruction be received from France or Scotland as to your disposal, I have here a warrant that you may be put under ward and guard, from this day onwards, in the King's Tower of London. *Take him*.'

There was a soldier at either of his elbows. Robin Stewart didn't heed them. His long face yellow, the grain exposed by the sinking blood, he stared, unfocussed, at the sheriff. Then his ruffled head, on its long neck, swung round to Brice.

No soldier stood at Brice's elbow; nor did Brice, in any of his languages, utter a word.

'I thank God,' said Sir John Atkinson, rolling up his parchment and passing it to the clerk, 'that a warning of this wicked plot was given by Master Harisson here to an emissary of the French Ambassador, so that the affair could be prevented in time. I have no doubt what your fate will be. The King of France will have a short way with intended murder and high treason.'

Stewart heard the first half of this; then, with a conscious suspension of understanding, stood thinking of nothing at all. A distorted picture, slipping glutinously from nowhere into his vacant mind, showed him Tosh, chatting amiably among the wood shavings, and a pearwood block with the Culter arms.

Then Tosh's asthmatic face gave way to Brice's, flat and white; and Brice's voice, higher-pitched than usual, saying, 'That's all, then. That's all, isn't it? I assume he can go away now. He had better go before Crawford comes back.'

Stewart missed it. Because understanding was only now coming dizzily into his brain, like the agony of blood refilling a limb long benumbed, he missed it and bleated, his own voice breathlessly tight, '*You gave it away!*'

Harisson looked quickly at the sheriff and away again, saying nothing.

This time Stewart's voice was louder. 'You went to the

Ambassador! You told them what we were doing! You sent for me just now! You pretended to go to Warwick and help, and all the time . . .' An impossible truth, a dreadful certainty, burst upon Robin Stewart, raking back wildly among Harisson's recent affairs. 'Ah, dear Christ send you to hell, you filthy tattle-bearing runt—*you're in league with O'LiamRoe!*'

'I really wish you would take him away,' said Brice Harisson angrily. He faced Stewart, the veins of his dark, high forehead standing out, his hands clenched behind his flat back. 'No one could have gone on with it, I tell you. My God, you might as well conspire with an elephant. Blundering in and out of boats in broad daylight, putting your horse in my stables. You never did one thing well in your life— Christ, not even killing that fellow you talked about. O'LiamRoe didn't persuade me to make a clean breast of it, Stewart. Only one man did that—tried to force me to tell the French Ambassador the whole transaction, and begged me to betray you. Not O'LiamRoe, you fool, you stupid, long, witless fool. *But your friend Crawford of Lymond.*'

There was a shocking silence. When you least expect it, the true, rending blow falls. 'He's dead,' said Robin Stewart, his voice bleached of colour.

'He was here in this room a few hours ago. Laughing,' said Brice Harisson spitefully. 'You and your vile plots and your deadly nightshade. They must be fair palsied with laughter in the Loire Valley by now. High treason! You poor, puking villain,' said Harisson, carried back in his nervous hysteria to the frightened defiance of boyhood, 'you couldna knock the head off a buttercup!'

The numb nerves were alive now. The blood was boiling in his veins; his head and heart were full as the stiff core of the earth with hard-packed purpose and power. On either side, the two men still stood, but neither crowded him; carelessly, they had left him his sword. He did not even think. As Harisson spoke, the Archer drew his blade and took a step forward.

Harisson backed, his voice choking off in mid-air. Stewart took another step. Harisson screamed, a dry, unexpected sound which continued for a long time; he was jammed, now, against the window, as far away as he could get. Through the window the apprentices' calls floated, thinly, like gulls. The sheriff said, 'Stop him!' in a loud voice. The clerk and the usher hesitated, and the two guards ran uncertainly forward.

They were far too late. Staring down into the sallow face, the grey hair wild, the braided epaulettes twisted—'It's about time I practised then, isn't it? Go to hell where you belong,' said Robin Stewart, his eyes stiff, his breath noisy as a man under drugs. And raising both hands with the long sword between, he brought the blade, like an axe in a shambles, upon the quailing body beneath.

*　　　*　　　*

That same Thursday night, Lymond returned from his fruitless journey to Islington, changed, and armed with de Chémault's authority and his own powerful insignia of office, went straight to Warwick to express his formal concern at the plot which had come to light involving a Scot in his custody named Brice Harisson, to request that Harisson should be permitted to visit de Chémault for questioning, and to ask English help in tracing and capturing Harisson's accomplice, the Scot Stewart.

It was the routine opening in a game imposed now on both sides: every move must be made in public, and its predestined course was quite clear. The French Ambassador had no doubt that the man Vervassal would handle it competently.

And aside from this competence, there was an understanding of the unseen balances of the situation which went deeper than de Chémault's own. When, unguardedly, he had spoken of Stewart to his wife and she had exclaimed, 'An assassin! Ah, not from John and Anne's own company! How he will feel it!'—he had felt, without seeing it, the flick of Lymond's attention. He knew that, convalescing from some injury, Crawford had been pressed into duty by the Queen Dowager in the absence of other accredited messenger—a thing not uncommon for a well-born younger son. He knew a little, even, of his past history, for Tom Erskine was an old friend. He would have liked to have known more. Jehanne, his wife, he guessed was afraid of the queer, catlike young man with the stick.

They had begun supper when Lymond returned, served privately tonight in the Ambassador's own quarters, the men moving quietly with the mutton and quail, their livery caps neatly laid on the buffet. On the tapestry cloth Jehanne's silver sparkled in the late April sun.

It was she who heard the step pass the door, and was driven by her housewifely instincts to rise and bring him in. He turned as she called after him, 'M. Crawford, we have kept supper for you!' and came in. But although he took his place courteously at their table and made conversation fluently, he crumbled his way absently through the meal, unimpressed by her cooking; clearly interested only in making an end so that he could inflict business on Raoul.

He began, in fact, before they had finished, when she had barely ended her best story of the baby's attack on the cat. Certainly he smiled at her, and said something she must try to recall next time she wrote to Maman. But the next instant he had turned to her husband and broached the subject of his interview with the Lord Great Master of the King's Majesty's most Honourable Household with no apology at all.

She did not, of course, fully understand the details. She watched him instead play with a silver cup filled with their best wine, untouched, while he said, 'Exactly the kind of story you would expect Warwick and his friends to concoct. According to him, three weeks ago Stewart came to them with an offer, but Lord Warwick was perfectly ignorant of what it might be until today. He is shocked, appalled, disgusted, and will do everything in his power to help us.'

Raoul did not seem put out at having his favourite meal interrupted; indeed his voice was less testy than she had often heard it, at the end of a long day of work. 'And Stewart and Harisson?'

'Harrison was arrested, of course, for reasons quite unconnected with this affair. The letters to the Queen Dowager. That is their story, and they are bound to keep to it.' The herald paused. The despised wine, beneath his spare fingers, rinsed the rim of the cup, and Jehanne tensed in her seat. The tapestry was expensive.

Then Vervassal said, 'I had no need to ask them to help find Robin Stewart. My talk with Harisson evidently had some effect, even if it was not quite what I intended. In his rather tardy efforts to pacify Warwick, Harisson sold the Archer to him instead of to us. In other words, Harisson confessed to the sheriff that Stewart had approached him to act as middleman in a plan to poison Mary of Scotland, and that he, Harisson, had betrayed the plot to the French Ambassador, who knew all. The sheriff told Warwick, who of course knew all about Stewart and the plot, but not that you were aware of it. From that moment the English Council, for the sake of their relations with France, were forced, of course, to sever all their connections with the scheme. In return for God knows what promises, Harisson was instructed by the sheriff to send for Stewart, who was captured this afternoon and bundled off to Ely Place for a complete confession— the poor idiot thought apparently he might still win Warwick's support and told them again, with some pride, all his qualifications as a hired assassin—and that, according to Warwick of course, was the first direct news he had of the plot . . .

'. . . I can imagine Stewart's feelings,' said Lymond, 'when his lordship, instead of opening his arms, began to shriek for every guard in the Palace. Stewart is in the Tower. Warwick has undertaken to have his confession written out and sent to us, and will send him to you or straight to the French Court for punishment. He will take that up with you himself.'

'It is for the King to say. I shall write him tonight. And Harisson?' Raoul asked.

'Harisson?' said the man Crawford, and got quietly to his feet, an appalling solecism, with the curious quick lurch he had which covered whatever was wrong with his leg. 'He and Stewart were brought face to face, for identification, at the sheriff's house, and Stewart killed him. No one, obviously, rushed nobly upon the blade. So there is no evidence against Warwick, and no evidence but Warwick's, and O'LiamRoe's, against Stewart, come to that. You must get Stewart's confession out of the Council. You can hardly act against him otherwise.'

Adding rudeness to rudeness, her husband had risen too.

'I shall take Stewart into my own custody. He will confess then.'

There was a fractional pause. Then, 'I think not,' said Crawford calmly. 'My advice to you, on the contrary, is to insist that Warwick keeps Stewart and is wholly responsible for sending him to France. England is desperately anxious to avoid an incident. That is already clear. The surest way of delivering Stewart alive to France is to let Warwick do it. He dare not let him die.'

You would think something ominous had been said. The two men stood facing each other, eye to eye, without saying a word; then Raoul, saying, 'Nothing would happen to him here,' suddenly grasped Crawford's arm and added loudly, 'Go! Go, go. You wish to go. I should not have kept you.'

Startled, Jehanne got up and looked at first the herald, and then her husband. Lymond, who had not in fact moved, went on as if nothing had occurred. 'If it did happen, you could not prevent it. You realize why we must have Stewart's confession: it is a weapon we shall have to use. He has a superior unknown, still living in France. You must make Warwick send him to Calais, and you must extract that written confession with every shred of power you have. They may seem willing, but they won't want to supply it. From Calais he will have a French guard to take him back to the Loire. I shall concern myself with him there.'

From his face, Jehanne de Chémault guessed, with uncharitable pleasure, that the prospect was anything but convenient. Raoul had thrown open the door. 'I understand you. We shall speak again in the morning. The urgency in all this, you must remember, is relative.'

Lymond, his weight on his stick, stood facing the door. '*Je vous remercie*,' was all he said, but she could see Raoul smiling with the undue warmth of relief, and then the herald, recalling his duty at last, turned and made her some sort of apology and withdrew making, as she saw through the half-closed door, straight for his room.

And all very well for that gentleman to burst in halfway through supper, leave Raoul with a deskful of work and then go off to bed; but the sooner he left Durham House, thought Jehanne de Chémault and wrathfully said so, the better she would be pleased.

Lymond did leave Durham House the following day; but only to visit the Earl and Countess of Lennox, from whose rooftree he had made up his mind to remove Phelim O'LiamRoe.

266

VI

The Nettle and the Venom

It is not the tooth of old age that merits it: it is not age that
shares the tribe-lands; it is not the age of nettles that gives them
venom.
   He is entitled to full honour-price out of his confidential,
talking or discoursing amus.

AS a child might toy with a squirrel, Margaret Lennox had
   played with O'LiamRoe in the three weeks which followed his
first critical visit to Brice Harisson's house, the heroic venture in the
bookseller's, and the visit to de Chémault which had ended his share
of the affair.

She played with him idly, softly, skilfully; and he knew it. Lazy to
the bone, he was also perspicacious. A few weeks ago, he would have
taken all the amusement he could get out of the situation, and at the
first twinge of discomfort escaped. This time he did his level best,
cursing wildly under his breath, to hit the ball back.

He had not gone to de Chémault again. Lennox, whose fair,
sagging charm O'LiamRoe could not find funny, came sweeping into
the great reception room one afternoon, flung his hat on a chair, and
said, 'Well, they've got him. They've got both of them. Now he can
damned well take his foot off my neck. . . .'

Then Lady Lennox had followed him into his study and they had
discussed the rest privately. But that evening as Phelim himself was
nicely launched on a favourite tale about the two little dogs and the
eggshell, the Countess of Lennox broke in, her robes as sheerly pure
in the firelight as they fell from the loom, the pearls milky in her
greenish-fair hair. 'I have news for you tonight worth more than
two dogs and an eggshell. You should go to Cheapside, Prince, now
and then; we can match Dublin, nearly, for excitement.'

'How so?' O'LiamRoe was busily interested.

'The Archer who took you to Ireland was arrested today at Cheapside, and has confessed to planning the death of Scotland's Queen
Mary.'

'Do you tell me?' O'LiamRoe's blue eyes were round. 'And myself
sitting easy on that deck, within a foot of the rail, and he might have
had me over in a winking. A would-be assassin!'

'An assassin in fact,' said the Countess. Across the hearth, her firm, well-made features were bathed in innocent light. 'As he was taken, he ran a sword through his betrayer—a man Harisson who had been his friend.'

'Ah, the devil,' said the Prince. 'That's the French for you. There was Harisson smoothing the way for them. The least they could do, you would think, is protect him.'

In the ensuing silence, Margaret Lennox's fine eyes fixed on his, within them the faintest spark of amusement. 'Now why ever should you think he confessed to the French? It was the English who took him. He's in the Tower tonight.'

He heard the story through, and wondered vaguely what had gone wrong. It did not seem greatly to matter. Robin Stewart had confessed, and justice could be done. The name of the herald Vervassal had cropped up briefly. It meant nothing to him, but thinking it over later he wondered if this was the man whom the Queen Dowager, on receiving his message, had decided to send off to London. He spent some time that night thinking about Margaret Lennox.

She had been interested, of course, in his visit to France. He had become used to that after Paget and the rest, politely questioning, had tried to find out what he had been offered, and what he knew. The January rumour had taken a long time to die: the rumour that a vast French fleet was preparing to invade Ireland and throw out the English neck and crop. He could have told them that since she had repossessed Boulogne, France was sitting back in comfort watching Croft and all the rest of the English Council's minions in Ireland crying wolf. He didn't say so. O'LiamRoe's feelings, to himself, were not at all clear.

Other people had done extremely well out of England. Long ago, Ireland had been ruled by English-born deputies, but all this had given way sixty years before to home rule by the great, noble families, and the great, noble families had feathered their nests like eider ducks in a snowstorm. They had ruled, Ormond, Desmond, Kildare, as if they were kings, giving state offices to their families and using state funds for themselves.

Old King Henry hadn't stood for it. The Viceroys came back, or the Lords Deputy as they were called, and after a cracking rebellion during which an O'Neill actually got himself crowned King at Tara, the whole drove of nobles had been killed, or had been deserted or been bribed over to England. The ten-year-old Gerald of Kildare, whose family's claim to rule had wrecked the Kildares for good, had fled to Italy, and the uprising had almost expired.

Then the earldoms flew like henfeed. Forty chiefs and lords submitted and got their English titles, renounced the Pope and promised to help the Lord Deputy's raids; got houses and land near Dublin for their horses and servants when they trooped into Parliament, and sent their sons to be educated in England, or in the Pale.

And now, as the whole upheaval began to settle, crumbling, only one name stood out among the unpardoned. Brian O'Connor, lord of Offaly, brother-in-law of Silken Thomas, done to death after the notorious Pardon of Maynooth, and the strongest supporter of young Gerald, had had all his lands confiscated and had been flung into the Tower, still defiant. But his son Cormac was free, landless, unpardoned, and swearing revenge.

O'LiamRoe thought of that; and he thought, too, of the oath sworn by the ex-rebel Conn O'Neill, once crowned King at Tara, as he knelt before the King of England to be elevated to the title of Earl of Tyrone. *'That I may utterly forsake the name of O'Neill. That I and my heirs shall use English habits. That I shall be obedient to the King's law; and shall not maintain or succour any of the King's enemies, traitors or rebels. . . .'*

And he thought of the dog Luadhas and did not mention to Margaret Douglas when she probed, sewing with her women one sunlit afternoon after that, that had the King of France offered him ten thousand men and the ring of Gyges, he would still have shaken his head, related the tale of the two dogs and the eggshell, and trotted obstinately back home.

He told her instead, when she asked, about the grand ollave he had had, that was called Thady Boy Ballagh; and the time he filled the quintain with hot water at St. Germain, and wrecked the river pageant at Rouen with a herd of elephants, and upset the tumblers and began a riot in a cellar and climbed the steeple of St. Lomer in a race after dark.

He was aware of his glib tongue checking here and there, for the story did not come lightly to him. But her questions went on for ever, and her women giggled. At the end she said, 'And your splendid Thady Boy, what happened to him? You told me he was still in France when you left.'

The ready pink moved up into O'LiamRoe's clean-shaven face. He absently pawed the short, silky hair that would not disarrange, patted his padded silk chest and said, 'No. . . . 'Twas a sad tale. In fact, the poor soul is dead.'

For a moment her eyes widened; then the lashes fell. Her strong fingers, idle for the moment, drifted among the silks in her alabaster box. 'You didn't tell me this. Of what?'

'I only learned of the thing recently.' Again the ready flow had stopped. O'LiamRoe said angrily, 'He was a crazy fellow, with a devil at him, and going the foolish way to his grave.'

There was an odd look on Lady Lennox's face: a look of astonishment mixed with a kind of satisfaction, as if he had confirmed something she had already suspected. In the midst of O'LiamRoe's uneasiness, a piece of information dropped suddenly into place. Once, Lymond and Margaret Lennox had been lovers, and she had betrayed him nearly to his death, to be tricked and mishandled in return when he redeemed himself. George Douglas was this woman's uncle. And George Douglas knew that Thady Boy and Lymond were one. Lady Lennox had made him show her Lymond, deliberately, through his, O'LiamRoe's eyes.

The same, blue, space-filled eyes were perfectly able to hide this discovery. He did not interrupt the little silence that fell. The ladies whispered, the silver dust from the silks moved and danced in the sun, and the Countess's monkey, slipping its tether, flew unnoticed along the long silken wall from shining table to table top and, reaching the end, hung poised from a painting and leaped, its pink fingers outspread, for the great stucco architrave above the white double doors. It was sitting there, its eyes bright, its gold chain tinkling, when the doors opened on the announcement that the herald Vervassal was waiting outside.

*   *   *

She had got rid of her women. Only O'LiamRoe remained by Margaret Lennox's side as the doors reopened and in the shadows a man came to stand, fair, lightly made and dimly sparkling, like crystal half-seen in the dark, a young page carrying a baton at his back. Then he moved out into the fine room and the monkey, shrilling, dropped on to the cloth of gold tabard, thick and dazzling as the sun on the sea. 'Hallo! A family welcome,' said Lymond. 'How kind, Lady Lennox.'

Contemplating all this cool symmetry, O'LiamRoe was pleasurably startled. Heralds, in his experience, rarely addressed ladies of royal birth with quite so much edge. He looked at the Countess. Her unusually bleached good looks which he had been admiring a moment before had given way to a sudden queer heightening of her splendour. She drew a long, unsteady breath. The air, which had been alive as an eel bath with brilliant unchosen words, became abruptly quite dead. Sensing it, on a queer Celtic wavelength of his own, O'LiamRoe felt his skin prick. Turning, he look at Vervassal again.

The shrillness of temperament you might have suspected from that opening sentence was not in fact there; rather there was, nearly concealed, a sort of residual power, clear as blown glass, piercing and concentrated as a needle of ice. O'LiamRoe became conscious that the man was looking at him, and turned away. The herald's gaze turned to Lady Lennox, who, O'LiamRoe could not know, saw none of these things: saw an untouched boy's face of eight years before

270

and another, more recent, with the new hammer-shapes of leadership plainly on it. And now here was a face she had never quite seen, circumstances she did not know, an intellect she recognized, an illness he could not easily hide, pressed and frozen together into a detachment as dark and icy as O'LiamRoe's, for example, was shallow and warm.

For all these reasons, for the surge of a blind force within her that she had throttled all these years before and abandoned for dead, Margaret Lennox looked back at Lymond and was silent. O'LiamRoe, glancing back and forth inquisitively, met the curious, direct gaze again, was taken and vaguely disturbed by what he saw, and smiled.

The blue eyes glinted. The herald, drawing the monkey gently on to his hand, said, '*La guerre a ses douceurs, l'hymen a ses alarmes.* You are forgetting your duties, Margaret, in all this excitement. Won't you introduce me?'

It was the quality of the voice, a timbre it had held even when most abysmally drunk, that held O'LiamRoe paralyzed where he stood. His heart gave a single loud beat that drove it straight into his stomach, and he felt his whole comfortable interior recoil, leaving his exposed skin naked and cold.

The words, miraculously, brought Margaret back her balance. Using her strong, steady voice like a weapon, 'Mr. Francis Crawford,' she said, 'The O'LiamRoe, Prince of Barrow, and lord of the Slieve Bloom in Ireland.'

'I am honoured indeed,' said this unknown resurrected Thady Boy Ballagh with exquisite courtesy, his gaze dropped to his hands. 'But, my God, it's a damned silly name for a monkey.'

And then, as he dizzily came to realize, except as a whetstone O'LiamRoe was forgotten.

Sitting straight, for once, in his chair opposite the Countess, Phelim saw the fair man take a seat, the monkey bounding from his fingers like a ball, and observed for the first time the passive right hand. Flurried speculation over that was broken by Margaret's sardonic voice. 'Pray don't allow the shock of it all to confuse you she said. 'Popular resurrections are a tedious pastime of Francis's. Had I known he would do this, I need not have played out our particular farce.'

'My dear, the shock is mine. *De par cinq cens mille millions de charretées de diables*,' said Lymond; and catching the monkey on his knee by the hairs of its chin, gazed from it to O'LiamRoe with bland enquiry. '—*Le cancre vous est venu aux moustaches*. Your whiskers, Phelim! Did your revulsion impel you to a general lustration?'

The Countess's voice was calm. She lifted her sewing and spread it flat on her knee. 'Don't work so hard, Francis. The Red Lion. He needed them off for his disguise.'

The only method of dealing with that was to look as if one had known the fact was public property all along. While doing this, O'LiamRoe, his senses raw as a burned man's on the side where Francis Crawford was seated, realized that in some way Lady Lennox had scored. In the second's pause before Lymond answered, the Prince of Barrow said apologetically, 'I was hard-set to look like an Englishman; a fine race but not as much hair with it as would furnish a Meath man with eyelashes.'

'God,' said Lymond. 'Would they want them? Any Meath man I knew had his eyes pickled like radishes; you could wipe your feet on them and never a blink. In any case. *Tu ne fais pas miracles, mais merveilles.*'

'He doesn't understand French,' said Margaret Lennox, lifting the little, precious box with her silks. She had recovered all her serenity. 'Don't you remember? Although from what I hear of your behaviour in France, your whole recollection is presumably blank. Someone gave you a slender excuse, and you drank yourself raving into the ditch. Degraded to the point of stupidity when you neglected the simplest precautions. How like you, Francis. And then, rescued no doubt by someone else, at considerable risk, you dress in diamonds, promenade the sodden pieces of your brain and wear your pitiful bruises soulfully like a cross. Are you even injured? Or are you walking like that for a wager?'

From his chair, in absolute disbelief, O'LiamRoe saw the alabaster box coming, cast with casual accuracy to pitch against the limbs so exquisitely exposed by the high cut of the tabard. It was a right-handed catch, for a quick man. Lymond flung up his left hand to intercept the blow, but it was O'LiamRoe's arm, shooting forward, which diverted the box. It brought him down on his knees, blundering unavoidably against Lymond's chair as he fell. The heavy case, grazed by his hand, shot off sideways, half-opening its alabaster mouth, and struck the monkey hard on the neck.

The blow was mortal. Without a sound, the furry thing dropped; and O'LiamRoe, crouching, caught it loose in his hands and laid it down, the winking chain dangling. Above him Francis Crawford, his face like a mask, bent too, but looked at neither O'LiamRoe nor the monkey. Lingering helpfully, after one curious glance, the Prince of Barrow looked at the white and tawny beauty of Margaret Lennox and thought of another animal and another death.

'He smelt,' said the Countess, and sitting back, watched O'Liam-Roe resume his seat. Lymond, scooping up the dead monkey, laid it on the table beside his chair. 'But at least we have enjoyed, my dear, the harrowing display of your impotence. What do you wish of me? Money? Or work?'

'. . . For to give good smell and odour to the Emperor, and to void away all wicked airs and corruptions? Margaret, this air of chaste reproof—you have joined the Reformed religion, I know it. No more transubstantiation and other naughtiness? Matthew has turned Lutheran?'

In some way, in his turn he had silenced her. He added chidingly, 'No?'

'No.'

'Then I should advise,' said Lymond gently, 'that he should give it serious thought. Meantime, to save you the trouble of asking him to leave, I have come for The O'LiamRoe.' And the Prince of Barrow, thinking fast, found his former ollave addressing him. 'Will you come to Durham House with me? I can wait outside while Piedar packs.'

They were involving him in something bitter and dangerous, in which he had neither responsibility nor concern. O'LiamRoe had no intention of spending a minute more than he need now at Hackney. But equally he was bent, single-mindedly, on shutting Francis Crawford's affairs out of his life. He had no wish to go to Durham House. He would go to an inn. He intimated this last, briefly.

Margaret smiled at them both, her ribboned sleeves slack in her lap. 'My dear man, your charming juggler, your Abdallah al Kaddah here, won't allow that. He wants you to help him take Robin Stewart back to France.' And holding the herald's eyes with her own, she laughed.

His bright head resting on the chair, Lymond watched her undisturbed. 'Would you care to wager?' he said.

'Wager with me.' It was a new voice: a grating tenor, breaking in from the open door at their backs. O'LiamRoe turned as Matthew Lennox came in, his pouched eyes glittering, something black and gold turning between his white hands. 'Your boy was loth to give it up, Crawford, but I felt you might need its support.' He threw the herald's baton lightly, and Vervassal caught it. 'Wager with me,' said Matthew Stewart, Earl of Lennox, standing hands clasped before the fire, his bright gaze on them all. 'I have more to lose.'

Then, smoothly, he moved to refresh their wine. 'If you set foot in France you will be arrested as the late Master Ballagh, who designed the treasonable accident in Amboise castle. George is no lover of yours.'

'George's son's wife is now the heiress of Morton,' said Francis Crawford. 'And however much anyone may suspect that Thady Boy Ballagh and I are one, no one can prove it.'

'Forgive me,' said O'LiamRoe. They all looked at him, and he twiddled his fingers. ''Tis over-curious I am, that I know—but tell me, why should any of us escort Robin Stewart to France? Has he not confessed?'

Lennox smiled; and after a moment Lymond acknowledged it.

'Yes, quite. Thus perishes a minor state secret, *que Dieus assoille.*— He has confessed, Phelim; but for his own manly reasons Warwick is unlikely to provide us with a copy of the confession, however expurgated. It is, after all, the only direct evidence against Stewart, and if Warwick withholds it, Stewart might be persuaded to be discreet in what he says about his lordship himself. And lacking that confession, my dear, Stewart might possibly prove hard to convict. Hence the desire for your testimony.'

'What a shame, now,' said O'LiamRoe blandly, his smooth face milk-warm in the sun, his shining elbows raised, smoothing his hair. 'The ill-lucky thing that it is; but I shall be needed straight back in the Slieve Bloom this summer, and time to travel to France I have not.'

'You needn't trouble,' said Matthew Lennox. 'You won't be needed. Stewart'll never leave the Tower alive.'

O'LiamRoe was tired of being regarded as foolish. 'Do you say so? I would say, from my reading of matters, that Warwick's whole standing depends on Stewart getting safely to France.'

It was the Countess who answered, out of the brittle silence, her husband knew so well how to induce. 'Naturally Lord Warwick wants him alive,' she said. 'No one is more concerned about this than his lordship. But Stewart, you see, has attempted suicide twice and is now trying to starve himself to death.' She rose slowly, a tall woman, splendidly built. 'Matthew, the Prince is leaving us. Forgive me; I have things to arrange.'

In this vast house, packed with servants, there was no need for her to go. Lymond's voice pleasantly said, 'Don't retreat, Countess. You are not being pursued.'

She halted, her head up; but her husband broke in. Where do you go, O'LiamRoe? To an inn?'

'The Master of Culter will maybe advise me.' In this bandying of titles he had remembered, suddenly, Lymond's own.

'*Who?*' It was Lady Lennox's voice. Then she laughed, a laugh of free and genuine amusement, her eyes not on him but on Lymond, his head back, his gaze perfectly unmoved. 'Prince, you have a good deal to learn. Did you think he was a gentleman's heir, with his borrowed tabard and his gems? Ireland has triumphed, O'LiamRoe—the traditional stab in the back. Mariotta, Culter's wife, has given birth to a son. A per robert, my dear. *Whose*, of course . . .'

There was a tiny silence. Then O'LiamRoe saw her take a quick breath, her eyes flying to Francis Crawford, but Crawford was not looking at her. Between Lennox and Lymond there passed something unsaid: a single, white-hot flash of enmity that could be felt. Then with a curious, smooth-looking twist, Lymond got to his feet. 'Do these things matter?' he said.

'*Dhia*, they matter to the lucky ones, so,' said O'LiamRoe placidly. 'There's Lady Fleming, now. The news came down from Scotland just yesterday, and the whole court agog. A boy, it is. A fine, bastard boy for the great King of France.'

It was well meant; but although he knew quite a lot, the reaction found him nonplussed. Standing still at his side, his clothes aflame in the sun, his eyes half-closed against the glare, Lymond turned, and laying the herald's baton deliberately down, stood empty-handed before the Countess of Lennox. Her face pale, her eyes sparkling, she laughed. '*The Flemings? Whores to a woman*,' she said.

Her husband, O'LiamRoe saw, had moved away. Francis Crawford said nothing. But his gaze, even and cold, continued to hold hers until, in the end, the woman's eyes shifted. 'Some love for a living,' said Lymond. 'And some kill.' And raising the corpse of the monkey in his jewelled hands, he laid it in her arms like a chrisome child, and bending the golden head, bowed.

*   *   *

They left together in the end; O'LiamRoe outwardly calm over a jumble of uneasy emotion, fidgeting to be free of this rare and troublesome ghost but chained, for the hour at least, by the burden of a vague and indefinable debt. In the street Lymond, his page dismissed, said, 'There is an inn not very far away. I don't suggest that you stay there, but we could rent a room for an hour and talk. I'm sorry you had to witness so much private unpleasantness, as well as my sudden resuscitation. I might have guessed she wouldn't have told you.'

He paused again and said, 'If you were enjoying your stay, I must apologize again. But they have fallen out with Warwick, and in fact would have found it unwise to keep you much longer. But you probably have gathered a little about all that.'

'A little,' said O'LiamRoe. After a moment he said, 'Is it far, this inn?' And when Lymond did not answer him, he said, 'Give me your reins.' But at the touch of his hand the other man, withdrawing suddenly, said, 'Good God, no. It isn't far. The chimney pots there, over the trees.' And they rode on after that, separately in silence.

It was O'LiamRoe who sent for food and wine and O'LiamRoe, in the end, who ate, discoursing at gallant length in his most prodigious blossoming of whimsy, on every topic in heaven and earth open to a literary-minded Celt in their private room at the Swan. In between eating, he scowled at Piedar Dooly who, in between serving, scowled at the bleached and resurrected ollave, blazing with undeserved riches that would have dazzled the Pope, who lay on his back before the jumping wood fire, his tabard off, his head sunk in a cushion, juggling absently, over and over, one-handed, with a crown and some testons.

O'LiamRoe, who had expected to find him a good deal less formidable lying flat like a schoolboy under his feet, became aware, as he ended his meal, that Lymond was merely waiting for him to finish. The Prince of Barrow got up, remarked, 'Piedar Dooly, let you look for a fine lady scowler somewhere else down below,' and as the door slammed, came and curled his comfortable unhandy person at the end of the hearth.

'Talk away,' he said. 'So long as this thing is quite clear. A week on Tuesday, 'tis the Slieve Bloom for me. Neither England nor France, I find, is quite to my taste.'

The little coins showered through the thin fingers. Trapping the crown piece, Lymond flipped it sideways into the flames and lay with one arm under his head, watching the silver run, the king's face sagging over his armour, miserably, until it mixed with his horse. 'What did they offer you for your goodwill and your horse and your kernes and your gallowglasses?'

'Enough,' said O'LiamRoe. 'Or even too much, depending on how you look at it. I didn't care for the look of the Irish pages they have. I admit the Slieve Bloom isn't Upper Ossory, but it would be a sad, unnatural thing to beget a silly foreign creature like those to sit at my fireside and table.' He paused, and then said, 'They are in a queer taking, surely, over this man Stewart. Why should they not wish him convicted?'

Lymond, who had turned, moved his eyes back to the fire. 'Because Warwick is working hard towards a closer alliance with France; and he greeted with just a little more warmth than he would have anyone know Stewart's offer to dispose of Mary in return for cash and favour and a nice little manor somewhere. He must, sooner or later, hand him over to France. But Warwick has probably offered at least to hold back all the English evidence against Stewart, if Stewart keeps quiet. There is no other proof worth speaking of, and Stewart can always claim that Harisson was mad. He might have a chance.'

'Well, God save you. Whether they can prove it or not, the French won't let him out of their sight,' said O'LiamRoe easily. 'There seems little need to chew up your tongue on that score, unless it's dead set you are on flaming swords and the like. Did you suspect Stewart in France, now? Was that why he poisoned you?'

An odd expression, half-understanding, half-rueful, rested for a moment on Lymond's face. Then he said, 'I did. But that wasn't why he tried to kill me.'

'Why then?' O'LiamRoe, speaking in idleness, recalled suddenly Stewart on his knees, in that bedroom in Blois.

'He had found out who I was. He knew, you see, that it was one of us. He guessed at the wrong one. . . . But you knew that, Phelim.'

He had known. Open-eyed, staring across the fireplace to the blank plaster wall, he saw the flaming curtains of the Porc-épic, the tennis court, the looming galliasse, the helmeted footpads jumping out of the shadows in a dark street in Blois. But his roused understanding showed him the edge of something else too, which fumblingly he tried to disentangle, his face blank as the wall. Lymond said quickly, 'But the point was that the attacks didn't stop when you and Robin Stewart left. They simply transferred to me.

'Since, at the end of it, I was supposed to be dead, I let it appear that I was dead. And to make quite sure that I should inconvenience no one any longer, the rumour has been put about that I was the author of the accident in the first place. Hence Lennox's kindly suggestion that I should find it difficult to re-enter France. We shall see. In fact, apart from the Erskines, the Queen Dowager and my brother, and one or two allies, only one person that matters knows for sure that I'm not dead.'

Lymond had not moved. He spoke into the fire, lucidly as O'Liam-Roe had heard him sometimes in the early days demolish some wild argument of Michel Hérisson's. Yet the Irishman, his soft hands clasped firm on his knees, felt his stretched nerves begin to play with his breathing. He said, striving to push it all aside, 'You are saying there is another man in it, who wished the little Queen dead?'

'I'm sorry,' said Francis Crawford, and turning, looked with reflective eyes at the flushed fair face of O'LiamRoe. 'I've given you no reason, I suppose, to think me other than bent on sport or revenge. But the facts are these. Robin Stewart had an employer. I hoped to draw him away from this man, and failed. Whether of his own accord, or because the two quarrelled, Stewart abandoned his principal and fled home to try to sell his services elsewhere. Whatever happens to Stewart, somewhere in France there lives still a man who has sworn to try to make away with the little Queen. Stewart knows who he is. So does one other person who might talk. I have to choose which to . . . persuade.'

O'LiamRoe didn't know that his face had suddenly grown white. Sharply he said, 'That great silly fellow would be wax in your hands. There he is in the Tower, and you a herald with all your great powers. What ails you to visit him?'

There was a little silence. Then Lymond moved, drew a sharp breath, and relaxed. 'I have, Phelim,' he said. 'He won't see me. And he is fasting to death.'

'The devil choke him,' said O'LiamRoe deliberately. 'I am not going to France.'

It was an admission; as the words left him, he realized it. But

Lymond took it no further. He merely said, staring still into the fire, 'I'm not asking you to. I'm asking you to visit Robin Stewart in the Tower, and either to get from him the name of his patron, or force him somehow to see me.'

Retreating wildly, bruised already by the forces gathering about him, The O'LiamRoe said, 'I thank you kindly, but I've had my true fill of secrets. With the whole force of these old Queens behind you, and Warwick half out of his skin in case the poor fellow dies, you can hardly fail, surely.'

'I think not,' said Lymond. O'LiamRoe could hear the hiss as the other man let go his breath; then with a movement on the surface perfectly easy, Lymond turned over at his feet and, lying still, his head invisible beneath his long fingers, said, 'Tell me. Why would you not go back to France?'

So this was how it was coming. With a grimness new to him, O'LiamRoe said, 'Let you be still. There is nothing more of this to discuss.'

'We shall discuss no more than is necessary,' the even voice said. 'Why would you not go back? You must know that she tried to protect you. She tried to keep you from returning to the castle that night. And she offered you . . . almost anything you desired, I would guess, to go away from Blois. Your face told as much.'

The name of Oonagh O'Dwyer, lying like a banked fire under their words for these ten minutes past, had never yet been spoken. There was no need. Illumination and despair equally in his heart, O'Liam-Roe said, 'After the accident . . . she helped you too?'

Bronze as a penny in the firelight, the head at his feet moved assent. Then without looking up, Lymond said, 'She knows for whom Robin Stewart was working—she was working for the same man herself. If Stewart dies, either you or I must go back to France and force her to tell us.'

'*No!*' said O'LiamRoe sharply.

The hands came down flat from Francis Crawford's face, but he stared still at the rug. 'No? Why not? She likes you. We must find out what she knows. Or the child dies.'

'I have told you.' O'LiamRoe's own voice was colourless. 'I will not go back.'

'*Why*, Phelim? *Why? Why? Why?*'

Blazing, blue, the eyes fastened on him like live things in Lymond's uplifted, white face. '*Why?*'

'Because,' said O'LiamRoe baldly and terribly, 'she is the mistress of Cormac O'Connor.'

In the face below him there died slowly both the anger and the light. Other changes were there, but in the shadows O'LiamRoe could not see them: only the top of Francis Crawford's head, held in his hand. Then Lymond spoke, without triumph, without indeed any emotion at all. 'I didn't know,' he said, 'whether you knew.'

The circle was complete. All the turmoil of feeling sown in him by the creature lying at his feet slammed and spouted in a gush of pure, boiling anger: the anger of abused innocence and hurt pride and stubborn blindness leaping back from the light. O'LiamRoe stuck out a booted foot, and with a jerk that nearly sent him on his own face, threw Lymond head and shoulders back to the light. 'You're so damned brilliant,' said Phelim. 'You know everything. It's hard-set you'd be to give yourself a dull Saturday afternoon. We're all puppets—not the old Queens only, but the rest of us, man, woman and child, looking the fools of the world.'

'Not of my making,' said Lymond. His eyes, in the full light, were animal-bright.

'Ah, no, my fine, busy fellow. But you have them there, on their strings, all curled tight to your littlest finger; and you little heeding as you swing them what soul you may bruise. Francis Crawford knows all about Oonagh, does he? Or enough to send her rocking on her dizzy bit thread, while he shifted the rest of us to and fro?

'I was sorry for the unchristian drouth on you, and the slack hand on your duty. When did you decide to put pity on me for that? And why? When you used the small girl herself, pricking Robin Stewart, or O'LiamRoe, to tumble them like sheep's knuckles the way you would want? I would not wonder,' said O'LiamRoe, his bitterness flooding his voice, 'did Robin Stewart kill himself this day or the next. You have roused your bright words before him the like of a king, and you a halflin gallowglass in the top folly of youth, with a tongue to make the blood leap from the bone only. . . . She nursed you well, did she?' The deepest place of his hurt, unaware, burst into words. 'And you two laughed over your secrets?'

'She held me bound and drugged in the Hôtel Moûtier for Cormac O'Connor to deal with. Nothing but violence would make her talk about her share or his.' Deeply breathing, lying still on his elbow, face averted, the other man hadn't stirred.

'And since you cannot cast me now in the role of lover, violence is what you are planning to use?'

There was a pause. Then in a voice unlike his own, 'I have my duty,' Crawford said.

O'LiamRoe swore. Swearing, he got stumbling to his feet, and striding over the floor, picked up his hat and his cloak and the bag Piedar Dooly had not yet unpacked, flung some coins on the table and returning, stood astride the golden head and the holland shirt and the long hose as Vervassal reclined still, watching his rings frosty in the light, his face groomed and inexpressive, pastured by the costly jewels in his ears.

'Robin Stewart was little joy ever to me, or to himself, I would suppose; but there is not the least heart in me to see him rolling fish-cold and choking in the great, godly stream of Francis Crawford's duty. I will go to the Tower. There is money on the table,' said O'LiamRoe, in one of the rare, consciously wounding attacks of his life, 'to pay for your keep this evening. I cannot afford more than one night of you.'

VII

London: Pledge to Fasting

He who does not give a pledge to fasting is an evader of all: he who disregards all things shall not be paid by God or man.

He is a man who has lost his patrimony, who does not possess anything visibly or invisibly, and the supply of whose stores is chaff. He is not entitled to be advised, in sickness or in cure; and his meals even are empty unless he steals, or unless he sells his honour in the same way. His green is empty to him too, unless a person gives him something for God's sake. His freedom too is empty; and his honour-price.

THEY had put Stewart in one of the tall towers, in a thick flagged stone room with a window and a fire, for he was an Archer, a political prisoner, and the citizen of a friendly power.

To The O'LiamRoe, climing the worn stairs with Markham, the Lieutenant, the place smelled less of despair than of a sort of threadbare vanity—the damask powder over the dirt. Markham was muttering about the conditions: 'He's suicidal. How do they expect me to keep him in a room like a boudoir? I've had to put one of my best men in to live with him, wasting his time.' Then, as O'LiamRoe was silent, the Lieutenant said irritably, 'I hope at least you'll have more success than the last man they sent. When we got in, the prisoner had slashed his wrists. Blood everywhere. The fellow had to leave without setting eyes on him, and we had all the mess to clear up.'

Lymond hadn't told him that. Heavily, his accustomed insouciance dead within him, O'LiamRoe wondered just how he had expected to rescue Stewart from the egotistical shadow of Francis Crawford when disillusionment itself was the reason for Stewart's despair. Then Markham stopped in front of a door and put his key in the lock.

Stewart had heard the voices, dreamlike, as a child in bed hears older children speak and laugh in the free air outside. He recognized O'LiamRoe's, but this time he was tired. For three days he had refused his food and on Friday half his blood had drained from him; he had no energy for the surge of passion with which he had heard the soft cadence of Thady Boy Ballagh's voice outside his door. Stripped of its brogue, he would yet have recognized it at the ends of the earth. Sometimes, after he had killed Harisson, it had come to him that

281

the little traitor was lying. For Ballagh—Lymond—was surely dead.

But he was not, and it was true. Afterwards, his wrists bandaged, a guard brought, sulkily, to watch the door, he had lain in the window and watched them leave, down below. Markham had come out first, half-turning, fussily expatiating; and then a silvery head he did not know. They had gone off together under the trees: Markham and his slender companion—the latter with a stick, Robin noticed, in his hand. Then unexpectedly the limping figure had turned, and in the uplifted face, drained of colour by the wide, pale sky, he had seen the ghost of Thady Boy Ballagh. For the moment, he had the illusion that the searching eyes looked straight into his; then presently the fair head had turned and the man he, Stewart, had poisoned walked steadily away.

He had sent O'LiamRoe now, presumably to gloat, perhaps to persuade him to tell the thing that Warwick had promised him his life to keep quiet, perhaps to try to force him to live until he could be gratifyingly punished, in France. Warwick's offer to suppress his confession had no meaning for Stewart; he was going to die anyway. But he saw no reason to oblige O'LiamRoe with that or anything else.

So the Prince of Barrow entering the small, lived-in room with its heavy table, its stools and its boxes, its camp bed set up in a corner, its barred sunlit window, its pale fire, was conscious of the worn, inexorable barrier of Robin Stewart's enmity even before the door was locked fast behind him, leaving them quite alone. But he spoke steadfastly; only his vowels were perhaps a shade rounder than usual. 'I want your help,' O'LiamRoe said, 'to trim a bowelless devil named Francis Crawford until there's a human place on his soul to put the mark of grace on.'

This was, of course, a trick. Sunk in his chair, his eyes fallen on bone, the folds pressed dark and moist in his wrecked face, Stewart lay without speaking while the Irish nouns buzzed in his ears like bees laboriously moving a hive.

For a long time he did not listen at all. The voice swung to and fro, like sealight on driftwood, without affecting him, crushed hard as he was in the blackness, his nostrils crammed with the endless, sliding rubble of his failures and his inadequacies. Robin Stewart had resented all his life the fact that he, of all others, was always imposed upon; that he had been forced to work hard for all he possessed, without the magical mercy of accident or fortune to make smooth the path.

Three times, from this undeserved isolation, he had found another man to broach the gap into the golden world of smooth affairs and easy friendships, and three times he had been abandoned and betrayed. And now he knew, with dry finality, that these things

282

happened, not because of what he was not, but because of what he was. He was a painstaking fool with less than average gifts, who had been led to believe that hard work would take you anywhere you wished to go.

It did, if you were a person of ordinary, likable disposition, whose talents could be made to grow. His lay stopped within him, mean and static and immalleable, and would never alter while he lived. He did not care to live. Then he realized, as the warm, patient rubbing of O'LiamRoe's voice went on, that the Prince of Barrow was relating, slowly, clearly and without expression, the whole story so far as he knew it of Lymond's mission in France. And as it continued, it came to Robin Stewart, with the first dull stirring of thought, that here was a fellow victim.

O'LiamRoe told him all he knew, all that a night's hurtful thought had made plain to him. Lymond had used him and had dispatched him, in his own lordly way, when his usefulness was done; administering a passing kick of adjustment as he went. All had been seized upon and used, even his friendship with Oonagh O'Dwyer.

O'LiamRoe brought out the name flatly. This tale, told to a man he had no time for, and searching into the personal minutiae instead of the great verities which were his proper concern, was the hardest thing—perhaps the only hard thing—he had ever done in his life. Stewart, listening, felt whisper within him, as in the old, difficult days, the sardonic, bitter flame of accusation and jealousy. He said, 'You were fair away with yourself over that cold-faced kitty, weren't you man? God . . .' And feeling again the strong hands holding him, that vital, glorious night on the rooftops in Blois, 'You and me—we're damned ninnies both. She's O'Connor's whore . . . she tried to kill you. You know that?'

Schooling the naked, baby's face, O'LiamRoe said, 'She tried to kill O'Connor's rival.'

'Ye should have whipped her,' said Robin Stewart, with a faint and sluggish contempt. 'Whipped her and taken the woman and O'Connor's place both. You have men and land and a name of your own; you're as good a man as Cormac O'Connor to rule Ireland, if rule Ireland you must.' From the stark threshold he was crossing, advice was easy and problems were light.

'There is no wish on me to rule Ireland,' said The O'LiamRoe with, astonishingly, the vehemence of utter honesty in his voice. 'I wish only to be rid this day of the devil on my back.'

The colourless grain of the starving man's skin moved; the lids lifted; the Adam's apple moved convulsively and the dry lips opened. Robin Stewart laughed. 'He's sucking the blood from out of you as well, the bastard, isn't he? What do you want me to tell you? I'd make a rare teacher, so I would, on how to handle Crawford of

Lymond. An empty sack won't stand, man. And I'm empty, scoured, drained and cast aside. Do you fancy the road? It's easy taken. You put faith in one other man of Crawford's sort, or maybe two, and you end up here.'

'You dealt with Harisson,' said O'LiamRoe.

Stewart's eyes, in their darkened cavities, were fleetingly bitter. 'Because I was meant to. They stood aside, Warwick's men, and let it happen. So that Harisson and his evidence needn't trouble him any more. D'you think I haven't had time to realize that?'

'But you settled the score,' said O'LiamRoe. 'If you did no more with the others who cast you aside, there'd be little in it to complain of.'

'It'd be grand, wouldn't it, if it were as simple,' said the sick man's slow voice. 'With me, ye ken it's never simple. If there's a man I would fain send to hell, there's another that would pluck cream and kisses out of the sending. God give him lack . . . My curse on Francis Crawford is my silence.'

Nothing showed in O'LiamRoe's blue eyes. He said, 'I am sorry. I had come to beg for your tongue. It seemed to me that once you and I were back in France, there are a powerful lot of people who would be shocked to know that the fine herald Crawford was the fellow who fooled the whole Court of France as Thady Boy Ballagh.'

Low behind the extinct spirit, something was burning. 'Expose him?'

'Why not? Himself will be waiting for you in France. And it would give that great champion,' said O'LiamRoe, 'some small thing to think about other than the moral aptitudes of his fellow men.'

With a sharp effort, the rickle of bones that had been Robin Stewart, Archer of the Scots Guard of the Most Christian Monarch of France, struggled up in his chair. 'Who would believe me? Unless yourself . . . Would you back me?' he said.

'With the four quarters of my soul,' O'LiamRoe replied. '*Provided that you denounce the man you have been working for, too.*'

There was a long pause. 'Whatna man?' said the Archer slowly.

'Father in Heaven, how would I know?' said O'LiamRoe. 'But it's an open secret, you may as well know, that there's someone, and I dare say you and he would soon do each other an ill turn as not. I've a mind to see that child safe, and she won't be, with another of your adventurous brotherhood abroad. I'm not asking you for his name. But denounce him, tell all you know of him once you're in France, and I'll support all you want to say about Thady Boy Ballagh.'

Halfway through this painstaking speech, he knew that he had won.

Then, 'Christ,' Stewart said. 'Christ . . .' His eyes starry, hooded

284

with bone, his thin chest pumping, he saw something beyond the stone walls that lit the seams and hollows of hunger in his long face and fired his dull eyes. 'I could soup them up clean. First the tane, and then tother. Christ, I'll have the two of them yet.'

The hollow eyes, shifting, found the window, dancing in the bright sun, with the smells of dust and greenery and horses and all the life of the great, living fortress bursting soft on the wind. Then Stewart turned, and his gaze, newly clear, rested on O'LiamRoe's pale, placid face. 'Sakes alive,' said the Archer, and stared. 'Whatever came to your whiskers? Man, man, you'd break the heart of a fresh-clippit yowe!'

*   *   *

Back at his inn, where he had booked a private room indefinitely, O'LiamRoe wrote a brief message for Francis Crawford at Durham House. It said simply, 'He will travel to France, and he has agreed to give evidence against his employer, but so far will mention no names. His only condition is that you should not travel with him but that both you and I should be at hand, if not present, when he answers these charges before the French King. This I have promised. It is for you to arrange. I can be found at this address when the time comes to leave.'

Then he settled to wait. His summons came in the end; but not for three weeks—weeks during which Stewart, aided by his gaolers, nursed himself back to health while both the French Ambassador and Lymond awaited instructions from France. On the 7th of May they came. Nestling among expressions of fierce delight and admiring pleasure in the stout English honesty thus displayed was King Henri's demand that the person of Stewart be delivered across the Channel forthwith (at English expense) and a signed confession with him.

The English King and Council, reiterating horror at the whole affair and favouring the severest punishment as an example and a deterrent, thought that the French Ambassador ought to take charge of the crossing. M. de Chémault demurred. The English Council argued. There was a polite and pointed wrangle, ending in agreement to send Stewart to Calais, under strong English guard, from whence he would be the responsibility of France. England would also obtain and hand over a written confession.

The written confession, however, never materialized. Twice approached on de Chémault's behalf, Warwick was both honest and apologetic but produced only promises. In the end, on a windy, grey morning in the middle of May, the Ambassador went himself to Holborn to see his lordship. Later on the same day, O'LiamRoe received his summons to Durham House.

The stick had gone, and with it any undue need to exercise the

285

humanities. 'I got your note,' said Lymond, inclining his fair head and crossing smoothly to the study fireplace where O'LiamRoe stood. 'How did you persuade him? A pact of resistance aimed at me?'

'More or less,' said O'LiamRoe steadily.

'Of course.' The steely, restless figure dropped into a chair. 'Well, think twice before you do anything piquant. Our nations, yours and mine, are exceedingly open to hurt, and I personally am not. You realize, of course, that O'Connor will be there?'

There was no smile on O'LiamRoe's likable face. 'Of course.'

'He and Paris, I am told, have asked for an army of 5,000 men to rouse all Ireland and even Wales. The Queen Dowager and my friend the Vidame think he should get them. The Constable is not so sure.'

'The Queen Dowager is still in France?'

Lymond was examining his delicate fingers. 'Her departure from Amboise is delayed, it is rumoured, by the King's fancy for one in her train. The first hints about Stewart have got to the Loire. The Dowaager will stay at least until that is settled. In fact, I fancy she is in trouble of another kind, too; but that is by the way. We shall arrive, my dear Phelim, in the vanguard of a large embassy from England coming to invest our good and gracious King Henri for his sins and ours with the knightly insignia of the Garter.'

'Good God!' said O'LiamRoe, taken unawares.

'Quite. At the head of it will be our good Marquis of Northampton. And in the large and glittering train will travel the Earl and Countess of Lennox. They are due at Châteaubriant on the 19th of June; and before the end of their stay, they will request the hand of Mary of Scotland for their King.

'. . . But since,' the light voice continued, forestalling O'LiamRoe's openmouthed intervention, 'since Queen Mary is affianced to the Dauphin of France, and no French party has so far appeared strong enough to break the betrothal, the King of France will with sorrow refuse and will offer his daughter Elizabeth instead. It is as well,' said Lymond, 'to have all this quite clear. Because the murder of Mary with a hint even of English backing would burst asunder all these beautiful overtures of friendship between England and France. You might even expect France, if sufficiently piqued, to be ready to stir up trouble in Ireland again. In which case Cormac will probably get his 5,000 men and a French blessing to kick the English out of his country.'

O'LiamRoe sat down. 'Meanwhile,' continued Lymond, ignoring him, 'Robin Stewart has confessed to Warwick, and Warwick has repeated to de Chémault, the names of the other men in the conspiracy. One of them is Lennox: a fact which Lennox has most strenuously denied. The other is the man we are after. I knew it, every sign pointed to it, but I must have Stewart's confirmation. It isn't in writing yet; but once in France . . .'

Lymond paused, eying the ceiling. 'The last thing Stewart wants is to afford Thady Boy Ballagh the chance of covering himself or anyone associated with him with glory. Once in France, he has plans, I take it, for the direst sort of retribution. Hence the scattering of these passing favours. Lennox will warn him, of course. Stewart's probably laying wagers, the bastard,' said Lymond, laughter aflame in his eyes, 'on who's going to kill whom. Is that fair?'

O'LiamRoe cleared his throat. 'You go too fast for me. Stewart named two men. One was Lennox, and he's denied it. Who was the other?'

Lymond rose, and O'LiamRoe watched him come, walking like a cat over the polished floor, his hands clasped, his fair head tilted, his face grave. There was no trace of a limp, and a world of malice in his eye. 'Oh, come, Phelim,' he said. 'You've spoken to Stewart. If he's going to France for your sake, he's surely bequeathed you some of his handsomer secrets.'

And the Prince of Barrow was silent, for Lymond was perfectly right. He knew, and had known since leaving the Tower, that the man behind the conspiracy was John Stewart, Lord d'Aubigny, Robin Stewart's own captain—the foolish sybarite who was thrown into prison and then inadequately soothed; the man with whom Robin Stewart had quarrelled, and through whose wiser, subtler, clever English relatives the whole wasteful business had probably started.

PART FOUR

The Loan and the Limit

The law of loan among the Feine: A loan with limit; viz, Yield me my property after this limited day. A loan without limit, its time not tied or determined, is the right of him who takes it. For the world even is the loan of a house to man; for from this is the world: God gave it to thee. Thou gavest it to me. Until God shall reckon whose right it is, I shall not take it.

I:	*Dieppe: Illegal after Screaming*	291
II:	*Angers: Boarshead and Apple*	299
III:	*Châteaubriant: A Bed-tick Full of Harpstrings*	317
IV:	*Châteaubriant: The Price of Satire*	349
V:	*Châteaubriant: Proof, without Love or Hatred*	370
VI:	*Châteaubriant: Satin and Scarlet*	402

I

Dieppe:
Illegal After Screaming

She is free to the man with whom she has made an assignation
until she screams, and after she screams. The man with whom she
has made no assignation is safe till she screams; but it is illegal
after screaming.

ON FRIDAY the 14th of May, Francis Crawford and Phelim
O'LiamRoe, Prince of Barrow, took ship for Dieppe, France,
for the second time together. Under the fond grey-green wind
of the west, the sea set to hissing like silk, the timbers dipped,
and the wheaten canvas ripe in the pod spilled cold air into the poop,
where O'LiamRoe sat and sneezed.

Intimations of doom had attended the Prince of Barrow at last.
There was a woman he did not intend to see; a hypocrite he meant to
see chastened; an autocratic courtier he wished to chastise. Grimly
bolstered by these evidences of his caprice, O'LiamRoe was being
hard pushed in private to deny he was going to France because, like
sawteeth on a crown wheel, his destiny was locked hard in theirs.

Lymond, ranging the boat, his neat head stirred by the wind,
tended rather to song. ('*Les Dames de Dieppe font Confrairies qui
belles sont.*') Presumably, he knew perfectly what was before him.
Nothing of violence; d'Aubigny's guilt would take care of that. But a
fine ripping of masks and shredding of tinsel: the awful denunciation
of the elegant herald as none other than their old drinking crony
Thady Boy.

He would be able, in his own defence, to quote all that he had done
to capture Stewart and expose d'Aubigny. A waste of breath. The
embarrassed rage of his lords and lovers would rise to him in his safe
place, thought O'LiamRoe lyrically, and tarnish every shallow spur
of pseudo-gold.

From Portsmouth to Dieppe, no responsible word passed between
O'LiamRoe and his former ollave. In the city of limes, the Prince

of Barrow and Piedar Dooly would take horse for the Loire, there to enjoy the hospitality of Scottish Queens and French King alike until Robin Stewart should arrive for his reckoning.

Francis Crawford was not travelling with them. Lymond, it seemed, had business first in Dieppe. He paused once to explain that the name of his business was Martine.

'Busy child,' said Phelim O'LiamRoe, and in his voice was the sharp derision of their earliest acquaintance. 'Do you not be plotting too hard, or the strings of your charm will fall down.'

They parted, with dry exactitude, on the quay; and by afternoon O'LiamRoe was on his way south.

*   *   *

La Belle Veuve, whose other name was Martine, took an open breath, the two dimples like fingermarks in her cheeks, and half shut the door on the princely dark blue silk on the threshold. 'Wait, monsieur. Do I remember you?'

'Let us see,' said Lymond helpfully. She had forgotten how quickly he moved. 'You remember me now. The travelling gleeman.'

The demonstration was brief and rather savagely efficient. Wrenching free, composed, bright-eyed, to lead him into her parlour she said, 'Well, Dionysus. You are yourself again.'

He was uninformative. 'Bathed overnight in a pan of new milk. And you needn't think I am here because of the manifest comforts. My mind is purely on commerce.'

'Mine also,' said La Belle Veuve placidly. She was a slender, clever woman, no longer young, who had been salaried *gouvernante* to the *filles publiques* in the old King's day, when a travelling army of young and distinguished prostitutes was by no means easy to rule. 'But pray be seated, none the less. We thought you had been roasted to death.'

'Singed a little, I must admit,' said Lymond. 'But you should have seen the Druid. . . . Has she come in?'

'A week ahead of time.'

He did not need to explain. The Flemish galliasse of that September attack on *La Sauvée*, repaired at her home port and dispatched then abroad, had been a care of Martine's for many months, and it was she who had found the one jettisoned matelot who had told them all they so far knew. She listened now to the particular oath Lymond used and said, 'Is it now of such moment?'

He laughed, his annoyance gone, and examined the fine rings on her hand. 'Have you seen the Three Queens and the Three Dead Men? You will, if this doesn't succeed. Did Mathhias come to you?'

Mathhias was captain of the *Gouden Roos*, which had had orders, all these months ago, to ram and drown O'LiamRoe. La Belle Veuve watched Lymond from under her long lashes. 'I went to him,' she said. He would not, and did not, think it necessary to comment on the magnitude of the service. She added, 'The *Roos* was financed by Antonius Beck of Rouen.'

'A French merchant controlling a Flemish trading ship?'

'His father came from Bruges. He has made a fortune in illegal trading and a second fortune out of piracy. That is Mathhias's work. The Spanish treasure ships don't begin to run until they see the cannon mounted. This is where he stays in Rouen. . . . Why are you laughing? Francis,' said Martine, who in her own way was a great and powerful woman, 'You are Hell's own Apollo.'

'Quetzalcoatl,' said Lymond, and shutting his eyes, crowed like a fiend. 'Ma belle, ma belle, you have rebuilt the walls of Rome.' And setting himself, lightly, to please her, he would explain nothing else.

From Rouen he sent her a little barrel, plated with gold, with a string of twelve-carat pearls in it, from which she guessed he had discovered the warehouses of M. Antonius Beck.

*   *   *

The presses were silent and the house empty of society when Lymond called at the Hôtel Hérisson, Rouen; for the sculptor was working, the chisel sweet as a dulcimer over the rumbling ground-bass of oaths.

The name Crawford of Lymond meant nothing to him. The chime of the chisel stopped and, waiting outside the cellar door, his visitor listened with amusement to a profane exchange between Michel Hérisson and the steward sent to announce him. After a moment, Lymond pushed open the door and wandered down the steps by himself.

The statue was of the giant Tityus, felled and twisted, with the vulture sitting on his chest. Lymond had seen it, hewn into half-detailed torment when gout, in classical retribution, had forced the sculptor to break off. The gout, you could see, had not left him. He was working in spite of it, his thick forearms knotted in his white fustian gown, an old dust-cap buttoned under his chin, the grooves in his broad, high-coloured face wet and silted with dust. Round his neck, as he turned, was visible a sad rag half stuffed into his collar. Lymond recognized it, shrunken and sweaty, as Brice Harisson's smart, braided doublet. He said quietly, 'I have a message from the Prince of Barrow, M. Hérisson. I shall not take up much of your time.'

Below tufted brows like his brother's, Michel Hérisson's hot, round eyes ran over his visitor, from the brushed yellow hair to the dark jewels and the thoughtful clothes. He said, 'My god, a Fatimite!' without undue force, and dismissed the steward with a thumb.

Francis Crawford's eyes were on the Tityus. There in the dust-filled cavity of the mouth, the arched ribs and splayed hands, the stony gougings of gut was all one needed to know of the mind of Michel Hérisson, whose late brother Brice had so gallantly served his country by exposing Robin Stewart's perfidy to the French.

'Damn you,' said Lymond pleasantly. 'I'm working like a horse treadle in an iron furnace. Look again.'

The big, dirty face glared, suddenly impatient. 'Christ—'

Through the haze their eyes met, and held. '*Christ*,' repeated the sculptor with an intonation totally different. '*It's Thady Boy Ballagh!*' And with a roar of joyous recognition, Michel Hérisson leaped to embrace him.

Unconstitutional activity was Hérisson's life-force. It was enough for him to be told Lymond's purpose in France and to shriek at his assorted escapades and at the whole inspired lunacy of his masquerade without requiring to know for whom, if anybody, he was doing these things. The visit had been worth the risk. Michel Hérisson's kind of morality was highly personal and was based on fierce and passionately defended convictions. He would have hounded to death for bowelless principles and shoddy thinking any man setting out to murder a child from some sort of distorted crusading zeal. For Robin Stewart and his hurried, muddle-minded expediencies, he had nothing but careless contempt, tempered by a fairly accurate understanding. In the fallen giant and the vulture were all that the sculptor would ever say of the sword stroke with which Robin Stewart had killed his brother.

Rumour had told Michel Hérisson what all France knew, that the Archer was on his way now to Court; the sad embassy from London with Brice's effects had told him part of that story. He now heard for the first time of Lord d'Aubigny's share, and his own hurt exploded into fury against Robin Stewart's corrupt master. Lymond nursed it, delicately, and introduced the name of Antonius Beck.

'Yon raddled neep-end!' said Michel Hérisson, overflowing joyfully into the doric. 'Keeps his lordship supplied with stolen silver at half the market price. Used to buy off me, too, till I found what he was up to. By God, I could tell you—'

'Do,' said Lymond; and at the end of a vitriolic recital, related what he knew of him. 'I want proof from him, Michel, that it was for d'Aubigny that he arranged to wreck *La Sauvée* last year.'

The sculptor, spread on a box with his swollen feet on a bracket, looked from under his eyebrows at the other man. 'Stewart will tell everything about d'Aubigny, won't he? D'ye think his lordship will wriggle out of it?'

'Yes,' said Lymond placidly.

The round eyes continued to stare. 'I see. Have you seen Beck?'

'He's not at home. I haven't managed to trace him in three somewhat rigorous days. And I can't afford to stay any longer.'

'Have you any other source of proof, man?'

'One. A last resort, only.'

'With that lamentable mess,' said Michel Hérisson tartly, 'nothing should be a last resort. If it's proof, use it. I'll look after Beck. I know enough about him to bring his scalp out in quills. He'll confess . . . once I find him. But if I were you, man, I would go and make sure of your witness.'

'With a bloody great chisel,' said Lymond.

At the tone, the sculptor's light lashes flickered. 'A woman, is it? Why get dainty over that? The alchemy's different, but the claws are the same.'

'Not my property,' said Lymond pleasantly. 'The alchemy, at least. I've had a taste of the claws. Right so came an adder out of a little heath bush, and it stung the knight on the foot. You confine yourself to tearing the God's truth in handfuls out of the elusive M. Beck.'

Hérisson got to his feet. 'Christ, I'm going to enjoy it. Let's go and eat. Man, I wouldn't have known you. You've—'

'—Sinned against my brother the ass. I trust the rulers of France are going to be equally deceived. My brother is at Orléans, waiting for me with the Court news. O'LiamRoe was to arrange that.'

'You think you can fool them a second time?' Michel Hérisson, his gaze critical, helped himself, limping, to Lymond's near shoulder. '. . . God, I'm glad I'm not your brother. If they find out you're Thady Boy and d'Aubigny's still in favour, then—'

'Then how happy we shall be,' said Lymond gently, 'to have the confession of M. Beck.'

*   *   *

In Orléans Richard Lord Culter, whom Michel Hérisson did not envy, awaited his brother in the inn called the Little God of Love; a choice on Lymond's part reassuring in its felicity. Elsewhere in the inn also awaited the main portion of Vervassal's considerable luggage, his page, his valet, his trumpet, his three men at arms and his groom, as supplied by the Queen Dowager, dispatched directly to await their master's arrival.

Richard, admitted late to the Queen Mother's confidence and owing the better part of his new information to O'LiamRoe, could find nothing either chastened or repentant in the image Phelim had drawn for him—an account in which O'LiamRoe had not seen fit to include any mention of Oonagh O'Dwyer.

With mild curiosity therefore, and no more, Richard from the

Dowager's side had noted the coming of another Irishman brought by George Paris to the hospitable Court of France: a burly man of great height, with filbert cheeks, black brows and a round calyx of satin-black hair trimmed just above. After his initial reception at Court, Cormac O'Connor stayed at Neuvy, with the Irishwoman Richard had already met: a retiral advised because he proved greatly given to fighting, a pastime which also appealed to the Queen Dowager's disgruntled Scotsmen.

The Queen Dowager approved of Cormac O'Connor; the Prince of Barrow did not. In his mind's eye Richard cherished a picture of the only occasion, to his knowledge, when O'LiamRoe and Cormac O'Connor had so far come face to face. O'Connor, from his meaty eminence, tanned shiny as horn, had turned narrow eyes on the washed and rose-pink person below him, and had said, 'My faith, but the Slieve Bloom have been hard put to it, surely, to pick up a prince. Did they feed you well, now, in London?'

'Nearly as well,' said O'LiamRoe mildly, 'as in the Slieve Bloom, in the one year in six that some bodach isn't making his hero's mark battle-marching across it.'

'Fair weather after you,' the big man had said, with something approaching a laugh. 'If slavery with a full belly appeals to you. You will excuse me if Cormac O'Connor is not in it.'

'Ah, the silly fellow you are,' had replied O'LiamRoe, opening his pale eyes wide, the growing hair silky over his brow. 'What for would I be wanting Cormac O'Connor any time of my life, or any possession of Cormac O'Connor's, or any ambition of Cormac O'Connor's, or any thing which he thinks he has and he does not have at all?'

And the big man, at that, had raised the glazed brown back of his hand as if to strike the other; but Richard had moved forward and Cormac, wheeling, had marched without speaking away.

'Ah, 'tis a Crawford,' the Prince of Barrow had said, an odd, breathless look on his tender-skinned face. 'Gallant champions all. If you catch sight of a girl called Martine, you might tell her to make short work of it; for the steam is fairly beginning to come off the darling situation here.'

Then Francis arrived, exactly on time. In the private room he had hired, sparing comment on either illness or recovery, 'You incredible liar,' said Lord Culter calmly. 'You promised to be out of the country by Lent.'

'Always excepting a *damnum fatale*. I had a *damnum fatale*,' said Lymond, settling luxuriously in a doublet as soft as a glove. 'I'll take you to Sevigny some day. Nick Applegarth looks after it for me—he left a leg on one of our common battlefields. And how is Robin Stewart, by nature privily mixed?'

'On his way to Angers, I understand,' said Richard. 'Throwing off confessions like a fire stick. His best so far was at Calais, so they tell me. A copy is on its way to the King now.'

Recently Lymond had acquired a direct gaze which his brother found vaguely disquieting. 'So O'LiamRoe's testimony will not be required,' said Francis Crawford. 'And where is the Prince of Barrow now studying the hazels of scientific composition?'

'He's going to Angers as well. He got an informal welcome, but not unfriendly,' said Richard. 'He and Dooly are in lodgings, but come to Court quite a lot,' And he related the tale of the great confrontation.

'Oh, God,' said Lymond. 'O'Connor will toss him one-handed from Neuvy straight into Tír-Tairngiri. And the Queen? D'Aubigny won't attempt anything now, of course. He must be sitting at home in quite a ferment wondering whether Robin Stewart will denounce him.'

Lord Culter said sharply, 'I thought he had already.'

'He has hinted to Warwick. But he's unlikely to amplify the hint. It makes no difference to him; he's going to die anyway. And where his dear John Stewart is concerned, the King as you know would believe nothing without proof; and probably nothing with it either. And proof is what I have come back to find. . . . Other people have been working for d'Aubigny, after all,' said Lord Culter's brother, his gaze limpid. 'I have hopes of tracing one of them already. Someone in Dieppe has found out for me a connection between d'Aubigny and the owner of the galliasse which nearly sank O'LiamRoe and myself on arrival—a man called Antonius Beck, who has probably done a good deal, one way or another, for d'Aubigny. I have a friend in Rouen who seems to think he can trace Master Beck without any trouble, and who is quite certain he can make him confess. And in addition,' said Lymond, doing his work thoroughly, 'there is a woman who knows at least as much as Robin Stewart about what has been going on. I shall deal with her myself.'

Answering amusement lit Richard's eyes. 'Rumours of the new herald have come from London already. From the de Chémaults, I believe,' Lord Culter said maliciously. 'Don't disappoint them. And for God's sake don't slip into the Coiniud, or the One-horned Cow, or they'll quarter you,'

Lymond smiled. He said, 'I have something for you to take home. You *are* going back now, I suppose?'

Richard's sense of complacency increased. He had already told himself that, with Francis back, and obviously better, his tour of duty could be concluded. The Queen Dowager, he knew, needed his steadying presence in Scotland. And he wanted to go back.

Thinking therefore of ships and packhorses, he took the box Lymond held out. On the lid was written *Kevin*. Margaret Erskine, he remembered, had chaffed him about that. 'An Irish name for a Crawford! What says Sybilla to that?'

What Sybilla had said, in fact, was a flat negative to his first choice: No to Francis and No to Gavin. 'He's black amber, child. Name him after Mariotta's people,' she had said. And Kevin Crawford his heir had become. Richard, his head bent, opened the box.

Inside was a silver rosebush, just six inches high; and on its stark, leafy stem bloomed a single, night-black rose, carved half-open in jet. Their crest, in blue and silver, was set in the base. Lymond spoke, as he sat staring at it. 'I hope you like it. Send him to me when he is eighteen and needs the money; and I shall direct him to a man called Gaultier who will give him a good price for it.'

They took leave of each other that evening—a definitive parting, because Richard suddenly decided that he could not leave France too soon. Lymond was to join the Court Richard himself had just left, on its way to Châteaubriant for the visit of the English Embassy. Lord Culter himself would ride on north.

In the hour or two they had left together they avoided matters of moment, and Lymond applied himself otherwise to marking the day. The Little God of Love, which had never before witnessed a dice game conducted on a forfeit system connected with clothing, nearly had to call in the watch. There was a good deal of verse making and some singing in the public rooms. And then Lymond, perfectly sober and dangerously playful, collected his grinning train and set off, declaiming.

His brother's voice, mournfully receding, rang in Richard Crawford's ears long after the irrepressible party had gone. Turning from the vanished shadows and the misty river, he walked indoors quietly and sat down, the silver rose tree in his palm.

II

Angers: Boarshead and Apple

> There are three periods at which the world dies: the period of a
> plague, of a general war, of the dissolution of verbal contracts.
> In like manner is fixed the contract by word of mouth, as Adam
> was condemned for his red fraud: all the world died for one
> apple.

"*ANOTHER* Scot! *Tête Dieu*, they're spreading like mildew,'
Louis de Bourbon, first Prince of Condé was remarking; and
baring his white teeth he enunciated grotesquely. 'A haile Karolus,
man—what's it worth? It's worth five pennies, nae mair, in Scotland
this day; and a hauf Karolus tuppence ha'penny. Corruption and
thievery, man! Sinful corruption and illegal thievery off the Queen's
puir hapless childer the Scots!'

He and his decorative brother, passing the time with backgammon in the Gran' Salle at Chinon, both laughed excessively, and
a large, healthy man with black hair, hanging restlessly behind
d'Enghien's gilt stool, exclaimed, 'Ah, wait you until we beat at the
gates of England, you and I, with thirty thousand Irish at our backs,
and the True Church rises and kicks her tormentors in the face.
Then the snivelling Scots in their backyards nursing their bent swords
can look at heroes and chew on their shame. . . . Is he the old Queen's
man? I thought the woman was due long since back home.'

Disposing swiftly of an excellent move, d'Enghien reached up
absently and patted the big Irishman's hand. 'How improvident you
are! Do you need money? Don't malign the Dowager, mon cher.
She is a staunch supporter of your designs. She will stay merely to
see the assassin Stewart hanged at Angers and the English Embassy
safely over without any surreptitious pact concerning herself and the
child. Then you may be sure she will hurry home. Thrones speedily
cool. Twenty crowns?'

'Faith,' said the big man, laying a broad hand on Jean de Bourbon's satin shoulder. 'There is no finer gentleman on Irish soil or
under it than the like of yourself. If you had thirty in your purse, it
would clear my honour of a sore offence of a debt. And he is with
the Constable, you say?'

'Who?' said Condé, who was losing, and willing to beguile his brother's attention from the game.

'The herald. Crawford of Lymond. The Scot you were discussing.'

'Oh.' D'Enghien was examining the contents of his purse. 'He carries London dispatches.—I believe so, yes.'

The Prince of Condé, sitting in the only chair with a back to it, leaned back and laughed. 'Ask him for forty, my dear. Then ask him what de Chémault's secretary scribbled under the report he sent the other week. *C'est une belle, mais frigide.* Une belle, vois-tu!'

For a second, the third man's narrow eyes, their contempt undisguised, ranged over the two careless, painted faces. Then, his voice flattened with effort, he said, 'A smooth-skinned bag of curds, brought up by an Edinburgh dominie and turned silly on a cup of pear juice. The red blood is all run out of the Lowlands, they say.'

'My brother,' said the Prince of Condé maliciously, 'has had a sufficiency, I believe, of red blood. Better make it fifty crowns, my dear.' The game was his, after all.

'—No dissensions, my lords, I pray you,' said an unannounced voice, of serenest reproach. 'Mother Church has enough to bear. *Faut-il que Père Éternel gagne Pater Noster, et Haile Carolus suit Ave Maria quandmême?*'

In the doorway, an elegant gentleman smiled at d'Enghien, and d'Enghien, to his own delight, blushed. Mr. Crawford, Vervassal Herald, had arrived.

Fate and Francis Crawford, in wary collaboration, had arranged that the re-entry of Thady Boy Ballagh should take place in two steps.

First, he was to deliver de Chémault's dispatches at Chinon, rocky fortress south of the Loire where King Henri and his favourite gentlemen were plunging through the forests and vineyards of the Chinonais in pursuit of venery. Thus in new dress, new colouring, new name and new accent, he would meet the King and the Constable, the Vidame and St. André, Condé, d'Enghien and the rest in a new setting also.

Then he would accompany the Court west along the Loire to Angers, where the Scottish Court and the rest of the French courtiers waited with the Queen. For Angers was the last station in the Court's pilgrimage to meet the English Embassy next month near Nantes. It was also the prison where Robin Stewart, nearing the end of his own abject journey from London, was being purposefully brought. Which meant that The O'LiamRoe would be there too.

Arriving at Chinon, its Plantagenet masonry thick on the sky, Lymond showed no apprehension, and his followers, unaware of past reincarnations, certainly expected none. Scaling the steep streets to the escarpment, he was received with courtesy at the castle, and taken presently to the Grand Logis, where the Constable awaited him. The King was out hunting.

The roebuck season had opened at Easter; so had the season for evaluating the current shifting of power, ecclesiastical and temporal, in the wealthier regions of Europe, and the chances of benefiting thereby. It was approaching the time when the well-fed, well-rested and well-exercised in the kingdom with ambitions to satisfy began looking for trouble; and old men turned up old antagonisms like truffles, and dressed them in valorous tinsel to lure on the brash.

It was approaching the time too when, sniffing cautiously, the old war dogs of England and France should cease their circling and approach. The Ambassage Extraordinary now setting out from London was to do much more than invest the French King with the highest English Order of Chivalry; and a similar embassy soon to leave the Loire for London under the Marshal de St. André would carry more than the St. Michael to England. A pact of friendship was afoot, a political and military alliance, and a tacit understanding that should my lord of Warwick, Earl Marshal of England, find it necessary to deal firmly with the Duke of Somerset, the English King's appointed Protector, Henri of France, would be in no way abashed.

On Anne de Montmorency, Constable of France, lay the weight of sustaining this relationship. Alone with Mr. Crawford and a secretary, the Constable broke the seal and read Raoul de Chémault's edited account, addressed to the King, of all that had happened in London. He then accepted with a shrewd glance and read a second report from de Chémault. This was addressed expressly to the Constable himself, and contained, for the Constable's ear alone, Stewart's hint that the Earl of Lennox and Lord d'Aubigny his brother were involved.

In his report, as de Chémault and Lymond both knew, lay the explosive crux of the affair. For the seigneur of Aubigny, high-born, florid, aesthetic, unstrung, was in the enchanted brotherhood of Henri II's cronies, whom another crony might touch at his peril. The Constable read the dispatch through, picking his nose, and then laying it down, spread his broad, swordsman's hand flat on the page.

'Yes. M. de Chémault did well. Such an accusation should not reach the ears of the King until better substantiated. Unfortunately, M. de Chémault's precaution was unnecessary. The charge against Lord d'Aubigny has already been made public. The Archer Stewart was questioned at Calais, and has made a full written confession implicating his lordship, which was sent on by courier ahead. The King knows of the accusation against his lordship.'

From beyond the desk, the herald showed no surprise. 'Can monseigneur say whether Lord d'Aubigny has replied to the charge?'

301

The Constable of France used, absently, a brief and forceful expression. 'As you might expect, M. Crawford, Lord d'Aubigny flatly denies it, and his highness the King fully believes him. Unless the man Stewart brings concrete proof of Lord d'Aubigny's guilt, the seigneur will not be touched.'

'If Mr. Stewart had such testimony he would have produced it, I feel, before now,' said the herald. 'Should my mistress the Queen Dowager obtain proof against his lordship, either independently or in communion with the Archer, would she have monseigneur's aid and support?'

To this, the Constable's reply was most cordial. Nothing in the well-anointed precision before him recalled a battered figure on the roadside at Rouen. As for Lymond, chatting in the Constable's company just outside the Gran' Salle door, he yet found time to register, in the docketed stream of his thoughts, that the Prince of Condé and his brother d'Enghien and someone else were having an interesting discussion inside. Presently, it was obvious from the brogue that the third speaker must be Cormac O'Connor. It was then that he prevailed on the Constable to open the door.

Throughout the introductions, d'Enghien's gaze did not leave him: moving slowly over the burnished head, the indolent face, the beguiling limbs. For a long time after that, without quite realizing it, he stared at Mr. Crawford's polished features until something the herald said, by the very fluency of its delivery, broke his train of thought.

'M. O'Cluricaun, you said?'

'Mr. O'Connor.' The Constable, who was taking a good deal of trouble over Lymond, wondered why the big Irishman had flushed. '—Cormac O'Connor. Offaly's son.'

The herald was apologetic. 'Of course—I have it. The Cluricaun is the fairy, is it not? Who makes himself drunk in gentlemen's cellars? On pear juice, perhaps?'

There was a light in d'Enghien's lustrous eyes; a familiar light, a light which the Prince of Condé noticed and understood.

'*Une belle!*' said Jean de Bourbon to the air, in sotto-voce delight. '*Une belle, mais pas frigide! Pas frigide du tout!*'

*   *   *

That evening, Lymond met the King and discussed de Chémault's report without incident. Lord d'Aubigny's name was not mentioned, and there was no flicker on the royal, black-bearded face of anything other than doggedly upheld hauteur. To every question the herald's response was detached, graceful and proper; and remained so throughout the stay at Chinon, at Montpensier's palace of Champigny, at Saumur and during the arrival, to trumpets, at Angers.

Within the feudal fortress with its seventeen hooped drum towers, tunnelled out of black Trélazé, were Queen Catherine and her guests the two Queens of Scotland, with Margaret Erskine in their train. In the stony cells of the western tower was Robin Stewart. And living in the crowded, painted town, all florid with stone and appled wood and sliced and medal-packed slate, were the Scottish nobles, among whom was Sir George Douglas; the humble lodging of the Prince of Barrow and his servant Dooly; and the pied à terre of the lively Mistress Boyle and her fine niece Oonagh.

All this Lymond knew from the Vidame and from the Bourbons' merciless chatter. And riding with his silken banner and his servants and his own blazing livery of red and blue and tasselled gold over the River Maine and past the monolithic bastions, tower after black tower rising two hundred feet high over his head, Lymond nearly allowed Cormac O'Connor to succeed in picking a quarrel with him at last. For his main emotion, approaching his friends, the Scottish Court, all those knowledgeable eyes which knew him for the former Thady Boy Ballagh, was one of anger: sheer, helpless anger because, prinked like a cake baker at a ball, he had condemned himself to a tawdry transformation which would label him juvenile, would label him apostate, as surely as The O'LiamRoe's silk suits and shaved chin had done.

Riding, then, across the north bridge into the castle of Angers, Lymond addressed his absent friends bitterly under his breath. 'Don't show your satisfaction too much. Don't smile; don't signal your congratulations. Or by God, ladies and gentlemen, you shall have Thady Boy Ballagh back for life.'

*   *   *

It was Saturday, the 6th of June, and on the 19th the English were due. That afternoon, Robin Stewart was examined before the King's Grand Council at Angers. Lymond, who was having a briefly momentous interview with the Queen Dowager, was not present, but The O'LiamRoe and his lordship of Aubigny were. All that emerged, and all that the attendant flock of lawyers and clerks were able to reduce from it, was proof after damning proof of Robin Stewart's confessed guilt, together with an utterly unsubstantiated accusation against Lord d'Aubigny which his lordship, high-coloured and angry, coldly denied.

O'LiamRoe, his evidence unwanted, was silent throughout. His most powerful memory of an unpleasant experience was the little silence after Stewart's diatribe against his former captain, when the Archer's eyes, passionate in his sunk, meagre face, had turned on him. The look had held a fearful triumph, and an accusation as well. Stewart had carried out his share of the bargain. It remained for

303

O'LiamRoe to support him in the other half, when he chose to call on him to expose Francis Crawford of Lymond.

His other recollection came at the end, when sentence had been passed. It was not a quick or dainty death they had devised for Stewart; but he must have expected that. What he had not expected, clearly, was the smooth jettisoning of the entire case against Lord d'Aubigny. It was then that he began to shout, and they took him away. O'LiamRoe, his round face pale, wanted to leave, but had to wait until the King rose. The hearing had been short because of the bearbaiting in the moat. Stewart had not even had time, at the end, to mention Lymond. It came to O'LiamRoe that Stewart would only do that anyway, if humanly possible, in Lymond's presence, and with the largest audience he could get.

It was at this moment that he heard Lord d'Aubigny, laughing, suggest to his grace that in view of the discomfort he personally had suffered, the Court was entitled to a little amusement, not to say revenge. He proposed that Robin Stewart should be exposed in the moat; and the suggestion, with some pleasantries, was accepted.

The Court, such as it was, rose. O'LiamRoe, looking grim, went off immediately to try to find Vervassal but did not succeed, being only just in time himself to take his place at the baiting.

*   *   *

Traditionally, at Angers, such shows were held in the ditch, a hundred feet wide and forty deep, which circled the castle. The tame deer this time had been cleared out, and for the time of the royal visit Abernaci and his staff had restored the moat and the castle gardens to something of the redolent vivacity of Roi René's time, when lions roared from the river bank, the pond was stocked with swans, ducks and wild geese, and there were ostriches and donkeys, dromedaries and ibexes, and lodges of boars, ewes, deer and porcupines in the moat.

Now a miscellany of instruments, somewhere, had started to play and Brusquet, the King's fool, had descended a ladder into the moat and was performing, in mime, both sides of an encounter between a very shy lady goat and her suitor. The townspeople, on the far side of the ditch, were amused to the point of hysterics; Brusquet, who had mistimed his programme a little, capered on, smiling harshly, while the royal stand remained empty.

Then the trumpets blew, drowning the viols; but for the entrance of the Queen Dowager of Scotland with her ladies and noblemen, pacing between the great doors of the castle and on to the canopied drawbridge where the gold fringe whipped in the wind, and the gilded chairs, neatly arrayed, had dust and grass seed caught already in their cushions. The thick clouds tumbled over the sky, jerking shadow back and forth, as if dispensing sunlight from a badly made drawer; and Margaret Erskine, as she walked between the Dowager and the child Queen, did her best to keep her eyes from the new face in the torrid, familiar crowd.

Reserved and correct, Vervassal had arrived that morning. They had all seen him enter and leave the Queen Dowager's cabinet. He had not sought their company since. She saw, from George Douglas's sudden halt, that Lymond's arrival was new to him. After a second Sir George, having failed to catch Vervassal's own gaze, turned and threw a vast query in her direction, suggestive of a reeling astonishment laced with malice.

She turned away. Mary, thank God, had noticed nothing. The Dowager, although a little flushed, was of the order of superb politicians to whom dissimulation was life. Her brothers, at her other side, obviously had met the herald fleetingly, if at all, and had dismissed him utterly. Lymond himself, looking like ice, had not put a foot wrong; nor had he looked at her. She found, without realizing it, that she was watching him again, and took her place hurriedly along the side rail of the drawbridge. Even two years ago, he had not looked like that.

Then the fanfares burst out afresh, and the long gallery on the castle face at right angles to theirs became filled. Henri. Catherine. The Constable. Diane. The courtiers. The Ambassadors, the mayor and échevins, the castle Governor, the guests. On one side, in an indifferent seat, was O'LiamRoe. At the other, much nearer the front, the man O'Connor. And next to O'Connor was John Stewart, Lord d'Aubigny.

He was handsome still; magnificent in his puffed and slashed doublet, the shoulder knots sparkling, the jewels on his slanting bonnet flaring as the flickering canopy admitted the sun. But he took no time to gaze down at the arena. Instead, fists in his lap, he turned his well-shaped, long-lashed eyes on the crowded drawbridge.

Margaret could have told the very second he found what he sought. His lordship of Aubigny drew a deep breath. Whatever, from his brother's warning, he had been expecting, it was clearly not this. Then slowly, as he gazed still at Lymond, the colour returned to his face and Margaret realized she was watching an open challenge. D'Aubigny was intent on capturing Lymond's gaze. Then, suddenly, he had it. Between gallery and gallery each man looked silently into the other's eyes and conveyed, not an ultimatum but a judgment. Then below, the first bear and the dogs were let in.

It was an old sport, a little run-down now, popular since the days of the Triple Goddess when lions by the hundred, elephants, bulls, giraffes, were killed in internecine combat in the Roman ring. It was a little difficult, now, to find new and interesting combinations. Once

305

the old King had cheered the Court for a fortnight by laying his drunken dinner guests in the lionhouse, à la Heliogabalus, and then introducing a very old beast with its teeth drawn, to shock them awake; it was not repeated, as the lion shortly afterwards went into a decline. Modern baiting was simpler: between bear and bear, or boar and mastiffs, or bull and lion; rarely between beast and man. The animals were brought in wheeled carts, pushed close to the arena gates. Outside, Abernaci and his staff stood waiting, with swords and spears and lighted torches, ready for accidents.

They were not needed. The first two combats took their course. The bear, ponderous and flat-handed, bare-rumped with disease, still managed to strangle one of the mastiffs pitted against him, and broke the spine of the second. They pelted his bleeding muzzle with flowers as he was led off.

The boar was a different matter. A bolster of fat and muscle, plated with spikes, he hurtled sud-strewn through the gates and stopped, skidding, under the straw dummies they had dangled over his head. This was not a sanglier, but a fresh-caught wild boar of the third year. The arms and grinders stuck dripping out of his mouth were nearly two fingers thick; and in the heavy head, sunk below the strong flesh of his shoulders, the eyes were needle-sharp and red.

He was angry, excited and frightened; and the grotesque, wind-jolted dummies catching his eye, he raced towards them and gored. There was a cheer, and a spatter of straw whisked into august faces. The two bigger tushes, contrary to appearance, were harmless; they existed only to whet the two lower. With these he kills. Grunting, the boar turned in its small feet and made for the next figure.

Amid the cheers Sir George Douglas at last worked to Vervassal's glittering shoulder. For a moment he studied the downcast lashes and the imprint of well-bred deference held, evidently without effort, on that harlequin face. Then he turned his own eyes to the boar and said, just loud enough for Francis Crawford to hear, 'It is a proud beast, and fierie and perilous; for some have seen him slit a man from knee up to the breast and slay him all stark dead, so that he never spake thereafter.—You know that Robin Stewart is about to take the arena?'

He got Lymond's attention then; all of it, except that the man's eyes in the event looked through him and not at him. 'Dear me, really?' said Lymond slowly. 'I wonder why.'

The answer to that was easy. Sport. They wouldn't permit him to be badly damaged; indeed, if he were skilful, he might make his kill and escape unhurt until his official disembowelling. Sir George was not fool enough to give Lymond the easy answer. He waited, alive with curiosity, and after a moment the other man said reflectively, 'Of course, a little public odium would be helpful,' and turned back

306

to the ditch as if satisfied. Resignedly, Sir George settled to watch.

Behind the gates, the keepers had launched into the *agere aprum*, the shouting and horn blowing calculated to rouse the beast and bring him to frenzy. The third dummy, exploding on the wet tusks, snapped free and flounced over the grass. The boar's head dipped, and with a rustle the dummy soared into the crowd on a flying carpet of straw rack and glitter. The King, glancing at Lord d'Aubigny, leaned forward and raised his baton. As the boar turned, dripping, and paused, the gates opened and Robin Stewart was pushed inside.

From the Archers lining the stands and the passages, there was rigid silence. From the townspeople, long since primed by rumour with tales of more deeds than he had ever done, there rose a clamour of shrieks, hissings and mock threats. He was the fourth dummy. They did not much care what he had done, if it made good gossip and good burning. From the Court, according to rank and nationality, there was impatience, anger and disgust, and ordinary pleasurable anticipation. The Dowager's features were set in their harshest mould; but then a great many people were looking at her. A trumpet blew.

A boar trusts to his strength and his tushes, and not to his feet, which are slow and less than nimble. To kill him, a man needs a spear of exceptional strength, razor-sharp, with a crossbar of great staying power. This is to prevent the spear, once driven in, from sinking so deep that the man is brought within range of the boar's last, formidable charge.

Robin Stewart had one of these; and in his other hand a sword. He had also, invisibly, the years of his profession, when from Christmas to Candlemas every year a chosen escort of Archers had helped the monarch bait, net and spear his boar. And more than these was a violent anger, driving out even fear, at the fate which could strip him of the dignity of death and the pleasures of denunciation at one stroke.

He did not suppose he would be left deliberately to die. Someone would intervene—if they could. But he was there to make sport, with the beast of this world that is strongest armed, and can sooner slay a man than any other. In the last resort, the man his life depended on was himself. And Thady Boy—Lymond—wherever he was, was still untrammelled, still fêted and free.

A gust of wind rocked the last dummy. The boar, hearing, started round at it and then paused. The heavy head turned again, and the small, thick-veined eyes hunted, stiffly, for the man-figure the delicate nose had picked out. The young boar, the animal gregale, the stinking beast born to rip, sidled, stopped, gathered his haunches and, shaking his leather hide, his shield and his straw-spattered spikes, launched into a straight charge at the Archer.

As if Beelzebub, god of Accaron, oracle of Ochazias, had dragged her by the hair, Margaret Erskine looked round. She met, disconcertingly, the direct gaze of George Douglas, who raised his eyebrows in even more exaggerated enquiry this time. Beside him was an empty seat. Circumspectly, controlling all her impulses, she searched the crowds, to realize presently that the Queen Dowager, calling on her herald for some service, had kept him at her side. Lymond was folded neatly beside Mary of Guise's chair, distracting the attention of several nearby ladies and enjoying an uninterrupted view of Robin Stewart sidestepping the first rush of the boar.

Robin Stewart's view being equally unimpeded, he glanced up, gasping, from this endeavour in which he had slit, but not impaled, the boar's hide, and discovered that Heliogabalus, fair, exquisite and untouched in cloth of gold, was in the front row, savouring him. He turned on the boar, and the boar backed.

Then, transfigured with anger. Robin Stewart fought, and fought well: well enough for the laughter and the drawled abuse to alter to excitement. A direct hit he could not get. But as time went on, the black mess on the animal's hide showed how near he had come; and Stewart's gashed left arm, the stained doublet and the sword split in the grass told of something stoical and persevering which had always been there, but seldom drawn out in other than low causes and grumbling.

Man and beast were by that time tired, shaken with effort and the loss of much blood. The boar, sustained more than Stewart now by stubborn anger, slid and threshed on the grassy tilth, and turning, lowered his head afresh.

Now, if ever, was the moment for Henri to end it: to drop the baton and let the Archer serve his days of waiting with honourable wounds. It was Lord d'Aubigny who stayed his hand, and his own passionate love of sport which left the baton untouched. For Stewart, in Roman style, was kneeling, his back to the castle wall and the shaft of the spear tight in both hands, waiting for the boar face to face. And for the flicker of a second, as the lumbering creature gathered speed, Stewart's eyes turned, searching, to the crowded faces above his head. Some of his audience, in this ultimate moment, had risen craning to their feet. And among them, suddenly, was the herald Vervassal.

Something happened to Stewart's face—an intake of breath, a grimace of hatred, the beginning of a smile, even. Then his whole attention, blazing, meticulous, was on the charging boar.

It was the boar's own weakness which made him falter in the last dizzying second before the spear. The point took him, not through the yielding, breathing flesh but near the snout, where the near tush caught it, deflected it, and left the ponderous body, stumbling side-

308

ways, to take the shaft askew in the shoulder and twist it, shuddering, out of Stewart's wet hands. The slobbering bulk crushed him, the stinking breath took him in the face; then he was on his feet weaponless, while the boar, grazing the wall for a dozen, staggering yards, turned and faced him, tusks chattering like glass, the metal in him vibrating in the wind. The Queen Mother of Scotland dropped her scarf.

It whisked into the arena with an efficient air and lay twisted in elastic abandon, sparkling. There was silver embroidery on the hem. 'Fetch it for me, M. Crawford?' said the Queen.

For an interminable moment, Lymond did not move. The ladder Brusquet had used to enter the ditch lay at his feet. Such an order, capricious and intolerable as it might be, was royal. It was a command performance of chivalry; and to disobey it in public was something no man there would have done. After waiting just long enough, the herald turned and bowed; meeting the cool gaze under his lifted brows, Mary of Guise smiled. Then he swung over the rail and down the ladder, thrown swiftly into place. He stood there, gripping the rungs, while Stewart, unaware, backed towards him, the boar trampling the far side of the square.

The boar had seen and smelled the newcomer if Stewart, dazed with injuries, had not. He sidled nearer, approaching the Archer in small runs and halting as the whickering spear twisted within. Stewart waited, hands spread, oblivious of all but the tusks, the eyes, and the quivering haft of his spear. All the strength of his badly knit body, all the grudging, drearily acquired skills, came to his fingertips. He waited, traitor, conspirator, confessed assassin, in his single moment of solitary public achievement; his one honest treasure found just this side of the axe.

With the low, snoring groan of his kind the boar charged. It ran onesided, furiously, pounding the mangled earth, spitting blood and foam as it went, the spear whipping at its side. It ran past Stewart, past his hands outstretched to grasp the shaft, past the embroidered gauze snake lying supine on the soil, and straight up to the ladder. Lymond left it till the last second. Then he leaped aside as the boar sheared clean with his tusks the bottom rungs of the ladder where the herald had been. Lymond let him pass, took a single step, and laying both hands on the spear stuck in the animal's hide, gave a powerful jerk. It caught the half-rearing creature off balance. Squealing, the boar tottered, lurched and tumbled backwards among the debris of the ladder, as Lymond pulled the spear free of the wound.

The herald got to his feet like a cat, his tabard washed with boar's blood, lithe and gravely intent, and faced the dripping animal, the red spear in his hands. Then as the boar charged heavily for the last time, Lymond sunk the spear upright, with both hands, between the broad shoulders. The beast screamed, and its naked, neatly turned knees suddenly shook. Then, shapeless, unshackled, spiritless as a sack of wet peat, it fell on its side, the tushes scoring the turf.

Across the bulk of it, as the dust seethed and settled, swaying, bleeding, Robin Stewart faced his daemon. The flowers were already beginning to fall, clinging to the wet tabard. Lymond caught one up and walked with it, slowly, past the dead animal. The broadsword, shattered in the early play, lay at his feet. Lifting it, Francis Crawford impaled the spray on its split point and, moving straight up to Stewart, offered the sword, balanced on his two palms.

The blood sticking about his burst clothing, his hopeless hair glued on his cheeks, his lip bitten, his eyes aching, his head ready to burst, Stewart stared at the graceful gesture, the cool splendour, the careless thief of success, and seizing the sword by its pommel, aimed at Thady Boy's face.

Lymond was fresh, and moreover knew exactly what he was doing. The message he had failed to transmit, walking steadily to Robin Stewart, had been a warning against just this. He ducked, and brought his foot up in the same smooth, practised movement and Stewart, tripped, ended his lunge on the ground where, buffeted and bleeding, he rolled over and lay.

To a casual observer, nothing had occurred except Stewart's collapse. Already the keepers were running on, and with them two or three Archers, in whose charge he nominally was. The cheering, except on the part of the townspeople, was dying away: excess in anything was ill-bred, and there was a need for collective speculation. The Queen Mother's herald, moving easily over the grass to retrieve her highness's scarf, was being given points like a greyhound, and probably knew it. Any hopes Lymond might have had of discreet anonymity on his second appearance in France had been decisively dashed. His second entrée, as it turned out, was quite as spectacular in its way as his first.

When he could walk, Stewart was taken to the King at his own request. Two tumblers were in the arena, along with a goat. From the height of the royal stand you could see plainly across to the drawbridge, where the sun shone on a cluster of admiring heads, the middle one yellow.

He had the King's ear: filthy though he was, prisoner though he was, he had fought well. And the Queen, the Duchess, the Vidame, the Court all about him, were watching and listening too; only Lord d'Aubigny, in the last moments, had risen and gone.

Robin Stewart raised his voice, aiming it at the King, and at O'LiamRoe sitting beyond. '*About the man calling himself Crawford of Lymond,*' said Stewart loudly and plainly, blood springing as the muscles jerked in his cut face. '*There's something this Court ought to know. The Prince of Barrow there will be my witness.*'

He had their attention, at least. Within sound of his voice, conversation drawled to a halt; there was a second's silence. The Constable broke it sharply. 'You presume, sir. The gentleman is a herald of her grace the Queen Dowager of Scotland, and is no concern of yours.'

'Is he no? Is he no? Then he's a concern of yours, monseigneur, and a concern of the King's, and a concern of everybody who doesna care to be made a fool of, whether he's a pet of the de Guise family or a dressedup tumbler with a chapman's tongue in his heid. . . . Ask The O'LiamRoe. Listen to the Prince of Barrow, then,' said Robin Stewart, his voice an uncontrolled shout. 'Tak' tent o' this!'

Mysteriously, like a simple-minded jack-in-the-box, O'LiamRoe's face appeared at his side. The kind, oval face glanced over over the arena before O'LiamRoe said, 'Death alive! Listen to what? The only soul I ever knew anything about was Thady Boy Ballagh, and him due for the block for mass murder now that our other suspect is proved white, white as the driven snow. Lymond? I met him in London. Aside from that, I know nothing of the fellow at all.'

In a single, ripe-vowelled breath out of Ireland, Stewart's one, sweet hope of revenge had thus gone. For a moment, as he stared dizzily at O'LiamRoe's steadfast, scarlet face, he was on the verge of denouncing Lymond regardless, in face of the ridicule and denial and the final, damning opposition of O'LiamRoe. He struggled with it, breathing heavily, while the translation was going on, aware that he was losing their attention. The King, his eye straying impatiently to the goat, said, 'Eh bien, monsieur?'

Stewart opened his mouth.

'Body of me, take him away,' said the Constable briefly. 'This is a man already half crazed. Who else would lift a sword just now against one who had just saved his life?'

The King said, 'Did he do so?' in the same moment as Stewart exclaimed, 'I could have turned off the beast by myself. Devil draw me to hell, I didna need that mincing mountebank—'

The royal brow cleared. 'Stole your audience, did he? And receives a fine reward, I see. *Below*.'

They cleared him away, shouting. He had let them bring him to France for two reasons: to implicate Lord d'Aubigny, and to expose Lymond as Thady Boy. Because of the King, Lord d'Aubigny was still free. And as a direct consequence of that, he had lost his only corroborative evidence against Lymond.

O'LiamRoe wanted Lymond exposed and degraded; but he was too soft in the guts, it seemed, to make him suffer for another man's crimes. Robin Stewart was not. He was not to face the wheel for the better part of a week. And before he died or after it, Robin Stewart would make sure that on Robin Stewart's behalf, if on no other, Thady Boy Ballagh would suffer.

*   *   *

Gossip, bright-eyed and smiling, brought the news of this exchange to Lymond later in the afternoon and went away empty-handed. The final verdict on Robin Stewart he already knew. It meant that the affair of the Tour des Minimes and the spurious thefts were still attached to the name of Thady Boy Ballagh, and he was finding the evidence, despite his own formidable efforts, to be of a vaguely damning nature very hard to disprove. If this disquieted him, nothing of it showed to his companions of the afternoon. In the logis he shared with two others he received visitors and abstractedly exercised his charm.

There was nothing else he could do. In casting her pearls so casually before the enraged swine, the Dowager had not only risked his life. She herself made no further demands on his time; he was free, and in the absence of his afflicted tabard, in ordinary clothes. But so successfully had she marked him that he could safely go and see neither Abernaci, whom he had not met since his return, nor O'LiamRoe, whom he had last seen at Dieppe, until darkness fell.

Black Angers, from which all England was once ruled, was overflowing with the French Court and its outriders; with Scots, Irish, Italians and assorted Ambassadors, with officials, couriers, huntsmen, wagoners and other staff of the toiles, with experts on foraging and requisitioning, with prelates and physicians, with lawyers, archers and halberdiers, people's servants, Gentlemen of the Household, musicians, pages, equerries, barbers, ushers, secretaries, hawkers, entertainers, prostitutes and officers of the college of arms. Among the throng, in a flattened way, were the Angevins themselves, making what profit they could out of the situation before the food supplies ran out and the Court passed from this grazing to the next.

It was a dark night, and the narrow streets, packed as they were, had only irregular lanterns: a discreet man who took care to avoid the liveried torch-bearing servants had every chance of escaping notice. Lymond arrived without incident at the small lodging where O'LiamRoe had taken a room; found the back door and a shutter which opened, and followed the sound of O'LiamRoe's voice, discussing elephantine habits in Gaelic with another which was almost certainly that of Abernaci. Without knocking, Lymond opened the door and went in.

O'LiamRoe, who had only been filling time anyway, stopped abruptly in what he was saying; and Archie Abernethy, incognito out of turban and without his Oriental silks, split his dark, dry-seamed face in a grin. 'I guessed you'd be here. Man,' said Abernaci, 'you're looking a sight better set up than the last time I saw ye. . . . Yon was a lovely stroke at the pig. . . . It's a case of finding proof against yon bastard of Aubigny, I take it?'

'Yes. Well done, Archie. I wanted to see you. I'll tell you why in a moment. Phelim—'

'D'ye think,' said Abernaci, who had something he wanted clear in his mind, 'd'ye think he'd really try to harm her again? He would have to be wud.'

'The smart answer to that,' said Lymond patiently, 'is that we are all mad. But in fact men who wreck whole ships and stampede elephants and destroy cavalcades of riders out of hand are probably less balanced than the rest. Lord d'Aubigny, if it hasn't already struck you, is a slightly stupid man of exquisite culture who has been living for years off the fat of his ancestors' reputations. Up until quite recently he assumed that being the King of France's dear friend meant that you became a Marshal of France like Bernard, or Regent of Scotland as Stewart, Duke of Albany, did. When Henri took him out of prison on coming to the throne, d'Aubigny arrived fully primed for his role in history as the man behind, beside and very nearly on the throne of France. Instead, he found himself merely a foundation member of the Valois old compère society, the circle of dear old friends whom Henri had rescued from the displeasure of his father. And inside, in an exclusive circle around the King were his mistress, the Queen, the Constable the de Guises, St. André. Lord d'Aubigny wasn't going to be the Great Man of Europe.'

'So that after a bit he goes seeking a different throne to support.' O'LiamRoe, his voice austere, tried a guess in spite of himself.

'Of course. Lennox, his brother, had a claim to the Scottish throne and even to the English throne though his wife. Mary's death would give Lennox at least a chance with the Scottish succession. And if the English King were to die, Catholicism would come back with his sister Mary—or even before, if there were a Catholic revival. The Lennox family are dear friends of Princess Mary Tudor. You can see—or at least d'Aubigny could see—a Lord Chancellorship waiting for the man who should put all this into motion by disposing of Mary of Scotland. He was going to make a new career of being brother to royalty—I shouldn't be surprised if the original hint even came from the Earl of Lennox. So Lord d'Aubigny set out to sweep aside Mary of Scotland—of course; but also to teach a lesson to the French Court he was attempting to despise. He devised his murders like a masque . . . a poor, perverted vehicle for all the ingenuity of his fathers. And I think he will want to end Mary's life with equal ceremony, now that he has the perfect theatre. I think he hopes to kill her during the English envoys' visit, before brother Lennox's very eyes. A triumph indeed.'

313

Lymond's soft, even voice paused a moment to give point to this, and then went on unaltered. 'Robin Stewart in prison is an embarrassment to him. Robin Stewart dead, as we have seen today, would be better. Robin Stewart free would be best of all. Phelim, have you seen Stewart?'

'Since the boar fight? No,' said O'LiamRoe politely. 'They're taking him to Plessis-Macé tomorrow, you know?'

'Have you tried to see him?' said Lymond directly.

O'LiamRoe flushed. Then he said, 'I have, then. He's in the north tower this minute, with a power of young men guarding him. No one is allowed through.' He paused, his lips pressed with uncommon firmness against their wreathing habit of irony, and then said, 'You may as well know this thing: that Stewart and myself—'

'Oh, the pact. I know,' said Lymond with brief contempt. 'God, did you think there was anything new in it? And you are going home now, are you?'

'You have the right of it.' It was amusing to note, said the Prince of Barrow's mind to him angrily, that whatever humanitarian impulse prompted him that afternoon, he was getting no thanks for it. 'I am for home after the execution,' O'LiamRoe continued, ignoring Abernaci's jerk of surprise. 'I owe it to the fellow to stay the length of that, at least.' He did not add, *You can live for seventy hours on the wheel.*

'And the woman?' said Lymond.

He had expected that. He had known, when Stewart's denunciation of Lord d'Aubigny failed, that all this pitiless excellence would turn against Oonagh. 'The woman is no concern of mine,' said O'LiamRoe. 'Nor of yours either, if you are wise.'

'If you won't go to see her, my dear,' said Lymond, ignoring the threat, 'you may be quite sure that I shall. Haven't you seen Cormac O'Connor?'

'I have done more than that,' said Phelim O'LiamRoe, and his pleasant voice was quite changed. 'I have seen Oonagh O'Dwyer; and I have written her a letter asking her would she say nothing at all about either Lord d'Aubigny or herself.'

'That was large-spirited of you,' said Lymond. 'And his lordship may now do as he fancies?'

'I am sure,' said O'LiamRoe on a deep breath, 'that you or some other busy fellow will find a way of stopping him. Go and sit in front of his lordship and show your little sharp teeth. He might even confess.'

'Oonagh O'Dwyer knew beforehand about the Tour des Minimes,' said Lymond. 'If she knows the name of even one man to connect it with d'Aubigny, it is enough. Your opinion of O'Connor is so high, I gather, that you are willing to concede him the lady and the run of

314

your native land? Or are you afraid that once you have her, you cannot hold her, so you prefer to resign? If she is any man's leavings, you may be right.'

O'LiamRoe was on his feet, the pale eyes shining. 'You have a delicate way with a lady's name, for a hired sniffer at chairs and a licker of footmarks.'

'It's damned picturesque,' said Lymond bitterly, 'but it doesn't alter facts. Is that cunning, crib-biting lout your notion of a prince or a lover? And if I'm warned off, what do you mean to do? Wait for the execution, and then leave for home? "You owe it to the fellow".' The mimicry was merciless. 'What do you owe to Ireland? To yourself? To Oonagh O'Dwyer?'

The Prince of Barrow, standing foursquare and steady, lifted his smooth chin. 'The grace to leave her alone, my deaf and blind apostle of frenetic employment. Alone with her chosen life *and her bruised face and the white and red weals on her arms*.'

It was a hit. He saw it, bread to his famished ego, in the flicker of Lymond's eyes. He let the silence lengthen and then said, 'Go and see her. They live quite near at hand. After all, you can't be after making a pudding without slitting a—'

'You *left* her with him?' said Lymond.

'She has no desire to leave him,' said O'LiamRoe simply. 'Whatever he thinks fit, she will accept.'

'And O'LiamRoe also.' For a long moment Lymond stared at him, then got up and with a rigid, exasperated gesture, laid both fists on the chimney piece. 'Phelim, Phelim—a normal man would be there making knife handles out of his bones.'

'And of her a keening vampire at a martyr's grave,' said O'Liam-Roe, his face pale. 'Or become any man's leavings.' His lids fell; he looked, with a familiar vagueness, at Lymond's flat back. 'I have some business to do. Stay and have out your talk with Mr. Abernaci if you wish. I leave you to whet your tools and to pluck up the weeds and to cut down the tree of error.' He stared at them both for a moment, then with Dooly behind like a shadow, he left his own room.

Lymond, his head between his arms, continued to look at the fire. After a while: 'He's sore in love with that one, the fushionless loon,' said Abernaci, not without sympathy. 'You're smitten a wee bit yourself, I shouldna wonder.'

'Maybe.' It was not the voice of a man in love.

'She was his father's before she was his; that's why she won't leave him.'

'I know. But if we give her up,' said Lymond, straightening, his white face full of mockery, 'as with Faustina, we give up her dowry the Empire.' He paused, smiling with charm, at Abernaci's chair. 'What would you give to change places with me?'

315

'A night in my lioness's cage,' said Abernaci calmly. 'Robin Stewart's skin is saved, but the lass is let suffer?'

'I have a spare card up my sleeve,' said Francis Crawford. 'In case of need. And if you are comparing the two, I did Robin Stewart no service today, and I shall probably do none for Oonagh O'Dwyer tonight. Thus I distribute my favours impartially.' A little later he left; and after a suitable interval, the Keeper also departed.

O'LiamRoe himself came back to the house very late and rather drunk. The next day, reporting thickheaded to the castle, he found the Court in labour, preparing yet another majestic move. Robin Stewart, under heavy guard, had already left for his last prison at Plessis-Macé, where the King was also due that day.

The news was given him by an Archer. Pausing irresolute outside the guardroom, where the blue-tiled city lay spread below him, the smooth Maine to his left, the cathedral spire lifting ahead, he heard the rattle of a hard-ridden horse on the cobbles and was there still, intuitively waiting, when the rider, dismounting, flung himself indoors to announce that Robin Stewart had escaped.

Liking or sympathy for that difficult man The O'LiamRoe could never find. But he did understand, in part, the mark left on him by Crawford of Lymond's careless hand. His first reaction to the news was relief and even pity: no sort of life remained now for Robin Stewart but the life of a failure and an outlaw. Then he realized, with a slow chill in his stomach, the one inevitable and Damoclean result. With Robin Stewart at large, the would-be killers of Mary had been given carte blanche to finish their work.

III

Châteaubriant: A Bed-Tick Full of Harpstrings

A woman who offers upon a difficult condition: she offers herself for a wonderful or difficult dowry; i.e. a bed-tick full of
harpstrings, or a fistful of fleas, or a white-faced jet black kid
with a bridle of red gold to it, or nine green-tipped rushes, or the
full of a carrog of fingernail scrapings, or the full of a crow's
house of wren's eggs. . . .
There is no fine for forcing these women.

BY this time, the English Ambassage Extraordinary, three hundred
strong, with its aching diplomacy and its groaning digestions,
with its cliques, its amateurs, its professionals and with the Earl and
Countess of Lennox, was already at Orléans, not much more than
two hundred miles away.

Except for the Lennoxes, they were all Warwick's men. Most of
them were familiar with France, because you could not be a soldier or
a statesman under Henry or Edward without sitting at a French
siege or a French conference table at some point in your career. By
the same token, most of them had also fought in Scotland.

None of these facts was at all likely to embarrass the Embassy or
its distinguished leader and chairman, William Parr of Kendall,
Marquis of Northampton and Lord Great Chamberlain of England,
and brother to the old King's last wife; a grand gentleman of limited
gifts who had never quite lived down his military shortcomings
during the recent rebellion.

So far, all had gone smoothly. A week ago, they had been met at
Boulogne by a charming and efficient Gentleman of the Chamber
who had escorted them to Paris and then further south with their
trains of horses and mules, their wagon teams and guard dogs and
their interminable luggage.

They had been fêted. They had been entertained. At each town on
their route, mayors and échevins had made their speeches of welcome; presents had been exchanged. The political factions in the

Embassy kept to themselves; the diplomats were diplomatic; the arguments—even the arguments in and on Greek—had been staid.

My lord of Northampton hoped to God it would remain so. For they were ahead of time. In a fortnight's time, the Embassy was due at Châteaubriant, and before them lay only a simple journey by boat down the Loire.

They were due at Châteaubriant for the symbolic service of Investiture. They were due also for other and momentous affairs: to arrange a treaty of strict alliance and defence between England and France; to demand the Queen of Scots in marriage with the King of England and in the event of refusal, to solicit the hand of the King's daughter Elizabeth instead. They were due to appoint commissioners to visit Scotland and settle all the vexed points not yet comprehended in their treaty there; and they were due to introduce Sir William Pickering, the new English Ambassador to France.

And now, the retiring Ambassador, Sir James Mason, wrote anxiously from Angers enjoining delay. The Marshal de St. André had not even left on his duplicate journey to England; the great preparations at Châteaubriant were unfinished still.

The Marquis of Northampton read this dispatch, ejaculating at intervals, with his gentlemanly face flushed. The Scottish Archer accused of attempting to murder the young Queen was at Angers, and had been condemned. He knew enough to be thankful that the affair was to finish, it seemed, without any awkward revelations implicating the Earl of Warwick more closely in the attempt. The Earl and Countess of Lennox, for whom he personally had little time, were attached to his Embassy, he well knew, in case such a thing happened. If England were accused, by Stewart or anyone else, of helping or condoning Stewart's murder attempts, Northampton's orders were to saddle the Lennoxes with the blame. Lennox himself was in no doubt, presumably, about the situation, but was in no case to protest.

They would not get the little Queen for Edward, of course. Or if they were offered her at all, it would be on terms so ruinous that he could not accept. But even so, the Queen Dowager of Scotland could not be too pleased about any sort of alliance between her enemy and France, even an alliance on paper as frail as this would be. And she and her family were a power in France. They could point to Edward, schismatic, excommunicated, as no fit bridegroom for Elizabeth or Mary. And they might seize any excuse, any false step on Warwick's part, to persuade the French King to drop these overtures of friendship.

On the other hand he knew from Mason, the faithful Mason, that Scotland was becoming restive under the French yoke; that they watched with mistrust the rebuilding of forts which might turn out to be as much for their discipline as their defence. And in France, the de Guises had their ill-wishers. The Constable, notoriously, wanted the proposed wedding between Mary and the Dauphin deferred, and even the King had jibbed at presenting the Queen Dowager with the whole of her annual fifty-thousand-franc pension to take home in gold. Last month, Northampton knew the Receiver General of Brittany had been heard to comment that nearly two million francs had so far been spent on the Queen Mother, and he wished that Scotland were in a fishpool. Northampton, irritable with his responsibilities and the delay, wished the same.

Sir Gilbert Dethick Knight, alias Garter Principal King at Arms, tried not to think either of fishpools or rivers. For twenty shillings a day, he had to take and deliver to His Majesty of France the two trunks with the livery of the Noble Order of the Garter, all wrapped in a pair of fine holland sheets with a couple of taffeta sweet bags inside. They had crossed the Channel safely. But it was with a heart chafed raw with anxiety that he contemplated confiding them for two long, slow weeks to the Loire.

* * *

Scattered between Angers and Châteaubriant, where grandstands, spectacles and temporary housing had been six weeks in the making, the French and Scottish Courts accordingly took their time, having purchased leisure, cheeringly, at English expense.

The Queen Dowager's party, although not Mary of Guise or her daughter themselves, spent two nights in the fields outside Candé and enjoyed it. Reclining in the garden of France under the soft sky of June with half the Privy Council given up and gone home, they slept, ate, read, talked, and did a little desultory hawking, denigrated their hosts and the English with some thoroughness and dispersed a good deal in gentle company. In the free air, the bickering sank and died.

Nothing could have suited Robin Stewart better. During the second day, moving quietly from cover to cover, he found where, among the cockleshells of buckram, Lymond shared his pavilion. Now, at leisure, you could see how pitilessly right had been the whirling impression of the boar ring, the distorted glimpse at the Tower. Under the honest earth of Thady Boy was somebody's precious gallant quite alien to the uproarious creature of the hunt and the race. It made it in a way quite easy to kill the one without even touching the image of the other.

Thady Boy—Lymond—had been called over by a group of his fellow countrymen. He was treated, Stewart saw, with the easy familiarity due his name, and with a certain guarded respect. What Lymond would do, in the end, with himself and his talents mattered,

319

after all, more to these men than to anybody. And this singular, if temporary, metamorphosis as a state servant of the Queen Mother's would have been analyzed from Chinon to Candé.

It was the first chance many of them had had of meeting Francis Crawford of Lymond. Stewart guessed, from the gravity of his face, that he was playing with them. He saw George Douglas, bland, ironical, his manner verging on the exhibitor's, abandon all his attitudes with a thud as some intellectual morass received him, leaving him to climb out with what dignity he could. Lymond was evidently not feeling patient tonight.

The day had been hot. Lying among the lukewarm grasses, stifling his hunger as dusk fell. Stewart watched the cones of marquees all silken yellow with candlelight; and beyond, the sprinkled windows of Candé, the village and castle all ablaze. In the meadows, there was still a whole tapestry of space-dwindled noise. Men spoke and laughed; pails clanked; dogs and horses responded, and the forked banners changed direction under the light evening wind with the soft night-noises of birds. A blackbird sang.

When the light had gone, and the fires gave gold and red to the eye like the jewels of an icon, Stewart held his stolen cloak tight at the throat with his one free hand, and walked forward from under the trees.

Somewhere, a company was parting. A tent flap stirred; hosts and guests, stooping, came out, rimmed and vesicled with flurried light, the words and laughter unmasked by the cloth. The clear, pleasant voice refusing escort was immediately recognizable, accentless though it was. Someone made a faintly edged joke. '—*Le monde est ennuyé de moy, Et moy pareillement de lui.* I would prefer, forgive me, to promenade my bad humour alone.'

And turning, his hair edged with silver and his face faintly amused, like some professor escaping a dull class, Francis Crawford walked steadily through the tented grass and out beyond, to the open flanks of the meadow. For a long time he stood there alone, his back to Stewart, his eyes on the ranks of tents, now extinguished and dim; and Stewart in the distant shadows waited, watching, his throat closed, blinded, exalted by the peerless moment of victory.

Then the longbow came, cool and heavy to his hand; the clothyard nocked, razor-sharp, the aspen with its grey goosefeathers smooth to the touch. Noiselessly Robin Stewart drew the cord to his ear, the lovely instrument aiming true, the even weight of the pull on each finger pad, every muscle answering by instinct the one skill above all others he had been made to acquire. He aimed, and shot.

The whine of the flight was no more than an indrawn breath in the night; the whicker as it buried itself as soft as a harp. Vibrating, the arrow sank into the ground a yard from Lymond's right hand and

Lymond himself, collected suddenly like an animal, turned his head.

In the broad, dark meadow he was alone. The tents were silent: no sentries had seen. With a puff of dust the second arrow, bracketing him, had arrived.

He might have shouted, or run, or drawn his sword, or done all three—all equally useless. There is no reply, in clear terrain, to an archer in cover. But Lymond made no sound, though his face, colourless in the moonlight, was turned to the trees whence the second arrow had come. Neither did he draw a weapon. Instead, silent on the grass, he began to run towards the source of the flight.

Robin Stewart's mouth was paper dry. Somewhere, for the first time, a tremor began within his worn nerves. But he raised the bow for the third time, nocked his bodkin point, with its four barbs and its sweet chisel head, and standing tall, rawboned, firm, aimed and let fly for Lymond's breast as he came.

It struck him true, in the centre of the breastbone, and fell to the ground. For an instant, the running man checked. Then, one hand firm on his scabbard, choking the rattle and keeping the bastard sword out of his way, Lymond came steadily on. Which meant only one, devastating thing: he was wearing shirt of mail. And he was coming now so quickly that Stewart halted with the shock, had no time left to aim. As Lymond hurled himself into the wood the Archer threw aside his useless bow, and drawing the sword singing from its sheath, plunged forward under the trees to meet and slice the vulnerable, pale flash of bare hands and face.

Lymond had not drawn his sword. For a second they confronted each other, Stewart's blade descending already. Then the other man swerved violently, the steel grating on his protected shoulder, sparks glinting blue from the mesh; and disengaging, ran on into the shadows away from Stewart, deeper and deeper into the wood.

He had no chance of escape. The Archer's long legs pounded behind him, losing ground sometimes a little, sometimes baffled by the echelonned trees; but always led, like a drumbeat, by the crackle and thud of Lymond's light feet. Then, a long way out of earshot of the camp, where the trees thinned for a space and the moonlight fell like frost on the grass, Stewart overtook him, and Lymond turned, his sword drawn, at bay at last. For a moment the steel glowed in the darkness, caught in the queer opal light like green fire; then Robin Stewart raised his own sword and cut.

They breathed like animals, the sweat streaming down Stewart's face, a moment ago so dry and cold. From the beginning, no word had been spoken. None was necessary. Lymond had expected him; Stewart knew that now. Equally, he supposed, Lymond realized that this was the end. The death of a herald could mean nothing to a man with nothing to lose. The chain mail couldn't save a man's legs. It couldn't save his hands, or his head, or his eyes. It couldn't save his neck. Using all the lying shadows, the floating beech boughs, the leaded moonlight, Robin Stewart, gaunt and invincible, crossed swords with his private devil at last.

He had never been brilliant, but he was thoroughly trained in a hard school. He knew the joy of the first sweet tingle of contact which taught you your enemy's calibre. There was a long, fiery exchange, the sparks red in the darkness; a pause; and then a briefer one. Stewart fell back, the dried saliva stiff round his grinning mouth. They were matched. And he, who had nothing on earth left to fear, had the stronger will of the two. He paused, on an involuntary snort of pleasure that closed the back of this throat, swallowed, renewed his grip on the pommel, and began to play, delicately, for one thing only: the pale skin of the other man's face.

And that, clearly, his opponent did not relish. An excellent parry suddenly appeared, to defend those thick lashes from a cut which would have sliced the bridge of his nose. Then Lymond's blade swept low to save himself from being hamstrung. In dumb and desperate battle, Robin Stewart realized elatedly, the golden voice was silent.

It was silent, had he known it, because in the midst of these very real difficulties, Francis Crawford was also wrestling with an urgent desire to laugh.

Swordplay in a wooded clearing at night has its own special hazards: you must turn your eyes up as well as forwards, or the annihilating blade may sink deep in some curtseying bough. Creeper and rabbit hole await you; a shocked bird blunders, and the hair springs cold on your skin.

As it was, they pranced knee-deep like player-goblins, their breath in the silence like saws, the soft palate registering each truncated, tight-mouthed gasp. Stewart's blade had touched once, near the beginning, and a thread of black showed from a scratch under Lymond's bright hair. Stewart himself was unharmed.

Fern and knotted root pulling at their feet, they tired quickly. Between Stewart, with the boar's marks on his skin and Lymond with his illness behind him, there was physically not much to choose. The ear became as important as the straining eye: where the enemy's glance delivered no warning, you gleaned news instead from the rustling shift of his weight.

To Stewart, his body slippery inside his doublet, it seemed that his opponent was becoming unnecessarily nimble, but he felt no inclination to laugh. High, low, to one side or the other, the flat blades cracked and crashed, wringing his arm. With grim exaltation he aimed the deliberate, maiming blows, and made the other man hop. The sparks blossomed, bright as smithy-work suddenly, as he touched the chain mail and very nearly the neck; Lymond drew a short breath and disengaged. Stewart fell back, his eyes joyous, his dedication a holy thing; and a girl's voice, high, shaky and French, said from beyond the clearing, '*Georges! Qu'est-ce que c'est? Ah, non, ne me laisses pas!*'

There was a shocking pause. Then the bushes parted. Through them bounced a half-dressed, half-drunk and wholly belligerent young man whom Stewart recognized in a single, hate-filled glance as one of those sharing Lymond's tent. 'What in the name's going on here . . . Crawford!'

For Lymond in three dancing steps had moved into the moonlight from under the lee of Stewart's high, arrested blade and said, almost stripped of breath, 'Thank God, George. Did you see him? He ran past over there.' And pointed, with his sword, to the trees directly opposite the shadows which hid Robin Stewart.

Stewart, girded with muscle and sick resolution which somehow were to help him fight and kill two men instead of one, stood, his chest heaving, stopped on the verge. The young man said short-temperedly, 'Who?' and Lymond answered: 'One of the *venturieri*—a robber. Or so I suppose. When he heard you, he ran.'

'*Aïe! Bertrand!*' The girl's voice scraped through the silence. '*C'aurait dû être Bertrand!*' She had appeared at the edge of the clearing, Stewart saw; a local girl obviously, her hair in a mess. The long gown was kirtled, country style; otherwise, unlike the lady who by tight-lacing bought hell very dear, she was singularly untrammelled. Neither she nor anyone else had glanced behind Lymond's back, where the bushes were comfortingly thick. The Archer hesitated, then stepped softly among them.

'Was he a stout man?' The enquiries of the hasty lover had suddenly become a good deal more cogent. 'Black-bearded, with a stinking jerkin half-cured?'

'Christ, yes,' said Lymond, after the briefest possible pause. His voice sounded odd. 'Not as the fragrance of him who walks according to the precepts. Her brother?'

'*Mon mari*,' said the girl, and moaned. 'He will follow you, Georges. He will kill you. Quickly!' She tugged at him. 'You must run!'

'Try that way,' said Lymond, and indicated the way they had come. 'It'll take you back quickest.' He paused. 'You fool, you haven't a sword?'

George, swaying very slightly, fired up. 'I'll kill him with my bare—'

'You won't get a chance. Here, take mine.'

The young ensign held out his hand, then drew it back. 'But what about—'

'He won't trouble me again. He's had a taste of the steel. Besides, he knows by now he had made a mistake. Hurry, you imbecile. Good luck.'

Pulled by the lady of his heart, George hesitated no longer. Seizing the weapon and the girl, one in each hand, he disappeared into the undergrowth, and Lymond, alone in the moonlight, collapsed breathless on to the ferns, helpless with laughter. '. . . The next lesson,' said Francis Crawford, sitting up at length, 'will be some Quick and Merry Dialogues. Before you cut my throat, dear Robin, may we talk?'

Much later, Stewart realized that fate had improved on some original plan. At the time he only knew, fumbling to recover the blind paths of his wrath, that Lymond had seized the chance neither to betray him nor to escape; but had made instead the one unanswerable affirmation of neutrality: he had disarmed himself.

But for themselves, the wood was empty. You could sense it, vacant around you after the running footsteps died away. Even the wild life, flinching from the metal and the angry voices, had abandoned the arena to Lymond and him. Shakily, cold with overstrain and post-battle nausea, Stewart walked out sword in hand to where his enemy was sitting.

Looking down at the long, exposed throat, 'What did you do that for?' said the Archer angrily, 'Something you want off me, eh? Something you couldna survive, just, without. I hope so. For you'll lack it and life both before I get out of this wood.'

'Hanged in irons within the floodmarks of thy pride. I know it. How did Lord d'Aubigny contrive your escape?'

'*Lord d'Aubigny!*' After a second, flummoxed both by the suggestion and the unexpectedness of the subject, Stewart exclaimed, 'I escaped with no man's help, thank you. Are ye wud? His lordship as you well know has more reason to want me executed than anyone.'

'Why? Your cannon misfired last time, my dear. Free, you can do him nothing but good.'

'How?' It was guttural in its contempt.

'By killing me, for one thing,' said Lymond gently. 'And when he kills the Queen, by taking the blame. Afterwards, your body will be found.' He paused. 'Someone in the escort was sympathetic, wasn't he? And made sure that after you had escaped, you would know how to reach him? Someone rather clever, by the way; for a man of mine who was following you quite closely saw nothing at all.'

No one had helped him escape. He said as much again, blasphemously, with André Spens's address burning in his pouch, and André Spens's bow lying back there in the wood. The man had been friendly, yes. But as to conniving at his escape . . .

His expression, as he worked it out from that point, must have told its own story, for Lymond said quietly, 'I thought you might prefer to know. Mary's death might make of d'Aubigny a very exalted person indeed. Do you want him to kill her?'

Success for that aesthetic gentleman was the last thing he wanted. But how, anyway, to prevent it? Stewart said coarsely, 'I forgot—you were raised in a coven. A bit juggle here and a puff of smoke there, and his lordship vanishes into a bottle—if I spare you.'

'I'm not indispensable,' said Lymond surprisingly. 'Not to you, anyway. If you want to kill me, I should find you hard to stop. No. The only certain way of embarrassing d'Aubigny—surely—is for you to give yourself up.' And, as Stewart's snort of disbelief grew into a single, outraged laugh, Lymond added coolly, 'Why not? What else in God's name did you escape for? You claim you don't want to live.'

But the Archer's mind was busy. 'Why didn't you have yon silly loon come and help take me, then? Ah, of course! For greed, come ben! Witness wanted against his lordship! Ye thought out of gratitude I'd help you trace my escape back to him!'

'Perhaps,' said Francis Crawford. During all this exchange he had remained seated, his weight thrown back on his hands, his expression obliterated by the dark, like a face seen through gauze. 'It seems likely that the man suborned for your escape might well have been used, or might be used yet on an actual murder attempt. You could injure d'Aubigny to my benefit by telling me who. The only way you can injure us both is by killing me now, and by giving yourself instantly up to the Constable, throwing in the facts about your escape for good measure. With you once more in prison, d'Aubigny really dare not try; and in the meantime, proof may appear against him through your helper.'

And having stated his premise, Lymond took out a square of linen, unfolded it, and removed neatly, by touch, the trace of blood on his face.

Stewart, staring at him in the milky light, the mild leaves still and undemanding about them, listened to the exposition of logic which, half an hour ago, in his blood fever, would have meant nothing at all. You had to admire the skill which had brought this about; you had to say, however unwillingly, 'If you'd taken me between you, just now, I'd still have overthrown Lord d'Aubigny, very likely, by telling the facts, as you call it, of my escape.' His first conclusions, obviously, needed amending. 'Why then do as you did?'

'I owe you a little free will,' said Lymond shortly. 'The crossroads may not be of your seeking, but at least the road you choose will be your own.'

Stewart advanced. It was impossible to see the other man's face.

Standing so that the sword threw its shadow across the white gullet, the Archer said, 'Take off that mail shirt of yours, then.'

The silence lengthened. Then Lymond, without speaking, untied and dragged off his doublet, and pulled off the mail. It rustled tinnily, a far-off tambourine, a far-off anchor chain spilling sweet in the locker: which last anchor had been raised? Lymond said, 'It's off. Are you happy?'

Commonplace words, to achieve what they did. But, straining, Stewart at last had made out his enemy's features. There was no fear in Lymond's face. The thin, long bones of it were set in thought, and there was a line between the shadowy eyes. It all said, plainly enough, that Francis Crawford did not know what he, Stewart, would do; and that patiently he was giving Stewart himself time to decide.

The sheer weight of the blade in his hand reminded the Archer. Tightening his grip, he lifted it afresh. The soft light, like strung sequins, spilled off its edge. Lymond said impersonally, 'Are you happy?' and the leaden 'angle between Stewart's ribs, where every bearing rein of his body was whipped hard and knotted, grew until his thin throat with its coarse tendons and its comic Adam's apple shut tight. He dropped to his knees, the sword falling flat and unheeded on the dark grass, and clapping his two bony hands to his beaten face, wept.

Francis Crawford, who had his own laws. did not move. '*Je t'en ferai si grant venjance Qu'on le savra par tote France,*' someone had once written. 'I shall wreak such a vengeance that all France shall know it.' It had a noble ring.

There was nothing noble about the dishevelled head snivelling harshly at his feet. After this show of cleansing emotion, Stewart would doubtless feel much restored. Already, wiping his smeared face with his hand, he had opened his eyes, glaring, on the earth and was catching his breath to speak.

It was going to be sentimental; the very cast of the mouth foretold it. The bloody fool could not realize, even yet, that anyone trained as Lymond was could have outplayed him, disarmed him and manhandled him back to camp shirtless, swordless and without intervention from half-naked young idiots with their mistresses or anybody else.

The Archer lifted his furrowed face to speak, and Lymond said, 'But really, bastardy is no excuse for all this. Look at Bayard. And who was *your* father? The last lord of Aubigny? Old Robert?'

The other man's face stayed upturned, the mouth half opened. The resemblance to d'Aubigny was not striking, but that would explain it. The great-uncle had been a vigorous old man. Stewart swallowed. Then he said hesitantly, 'I canna prove it. Anyway, she was out of the bakehouse; they didna marry. Had they married—'

'You would have been Lord d'Aubigny. Not, I suppose, an uncommon trouble really. Would you have made a good seigneur, do you think?'

Stewart, who had been caught on all fours, crept to a log and sat down. He said roughly, 'As good as him, then.'

'Do you think so?' said Lymond idly. 'You might have harried your Protestants—yes—but would you have cherished your beautiful buildings and dressed them with works of art? Would you have spent your money on jewels and fine clothes, on music and tapestries? Neither of you can lead. Neither of you has made a wild success of the profession of arms. If you are not going to be practical, you must perfect the lusty arts of leisure.'

'Living on what?' With the tingling resurgence of anger and prejudice the Archer stiffened like a hog. 'John Stewart of Aubigny will live on manchets and muscatel all his days, out of his parents' marriage lines. The same as you did. You treat life, all of you, as if the world was a tilting ground. *The lusty arts of leisure!* When you're born to a mean spoon and a worn thread, when the only food in your mouth and the only clothes on your back and the only turf on your roof is your own bloody sweat, you get good heart out of all your braw hours of leisure, I can tell you!'

'In other words,' said the voice in the darkness, profoundly unimpressed, 'your enforced métier was to be practical. Very well. When you ran that roof race with me you started with one stocking marked, a loose row of bullion on your hoqueton, and your hair needing a cut. Your manners, social and personal, derive directly from the bakehouse; your living quarters, any time I have seen them, have been untidy and ill-cleaned. In the swordplay just now you cut consistently to the left, a habit so remarkable that you must have been warned time and again; and you cannot parry a coup de Jarnac. I tried you with the same feint for it three times tonight. . . . These are professional matters, Robin. To succeed as you want, you have to be precise; you have to have polish; you have to carry polish and precision into everything you do. You have no time to sigh over seigneuries and begrudge other people their gifts. Lack of genius never held anyone back,' said Lymond. 'Only time wasted on resentment and daydreaming can do that. You never did work with your whole brain and your whole body at being an Archer; and you ended neither soldier nor seigneur, but a dried-out huddle of grudges strung cheek to cheek on a withy.'

He stopped again, his eyes running over the rigid, tattered figure on the log. 'I wish,' said Lymond with the same surgical incisiveness, 'I wish you had come to me five years ago. You would have hated me, as you do now, but the Stewarts might have found themselves with a man.'

327

'Created by *you!*' Rising, Stewart's head blocked out the moon.

Lymond's voice sardonically deferred. 'You don't need to excel at anything in order to teach.'

'Except hypocrisy,' said Robin Stewart. 'You taught me to respect you, and all the time you were a spy. What did you teach O'Liam-Roe?' He laughed, quite out of his usual key. 'I notice he's shaved. He broke his oath to me without a backward glance the day you got hold of him again. He's neither the seigneur nor the practical man either, is he?'

'On the contrary,' said Lymond, 'he is very nearly both.'

'And by the time Francis Crawford has finished with him he'll be neither,' said Stewart. His hands swung loose at his sides, unregarded, like rough-tackle. 'He'll be kneelin' greetin' at your feet.' The thick voice choked, cut off with self-loathing, then with a new breath Stewart said, 'You're gey unsympathetic with bastardy, aren't ye, man? Gey unwilling to let us crawl over the clean floors until our manners have been trimmed? What does Richard Culter say to that?'

Silence. Then—'To what?' said Lymond quietly.

'To the habits of his famous grandfather. By all accounts a grand family man, if a mite careless where he slept. How does his lordship enjoy all the rumours?'

Lymond rose. Not quite as tall as the Archer, he had a voice which cut the space between them to ribbons. 'What rumours, Stewart?'

The Archer, fleering, did not answer directly. 'The new heir to the title's cried Kevin, is he not? I heard the Erskine woman talk of it once. The old lady wouldn't have Francis, and she wouldn't have it after your da. You can understand it, right enough.'

He didn't see Lymond's right arm go back. He only felt the brutal snap of the blow on the ridgy bones of his face. The moon dissolved into a powder of planets and the air swept his cheek as he fell.

When he woke he was alone, in the thick of the bushes, with his sword and his bow at his side. The bow must have taken some time and trouble to find.

Robin Stewart rolled over, and pressing his fists to his face, cursed Francis Crawford with hate and yearning raw in his voice.

*   *   *

It was hot. At Châteaubriant, in the new palace and the old feudal fortress, with their gardens and parks, where the old King's mistress had lived until her husband had opened her veins, where the poetry they wrote each other spoke still in the air, the garlands drooped and the new paint boiled into tremulous cabuchons. Here, in one of the Constable's splendid castles, the Court was to gather and the principal members of the Ambassage Extraordinary were to stay. In hall and audience chamber and arcade, outside in the new tilting ground, the new lake, the tone was one of severe efficiency: ceremonial inventiveness stiff-corseted—propped up sometimes, indeed —by precedent and etiquette.

The Marshal de St. André, bound for London with a train of seven hundred, several shiploads of wheat, a band of the King's best musicians, a kitchen staff of vast proportions and Boisdaulphin, the new French Ambassador, with a hundred barrels of wine for his own use alone, called and was fêted, before setting off in a leisurely way to present the Order of St. Michael and a number of interesting propositions to His Majesty of England.

If he regretted leaving his own newborn son, he did not show it. If there were more reasons than appeared on the surface for the recall of de Chémault, the Constable did not explain. The Marshal de St. André went on his way, and called on the English Embassy at Saumur as he passed. Sir James Mason, thankfully nearing the moment when his year's French embassy would end and he could pass the two thousand seven hundred ounces of silver and gilt plate on to his lucky successor, left likewise to join his fellow countrymen on their slow journey to Nantes.

At Châteaubriant, the preparations drew to a close. This was what France did best. The guests on her soil, willing and unwilling, were forced to admire as the splendid, costly machine blandly continued to work. O'LiamRoe lingered, smitten with uncomfortable awe.

He had stayed, in spite of himself, because of the little Queen. Stewart was still at large. Since the cheetah hunt, O'LiamRoe himself had been amiably received at the Queen Dowager's little Court, but he kept in touch circumspectly, lest he compromise Lymond.

His feelings towards Francis Crawford were still close to bitter; but he could not bring himself to see him denounced for something he did not do. Moreover, it had to be recognized that in this one man, however pagan, however despotic, however lawless, lay the little Queen's main hope of safety. It had also to be recognized, with a pain at your vitals that grew as day followed critical day, that Lymond's surest means of doing just that lay to hand, in the person of Oonagh O'Dwyer.

O'Connor was not to be at the castle for obvious reasons of diplomacy from which the Prince in his state of registered neutrality was exempt. Mistress Boyle and her niece likewise, harmless residents, were permitted to attend, and had rented lodgings for themselves in the town, which O'Connor would doubtless inhabit until the Embassy had gone on its laborious way.

They had not arrived yet. But the Queen Dowager's train had. Presently O'LiamRoe went off by Madame de Paroy's permission to visit Mary—Madame Françoise d'Estamville, Dame de Paroy, the plain martinet who had replaced Jenny Fleming at five times Jenny Fleming's (ostensible) salary; and had heard a familiar, pleasant voice behind the door.

'King and Queen of Cantelon, How many miles to Babylon?'

A young voice laughed. 'Go on,' said Lymond; and the young voice obediently, strongly French, continued.

'*Eight and eight and other eight*—Don't,' said the young voice warningly, 'pray me to add them.'

'I don't need to,' said Lymond, affronted. 'I can do it myself.'

There was a long pause. 'You're taking a very long time,' said Mary.

'Don't hurry me.'

'I can do it quicker than that,' she said. 'It's twenty-four.'

'Unfair! Unfair! Bestiall and untaught,' said the pleasant voice, ringing like a wedding bell. 'I have ten fingers and ten toes, and beyond that I must rely on my good and noble princess Mary. Again?'

'Again.'

'King and Queen of Cantelon, How many miles to Babylon?'

'*Eight and eight and other eight.*'

'Will I get there by candlelight?'

'*If your horse be good and your spurs be right.*'

'How many men have ye?'

'*Mair nor ye daur come and see.*' And both voices laughed.

Then a page opened the door.

On the way out, Lymond spoke as they passed each other, lingering, in the doorway. 'Hallo. Minerva covered with sweat. No attempt so far, as you see. Smile, Phelim. I called on your lady and she was not at home.'

Taking a deep and painful breath, O'LiamRoe said, 'Is there nothing I can do to stop you?'

Lymond's face closed hard. 'Go in there,' he said, his hand on the door. 'And then ask me again.'

O'LiamRoe did not drop his pale gaze. Instead he said, 'And Robin Stewart? Is there any news?'

'It depends,' said Lymond evenly, 'on what you call news. I saw him yesterday. . . . The interview was interesting but indeterminate.'

'My faix,' said O'LiamRoe a little blankly. 'Did he *speak* to you?' And added quickly, 'Then how did it end? Where is he now, then? Did he get away again?'

Lymond did not answer at once. Then he said, looking consideringly at O'LiamRoe's agitated face, 'It ended in my knocking him unconscious and coming away. He's free still, so far as I know.'

'But—' began O'LiamRoe loudly, and hurriedly modified his

voice. 'But that leaves the child exposed to Lord d'Aubigny... unless you've found real evidence against him?'

Lymond shook his fair head. 'I have told you. Our mutual friend is proving hard to trace. Mistress Boyle's doing, I should guess. But she will have to come to Court for the Great English Lupercalia.'

In the single moment he, O'LiamRoe, had had with her, Oonagh had flung her head up, a bruise yellow under the stretched white skin, and had said, 'What comfort do you owe there, Phelim O'LiamRoe? Are you away in your head?' And later, grimly, she had said, 'All right. I tell you, he is safe from me. Were I to name him Thady Boy Ballagh I should have a question or two to answer myself. But let him try to lay his harness on me while better men are breaking their hearts and I will scorn him clean out of France.'

And now Lymond was telling him that he had spared the Archer at Oonagh's expense. 'This sudden tenderness for the unfortunate Robin,' said O'LiamRoe, 'would fairly bring you out in the purples. You prefer to sacrifice Oonagh?'

'I hope,' said Lymond precisely, 'not to sacrifice anybody. As far as Stewart is concerned, I preferred not to deliver the log to the sawpit, that's all.'

'And Oonagh?'

'My dear Phelim,' said Lymond, moving away. 'Cease to worry. You know my tenets. The mind is the origin of all that is; the mind is the master, the mind is the cause.'

'Try telling that,' said the Prince of Barrow grimly, 'to Cormac O'Connor.'

*   *   *

The Court waited. During all this time, its manner to Lord d'Aubigny had never changed. Only the charges against him were mentally docketed against future indiscretions, and the suavest exchanges invisibly edged with black. D'Aubigny expected it. Despite the graceful attentions shown him by Henri, the added courtesies and warmth, Lord d'Aubigny travelled in childish fury from Angers to Châteaubriant, and on his first off-duty day, rode to Nantes and brought back some smoked crystal and an authenticated statue by Phidias, eighteen inches high.

Examining its dry ivory and gold, his fellow-courtiers were polite, but he was in need of a therapy deeper than that. It was Francis Crawford, Vervassal Herald, bending over the lovely carving, who said, 'There is one like it in Rome. But I never saw a finer. This, and this, for example.' And, his manner lyrical, Lymond expounded, while his lordship with angry reluctance feasted on these tainted sweets.

But then, neither now nor at any time could you have told that

331

they were enemies. For a week now, the herald had attached himself to John Stewart of Aubigny and had sat at his feet, a fellow Scot and admirer. There were many times—at night, and when his lordship was on duty—when he and his acolyte were forced to part. But for the rest, it was surprising how often John Stewart looked up from cup or gem or manuscript to find the lazy, well-dressed person of the Queen Mother's herald somewhere nearby. Even to Lord d'Aubigny, who had no keen sense of the ridiculous, this was trying, but he did his best to keep his manner both placid and cool. After all, it was not for long.

In the intervals when Lymond was free, Margaret Erskine sometimes saw him. From Richard, before he left, she had learned a little of what to expect. Francis himself, at their first encounter shortly after the episode of the boar, had described O'LiamRoe's brief embrace of Saxon culture until she was speechless with laughter, and had been otherwise uninformative. His eyes were clear, his movements resilient as a whip. What had cured his broken bones had mended, clearly, the damage other things had done. He made no reference to that.

On the Friday of Northampton's arrival, Lymond swept through the Queen Mother's empty rooms airily. 'My sweet, the pennants are hanging like gutter cloths and they are *writing sonnets on the statues:* will the cool northern blood be enchanted, do you think?'

'According to O'LiamRoe,' said Margaret placidly, 'every statue in Westminster has its bottom covered with verse.'

'But in France, my dear, they *sign them,*' said Lymond. He had come straight from somebody's perfume room and was furled in attar of roses and expert goldsmith work; clearly he was going to the ball. Sir George Douglas, also exquisitely dressed, smiled as he passed by. 'Such élan, my dear. Lady Lennox will worship you,' he said.

But it was Matthew Stewart, Margaret's husband, he saw first at the ceremonial meeting between Northampton and the two Scottish Queens. This Lymond attended, inhumanly grave, while Mary of Guise, mollusced like a sea wall with jewels, acknowledged the triple obeisance, and the young Queen and the Marquis touched hands. The child's face under Moncel's fine pearl cap was scarlet, less because of the Latin sentence she had to recite than that the tight lacing, the gartered stockings, the long sleeves and silk attires, and the floor-length soieries de luxe were throttling them all.

Nor were the gentlemen, with chemise, camisole and pourpoint, with tracé tunic and high bouffant breeches and pushed-in waists, better off. Even the Duke of Guise, godly in his calm, was leaving dark fingermarks on his scabbard and the crisped point of George Douglas's beard sadly hung. Afterwards, when the Queens were

332

greeting the chosen few brought up to the dais, the Earl of Lennox strolled over to his wife's uncle.

Matthew Stewart, Earl of Lennox, was at home here, as Douglas was at home. For eleven years he had lived and fought in France; had indeed left for richer pastures only eight years before. For his defection to England he had been anathema to the old King of France; d'Aubigny his brother had been imprisoned because of it. But that was over. England and France were about to become allies; d'Aubigny was one of the present King's dearest friends; and if Warwick, so hastily Reformed, was not a very dear friend of Lennox at present, all might be well if Margaret were circumspect in her encounters with that shifty gentleman Crawford of Lymond; and if nothing untoward happened to the young Queen of Scotland—or at least, so ran his prayer, nothing that could be traced to Matthew Stewart of Lennox. For since that first, delicate conversation with brother John long ago, he had been horrified to notice how the sparks from the d'Aubigny activities in France kept flying towards the Lennoxes in London. Whatever was happening, he wanted nothing to do with it; as Catholics, he and Margaret found life risky enough.

In defiance of all these morbid shadows, Matthew Stewart was wearing all his portable wealth. Sir George, not patently impressed by gold lace, watched his approach, amused. When he was within earshot—'What surprising encounters one does have,' he said. 'Is this visit wise, Matthew? I thought the French had taken a little against you.'

The washed-out, over-relaxed eyes were angry. 'I bow to your definition of wisdom *of course*; but a little leavening among the dogmatists might not come amiss on this Embassy. You heard about the scene at Saumur where none of my Reformed colleagues would bow to the pix. At Orléans, they distributed consecrated bread to the populace; and at Angers the whole legation would have been massacred if the dear Marquis had not intervened.'

'I didn't hear,' said Douglas, interested. 'What did they do?'

'Abstracted a holy image from the church,' said Lord Lennox bluntly. 'And carried it about the streets with a hat on its head.'

Sir George laughed.

'It was not, at the time, very mirth-provoking,' said Lennox. 'At Nantes they had to hide the statues in their houses from the Commissioners who have, of course, eaten flesh regularly throughout the whole trip. It is not,' said Lord Lennox, a red spot on either dry cheek, 'really the best of times to try how far French patience will stretch. Jokes about the Hollow Father do not always appeal.'

'Then you must make jokes about my lord of Warwick instead. How fortunate,' said Sir George, not at all to be put off, 'that Robin Stewart is no longer with us, at least. Your brother has been looking out for you quite assiduously ever since you arrived. Have you seen him?'

'No,' said Matthew Stewart briefly. 'I find John's passions a little irksome.'

'*Do* you now?' said Sir George, his eyes opening in delighted surprise. 'Not drawn to our dear d'Aubigny, are you? Then what about the Queen Mother? The lady doesn't bear grudges. After all, she turned down Bothwell's marriage offer or well as yours. And she has a charming Officer-at-Arms. Make a point of meeting him.'

But long before that, as Sir George well knew, the faded blue eyes had made their exploration. The Earl of Lennox turned his back on the very presentable Court of Queen Mary of Scotland, in the middle of which winked the blue and red and gold tabard of Vervassal, now restored, and said thinly, 'If you mean Lymond, I have met him already, in London. These men's lives are very short. I should not pin my faith, Douglas, on a giddy gentleman who will carry a hod for anyone willing to pay.'

'Usually, in my experience, to use in browbeating his would-be patron. And giddy?' said Sir George. 'We are all giddy, loitering here begging with a golden cup. But certainly, like Jack Straw, our friend is enflamed with presumption and pride; and I for one will applaud his first serious mistake. So, I am sure, will Margaret. I should even trust her to help him to make it.'

The wandering gaze of Margaret's husband, like a ball from a racquet, slapped back into Sir George's bland face. '—In which case,' Sir George added, smiling more broadly still, 'I should say, more power to her elbow.'

In this last speech, the hesitation between one word and the next was fractional. But it was enough to turn the Earl's pale face paler, as he gazed after the retreating speaker; and to make the more informed of the bystanders wince.

Sir George, whose son was married to the heiress of Morton, was undisturbed.

*   *   *

After the receptions the banquet; after the banquet, the masque; after the masque, the ball, in the great courtyard where new fountains were filled with rosé wine and drowned insects, and the trellis between dancers and stars was hung with muscatel grapes.

The formal music for the branle and galliard, the charconne and allemande and pavane and the Spanish minuet blew pattering like tinfoil through the peach trees, suffocated by the drawling French of English thoraxes and the polite, beautiful French of the most highly cultured courtiers in the world. In the long arcade adjoining the Château Neuf, Queen Catherine watched with her ladies, Margaret

Lennox among them, and the pages glinted like rudd in between.

Moving in the dance, pair by pair in their worked satins and Tardif velvet and their gem-embroidered silks, in silver lace and cloth of gold, the ostrich feathers tilting the grapes; with the men with their bleached hands, long-legged, broad-shouldered, smiling and negligent; the women with their jewelled breasts and high, plucked brows, the long oversleeves glinting, the train lifted to show an inch of stocking and Venice satin pump—the high blood of three nations bowed, swayed, paused, dispersed and re-formed as time dallied past.

Cupids filled the cleared floor and danced a moresca with torches. Veiled ladies sang flattering verses and masked knights recited. There were tonight no gigantic pies, no lions, no living statues . . . fantasy would come another day. Instead, the pages brought garlands of flowers, and wine, and wicker baskets filled with cat masks.

They were beautiful. Oonagh O'Dwyer, her black hair cauled and jewelled, her long limbs hidden under stiff damask, was masked in the ash-grey fur of a Persian, the emerald eyes drawing fire from her own. Below, the spare, smiling lips with their thumbnail soffit underneath, drawn in silver with sweat, were holding the attention of Black Tom Butler, tenth Earl of Ormond, one of the smooth boy Irishmen who had entertained O'LiamRoe in London, and a member of the English Ambassage. Ormond had been brought up with Edward of England, knew no other nation and, so far, desired to know none.

Oonagh, watching him through her mask scrutinize her body at leisure, continued with the sly and slightly malicious story she had embarked on. As Aunt Theresa had said, he could be quickly attracted. And Cormac, his eyes sparkling with the sheer joy of planning, had said, 'But can she keep him so? There's the challenge, my cold, black darling from the sea. My cold, black, ageless darling, you will need a charm, and another charm, and all the spells there are to bind that soft, oiled puppy kicking from his English nest. But—' And, lifting a lazy finger, he had drawn it round her fine jaw, where the skin was tight drawn at the edge, and under the heavy eyes, where lack of sleep had stepped like a bird. 'But for love of me, you will do it. It will be hard, but you will do it, my heart.'

So she had hidden the marks of his disapproval under her mask, and accepted a dance with the tenth Earl of Ormond, knowing that somewhere under this awning, in the warm, scented night, was the man who had come to France solely to challenge her. She was dancing, and for a moment she had forgotten that he might be there— among the dancers, in the spangled darkness of the gardens, in the mellow lights of the château and arcade. She did not even see him, as **she and her partner moved up the line, until a voice of virgin honey** spoke in her ear. Moved by the exigencies of the dance it died away, returned, shifted focus but remained always just audible through the music and talk.

Then she turned, against her training, and saw him.

He was not even masked, the man she last remembered as the drugged and bandaged prisoner at Blois. And of all the knowing eyes that looked at him, as on the ride to Angers he had foreseen, hers alone did not change. As she turned, the music stopped, the dance was stilled, and her partner, turning, came face to face with Francis Crawford, who continued speaking as if nothing had happened, his blue eyes lit with untrustworthy joy. '*C'est Belaud, mon petit chat gris. C'est Belaud, la mort aux rats . . . Petit museau, petites dents.*'

Butler, who had no French, said now in his high, cold English lisp, 'Pardon me. You are a herald, sir?'

'To the Right High and Excellent Princess, the Dowager of Scotland's Grace. My name, my lord, is Crawford, and I seek your permission to lead this lady to my Queen.'

There was a little pause. The high voice was annoyed. 'The Queen Dowager wishes to see Mistress O'Dwyer?'

'If it please you—and her.'

'Just now?'

'As soon as I may lead her there.'

Discontentedly the Irishman who had spent most of his life a page in London said, 'It is not an opportune moment, but naturally . . .'

'Naturally,' said Lymond with tranquillity, and offered the lady his arm.

She took it, not because she believed for a moment that the Queen Dowager wanted her, but because she could do nothing else. They moved off, the lovely woman and the fair-haired man at her side, leaving the Earl of Ormond irresolute in the middle of the floor, and Mistress Boyle starting out wildly from the distant arcade, where Margaret Lennox, blank-faced, sat and watched. Then the music struck up, the dancers linked hands, and fifty couples slowly weaving a pavane barred Aunt Theresa's desperate way.

By the time she had stumbled through the crowded grass of the gardens, Lymond and her niece had both gone.

*   *   *

By whatever munificence of bribery, the unlit room to which he brought her had no guard at the door, nor had it any signs of occupation at all, although its windows gave on to the latticed ballroom below. It was a bedchamber, small, orderly and smelling of some heavy and unidentifiable scent.

Tomorrow, her arm would be bruised where he had held it, chatting, smiling, drawing her smoothly through the crowds. As they

336

both knew, she could not afford a scene. She was trapped, and behind the soft mask was responding like an animal to the challenge, her eyes wide and dangerous, her breathing quick and hard. In the dark room in the Château Neuf, facing him silent at last, she was able to clear her mind of all but what she had long ago primed herself to do. His face, like hers, was obscured; his skin and sparkling clothes blemished by the fountain drops strewn on the panes. As soon as they had entered the room, he dropped his hands and stood still.

She had moved instantly to the window. There, now, she looked out. Among the politely discoursing spectators, an eddy betrayed Mistress Boyle's purposeful grey head, making for the château. She would not be permitted to enter; and even if she did, it was too big to search; and Lymond, moreover, had locked the door.

Among the dancers, the Earl of Ormond had found another escort and was smiling again, his polished English smile. Her task for Cormac had had to be abandoned too. But she could handle Cormac. In the last resort he might use his fist, but that was because he had already conceded the case with his brain. Anyhow, she was prepared for this encounter, schooled like an athlete about to take the arena, the muscles of her mind firm and hard. She turned sideways in the faint glow of the window, and lifting her hands, she took the mask from her marked face.

Dim in the shadows by the door, Lymond showed neither alarm nor surprise. Instead he said sardonically, 'It's quite a price to pay for being the Petite Pucelle of Ireland, my dear. There are worse things than passing from hand to sweaty hand, much as the prospect appalls you.'

She did not make the woman's answer: 'Who told you so . . . Martine of Dieppe?' Instead she said, 'Before you spend yourself loosening my chains, you had better find out what they are. I never did anything yet out of fear . . . even fear of common harlotry, Francis Crawford. The O'LiamRoe, you must remember, is a sentimental man. If he told you I am tied to Cormac's side by any fear of the future, he was wrong.'

'Was he? What was Cormac like as a young nobleman, Oonagh, ablaze for Geraldine Ireland? The splendour there must have been.'

'The young man is there in him yet,' she said, and went on quickly. 'What would you have him? A spectator, or a spy?'

'A man,' said the pleasant voice, undisturbed, 'who does not need a woman to lead him.'

Two of her fingers were at the bruise on her cheek; she did not know how they got there. Dropping them, she said with soft bitterness, 'Do you think I want power?'

'I think you have staked your life on Cormac O'Connor,' said Lymond. 'And have kept his young love and his young crusade

337

green under the ice while the reality has rotted. He is not ambitious for Ireland, he is ambitious for Cormac O'Connor. He may still love your body, but he keeps you for your brain.'

Her throat closed; but through the anger rising like thunder through her head she managed to speak. 'And what would *you* keep me for? The graveyards and prisons of Europe are full enough of half-made souls created by Francis Crawford and loneliness and God.'

When he spoke, his voice was dry. 'I was not proposing, my dear, to support you for life, or even to seduce you in lieu of a fee. I am offering you a chance to define and revise your ideals. It is impossible that they should quire with mine?'

''Tis a lavish offer, if a trifle obscure,' said Oonagh O'Dwyer. 'If in my burning patriotism, I betray someone else's scheming, you will refrain from the cruder gestures of appreciation. You return triumphant to Scotland, the golden stripling; Cormac languishes no doubt in a French prison for attempting the life of an Irish rival and I, with my eyes averted from this unworthy Messiah, am cast into a dull but healthier void.'

'It is still an improvement,' said Lymond, 'on the Tour des Minimes. What aspect of Cormac's homely charm made that experiment worth while? Lord d'Aubigny had found out, perhaps, that Francis Crawford was not O'LiamRoe, and began to suspect that you had been helping him kill the wrong man for your own ends? And as she moved suddenly, before she could stop herself—'Oh, yes,' Lymond added calmly. 'We know that d'Aubigny is the villain. Don't let's labour the point. So when Stewart told him who Thady Boy was, his lordship realized you had deceived him?'

She said shortly, 'Give me credit for sense. I had discovered long ago that Phelim O'LiamRoe was no rival that Cormac need fear.' Then, as he was silent, she said, 'I risked my safety to pull you free from the Tower that night. What more are you worth? It was Cormac or all of you.'

'Cormac, or all of us,' said the voice from the darkness, reflectively. 'Cormac's ambitions, Ireland's future, to be bought at the price of our lives, and the life of Queen Mary as well. . . . You know that Lord d'Aubigny meant her to die? But of course you did. He had been in your confidence and your aunt's for a long time, I suspect. He was trying to kill me because I had been induced to come and protect her . . . how did he know that, I wonder? From someone in Scotland who was haunting the Queen Dowager hoping for favours—and not receiving them; someone who has an excessive interest in the Culters and with relatives in both London and France . . . someone like d'Aubigny's own relation, Sir George Douglas?'

This time she did not move; and wondered afterwards if her very stillness had given her away, for he laughed and went on. 'And you, of course, knew from George Paris that the Queen Dowager at just this moment had proposed the unknown O'LiamRoe's visit to France. There was no time to attack him in Ireland, but it seemed easy to have an accident at sea. Then Robin Stewart encouraged Destaiz in his little piece of fire-raising at the Porc-épic: a foolish move, not at all easy to explain as an accident, for which d'Aubigny duly berated him. And the next attempt to get rid of him was yours, at Rouen, when you arranged for O'LiamRoe to make a fool of himself at the tennis court, when he was nearly sent home. But by then, of course, you had guessed the truth. . . . What gave away Thady Boy's identity, I wonder? Bad acting or bad grammar, or a certain aura which is neither flesh nor fisshe?'

'An Appin man taught you your Gaelic long since, and a Leinsterman has recently corrected you well; but you still forget to lay stress on the first syllable instead of the second, now and then. It is not a thing a Scotsman would notice.'

'So Stewart and his lordship continued to believe that O'LiamRoe was their proper victim, and you allowed them to think so. . . . D'Aubigny took poor Jenny Fleming to the Croix d'Or and confronted them with each other. He must have had the highest opinion of their dissimulation. How foolish he must have felt when he learned the true facts. And how angry he will be, my dear, should he ever find out that you knew these all the time.'

'My life is my own,' she said, her voice thin in her own ears. 'You asked me last time to leave you to deal with this man. What ails you? Deal with him!'

'You know what I want,' said the quiet voice. 'Evidence against Lord d'Aubigny. Destaiz is dead. Someone besides Stewart must have helped him at times. He didn't tie that rope at Amboise himself. One name would do.'

She thought, her hands gripping the windowsill, the dim, merry lights on her grazed face. She thought of the organ at Neuvy, made to magnify her breath, her heartbeats, her fears, instead of the Almighty; of the humiliating serenade at the Hôtel Moûtier, so mercilessly timed for the one space when she had hoped to reach Lord d'Aubigny's ear with the news of Cormac's arrival. For two days she had waited at Blois for the Court to return, so that she could warn d'Aubigny that O'Connor was coming, and that it was time for him to keep his promise and influence the King in Cormac's favour. And Lymond, she now realized, had waited too—had he had her watched? —to see if her sudden departure from Neuvy had to do with Cormac, and if so, whom she might meet when the Court came back to Blois, for she had to meet someone that night, if at all. Next day the Moûtiers would leave, and she must return to Neuvy.

He had not only waited, damn him. He had taken half the Court to her. Transfixed on her balcony, full in the public eye, she had been forced to ask O'LiamRoe's help. Piedar Dooly, unwatched, had slipped from the Hôtel Moûtier to the castle, and in response to her message, Robin Stewart had come to receive her news and bear it to d'Aubigny. And even that had played into Lymond's hands, for it had brought the Archer to run with him on the rooftops and had nearly suborned him from his purpose. She wondered, briefly, if her borrowing of Piedar Dooly that night had been mentioned by O'LiamRoe; and then dismissed the thought from her mind. It was the hour for harshness and for strength: neither symptomatic of Phelim O'LiamRoe. She said, 'There is nothing I can do.'

The whole width of the room lay between them; there was no sound. Then Lymond said calmly, 'Let us try a little sentiment, then. Queen Mary is eight years old.'

'She is eight, and has food in her mouth and down in her bed, a nurse to dress her and a great chest for her jewels. The jewel of an Irish child is a handful of meal.'

'And a rebellion under Cormac will bring plenty?'

'It will bring freedom. The rest will come.'

'You talk as if Mary were free,' said Lymond. 'Her death will set brother against brother in Scotland as it has already with you. Can you look no further than one nation and one man?'

'You do not know me,' she said.

'I know your pride. As your lover shrunk in stature his cause had to grow. A humbler woman would have knifed him.'

She stared at the blur of his face in the twinkling dark, her rage bursting its self-imposed locks. 'Then there are two of us,' she said hardily. 'A man of smaller vanity would have killed him before she had need.'

'Thinking death the only division. I could not imagine,' said Lymond, 'ever so insulting you. In any case, you are committed to your cause, are you not? You would need only another Messiah. The Prince of Barrow, perhaps.'

'Perhaps.' Under the heavy damask the sweat was cold on her skin; her eyes, open in the scented darkness, ached with the strain of the fight; her lashes dragged like fire from their roots.

For it was a struggle. She was under no illusions. He meant to have the help she could give. His moderation was a debt he owed to other women, not to her, and eventually it would break. . . . Placed between these steely levers, face to face with her own mind, she must use what weapons she had. Choosing her words, she said, '. . . But that you would frighten him out of it. No matter. Ambitious princes in Ireland are as thick as the sands of the sea. Any one of them will do.'

Deeply she had planned this inevitable duel of theirs; her blood heavy in her veins she waited to hear him reply. The silence went on, drowning the shallow murmurs of talk and laughter, the remote beat and pipe of music outside. Then Lymond said, 'So you have never loved.'

Oonagh said, 'Have you?'

He did not answer. Instead he said, his voice attuned to a deeper breath, so that her hands closed suddenly, 'There is a man already half-awake in O'LiamRoe. I should not prevent you. How could I?'

She let him hear the contempt in her voice. 'And in the loving leaf-beds of France I should let drop the starved skull of a nation, and watch it roll into the weeds? Show me the man, awake or half-awake, whose lips could teach me to do that!'

Her own words chimed in her head. They sounded unconvincing, the words that were meant to persuade as the spade persuades the deep earth. Standing in that dark room, gambling mind and body against this silken, disembodied voice, she had begun, strong as she had made herself to be, to tremble. She had to wrench from him her secret, her identity, her pride all intact, and to buy security for Cormac in the future. Oh, God . . . she thought furiously, shaking. How frigid was he? Mary Mother, how much wooing must she do?

She had thought herself open as a sounding board to every move of his body; she had killed her sight on his dim, jewelled dress. But blind with stress she missed the move when at last it was quietly made; was aware only of his perfume behind, and of two peaceful hands lying under her throat. His voice in her ear said, 'I gave you my word, a while back, that I proposed to be continent . . . but are you and your song, my green-haired morrow, attempting by any chance to seduce me?'

Before her, his shadow lay superimposed on her own upon the empty tiles; his breath was sweet; his smiling lips in her hair. Her chin lifted. Staring open-eyed before her, 'Are you afraid?' she said. And raising her hands, slid apart his light ones and turned.

She had studied his sleeping face, exposed under the dye. Lymond asserting his full powers she had never met at close quarters before. Without touching her, he was so near she could feel the warmth of his skin; the lamps from the garden struck a sudden, dense blue from under his lashes. In the broken light, the short hair clasped his head like lit silver. He spoke again, his voice steady; but she could hear that, at last, he was controlling his breath.

'The star of Gormluba was fair. White were the rows within her lips, and like the down of the mountain under her new robe was her skin. Circle on circle formed her fairest neck. Like hills beneath their soft snowy fleeces rose her two breasts of love. The melody of music was in her voice. The rose beside her lip was not red: nor white beside her hand the foam of the streams. Her eyes were bright as sunbeams; and altogether perfect was the form of the fair. . . . Maid of Gormluba, who can describe thy beauty!'

In the timbre of the Gaelic, you remembered his gifts, his hands on the strings and his thoughts in them. She answered him in the same tongue and kind, her body graced by his voice, her glimmering face and shoulders and breasts small and deep in his eyes.

Without looking, he put out his hand and drew the great shutter slowly closed. Behind her, the lit square dwindled on the fine tiles and was gone; in his eyes the last spark of light, reflected from her own, flamed and was extinct. In the soft darkness, smoothly, he found her two hands and brought them high under his own before gathering her for his kiss.

Within the boy's frame and the armoured violence of her soul came a response stronger than her will: a surge of triumph so great that she would have stopped him, if she had been strong enough, in that moment before the glory could be dimmed. Then she was held fast in a sudden turbulence as suddenly leashed, as if an iron door had closed on a fire. Attentively, his lips visited her skin, exploring the way to her dry mouth, and found it.

He spoke, in the end, lifting his lips from hers; but she did not hear. Consumed like a spar in the flame she had incited, born like some parched changeling on the white bed of its heat, she was sealed by that spare kiss from words. When she came to herself she found him kneeling, and herself taut in his hands. 'My dear, you are weeping,' he said. 'Welcome with hautbois, clarions and trumpets, noble lady. Welcome to the company of those who can be hurt.'

She had guessed, and she had gambled on one fact: that Francis Crawford's ultimate stake in this war between them, unsought by either, would be the same as her own. And in this one thing she was his equal, and thought to find herself even his peer. She had almost loved O'LiamRoe for his innocence. She had come tonight, sure that Lymond would try to assail her mind in the end, in the long run, by trying to captivate her body. And grimly, icily, she had come prepared to show a conceited trifler ten years her junior a glimpse of what he had never known. She had come ready to serve him well, her anger cloaked, so that by morning, wordless, he would know that he had nothing of this coin with which to bid. And then, perhaps, he would let her and Cormac go.

Her plan was ashes. Braced for the torrid and the fanciful, she had met instead a strength steady and firm, easy in its ways and controlled—*a mhuire*, why had she not expected it? She had known it when his hands touched her, long before that blinding, terrible kiss—controlled as any other instrument he used, his hands subtle on the keys. It was little she knew of him, after all, and less of herself; and the slow tears felt their way down her skin as she said, 'My heart is scalded.'

He had become very still; the warmth from him was like the smell of a meal on a frosty day, at the end of a hard ride. He said, 'Yours is not to lead now: we go side by side. Rest from your travels.' Then the soft silk of his shoulder closed her eyes. He caressed her, smoothing laces and clasps from his way so that her body, unimpeded learned his hands; speaking softly, until her mind sank back numb, the pressures in the room, in herself, in him, stealing her breath.

His hands searched her, touching her passions one by one and shaping with his musician's fingers the growing, thunderous chord. The darkness shook, like the bursting crust of the earth, fissured red with the wildfire within. Under a discipline she could not bear to contemplate he drew together in her and united in a single, raging anthem, all the craving strands of her sleepless years. With all the life in her between his two palms, he slid wide his hands and quickly lifting her, swaying, like warm wine in too tender a lapping, took and laid her on the dark bed where, crudely, she had always meant to surrender.

Outside, the dancing had stopped. For a while, the voices scratched the night air, coalescing, thinning, joining again in wine-eased laughter. Then they dispersed, and you heard only the pad of servants' feet, aching for bed, the chink of cup on tray, the pang of moved lutes and the hiss of brushes, and finally, in the dark Château Neuf and Château Vieux, only the harp-fall of the fountains, and silence.

Behind more than one window the satins lay strewn in the moonlight, and the night passed sleepless, playing at love. For one person only the music stayed all night long, losing no magnificence, demanding more sometimes than she could support. She knew neither where she was nor whom she was with; for Lymond had given her the greatest gift in his possession. For one night he had severed Oonagh O'Dwyer's soul from her mind; for one single night, she was free.

It was the first time; and the last. They did not know each other when it began, and when it was over they knew nothing still, for they embraced visions and not flesh; his eyes lifted, considering, to wider horizons, and her soul, a stranger to warm earth and harvests, bent on snatching its hour.

Oonagh woke soon after dawn, the blackbirds loud in the orange trees and turned her head, not remembering, against the black swathes of her hair. It was not Cormac's head, pillowed and assuaged, lying beside her. Francis Crawford was watching her, the sheet pushed back from his shoulders, his chin on his folded arms. He looked as if he had lain a long time, quietly thinking without sleep. He smiled now instantly, a brilliant, fleeting smile of mischief and friendship, and said in her own tongue, 'It is superb you are, my lady; and a gallant night we made, you and I. But if you would have me lay stress on any syllable at all, I shall have to pray God for the strength.'

She saw the long-nailed hand, lying at ease under the tilted chin, the pale, ruffled hair, the thinly timbered face with its inbred austerity giving the lie to his words; and through the dawnlight and the peace and the unturned memories, like drowned jewels, of the night, she remembered why it was done.

She had meant to show him that he had nothing to barter. He had given her instead the price of her secret, her pride, herself twenty times over. And defying all the great laws, the laws of hospitality, the laws of humanity, the laws of her own people, being what she was, she must fling it back in his face. She looked at him, and for a long moment he answered the look, before turning away. He buried his elbows in the down, and cradling his brow in his laced hands, closed his eyes. 'Well, Oonagh?'

With bitter smoothness, she sat up, the heavy silk of her hair falling straight by her straight arms, and answered. 'There was a King called Cormac,' she said flatly, 'who knew women. Forgetful in love, he called them. Not to be trusted with secrets; ever ready with an excuse. Scampers of work; feeble in contests; termagants in strife; deaf to instruction; futile in society; dumb on useful matters; eloquent on trifles. To be feared as wild beasts. Better to be whipped than humoured, he said; better to be crushed than cherished.' She paused; then went on evenly. 'They are true words, and better in my mouth than yours. It is not well, so. It will not be well until Temair is the habitation of heroes once more.'

His disordered head did not move, but the profile fretted, as if his closed eyes had suddenly clenched. It was the expected answer, made no sweeter for being defiantly florid; never tender with words, she was dragging them at her wanton plough tail anyhow. Without condemning anything she had said or done, he said only, 'I have failed, then. I thought so.' His voice was dry.

She said, turning to clasp her knees, her voice low. 'We are both traders in snow. It is our kind, Francis.' His mother had used these words to her once: she did not tell him. Nor did she tell him the other thing he did not know. With a quick movement he slid on to his back. His face looked merely thoughtful; she could see on his brown skin the scars of the Tour des Minimes. He said, 'I do not feel like Diogenes.'

'Nor I like—' She broke off, her voice failed. And then a moment later, whipping herself for the weakness, she said baldly, her voice vacant of colour, 'I will sell you the information you want for five thousand Frenchmen out of Scotland.'

344

He took so long that she thought he would not reply at all. Then he said, not quite in his usual register, 'And if I discredit you and Cormac by exposing d'Aubigny, who will lead your wonderful army?'

'Be at ease. I would not ask O'LiamRoe to destroy himself on the bare rocks of my little liking. I should find some man else.' She turned. 'Would the Dowager not contrive it, to save her daughter? The whole of Scotland and half France wishes the French occupation ended. Or is your heart set on being one of the Dowager's new pensioned pups?'

'Be still,' he said; and putting his two hands on her arms, brought her to lie on the pillow, white and quick-breathing, the circles dark under her eyes. 'Be still. I owe no allegiance; I have no ambition; but what you ask is impossible. The throne is too insecure. Without the Queen Mother's good credit here and in Scotland it would topple, and the child might as well die.'

Sharply she turned her head, and caught the wry amusement still in his eyes. He did not hide it. 'Stop tormenting the morning; lie with me and be still,' he said. 'My bed is not a market place, whatever you may think. I had nothing, ever, but a little self-knowledge to offer you. If you will not tell me for that, I have nothing more I can sell.'

And it was then, strangely, in the face of this calm and undramatic statement of truth, that Oonagh O'Dwyer's composure broke down. Turning her black, weary head into his arm, she closed her green eyes and wept, and he lent her his comfort for, like Luadhas, she had been pitched against something too fierce for her race.

He had one more hurdle for her to cross. On her way home, by back stair and postern, planned with practised adroitness to arouse, at another time, her ironical smile, he stopped before a stout door and turning, said, 'I have no wish to distress you. But you owe it to your crusade to see clearly the bodies on which you build. Will you come with me?'

Then she knew he was taking her to Mary. The helpless child Queen was to be his final weapon. And the very triteness of it made her look at him afresh. She did not understand him: she had assumed he understood her surprisingly well.

There were three doors to pass, and an attendant before each, unobtrusively armed. The last, she saw, was young Fleming himself, with the page Melville beside him. Inside, Margaret Erskine admitted them, her manner quiet, her intuition busy. The early light on Lymond's face left her with an impression of swift assurance; his voice and his bearing had an exceptional clarity. The Irishwoman with him she remembered most clearly at the start of the cheetah hunt, snapping her fingers at O'LiamRoe's lovely dog. And she, on the other hand, was quite different. Under the long cloak she wore you could see last night's damask. Defiantly, on entering, she had flung back the hood from her heavy, undressed black hair. Within it, her eyes looked half-dazed. Margaret's own eyes dropped, hiding her exasperation, while Lymond was speaking. *You fools, why do you let him?* Another lesson; another experiment; another flawed vessel that would break.

He was saying, 'During the night she is safe, and part of the day. We cannot guard her fully in public. Today she need not go out at all until afternoon; she is safe therefore until then. In the afternoon she goes with her retinue and her mother's to watch the Breton sports and the jousting in the tilting-field. All the people we can trust will be about her, but she will be in public, and therefore exposed. At night she will be unwell. In that way the torchlight hunt will be avoided, and the alfresco supper later on. Tomorrow—'

'Tomorrow she will be on view all day as a courtesy to the English. The King has just ordered it. You can do nothing about it,' said Margaret wearily, 'without drawing attention. Do you want to see her now?'

'If Janet will allow,' said Lymond. Oonagh, behind, thought, Now it comes. The curving cheek, the nestling hand, the red-gold hair on the pillow. The charming snap at the heartstrings . . .

'*Wait.*' It was Lymond's voice again, edged. 'She isn't asleep?' And as Margaret nodded, 'Oh, for Christ's sake . . . is the girl a turnip? We haven't come to dote on her levée.'

And he meant what he said. When presently they came face to face with the child Mary, she was nearly dressed, sitting grousing like a harridan at having her tangled red hair combed. Janet Sinclair, annoyed at the interruption, sagged in a brief curtsey and stood back. Two maids of honour, one of them Margaret's own sister, were put outside the door with a groom. Lymond said, 'Your grace, this is Mistress Oonagh O'Dwyer of Ireland, whom you may have met. My lady your royal mother knows her quite well.'

Below the enraged brow, the hazel eyes had become quite clear; between the child Queen and the herald was seen to exist an amiable affinity with a faintly ecclesiastical air. Disbelieving, Oonagh heard him address his monarch again. 'The lady wishes to drive out the English from Ireland, and suggests that your noble grace might assist by transferring all the Frenchmen from Scotland to an Irish rebel command. Do you agree?'

Oonagh thought, impatiently, The child is eight, God help us. He has already told me—and heaven knows I knew it before—that the Dowager would never want it. The young face, she saw, had gone scarlet; head up, the child confronted her. 'My Frenchmen are protecting my domains from the English.'

'I don't see the force of that,' said Oonagh, 'when you're at peace with the English.' There was no point in making much of this. 'The treaty itself was due to be signed a week ago, and England is the weaker party now. There is no threat under Lord Warwick.'

'You are at peace also, are you not? And my Frenchmen keep the law between lord and lord, for many jealous nobles weaken a nation.'

'We are occupied,' said Oonagh. The sense of the ridiculous faded a little. 'We are wanting to drive the usurpers out. So should you wish the foreigners to leave your soil.'

'They are my mother's people. And mine,' said the girl.

'True enough,' said Lymond judicially, speaking for the first time. 'Your Norman lords went native enough, Oonagh, and gave the English their thorniest problem in the end. Just wait and see what our Norman-Scotsmen will do.'

Over the child's head, Oonagh's grey-green eyes met his. 'Children are dying; freedom is failed, while this child on a foreign soil clings to luxury like two cold crow's feet on the back of a ewe.'

'She is insolent,' said the girl, and turned her straight back. 'Tell her, M. Crawford, that I came here to find safety from the English.'

'But Lord, child!' said Oonagh, suddenly forgetting her state. 'The English are here this minute, in solemn embassy, to ask your hand in marriage for their King.'

Mary swung round, the creamy skin hot, the eyes angry. 'Because they cannot seize and wed me by force, as they so often tried! We are too strong, we and our Frenchmen!'

'And we are weak,' said Oonagh, and stopped short. How in five minutes had she passed from anger to appeal?

Mary was watching, clearly thinking hard. Her face was grave. 'But my mother wishes you to have help. She constantly asks the King my father to help you. But not with soldiers from Scotland. That would be—'

'Robbing a sea wall to build a byre,' said the dry voice of Francis Crawford. 'You won't persuade the lady, your grace. She would hold even your life cheap.'

Docile in the dark gown, the tangled hair bright at her ears, Mary listened, her eyes on Oonagh. Then shatteringly she smiled, her cheeks round. 'Did she tell you so?'

'Yes.'

The sparkling smile became enormous. 'Do you think she has a dagger there? Do you? Ask her, M. Francis? For,' said the most noble and most powerful Princess Mary Stewart, Queen of Scotland, delving furiously under all the stiff red velvet, showing shift, hose and garters, shoes, knees and a long ribboned end of something recently torn loose, and emerging therefrom with a fist closed tight on an object short and hard and glittering, 'for *I* have!'

And breathlessly, flinging back her head, with the little knife offered like a quill, 'Try to stab me!' she encouraged her visitor.

There was a queer silence, during which the eyes of Oonagh O'Dwyer and her love of one night met and locked like magnet and iron. The child, waiting a moment, offered again, the ringing, joyful defiance still in her voice. 'Try to stab me! . . . Go on, and I'll kill you all dead!'

Her throat dry, Oonagh spoke. 'Save your steel for those you trust. They are the ones who will carry your bier; the men who cannot hate, nor can they know love. Send away the cold servants.'

The red mouth had opened a little; the knife hung forgotten in her hand. 'I would,' said Mary, surprised. 'But I do not know any.' And, anxiously demonstrating her point, she caught Lymond by the hand.

Between Oonagh's closed lips was forced a sound—a cry, a sob, a laugh—no one present could tell. She stopped it herself, her teeth clenched, and turning swiftly left them, walking fast. The door opened and closed. She had gone.

'Quoi?' said Mary, her round brow wrinkled, peering upwards past their clasped hands to Lymond's still face.

'Excellent,' said that comely person smoothly. 'She becomes easily upset. But was it necessary, my Queen, to prove me warm-blooded on the spot?'

The cut, made in her forgetfulness, was small, but the child, all contrition, rushed for wrappings. Silently Margaret Erskine held open the door. Lymond's eyebrows shot up. 'My dear, have patience. My wounds are to be salved.'

'Go away and bleed to death,' said his onetime saviour sharply. 'On behalf of the female sex I feel I may cheer every lesion.'

The laughter left his eyes. 'It was necessary.'

'But it failed,' she said. '*Didn't it?* —I sometimes think that dull, deformed or even wittingly vicious, you would be of more use to the Queen. Go. . . . Go. I don't want you here.'

And as he followed after the Irishwoman, Margaret Erskine, most levelheaded of women, picked up a Palissy vase, looked at it earnestly and smashed it clean on the floor.

IV

Châteaubriant:

The Price of Satire

Is payment for praise, or satire, commanded in the laws? If
according to the law of the divine house, there is no command
but for the praise of God alone; and heaven is its price.

FROM then onwards, it was possible to trace the altering atmosphere, as Lymond caustically observed, by the periodic ringing of
bells, and the deliquescence of O'LiamRoe.

Barred by conscience from denouncing Thady Boy, who would
then pay for Lord d'Aubigny's lapses, he found himself uselessly in
France, in the same town as Cormac and Oonagh, whom he had
forbidden himself to see, and without even his sour kinsman in
misfortune, the Archer Stewart.

It was Piedar Dooly, who had no delicacy in matters of the heart,
who informed him that Oonagh O'Dwyer had been at the château all
night, and that her aunt was fit to swell up and blacken with rage.
Châteaubriant was a small place. Issuing to seek balm for his raw
soul, he met Lymond, on his way back from escorting his night's
companion to her home.

The fair, agreeable face and modest fortune about the clothes
inflamed the Prince of Barrow beyond the point of caution in a public
street. He said, 'And had she any good in her now, or did she deserve
the pasting she will be having from her other lover this morning?'

He expected a blow; he urgently wanted a fight. But after a
second's hesitation the other man only said, 'She has told me nothing.
Unfortunately. Phelim, go and get drunk.'

And he did.

There were a number of others at the Cher Saincte on the same
errand. Its rooms, public and private, were filled with refugees from
the nerve-storming, playing-card propriety of the Ambassage. The
Archers not actually on duty, of which there were few, were forced
indeed to share the same parlour as the Swiss Guard off duty, which
had already led to some stridency.

Newly returned from a mission to Nantes, and by no means the quietest of that company, Lieutenant André Spens hardly noticed the beggar's urchin at his elbow at first. It was not until the all-important words pierced the din that he jumped a little, thought, and after excusing himself with a few well-chosen oaths and a telling improvisation, followed the child out of the inn.

Half an hour later, in someone's tumbledown shack outside the town, Lieutenant Spens came face to face with Robin Stewart, whom he had been instructed to befriend, keep in touch with, and eventually to kill. The delight on the lieutenant's well-shaven face was only equalled by the pleasure on Robin Stewart's, who was about to forestall him.

It was typical, even at this hour, of Robin Stewart's farcical and humourless affairs that some two hours later the same urchin should return, with the same errand, to the crowded Cher Saincte; and finding the Prince of Barrow totally senseless in drink, should persuade Piedar Dooly to accompany him instead.

For his final dramatic intervention in the world's affairs, Robin Stewart had taken residence in a stone and turf erection he had found in a forest clearing near Béré, just outside Châteaubriant and a little to the northwest. There, untroubled by monkish ghosts, dragons or nymphs, he had lived by his bow for ten days; a thing which gave him no trouble, but which gave a little extra savour, like garlic in the bowl, to his present relative affluence.

To Piedar Dooly, however, grim and silent, locked in his passionate Irish soul, the journey through the tepid summer trees with their market-day smell was something to get over quickly, so that he could return to where his master lay curled like a record roll on a rented table pushed in a cupboard. Storage of the eminent incapable was routine to the Cher Saincte.

He gazed acidly at the balding ground, the patch of sky, the fence, and the crumbling house, built for a hermit or a herdboy at acorn time; and when Stewart came to the door he observed nothing significant about his person or about the single room into which he was ushered when the Archer with a coin and a word had sent off the boy. Dooly said, 'It's cosy you are for a dead man, surely, and will make a beautiful corpse. Himself is busy.'

Gently Stewart hitched his long bones on the deep windowsill. 'The lad says he's fou',' said the Archer without rancour, but with a thread of contempt unconcealed in his voice. 'It's not to be wondered at. Anyway, you'll do. I can't get hold of Mr. Crawford . . . that was Thady Boy, ye ken. Him. He's not at the castle. And I've a message for him about the Queen.'

The little man, barely listening, hopped to his feet. 'Am I a pageboy, then? That man may learn it another way, or not at all.'

'Do you want to go home?' said Stewart quickly. And as the little servant stopped, watching, Stewart went on. 'He's staying, isn't he, because of the brat? Then he'll want to know this. It'll be all done by tomorrow. They're to finish her on the lake, while they're all in their flichtmafleathers getting the Garter in the morning.'

'How?' said Dooly, his black eyes sharp. 'And did you learn of it in this world or the next?'

'I got it from an Archer, a fellow who helped me escape. It turns out,' said Robin Stewart reflectively, 'that he's Lord d'Aubigny's man. Or was.'

'Goodness be about us.' It was a sneer. 'Has the poor man told all and perished?' It was not long after midday, but his beard was there already, black under the skin. Until May, like his master, he had been whiskered.

'Unhappily. Knifed in the back, I think,' said Stewart complacently. 'At least, dead with a knife in his back, a long way from here. The girl will be killed by the man who arranged the accident at the Tour des Minimes. D'Aubigny is as good as condemned. The man can be caught in the act. The ceremony's at ten; she'll go out on the lake just after. D'Aubigny himself will see she gets the idea, and they won't oppose it. Provided the boat's safe—and it will be—and she's surrounded by friends—and she will be—they'll see no possible harm. It'll look the safest retreat there can be: the Lake of Menteith all over again.'

'I wouldn't know,' said Piedar Dooly, 'what you're blathering about. If it's that safe it is, how is she killed? There's only little boats on the lake, with poppin's in them, ready for tomorrow night.'

'That's right,' said Stewart cheerfully. 'Clods, squibs, fire darts, bombards, and a floating ordnance store of gunpowder, packed in a full day before. She'll be sent off birling like a wheel at a fair; and no one to know there was powder in it at all. A wee thing wasteful, but bonny to watch. It's got to have pigment in it, and plasterwork, and a Latin verse or two to set it off, before his lordship can get cosy with a murder.'

His cheeks brown as two uncured hides, his eyes hollow, his mouth thin as a twig, Piedar Dooly heard, repeated over and over for clarity, all Robin Stewart had to tell him. And as he spoke, Stewart thought of the news reaching Thady Boy-Lymond; of Lymond's quick grasp, his private surprise, his recognition of something vital, well done. He doubted if Dooly would read English, but he had written it all out, too: the times, the places, the name. Only when he was satisfied that the Irishman had grasped it all, did he come to the point of the highest importance.

'And you must say,' he said carefully, 'that in giving this information I trust Mr. Ballagh—Mr. Crawford—to see I take no skaith and

351

no blame for it all. I shall need to give myself up, and before the explosion takes place. Mr. Crawford must come here, with a proper guard and officer, and I will put myself in their hands. Otherwise, he doesna need to be told, they'll shoot me on sight. . . . I'll wait here at nine tomorrow morning. Tell him I'll expect him then, to share my bread. He won't be disappointed in my table.' He had written that, too, at the foot of his notes. And he had added, 'I have been unfair no less than you; I can see it now. As one gentleman to another, I offer apologies with my meat.'

There was no understanding in Dooly's fixed eyes, only contempt. 'I'll tell him,' he said. 'If he's risen from his kissing couch yet.'

Suddenly Stewart was still. 'The O'Dwyer woman? What did she tell?'

A chuckle, creaking and eerie, rose from the black Firbolg's throat. 'The darling devil that's in her, she took all and gave nothing. She would not tell.'

The bony jaw-strings relaxed, the thin cheeks wrinkled, and Stewart smiled. 'Women. . . . They'll thin him like poor cloth, body and soul. Give him the message.'

'There will be no trumpet in the country earning his shilling that will be equal to me,' said Piedar Dooly, and spat.

When his servant got back to the Cher Saincte O'LiamRoe was already groaning. They needed the table for other gentlemen and were glad when Dooly dragged him, stumbling, to their lodging, where he applied various sobering agents at no great speed. Presently, soaked and silky head in his hands, The O'LiamRoe enquired the time, which was three o'clock, and swore fuzzily, getting to his feet. To him, but not to Cormac had been extended an invitation to the jousting that afternoon.

'I must have slept in that damned inn for hours.—Holy Mother, my head. And do you tell me you sat beside me and made never a move? Did it never hit you to push me on a mattress, at least? I have the graining drawn on my haunches of every knot in the deal.'

''Twas a long, drouthy wait, and that's no lie,' admitted Piedar Dooly, his black eyes unwinking on the gold head. 'But there'll be a grand reward for my patience in heaven, since there's no thanks for it here. . . . You will never take yourself to Court, then, in that state. Lie back, so, and sleep it off. I doubt will they miss you.'

'No.' Like a visitor at a sickbed, he had to be there, although he knew that under that caustic blue eye his detachment would become dense and dusty, like a stuffed owl foolishly glasseyed in its case. The birds of hell shall devour them with bitter breath; and the gall of the dragon shall be their drink, and the venom of the dragon their morsels . . . 'No. The morning seems to be lost on us; let the devil do us good with the afternoon.'

Dooly did not try again to dissuade him. It would do no harm. By tomorrow the Scotch Queen would be dead and The O'LiamRoe on his way where he belonged, in the heather breasts of the purple Slieve Bloom, untroubled by all but the squirrel-hoarding of knowledge.

To Stewart and to Lymond he gave no further thought. He disliked them both, and found much stimulation in tearing up the Archer's long message and sealing it inside his bags, in between attiring O'LiamRoe for Court. O'LiamRoe, noting a slight lift in the customary dourness, put it down to a willing wench at the Cher Saincte, and was aware, in passing, of a crabbed sliver of envy.

*   *   *

The French Court meanwhile was engaged, as ever, in a competition in courtesy, in etiquette and riches, in intelligence, accomplishments, in knightly prowess, in sport, and in the exercises of the mind. The King, carefree amid the hubbub of diplomacy, civil, legal, international, leaned as always on his dear confrères and amies the Constable, the de Guises, his distinguished mistress and his pregnant Queen, and his cherished sister of Scotland whose visit, surely, was drawing to a close.

He might, and did, feel impatience at times with them all; but he was a man whose love ran in deep channels. Not one of his dearest cronies would have seen a denouncement of Lord d'Aubigny or any other of that trusted circle as anything but suicide—social, financial and very likely actual as well.

Sir George Douglas, with whom the Lennoxes were staying, recognized the dilemma very well, and got a good deal of entertainment from it. The circle of the Queen Dowager did not.

Mary of Guise herself had had no interview with Lymond in recent days; so much Margaret Erskine knew. Of what went on in her mistress's mind she had no inkling. More than ever she was missing the sane interpretations of Tom, now on his way to the English Border to conclude the formal peace between Scotland and England, with all the tangled and difficult issues this involved.

Tomorrow's conference concerning Mary's marriage appeared, of course, to be the crux of the stay; that and the money promised by the French treasury for the security of Scotland, over which daily haggling continued.

Once only, twisting the rings from her swollen fingers, the Dowager had said to her lady-in-waiting, 'Why does that man believe the attack will be so soon? The guard for Sunday is prodigious.' And then, hardly listening to Margaret's answer, she had added suddenly, 'If the child dies, every hour I have spent on French soil has been a folly, and every transaction a waste.'

353

In her carrying voice, more French even in its Scots, the weariness and the flat foreboding were plain. She was vain of Mary, and skilful in ready-made relationships: mother-daughter, mother-son. With the puppylike magnetism of the toddler far behind, Mary's mother had found reborn no inconvenient torrent of warmth. In France the princes drugged the child Queen with gifts; her mother had no need to court her. 'A folly,' she said, and frowned, pinching her nose; then spoke incisively about something else.

The English were enjoying it rather more than they had thought. The technique was much the same as in England, though the monarch was older: show respect for his toys. And the food was good.

*   *   *

By Saturday afternoon, when The O'LiamRoe had joined them, pink-nosed, his eyelids half-fixed like a boa's, the daily exhibition of craft, dexterity and brawn was well under way. Like a man answering the beat of a drum he made for the jousting ground laid out along the great lake in the parks of Châteaubriant, followed by the silent Piedar Dooly; and pressing unhandily past the ranked knees, joined the Scottish Court in the streamered pavilion.

To reach his vacant place he had to pass George Douglas. 'Smile, my prince,' said the lazy voice. 'You have the better part. *Samson en perdit ses lunettes; Bien heureux est qui riens n'y a!*' Beyond him, a woman laughed; he did not need to struggle with the French to divine the subject of the joke.

The woman was Margaret Douglas, Lady Lennox. Passing, he bowed, his oval face blank. By the holy cross of Jesus, how did these things become known? She was dressed in a light, blowing robe, in white, her splendour bold in the sun. 'Samson is below there'—her voice, gay and fresh, followed his buffeting scabbard—'if you desire him. His own desires are humble today, I am told.' During the preposterous journey she had had time to shape her attitude, both to Francis Crawford and to O'LiamRoe.

He turned. 'There is a laughing time, and a time for speech. I am in my hour for breathing only.' She laughed again, but not with her eyes.

When he sat down, not six rows behind the Scottish Dowager, with her daughter and Margaret Erskine at her side, he found the airy yellow head a little below him on the right; and from all the poisoned corridors of his lazy senses, dislike ran fuming.

Because of Francis Crawford he was here, tail docked, pepper in the nose, turned loose for minstrels to pursue. Watching, with vacant mind, the impact of metalled monsters, feathered, gauntletted, on aproned horses, flying past the coloured barriers, he wondered what Lymond was thinking. Round the little feathered hat bobbing on the

Dowager's left was a thicket of Fleming heads; beyond the ladies, the Dowager's own suite pressed closer. The little Queen was well guarded.

But in George Douglas's voice had been a chord of something other than mockery; in Lady Lennox's, a glitter of tension. Fear was in the air: fear of nothing so explicit as a single killing, but an almost pleasurable fear that somewhere, this day or the next, a wanton hand would snip, and the whole frail net of treaties, understandings and expediency over states German and Italian, over England, Scotland and Ireland, over divided France herself, would sink to the ground.

Bruised with loathing, O'LiamRoe could yet comprehend the real issue; and through the tilting his eyes were on the man on whose shoulders the whole burden lay. Lymond was half-turned, his wrist on the rail, listening to Chester Herald, leaning over to comment. Phelim could hear Flower's Yorkshire accent from where he sat. Lymond said something, and the herald laughed. On the tilting ground, there was an English victory. Sir John Perrott, brawling bastard of the English King's father, flung back his vizor, grinning, and stuck a foot in mock heroics on his fallen foe, while the French politely cheered. He allowed a page to unhelm him, loosing the rough chestnut hair to the breeze, and strode off bellowing: bluff King Hal, wearing out his ten horses a day.

A Gentleman of the Household, smiling, left the royal benches and sidling along the packed seats, addressed the Queen Dowager. The King wished her Scottish lords to show their skill now against these Englishmen. 'He hears,' said the gentleman affably, 'that your herald Mr. Crawford is a notable warrior and would have him take the field, if you will permit, at the quintain.'

Along the bench, Flower's laugh rang out again. The straight, plump back of Margaret Erskine had become quite still; and O'LiamRoe, his attention cuffed into place, thought of a fat black figure at St. Germain, flying like a witch on a broomstick at a barrel of hot water, lance couched.

They had seen Thady Boy's style then; and how often since? 'Pray tell his grace,' said Mary of Guise kindly, 'that our herald is notable for much, but not as a performer in the field. If he will allow us, we shall find another.'

With enviable polish, the emissary hid his surprise. 'He excels perhaps at national sports? The King would willingly see him matched at putting the stone, or the bar of iron perhaps?'

A long hand touched the King's Gentleman on his stooped shoulder. 'My mistress the Queen feels perhaps that she has tested her herald's valour sufficiently in the boarpit at Angers. Allow me to take his place.' And bowing to the Dowager and to the envoy, Sir George Douglas strolled down to the field, his attendants struggling after.

355

Chester Herald, drawing out of his story, laughed again, clapped Vervassal on the shoulder, and turned off. Lymond, swinging back in his seat, caught Sir George's eye and with perfect naturalness bowed. The Douglas, well-built, handsome, a notable knight in his day, returned the smile, mocking, and went off to pay his self-imposed debt to the Queen.

He was joined by others. Uneasily O'LiamRoe watched the grim playfulness with lance and spear and blunted sword, with iron and stone, between the great houses of Scotland and the soldier-diplomats, the soldier-scholars, the knights of England: Dethick who had marched with Somerset to the bloody massacre of Pinkie and Throckmorton who had been knighted for taking news of it to the King; Rutland who had demolished the walls of Haddington and Sir Thomas Smith whose historian's voice had helped form the English claims of feudal sovereignty over Scotland; Essex whose son had been killed in the Scottish wars. The blows were hard and the laughter loud, but nothing unseemly occurred; Mary of Guise just then had power to ride them hard. And Lymond, at ease, chatting soberly with his neighbours, hardly watched.

It was nearly over when the cold-eyed face of Sir John Perrott laid itself, like a prime kill on a slab, on the ledge of the Queen Mother's stand, and addressed Crawford of Lymond. 'Sir, they tell me you wrestle, and I have much surplus energy and some skill at the craft. If your mistress permits, will you try a fall with me?'

Cool under the awning, the herald rose. Knightly pursuits were, or should be, part of his calling, temporary though that calling might be. Neither he nor the Queen Dowager could ignore an invitation twice. For a fleeting moment, O'LiamRoe saw the pale head lift to where, among his Queen, his mistress, his great officials, his courtiers and his friends of the heart, Henri King of France waited, with Lord d'Aubigny, beautiful, modest, detached, at his side.

Then Lymond said, 'With pleasure; if my lady will allow?' And the Queen Dowager, her eyes not on him but on some angering sight at his back, gave her slow nod. To protect him with her refusal would have argued complicity; he had accepted to save her that, as it was. For plain as the white sun in the purple-blue of the lake, as the green grass and the red dust and the jingling colour of shield and standard, flags, pennants and canopies, as the Court robes, serried, bright as bolsters in a sultan's rich playbed, was the truth, plain to them all, that Lord d'Aubigny had chosen today, here, now, to open his war, his series of broadsides which would reveal Francis Crawford and Thady Boy Ballagh to be one and the same man.

Jacketless in the sunlight, the Queen's herald stirred no meaty chords of remembrance; there was no whiff of Thady's highhanded flavour in all this pale precision. But to O'LiamRoe, his heart beating sodden inside its pink cushion, the dilemma was without solution. Fight well, and Lymond would invite comparison, by every trained move that he made, with the twin moves of Thady Boy. Fight badly, and he brought his Queen into ridicule, invited suspicion, offered himself even to injury. And in his freedom and mobility lay their last hopes.

He had stripped quickly. As they waited for Perrott, the trumpets soared; the talk and laughter rushed round. It was the last fight of the day, and already the pleasures of evening were pressing on them: the torchlight hunt of red deer, the midnight supper. There was a ripple of movement in one of the passages, and a lady-in-waiting bent down and spoke to Sir John Perrott's page, who trotted off. A moment later Perrott himself reappeared, and the English stands were restrainedly enthusiastic.

'Happy mortal,' observed Sir George Douglas, his eyes on Lymond, his neckband black with sweat, sliding into the vacant seat at O'LiamRoe's elbow. He had used his lance more than adequately, enough at any rate to match any of the late King Henry's illegitimate sons. 'Happy mortal, invariably licensed to lechery, forced by duty like clockwork into sin and indulgence. . . . Even here, all he need do is fail.'

'After the boar fight?' said O'LiamRoe sardonically. But the two men on the field had closed with one another, and Sir George Douglas, his hands unconsciously fast on his chair, said nothing at all until some long minutes later, when releasing his pent breath softly, he observed, 'Well, Irishman, if he is wise he will get himself thrown, fast. I fancy Sir John has had a little advice. He is following the same moves exactly as our friend the Cornishman.'

If the same thought had occurred to Vervassal, it was obvious that, short of throwing himself abjectly on his back, there was very little he could do about it. Sir John Perrott was built on the same scale as his father, and to weight was added training and temper. Perrott was angry, he was out to do damage, and he was being very careful indeed not to throw his opponent too soon.

This left Lymond, clearly, to improvise a series of defences which should be safe, unspectacular, and quite unlike his habitual responses to the recognized moves.

There are not so many ways of solving a sudden problem of leverage; especially when the problems are presented in prearranged sequence. The Englishman, his fringed jaw like a quarry block, hugged and hoisted, heeled and thrust with knee and foot, and was parried with an adequacy which was less than enthusiastic. After a good deal of this, when both men were blotched with bruises but otherwise unimpaired, Sir John Perrott released the Queen Dowager's herald, rasped, 'Well, here is a bastard, sir, who will dirty his hands on *you*,' and opened his thicketed hands.

Arrested for the second, whether in admiration for Lord d'Aubigny's inventiveness or in a kind of silent snort of hysteria at the prodigies expected of him—a condition, O'LiamRoe recognized, to which Lymond was all too prone—Francis Crawford was off guard for the one moment that mattered.

In the pavilion, attention already weakened by the Breton sports, the tilting, the jousting, was left cold by the undistinguished contest, spiderlike on the big field to all but the nearest benches. People were moving, tongues were chattering. Although no one physically could leave until the King rose, mentally most were by now back in the castle and climbing into their next change of clothes.

So perhaps only those who had heard Lord d'Aubigny mention Vervassal's supposed prejudice against bastardy, only those sharing willy-nilly the King's diplomatic engrossment, and those, finally, who knew who Thady Boy was, saw the quick succession of moves that brought Lymond to the ground under hip, knee and calf locked in a tightening wedge intended to crush.

For an agile man, there was one feasible retort: the move which had put the Cornishman's neck under Thady Boy's hand and then broke it. Watching the two immobile, straining figures, O'LiamRoe in his anxious ignorance jumped to hear Sir George Douglas swear. 'He can choose,' said Sir George informatively, 'between having his leg snapped and declaring himself to be Thady Boy. Full of interest, isn't it?'

In the rows about the Queen and the Queen Dowager silence had fallen. Across the passage, the faces in the King's pavilion, sewn like freshwater pearls on its tapestry, were turned also on the Englishman's broad back, straining pink through the oiled film of his shirt; on the rough russet head and fat hips, sinuous under the cloth; and on the jagged line of pelvis, elbow and throat belonging to the Queen's herald, gripped fast underneath. And Lymond made no move, for the only one he could make would have branded him, like a confession, as Thady Boy Ballagh.

At the edge of the field, someone in the de Guise colours moved quickly; a man bent over the King. Then, unexpectedly, a trumpet blew, and the rattle of conversation hesitated and stopped. The King's baton fell and rose again; the King got up. The fight had been ended.

Sir John Perrott had not noticed, or hearing, had decided to ignore. He lifted his body a little, giving them a glimpse of his ripe, beaded skin, the splendid teeth bared in stress and eagerness. Lymond's hands, resisting, were white to the bone and O'LiamRoe said, 'Mother of God, that leg—' and stopped.

From in front, Will Flower, Chester Herald, turned round, his plain Yorkshire face animated with knowledge. 'A good fellow, that is. His own people sent to stop it, and I can't say I'm sorry. He has some war wound, they say, and he's not just himself again yet; and you'd want to be at your best, my word you would, to stand against Perrott. A brave effort, I'd say; and no shame to the lad—no shame at all.'

Into the silence: 'No shame to him; but a very great pity. Since he was at it,' said George Douglas succinctly, 'he might as well have broken Sir John Perrott's neck.'

It was true. Watching as the Constable's officers smoothly prised the combatants apart, O'LiamRoe realized that this opening round Lord d'Aubigny had won. For in spite of all Francis Crawford's care, the association of Lymond with recent injury alone was enough to make an observant man think. In saving him, the Queen Dowager had opened the breach.

On the pavilions, everyone had risen, shaking their skirts, re-grouping, embracing. Perrott, dragged up, had marched off across the clearing field without a salute. Vervassal, after waiting a moment, rose in one collected movement and was standing, with extreme care, looking towards the King's bench.

There, among the baring seats, someone else stood, the sun, through a chink in the awning, proclaimed the day's blue dress of the Household. To John, seigneur d'Aubigny, Lymond raised his left arm in formal salute and then, moving smoothly, walked off the field.

Mary was still safe.

*   *   *

They returned to the château. Mary was still safe. She looked from her window at dusk as the long cavalcade left, apple-green under an apple-green sky, the torches like embers amongst them, to hunt the red deer in the forest.

You would not think it possible to isolate one man out of hundreds, to illumine him with accident, admiration, solicitude, so that in every episode of the hunt the French Court was made aware of Lymond. He dropped back finally, melting into the darkness in preparation for a quick return home; and d'Aubigny's Archers blocked the way with an unanswerable request. The King desired his presence, with the Queen Dowager's, at supper.

Douglas, never far away, touched Lymond on the shoulder then. 'Christ, get away, man. Feign sickness. You mustn't think of going. They'll take your ashes away in a tigerskin sack.'

The voice of Quetzalcoatl answered him. 'Be calm! Be calm!' said Francis Crawford soothingly. 'To dispel doubt and error, one must exercise the light of supreme wisdom. If his lordship is really deter-mined to expose me tonight as Thady Boy Ballagh, nothing I can do will stop him.'

'You can escape,' said Douglas.

'To do what?' In the torchlit darkness, under the green and black trees, the jewels bright in his ears, Lymond laughed. 'Mary is as well guarded as love and duty can make her. The information that will save her will save me. Three people can do it—Oonagh O'Dwyer, Robin Stewart, or Michel Hérisson from Rouen. Perhaps they will do for me on my prison pallet what they would not do for me in my—'

'You're a naughty, cold-blooded devil named Jeroboam, son of Nebat, who made Israel to sin,' said George Douglas dispassionately. 'And you know that if they recognize you as Ballagh and convict you of the Tour des Minimes and the rest, they'll light a large fire and toast you brown on a dungfork.' He looked curiously, in the torchlight, at the other man's unrevealing serenity. 'What do you hope for that you haven't got? What can that child give you?'

There was a little silence. 'A virgin audience for my riddles, I believe,' said Lymond thoughtfully, at length. 'But it certainly poses an ungallant question. Shall we join his grace?'

And riding off through the long layered ranks of warmcoated kill, he reached the wide spaces, filled with firelit satin and jewels, where the supper was; and as lute, rebec and vihuelas played like unborn voices through the trees and gilded Pan children danced, he fumbled the scented oranges they threw him, or tossed them away, and defended his long-fingered dexterity from the charms of legerdemain. And yet, as the bright, tempting fruit left his hands, the Vidame, stretched loose on the grass, looked nowhere from that moment but at the profile above him; the Duchess de Valentinois, at the King's side, broke off once or twice to watch, and the Prince of Condé and his brother exchanged looks.

It was the Princess de la Roche-sur-Yon, no friend of the Constable's, whose very castle of Châteaubriant he had filched from her hands, who leaned over at last, and laid a lute on his lap. 'M. Crawford, you cannot deny that you play. Honour us.'

They had hung arras between the barks of the trees, and laid velvet over the dried roots and beaver tracks; in this forest clearing in the exhausted heat of midnight, every accustomed artifice was imposed. From their wreathed tables the Embassy, slackly comfortable, shifted a little, sensing a change, sniffing at abature and blemish to distinguish the prey.

O'LiamRoe, watching, wondered fleetingly, since exposure had to come, if Lymond would not have preferred to stand on his scholarship: to reveal himself in argument with Pickering or Smith or Thomas rather than as a tumbler, a clown, a singer.

Lymond himself gave no sign, but took the lute and touched the strings, thinking. O'LiamRoe became aware of many eyes watching:

of Catherine, of the Dowager, of her brothers the Duke and the Cardinal, of the Constable himself. By now, surely, they knew or guessed. Refusal itself was an admission by now.

Couched within the torches they had brought him, head bent over the dark lute on one knee, Lymond struck one scattered chord. The sound of it attracted wandering eyes, and silence enough. The first phrase with its unaltered texture named the singer, and to a blind man had described the proper contours of his face.

> '*My lute, awake! perform the last*
> *Labour that thou and I shall waste*
> *And end that I have now begun:*
> *And when this song is sung and past*
> *My lute! be still, for I have done. . . .*'

Easily, bright with irony, the voice rose and fell, and the lute lapped it like water.

Relaxed after the hunt, warm under the limpid trees, a little stirred by the romance and the artifice, the English Ambassage lay listening, smiling, and watched the young man who had given Sir John Perrott a poor game, but had clearly been selected by the Scottish Queen for quite different talents.

Lord Lennox, thumb to cheek, heard the opening and then found matters to discuss, low-voiced, with his neighbour. Beside him, his wife's eyes, leaving the singer, explored the cushioned groups on the spread tapestries and the faces turning like leaves in a light wind to watch. Then, pulled by another gaze, Lady Lennox looked round and in her turn met the wordless challenge of Margaret Erskine's flat stare as the song ended.

> '*Now cease, my lute! This is the last*
> *Labour that thou and I shall waste*
> *And ended is that we begun:*
> *Now is thy song both sung and past*
> *My lute! be still, for I have done.*'

He did not allow them to applaud him. As the notes died, he forced his thumb through the strings, then again, then again, hurling them into a fury of sound, and launched like an armed man into battle, into one of the paramount Irish epics, the greatest perhaps of all, which he had given them again and again unstinted from his extravagance. O'LiamRoe, drunk, had listened to Thady Boy, drunk, creating this passion and had wept, snorting unawares, the oval face caged with tears. Then he had wept for himself; for the human pain and valour and grief he knew and recognized in the song. This time he did not weep, but pressed his lips on his clenched hands with a stubborn pain in his throat, for he had never heard it as, cold sober,

Lymond created it now. And about him, involuntarily, each listener tightened as if called into tune. The double pull on sense and intellect was final, exposing the small places of self to universal challenges. The Queen Dowager of Scotland looked away; George Douglas, his brows raised, studied his knees; and Margaret Lennox, her eyes wide on the singer, sunk her teeth in her lip.

Lymond himself flung what he had made at John Stewart of Aubigny, standing broad and still by the King, ornamental as some Ionian pillar, perfect in column and capital, waiting.

The paean ended, properly served, dying until the brush of the forest leaves hid it. There was a vacant quiet into which all their bruised emotions pooled and ran, filling it, splash by splash, with exclamations and the stir of revived movement, and the mounting dash and eddy of applause. From his stance behind the King, Lord d'Aubigny moved forward smiling and dropped on one knee. No one in the Scottish Court heard what he said, but it was cut short by the King's own hand summoning the singer.

Only Margaret Erskine, close to Lymond, saw that he was shivering. He waited a second until the fires of his own making left him; then with a minimum of gesture he rose, laid the lute neatly down and walked across the soft dunes of tapestry. The torchboys followed the tabard, bright as a wave breaking at night, their shadows chequered in the cross lighting. Lymond knelt.

From Northampton's circle, it looked merely like a called-for bestowal of praise. King Henri, keeping his voice level, preserved the illusion. 'M. Vervassal. How are you called?'

'My name is Francis Crawford of Lymond, your grace.' The reply also was sober. 'I commend me to your justice.'

'Francis Crawford of Lymond. You are known also as Thady Boy Ballagh?'

'I have been so,' said Lymond. Beside the King, the sieur d'Enghien looked suddenly up and away again; the King's sister had not removed her gaze throughout. D'Aubigny smiled.

The bearded, fine-drawn face of the King studied the other man at his feet; and in Henri's hardened muscles and pressed nostrils was plainly the temper he did not propose to unleash. 'Here is a matter for judges,' he said. 'My Archers will bring you before me tonight. Go.'

And Stewart of Aubigny, bending, raised the former Thady Boy Ballagh to his feet and drew him among the guard with a grip framed expressly to cripple. Lymond sustained it, his eyes alight, while the applause broke out again, and across the carpet someone held out his lute. But Henri, smiling briefly, indicated the interval closed. It was time to stir, to leave the night and prepare to return.

Francis Crawford turned his fair head on Lord d'Aubigny's

shoulder and looked up at him, with his right arm hanging numb and the bog-gravel irony of Thady Boy plain in his face. 'A bull for the cows in time of bulling; a stallion for the mares in time of covering; a boar for the sows in time of their heat. A foot for a foot; an eye for an eye; a life for a life,' said Francis Crawford. 'So says the Senchus Mor, my darling. And Robin Stewart is still free, and hot bent on revenge.'

Piedar Dooly heard, and spat, grinning, as the yellow head in a huddle of Archers took to horse. Far through the forest, on the flank leading to Béré, Robin Stewart, he supposed, was waiting patiently for his fine guest tomorrow. O'LiamRoe heard too, his mind busy. As Thady Boy's master, he would have some explaining to do. But not as much, Christ, as Lymond. With thought working, cold as acid, on the stately procession home, the King would not rest, nor would his lords, the perfect image of learning and chivalry, until this small and festering dart was removed from their side.

*   *   *

It was done in the King's cabinet at Châteaubriant that night.

When they brought O'LiamRoe into the brightly lit room, lined with bitter night-faces, the Prince of Barrow's tongue was creaming over with quip and insult to let fly at the master figures. It was for this that he had stayed.

—Of course he knew Thady Boy was no ollave; what of it? he would say. Thady Boy only existed because the Queen Dowager of Scotland desired it. Lymond had risked his own safety to remain and protect the child and draw off her enemies so that the Franco-Scottish talks might proceed unimpaired, and no dire change of crown or impolitic accusation might destroy them.

That in exposing himself, Francis Crawford had foundered— that, surely, they could understand. If he had no positive evidence of another's guilt, he had indirect evidence of his innocence: the elephants at Rouen, the impressive performance in London, the injuries he had received in the Tower at Amboise. Jenny's son could speak of the arsenic. . . . But no, Jenny's son was perhaps better left out. And to summon Abernaci would destroy his livelihood; to call Tosh would be to endanger his safety. And Oonagh . . .

Thought stopped, and restarted, freshly armoured. They would laugh at the old women, he and Lymond. He and Lymond, outside the fence together, shrugging off involvement and the poison all run out.

Then Phelim O'LiamRoe, Prince of Barrow, was ushered into the little cabinet, through the heat and the drawling, arguing voices, to find Lymond standing tabardless, his hair in his eyes, his scraped hands lashed tight behind him; and saw foolishly that there are

363

circumstances under which it is a little hard to sparkle with provocative wit. 'Et dis-donc', said the King, his voice flat with distaste. 'Whom do you serve?'

With a slow and studied exasperation, Crawford of Lymond shook his head. His eyes, brilliant in his pale face, passed over O'LiamRoe, ignoring him; rested for a second on the Queen Mother, and flickered back again. What message he had received or conveyed, O'LiamRoe could not tell. 'I sell experience . . . and buy it; and pay due tax on the merchandise as you see. I serve my own whims, that is all.'

'You are here,' said the slow voice, 'as an accredited herald to Madame ma bonne soeur, the Queen Dowager of Scotland. It would appear to us that Madame my sister is your mistress and that the Prince of Barrow was your knowing accomplice.'

No one spoke. In the recesses of the silence crowded all the weary weeks of this sojourn in France; the gold almost promised, the marriage contract almost confirmed, the regency almost achieved. In it lay coiled the absent power of Cormac O'Connor, the beckoning fame and treasure of the Italian wars, the sweet compliance of England, balm to smooth minds overfretted by Scots.

Lord d'Aubigny had less patience than the others. Stretching his well-kept hand, he removed the whip from the sergeant beside him, and with an easy snap, touched the flat back across and across, like a lion tamer.

Lymond turned, so fast that he almost took the last lash in his face, and d'Aubigny, taken by surprise, stepped back.

'If you have a case, make it. If you have a question, put it. It is interesting, I admit, but it would take more time than you can spare to thrash me into compliance.'

A whip cracked again, a small whip, razor-sharp across the legs, and one of the Queen's dwarfs, hopped back sniggering, 'Keep a civil tongue in this gathering,' said Catherine de Médicis coolly in the Italian-French she had had to learn so quickly after her marriage, together with the patience she had afterwards taken so long to master. 'You cannot deceive us. The Queen your mistress is here.'

Her long chin sunk on her chest, Mary of Guise shook out her sleeve smartly, and laying her wrist on her knee, engaged Catherine and then the King with her strongly marked brows. 'The old women that are in it,' said O'LiamRoe's mind to him softly; and his memory said, '*You'd better play tennis with them on Tír-nan-óg, my dear, if you're going to call thirty-five old.*' And it added, 'The Queen Mother isn't going to stir a little finger in this affair . . . and I'm not at all sure that I want to meddle in hers.' The whip cracked, thoughtfully.

'I love a brave man,' said the Queen Dowager of Scotland. 'And the Crawfords are brave men who have served me well in the past.

364

But a sly, high-stomached swaggering man I cannot abide. Had I known a Scot of mine was engaged in this mummery I should have sent you his tongue and his hands. As it is, you are welcome to pluck your restitution from him as you wish. I cannot believe him guilty of theft and prodigal of murder. I do find he has mocked both you and me, gentle brother, in deceiving us boldly not once, but twice in this fashion. Do as you wish with him.'

She had repudiated him. The unspoken words filled O'LiamRoe's mouth. In Lymond's face there was no line of anger or surprise; even dusty and uncombed he contrived to look acidly collected. He gazed at Mary of Guise through half-shut, lazy lids and said, 'Madame, what king should I sing to in Scotland? Even Lyon is old.'

She had repudiated him and he had accepted it. Drawing breath, the Prince of Barrow felt the warning pressure on his arm. Margaret Erskine had moved up beside him. The Queen Dowager icily answered. 'Had you come as Francis Crawford, you might have done your country honour. Instead of taking all Ireland in your mouth and spitting it at our feet.'

'But Francis Crawford,' Lymond said simply, 'was not invited.'

'And Francis Crawford is known,' said Lord d'Aubigny. The late hour had made no hollows in his well-furnished face, but the spread of pink was uneven from cheek to brow; he was, after all, breaking a desirable vessel.

'We are not forgetting the jewels he had ready to take, the rope in his room, the friendship with my wretched man Stewart. Robin saved his life, climbing—many of you saw that. They worked hand in glove over the pretended accident of the cheetah. Only because M. d'Enghien held the reins was he made to run in the forefront of that ride downhill in Amboise—he intended, I am sure, to be safe behind. And Crawford and his friend O'LiamRoe between them, I am told, rescued Stewart yet again from near death in the Tower and persuaded him that he should do better to live and return to France. And mysteriously, as soon as he reaches the Loire, Stewart escapes. If his Irish disguise was simply a discourteous and foolish masquerade,' said Lord d'Aubigny, his voice shade high, 'why did Lord Culter his brother, of that brave and so serviceable family, refrain from halting these excesses, or at least informing the Queen his mistress of Mr. Ballagh's real name?'

The prominent brown eyes of Queen Catherine, tight-rimmed in the sleepless white skin, moved to stare at the Dowager. 'Why, indeed? Look to your lords, my sister. The family appears to be less reliable than you thought.'

The old women! For the second time, O'LiamRoe opened his mouth. To his left, Piedar Dooly, his strained black eyes intent, stirred at his side. At his right, Margaret Erskine moved, her body blocking his view of the King, her eyes nearly level with his own. 'He does not want it,' she said, in a voice which carried only to him. 'He does not want it. How can you help him unless you are free?'

Lymond laughed. Shivering round the small room it sounded indelicate, like the rubbing of crystals over some robust Arabian couch. 'The worthy Prince of Barrow left France on the day he discovered my identity, and has been trying to make amends for me ever since. Do you suppose any accomplice of mine would have risked total exile from France as he did within the first week of our stay? M. O'LiamRoe, as you have found for yourselves, despises diplomacy, laughs at statesmanship, pokes fun at pretension, ridicules wealth. You did not know what a jewel you had. A man who wanted nothing from you but fuel for his wit. *Phelim is welcome,* you should have said—' The light voice indulged in cool parody:

> '*Phelim is welcome*
> *Phelim son of Liam*
> *Place where dwells a champion*
> *Heart of ice*
> *Tail of a swan*
> *Strong chariot-warrior in battle*
> *Warlike ocean*
> *Lovely, eager bull*
> *Phelim son of Liam* . . .

'*Lovely, eager bull,*' said Lymond lingeringly again, this time in Irish; and O'LiamRoe, the ducts of his brain half choked by the mud and gold Lymond had flung him together, said clearing his throat, 'Bad scran to it. What about you? There is great music in you, I can tell you now. A new-made angel put beside you would sound like an old nail scraping on glass. . . . What call had you to name yourself an Irishman, and use the first chance to let drink and decadence murder your gifts?'

The innocent, deceiving eyes turned to the Prince. 'Art cannot live without licence.'

There was a little silence. O'LiamRoe grasped that the barbarous spectacle of accusation and blow had somehow been replaced by a match of quite another kind, to which the Court was tacitly granting a hearing. He hesitated only a moment before letting his own worn-out theories slip for the last time through his hands. He said, 'Ah yes, my fine *gean-canach*, but how much licence? A man's art is only as good as his liver. Who decides when to stop?'

'The artist?' said Lymond, his voice grave, his eyes nakedly derisive.

'He knows the inspiration he needs to begin, but after that you'd be hard set to halt his little indulgences. Death alive, you know that.

Then you'll have nothing out of him but bad art and worse manners, fit to be copied by every journeyman who can dip his brush in a paintpot or stitch together a tavern lampoon.'

'Does that trouble you?' said Lymond. 'It won't trouble posterity. *Nous devons à la Mort et nous et nos ouvrages,* you know. Both ourselves and our creations are a debt owed to Death. If you sober us and church us and rob us of our Bella Simonettas and our Vittoria Colonnas at this pace, there will be no inspiration and no works of art left to hand on.'

'Not every artist that's in it must find balance in drink or drugs or nameless indulgences.'

'But those who do? Must they be stopped? Must posterity suffer in the cause of the corruptible present?'

O'LiamRoe was silent. Here lay the core of the matter. The accusations of theft and treason Lord d'Aubigny had made were without real foundation; however eagerly the Court had seized on them to salve their raw pride, it was not on these counts that Lymond would be condemned.

He would be crushed for the trick he had played on them, for the power he had held over them, and for the attentions he had forced them to pay him. To save his skin, since he would not call on either the Queen or O'LiamRoe, Lymond was salving their pride. For that, he had turned against O'LiamRoe just now every argument O'Liam-Roe himself had used in order to show the French Court to itself in a new light: not as his companions, his victims in some deliberate essay in decadence, but as ministers to his art. And arguing against him, playing his part, O'LiamRoe heard his own philosophy in another man's mouth, and found it lacking. '. . . Feeling,' Lymond was saying, ending his exposition on the inspiring properties of drink, debauchery and general freedom from convention, 'feeling needs a respite from thought, and thought returns refreshed after.'

'Yes, M. Crawford.' It was Catherine, her fine ankles crossed, her ringed hands still. 'But example kills, and the example of genius kills quicker than any.'

'And the artist with them,' said O'LiamRoe. 'The holocaust which nearly sieved your flesh through its bones at the Tour des Minimes was your salvation, and you know it. When you kicked out your self-control, your art walked out after it.'

'I came to France to find freedom,' said Lymond. About him, the Archers had fallen back, leaving him standing alone, his arms bent to the lashing. Impatience had gone; he looked alive and alert in the soft light.

'You have found a prison, it seems,' said the King, and let his eyes rest for a moment on the still face of the Constable, his old compère. Then he drew a long breath and let it hiss as a sigh in the quiet room.

'Is this not the truth then; that such a talent, working only when freed, must also be caged? From adversity, illness, poverty, persecution, comes the discipline necessary for perfect creation? ... And yet,' said the careful voice thoughtfully, 'you do not appear a man lacking in self-control. This is, perhaps, a man who studies other men, and himself in relation to other men? An amateur of modulated conduct; a man who traps mutations, freakish properties of the soul and sets them in conflict; a keeper of menageries ...'

He paused. 'You did this, intending theft or worse, for which your doom will be death; or you did this with no purpose other than mischief inspired by the devil. I should condemn you if you had meddled with potboys on these terms. It may please you to think that, had you not succumbed yourself, you might have pushed apart the fabric of a nation and turned our very greatness against us. I regret,' said Henri of France, turning his dark eyes to the Dowager, upright and still in her chair, to his wife, the Constable, the silent faces of all his courtiers and the pale oval grimness of O'LiamRoe and addressing at length the contained presence of Thady Boy Ballagh, who had been their treasure, 'I regret; but art without conscience is a hunting cat no mansuetarius alive should be expected to tame. At a place appointed you will be broken; and your music with you.'

With no purpose other than mischief! 'Mother of God!' said O'LiamRoe furiously, and took three thrashing steps towards Mary of Guise. The big, passive face did not even turn.

'My dear Phelim.' It was Lymond who had moved, his voice prosaic, a shade of irritation and something else in his face. 'I appear to be committed, even though you may not be. Since you cannot improve matters, at least allow me the fruits of my own husbanding. Go and get drunk.'

It was said quite kindly. Phelim O'LiamRoe and his ollave stared at each other for a long moment, blue eyes meeting blue; then the Prince of Barrow turned and, uncaring whom he buffeted, strode headlong from the room.

Piedar Dooly had been caught unawares. Unfolding hastily in a pentagon of angles, he jumped behind his master, whistling under his breath. 'Heaven protect us, there's some sense in the creatures,' said O'LiamRoe's familiar, scurrying along. 'And where now, Prince of Barrow?'

The face that turned on his he hardly knew for Phelim O'LiamRoe, Chief of the Name, so angular was it with purpose and a kind of harsh and miserable anger. 'The likes of you, fortunate man, will be going home to your bed,' it said.

For a moment, in his surprise, Dooly dropped back. Then catching up, he put his question cautiously. 'And yourself, Prince? Where do you be going?'

368

'To the house of Cormac O'Connor, fellow. Where else?' said Phelim O'LiamRoe, artist in living, the very core and prototype of detachment.

It was already Sunday, the 20th of June; and the first grey-veiled light of the new day would hint soon at the trees in Châteaubriant park, and breathe on the dark confines of its lake.

V

Châteaubriant: Proof,
without Love or Hatred

Test is not easy without proof. Proof of certain necessity may
be demanded with the Feine, without love or hatred.

What is the reason that there is more for them as foreign
slaves than as Irish slaves? Is it that the Irish slave has greater
hope of becoming free than the foreign slave has, and so it is
proper, though there be more for him as a foreign slave than as
an Irish slave?

THEY would not admit him: who would unlock to a foolish
Irishman, a moonstruck compatriot, at half-past three in the
morning? Mistress Boyle's hollow-faced steward slammed the grille,
and O'LiamRoe climbed two walls, forced a shutter and tumbled
into the parlour where Cormac O'Connor lay felled and snarling in
sleep among all the spilled ashes, where the night before he had
rustled drunk from the table.

O'LiamRoe gazed at him with interest; then stepping over his
buttocks, threw open the hithermost door.

Green moonlight filled a bedroom, unperfumed, undecorated,
filled with a woman's clothes and the scoured, herbal smell of the
schoolroom. Without stopping, Phelim strode to the wooden
travelling-bed, dim in the corner, where the sleeper, cramped under
thin sheeting, lay drowned and veiled in the black weeds of her
hair.

Next door, a candle still guttered. With a taper deftly lit, O'Liam-
Roe walked from bracket to bracket, from lamp to torchère in both
bedroom and parlour, binding light upon light until the air gasped
and glittered in a tourniquet of searing dazzle and Oonagh O'Dwyer,
white face and black brows, white pillow and black hair, white
elbows and black, sodden shadow where the sharp bones, urgent,
pressed down the limp bed, stared at him in her dazed, with distended eyes
black as flowers in her white face, and said harshly, 'Is he dead?'

'*Tres vidit et unum adoravit.* He's before the fire, my dear, like a

370

pricked pudding . . . if that is the he you mean.' And his eyes, round, pale, innocent, dared her to deny it.

She obliged him, direct and stormy, without a second thought, both palms flat on the bedclothes. 'You know what I mean. Why are you here? Is the Queen killed, then? Why has he sent you?'

''Tis pigeons you have got in your head. Sweet, fat pigeons,' said O'LiamRoe warmly. 'No one sends me, and the Queen is not killed yet. But Thady Boy Ballagh, *ochone*, is sent by royal command to be broken as whipping boy for his lordship of Aubigny, of unsullied fame, and no one but you and I, my love, no one but you and I can save that child now.'

The blurring of sleep was leaving her face; her eyes and brow and wide cheekbones clearing, precision restored to her spare, warm lips. He remembered them, as she threw a bedgown over her robed shoulders, her gaze going beyond him. 'Mary Mother . . . Put out those lights! The child is nothing to me, and will be as easy in the grave.'

'I put them on,' said O'LiamRoe agreeably. 'I want O'Connor's fine brain to help us convince John Stewart of Aubigny's royal patron that the man is a would-be assassin and, I should wager, half-mad.'

Slowly Oonagh spoke. 'Aubigny has exposed Lymond as Thady Boy Ballagh?'

'Yes.'

'Then accusing d'Aubigny won't save him. His offences as Thady Boy alone would have him ended. You know that.'

'Not,' said O'LiamRoe, 'if he could prove that his masquerade had the purpose of saving the Queen.'

'Then go to the Dowager,' said Oonagh O'Dwyer. 'Or has she denied him?' And as O'LiamRoe's silence answered her, she widened her queer eyes and smiled. 'And so do I. He is unlucky, our amateur, our sweet ollave.'

'I would not have said that thing,' said O'LiamRoe and, startlingly, she flushed. 'In small things, yes. He will not ask the Queen Dowager to admit she called him to France to protect the small Queen. He will not call on me to admit I knew he was in France because of the Queen. That would be merely my word against theirs. He cannot suggest he came to France as his own master to do this work without accusing d'Aubigny, and he has no more proof against d'Aubigny than they have against him. So the word you and your friend here are going to give me will damn John Stewart and save the girl and deliver our sweet ollave, as you call him, all at once. As neat a conclusion as ever I saw.'

'And when,' said the woman in the bed, 'did Francis Crawford become the friend of your soul?'

'I was wondering myself.' O'LiamRoe's reply was perfectly

equable. 'I rather fancy 'twas when it came to me that the black roaring Irishman we had there was only half the actor in Francis Crawford; the rest was that unnatural animal being human for once.'

'Do you think so?' For a moment the green eyes, diverted, looked at him curiously.

'I think the rope at the Tour des Minimes—and your regard for him—saved him. You have protected us both, hate us though you may. There is one thing still to be done.'

'I do not hate you. Nor do I delude myself I can read his mind, human or otherwise. . . . Go over,' said Oonagh, her voice, clear and low, reaching his ears on a note of sudden, desperate anger. 'Go over; *go home!* Whatever my body may be, my mind is my own. Let him pat and prick your soul as he wishes. *I will not be touched.*'

Exasperated, O'LiamRoe raised his voice. 'He has no wish to involve you.'

'He is involving me this minute, fool that you are. Why else are you free? The rest of that person was human, do you say? *A mhuire!*' said the black-haired woman, her dry eyes wide and bitter. 'Dacent crathur, go home. He is beyond you, that sweet ollave with the love of every girl in the breast of his shirt. . . . We are the fools, struggling, planning, begging at foolish doors, giving suck to the craven from all our sunken stock of force and eagerness and passion, while you court a strange brat and pare rhymes in Latin.'

She stopped, and for a moment O'LiamRoe faced her in silence. Then, 'Wait you,' he said evenly. 'Since you are so hearty in handing forth blows, let me slip in a small dab of a word. To watch you would be sorrow's own fun; but it is coming to me that I would not at all fancy being ruled by King Cormac.'

She studied him, her mind only half arrested. 'The French King would be your monarch.'

'You're complete,' said O'LiamRoe heartily. 'The first thing Cormac O'Connor will do when he kicks out the English is to kick out the Frenchmen who helped him. Cock's bones, if England can barely keep off her elegant knees, what hope has France, with Scotland to look to, and the Pope and the Emperor gnawing at all her fine frontiers?'

'You would rather have England?' said Oonagh with contempt. 'Or your own self, perhaps?'

'*The Cross of Christ*,' said a rolling voice, a round-bellied orator's organ, just a little hoarse with drink. O'LiamRoe backed. The sleeper had been roused at last. In the doorway, swaying gently, thick-veined brawn enclosed in soiled shirting, his smallcut eyes sparkling, hung Cormac O'Connor.

'The Cross of Christ about us. . . . Are we having visitors, girl, and meself not advised? Have you pleased my dilsy, Phelim O'LiamRoe?

She's hard to please, but the kernel's sweet—as others know. . . . Ah!' said Cormac, and strode forward to the woman straight-backed in the bed, the classical, obstinate jaw plain as a melon from ear to chin. 'Ah, is it your old nightgown you have . . . will you not make the least set to please us . . . and the fine, white jewels you have?'

And bending, in one jerk he ripped apart bedgown and robe, baring her from elbow to elbow between his two fists.

She was made small and white, like the green-eyed morrow Lymond had called her, and on the veined skin the week-old bruises were faded yellow. 'The darling you are!' said Cormac easily, and turned. '*A mhuire.* . . . *Look at his face!* Sure, I woke up too early! Have you had none of the cream, Prince? . . . Have I given you an appetite?' And looking from O'LiamRoe's witless face to the stony one of the woman, he exploded into mirth.

She did not move; even when he flung the two torn edges of her nightrobe crossed and closed, and sank sprawling in her bedside chair, his beard stuck writhing skywards, his black head dug into her thigh. He said, still in a voice of laughter, 'Or must you wait for a unicorn?' and twisting, upside down, gave Oonagh a wink before returning to O'LiamRoe.

'She sent to me—did you know, fine prince?—to set my mind at rest. She said "Cormac love"—and drawing her docile arm over his shoulder, he laid its long palm against his wet, bearded cheek— "Cormac, love, life is an illusion. The great lord of the Slieve Bloom is a blushing small virgin, one of nature's doorkeepers. You have no rival to fear."'

'Faith, you're a modest man,' said Phelim calmly. Throwing his battered cap on the nearest chest, he folded his arms and gazed at the two, his round shoulders comfortable against the wall. 'Do you fancy that your fists will preach better than the honey tongue in your head? We are two reasonable men; and if you have the right of it, I just ask to be convinced.' He stood at ease, the high collar hiding the slide of his gullet, and the folded arms over the fluttering ribs. 'It would take a bold man, would it not, to claim the Six Titles?'

From Cormac O'Connor's upturned throat came a fanfare of derision. The beard dropped, and the two knowledgeable eyes surveyed O'LiamRoe. 'Ten years since, Henry proclaimed himself King of Ireland, and annexed us like a glove to the Imperial English Crown—"*From henceforth, Irishmen be not enemies, but subjects.*"' Cormac swore, and laughed again, looking at O'LiamRoe. 'It hardly stirs your thick blood, does it, it barely lifts your snout from the bog to see the Lord Deputy mouthing orders at Kilmainham, and the bought earls meek as mice in Dublin Castle hall?'

'Three hundred years under England is a long time,' said O'Liam-Roe. 'Even a French invasion, save you, is only an old tune in a different key. Desmond tried to bring in the French thirty years ago, poor silly Ireland, to make war on Henry VIII, and Kildare himself boasted that he would do the same with twelve thousand Spaniards in his tail. Well, the great Earl of Kildare is dead, his family attainted, his heir a child with an Italian accent living in Florence these ten years. True for you, your own mother was daughter to the ninth Earl, your lands are gone, your father fast in the Tower, your ten brothers and sisters homeless or on alien soil; but 'tis fifteen years since the English took Kildare's son Tómas at Maynooth Castle and broke their pledged word to him; and three hundred and fifty years since an O'Connor was supreme monarch of Ireland.'

The black head had lifted, and Cormac's brosy gourd of a face stared at the Prince. 'There speaks the creeping son of the swamp. Fifteen years since Tómas an tSioda, my own mother's brother, and five Geraldine uncles were murdered at Tyburn after they had surrendered in all good faith at Maynooth; and the heir to all Ireland escaping like a trickle of dirty water into the sea. 'Tis a throne for Gerald of Kildare that I and the woman there are after making.'

'Does he speak English?' enquired O'LiamRoe neatly.

The snarl of impatience echoed in O'Connor's throat; but from behind him, Oonagh's cold voice spoke for the first time since her lover had entered. 'As much as the child Mary will speak,' she said.

'And will rule as freely, I take it,' said O'LiamRoe. 'We're become a nation of uncles. All Europe is a cradle of naked emperors lulled by a jackboot; Warwick and Somerset in England; Arran and de Guises in Scotland; the last of the Geraldines with us. Faix, two Earls of Kildare were Lords Deputy for England, and sore lords they were for both Ireland and her masters. "All Ireland cannot rule this Earl," they told the Council, and "Then in good faith, this Earl shall rule all Ireland," the Council replied. Young Gerald would be off the throne in a fortnight, in favour of some grand *buailim-sciath* such as yourself; and we should be tossed straight back into the midden of anarchy. Our royal tradition is broken. There is no living vein of divinity with us; there is no heritage but one of wind-seeded vivacity. Can you not rest,' said Phelim O'LiamRoe, his oval face damp and rose-coloured, 'and let the corn hear itself grow?'

Like sword cutting through glass, a high, hard voice said, 'He loves them, the household of hell.'

Bundled cabbage-like in creased linen, the iron hair stiffly upholstered in two angry plaits, Theresa Boyle straddled the doorway, and her eyes on O'LiamRoe were shining with anger and hate. 'He would kneel in his basket at an English lord's hearth for a joke and a kind word; he would take the scarlet cloth and the silver cups they bring us wooing like savages, spurn the old Apish toys of Antichrist,

374

yoke malicious mischief to his heart, reject the laws of six hundred years and customs eleven centuries old—'

'Were I eleven centuries old, I would follow them,' said O'Liam-Roe. 'Today I would follow the man who raised good beasts and crops, who mined his own land, and cut passes and made roads and ploughed up moor and bog and barbered the woods. I'd follow the man who carded and weaved and brought in new seed, who used his own dyes and set his own silver and made old men as well as laws and medicine and poems in Latin: old men in good, decent houses, making fellowship with their neighbours whether Celt or Irish-Norman or Irish-English; whether in the sea ports or in the Pale. We are a million people lightsome from birth to death as the froth of the sea, and leaving no more behind us. . . . Seize your battleaxe and lead out the MacSheehys,' said Phelim O'LiamRoe, Prince of Barrow, hardily, his fists nail and bone at his sides. 'Turn kern against kern, gallowglass against gallowglass, live the past, murder the future; and I promise you, when you have extorted your living tax of cracked pride and savage frivolity, France or England or Charles in his little suit of Florentine serge will stroll whistling across the bare fields, kicking the stones.'

"Tis a glorious poem, so,' said Mistress Boyle. 'And yourself, Prince, has cut off your fine whiskers to make bowstrings? You'll oppose us, Lackpenny?'

'He is deserting us. Alas, the loss of it!' said Oonagh coolly. 'He is Francis Crawford's new lover.'

O'LiamRoe did not even look at her; he answered Mistress Boyle direct, his mild face sober. 'I am opposing you.'

'In the name of God, what with?' said Cormac O'Connor, and turned to Oonagh, and barked.

'With force,' said O'LiamRoe mildly. 'I have sent word to the Slieve Bloom today. Do you land, with your French or without, you will get such a blow you will never need another.'

Nobody laughed. In the white, stark glare of the lights, in the antiseptic heat of the air, Mistress Boyle drew a sharp breath and was still; Cormac, his thick wrists outflung on the counterpane, lost his smile and Oonagh, behind him, rising to her knees with the night robe paged taut by the pillow, said 'Phelim!' and tugging the heavy stuff free, slid astonishingly to the ground and moving swiftly, caught his shoulder.

Swung round, he looked down into clear, grey-green eyes searching his own. 'But Phelim— The meaty haunches who grunt and whack while the knowing ones smile and bide their time. . . . The world to be fairly divided among the small, calm men who watch and think . . . ?' They were his own words. 'This is Francis's doing?'

'Equally I oppose Mary Dowager of Scotland,' said O'LiamRoe

quietly, 'should she lean her elbow on Ireland. Though I will help her to know what Francis Crawford would do for her daughter. Sad, sad is a recusant. I was the world's bully at four, so they say. I have been made to learn a thing: that like a garden of windflowers, our nature is talk. But good talk has its roots in the earth; like a turnip it thrusts its feet in the soil and its head in the clear air, thrusts with vigour, moves, swells, ripens and is harvested. . . . I, a miscast, rambling thing, am ready to plough up this field.'

She had dropped her hand, holding his gaze with her own. 'There is a death in it,' said Oonagh.

O'LiamRoe smiled. 'There was always death in it, since *La Sauvée* sailed. Your fears have come true, that is all.'

'There is death in it. She is right.' The harsh voice of Mistress Boyle spoke not to Oonagh but to Cormac. 'God show you your duty.'

''Tis no duty with our philosopher's maidservant here, but a pleasure entirely,' said Cormac O'Connor, and he rose to his feet.

'Get back, Phelim,' said Oonagh.

O'LiamRoe did not move. 'It's this way will be best. My cousin is tanist heir, so. I have sent word, and he will do as I would. You can tell the King of France that Ireland is lost to him.'

She had her back to him, her eyes on Cormac, moving slowly from the bed. Her aunt stood still in the far doorway. 'Escape while you can. Himself will kill you.'

'Maybe,' said O'LiamRoe.

Standing full in front of him, her voice sounded oddly dry. 'Francis Crawford depends on your help.'

'No offence in life,' said O'LiamRoe, 'but he depends on you, not myself. I am at my extreme end. Will you move, now?'

Cormac took another step, smiling. 'Yes, move now, me darling slut,' he said. 'God bless you kindly, my brave black bitch, with no sweet oasis in her white body she would not have ready to bless the thirsty traveller with. Move, my delicate whore, and let me kill him.' The steel was out of his scabbard, but O'LiamRoe had not drawn his sword—the mishandled, miswielded blade which he had never mastered and never bothered to use.

'Why do that?' said Oonagh. Her face was dry and grey as earthenware in the kiln, but the clear voice was cold. 'You will save nothing and have the King at you, only.'

Within touching distance, Cormac stopped. In the coloured rind of his skin, the red lips parted and smiled. In his hands the blade lifted and stilled. 'Kill him,' said Mistress Boyle from behind, and the grey plaits jerked, like bell ropes weaving an echo. 'Kill him and the woman too. That is something the French will understand.'

Oonagh had been leaning a little against the Prince of Barrow, her black hair caught in his shirt, the soft robe brushing his feet. At that, she flung up her arm, and then collecting herself, moved a step forward and faced the great black bull-shape of O'Connor, her pride, her king and her lover. 'Leave troubling, Cormac. Let him go.'

Her voice was sane and quiet. The stab of the sword cut across it like a battle cry, as Cormac raised the blade, high and true, and drove it at O'LiamRoe's heart through hers.

O'LiamRoe was made badly by unresented ill-luck—strung stiffly, knotted wrongly, animated faultily. But he had a brain; and he had seen that move coming. As the sword flashed, he gave Oonagh a great shove, and as she struck and rolled on the floor he threw himself to one side so that the missed blade pulled the swordsman staggering past his quarry and brought him up short beside Theresa Boyle. Then as O'LiamRoe recovered, Cormac O'Connor jumped forward again.

O'LiamRoe fled. He did it hastily, and with a frantic lack of address which was its own grace. Chairs rocked and tumbled in O'Connor's way. The bed curtains ripped, dropped and draped him as he followed the others over the counterpane; kicked pillows tripped him; the jogging end of O'LiamRoe's own scabbard at one point caught the big man and nearly felled him. Oonagh, rising, was crouched hard in a corner; Mistress Boyle, eyes wild, had retreated to the parlour and watched from there. No one attempted to fetch help. If this was to be a crime passionnel, the fewer witnesses the better. And no servant, knowing Theresa Boyle and knowing O'Connor, would dare intervene.

In the crowded space, the sword was not easy to use. It stuck, became impaled on the panelling, or impeded the wielder with its weight. O'LiamRoe, jumping on a fine marquetry table, had it knocked from under him by Cormac's boot and falling, found a shield quite by accident as Cormac's steel sank deep in the wood.

Cormac left it there and jumped on the soft somersaulting body of the other man. As he hit him, O'LiamRoe's arm shot out with the impact, found the poker laid in the nearly dead hearth, and swinging it over the big Irishman's back, branded him like a heifer. With a screech O'Connor flung free, and in the stench of wool and hide his curses found habitat.

O'LiamRoe got out his sword and scrambled to his feet as the other man, his fists opening and shutting, rose likewise and faced him. In the parlour there sounded, briefly, a sharp crash. O'Connor's attention left his victim for a second; long enough to catch the broken-necked glass tossed to him diamond-bright by Mistress Boyle. Holding it queerly before him, flashing, pure as a bride's bouquet, he feinted neatly and leaned to stroke the jagged glass down O'Liam-Roe's face.

O'LiamRoe was not even looking. His kind face, printed with surprise and dislike, was turned to Theresa Boyle. He opened his mouth, shifted his weight, and with perfect simplicity sat down, just as the arched blow approached him. It passed over his head, stirring the marmalade hair, and Oonagh, moved beyond even her steely strength, let out a high sharp note of laughter.

O'LiamRoe had dropped his sword. On all fours he was fumbling to lift it when with a rustle Mistress Boyle swept through the doorway and bent down to seize it.

'Ah, no!' said Oonagh O'Dwyer. 'Ah, no, wild hag, we are not heeding you this night at all.' And laying hands on the two wiry grey plaits, she made to drag the older woman like a drowned thing to her feet.

In that moment, for the second time, the bright glass aimed at O'LiamRoe descended. Like the grey shears of Atropos, grim among the late flowers in Jean Ango's garden, the needle edge dropped, cleaving the thick plait with a tug clean between hand and scalp; and falling, bit into Theresa Boyle's neck.

The scream, when it came, was like a man's, gross and brutal, and all the folds of the bundled cabbage, screwed featureless on the floor, had become poured over with red. His mouth open, the upwrenched bottle still fast in his hand, Cormac O'Connor bent over the woman while O'LiamRoe rising backed, his face sick.

He turned and ran.

He had reached the parlour door when Cormac came back to himself. O'Connor said nothing; the curses and threats all cut off by the weight of the shock. Then rage came. Like a man spiritually harmed, like one who has looked on the symbols of a diabolical Mass, he put out his hand and armed himself, lifting the heavy sword from its deep cut as if it were paper and presenting it, across the width of two rooms, at O'LiamRoe's unarmed body.

Oonagh saw it. Rising stony-faced from the fallen woman's side she jumped at O'Connor, her two hands firm on his arm, and without looking he hurled her off like a cur. As she crashed clutching into the far wall, O'LiamRoe's hands moved.

It was only a small sling, and the stone was small too, round, silvery and warm from his pocket. But slinging was an ancient art, a lost custom, a piece of erudite and unnecessary knowledge which only O'LiamRoe would have bothered to gain, and an art which only O'LiamRoe would have thought it worth while practising. With the soft, craftless fingers which, right hand or left, could split a held hair, the Prince of Barrow fitted his little stone, lifted the sling and let fly.

The first struck O'Connor in the mouth, breaking in the fleshy lip and like a wrecked forum razing his teeth. The second, stinging sharp in the middle of the round, suffused brow, felled him like a tree; slowly, buffeting shrub and sapling and undergrowth, flat to the ground. Holding hard to the wall, Oonagh watched him.

Above the old woman's harsh moaning, 'Never fear,' said O'Liam-Roe breathlessly. He cleared his throat, gasped, and moving stiffly nearer, ran a dirty hand through his hair. 'He won't be dead.'

In her white face the younger woman's pale eyes looked almost black. 'And if he were?'

Still breathlessly, he spoke at a tangent. 'The woman will need help.'

Again she faced him without moving. 'She is past helping.'

He said, 'It had to be done . . . and at this minute I do not know yet if it is done.'

'It is done,' said Oonagh O'Dwyer. The woman moaned, and was quiet.

His oval face had no smile. 'Twenty years of my thinking life have said their seven curses over him. He has won, too, in his way. It is a triumph of violence over culture, force over thought. . . . I have come to the crossroads you feared, and passed them. It may be a true road, or it may be the first step into all the kind, easy turnings of decay.'

'Maybe. There is no knowing for either of us until judgment day.' She passed him, remote as she had always been, dreamlike with her white face and her streaming black fall of hair, the stained robe dragging the floor; and opening the door, turned and faced him. 'The back door is quiet to unlock, and not overlooked. Go quickly. The light is not far off.'

He came beside her, but no nearer than that. 'I will not leave you with them.'

She turned her head. Raw, rumpled, stiff as an ox on the spit, Cormac lay in the smashed room, and at his feet the woman lay still, her thick hands at her neck. 'It is time to go,' she said. 'I must take my road, too. From this out you will hear nothing of me, and will do nothing to search me out. That is my price.'

He did not reply all at once. Then, 'For what, *mo chiall; a chiall mo chridhe?*' he said steadily.

But he knew already what his ignorance was to buy: the name he had wanted, the name of the man serving Lord d'Aubigny which was to deliver both Lymond and the Queen.

Telling him, her eyes were compassionate. 'Leave me go kindly,' she said. 'My body will not want, and my thoughts you will have. There is a strong path before you, and a forced door you need not be ashamed of. Only violence could have sundered this man and myself, and the violence which parted us was the force that was born fresh in your mind, not the coarse work it has had to put its hand to tonight. It will find nobler tasks yet to do.'

Her hands lay cold in his. Searching her empty face he said, 'We shall meet?'

'At the fall of night, on the far side of the north wind,' she said. 'Love me.'

'All my days,' said Phelim O'LiamRoe, Prince of Barrow, dropping into the tongue of his land. 'Dear stranger, dear mate of my soul: all my days.'

And walking quiet and blind, he let slip her two hands and left.

*   *   *

'His name is Artus Cholet, Lord d'Aubigny's other henchman,' Oonagh O'Dwyer had said. 'He is of the district, a master gunner who has fought for any well-paying captain in his day. He will not show himself at Châteaubriant, but if he has been given work to do, he won't be far away. Take the Angers road, and at the Auberge des Trois Mariés ask for Georges Gaultier, and tell him what you want.'

Dark in the misty June morning, Châteaubriant was still. Dim through the painted shutters, the hoof beats of a single horse burst, applauding the cobbles, and were gone.

No one saw O'LiamRoe go. He had not taken time to find Dooly, curled on the straw in his dark lodging, watching the lightening sky. In another street, handsomely lodged, Lord d'Aubigny slept, ready to wake fresh and serene to his harvest at last. The English, courtiers and servants, lay exhausted by heat and diplomacy in rooms and lodgings, hospices and barns all through Châteaubriant. At the Château Neuf Northampton slept, well bedded, well content, under the three flags of Scotland, England and France. The Court of France, King and Queen and Constable, de Guises, Diane, fulfilled the allotted hours of slumber, precisely as automata, as part of the long-learned, accustomed framework of rite.

A heap of red hair in an immaculate bed, the Queen of Scotland slept; but in her mother's room the candle burned and spluttered by the outflung arm of a sleeper who had counted most of the night hours away. Beyond, Margaret Erskine lay still with open eyes.

In the Vieux Château, Lymond's two warders, both Constable's men, were having an unexpectedly tedium-free night. The tall one, rattling the dice box, was the more impressionable. 'That's a good song.'

'This is a better,' said Lymond; and sang it, while they listened to each bawdy verse, whimpering. At the end, sitting curled on his pallet, Francis Crawford spoke idly. 'Anton, why does a man leave his mistress?'

'He loves another,' said the tall gaoler promptly, and threw.

380

The short one chimed in. 'Or *she* does. Or she grows fat and ugly, or pesters him for marriage.'

'Or has too many children,' said the tall gaoler gloomily.

Lymond's face remained grave. 'And why, do you think, might a mistress part from her lover?'

'Your case?' asked the tall man, and laid down the dice.

Lymond shook his head. 'Another's.'

'She leaves him for a better lover,' said the short one aggressively.

'No,' said Lymond gravely. 'That has been tried.'

Curiously, the eyes of the tall gaoler searched the cool face. 'For money, then? Marriage? Position?'

'That has been tried, too.'

'She's not a mistress, that one; she's a leech,' said the short gaoler, and he picked up the dice.

'She suffers the child in man,' said Lymond. 'I would guess, because she thinks with his shoulders in the clouds, his head must see further than other men. But in time—'

'She finds his eyes are shut,' said the short man, and threw.

'Or that she has been invisible for so long that he has forgotten she is there. The clear skies above all that cloud no longer bewitch her. She looks for a man with a God-sent vocation, a brilliant vocation but a different vocation, who will either put her before it . . . or change it for her.'

'And then she will leave her first lover. It sounds unlikely to me,' said the tall man, and threw in his turn.

'It is beginning to sound unlikely to me,' said Francis Crawford after some thought. 'What about another song?'

Much later, when the short guard was asleep and Lymond, stretched prone on his face, lay open-eyed and abstracted in bed, the tall man swung his chair to the floor, saying, 'But would she be happy with him?'

The fair, bloody head jerked round. '*What?* Who happy with whom?'

'With the other. If he altered his ideals, would the woman stay even with him?'

'Christ,' said Lymond. 'Mild and eloquent Balder, the woman would never even think of him. His office is purely to sunder; neither he nor any man has power to do more than that.'

'Then where is his reward?' said the tall gaoler, and began to swing rhythmically again.

'Round as Giotto's "O",' said Francis Crawford. 'His reward is nothing, nullity, negation, an absence, a lack. His golden reward, equal to its own weight of shaved beard, is this, that the lady did not accept him.'

'She is ugly?'

'She is beautiful as the tides of the sea,' said the pleasant voice from the bed. 'Warm, silken and fathomless; and familiar with mysteries.'

'They all are, the bitches,' said the tall man, and went on rocking, slowly, in silence.

*   *   *

The Inn of the Trois Mariés, outside St. Julien-de-Vouvantes and nine miles from Châteaubriant, had brought Maître Gaultier as close to his clients at Court as the congested billeting situation would allow. He was not disturbed, confident in the belief that a needy gentleman will sniff out a usurer, as the mastiffs of Rhodes were said to distinguish Turk from Christian by the smell.

The O'LiamRoe, launched upstairs with the first sunlight, was given audience without question; but Georges Gaultier's listening face was vacant. He heard the Prince of Barrow through, hummed a line of some obscure monody, his patched eyebrows scaling his brow, then disappeared without excuse.

Ten minutes later O'LiamRoe found himself greeting the tall, brooding figure and eaglet face of the Dame de Doubtance, seated at a little spinet and picking out with one thin, tight-cuffed claw the notes of an astonishingly bawdy song O'LiamRoe hoped she had never heard sung. Clearly Gaultier had conveyed all his news. The flat, downturned mouth tightened, then moved as she swung round for his bow. 'The woman is a fool.'

He faced her out, all his clothes whitened with dust, and dust in his wild golden hair. 'You will never see a braver,' he said.

'And you are a fool,' said the Lady harshly. 'She has the gift, that black-haired woman, and she gave herself like carrion, to feed her own pride.'

'She has left him.' His face thinned with sleeplessness, O'LiamRoe kept his temper.

'*Left him?* Dotard, schoolboy, unleavened bread, can you believe I speak of Cormac O'Connor?'

Erect, drawn to her full height, she peered down at him from her archaic headdress, the golden plaits thonged on her breast. 'Ah, you are pleasant,' she said. 'Many a starving man will come to you, seeing you starving and able to laugh. You appear pleasant, as drowning leaves in a pond.'

Anger had gone. 'He has shown me,' said O'LiamRoe.

'He has shown himself; that is all that matters,' said the Dame de Doubtance. 'Artus Cholet lives with the woman Berthe at St. Julien. The house is thatched; with St. John over the door.' Still speaking, she reseated herself, the long robes shifting, and resumed at her spinet.

Stiff-backed, O'LiamRoe stood and watched. 'If man can do it, I shall save them both.'

'Run, then,' she said encouragingly. 'And try hard. I would have told this sooner . . . I might have told this sooner, but Artus Cholet is my sister's son, though a fool. You may kill him. He has come to the end.'

He left her, predatory, frowning over her fingering hands. As he closed the door he heard her address them: 'Sleep, mes enfants—but can you not sleep? This day you must wake fresh as a rosebud. Right hand, you have left hand to meet in the lists.'

Out of the inn; through the stirring life of a country road, and past the unlocked door of a cottage with St. John over the threshold.

Berthe, fat, frightened and wary, had been sleeping alone, but another head at some time had crumpled the pillow and, outside, a horse had recently been watered and fed. He threatened her, hoarseness and tension disguising his lack of skill, until she spoke.

Artus had left early for Châteaubriant; where and for what purpose she did not know. She knew nothing of use, it appeared, but his description; and this, cringing, she gave.

There was another mare in the littered stable. O'LiamRoe changed saddles and, freshly mounted, started back. He had had to beat her, in the end; but it was plain she knew nothing more. After all his efforts, after the agony at Mistress Boyle's, after the ride to the inn and to St. Julien, he was no further on. The man he wanted had vanished into Châteaubriant, and by the time he came back to his Berthe, it might well be too late.

Flying through the first heat of the morning, double-printing the track he had taken such a short time before, it came to O'LiamRoe that it was no longer one man's work. Lord d'Aubigny notwithstanding, the English visitors notwithstanding, despite the Queen Dowager and the delicate balance of power she had betrayed Lymond to preserve, his share in all the bitter complexity of the day's work was to beat the drum; to rouse the jungle; and to call friend and enemy alike into the open.

His bones ached, under the sun; and when carters cursed him, he did not turn.

*   *   *

On the new lake, the painted boats moved no more than a mirage, barring the satiny water with candy-bright troughs. Mary, solid and rosy with heat, was being dressed by a cat's cradle of nurse, governess, maids of honour, femmes de chambre, valets, pages, grooms and a drum she had fallen in love with the previous evening and had demanded, screaming, to attend her at dawn. Quickly, and with tact, Margaret Erskine got rid of him before he passed the outermost door of the suite. Today, none but trusted faces were allowed in these rooms; no food or drink passed the child's lips that one of them had not tasted; none but friends and servants would surround her when she walked abroad.

The Queen Dowager came in, the Cardinal cool and fair at her back; kissed the child, and went out. This morning, her rôle was to wait.

* * *

In the darkness of the Vieux Château, Lymond waited, too, with tired patience. Miraculously, after a while he slept, in the shirt of coarse wool which was all they could bring him.

He was sleeping when the Countess of Lennox came upon him, his head buried in his bare arms. She had come prepared to bribe handsomely for the ten minutes' pleasure she wanted, but had found the tall gaoler surprisingly modest in his needs. His smile had puzzled her, too.

Then the cell door closed behind her and locked, and she watched but could not tell what second he woke, for he looked up lazily after a moment and said, 'Welcome, Countess.' And added immediately, swinging with grace to the floor, 'Lady, this is most indiscreet. Warwick's brutish eye is everywhere, you know.'

'They are gathering for the ceremony.' He looked neither anxious nor angry, damn his kingfisher soul. 'I feared we might not meet before you suffer at last for your crimes.' She seated herself on the bare bed he had vacated, arranging her gown. 'You see what happens when you lose your head.'

'You warned me.' He bowed in acknowledgment; the odd shirt over his long hose recalled, involuntarily, the cloth of gold tabard at Hackney. He said dryly, 'Don't look so surprised. *Coronez est à tort*, granted; but not for the first time in the world. Let's not sing a fourpenny dirge over it.' He twitched up a stool and perched on it, patiently embracing his knees. 'Well. On which aspect of our ill-advised doings are we about to lecture each other? I have very little to say. As I recall, I exhausted the matter on several other occasions.'

'But this godlike magnanimity is new.' Under the high-dressed, green-wheat hair, Margaret Douglas's eyes were wary. 'Such forbearance, when your own Queen has forsaken you!'

'Identify your Queens,' said Lymond promptly. 'You forget, we have a pack. The cells are bearing Queens as if every one were a coining iron, with a fat, laurel-wreathed face in the wax. If you mean the Dowager—'

'Of course I mean the Dowager,' said Margaret.

'—She is a tough lady to woo. Matthew will tell you. Jenny Fleming's stepfather, even. King Henry of England—'

'I had not supposed,' said Lady Lennox sarcastically, 'that you were asking her hand. Your practices are quite other.'

Abruptly Lymond got up. 'Oh, no. Not this. Not again. If you must dispute, dispute the living issues: Rome and Mary Tudor, Lutherism and Scotland, Spain and the German princes, France and Suleiman's new empire, the rich new world and starving Ireland, and everywhere the new steel-founder's war. These are the events you and Matthew are moving. I don't want to know how small the mainspring may be.'

She had risen as well. 'Then you would have done well to have found out. For that is why you are here, my dear: because you will not learn that in each of us the mainspring is the smallest thing in the world—is just the single word "I".'

In the dim light they faced each other. 'God help us both,' said Lymond, his mouth straight, his eyes level for once. 'But if I live, and if you live, I will bring you a nation of souls that will give you the lie.'

But he recovered his good humour, it seemed, quickly; for as she left she could hear his voice, at ease with villancico, carolling *Ninguno cierre las puertas* behind the grille of his door.

* * *

Muffled under the tinsel of birdsong, the bells for Tierce ran their oiled course. Robin Stewart heard them at the door of his cottage, the green light flecking his groomed hair and the painstaking white of his shirt; in the deep grass his boots shone, nutbrown, vigorously tended in their turn.

Inside, it was the same. Hard work had turned a hovel into a soldier's room, clean, orderly and shining; the one chair mended, the bed folded, the scrubbed table spread with the best food he could buy or steal: farm butter and milk in a crock, a cheese, a board of patties and a thick jug of wine. In the corner, his canvas bag lay, packed like a surgeon's, with his spurs and sword like silver beside it. On the long, rawboned unshackled frame as he waited lay pride and confidence and calm expectation. The scrubbed hands hung at his side and the angry eyes, sunk in skin darkened by harsh work and harsh purpose, were serene.

The Queen was to die during the Investiture, which would open at ten. An hour earlier, he had asked, Lymond should bring the King's troops to take him into the custody which would prove to the world that of this, at least, he was innocent. And through his information, Artus Cholet would be taken in the act; d'Aubigny would be inculpated and the shadow of Thady Boy's guilt removed from Lymond himself.

He would bring perhaps a dozen Archers; or perhaps only a few of the Constable's own men from the castle, with an officer. There must be an officer, so that the testimony would be quite clear. He would hear them coming: first the pealing alarm of the birds, then the drum and rustle of hoofbeats; and the trees would lift above the helmeted heads, toss and curtsey and lift again until they were all past. Then Francis Crawford and the officer would dismount and come forward, and he would offer them food.

He would say nothing, but the new face of Thady Boy would note everything, the clean shirt and the hard work; and as they left, they would walk shoulder to shoulder, sure of each other, as they were on the tower at St. Lomer.

The bells for Tierce stopped ringing, but Robin Stewart stood and watched by the door.

*   *   *

Dethick had lost his temper. Hearing the thick Dutch-French ringing from the Privy Chamber the Constable banged with his blue-robed thickset shoulder through the tambours and fifes, the silver-tissued Gentlemen nursing axes, the Audiencier and the Commis du Controlleur de l'Audience in black velvet, the heralds at arms, lined up uneasily in silk and gold fleurs de lis, the mob of silver-hoquetoned Archers and the ground-matting of pages into the King's room.

He was not there yet. Garter, his crown pushed back, his beard limp as a lapdog's front paw, was demanding the upholsterer. The French heralds hung by uneasily and Chester, embarrassed, was on his way out to fetch help. There were, he saw, only two tables instead of three, and the carpet had not been spread. He silenced Garter, his courtesies a little belated, and got a third table in.

There was half an hour yet before the Investiture. He opened the door of the French robing room; the dresses were blinding, and so was the scent. Three Knights of the Order of St. Michael jangled together in their shells and white velvet; he missed the red velvet hat of the Chancellor and came away dissatisfied. His white ostrich feathers bobbed, and the thirty ounces of gold, troy weight, round his neck clinked garter to garter as he strode along.

The English Embassy Extraordinary, similarly dressed, waited about rather silently in a room nearby. Anne, Duke de Montmorency and Constable of France, sent a page to tell the drummers to begin, and all but trampled on the boy de Longueville, Mary of Guise's French son, with extraordinary news.

Waving a thick hand at the plaintive business around him, Montmorency heaved about him his blue robes the colour of heaven, and hurried off.

*   *   *

'Witness against Lord d'Aubigny is clear,' he was saying ten minutes later, standing again, his clothes gathered ready to leave. 'And this man Cholet, when we can trace him, will no doubt be made

386

to confess. But until that moment, remember, there is nothing to say that the Tour des Minimes was d'Aubigny's doing. I cannot release Crawford without clearer proof. As it is, the affair of d'Aubigny, evidently, will require the most gentle attentions. . . . Madame, I must go.'

He had no special liking for the Queen Dowager of Scotland, but he could admire her gift for negotiation; he had never before caught her with her timing at fault. Hurried by the boy, he had found her with only one of her ladies, the mad Irishman O'LiamRoe who had insulted the King, and a big man he recognized vaguely as some sculptor.

Listening to the tale, he realized that the unfortunate was happening. The sculptor Hérisson had evidently in his keeping a man called Beck, a Flemish merchant who would swear to d'Aubigny's guilt at Rouen. On top of that, the Irishman had just come in with a tale of a man loose in Châteaubriant who meant to do the little Queen harm.

If he were caught, it meant the convenient scapegoat in the Vieux Château must be freed, and the King must be coaxed to put aside the friendship of d'Aubigny. While his heart could wish for no more, the Constable knew this particular diplomatic labour was beyond him. He said, staring at Mary of Guise, 'We can do nothing while the Embassy is here . . . corbleu; envisage the Commissioners sent to ask our princess's hand watching the grounds being combed for a French assassin intent on killing the girl . . . especially if the assassin is inspired by some English minority. —You have no firm reason to believe the attempt will be made today?'

O'LiamRoe answered. 'Only that the man has left his home for Châteaubriant. And it seems likely that it will be done while Robin Stewart is at large and while Lord d'Aubigny himself is plainly on duty. A house-to-house search, monseigneur—'

'No. Unthinkable,' said the Constable. 'No. I must go. And you, M. le duc. Thank you, M. Hérisson, and you, my lord of the Salif Blum. My officers will call on you after the Investiture and M. Beck will be taken *au secret*. Meanwhile, the child must be doubly guarded. My lieutenant will present himself to you. Take as many men as you need, and surround her. She need not be frightened; they will hide their arms. You will give my lieutenant also your designation of Cholet. One may not search, but all men may observe. Between the banquet and the conference if I can, I shall return to the matter. Madame . . . messieurs.'

The grand rabroueur had gone. His leaf-gold tresses on end, his eyes in baskets from the long night without sleep, Phelim O'LiamRoe smacked his two fists together and cursed. The Queen Dowager, hardly aware of him, had turned her erect body to the window, followed by Margaret Erskine's wide eyes. But Michel Hérisson, who had arrived so unexpectedly on the Irishman's heels, ran his hacked and gouty hands through the wild white hair and said through his teeth, 'Liam aboo, son, Liam aboo! My Gaelic's all out in holes, the way my arse is ridden out through my breeches; but if you are saying what I hope you are saying, Liam aboo, my son, Liam aboo!'

*   *   *

On the lake, the early mist had all gone and the little boats had been moved into the middle. A small gathering of musicians, moving tenderly about a flower-decked raft, were tuning rebec, lute and viol for a rehearsal, thin as oyster-catchers in the still air. Elsewhere, on the shore, in the tilting ground, about the pavilions and stands, men were busy.

It was magnificent, if not very new. The theme and costumes for today had been used before: they did the English Commissioners sufficient honour. Industriously classical, Sibec de Carpi's stands lining the tilting ground were redecorated with vine garlands and busts, cartouches and winged genii bearing the three royal flags; for after the Investiture, after the banquet, after the conference, there would be jousting that night.

And later still, a water pageant. Round the lake, low gardens had been laid out, a fountain erected at each end and a pavilion put up overlooking the water, draped with eye-blinding cloth of gold and fitted with lamps and torch sockets. From here, where the painters worked stripped to the waist, the Court would sit after dinner and watch the spectacle of Ida, *la bergère phrygienne*, driving cautiously round the lake, her chariot harnessed to geese and nymphs and satyrs, Pans and centaurs gambolling round. Some of these, lured by the sun and an authorized negligence of dress, were already there, spread on the dry grass: a Victory with gold wings sat under a pear tree playing a whistle, and two priestesses crowned with snakes chaffed a Bacchus in purple sitting on the paving, knees akimbo, and feet spread green in the cool pond.

Behind the gardens, the accessories were stacked: the hero's flask of leopardskin destined to spray the paths with cheap wine; the chariots to be drawn by elephants, ostriches, deer; the Fortune forwarded from Angers, wheel and apple in hand; the carts with statues of kings and gods stacked inside. Among a group of forest maids admiring them was Diana herself, Madame de Valentinois, in black cloth of gold sewn with silver stars and amazingly brief, though not as short as the nymphs' dresses, turned up to mid-thigh. Their bows and darts, of carved and gilded hardwood, were piled among the crowns and the torches and the cages of doves. Her ladies, in violet lustring, looked hot and rather cheerful: the workmen were not shy of tongue.

'The auld quean,' said the Keeper of the Menageries, watching mask-faced from under his turban on the distant side of the lake. Hughie the elephant, half-dressed in expensive gold harness, eructated with sonorous calm, and Piedar Dooly, his bees' legs in fustian black hating the ground they stood on, said coldly, 'It's the King's woman. Would you need three eyes to see it? And if he isn't here, where is he?'

The brocaded figure, cross-legged before the biggest pavilion, watched keepers and cowardies move about the tents and cages, listened to the soft animal sounds and breathed through bean-wide nostrils the pattern of smells that reveal the well-regulated menagerie. He did not turn his head. 'If ye dinna know, then likely you're not meant to ken,' said Abernaci. The camel, which was suppposed to carry the incense, had thrown a fit in the night. Mules would have to do; he wouldn't trust any more cats. The grass rustled to approaching feet, and another figure slid on its haunches beside him. 'If you mean the Prince of Barrow, he's at the castle,' said Tosh. 'Christ, what does it remind you of?'

'Paris. Lyons. Rouen. Dieppe. Amboise. Angers,' said Abernaci. 'There's a kind of sameness. Only this time we're untying our very own purse, so we're a wee thing skimped as to hay. D'ye mind Hughie upsetting the— No. Ye werena at Rouen.'

'They play at gods,' said Piedar Dooly, and spat. 'French and English alike. Gods out of hell would you say, harrowing green land for their tennis courts and dressing lapdogs in treasure that would keep half Ireland in bread for a year. The heroes of Tara would have put them face to schisty face and used them for millstones.'

Dropping back on the burned grass, Tosh stretched his arms under his head. 'Ye needna miscall the French. They drove the English fairly out of their country.'

In two wiry steps, Dooly lowered over the funambulist. 'With eight thousand Irishmen to help them!' he exclaimed. 'Are you saying that Ireland won't send the English off her shores with a blow that will make these fat folk look seven ways at once—and the Scots too? Doesn't every man know that the great Scottish nation has got so soft all out that France has to fight all her wars for her? Women ruled by women . . . and there's the great war-lord chief of you all, in her petticoats, scarce off the breast of her nurse, come to preside at the weapon showing there.'

Tosh, an even-tempered man, caught Abernaci's eye and rolled over. 'Oh, aye, there's great bullocks in Ireland,' he said. 'But they canna get them shipped for their long horns, they say.' Abernaci, having observed that the child Queen had indeed come to the far edge of the lake, hopped to his feet and stood astride, shading his brown cracked face with his hand. 'Christ. The governess. The

Erskine woman. The Fleming boy. Two of the children, and six men-at-arms. They're examining the boat the way it was a good case of beggar's leprosy. . . . They're getting in.'

'They'll be as safe in mid-water as anywhere, if the boat's all right,' said Tosh. 'What's the rest of the armada?' In the middle of the lake, twelve little boats bobbed, roped to each other and then to a buoy: gondolas, brigantines, galleys in small.

'Nothing to harm her,' said Abernaci. 'Brigantines and galleys for the mock fight, the state barge, and boats with squibs and canes of fire darts and clods and moulins à feu. Even were they all set off at once, they couldn't hurt; and they can hardly be set off. There's not a lit torch been allowed near the lake. You'll have heard— Man,' he broke off, turning on Piedar Dooly, craning at his elbow. 'Are ye not for finding O'LiamRoe, now ye ken whaur he is?'

'Ah, get comfortable,' said the Irishman contemptuously, and turned his back on the water. 'I was there when they threw the ollave into prison, and a better thing the fools never did. It's no news to me.'

For the second time, the eyes of the other two met. 'Nor to me,' said Tosh briefly. '—I hear also that Cormac O'Connor is sick.'

Piedar Dooly dropped to the grass. 'O'LiamRoe—would you know it?' he said. 'I tell you, were I not to let the wind out of him this while and that, we would never see the Slieve Bloom again.' And he hugged his knees, his raw face complacent.

It was Abernaci, used to reading the speechless, who stood as if graven, receiving the first signals of danger; then, like a snake striking, flicked into the grass and came up with Piedar Dooly's shoulder pinched flat in one hand. Tosh, jumping to his feet, took one look and gripped Dooly's other arm, a question on his broad Aberdeen face. 'Would you say,' said Abernaci kindly, 'that he was waiting for something?'

Piedar Dooly was too wise to shout, and too stupid to keep his mouth shut entirely. '*Stad thusa ort!*—It's too late, anyway,' he said smiling, and spat.

The King's Keeper looked over his head at Thomas Ouschart, and then spoke aside briefly in Urdu. Then, holding the little Firbolg very carefully between them, they carried him silently into the pavilion.

*   *   *

At five minutes to ten the King, hatless in white, entered the Privy Chamber, and the Archers of the Guard, the gentlemen and princes lining the walls uncovered and bowed. The music stopped.

Outside the far door, the Garter procession had been formed for ten minutes, talking in low voices, sweating in velvet. The Constable, ncongruous among all the English faces, had arrived, a little late, to take his place next to Mason. Ahead of him was the Bishop, Sir Thomas Smith and Black Rod; in the middle, Northampton was talking to Dethick, a Christian act for all concerned. The file of servants stretched in front up to the doors, not speaking at all. Their necks were clean.

The trumpets blew, and they moved in.

You had to grant they were good at it. Like machines, the Lord Ambassador's staff paced into the Presence, lined with diamond-tudded foreigners, moving straight up to the tables to let the tail of he Embassy get in. The door shut, the three reverences were made, nd as the trumpets burst into a fantasy of sound the two ranks eparated, exposing the advancing officers of arms: Flower, tramping teadily in Chester Herald's brilliant coat, his arms full of material, nd Garter King of Arms, his beard combed, his crown straight, in is furred robe with the blue and red quartered tabard V-necked over t, gleaming with gold lions and fleurs-de-lis. He carried the cushion f purple velvet, tasselled with gold, on which sparkled the Garter, he Collar, the Book of Statutes in gold lace and velvet and the croll with their Commission of Legation—most of which must be inned—nothing slid or even moved.

With a marvellous bow to the sovereign's state, Dethick deposited he Ensigns on the long table beside the Mantle, Surcoat, Hood and Cap, and made way for Northampton. The oration began. The Commission of Legation, handed over to Henri, was read aloud by is secretary. 'Edward VI, by the grace of God, King of England nd Lord of Ireland, Defender of the Faith, Sovereign of our Most Noble Order of the Garter, to our right truly and right entirely be-oved Cousin, the Marquis of Northampton . . . will and authorize ou . . . accept and admit to the said Order, and receive his oath. . . .'

Extraordinary how well their robes became them. Parr, who hadn't he wits of a trumpet on the field, could pass for a King. There was 'Aubigny. Henri looked nervous. Devil take the de Guises, thought he Constable. He would like to see the Dowager's face if Edward greed to hand over Calais in return for marrying her daughter after ll, compensation or no compensation.

He suppressed a sigh. It wasn't likely to happen; merely an inter-sting gambit, nothing more. But it was a triumph for his own party hat the thing had even been agreed. He hoped to God that St. André would be circumspect. The last marriage embassy they had ent in old King Henry's day had nearly ruined their mission, selling ff the contents of their baggage at cut prices to their hosts before he puddings were set on the table; the Tailors' Hall had looked like market stall, and the guilds had all been up in arms, and quite ghtly too. However, he could trust St. André. Unlike the de Guises.

Pasque-Dieu, the Duke wasn't here. No, he was; come in late. . . .
God, it was hot.

*   *   *

It was the short guard who came at a run and unlocked and flung
open the door; the men behind him were de Guise's. Lymond was
amongst them in a second, his hand on O'LiamRoe, white and
breathless at their head. '—She told you?'

'Robin Stewart sent word. Dooly held it back. It's only reached us
this minute. The attempt is now, on the lake.'

They were running, the armed men rattling behind. As they ran,
O'LiamRoe managed to speak. 'We must go quietly. Your release is
unlawful. There's no proof as yet, and the King would never agree.
. . . Tosh brought Piedar; Abernaci's gone back. The Queen's on the
lake, but even if the explosive is there, Cholet has no means of firing
it,' said the Prince of Barrow, reaching dizzily for some sane element
in a rocking world. 'And listen—Stewart is wanting you. He was
after you to come for him this morning at nine, to keep the blame
off him for all this. There's a message.'

'Oh—Stewart,' said Lymond. 'He'll bustle in with a knife and a
bloody lecture, both wide of the mark, when it's all over. To the sea.
To the sea, thou that art initiated!'

Running past the tiltyard, the sweat dripping from the chin—
'Michel Hérisson is there,' said O'LiamRoe. 'They've got Beck. . . .
The man we're looking for is fortyish, small, thick, black haired, with
a ginger beard.'

'God!' said Lymond and laughed, panting; to O'LiamRoe he
seemed vibrant with life. He ran like a dancer, outstripping the
other man's stumbling feet, the soldiers in their leather jerkins at his
elbow. But at the lake he stopped dead. 'My God, what are they
doing? *She's still there*. Look!'

They stopped. It was true. The Queen's barge, gaily painted and
stuffed with children and men-at-arms, was tied up in the centre of
the lake, with the twelve little vessels alongside.

'No boats,' said O'LiamRoe, a shade late. 'They took the last for
the Queen. And the musicians are drowning the shouting.'

'If there's a slow match . . .'

'There isn't,' said O'LiamRoe. 'Abernaci swears no one has been
out to these boats since last night. There isn't a master gunner alive
who could judge a slow match for that long.'

'Then it's going to be a fire arrow,' said Lymond, without
apparently taking any thought at all. 'The menagerie is clear of
strangers?'

'We can depend on that.'

'Then it must come from the pavilion, or the end of the lake where the chariots are. You can see this end is empty. Take three men and scour the carriages. I'll do the—'

It was Michel Hérisson, without greeting, who interrupted him. 'Thady, there are Diana's bows over there, and flint by the stand—'

'Find the fountains and put them on. Can you swim? No? Phelim? God—no, look. Abernaci is in.' The file of running men, stringing out, began to spread round the box paths. Lymond, Hérisson at his side, started up to the lakeside stand, glaring cloth of gold, with the workmen resting, staring, on its roof. One of them began to run.

Lymond whistled. The high, sweet call stopped O'LiamRoe in his tracks, halfway over to the carts. The de Guise men below halted and looked up. By now the men-at-arms in the Queen's boat had caught sight of the flurry. From the shore their sun-reddened faces could be seen gazing distrustfully towards land. They had raised their shields in a kind of barricade; behind it, not even Mary's red hair could be seen. They must have thought, with relief, that she was quite safe; they made no move to row to land.

The man on the roof disappeared. But not before they had seen the small barrel body, and the chestnut grizzle on the chin. It was Cholet. Lymond seized one of the stout Roman pilasters and began to climb like a goat—O'LiamRoe could see the flying black coat of the ollave, racing up the mast of *La Sauvée*, knife in his teeth. He had no knife now. To free his arms he had stripped off even the wide canvas shirt; against his brown, scarred back his hair looked less yellow than silver.

Cholet reappeared, bow in hand, on the thick cartouche crowning the front of the stand. Against the white disc of the sun, flame was pale as air, but they could see the grey smoke rising, thin and wandering, from the flaming arrow as he nocked.

He shot three burning arrows swiftly, one after the other. The first dropped hissing into the water. The second and the third sank firmly into the wood of the ninth vessel in the lake, the small galley next the canopied barge of state. Then Artus Cholet threw down the bow and kindling on the flat roof beneath him. The varnished wood and baked metal cloth of the stand received it like some worldly friar his martyrdom, and laid between Cholet and Francis Crawford, racing towards him, a suddden lurching barrier of fire.

*   *   *

The Latin was over, thank God, and the worst of the affair: Ely with a cursed long-winded oration and de Guise replying, silky in red camelot—a foreigner; one would say English himself. Now Henri, in plain white sewn with silver aiglettes, his black hair shining, looking well, touched the Book, kissed the Cross and was taking the oath.

It was going smoothly after all. Garter, well into his stride, took the blue silk Garter with its gold letters and buckle from the cushion, kissed it and gave it to Northampton. Flinging back his own mantle the Marquis took it and, kneeling, bound it round the muscular left leg of the King, combining reverence with deftness in a way that betrayed well-spent time with an equerry.

D'Aubigny was looking smug. Why had François de Guise been late? That fellow who played the Irishman had been his sister's spy; you could tell that. The play acting over the boar had been typically *à deux visages*—a disclaimer of her interest at the time, and an excuse for her to be lenient later, if she needed one. And she had cast him off pretty sharply in the end. It was surprising that he permitted it. Not that you could blame her. As events proved, she had been right.

You could guess, too, the kind of game she would be playing in Scotland. A de Guise Regent of Scotland; a de Guise Pope at Rome; a de Guise virtually King of France. . . . Well. They would see about that. But with this fellow at her back. . . ?

Well, they would see about that, too. The King had liked him; he would give the Médicis something to think about, too.

Capito vestem hanc purpuream. . . . God, it was hot.

*　　　*　　　*

The ninth galley was on fire. On Mary's boat they had seen it. Someone, head and shoulders over the gunwale, was hacking at ropes. Then the whole linked cluster of boats rocked, and began to drift slowly forward. In his haste, the would-be helper had cut all the vessels free of the buoy, and the dozen roped boats were still drifting shoulder to shoulder in the same moving mass with his own.

Cholet, on the far side of the roof, had started to slither down. Beyond, O'LiamRoe with his three men were running back. Lymond called to him; then turning, slid to the ground and made fast for the lake. The fountains came on, two delicate blizzards of light on either side of the water.

The Duchess de Valentinois had long since gone in; the nymphs had absented themselves, with Bacchus, at the first sign of trouble; the men-at-arms in Mary's boat, still obviously fearing nothing worse than an illicit fireworks display, were fending off the empty fleet with their oars. The brigantines, the painted galleys with their dragon prows, rocked; and a spurt of flame showed at the side and deck of the ninth. A sudden gift from heaven: the musicians, gaping, had fallen silent. Lymond, already running in water, cupped his hands. '*Gunpowder in the boats. Row away.*' And turning quickly, caught the knife someone tossed him.

Abernaci, halfway from the menagerie shore, was treading water. Already the drifting boats were nearer Lymond than himself. He heard Lymond shout again, this time in Gaelic, just before he struck out. It was an instruction to harness the elephant.

It was meant for Abernaci, but it was O'LiamRoe who heard and acted on it, shouting to the cowardie, thonging new rope into Hughie's harness. He stood at the water's edge, hemp in hand, and threw it in unfolding yellow fakes into Abernaci's wet hands as Francis Crawford slid through the water, green and white, to the boats. Under the sudden, urgent drive of two pairs of long oars, the Queen's boat shot towards him, and the flotilla, sucked by the wake and the rush of fire near its tail, curtseyed after.

*   *   *

The white surcoat was off, and the new crimson gown on, the sword girded without incident; and Garter was kissing the Mantle and Hood. 'Accipe Clamidem hanc caelici coloris . . . Take ye this Mantle of heavenly colour, with the shield of the Cross of Christ garnished, by whose strength and virtue ye always be defended. . . .'

The fresh-tied tassels hung still; the powdering of garters on the blue shone steadily, silver-gilt in the bright light. Henri was becoming bored.

There was only the Collar left, and the usual homily; then Chapel; then the meal. There was this: Scotland no longer had such value to France, now the English threat was so weak. If the girl died, the Dauphin would be free to marry elsewhere. For example . . . By God, it was hot. A man might go to sleep, heavily robed in this heat.

*   *   *

At the last moment, the cowardie would not go. So the big male elephant, moving lazily through the lake, had O'LiamRoe on its back, O'LiamRoe who could not swim, with his ears clouded with water, clinging to the sodden leathers on big Hughie's brow and watching Abernaci, ahead, continuing steadily towards the burning boats.

Lymond got there first. Margaret Erskine saw it, holding Mary loosely in her arms behind the rattling barricade of shields, tossing everyday conversation between James, herself and the children, bracing herself against the great tug of the oars as the four men drove the boat through the water. The smoke behind them smelled acrid. 'What a shame,' she said brightly. 'All the beautiful feux de joie meant for tonight. I fear, chérie, you are about to have the most costly display of squibs ever set off in broad daylight.'

'M. Crawford will stop it,' said the girl, and poked her ruffled red head out between the lattice of arms. She was afraid—Margaret could sense it—but gallantly she too subscribed to the fiction. What a pity . . . the squibs would be put to waste.

The fair head, the dark chevron in the water, were almost level with them now. He must have known, halfway there, that the fire was now too strong to put out. His eyes lifted every few strokes gauging distances, watching O'LiamRoe and Abernaci drawing close from the far side of the lake. Once, perhaps hearing his name, he turned and lifted an arm quickly, in a shower of sunlit drops, in brief salute to the Queen. Then he was at the first of the boats, and pulling himself, wet as a starfish, up to its flanks.

It was one of the display boats. Smoothly though he climbed, the hull kissed the brigantine tied poop to prow, and the little shock ran jarring down the flotilla. The boats danced and for a second even the stranded players, clinging hoarse to their raft, were quite still. A cloud of sparks sprang from the burning galley, two-thirds along the swaying pack, and fell radiant against the rush of black smoke, thickly metallic with the smell of burned paint. The shadow of it netted them all: the clutter of boats; the Queen's barge straining to burst free at one side; and at the other, Abernaci's brown arms whirling nearer, with O'LiamRoe beyond, the bull elephant halted just within its own depth, hauling and barking at it in Gaelic to make it turn.

From the paved shore, as the startled water bumped and splashed at their feet, the men-at-arms and the workmen, streaming down to the edge, joined moment by moment by men and women from the castle, saw the sparks drop soundlessly into the smoke. The galley's carved rails were crowded with fire. All her detail was printed black on burgeoning gold, and her pennants, pointing to the blue sky, were run up afresh by the flames.

With a crack, the fire wheel on the ultimate barge burst into light. The pale gold head of Vervassal, slipping fast through the smoke, was haloed suddenly with coloured fire. The great wheel, near enough to touch, began to turn with gathering speed, and with crack after crack the little charges within it began to fire and revolve, sparkling within the grey haze, jewelling Lymond's glittering skin as he hopped through.

On the sailyard a second wheel began to whirl, and in the foreship another. On the flaming boat, the fire had reached the deckhouse, and the little brigantine in front had begun to show a pilling of flame. Lymond crossed from the last boat to the next, his feet like velvet, slid from there to a barge, and moving from boat to boat with unbelievable softness, had reached the burning galley before the wheels behind him had gathered full speed.

He must have checked each boat as he passed. Margaret Erskine, her light sleeves flying with their own gathered speed, realized it as she saw him poised on the eighth, the burning galley before him. He was standing on the barge of state. The cloth of gold draping the top castle had caught. Lymond ripped it off in passing, flinging it to hiss in the lake. The painted windows of the stateroom whirled and glowed, eye to eye with the spitting feux de joie in the rear. Then he jumped on to the blistered deck and, blazing prow and port rails bright at his back, cut the lashing to set all the boats he had just traversed free.

It was just possible to pass to the foreship with the deckhouse giving shelter between. Lymond stopped once, to glance in the well. Then he was gone, darting like a dragonfly down, up, along, regardless of caution, crossing three boats to where Abernaci, flying turbaned through the water, was ready with the rope.

The mahout lifted himself up, his scarred face enamelled with light, and raising one thin, powerful arm, sent the hemp flying. Lymond caught it. He had found a belaying place. He lashed the cable to the leading prow, raised an arm, and as O'LiamRoe kicked and Abernaci called, saw it tighten as thirty-eight hundredweight of elephant took the strain. It was all he waited to see. As the truncated convoy, heavy, squinting, stirred and started to move, Lymond made his way back to the fire.

O'LiamRoe looked back. Bleached as a raisin inside his pulped clothes, clinging to the horny grey loins with numb hands, his legs pumping awash, he could feel the big bull beneath him walking steadily and well, brow, trunk and back breaking the water, obeying the odd sounds of his mahout's distant voice.

It was a long way to the shore, but the water was empty, and the ground before them was vacant of buildings, or men or even animals to take harm. The musicians' raft, never very close, was now far away; between the four boats he was pulling and the rest of the flotilla the swirling debris-flecked gap grew and grew. Beyond that, the royal boat had pulled clear at last, skimming out of the shadow with the helmets of the rowers alight in the sun. The children's gowns showed, red and blue beyond the woman's encircling arms, and, bobbing and tousled, an excited red head. How much gunpowder was there? Christ. . . . Well, even if all four boats were full, in another few minutes the children would be safe.

Abernaci, nearer, had seen Lymond scan the leading boat as he passed. He saw something hit the water from the second, and sink gobbling; Lymond had found powder there. He saw, in between the queer cries to Hughie, that Lymond was back now on the burning ship, using his knife to get under canvas, the moving air of their passage fringing every yard and tassel with flame. He also saw that, gathering momentum, the four ships, like four coals in their pall, were beginning to swim free in the water, answering the pull of the rope merrily, skimming the glassy water faster than the elephant could pull. The ships were overtaking their pilot.

O'LiamRoe turned and saw it too. He saw two packets spin from the burning galley, followed by Lymond himself, moving swiftly, passing from ship to ship calling. What he said was not audible to O'LiamRoe, but he saw Francis Crawford raise his knife so that the wreathed sun shone on the blade, and throw it accurately and fast into Abernaci's outstretched hand. The mahout gripped it and slashed.

The cord tied to Hughie's harness sank, free. At the same moment Abernaci's voice, in Gaelic, roared 'Hold tight!' and followed with something else bellowed in Urdu. The elephant turned beneath O'LiamRoe's knees and ducking, started to swim.

Green water hit the Irishman like a scarf across mouth and teeth. Cramped fingers knotted hard in the leather, he hung on, deaf and blinded; it seemed that every box and tube in his guts was stretched and swollen with water, such was the pain. Then he broke surface, took a great, foaming mouthful of air, and saw Lymond reach the foremost boat and dive. He saw, too, Abernaci throw his wiry body kicking along the water, the cut rope fast in his fist. The mahout swam till he saw the boats veer, clear of O'LiamRoe, clear of Hughie, moving away from the rising wet head of Lymond; then he dropped the rope, took a deep breath and dived.

Before he dived like the murdered Hugh of Lincoln, he yelled. O'LiamRoe heard the call, but Hughie understood it. He squealed once, good-humouredly, because as he knew it, this was moderately good sport; and rolling flat over sank, taking O'LiamRoe with him, just as the four boats blew up—squibs, fusillades, gunpowder and all.

*   *   *

'Take ye and bear this Collar, with the image of the most glorious Martyr St. George, Patron of this Order, about your neck, by the help whereof you may the better pass through both the prosperity and adversity of this world. . . .'

The Collar shone round Henri's shoulders, the twenty-six Garters with their white and red roses and the Great George blazing below. Northampton, faultless to the end, had congratulated the Stranger in the name of Edward and all the Knights Companion, and had delivered the black velvet cap, diamonds winking at the base of the plume, and the Book of the Statutes in its red velvet cover . . . '*non temporariae modo militae gloriam, sed et perennis victoriae palmam denique recipere valeas*. Amen.'

Amen. The trumpets had piped faintly out, everyone had bowed, and there was the guarded ruffling of a gathering, stiff, thirsty, and overclad, which had a Solemn Mass to get through before food.

398

Sensibly, no one began to orate. Henri, smiling, summoned both Northampton and Garter to his side and addressed them courteously; in a moment, Mason and Pickering also went. Behind, someone had opened the doors. There was an attentive rustling among the Archers, among the servants and the gentlemen with axes. The Constable, with an eye on the sun, guessed that they had kept well up to time. He caught Stewart of Aubigny's eye, returning from the same survey, and knew a moment's unease, allied to a kind of defiant unconcern. Let the Gods, Popish, Classical or Reformed, take care of it. Warwick was no fool; Warwick had included Lennox and his royal wife in this Embassy just in case of accidents, and would slough them as fast as the de Guise woman had put down that fellow, should the occasion arise.

And France in his view should do the same. There was nothing in Ireland for France: let England pour her own money down that open drain. And let England think France her ally. . . . What could the Emperor do against both?

The King was talking a little too long. Pasque-Dieu, that fellow d'Aubigny looked green. Something was afoot, then. Montmorency, observing with small eyes, caught the Duke de Guise's limpid gaze and sustained it warily, for a long moment.

With a sweet and tintinnabulant crash, every window in the room cracked and blew in. The great boom which had followed the crash split into a chain of detonations, ranting like brother cannon breaching a town. Round the crackling centre of sound rose its echo, a great, sonorous wall of air which seemed to seep in through the shattered glass and fill all the stuffed room.

As puppets, every plumed head jerked round. Alone, among every pinched and startled countenance, the handsome face of Lord d'Aubigny looked at ease.

The Constable, absorbing the sense of the room in one glance, noted it and sighed. The clamour broke; it sounded like a boxful of geese. Deep in the heart of it, he heard the King's voice.

Not unpleasurably, Anne de Montmorency heaved another sigh.

The noyade was over. Queen Mary of Scotland, presumably, was dead. His wife had dressed her dolls. A pretty child, last of her race, born within days of her royal father's death. The Constable was fond of children; he had seven daughters although, of course, now all grown up.

Thinking hard, he moved forward and took his King by the arm. 'Some accident, Sire, which should not be allowed to discommode our friends. With your permission, I shall send to find the cause while we proceed to Chapel as planned.'

'John Stewart will go,' said the King. For a second only, the

Constable hesitated; he saw the Duke de Guise's eyes narrow like his own. Then—'As you desire, Monseigneur,' he said.

* * *

The wall of shock, moving through the turmoil of water, saved O'LiamRoe's life. Turning even the great elephant back to belly, it lifted Phelim and wheeled him like a dolphin into the air, air scarcely less dangerous with falling wood and flaming fabric, with random fire shells and lights white and coloured, and in the midst, the white coalesced furnace of what had been four ships, blustering and hissing, hammering like a molten mallet on the jerking black waves.

Far away, an untouched boat was reaching the shore, an untouched royal head in the bows. Nearer, a raftful of prone musicians trotted and leaped with the water as they lay, eyes squeezed tight, heads helmed with pocked lute and snake-gutted viol.

Nearer still, converging towards him through the splashing water, their heads rimmed with light from the conflagration, were Lymond and Archie Abernethy, swimming matched side by side. Hands gripped his arms, a naked shoulder bore him into the air, and as Abernaci, smiling, slipped past, calling to the rearing waterfall of trumpeting anger which was Hughie, Francis Crawford held O'Liam-Roe, vomiting water, firmly under his arms and set off with him to the shore; set off shearing through the smacking water like a honed blade as the feux de joie danced and sparkled, pink and blue and gold under the pall of black smoke between themselves and the sun; and crooning under his breath into O'LiamRoe's blocked red ears.

And he did not need, after all, to swim all the way. O'LiamRoe, emerging from his stupor, found himself brought to a little rowing barge, one of those Lymond had cut free, rocking gently on its own with two pairs of oars for cargo. In a moment more he was amidships, with the shafts in his soft hands, trying to match Lymond's unthinking, professional pull. The boat bucketed over the settling waves, making straight for the menagerie. Abernaci and the elephant, he noticed, were already halfway there.

Lymond was singing:

> *Un myrte je dédierai*
> *Dessus les rives de Loire*
> *Et sur l'ecorce écrirai*
> *Ces quatre vers à ta gloire. . . .*

O'LiamRoe, for the first time in what seemed like hours, essayed human speech. A quack burst from him, with a good deal of spit. He hiccoughed, his green face returning to pink. 'The intrusive C,' said Lymond's voice like a lilt over his shoulder. 'Did the Slieve Bloom and your sitting-skins seem dear to you just now?'

Over his shoulder, half choked, 'Last night, they seemed dear to me,' said O'LiamRoe.

The abandoned voice behind him, speaking beat for beat with the rowlocks, altered arbitrarily in timbre. 'I dreamed,' said Lymond, 'that . . . Cormac O'Connor was alone.'

'He is,' said O'LiamRoe, his eyes on the festival of lights. 'And the woman Oonagh O'Dwyer, she is alone also.'

For a moment, the boat glided in silence. Then—'We are two pedants, Phelim, guarding the moon from wolves. But better—I suppose better—than electing to be of the moon, or of the wolves.'

They had pulled out of the smoke. The sun struck them, cosy as an old nurse, happing them with heat and stillness and lazy security. Above, the sky was measureless, blue upon blue.

'What now?' said O'LiamRoe suddenly, catching something of the power and gaiety struck from the pure light and the mood of the man sitting behind him. 'The *menagerie?*'

'Certainly the menagerie,' said Lymond. 'Where are your ears? The menagerie, where Artus Cholet has been trying to escape from a fat Rouen sculptor ever since you began to swallow the King of France's new pond.'

VI

Châteaubriant:
Satin and Scarlet

In the distraint of a chained dog, let a stick be placed across his dog-trough and a prohibition made that he be not fed; if he is fed after this, there shall a man trespass upon him.

As to the distraint of a poet: let his horsewhip be taken up, and a warning given that he is not to make use of it until he cede justice to thee.

Satin and scarlet are for the son of the King of Erin, and silver on his scabbards, and brass rings upon his hurling-sticks. The son of the chief is to have all his clothes coloured, and is to wear clothes of two colours every day, each of them better than the other.

SCANDAL, outrage and unauthorized bedlam were the comforts of Michel Hérisson's gouty years.

When the three arrows arched flaming into the centre of the pond and the water filled like Palissy's crayfish with swimming forms, when the workmen and the men at arms and all the openmouthed spectators stood limply gazing after Lymond's vigorous head, or else scrambled with filled helmets to the flaming stand, Michel Hérisson hopped and hobbled and finally hurtled, forgetting his gout altogether, after the thickset scampering form of Artus Cholet.

Gingerbeard, to begin with, did not see him. Gingerbeard flashed down the far side of the stand like a lizard and set off, twisting and dodging, round the end of the lake where the stacked baubles and accoutrements for that evening's pageant offered unusual cover. Past the chariots and the plaster gods lay the way to the menagerie; beyond the menagerie was the edge of the forest and freedom.

Artus Cholet ran, head down, round the wreathed wheels, past the gilded lamps for the Satyrs, into and out of a grove of grey deities. A Jupiter rocked and Hérisson, heaving his knotty bulk on to a cart-shaft, roared from his vantage point: 'Aye, shoogle, ye pie-maker's huddle of ooze, take to the skies! Ye'd best get back to the Nymphaeum, for by God, ye havena the tibias for a socle on earth!'

And as the maligned King of Heaven fell with a crash, disclosing the black head and ginger beard arrested popeyed behind, the sculptor let loose a bellow that roused all the keepers, and leaped from the cart. 'To me! To me!'

A cage of doves crashed, and a frightened turtle, wings ajar, clung to his chest. He clutched it. 'A sign! Noah, we are saved! To me! To me!'

In the distance, a lion roared. 'Ah, puss!' said Michel Hérisson, running like a hare, hearing ahead of him the frantic crash of Cholet's escape and beyond that the first questioning calls of Tosh and Pellaquin and all Abernaci's subtle crew. 'Sing. Sing like one of Hero's own birds piping out of a siphon. I have a naughty man here, meet to be skewered.' And laughing like a fool at his own doubtful wit, he plunged after Artus Cholet past the first of the cages.

His broad back was the first thing O'LiamRoe saw when, already half-dried with the sun and exertion, he and Francis Crawford reached the shore. It was the first thing Abernaci saw as, comfortable on Hughie's mighty back as a lotus erect on its pad, he bade Hughie drink his fill and bless Michel's cotton poll with his trunk.

By then, the noise was prodigious. The explosion had rocked the menagerie, already distraught with scampering men. Among the loose animals, the Keeper's sick camel, a lady of brittle temper, had bobbed her tassels and sunk her yellow teeth three times into unguarded flesh; the dwarf ass brayed itself hoarse and the lion cubs, dear to Abernaci's heart, had shambled off, humping their fat, sandy rumps, to feast among the spilled milk in the wrecked kitchens.

Amongst it all Cholet ran, no longer the compact bully, the master-gunner, the man who had snored last night in Berthe's hot bed. Trapped in a labyrinth of tent, cage and pavilion, of sudden foot-encumbering messes of food and straw, of alleys which ejected liveried men with pitchforks, black men with horsewhips, bears, drunk on rice and reeds and primed for the arena; distraught with chained leopards whose leap checked a yard from his face, by stones accurately thrown by caged apes, by the roaring bulls and trampling, screeching elephants, by the whorls of black smoke and impossible blossoming of fire and squibs and fire darts and bombards booming, cracking and detonating in the quiet lake behind him, Artus Cholet finally came to the most wilful challenge to his resources. He came face to face with a lion.

It was a very large lion, shaved to a tawny velvet, tail to ruff. The frenzied mane, fit for a Cardinal or a Chancellor and thick with gold dust, framed a blunt tulip muzzle, a seamed mouth and two pale golden eyeballs. The mouth opened, showing the pink ridges of arch and palate; the lion roared.

There was a cage at his elbow. His wet hands slipping on the metal, Cholet jumped for it and started to climb. As he struggled upwards, he could see that the stinking little alleyways of box and cage immediately around him were empty. Further afield, he discovered the reason: the menagerie itself was surrounded. Someone had organized the frolic and dispersed the volunteers; and a ring of men, keepers, mahouts, waterboys, was moving inwards quickly, the bright sun on their weapons. Nearer still was the white head of the big man who had chased him, and not far from that the turbaned head of the Keeper. Two others, fair and auburn, followed.

Over his shoulder, Michel Hérisson, avidly following every development, was addressing Lymond as he stalked forward, breathing hard, his white hair blush-pink at the roots. '*Ha!* Ye can swim like a blue-bellied viper, but what have ye done about Robin Stewart?'

His drying hair lifted about his head, someone's short sword ready in his hand, Lymond was not responsive. 'Left him to go his own gait for five minutes. . . . Christ, Michel, my leisure in the last half hour has been a little circumscribed. What does it matter? Cholet's as good as caught in the act. D'Aubigny can't make Stewart take the blame now, can't do anything against Beck's testimony, and Cholet's, as well as Piedar Dooly's account of what Stewart told him. Lord d'Aubigny's guilt is clear.'

Michel Hérisson, a spear in his horny hand, dropped suddenly back. 'But Stewart doesn't know that. He summoned you, and you didn't come. In Stewart's terms, that means a knife in your back. If you don't want three Queens mourning their darling boy, my advice would be—go and find him first, fast.'

On his other side, O'LiamRoe's damp head unexpectedly turned. 'There's truth in that. He's a queer, violent fellow, Francis; and he's rightly vexed. You'd look the world's fool if you or your precious Queen had a little accident in that quarter now.'

'All right, give me a jacket,' said Lymond. 'Since you're all so damned glib . . . I was going, naturally, as soon as we have Cholet; but not naked, for preference.'

He was pulling on Michel's elephant-drenched taffeta when the lion roared. The mouth of Abernaci, stump-toothed in his sun-blackened face, unclasped in a charming smile of pure pleasure. 'Per Dinci, it's Betsy,' he said. 'Betsy, ma doo! Betsy, ma cabbage! Do you have him, Betsy, love?'

Artus Cholet, three-quarters way up the chimpanzees' cage, and pinned there forever by two hairy hands tight on his buttons, saw the little turbaned figure dance into the alley, saw the lion at his heels turn its great head, and saw the Keeper walk up and scratch it cheerfully under the ear. The lion purred. 'Ma bonny wee flower,' the Indian said. 'Hae ye a buss for your auld mither today?' There was a sound of a dreadful embrace.

'My God,' said Lymond, halting with Hérisson and O'LiamRoe at his side. 'Mother and daughter.'

'Eh, tiens—and there's Cholet like a side of beef on the cage there. Hi!' Hérisson, pleased, waved his arms to attract his victim's attention while Abernaci, catching Lymond's eye, blew his whistle. The beaters began to run in. The monkey startled by the blast, dropped its hands. Cholet, dizzy with chagrin and exhaustion, clung, hesitated, then collecting himself suddenly, clambered to the cage top.

At its foot, Michel Hérisson spread himself in luxurious stance, arms folded, head back, eyes surveying the multiplying audience and finishing, at last, on Lymond's calm face. For a moment, under the splendid hair, the florid brow creased. 'With the compliments of . . . the Hérisson family,' he said.

Round him, his friends were silent. Above him, squat against the dying pall from the lake, Artus Cholet stared speechlessly at his fate. He had nowhere to run to; he could make nothing worthy now but sport; but unreasoning, nevertheless, he twisted suddenly and made to run. And silent through the noise of the square came a shaft of grey feathers which said that he would not run anywhere, any more.

The arrow, shot from beyond all the crowding heads of keepers and friends, took Cholet full in the throat. He turned, bent like a withy, and fell; and the monkeys clawed at his buttons in passing. Then, like a dam, the space between the cages was filled with white and silver, girded with steel. It poured amongst the livery, the wet and turbaned heads, turning them aside; it cleared a path sheer to the little group around Cholet's dead body and surrounded it. Then practised hands fell like levers on Lymond's damp arms, wrenched the sword from his grasp, gripped him neck and body and turned him, held fast, to face the oncoming flood. The sun glittered on white plumes and on drawn steel, and on the silver-gilt crescents of the Archers of the Royal Guard, still now, filling all the paths, crushing out the royal livery of the menagerie and leaving just room enough for their lieutenant to come forward together with a Gentleman of the King's Household; broad, handsome, his fine dress immaculate, his face set like lard. 'In the name of the King,' said John Stewart of Aubigny, his voice pleasant, his bearing that of a temple god condescending to a ragged recalcitrant. 'The King whose despicable prisoner you are . . . Return to your cell to await his good justice.'

And Lymond, his eyes sparkling, called clearly and cheerfully to the Keeper, 'Here is a mate for your camel, friend.'

It was Michel Hérisson who lost his head, because in this matter more than his head was engaged. As Lymond spoke, Abernaci played to his thought with the ease of old experience and, stepping forward, exposed the lion. The lion roared. The grip on Lymond slackened, and he might have taken his chance had not Hérisson also seized the moment to whip the sword from his neighbour's scabbard and brandish it in Lord d'Aubigny's face.

'You mis-hacked boulder of butter rock, did I trap that man Cholet with my brain and my guts and my two gouty legs for you to kill off like pigmeat? I'll split ye! I'll smash that fine neb like a cup handle, if I have to seethe quick in a pot for it!' And elbows flailing, he leaped, blind with fury, at his lordship.

The guards dropped their grasp and started forward, but Lymond got there first, swiftly, from behind, wrenching the sword from the sculptor's furious hand. 'For God's sake, Michel, in law he is right. It would suit him to kill.'

He was too late in one way. Hérisson fell back, fuming, without drawing blood; but d'Aubigny, ready to fight for his life, was in no mind to let any man off so easily. As Lymond wrenched away the steel, John Stewart stepped forward, in all the avenging grandeur of his dress, and cut low, hard and deliberately at the sculptor's legs.

The sword was still in Lymond's hand. He drove it straight between the sculptor and the oncoming blow, the blades meeting flat on flat like the hammer of a bell. Then, disengaging, he jumped back, the sword steady, a threat as plain in the blue eyes above. Lord d'Aubigny hesitated, halted, and before they could try to disarm him, Lymond raised his sword and threw it from him, rattling on the ground. Hérisson stood panting, O'LiamRoe's hand on his arm, but no on touched him.

Then they lashed Lymond's arms, as they had once before; and the seigneur of Aubigny looked about. The crowd was increasing. So far, what had happened within the tight circle of the Archers had not been public; only the killing of Cholet had been seen by all, and that could be justified, to those who did not know, as d'Aubigny had known, that the man had no chance of escape.

Likewise, it was reasonable to restore an escaped criminal to custody, whatever he had achieved, to await the King's pleasure.

But still, the fellow had achieved a dashing performance; men admired such things. 'You,' said Lord d'Aubigny to Abernaci. 'Is there a tent here we can use?'

The nutlike face cracked. The Keeper answered fully in Urdu; then led his lordship, his lordship's Archers and the prisoner to the great tent where the elephants stood. 'Good. We shall stay here,' said Lord d'Aubigny, running his eye over the orderly, mountainous backs, 'until the menagerie and lakeside have been cleared. Then, Crawford, you will be taken back to your cell.'

Lymond's eyes were direct; his voice unmoved. 'Play it out,' he said. 'But we have Beck. It makes no matter now.'

Hérisson had gone, hurried roughly by the guards. O'LiamRoe likewise had been forced to go; but first he had said something in

Gaelic. '*Leig leis*. Do not answer provocation. He is in sore need of a chance to kill. I shall find Stewart.'

And then only Abernaci was left, cross-legged in a corner in a freshly glorious coat, bent over a block of wood. Leaving Lymond deliberately to stand, Lord d'Aubigny sat on a stool specially provided, twisting his fingers, and his personal bodyguard patiently waited, the canvas hot at their backs.

Then, obsessively as a man opening box within box who knows that, irrevocably, he has come to the last, and that the last will be empty; obsessively, he began to revile the man standing before him, because he had deceived him, because he had cheated him, and because he was a man and not made of ivory and gold. And also because, as O'LiamRoe had guessed, he intended to kill him if Lymond gave him one reasonable excuse.

*   *   *

The outcome of that would depend on Lymond himself. The matter of Robin Stewart, Phelim O'LiamRoe had taken on his shoulders. And since there seemed no possible means of tracing, in this seething town, one furious man bent on mischief, O'LiamRoe concluded that his only hope of success was to make first for the cabin in the forest where Piedar Dooly had been taken, and try to trace him from there.

The instructions Dooly had given were quite explicit, and they were written again on the handful of torn-up paper he had recovered from the near-unconscious Firbolg. Neither Abernaci nor Tosh had been gentle with Dooly. He himself, before they got all the truth out of him and after, had thrashed him until the stick broke. The thought of it curdled his stomach yet.

For he was tired, more tired than he remembered being ever in his life. Even Lymond's trained body, he guessed, after the double swim, the nervous work of the boats, the hard row, must be bone-weary by now.

To find his horse and mount it, to shake off the well-meaning offers of Hérisson and Tosh, to jolt cantering through the park and into the village, and then beyond the village on to the forest road, was a triumph of unreasoning instinct over the sedate, ironic soul which had lounged in the Slieve Bloom commenting with some wit, every now and then, on just some such dramatic embassy.

At one hour past midday, when at Châteaubriant the French Court and the English Embassy, both thickly robed, both smiling, both primed, in private, with the news of what had occurred and both ignoring it, were ending their banquet, O'LiamRoe rode through the vacant trees and saw the cabin before him.

Dismounting, he tied his horse to a tree and paused. He was not, after all, armed; and Stewart was no crony of his. If not already in Châteaubriant, sharpening a knife for Lymond's throat, Stewart could be here, bursting with understandable anger and waiting to show it.

Circumspectly O'LiamRoe walked over the mounded grass, his shoes shivering last year's oak leaves, rattling pebbles, snapping slivers of wood. The windows of the hovel, clear and glossy as jet, remained black; from the chimney rose a snatch of spangled grey ash. O'LiamRoe walked to the window and looked in. On the verge of cupping his eyes, boylike, to spy, he thought better of it, and turned at last to the door.

It was a little ajar. He said 'Stewart?' and knocked, at the same time, on the wood.

He was out. Or asleep. Or behind the door with a sword.

'Oh, well,' said O'LiamRoe, in speechless benediction to himself, to Stewart, and to the general situation at this ultimate moment. 'God save all here.' And pushing the door, he walked in.

He had waited a long time, in his swept and mirror-bright cottage, with the food set out as best he could on the table, and his new life and his new resolutions waiting, painfully created and painfully offered, for his last, jealous trust; his last friend.

He had waited a long time. The hours had passed, unmarked by the birds. The fire, raked out and raked out again, had begun to sink into ash; the fresh bread to stiffen; the wine to swim, greasily warm, in the jug.

When the explosion came and the birds were silent, then left the trees in a calling cloud of alarm, he had received notice of his ultimate failure. Then indeed, Robin Stewart had taken out his knife and held it high in his fist; but not to use it against Lymond. To use, instead, conscientiously, doggedly, steadfastly, against the man even a Lymond could not befriend. He had killed himself.

*   *   *

'Ma mie . . .' said the Queen Dowager. It would not become her to run, even with her child's life at stake. She had walked to the lake with her ladies unobtrusively, getting there just as the first fireworks went off. It was later, with the noise and then the explosion, that all the castle people who were free and many from the town, including her own Scottish lords, had crowded with her to the shore.

By her side, as the long boat with her daughter pulled to the shore, Lady Lennox was standing, and beyond her, Sir George Douglas her uncle. Lady Lennox: half-Tudor, half-sister to Mary of Guise's own late husband the King; Catholic, and dangerous. Without shifting, the Dowager took note.

But Margaret was watching the flaming boats, not the red head flying to safety: the boats, and the man who dived, like a gannet, just before the great white explosion came. Then—'Ma mie!' And the Dowager had bent to plant a soothing kiss on the child's hot, splashed cheek, to receive Mary's curtsey and to see her rush off to Janet Sinclair, waiting grimly behind. 'Did you see? Did you see? The boats go bang, and all the fire darts are gone!' And, true emotion suddenly tapped, the brittle excitement came all untied, and fatigue and fright bursting through, spent themselves on Janet's broad chest.

'Ma'am . . .' There was nothing to say. Margaret Erskine faced the Dowager and curtsied, seeing in the big-boned fair face a strain at least as great as her own; but for different reasons. Behind, tight in her nurse's embrace, Mary was being taken away. Margaret held her own little sisters by the hand. They had understood less, and they had James on their other side, his eyes sparkling.

'You did excellently well. The assassin was caught, it seems.'

'If not, he will be soon.' Sir George's voice, breaking in, was urbane. 'Lord d'Aubigny and half a company of Archers went by a moment ago.'

There was a little silence. Then—'Indeed,' said the Dowager. 'In that case, events may be worth watching. We shall wait. Margaret, you may take the children.'

What did she fear? Collecting Mary and Agnes, curtseying, walking over to James, Tom Erskine's wife became aware of someone addressing her.

'You are Margaret Fleming, otherwise Graham, otherwise Erskine? Is that right?'

The woman she disliked above any other blocked her way smiling.

'Yes. I am Margaret Fleming,' she said.

The tawny eyes which had studied her last night in the wood did so again, to the verge of impertinence. 'Jenny's daughter. One would never suspect it . . . I wondered,' said the other Margaret. '. . . But you are a sensible woman, I can see.'

The clear, unremarkable eyes turned up to hers. 'We cannot all think of nothing but ourselves,' said Margaret plainly and, curtseying, turned.

'*A sensible woman*. Yes. And lucky, lucky for the man you were watching there that sensible is what I am,' said Margaret Erskine to herself, angry tears in her eyes, as she marched to the Château Neuf, her sisters and brother at her side. 'Or neither he nor the child Mary would be here this day.'

Those who stayed by the lake had not long to wait. The news came, faster than Lord d'Aubigny would have liked, like an infection out of the empty blue sky.

'The assassin—'

'He is caught?'

'He is dead.'

The musicians were ashore. The loose boats, their squibs all spent, their deckwork flaked and blackened with sparks, were being collected and tied. In the middle, the burned-out galleys sagged, half-sunk, black on the satiny blue, smoke climbing sluggishly still over the sun. And beyond, from the menagerie, the press of many bodies, the glitter of pikes, the voices of a vociferous crowd, pierced by the small, sharp voices of command. Then, news again.

Sir George collected it and brought it, together with his niece, to where the Queen Mother was sitting with her ladies in the gold-hung stand. Around her swarmed the workmen, already cutting, hanging, painting, repairing, removing traces of the fire. It was not for them to decide whether royalty would come after all to sit and stare at the empty boats. Arms on the fine cushions, she watched Douglas come. 'Well, sir?'

'My nephew has, happily, apprehended the assassin, but unhappily has also seen fit to kill him.' He paused. 'He has also seen fit to place Mr. Crawford under arrest. His friends, foolishly, even fear for Mr. Crawford's safety.'

Margaret spoke. 'Whoever fears for Mr. Crawford's safety is a fool.'

'I have also heard,' said Sir George tentatively, 'that testimony of some kind has appeared which may even connect my nephew d'Aubigny with these attempts against her grace your daughter. If this is so, then Mr. Crawford is clearly innocent, and may indeed be in danger.'

'If so, the King will see to it.' It was Lady Lennox to whom this challenge was being directed, and it was she who spoke. The Dowager, understanding, waited her time.

'The King is engaged. Action is necessary now.'

'But who,' said Mary of Guise, her hands helpless before her, 'who can command his lordship of Aubigny? I have no powers.'

'His brother,' said Sir George, and in the long pause that ensued, gave an avuncular squeeze to Lady Lennox's arm. 'My dear, I know how hard you have struggled against Lord Warwick's conviction that the Protector Somerset has all your loyalty. He knows your love for Mary Tudor, your loyal love for your Church. Since the Archer Stewart babbled in London he must have wondered—unreasonably, I know, but nevertheless wondered—if Matthew was by any chance involved. . . . How awkward if, at this very moment, while the amity of France and England is being sealed over a chivalrous capon, on this very day when an English embassy is to ask for Mary's—or is it Elizabeth's?—hand, it transpires that Lennox's brother has attempted murder, and that Lord Lennox is by no means dissociated with the act.'

Silence. The Queen Mother, watching, added nothing. Sir George's suave voice, after a space, said only, 'You must disown d'Aubigny,

410

Margaret, quickly, publicly, now. Or your hopes . . . your most legitimate hopes . . . are as dust.'

He knew those eyes. He had looked into them often before; the magnificent, formidable eyes of Henry of England. She waited to force his gaze down, and succeeded, before transferring her regard to the Dowager. 'Mr. Crawford has performed a service for us all,' she said directly. 'My Lord of Northampton will certainly wish to congratulate him. I shall desire my husband to relieve Lord d'Aubigny of his . . . misapprehension.'

'So kind.' The Dowager's eyes, of cold Lorraine blue, were the masters of anything a Douglas could offer. 'And there is not the smallest need for you to leave us. As it happens, I sent to wait on Lord Lennox quite some time ago now . . . and here he is.'

*   *   *

It was true that he was overtired; but even standing you could in some measure rest, if you knew how. And it took the edge off the other sort of strain and dulled the smell of decay.

A mind responsive to beauty is a storehouse with many rooms; words, sounds, textures, all the nobler exercises of the senses leave some image filed and folded to be summoned at need.

There, too, the brutal images are kept: the sights and smells and hurts, real and imagined, which the responsive mind accepts and has bedded deep.

All these, the uglinesses that other men forget, were there waiting when Lord d'Aubigny turned the forbidden handle and, half-licensed by logic, opened the door. Upon Lymond, standing exposed before the Archers, the cowardies, before Abernaci crouched in his corner, this poured in a knocking downpour of insult, sneer and obscenity, noduled with bitter fact and relentless incident, thick with the combings of every rumour, gross and foul, which had ever played about Lymond's habits and deeds.

Facts were there: facts he recognized as half-true, built up out of the legend other people had created for him; facts he had never troubled to deny. Conjecture was there, and in this also, distorted, one could see the original image, the original flaw from which it sprang. He stood still, in the presence of other men, and heard applied to Sybilla his own mother a string of terms he had learned long ago in the galleys, but had rarely heard since.

And still, he managed to keep his temper. He could not move, unless he wished to commit suicide. He could only speak, and hope to channel the dirt. He waited until the big man paused for breath, his face yellow with loathing, his fine-cut lips wet. 'Don't stop,' said Lymond pleasantly. 'You've my father, my brother, my late sister and a whole clecking of aunts to get through. Auntie May is a good one to start with. Fifteen stone, and every spring she goes broody; and we find her out in the hen run on a clutch of burst yolks; except the year mother got there first and hard-boiled them.'

No one breathed; but under the bent mask of Abernaci's face, something cracked.

Lord d'Aubigny said, 'So they're mad in the whorehouse as well, are they? And how many mad brats have you sired?'

'Ask your sister-in-law,' said Lymond. 'Do they ever rule England, you can be proud. . . .' But before he finished, he felt the silence alter, and turned. Framed in the doorway was Matthew Stewart, Earl of Lennox, Lord d'Aubigny's dear older brother, white hatred in his face. Behind him, shadows outside his tent, were his men. Slowly, unshackling his white hands, Lord d'Aubigny rose.

They had been brought up as boys together in the long exile in France. Because of Matthew, three years of John's life had passed in the Bastille. Nine years since, John had elected to stay, his great-uncle's heir, and Matthew had gone to betray France, to betray Scotland, to marry England in his frantic search for a crown—a crown which had seemed within reach, but for one weak child's body; a crown a younger brother, surely, could share.

'I have come,' said the Earl of Lennox, ignoring Lymond, staring straight at the bright-fleshed face of his brother, 'to escort this man to receive the praise and thanks of all good citizens, whether of England, Scotland or France. It is plain that you serve no one in keeping him in custody, and I take upon myself the duty of release.'

'The King has sent you?' The cultured voice was harsh.

'No one has sent me. The banquet continues. Sergeant, untie him.'

Fast-moving in spite of his size, formidable in spite of his dress, John Stewart strode forward and placed himself, his hand on his hilt, between the man-at-arms and the prisoner. 'Are you crazy? No one has sent you? Then, by God, you'll have to use force first. You've no right to take this man!'

'I am taking him by right,' said Lennox coldly, 'of the grave doubts now expressed about your own past conduct, and my judgment, as a citizen, of your unfitness to continue in this post. *For God's sake, are you tying or untying him?*'

The sergeant, who had simply sidestepped Lord d'Aubigny to go on with his task, stepped back, rope in hand. 'He's free, sir.'

And free he was. Bare, dirty, unsteady with fatigue, Lymond looked from one brother to the other, brows raised, as he massaged his arms, and glancing beyond, to the Keeper's dim corner, allowed one heavy eyelid to droop. Lord d'Aubigny, rigid, remained where he was, all the implications of the events dizzy in his brain. He was outnumbered. And in any case, what use to resist? This, before him, was Matthew disowning him; draining his future, like blown

412

bladders rupturing his hopes. There was no purpose in anything now, except revenge. He said harshly, 'Leave him. Damn you, leave him. The King will take you to law over this.'

Silence.

'He can deal with foreigners who interfere with his justice. You'll find *yourself* in the Bastille—you, next. And what will Warwick make of you then?'

Silence again.

'Did I ever tell you,' said Lymond pausing on the afterthought, on his way to the flap, 'that that aunt of mine once hatched an egg?'

He paused, deep in thought, and walked slowly to the door before turning again. His lordship of Aubigny, staring after the vanishing form of his brother, received the full splendour of Lymond's smile.

'It was a cuckoo,' said Francis Crawford prosaically, and followed Lennox out.

He rode with him, in borrowed clothes, as far as the town so that he and Lennox could be seen and the rescue, as Lymond pointed out with some irony, should not have been made in vain. Once, outside the tent, Lord Lennox had betrayed a leaning to violence . . . and had stopped short, halted by the hilarious blue eyes, and the recollection of what he was doing. Thereafter he said not a word.

Outside the grounds they parted, by Lymond's desire; Lennox riding tight-lipped back to his royal wife. Fate, this time, had been rough-fingered with the Lennoxes.

Lymond rode on, and in a leisurely way set about keeping his belated appointment with Robin Stewart.

*   *   *

Phelim O'LiamRoe saw him come; and before he saw him, saw the avenue of trees lift and curtsey to the passing of his horse. There was no one with him.

He had taken all the time he needed, O'LiamRoe saw, to change and wash; to call on Michel Hérisson, probably, and discover O'LiamRoe had not returned; to obtain directions and follow them competently, well-dressed, beautifully mounted, his affairs now doubtless fully in order. How he had got out of d'Aubigny's jealous grasp, O'LiamRoe could not guess, and at the moment did not care.

Lymond noticed him, smiled, and dismounting, strolled across the humped grass. 'Hullo. You needn't have waited. The man will be prowling his tedious way round Châteaubriant, muttering threats. To tell you the truth,' said Lymond, dropping full length on the sweet grass and rolling over, face to the green light, 'I've had a surfeit of Stewarts, one way or another.'

There was a pause. 'I expect,' said O'LiamRoe grimly, 'that one or two of the Stewarts might feel the same way.'

413

Lymond's eyes were shut. For a while they stayed shut; then he opened them very slowly, his blue gaze heavy and firm on O'Liam-Roe's. 'Well?'

Standing still and sturdy in the little clearing, the triphammer of his heart beating the bones out of his flesh, O'LiamRoe inclined his head to the blank and glossy panes of the cabin. 'Robin Stewart is in there,' he said.

The movement that brought Lymond to his feet was so immediate that O'LiamRoe missed its component parts. He only saw him running, neat-footed over the grass, as fast as he had run today from his prison to the lakeside; running to the shut door, where he fetched up short, silent, a hand on either post. He raised his fingers to knock, but dropped them; and instead, pressing the handle slowly like some living thing he might crush, Francis Crawford opened Stewart's door and went in.

Mice had been at the table. The new cheese and the horny bread were half eaten, and the scrubbed table was scattered with mice dirt and crumbs. The fire was out. But all the rest of the room was as Robin Stewart had left it: the mended chair and the clean floor, the perfect pack and the shining sword; the signs of thought and decision and a painfully meticulous striving. 'As one gentleman to another,' had said the neatly penned note O'LiamRoe had pieced together in his sick time of waiting, 'I offer apologies with my meat.'

He lay before the hearth, the author of it all, the scoured hands idle on the floor, the dagger fallen, his lifeblood jellied on the blade. The loose-jointed sprawl was Robin Stewart, characteristic, not to be helped, outwith his last desperate control. But from the burnished hair so laboriously cut to the straight hose and waxed boots he was Lymond; Lymond in a last furious attempt to defy his stars; Lymond even in the privacy of his failure.

That O'LiamRoe had recognized also, in the two hours he had waited. He sat down now heavily, with a fierce emotion that was very near pleasure, and watched Francis Crawford pass in through the door.

Mors sine morte, finis sine fine. . . . Dim through the mesh of birdsong in the trees, the bell for Nones boomed and stopped. No sound came from the hut. What was he doing?

At Châteaubriant, the conference must be under way. Soon it would be over, and Lymond, the hero of the day, Lymond would be missed.

What was he doing? Contemptuous, angry, defensive, whatever his mood, you would expect him to turn and come out, and make of O'LiamRoe his first audience. But still he did not come.

Presently, his own heat gone, his heart shrunk in his throat, his hands cold, O'LiamRoe got up and went in.

Nothing was changed. Stewart lay in death as he had fallen; the

414

man for whom he had waited was not likely to rouse him now. The carefully spread table was the same, and the pack. Then he saw Lymond, at the deep side window, his hands clasped before him on the sill. On his face, a little averted, were none of the more dramatic aspects of anger or remorse. He stood staring down at his linked hands as a man might, merely considering a disturbing problem, had you not seen Stewart's blood on his shirt, and his knuckles and nails yellow-white with presssure on the cold whitewashed ledge. He did not move, although aware surely that O'LiamRoe had come in. The Prince of Barrow, suddenly in deep water, hesitated, his well-fed body too tight an envelope for his lungs and his heart.

Once, philosophy in hand and irony buried as best he could, he would have walked forward confidently and dealt with this. As it was . . . What Lymond's philosophy might be, he did not know. In irony he could outmatch himself, in width of vision he was, he suspected, his peer.

What was there left to say? Take him by the shoulder, said the O'LiamRoe of a year ago, the small parchment figure, complacent in its two dimensions, and say, kind but firm, 'When you got his message, it was already too late. There was nothing before him, anyway, but exile and the gallows. He was not even worth saving. He was a murderer. He was a man who thought of himself only, who, if it suited him, would brush anything from his way, busy, unthinking—even a child . . . even his friends . . . even you.'

It was the new O'LiamRoe who answered grimly. 'But the issue is quite other. The issue is that Francis Crawford set out to capture the mind of this man, and having used it, dismissed it like one of his whores. Had the message come in time, he would quite probably have ignored it. To say that he did not realize how far Stewart was his was no justification; he should have made it his business to know. *Nous devons à la Mort et nous et nos ouvrages.* That, thought O'LiamRoe bleakly, was one piece of French at least he had learned to understand.

'Thinking hard, Phelim?' said Lymond suddenly, and turned.

'Lo! said the King; now ye may see that there is no default in me. There must be *some* excuse you could mention.' His face was brutally composed, his eyes wide open in the gloom.

'You learn,' said O'LiamRoe's voice quietly, of its own accord.

'*I do not*,' said Lymond without expression, his eyes on the thin, sadly jointed shoulders on the floor. Presently he said, 'I seem to be armoured with scythes no one can see. Every breath I draw seems to twist some blameless planet from its orbit.' And after a moment, 'I suppose you are right. A cell is safest; or a tower, or a bog. To discuss the world of men, and laugh at it, or even pray for it. But not to meddle with it.'

415

O'LiamRoe braced his tired bones. 'Pause,' he said, 'for a sympathetic groan of assent. From Will Scott of course, at the very least And from the shade of Christian Stewart. From Oonagh O'Dwyer And certainly, the man at your feet.' And cutting short, again, the blank pause which followed, he said sardonically, 'You won't have noticed, but the argument you've just used used to be mine. I'm a graduate of your academy too. You might have the grace to wince at my little, fledgling scythes.'

Lymond, still resting with his back to the window, put up a hand suddenly for no obvious reason, and dropped it again. He said coolly, 'How did you know about these people?'

'Margaret Erskine,' said O'LiamRoe dryly. 'She made sure from time to time I knew exactly whom I was damning to hell. . . . God knows why I should cosset your conscience, but I could tell you, as a last piece of interference, some advice that the same sensible woman gave me once about you.'

'Spare me,' said Lymond briefly.

He had said already, in spite of himself, more than he wished; no one but himself need be obsessed by the clever decision to lay by soft handling, so that Stewart might stand up for himself. *I wish you had come to me five years ago. You would have hated me, as you do now, but the Stewarts might have found themselves with a man* . . . God. . .

Then it struck him that O'LiamRoe deserved to know something and he said, 'I could have forced him to tell me all he knew the other week, but—Christ, how bloody pompous can you be?—I thought he would hate himself so much. . . . He ought to be left to tell me out of his own conscience and conviction, not out of—'

'—Love for Francis Crawford,' said O'LiamRoe quietly.

'It wasn't love,' said Lymond in a queer, rather desperate voice. 'It was a kind of . . . oh, God, I don't know. Hero worship, I suppose. It's the only oozing emotion I seem able to inspire. It leads to nothing but misery.'

'Yet but for that,' said O'LiamRoe concisely, 'Robin Stewart would be alive, and none of this need have happened. I should be back in the Slieve Bloom with no past and no stake in the future. And Oonagh O'Dwyer would be with O'Connor still. *You see, you did right.*'

He paused. Lymond, breathing shallowly and fast, lifted his chin suddenly but did not speak. O'LiamRoe went on. 'You were angry with Margaret Lennox because she mocked my first, stumbling steps in the way of human responsibility. And an hour later, you had to draw me a picture of your duty as you knew it, that you believed would poison the very word in my mouth. I am telling you now that you did right with Robin Stewart and I am telling you that the error you made came later, when you took no heed of his call. It was to late then, I know it. But he should have been in your mind. He was your man. True for you, you had withdrawn the crutch from his sight, but still it should have been there in your hand, ready for him. For you are a leader—don't you know it? I don't, surely, need to tell you?—And that is what leadership means. It means fortifying the fainthearted and giving them the two sides of your tongue while you are at it. It means suffering weak love and schooling it till it matures. It means giving up your privacies, your follies and your leisure. It means you can love nothing and no one too much, or you are no longer a leader, you are the led.'

'And that, you think, I should find easy,' Lymond said; and even to himself his voice sounded odd. It was cold. O'LiamRoe said something and it came to Lymond, only then, that something was happening to him, and that he did not know if his eyes were closed or foolishly open, or even if he were moving or not. It was the last, bloody, squeak-gutted, pusillanimous straw.

As O'LiamRoe began to run towards him, Lymond swept round to the window and with a force that jarred the hair loose on his brow, smashed his fist clean through the glass. The mild, herbal airs of the forest welled through the space, and O'LiamRoe stopped.

For a long moment, neither man moved. Then the air, or the pain, did its work. Lymond opened his eyes, straightened, and after hesitating for a second, walked past O'LiamRoe to the table. He sat down, holding his injured hand tight with the other, Robin Stewart's blood and his own mixed on his sleeve.

'That is the work of a child,' said the Prince of Barrow, and opening the beautiful pack on the floor, began to search it for bandages. After a moment he got up from the litter and came over. 'Here.' Lymond, his gaze on his hand, had not moved.

There were flies in the warm wine. O'LiamRoe tipped them out and slapped the jug back on the table. 'He got it for you, so you might as well have it. Give me your hand.'

The thinned mouth tightened. Then Francis Crawford gave up his wrist, pushing the jug untasted away, and said in his ordinary voice, 'Yes, of course. Pure melodrama. How my brother would agree.' And added, after a moment, 'Thank you, Phelim. It was all well intentioned, I know . . . and very likely true.'

Two of the cuts were deep, but nothing was severed: the old bands round the thick glass had given way. By the time he had finished, Lymond was sitting quite collectedly, watching him with a sort of desiccated courtesy. 'Now what?' said O'LiamRoe.

'Now for the funeral,' said Lymond flatly, and got up.

The forest floor was soft. They dug in the small clearing; with stones, with their hands, and finally with a shovel O'LiamRoe unearthed from an old midden. In his pack was the Archer's cloak they wrapped him in; and the twined crescents of Henri and his mistress glittered up from the rich dark mould.

Lymond, looking down for the last time, saluted, as O'LiamRoe had done, the meticulous shadow of himself, then bent, with O'Liam-Roe, to obliterate it for ever.

It was a pleasant grave; gentler than the gibbet, or the town spikes, or the cold yard of uncaring, distant kin. They buried his pack with him, and put his hands on his sword, and put the turf like a living mosaic where he had been.

'Let us be tidy at all costs,' said Lymond. He came to where O'LiamRoe had flung himself, the last task done, and stood swaying a little, his face emptied of emotion, the blood drying on the soiled bandage round his hand. 'What, in the event, did Margaret Erskine say? Now, if ever, seems the time to tell me.'

O'LiamRoe looked up, sweat spilled in the soft cup of his throat.

'Ah, *dhia*. . . . Have I not attacked you enough? It was a piece of advice only, and aimed at myself as much, I suppose, as at you.—For those of easy tongues, she said. Remember, some live all their lives without discovering this truth; that the noblest and most terrible power we possess is the power we have, each of us, over the chance-met, the stranger, the passer-by outside your life and your kin. Speak, she said, as you would write: as if your words were letters of lead, graven there for all time, for which you must take the consequences. *And take the consequences.*'

Bringing down his gaze from the still, golden-green of the trees, Lymond was for a long time silent. Then he turned squarely to meet O'LiamRoe's blue eyes and in his own, remotely, a familiar irony showed. 'Now, that at least I seem able to do,' said Lymond dryly, and dropping beside the Prince of Barrow, rolled like a weary animal on his back and lay still.

Now the sounds of labour had ceased, birdsong had come back to the wood. You could even see them, high up: a dove, a couple of finches, the swinging flight of a tit. In the trees, the light had changed and ripened; it must be midafternoon by now. Their horses, content with the shade and the deep grass, cropped complacently, the un-strapped bits tinkling like Mass bells. Otherwise the quiet was absolute; the peace heavy as wine.

Out of a warm and billowing mist of some comforting colour, O'LiamRoe realized suddenly that, beside him, Lymond's breathing was making no sound. With a grunt, forcing his strained eyes open, he lurched to one elbow and looked.

He need not have worried. Francis Crawford and Thady Boy Ballagh were both asleep, noiselessly, the clever hands quiet, the ruffled head sunk in the grass; as still as that other, unendowed face they had just laid to rest.

'I want your help,' O'LiamRoe had said to that face, 'to trim a bowelless devil named Francis Crawford until there's a human place on his soul to put the mark of grace on.'

The living Robin Stewart had failed. But the dead, thought O'LiamRoe, sinking back, his eyes on the green grass and the cottage from which now no smoke came—Perhaps the dead Robin Stewart would achieve it one day.

*   *   *

'Lord d'Aubigny,' said Henri of France, 'will not leave this realm. Is that sufficiently clear to you all?'

Anne de Montmorency, Marshal, Grand Master and Constable of France, avoided looking at the Queen; by a stroke of good fortune they were without Madame de Valentinois just now.

The conference was over. They knew where they stood, though the arguments over dates and dowry would go on for a long time yet. Magnificent, manly and frank, my lord of Northampton on his King's behalf had demanded the Queen of Scotland in marriage with his master Edward of England, and had introduced the subject with a short homily of the kind familiar to all diplomats abroad.

His Majesty daily showed himself the towardest prince that ever England had to be her King. The estate of the realm was in good case, and quiet. The Commissioners on the frontiers of Scotland, as they knew, had concluded peace with the Scots. Ireland grew daily towards a good policy: justice and law were being set in good hand in parts where before they were unknown; the base money had been called down and commercial exchange had been reformed. Now, said the Marquis, looking King and Constable straight in the eye, now was the ripest time to carry out the age old promise between his nation and the Scots, and join their two monarchs in promised matrimony.

'No,' said the French monarch politely and at even greater length. She was affianced, as everyone knew already, to the Dauphin. 'We have been at too great pains and spent too many lives for her,' the French King replied.

And that was over. Northampton, withdrawing without ever having advanced, asked for and was granted the hand of the Princess Elizabeth, Henri's daughter of six, for his junior King. Provided a suitable dowry could be agreed.

The matter was at length finished. The compact of mutual alliance and defence was virtually sealed. And here in the privacy of his chamber was his Constable, producing witness after witness and argument after argument to demand that Stewart of Aubigny should be put under arrest.

419

The accusation was true. Even the wronged boy of the Spanish prisons could understand that; its very obstinacy in being blatantly true blinded him with rage. However the Constable gentled him, however calmly Catherine reasoned, the hurt pride was there. Stewart loved him. . . . Had loved him, once.

'You have appropriated Scotland today for your son,' said the Constable painstakingly. 'To keep by your side Mary's murderer would be an insult no nation would bear.'

'Let her leave, the Queen Dowager, if she does not like it. Let her take her begging train back to Scotland.'

'Insult her people?' asked the Constable.

'Insult her family?' said Catherine's collected voice.

'Then,' said the Constable thoughtfully, 'there is the charming M. Thady. He will wish satisfaction, and no doubt will expect a reward. My men are daily discovering interesting news of M. Crawford of Lymond. You know he owns the manor of Sevigny?'

'He is my dear sister the Queen's,' said Henri.

Catherine smoothed her fine dress with small, thickly ringed hands, and pursed her big mouth. 'My guess is—not yet,' she remarked.

There was a little silence. 'Then we shall make of Sevigny a comté,' said the King; and Catherine, smiling, played with her jewels. 'It is in my mind also to give his lordship of Aubigny work for his company of lances to do, on the frontiers.'

The Constable shifted his elderly bulk. 'Yes. But he must be shown, Monseigneur . . . It must be publicly understood that . . .'

'As you know,' said Henri abruptly, 'we have placed a ban on duelling in this kingdom. A ban not as perfectly kept as I should like. . . . It does not apply, of course, to sport in the tilting ground, with blunted steel. Before supper, we had planned a display of this kind. It shall be held in place of the water pageant. Advise Lord d'Aubigny and M. . . . M. de Sevigny that they will be permitted to relieve any hard feelings between them harmlessly in this fashion . . . and that Lord d'Aubigny, since he, I understand, received the first blow this afternoon, is in the position of challenger.'

Silently the grizzled face of the Constable turned to the Queen and silently, without lifting her eyes from her lap, Caterina Maria Romola smiled acknowledgment.

The Constable would take the news to Francis Crawford, Comte de Sevigny; the Constable, not Diane nor the de Guises, would report the King's wisdom and clemency.

A new star was being born. Not a star of Lorraine, or of Stewart, or of Douglas; and she and the Constable were its sponsors. She looked on her husband's black head, and in the shallow, prominent eyes was love.

*　　　　*　　　　*

The hot, brilliant day was sinking at last. In Châteaubriant, the lights sprang small and pale; in the castles, new and old, there were more; and a beading of lamps lined the walks. In the parks, the lake shone like a scale from the sky, buttoned with unwanted boats, black sitting on black without motion. Next the water, the great stand was unlit and silent, gazing emptily at the moving lights from the menagerie, where the small, clear jungle sounds, the chink of chains, the easy phrase of command, dwindled in the still air.

But between the lake and the châteaux, an arena sprang to the eye. The tiltyard, twenty-four yards long and forty wide, was garlanded with lights. Pale as new stars under the rosy sky they wreathed without illumining the great rectangle: the long, flower-packed stands for the Court; the tents to right and left for the champions; the striped silk raised like panniers to display the gilt stools; the gilded towers at the four corners for the pursuivants-at-arms.

Rose and pewter, flat as puppets under the great, dwindling sky, the audience bobbed and gestured and swarmed under the dark eaves, their splendours drained to grisaille; grey and grey among the small lights. Flatly the morions shone, pearly in the dead light; the silver trumpets, greyly flagged, were grey as water. Into all the riches of tissue and gems, into the silver brocade of the Archers edging the stand, into the bullion of the canopy, the cloth of gold on the champions' table, the armoured squires in the lists, sank the thin, pellucid light, levelling as ashes, ancient as the dry air from some staring rock.

Then the long day exhaled its last, and blue, liquid night rushed in. Then the clusters of lights shone golden as fruit, and the diamonds blazed. Then in the bed of each light, colour—living, vibrant—was suddenly reborn; then the warm, painted faces nodded and laughed; then the drums beat and rolled. Lovely night had come; and the lists were open.

They opened gallantly, gay as France could make it gay. The laughing companies came and went in their plumes and bright skirted armour: the side of youth, flamboyant, vicious against the side of riches; the side of the Bretons against the teams of the Loire. They shot at an inch board under the flaring torches and tilted at the ring in their ballroom dress, with diamond rings in their ears. Black-bearded, smiling, the King watched from his tribunal in the middle, the English Commission on his right.

Since the royal summons directly after their return, O'LiamRoe had not laid eyes on Lymond. The story he heard was the story put about all the Court: that after some unfortunate breach of conduct, Lord d'Aubigny and Mr. Crawford were to settle their differences formally in the arena, for the sport of the King. The charges of theft and treachery laid against Mr. Crawford, it was understood, had been dismissed.

That being so, it seemed a queer way of congratulating the quick-witted swimmer of the morning. It was, perhaps, more in the way of a last, sour riposte to the memory of Thady Boy. So thought The O'LiamRoe, sitting cautiously where he was placed, alarmingly near the lockjaw splendour of the Ambassage Extraordinary. Queen Catherine, to the left of the King, caught O'LiamRoe's wandering blue eye with a flutter of her fan, and smiled. The Prince of Barrow, amazed, produced a bow. He at any rate, it seemed, had entered the fairy circle.

The Queen Dowager's ceremonial thanks he had already, for the second time, received. Faith, thought O'LiamRoe. And not a decent creature among them thought to say that the only rule in it is for a man to have a fine, steady seat for an elephant.

Lennox sat stiffly, blond head facing front, sagging mouth pursed; looking neither to Warwick's fool Northampton nor to the Scottish seats, where Sir George's smooth face was turned, feasting on subtle discomforts.

The voice in Lennox's ears was not that of his brother; it was the voice of Robin Stewart, an unknown Archer now, pray God, dead, who had bleated to Warwick. Who had told Warwick that they could easily enter Scotland, having at their hand Lennox, nearest the crown after the Queen.

But Warwick had settled for alliance with France. And he and Margaret had saved their necks—*if* they had saved their necks—at brother John's expense. He hated them both: John Stewart, who had put him in this ludicrous quandary; and Lymond, of course, Lymond, But if the fight had been real, he would have wished his brother first dead.

The jousting was over, with all the buttoned lances; the foot matches with vizors open, with blunted lances and swords, had ended too. Pages were running; horses trotted off, tassels swaying; sheared plumes were recovered, sand reswept.

Music replaced the trumpets for the space of the interval, and there was a tumble of dwarfs. Brusquet, a little wary, not now so carefree as of old, was among them.

'Well, my dear,' said Sir George Douglas to Margaret Erskine at his side, 'this, I believe, is when the holy relics at St. Denis are usually taken down and exposed, by all right-minded people, against fiends, bogles and your friend Mr. Crawford. The fatal cartels have been exchanged by heralds, I hear, no less. And his Most Christian Majesty in his desire to look all ways at once, has forgotten the most vital thing of all, which is—'

'*What?*' Pushed into this extended strain, angry and worried, as she had been angry and worried for eight months about her wild, wayward protégé, on top of the shattering relief of knowing that at last Mary was safe, Margaret Erskine had begun to feel above all else the need to get out of France; to fly back to her own cool, green country, her baby, and the gentle, loving steadfastness of Tom.

She had sat by the hearth, as she had promised, but the other promise she had made to Lymond she had never meant to keep. He was afraid of his power; he had had to learn to live with its effects. Three people had suffered by his presence in France, and she had done nothing to help them or him, for the strength to sustain this burden was the very backbone of leadership, and he had to acquire it.

She knew now, from O'LiamRoe, how Lymond had been forced to face this issue at length. She knew, too, that other barriers had gone. He was free at last of all constraint with herself; and free too of Sybilla his mother, whose wits were as sharp as his own, and whose company he had precipitately left because it was so congenial and safe. Thinking of something else O'LiamRoe had once said, she had asked Francis Crawford that afternoon, 'And now will you marry?'

He had looked startled, and then amused. 'And whom do you suggest?'

'Is there no one?' she had said.

'A name has been put forward,' he had answered, looking even more entertained. 'If I could remember what it was.'

She did not know what he meant; she did know that he was not interested. At her expression, evidently, he had laughed aloud then. 'Better to be whipped than humoured; better to be crushed than cherished. . . . It was a woman told me that. I live in a world of men, my dear,' Lymond had said. 'I love you all, but I shall never marry you.'

And so, looking up at Sir George, Margaret Erskine snapped. 'He has forgotten what?'

'My dear, never underestimate a Stewart. He has forgotten that my dear Lord of Aubigny can prescribe the choice of weapon. As defender, Lymond has got to supply every piece of armour, every weapon, every item of horseflesh that his lordship conceives he might need to fight with. And if I know d'Aubigny, his requirements will be so large and so elaborate and so inordinately, impossibly expensive that Lymond will be able to do nothing but ingloriously retire. Sad,' said Sir George cheerfully, 'but as Periander and your friend Francis also once said, "Forethought in all things. . . ."'

*　　　*　　　*

'*When* is he coming?' said Mary, Queen of Scots. 'And will he have the black hair again?'

423

'How did. . . . No,' said Mary of Guise, a little helplessly. 'M. Crawford has no black hair now. You must watch.'

The dwarfs had gone. 'Will they kill each other?' asked Mary.

'No. Naturally. This is mock fighting only, my child. Be quiet,' added her mother.

There was a brief silence. Then—'Do they fight for a lady?' the girl demanded.

The impatient reply did not leave Mary of Guise's lips. She hesitated, looking down. 'In truth, no. But if you wish it, one of them might wear your gauge. Do you wish it?'

'Oh, mon dieu yes!' said Mary, carried slightly further than she intended, her hazel eyes enormous. 'A scarf! Maman, I have no—'

'Tais-toi. Your glove. Madame Erskine, procure me a large pin,' said the Queen Dowager of Scotland. 'I have yet to meet a man who can lay hands on a pin when there is need for it.'

*   *   *

The banners came first, as the trumpets proclaimed them down the lists to the royal tribune: Stewart of Aubigny and Crawford of Lymond, never before side by side.

And after them, the double line of servants: d'Aubigny's lances, steadily marching in the Stewart livery, halberds precisely angled, glittering in the streaming light; and Lymond's retinue, in new colours, in dress which Margaret Erskine found vaguely familiar and which Lord Northampton wakened up slightly to admire. They reached the table and there divided, so that the two protagonists stood revealed, walking steadily forward to the King.

John Stewart of Aubigny, on trial as he knew before his enemies, succoured as he believed by the clemency of his King, stood before him in all the riches of his heritage and estate. Below his justaucorps his shirt was embroidered and re-embroidered with gold; his dress of satin was sewn an inch thick with oystered pearls, and diamond-fire leaped on his shoes.

Beside him, Lymond had the desperate expression which more spectators than he knew in that audience recognized as a devastating impulse to laugh. With d'Aubigny's imperial grandeur he had simply not troubled to compete; either that, or had shrieked down all efforts to compel him.

He had no need. Lymond wore black silk, the shirt edge at neck and cuffs snowy white, and a twelve-thousand-ducat diamond on his shoulder, pinning a little girl's glove. On the glove, specific in the dazzle, the crown of Scotland was plainly embroidered. They bowed, the heralds stepped forward with the Master of the Lists, and the ceremony was under way.

Lymond lifted his eyes. All over the stand were faces he knew: the

Dowager and her lords, who had so busily courted him at Candé; the child—he smiled and bowed, hand elaborately on heart; Margaret, the quiet, deep woman who was older now than her own mother ever would be; George Douglas, whom France had treated kindly, and who might not find Scotland so kind.

The Lennoxes, Margaret blanched in the light, staring at him; he bowed lightly to her too. Diane, enemy of the Constable and of Jenny Fleming, who had not unbent. The de Guises, who had freed him—how Mary of Guise had laid her subtle stress on that point— but who had lost the diplomatic threads, in the end, to another faction.

The allies and good companions: O'LiamRoe, grinning sardonically, his new-grown whiskers gold in the lamps; Michel Hérisson, squashed in a corner, shouting something and being silenced by a Guard; and lurking among the performers, the flags, the tents, the stands of armour, the rare crooked smile of Abernaci and the shameless stare of Tosh.

Inescapable in the herald's strong, trained voice, his extraordinary title. Francis Crawford of Lymond, Comte de Sevigny. No longer Master of Culter as he had always been. . . . Well, that was an old story now. Mary of Guise, too, had heard. He had accepted from Henri the title he would not have from her; and that only for his brother's sake, she had guessed. His loyalty, if loyalty he had, was given to the lions, not to the Crown. He would not join, he had said politely, handsomely and finally, as a satellite of divinity, even for sweet Mary's sake.

He had said a great deal else that afternoon, and so had she. She had been so sure. It was true, she had hoped for his craft and strength only; she had refused him, out of very fear for her own eminence and her own policies, any exercise of his other abilities.

Thirteen years before, she had been married by proxy here on the Loire at Châteaudun to the King of Scotland, and for thirteen years had made Scotland her home. Châteaudun had not changed; but coming back, long-widowed, hungry for troops, for money, for power to fashion and maintain an undisputed and orderly throne for the grandson who one day, surely, would reign over Ireland, Scotland and France, she had found that in thirteen years France had altered.

With her eyes on the riches of Italy, and with her old enemy England weak and busy with internal struggles for power, France was no longer so tender towards Ireland or towards Scotland itself. France would have been content, she found, to have her abandon her self-imposed, stormy exile and stay with her child, while a Frenchman governed in Edinburgh in her place and Frenchmen remained inexpensively garrisoning the country's best forts, without pouring gold and promises, as she was doing, into the pockets of her Scottish nobles to buy their allegiance for their Queen.

Her brothers opposed that; but her brothers' power, though great, was not unlimited. The King was obstinate; there were times when neither the Duke nor the Constable, when not Diane herself, could move him. She had been right, whatever happened, to take her own measures, in secret, to safeguard Mary; there had been no one in this, her own country, to whom she could give absolute trust.

And few enough in Scotland. The Erskines: plain, honest, undemanding—she did not need to be told what she owed to her Chief Privy Councillor and Special Ambassador. Ten days ago at the kirk of Norham in England her well-beloved Thomas, Master of Erskine, with Lord Maxwell and the Bishop of Orkney and the French emissary de Lansac, had concluded a peace treaty between Scotland and England with the Bishop of Norwich and Sir Robert Bowes. In it, England contracted to give up the southern fortresses and her Tweed fishings within Scotland; had engaged that the debatable land in the west marches between the two nations should be neutral as before; and had agreed to release without ransom the hostages lying in English prisons since the fateful battle of Solway Moss nearly ten years before. Erskine, writing wryly, had quoted the English preamble. 'Though England, by conquest might justly claim enlargement of its own limits; yet the King agrees to a friendly and indifferent view of the old, true bounds; and that these should be the same as before the late wars.' Thus England in four years had shrunk.

But at the same time, England had become the refuge of the new religion, and a greater temptation to her own unsettled nobles—for intriguers like Balnaves, for so long a prisoner in Rouen himself; for Kirkcaldy of Grange, whom she knew to be in France, earning English pay. Douglas's allegiance she had, temporarily at least. Maxwell, though discomfited, was at the moment hers. Lord Chancellor Huntly was staunchly Catholic and a present support, but his ambitions were great. The Governor had been soothed with a dukedom, and a post for his young heir in France, but it would be hard to reconcile him, she knew, to abandoning his title to her.

The Earls of Glencairn and Drumlanrig were both of uncertain loyalty, and both had been displeased with their stay in France. Cassillis also was unhappy with his rewards, but might have enough to do, together with Maxwell and Huntly and the Douglases, in settling their own long-standing feuds at home. Livingstone, the stalwart guardian of her daughter, had died in France. Lord Erskine, her other guardian, was ill. Her husband's bastard sons, growing up, were restless already. . . . If Edward of England died, his successor would be the Catholic Mary Tudor, and her nobles could look for no sympathy there. On the other hand, Mary Tudor had the Emperor her cousin's support, and England might well be forced to break her new friendship with France, thus cutting off Scotland again. And the Lennoxes, Catholic, royal, and potential usurpers, were Mary Tudor's dear friends.

So Mary of Guise had come to recognize that she needed help. 'If he is in France for the term of my visit, I shall be satisfied,' she had said of Lymond, without pretending to mean it. 'In one year's time, his allegiance must be mine,' she had added, and had meant every word.

But she had cast him, in her mind, simply as a picturesque adventurer; and that, grimly, was what he had shown her from first to last. Only in London, after O'LiamRoe's message had come and her hand had been forced had he sardonically accepted and brilliantly played the role which at last had come fitly to his hand. And then, that done, had come back to the confines of his undertaking.

His undertaking was to save Mary, and that he had done. What secrets he had listened to on the loving shoulder of France she did not know; what the cajoleries of the Constable and the Queen might lead to she could only fear; what the flatteries of her brothers and the growing attention of the King might stir in him she could only guess.

She had designed the incident of the boarbaiting for her own ends: to prove to the suspicious her lack of regard; to give her, if need be, an excuse to beg clemency in the end, were he to be exposed; to present to him a stage on which he might exhibit himself, as he seemed to delight, to the best advantage, a promise of the applause and admiration in store for him, a favourite at her side.

And when she had read the disgust in his eyes she had known, again, that she had been wrong. She had been wrong; and she had lost him. He had saved Mary and he had safeguarded England's new burgeoning relationship with France. He had discredited the Lennoxes and won the attention of the French Council. He had George Douglas's admiration, for what it was worth; had he come in time, he could have swayed Jenny Fleming, she knew. What he had been busy about in the affairs of O'LiamRoe and Ireland she could only suspect. He had only to exert himself and he could make a following in Scotland; he had only to stay, and he could draw together for her all the Scottish allegiance in France.

In that queer afternoon audience, she had said none of this. Instead, she had spoken with feeling of all he had done, leaning lightly on the performances and the risks, stressing heavily the political sense and perception, coming as near humility as a Queen and a princess of Lorraine might safely do over the stupidities and exigencies of her station. And all the time she knew that it was not for her sake that he had kept quiet, when she denied him, but for her adopted country.

She had spoken of her plans. Soon she would return home. Only, meantime, her son was not well. And she waited to hear, with anxiety, what news the Marshal de St. André would send of his offer to England of her daughter in exchange for the English possessions in France.

He had known about that. It shook her, again and again, to discover how much he knew. 'They will never give up Calais on a promise as vague as that,' he had said. 'You need have no fear.'

And then she had asked him to stay in France. 'Men fall short of your desire, and so you abandon men. The Crown falls short of your expectations, and you abandon the Crown. A leader with no following is an aerolite unloosed, M. Crawford, its power blinding and blistering where it wantonly falls, until it burns itself out. To take a puny man and make him great is your gift. I offer you a child to fashion and make worthy of your soil.'

She had added much more. There would be a knighthood. His estate of Lymond should be made great: French architects would rebuild; the storehouses and purse of a grateful state would be his. In Scotland, when he chose finally to return, he could re-create the beauty and brilliance of France.

Not even her ladies had been present at this interview. She had dressed herself with care; she had given him her hand and permitted him to sit. And it was she, accustomed to dealing with male minds, barely aware of her sex, who found herself irritatingly aware that, sitting motionless, answering laconically and fast, he had formed his opinion long ago about her mind and her abilities, and was addressing himself solely to the pitch of these . . . as he might have done to a bullfrog similarly endowed, she thought with a sudden flash of anger, who had happened to be the Queen Mother of Scotland.

'I offer you a child to fashion,' she had said; and his tone, even and courteous, did not change. 'Then you must send her to Scotland—for that is where I shall be.'

After a long while she said slowly, 'I do not think you understand what I offer.'

And he had answered, rising as she rose, his eyes clear under the smooth brow where youth sat; the youth she would close in her fists if she could, the youth she coveted, raging, to fling against the mewing pack of wild creatures, the Douglases, the Stewarts, the Hamiltons, the ambitious sons and the kingly bastards and all young, young, young who would one day snap at her vacant throne.

And in all his enviable youth he stood before her and said, 'I have understood and I have refused. If you wish me to lead, I shall lead. In Scotland I shall make a company of men who can match any fighting men in the world; and for twelve months in Scotland they and I shall be. If you want me, send. . . . But I may not always come.'

'Even for the child?' she had said.

'Even for the child.' And his eyes had betrayed for one moment the life she knew must be there, but did not know how to reach. 'The brilliance and beauty of France were all ours, and more, forty years ago. They ended with Flodden, and they cannot be pinned on afresh, like a decaying rose. They must grow again, and in security. It has been merry,' said Francis Crawford. 'But the time for follies is over.'

He was waiting peaceably now, the child's glove on his shoulder; but d'Aubigny was watching the Master of the Lists, was waiting for the paper which the Master took now in his hand, and adjusting the spectacles which, to his sorrow, he could not do without, perused and then read.

'To messire Jean Stewart, Chevalier, Seigneur d'Aubigny, la Verrerie et le Crotet, fell the choice of arms to be used in this match, the fullest choice as the said seigneur demands to be provided, under pain of forfeiting the match.' And, licking his lips, he proceeded to read out the list of arms from which Lord d'Aubigny desired to choose.

And the quick Douglas mind had guessed right. Notorious among the malicious, sometimes done in sport, sometimes for a wager, this shift was the most ill-mannered and peremptory in the whole game of arms. The injured party had this right: to force his opponent to bring together an adequate choice of weapons, such as gentlemen might use. He had the right, if he chose to exert it, of stating sword by sword and plate by plate from what weapons and what armour and what horseflesh he desired to select.

Stewart of Aubigny had done just this. As the Master's voice launched forth, spoke, and then rolled on through phrase after phrase, first exclamations and then gathering laughter answered him from the stirring stands.

'Item. Horse. A pair of Turkish mares in harness, with ears and tails clipped, and furnished with military saddles; a pair of cobs, saddled in plaited armour and a pair of Spanish jennets with leather saddles and clipped tails. Two asses, caparisoned in velvet, with têtières of brass.

'Item. Two partisans, damascened in gold. Two halberds, with silk tassels; two pikes. A pair of the new Italian pistols. Two hand arquebuses, furnished with balls. Two cutlasses; two poniards with double edges and St. Hubert in the hilt, and two single-edged, with a honed point. Two rapiers, and two Swiss bastard swords with plain quillons, double-edged.

'Item. Two suits of goffered leather, with chain mail over. Two engraved corselets, damascened gold and silver. Two brassards in

Milanese steel, and two in German. Two cuirasses the same. Two bucklers, decorated in silver, with leather straps; and two with steel. Two pairs of gauntlets. Two morions, plumed, with . . .'

Long before the list ended, the laughter died. The form of mockery did not seem particularly witty; and they had all at least expected to witness a fight. In silence, the Master reached the end and folded the paper. D'Aubigny's eyes, large, flashing with life, looked at Lymond and then, head high and smiling, his lordship turned to the King. The trumpets blew.

'Do you produce these arms, M. le Comte?' asked the Master, of Lymond.

And—'I do,' said Francis Crawford, with the clarity, the abandon, the felicity of some royal bridegroom; and you could hear the sound, throughout all the pavilions, of the torches burning. Then, two by two through the barrier came the men of his short retinue in their brilliant dress which you remembered seeing, suddenly, on the King's pages a day or two before, with other servants to help them. And two by two they paced to the cloth of gold table and laid on it the most precious armour in Europe.

Gamber made the engraved armour Henri had worn at Blois; the golden cuirasses were wrought with lions; the morions with rams' horns and ostrich feathers, with diamond buckles at their roots. The swords had each their own scabbards, rubies on velvet, pearls on silk. The pistols lay in leather cases, the hackbuts with damascened stocks lay each with its pile of balls. The horses were brought on, shying a little at each other and the queerly muted noise, their housings sparkling with gold, their saddles waxed.

The English Embassy sat up, and made brief and privately astonished noises of admiration. Every Frenchman round the King was prudently silent. For every courtier there recognized the armour, horses and weapons of Henri, King of France.

It was the greatest rebuff John Stewart of Aubigny had ever received in his life; and the greatest he ever would receive until he ended his days in undistinguished obscurity after undistinguished service far from Court. And it was public as a proclamation to every French courtier there. Death, to Lord d'Aubigny, might have been less unkind.

He stood, his gaze on the King for a long time, sparing only a glance for the glittering arms on the table, and none for Lymond. He said, his voice a little high, 'I am satisfied,' and the Master of the Lists, looking in vain for guidance from the King, the Constable or the defendant himself, said desperately, 'State, then: what is your choice?'

He was a captain of lances, and he tried, at the end, to gather about him some tatters of pride. The handsome face, ignoring the Master, looked again up past the cloth of gold and the embossed fleurs-de-lis to the royal tribune, its crest the same as the one he had worn once on his own breast and back. Lord d'Aubigny, his eyes on the King, said, 'I make no choice. I forfeit my injury and withdraw my cartel of challenge.'

Above him, Henri's schooled face did not change. He said, 'Pray do not disappoint us. We and our friends here had hoped to see some sport.'

'The sport is done,' said John Stewart, his voice faded, and received the King's permission to go.

He walked firmly, in the midst of his retinue, banner high, and the glittering procession threading the undisturbed sand received neither cheers nor catcalls as it became dim in the night distances and dissolved. The fall of a favourite is celebrated with discreet music at Court.

On the field the Vidame, his hand on Lymond's shoulder, gently caressing, was inviting him to fight; and the English delegation, shifting a little in their seats, were careful not to meet each other's eyes. Northampton was smiling again.

They fought on jennets, for exhibition only, and the bout was pretty to watch. The Vidame, not unaccustomed to doing his courting with a poniard, talked all the way through

Francis Crawford fought delicately, like an automaton, his eyes largely elsewhere, and won. At the end, kissed, congratulated and bewreathed, still preoccupied, he took his jennet past the cushioned ledges where the Scottish Court was watching, and pausing, his little horse stayed between his knees, he unpinned his gauge.

Then he looked up, the light striking gold from his hair and resting on the high planes of brow and cheekbone and nose as he studied the child's face.

Mary unseated herself and sat again angrily, one fold of red hair fallen down the outside ledge of the box. 'But you didn't fight M. d'Aubigny!'

'No. . . . The King your father did that,' said Francis Crawford.

Her eyes opened. 'I didn't see him!'

'It was done another way. But I did fight someone, you know. Will he not do?'

'M. le Vidame?' It was the voice of proprietory scorn. 'He brings me cats!'

'Oh. Does he?' said Lymond with interest. 'It's one thing he hasn't brought me yet. How difficult it is. Then if he will not serve, I fear I must keep the glove until I find someone who will. What about that?'

'But yes, excellent. Do you keep it, M. Crawford. For someone truly dangerous. Such as the Irishwoman who wished me some harm?'

'No. We were wrong, you and I. The lady is a friend.' Lymond, no doubt sensing the Dowager's sharpened interest, changed the subject. 'I must go, your grace. There is word that The O'LiamRoe is to show the Court how to play hurley, and they will need a few sober men, and a physician and a priest too, before they are done. But if I am to take your glove, I ought to leave you some token at least.' And, reaching up, he laid something on the little Queen's outstretched palm.

It was the enormous diamond. The Dowager caught it from her. 'Ma mie, no! M. Crawford, she cannot accept that. It is greatly too much.'

'It is the King's,' said Lymond cheerfully. 'I understand that, unlike the pots and pans, he does not expect it returned.'

Under his own gauntlet, the edge of a bandage showed. She understood him too well. No duties; no obligations; no responsibilities—except to himself. And yet . . . he had kept the glove.

'Say me a riddle,' said the Queen.

The jennet was becoming impatient; he had paused long enough. 'We are not private enough,' he said. 'Your servant, my lady.' And smiling, tightened the reins.

'Sing me a song, then,' she pressed. He was hers; he had worn her gauge; others should see how pleasant they were together. But he only smiled again, and bowed, and moved off, the applause rattling down the stands, and the equerries closing in behind, his banner held high over his head.

Mary, watching half-annoyed, half-absorbed, raised her voice chanting; hardly heard, Margaret Erskine was thankful to notice, in the noise and movement around. Then she broke into full song, taking both parts herself, in a very good imitation of the famous voice: the voice which through a long winter had sung to the King and courtiers of France, and had played with her Queens.

'King and Queen of Cantelon
How many miles to Babylon?
Eight and eight and other eight.
Will I get there by candlelight?
If your horse be good and your spurs be bright.
How many men have ye?
. . . Mair nor ye daur come and see.'

August 1961—October 1962
Edinburgh and the Isle of Skye

432